SON OF A LICHE

SON OF A LICHE

BOOK TWO OF THE DARK PROFIT SAGA

J. Zachary Pike

Edited by Courtney Rae Andersson
Book Design by John Corsi
Cover design by James T. Egan of Bookfly Design
Published by Gnomish Press, May 2018

Version 2.0.1

Gnomish Press, LLC
P.O. Box 64
Greenland, NH 03840
GnomishPress@gmail.com

GNOMISH
- PRESS -

Acknowledgements

Writing a garbled first draft is a one-man task, but transforming it into a book I can be proud of takes the time and effort of many people. I'm grateful to every one of them.

Courtney Rae Andersson is a fantastic editor, with a deft touch and a deep knowledge of my particular niche genre (and financial fantasy humor is about as niche as niche gets).

Brittany Yost is a great sensitivity reader. Her perspectives on race and gender dynamics were both invaluable and gently delivered, and they made this a better book.

My beta readers offer edits, perspective, and encouragement in equal measure. Thank you to Cory Anderson, Nate Bates, Kristin Boucher, Josh Cole, Gary and Hilary Poisson, Erin Wallace, and Kayla Zagieboylok. Thank you also to Ariele Seiling for proofing this work, and to Chris Douglass and David Lurie, whose feedback made this a better book. And a special thank you to Mike Tibbals, who remains my most thorough fan. Over the course of his review of *Son of a Liche*, he remade a complete wiki on Arth, attempted a more thorough translation of Shadowtongue, and challenged my calendar based on lunar cycles. Mike is truly a red shirt in the fantasy MMORPG sense of the word (and not the space diplomacy sense of it).

My daughters have almost nothing to do with this book, but they've enriched my life so much that I'll tell anyone willing to listen about them. Case in point.

And none of this would be possible without my wife's support. From her words of encouragement to her tolerant sighs when I've neglected a to-do list to write just one more scene, she makes my work possible. Thank you, Becky

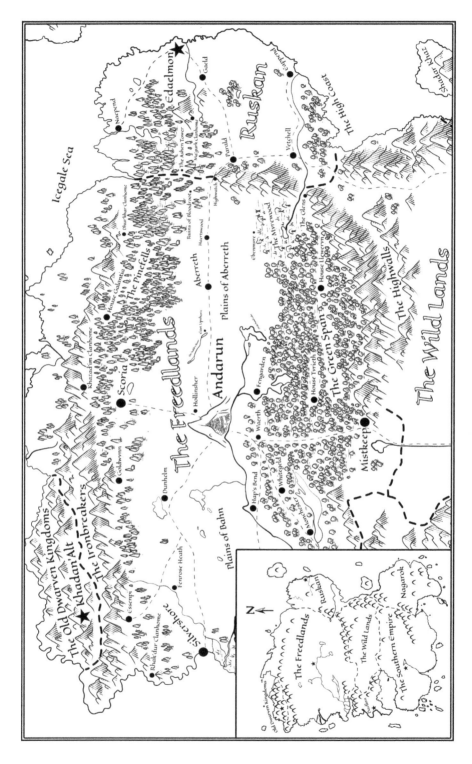

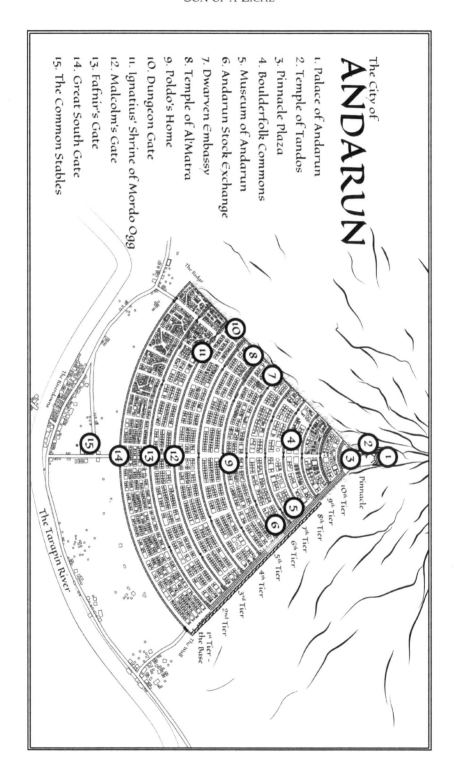

The City of
ANDARUN

1. Palace of Andarun
2. Temple of Tandos
3. Pinnacle Plaza
4. Boulderfolk Commons
5. Museum of Andarun
6. Andarun Stock Exchange
7. Dwarven Embassy
8. Temple of Al'Matra
9. Poldo's Home
10. Dungeon Gate
11. Ignatius' Shrine of Mordo Ogg
12. Malcolm's Gate
13. Fafnir's Gate
14. Great South Gate
15. The Common Stables

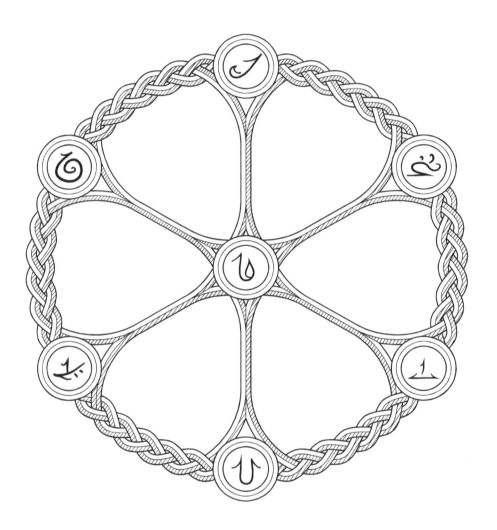

To
My Parents

Prologue

The raven prepared to settle in for lunch at the Glens.

Being a bird, the raven didn't understand what the Glens were; it just saw a massive stone nest built by the pink and brown apes that infested the ground. The entire concept of a fortress, let alone the strategic importance of a fort that controlled a narrow mountain pass, remained lost to him.

Yet, as a member of the genus *corvus,* the raven was intelligent, as birds go. Along with most of his flock, he had learned that large groups of the green and olive varieties of ground ape left food in their wake, especially when they wore shiny clothes and carried sharp tools.

The band of green apes below—Orcs and Goblins, though the raven didn't know those words—had lived up to expectations. Now that the battle was over, the victors were stacking their own casualties outside the walls, onto makeshift pyres built from old furniture, and setting the possessions of the departed around the grim piles of corpses.

The raven also had little concept of ceremonial cremation. From its perspective, the strange apes were wasting food by throwing it on ridiculously decorative fires. But it didn't matter. The tantalizing corpses of the pinkish apes still waited in the courtyard for the raven and its flock.

It took longer than the raven liked, but eventually the green apes finished the business of burning their dead. They departed in an organized stampede, thundering down the mountain path and into the forest below. They left behind enough food for a week, by the raven's primitive estimations.

The raven selected his meal as the raiders retreated, but he waited for them to be well out of earshot before he swooped to land next to a large, pink ground ape with a shining breastplate on his chest and a great axe embedded in his skull. It took some investigation to locate the perfect spot, and the raven had to pause and bark at a crow that kept creeping too close, but soon enough the raven moved in for the first bite of flesh. Its timing was unfortunate, because at that moment the dead man, against all odds and most of the laws of nature, sat up.

The raven flapped back into the air, squawking as its uncooperative meal moaned and hauled himself to his feet. Across the courtyard, more corpses were rising, prompting a flock of startled carrion birds to launch themselves into the air.

"Braaaains," groaned the dead man, swaying as he stood. "Braaaaaaiinnns."

"Oh, allow me," said another walking corpse. It stepped over and pulled the battleaxe from the first man's skull. "Better?"

"Cor, yeah! Thank you," gasped the first soldier. "Hard to do much with an axe buried in your brains."

"I'd imagine so," said the helpful zombie. "But it's all better now, and we'd best be going."

"Yes," said the first zombie, scratching his chin. He held his other hand to the side of his ear as if to hear some inscrutable sound better, or perhaps just to hold his head together. "Yes, we need to go."

"Funny thing, you speaking of brains," said the second as they shambled toward the gate.

"How's that?" asked the first.

"Well, I was just thinking of brains." The second zombie clutched his stomach, either in hunger or to hold his innards in. "Hard to think about much else, actually."

"They do hold a certain appeal, now that you mention it," conceded the first.

With that, the two zombies joined the herd of the undead shambling out the gates of the Glens, heeding an inaudible call, and leaving a very confused—and hungry—raven behind them.

Chapter 1

Gorm peered into the remnants of the funeral pyre. The wind blew snow into the pile of charred timber, dusting the remains inside with frost. The same wind blew the ashes from the pit onto the jagged slopes of the Highwalls, forming gray trails in twisting patterns over the stones and snow. This wandering soot mingled with remains from the other pyres scattered around the fort.

"It was the Red Horde," said Burt, shivering in the cold. Like most Demi-gnolls, Burt had a coat of canine fur, but as a Kobold, his grew in odd patches that didn't offer much warmth for his small, spindly frame. He wrapped himself in the fragment of a scavenged blanket and glared up at Gorm with his bulbous eyes.

"How can ye be sure?" asked Gorm. He peered at the fragments of charred bone left after the fire, but they held no clue he could see.

Burt stuck a claw out of his blanket and pointed at a string of beads among the weapons, trinkets, and carvings that decorated the area around the pyre. "See the complex pattern of color on that necklace there?" he asked.

Gorm looked. "All right—"

"Note the interaction of the different hues," said Burt.

Gorm sighed. "It's all red."

"Oh! I guess it must have been the thrice-cursed Red Horde!" snapped Burt.

"But what tribe are they?" Gorm said.

"They don't have a tribe. They joined the Red Horde."

A Shadowkin or monster foreswore any former identity upon enlisting in the endless ranks of the Red Horde. Yet, for the droves of former noncombatant paper carriers, or NPCs, who had lost their papers—voluntarily or otherwise—after the fall of Bloodroot, an identity was a small price to pay for survival. The movement had started out peaceful, when it was too small to be otherwise, but one by one the Shadowkin tribes were being absorbed into the crimson tide, and there was strength in numbers. Now the Red Horde was running regular raids across the Freedlands, pillaging small villages and robbing merchants on the road.

Gorm sighed and kicked at the ashes. He'd heard whispers that the Guz'Varda had fallen under the Red Horde's sway as well, but other sources said that Zurthraka's tribe had resisted joining them. But rumors went a dozen for a silver shilling these days, and he couldn't afford to rely on anything but evidence and hard facts.

"Ye know what I meant," he said. "Who were they before they joined the Horde?"

Burt glowered at the carved totems and teeth that littered the ground. "Hmm... There's Gnolls, a Kobold family or two... and a Goblin clan, though I could never keep all of those straight. Oh, see all the jawbone totems with the swirls carved in 'em? The Orcs here were the Zabba'Nuktar. The Great Beard Tribe."

"So, not the Guz'Varda," sighed Gorm. He wasn't sure if he felt disappointed that he still hadn't found the Orcs of Zurthraka's tribe, or relieved that they weren't yet a part of the Red Horde.

"Hey, if you're gonna stand around stating the obvious, at least let me get back inside," growled the Kobold. "I'm freezing my whiskers off out here, and I only say it that way because you get so sensitive when I talk about my—"

"Fine. Get back in the bag." Gorm sighed as he set his rucksack down. "No smokin' in there. I don't have a spare pack if'n ye start a fire in this one."

"Hey, they call it the Freedlands for a reason," said Burt, scurrying into Gorm's pack. "I'll be careful."

"It stinks up all me clothes!"

"Yeah? So do you." Burt pulled the drawstring shut. A light flared within the rucksack, and thin wisps of pipe smoke trickled out through its seam.

Gorm cursed stubborn Shadowkin and cheap pipeweed as he hefted the rucksack onto his shoulder. He grabbed the crimson beads and headed back toward the fortress at the Glens.

The Freedlands kept a detachment of bannermen in the lonely outpost to watch for invaders from the southeast as a longstanding tradition. The isolated fort had earned a reputation as a tedious and uneventful tour of duty. Looking at the charred and twisted gates, Gorm imagined the last crew of defenders would have preferred it that way.

An old spear pinned an ancient skeleton to the wall by the gates. It was missing the arms and head, and the bleached bones were connected by just enough ancient clothing and toughened sinew to keep it together as it rattled in the breeze. At some point in history, a disgruntled soldier had nailed a small, wooden sign to the dead man's sternum. It read "ABANDON ALL HOPE, YE WHO ARE STATIONED HERE."

Gorm passed Gaist on his way into the fortress. The weaponsmaster's clothes and hood were black leather, and his skin was the dark complexion of the southern Empire. Gorm might have mistaken him for a shadow were it not for the crimson scarf he wore over his face.

"Ho, Gaist," said Gorm. "Are the others still searchin'?"

Gaist's eyes flicked to the courtyard before returning to watching the mountain pass. It wasn't much of an answer, but by the silent weaponsmaster's standards, it was downright chatty.

"Thanks," said Gorm, and he headed inside.

The other heroes had built a makeshift cookfire in the middle of the ruined courtyard. They sat on the stones and fallen beams that littered the ground, waiting for lunch. Gorm trundled up to the circle, where Kaitha was stirring something gray and bubbling in a dented pot.

"That smells… edible," the Dwarf said.

"You're too kind." Kaitha made a face as she struggled to pull her spoon out of the sucking muck. "Really."

Life as a ranger had prepared Kaitha for extended trips into the wilderness, and her birthright as Elven royalty gave her a gift for looking elegant anywhere. She wore her auburn hair in a neat ponytail, her face was radiant—if a bit grimier than usual—and her armor, all green leather and jade and drake-hide, looked as new as the day it was looted from a dungeon.

"What is that anyway?" A trademark smirk curled Heraldin Strummon's thin mustache. His wide-brimmed hat was frayed around the edges and his costume had faded from bright yellow and crimson to taupe and rusty brown, but the bard beneath the outfit had unfortunately remained otherwise unchanged by over a year in the wilds.

"Just some scavenge from the larder," said Kaitha.

"I was certain that the Shadowkin looted the larder," said Laruna Trullon, closing the book she had been reading. The ruby and gold trim of the solamancer's brilliant orange robes shimmered as she pushed herself to her feet; a mage's garments served as enchanted signs of rank, and magical glamours kept them neat and new. The woman wearing the robes, however, enjoyed no such enchantments, and a year running from the law had taken its toll. Her raven hair fell unkempt around a handsome face that had a hard edge to it.

"They looted it clean," Jynn Ur'Mayan confirmed. Life on the road had been hardest on the noctomancer, who had a physique best suited to long hours of reading in dimly lit spaces. His neat goatee had been overtaken by a creeping, haggard beard. His head, once clean-shaven, now sported a crop of stubble that exposed a large bald spot. "There's not a single crate or barrel left down there."

"Right," said Kaitha. "There was nowhere in the larder for the rats to hide."

Gorm stared at the bubbling pot, then shrugged. "I've eaten worse."

Kaitha's face was grim as she ladled out the first portion of the sludge. "There's worse in here."

It has been said that necessity is the mother of invention. In the same vein, desperation is the father of compromise, panic is the sister of slapdash improvisation, and despair is the second cousin of quiet apathy. By that reckoning, dinner was a dismal family reunion.

The ex-heroes ate in sullen silence, wrestling with dour thoughts and noxious plates. The more Gorm consumed, the more he could see his reflection in the tin bowl he ate from. His long, red beard was frayed, his skin ruddy and pocked, and there were dark circles under his eyes after the long hike through the mountains, but he was no stranger to looking unkempt. Gorm had spent years on the open road, and years more in the open road's ditches, before he'd met any of his current companions.

Still, something about Gorm had changed. Some spark or light had faded enough that he looked more like his shadow than himself. It was that thought, and a dangerous rumbling in his stomach, that prompted him to set his foul meal aside and attempt to strike up a conversation. "Anyone find anything good?"

"I think we just ate the best of it," said Jynn.

"How did you and Burt fare?" asked Kaitha.

Gorm sighed. "We found signs that it wasn't the Guz'Varda."

The other adventurers shook their heads. Heraldin groaned. "So we came all the way up here for nothing?"

"Well, we know another place that the Guz'Varda ain't," Gorm ventured.

"We know a lot of those," said Laruna.

"Do we know anywhere else they might be?" asked Heraldin.

"Wouldn't have come to the Glens if we did," Gorm said. "Burt will have to gather more information."

"Easier said than done." Burt reclined in the warmth of the cookfire, picking his teeth with a twig. "Word spreads, and I'm getting a reputation."

"For asking too many questions?" asked Heraldin.

"Uh… more for associating with all of you," said Burt. "People are reluctant to help any Lightling, but that goes double for this crew."

"It's really that bad?" said Laruna.

"Of course," said the Kobold. "They hold you personally responsible for the business at Bloodroot. And since they pinned Niln's death on the Orcs, the guild's been way more aggressive about revoking NPC papers. Why do you think the information costs more gold every time I ask around?"

"I'd always assumed you were taking a large cut of it, to be honest," said Jynn.

"Ain't saying I'm not," said Burt with a shrug. "But with your reputation preceding us, any Gnoll or Goblin who's heard of you takes extra, uh, convincing to talk about the Guz'Varda. The Red Horde have a term for you guys."

"Us specifically?" said Jynn.

"Oh yeah. They call you *barg'hegga spi'nix'hest*," said Burt. "Roughly translated, it means 'a dog that befriends you so it can try to kill you.'"

"Ah," said Kaitha.

"It's like a traitor without the dignity," said Burt.

"We get the picture, thanks," said Gorm.

"Well, I hope you didn't spend all this time thinkin' the Shadowkin still liked you," said the Kobold. "I'm not saying they're right, you know, but some of you already had reputations for killin' Shadowkin before you met the Guz'Varda, eh, Pyrebeard? Those Orcs knew they were takin' a big chance trusting you, and just when it looked like it paid off, they got wiped off the map. That sort of thing drives up the price of information. I don't think you can afford it any more."

"If we could afford much of anything, we wouldn't be eating garbage," said Laruna, prodding at her plate with a spoon. It burbled in response.

Gorm grunted and looked back to his stew.

"Perhaps it's time for a change in strategy," said Heraldin. "As in, we should have one."

"Not this again." Gorm set his spoon onto his plate. "I'm gettin' sick of havin' this conversation."

"My sentiments exactly, my friend," said the bard. "Perhaps this time you'll listen. We all want to help the Guz'Varda, but we can't do much running around the wilderness and scavenging the Orcs' leavings. Maybe if we were a little more established, we could talk to a local lord or lady about opening diplomatic relations with the Orcs. Maybe we could find them a place in the Empire."

"And given that King Handor wants us dead, the Heroes' Guild branded us traitors, and someone keeps sendin' assassins to kill us, how are ye proposin' we establish ourselves?" Gorm asked.

"There's plenty of mercenary bands in the pirate towns of the High Coast," suggested Laruna. "They'd leap at the chance to take on a band of ex-Guilders with our resume."

"We could start over there," said Kaitha.

Gorm leveled a suspicious glare at the Elf. "Sounds like you've been talking about this idea a bit, then."

The Elf wore a guilty expression. "We've been discussing our options."

"And what are the other ones?" asked the Dwarf.

"Starving to death in the wilderness, it seems," said Jynn, setting aside most of his food.

Gorm shook his head. "I ain't one for quittin'. Besides, it don't feel right abandonin' the Orcs to go seek our fortune in pirate towns."

"More like our survival," said Heraldin.

"Just about everything feels wrong these days," said Kaitha. "Maybe we have to settle for a compromise here."

"Ye don't compromise on some things," growled Gorm.

Heraldin held out his plate. "Perhaps you'd like another helping of Rat Surprise while you lecture us on standards?"

"I…" Gorm stopped for a moment, distracted by the plate of alleged food bubbling in front of him. "I don't know," he confessed. "We're supposed to be out here seekin' justice, protectin' the weak."

"We still will be," said Kaitha.

"Just with a paycheck," said Heraldin.

"And maybe a warm fire to sit by," added Burt.

"You too, Burt?" Gorm could feel them slipping away from the mission, and if he was honest, he was slipping with them. "What about helpin' those in danger? Defendin' those who need it?"

"We can still do that if we see anyone who needs help," said Jynn.

"We wouldn't just walk away from people in need," Laruna agreed. "We may become mercenaries, but we'll always be heroes at heart."

"Killing people is a job. Saving innocents is a passion," said Heraldin.

"And we'll still work toward helping the Orcs," said Kaitha. "We're not backing off."

"Right," said Burt. "We're just open to finding new ways forward."

Gorm stood and hefted his pack onto his shoulder. "Give me some time to think about it," he called back to them as he headed out toward the gate.

"What is there to think about?" he heard Jynn ask. "I don't see a choice here."

"That's what he must make peace with," Heraldin told the wizard.

Peace is a difficult idea for many Shadowkin. Shadowtongue has no word for it; the closest concept in the language of Orcs and Goblins is the somewhat cumbersome term *dapitto'noddin appa'dad*. Roughly translated, it means "a short time for rest between fights."

This linguistic quirk ensured that praying for peace was a long and awkward process for an Orc, but Asherzu Guz'Varda did so anyway.

Within the chambers of her salt-bleached hut, the Orcess spent much of her afternoon gripping her holy symbol and whispering pleas to a Dwarven god that never spoke. Her fingers worked over the silver charm, fashioned into the shape of a glowmoth, until it was warm in her hands.

Lambskin canvases brimming with graphs and charts lay scattered around the crude furnishings of the hut. On any other morning, they would have completely engrossed her. Today, they didn't matter. She spent the high-sun meal in prayer, and might have missed the evening one as well had Jorruk not knocked on the rough pine column outside of her chamber.

"*A thousand pardons, but you should take food, my lady,*" said the wise-one.

"*Is there news?*" asked Asherzu, ignoring her mentor's advice.

"*There is roast pig. That will have to do,*" said Jorruk gently as he stepped through the curtain of beads and teeth that served as her door.

"*How can I eat when our eldest brother is in danger?*" asked Asherzu.

"*You can trust in the might and power of our chieftain. Char is on his own path now. We must find our way forward.*"

"*Char's only path has been his own,*" said Asherzu. Her eldest brother, the firstborn son of Chief Zurthraka daz'Guz'Varda, had long held a reputation for being headstrong and impulsive. Yet when the Lightlings razed the town of Bloodroot and killed Chief Zurthraka, Char helped gather the sacred treasures from the Orcs' High Vault and led much of the Guz'Varda Tribe, along with many other Shadowkin, to safety.

Through his heroism and might, Asherzu's brother had been made chieftain. But their father's throne had not imparted their father's wisdom, and Char remained impetuous and overconfident. He never should have ordered the last hunt, let alone led it. A pit had opened in Asherzu's stomach when his warband had come back through the gate without him, and that pit hadn't closed since.

Jorruk put a bony hand on her shoulder and tried another tactic. *"Your youngest brother eats."*

"I cannot dream of such a time that Darak would not find the will to eat," said Asherzu. A small smile flashed her tusks despite herself. *"I will not keep him waiting. Let me put on my beads."*

"I shall await you there, lady." Jorruk bowed and stepped away.

Asherzu draped two necklaces of green and orange beads around her neck; her father's favorite colors were those of truce and trade. She added a necklace of violet and yellow beads as well; her personal colors stood for wisdom and knowledge. She also took a string of blue beads over black and yellow, colors for feasting with one's clan or tribe. Finally, she added a few red beads to her blue-black hair, both to please Char's wise-ones and because she liked the way they looked.

She stepped out of her small wooden hut, nestled with two other yurts in the shadows of the pines near the edge of town. The air was crisp and salty. Broad patches of white, pillowy snow blanketed the forest and the Orcish town, but the rocky beach nearby was kept bare and wet by the crashing waves. A persistent chill hung in the air, and she pulled her silks closer as she made her way to the great house.

The center of the town was a monstrous nest of red canvas and beaded ropes spider-webbed between thick pine timbers. The Goblins of the Dark Raven Tribe had helped set it up and, typical of Goblin workmanship, the tent was tenuously strung together and riddled with useless additions. There were lookout towers with no stairs, balconies set just above the ground, and random banners and totems stuck everywhere. But it was large enough to serve the Guz'Varda and the members of the Red Horde they traveled with, and that was all they needed.

Most of the village had already gone home when she stepped into the tent. The end-of-day meal was drawing to a close, and there were precious few hours between sunset and the point at which sleep would claim exhausted laborers. But near the back of the tent she saw a few Orcs scattered around a small mountain of olive flesh and raven hair. Darak.

Her younger brother leaned against a post that may or may not have supported the roof. He glowered out the windows facing the beach, ever watchful, but his face lit up as Asherzu approached. *"Ah, my flesh and blood has come!"* he said, straightening as she approached.

"Good day, lady. I see you've chosen to wear the beads of your old tribe," said a thin, gap-toothed Orc in the tongue of Lightlings. His mustache and beard was short and oily, his head clean-shaven, and a multitude of crimson beads draped over his evergreen frame like poison berries on a scrawny shrub.

"As our people have for centuries, Grignot." Asherzu took the seat Darak offered her.

"Times change, lady," said Grignot. "In the Red Horde, we wear only the beads of our fellowship, as we did in the ages long past. We have no tribes."

"I am sorry for you, then," said Asherzu. "I, for one, could not bear the loss of my tribe."

"I fear we are all lost without unity," said Grignot with a reptilian smile.

"Leave her be, Grignot," said Darak. "It is only beads. Can you two not honor each other even in these troubled days?"

"Perhaps," said Grignot, standing. "But I imagine you two have much to discuss. I leave you to your dinner, Lady Asherzu. Farewell, mighty Darak, wise Jorruk."

Asherzu watched him scuttle from the tent, flanked by the warriors of the Red Horde. *"There goes a snake among the reeds."*

Jorruk nodded, but said nothing. His stern gaze told her she should keep quiet as well. She shot him a smile that said she'd take his advice under consideration.

"Brother Char trusts him," said Darak. *"He is the highest of the chieftain's wise-ones."*

"I have never seen a wise-one with a beard," Asherzu snorted.

"Brother Char says he has the heart of a warrior," Darak countered.

"And the head to match it," said Asherzu. *"A pity Grignot has the body of a wise-one, then. It leaves him unworthy to be either."*

"Your wisdom and knowledge are always sound, my sister. I will not argue with you. But a chieftain chooses whose council to take, and Char has chosen Grignot's." Darak shrugged. *"We should not question."*

"You always were dutiful, Little Warg," said Asherzu, batting at one of the braids in his beard.

"I know my strengths, wise sister," said Darak. He nodded to the massive warhammer set across the table.

"*But look where Grignot's council has taken Char now,*" said Asherzu. "*Who knows what the Lightlings will do to our brother if the rescue fails? What if they cannot find Fulgen's Rest? How will they return?*"

Darak shook his head. "*Brother Char will not falter,*" he said, despite all evidence to the contrary. "*We have already lost Father, and Challu, and Derdod'zu, and Frak. And Brother Char has said this will be his last raid before he sets aside his axe. Surely the gods would not be so cruel.*"

"*Surely they should not be so tempted,*" said Asherzu, taking a bite of cured ham. "*The Teachings of Phrek tell us to never say such things, lest we dare fate.*"

"*He will not...*" Darak trailed off.

Asherzu looked at her brother's face, a mask of shock and sorrow. She followed his gaze to the far door of the tent, where a cluster of Shadowkin had shuffled in. Grignot was among them, his usual smirk replaced with a deep frown. Asherzu paid him no mind as her eyes fell on Fradak, the leader of the rescue party. Strings of black beads dangled from his beard.

Her stomach plunged as her food dropped to the dirt floor. Jorruk was saying something, but his words fell away along with the rest of the world. She already knew the message.

Char Guz'Varda was dead.

"Just like that?" asked Duine Poldo. "Gone?"

"Bought out, chopped up, sold off. Nice and neat," said Samel Fitch, dabbing his napkin to his thick lips before brushing crumbs of spice cake from his ragged stubble. He had the bright eyes and curly hair typical of Halflings, and his fine red vest struggled to contain his unusually generous girth. "That's business."

Poldo shook his head in disbelief. "But Wysdon Cheque? I saw their numbers. They had good growth, for a hedge fund."

"Good isn't good enough anymore," said Fitch with a shrug. "The market's strong. With the Red Horde and other Shadowkin foes about, loot yields are way up. If you're not posting amazing returns, you're on the chopping block."

"Indeed," said Poldo, feeling sweat bead on his forehead. He discreetly took out a pocket mirror to check himself. His suit was sharp and impeccable, his thick mustache waxed and shaped to perfect tips, and the gold-rimmed spectacles perched atop his bulbous nose were polished to a brilliant shine. He looked like a Scribkin in command of his own destiny, a powerful man of industry. Once he dabbed the perspiration from his brow with a violet handkerchief, anyway.

"But you don't need to worry about that!" said Fitch, waving his arms at the verdant garden surrounding them. "You made it! An office at Boulderfolk Commons! The big mansion for little people!"

"Ah, yes," said Poldo, taking a slow sip of his tea. The Terrace Cafe sat on a mosaic patio in the Commons' largest gardens. Built by Tuld R. Boulderfolk at the end of the Sixth Age, the renovated mansion on Andarun's eighth tier had become the city's premiere multi-office business center.

"Speaking of which, when do I get to see your office?" asked Fitch.

Poldo held up a finger as he continued to drag out the single sip of tea.

Though its architects built Boulderfolk Commons to Scribkin scale, an office on the premises was still a sign of prestige to anyone in the business community of Andarun; even Elves would overlook the inconvenience of desks that only reached their knees for the status that a Boulderfolk office afforded. Everyone wanted to work in the big mansion for little people, which was precisely why Poldo couldn't afford to. Boulderfolk's high rents were even more well-known than its low ceilings, and just as likely to knock a prospective tenant out flat.

Unfortunately, a hot drink could only buy so much time. Poldo tasted the grit of the tea leaves before he cleared his throat and set the cup in its saucer. "Now, I believe we were going to discuss the outlook for Silver Guard Securities," he said.

"Right after you show me that office." Fitch's grin was unwavering.

"Yes, of course," said Poldo, his spirits sinking. He set a few glittering giltin on the table and stepped down. "Well, then."

Fitch gulped down the last of his coffee, then followed Poldo off the terrace and onto a cobblestone walkway. The Halfling stopped with some confusion as Poldo walked away from the Commons' main house. "Where are—"

"Right this way," said Poldo, taking a left into a topiary maze.

"Oh! Is the office in one of the old guest houses?" Fitch gasped the words as he struggled to keep pace.

"Something like that." Poldo briskly wove his way through the green walls of the maze.

"The carriage house? The falconry? The servant's quarters?" breathed Fitch.

"And here we are," said Poldo.

Nestled between the back of the maze and the Commons' brick wall was a small brick gardener's shed. Poldo stepped up to the doorway, straightened a small sign on the doorpost that read "SILVER GUARD SECURITIES," and knocked three times on the door as he fished in his pockets for the key.

"Aw, geez, Poldo. I had no idea," said Fitch, running a hand through his curls.

"It's a Boulderfolk address," said Poldo as he opened the door. "I can conduct meetings in the Cafe, and I can access all the facilities." He stepped onto the reed mat inside the door and turned around in place three times.

Fitch shook his head. "Yeah, but once someone wants a tour or… wait, what are you doing?"

"Beg pardon?" Poldo found it difficult to look casual caught mid-spin.

"Are you spinning because of Domovoy?" Fitch's eyes grew wide as he pointed. "You've got Wood Gnomes, don't you?"

The Gnomes are the most disparate race of Man. A Scribkin looked as far from a Halfling or a Tinderkin as a Dwarf looked from an Elf. But among all of the Gnomish clans, none was more different or odd than Clan Fengeld, the Wood Gnomes.

Most legends said the gods cursed Clan Fengeld with tiny stature back in the First Age. Wood Gnome lore held that the gods actually cursed all of the other peoples of the world to be giant monsters, but as they usually spoke in their own bizarre tongue, nobody paid much attention to their perspective. Regardless of their origins, the Wood Gnomes had stood no taller than a Human's thumb for as long as the Agekeepers had records. They were widely known for a tenacious work ethic and supernatural efficiency. Unfortunately, they were also well-known for moving into offices and living spaces uninvited, where they set about modifying the premises to their own liking.

Worse, Wood Gnomes insisted that their co-inhabitants adhere to strange customs. Any neighbor of Clan Fengeld was expected to knock three times at the door, turn around in three full circles upon entering a room, and leave a bowl of milk at night, among other rituals. Those that failed to observe the rituals quickly discovered that Wood Gnomes have an outsized capacity for property damage.

Wood Gnomes' habit of showing up unannounced, the wanton vandalism they committed whenever anyone violated their social mores, and the tenacity with which they remained entrenched on a property earned them the pejorative name "Domovoy," which was Ruskan for "rat men." Most people considered them to be a horrible nuisance, and it wasn't until almost halfway through the Seventh Age that the Wood Gnome Defense League successfully petitioned to have them removed from the Heroes' Guild's official list of designated Forces of Evil, or F.O.E.s.

"It's just a small tribe of them," said Poldo, trying to hide his embarrassment. "But I keep up with the customs well enough, so they shouldn't—"

"Yeah, yeah, sure, I'm sure it's fine," said Fitch. "Listen, I've seen enough, Poldo."

"Oh, come now, Mr. Fitch," said Poldo, rising panic sweeping away his shame. "You haven't looked at the numbers." He held up his briefcase as an acolyte presents a supplication to an angry idol.

"You don't want me to look at the numbers. And you don't want me to write a report on you," said Fitch, nodding for Poldo to follow. "Come on."

Poldo hurried after the Halfling, his hands shaking as he locked the door behind him. "Oh, but I do, Mr. Fitch. Without your endorsement, I'm going to have a hard time finding buyers for my funds. I was hoping you could do me a favor…"

"Yeah, exactly," said Fitch, stepping back into the topiary maze. "Anybody else, I'd be going home and writing a review that says their hedge fund is literally in a hedge, and their office is actually a Domovoy-riddled garden shack!" He stopped and looked between two paths, confused.

Poldo guided him to the left. "But if you'd just look at the numbers—"

Fitch cut him off with a firm grip on his shoulder. "Look, I'm sure the numbers are fine. Good even. The asset blend is probably solid. And you've got a degree from Hardvaark and a Goldson Baggs pedigree, which is going to look great for any fund you manage. Even with a Domovoy-infested dump for an office, I could probably give you a good review," said Fitch. "But listen, Poldo, with the market rolling hot, good isn't good enough, all right? Good is the new awful. A good report is going to get Silver Guard Securities bought out, chopped up, and sold off."

"Ah." Poldo's shoulders sagged. "Nice and neat."

"Right," said Fitch. "Which is why, as a friend, I'm going to give you some friendly advice and say you don't want a report from me unless it's amazing. And if you can't afford an office that isn't used to store garden equipment, it's not going to be amazing. Trust me."

Poldo sighed. Halflings and Scribkin seldom worked together, mostly because Halflings seldom worked at all by Scribkin standards, but over his career Poldo had found a friend and confidant in Fitch. Besides, he knew his old associate was right.

"Look." Fitch glanced around. "I'll tell my friends that the sandwich from the cafe didn't agree with my stomach. It's not that much of a stretch—those Imperial flame olives are murder. I shouldn't order them, but they're never in season anymore. Anyway, that's why we canceled today's evaluation, right?"

"Thank you." Poldo nodded gratefully.

"With my schedule, I can probably find excuses not to conduct another review for a month." Fitch threw his hands up in the air. "That's all I can do. As a consultant—"

"Your reputation is your livelihood," Poldo finished for him as they strolled out of the hedge maze. "Of course, Mr. Fitch. I shall... I shall try to see what I can accomplish."

"Speaking of which, have you looked in to what Lamia Sisters is doing these days?"

"Collateralized threat obligations?" Poldo said in hushed tones. "I've heard they're risky."

"Not for the firms that are bundling them." Fitch shrugged as he walked along the manicured paths of Boulderfolk's expansive lawns. "Lamia Sisters can't buy those things fast enough. Goldson Baggs is getting in on the game as well, and it's only a matter of time before Citistate and J.P. Gorgon follow suit. But there may still be time to get in early."

Poldo's brow furrowed. "I'm just not sure I'm comfortable with a product that's so... experimental."

"Oh? Huh," said Fitch airily. "I was over at Hylian Crest last weekend, and they seemed comfortable with it. But maybe it's just easy to be comfortable in a posh office on the top floor of an old Elven palace. At least, more comfortable than in a garden shed."

"I see your point." Poldo tugged at the edge of his mustache.

"Think about it," said Fitch, extending his hand. "And send me a messenger sprite if you're looking for a partner. I know a guy who can help."

Poldo thanked the Halfling and bade him farewell with a heavy heart and a spinning mind. He moved in a rote, almost mechanical fashion as he returned to the toolshed-cum-office to lock up for the night, going through the Wood Gnomes' rituals like a golem about its duties. He was still lost in thought as he tramped down the familiar path to Boulderfolk's service entrance, slipped into the back alley, and headed for the main street overlooking the seventh tier.

He stopped before he reached the main road, however, when he heard a commotion down a side alley. There were shouts of anger followed by the clattering crash of breaking pottery, and then a scrabbling sound from the back of one of the nearby restaurants. He peered around the corner just in time to see a shadowy blur of fur and claws before it knocked him to the ground.

A cloud of dust rose from the planks and splinters of wood rattling on the floorboards. Kaitha kicked at the remains of the box with her toe.

"You don't have to smash the chests like that." Laruna looked up from a ransacked bookshelf.

"There's nothing inside." The Elf shrugged. "The Shadowkin took everything."

"You don't know that," said the solamancer.

"I know Heraldin and Gaist searched in here." Kaitha pushed the remnants of the chest aside and tapped the floor beneath it. "The bard would have found anything obvious."

Laruna glanced irritably around the captain's quarters of the Glens. It had likely been well decorated once, but now the room was sparsely furnished and littered with boards and kindling. "Well, then what are we even doing in here?"

"Looking for anything that's not obvious," said the Elf, straightening. "Besides, it kills time while Gorm does some soul-searching."

"Fine. But you still don't have to smash all the chests," said Laruna.

"True." Kaitha hefted a table leg that could serve as a sledgehammer in a pinch. She set her sights on the footlocker at the end of the bed. "But it's fun."

Laruna considered this. Then she immolated the bookcase.

Kaitha's first swing smashed in the top of the footlocker. Her second and third sent a long crack down the side of its wall. As the wood buckled, she caught sight of something amiss. Two more precise blows with the table leg confirmed her suspicions. "Ah, see?" she said to Laruna. "False bottom."

"What's in it?" asked the mage, snuffing out the burning bookcase with a wave of her hand.

"Let's find out." Kaitha crouched and pulled several items from the footlocker's secret compartment. An old purse was the big find; more than a hundred giltin in coins and large notes were tucked in the leather pouch. There were also several pieces of personal memorabilia that might be worth a few giltin to a tinker: three silver medals wrapped in a yellowed letter of commendation, a woodcut of a young woman, and an ornate letter opener in a cherrywood box.

Kaitha noticed the glint of a glass vial in a dark corner of the ruined compartment. She handed Laruna the letter opener for evaluation and slipped the vial of elixir into her belt pouch while the mage was distracted. Then she dumped the last of the footlocker's treasures onto the floor.

A few loose coins and an icon of Musana spilled out, followed by a small sculpture of a knight cast in painted pewter that bounced on the floor.

"What is that?" asked Laruna as Kaitha held up the armor-clad figurine.

"I think it's a toy," said the ranger, examining the tiny knight. Its armor was violet speckled with white and silver where the paint was chipped. It still had a faded velvet cape tied around its neck, and in the center of its chest was a piece of cloudy purple quartz cut to look like a gemstone. One hand held a bent sword high, the other gripped the handle of a shield that had gone missing. "I think he's supposed to be Davon Royalheart."

"Who?"

"An old hero from before your time," said Kaitha. "Paladin running out of Silvershore. He led the party that took down the Gorgon Lord of the Eboncrags."

"I've never heard of him," said Laruna.

"Well, you've heard of Vorpal Corp."

"He's connected with Vorpal?"

"He founded it with a few investors after he retired from adventuring." Kaitha wiped the dust from the toy paladin's gemstone. "Had a great career. I think he passed on a few years back."

"Do you think we can get a few coppers for it?" Laruna asked.

"I'm not going to sell it," said Kaitha.

Laruna's brow furrowed. "Why not? It won't help us kill anything, and it won't help us survive. If you can't get a fair price, we should leave it."

"It's purple," said Kaitha.

"Oh, gods." The mage rolled her eyes. "Not the King in the Wood again."

The ranger shrugged as she stood. "You don't have to believe in him. He's there. Spirit or Elf or... whatever he is, I'm certain he's watching over us. Protecting us."

"All I'm certain of is that our ranger keeps sprinkling loot behind us if it's the right color," grumbled the mage as she gathered up the rest of the goods.

"You can't deny we've encountered very few monsters out here," said Kaitha.

"I can deny that it has anything to do with leaving toys in the woods," Laruna shot back.

"Oh, stop worrying about the toy. It wouldn't fetch more than a silver shilling," said Kaitha.

"It's the principle of the thing," said Laruna.

Now it was Kaitha's turn to roll her eyes. People fell back to principle when they lost ground on the facts. "Come on," she said, tucking the figurine into her pouch. "You can have two cents' worth of my share to make up for it."

"I'd pay a sovereign to see you get over this forest spirit," said Laruna. "We all see the way you stare into the woods. It worries me."

Kaitha smiled. "We've all got bigger things to concern ourselves with. I like the idea that there's someone out there helping us. I like the feeling I get when I know he's close. Allow me that small happiness."

Chapter 2

Gorm sought comfort in a small alcove on the Glens' ruined ramparts. The nook provided a dry patch of ground, a modicum of shelter from the frigid wind, and a truly impressive view. The Highwalls rose all around him, their icy peaks towering over the vale below.

The Dwarf rummaged around in his old rucksack, his nose wrinkling at the odors of cigarette smoke and wet Kobold. Beneath Burt's personal effects and his own supplies, a thick leather packet was bound with thin black rope. He unpacked it slowly, taking care not to spill the heartseeker beads. The small stones were inert in his palm, their magic long dormant. The beads were enchanted to orient toward the Guz'Varda Tribe whenever one of them gripped the Heartstone. Nobody had gripped the stone in months, and now they were little more than a momento of the Goblin whose grave he had taken them from.

There was too much to do to mourn Tib'rin again. Gorm packed the beads up, set them aside, and pulled an old book from the packet. Sheltering the pages from the wind, Gorm opened the collected works and notes of Niln of Al'Matra.

His calloused fingers traced the edges of the worn, leather journal. The ragged book reminded him of the thin scribe who penned it; both a wise man and a fool boy. He smiled at the thought of the priest.

"Let's see if ye can offer any insight today, Niln," he muttered to himself. Gorm began to read.

And I saw a bird, or maybe three, or maybe one that burned three times,

He was a babe, and then a beast, and then a dark king rising in blood.

The maiden of tears loves him, fears him, mourns him.

Her tears end, the vessel fills, once more rises the traitor god.

"Totally barmy," murmured Gorm, though he wore a fond smile as he said it.

The passage was from the prophet Rebik's first and most coherent book. According to Niln's commentary in the margin, the First Book of Rebik was completed just before the ancient scribe descended into the madness that claimed most of Al'Matra's chosen. After his breakdown, the prophet's writing turned exclusively to sonnets addressed to various species of caterpillar.

The margins of the scriptures overflowed with notes and cross-references, all written in a neat, tight script. Niln had studied every passage in great detail, slicing each verse into discrete parts for examination as a naturalist might dissect a frog. This particular passage had clearly puzzled the late High Scribe of Al'Matra.

A burning bird is a phoenix. Does it represent the Dark Prince, as he resurrects AlThadan? But where are the Seven Heroes? Is this a vision of what is to come, or a vision of the world if the heroes fail? If the Prince is destined to bring back the Sten, whence hope? If the heroes are destined to stop him, whence this prophecy?

"Ye never could make any sense of this claptrap either, could ye?" The Dwarf traced the text with the tip of his finger. After Niln's death, the scribe's scriptures and notes were all he had of his old friend.

It wasn't much, but it was enough to remind Gorm of why he was out here. When he felt hopeless, when aimlessness threatened to extinguish the fire at his core, it helped to remember Tib'rin's courage and Niln's faith, and the slimy bastards who brought both of them to untimely ends. Gorm's grip tightened on the page as he exhaled a ragged breath.

"Ye two are the only things keepin' me going," he grumbled, tracing his finger down the page. As he did so, his finger passed a hastily scrawled comment in the margins, the ink smeared in careless urgency.

This cannot be accomplished by mortal hands, least of all by mine. Marqwice, chapter 3, verse 3

The Dwarf was still considering the scrawled note when a large rock hit the side of the fortress with a crack and a thud. He stared at the stone for a moment before he carefully closed the book and placed it within the leather parcel. A second rock hit the ramparts as he tucked the package back in his rucksack.

"I'm comin'," Gorm grumbled as he stepped up to the edge of the ramparts and peered over the edge.

Below him, atop the narrow ribbon of rock between the fortress' wall and the jagged slopes of the Highwalls, perched a hulking figure with a grin full of daggers.

Gorm smiled, which was an unusual reaction to the arrival of a Troll. Thane, however, had proven himself to be unlike other Trolls in many important ways—most notably that he would interact with people without trying to kill them.

"Anything to report?" asked Gorm, clambering down a trail of rubble and stones.

Thane shook his head. "Nothing to speak of."

Gorm nodded. The monsters and villains that threatened the party came in two varieties: those that could detect a Troll well enough to steer clear of Thane, and those that quickly came to wish that they could.

"Come over here," the Troll urged, ushering Gorm around a piece of jutting granite that reinforced the fort's wall. "We're still visible from the gate."

Gorm looked at the tapering pass around the jutting stone and the sheer drop on the other side of it. "I can't believe we're still goin' through all this effort to keep ye hidden," he grumbled as he navigated around the ridge to privacy.

"You know I still can't show myself," Thane said.

"Why not?" Gorm barked. He always felt a little off-balance in talks about relationships, and the edge of a cliff was a bad place to be off-balance. "She knows you're there. She still stares out of camp at night. I hear her trying to talk to ye when she thinks nobody's listening. She can tell you're watchin' over us, Thane."

"She knows *something* is watching over you," Thane countered. "But to her, I am the King in the Wood. I am still as she imagines me to be." The Troll looked at his gnarled, hairy hands. "I doubt she'd be as happy with the truth."

"Stranger things have happened."

"Probably not many of them," countered Thane.

Gorm shrugged. "If a Troll can get all loopy over an Elf, I don't see why it can't be the other way around."

"Unfortunately, I can think of a few reasons," said Thane. He attempted to give Gorm a warm smile, and managed to not look too menacing. "Perhaps I'll show myself someday, but for now, keep my secret."

"I will," said Gorm. He looked out over the crags of the Highwalls and the baroque shadows they cast in the afternoon sun. "But I don't like it. How long are things between ye going to be this way? We've been travelin' together for over a year."

"It's been a rough year," said Thane. "There wasn't really a good time."

"There's never a good time to say ye've been keeping a big secret."

"Some times are worse than others," the Troll countered.

"Aye, but we don't have forever to choose from," said Gorm. "Parties of heroes don't stay together this long without a quest. Something always starts a fight, be it a spat over the best loot or a full-blown feud for party leadership. Fights become rifts, and then the party splits in two or three, or falls apart altogether."

"Surely it's not always like that," Thane said.

"It is often enough," said Gorm. "And that's assumin' you're on someone's payroll. We've been hunted like dogs by the guild, and even Burt is talking about the good old days of livin' in some poncy Elf's purse. Nobody's left yet, but it wouldn't take much."

"But after all you've been through together?" said Thane. "What of loyalty and friendship?"

"Not to put a tarnish on friendship, but a party of professional heroes is a group of well-paid killers for hire," said Gorm. "Every one of 'em's got their own agenda, their own dark past. And when all the secrets start comin' to light, parties split. And we can't split the party."

"You're not like that," insisted the Troll.

"Perhaps. We're a bit lighter on the killing, and we definitely ain't well paid," Gorm said. "But long kept secrets still have ways of doin' damage."

"You're worried that I'll divide them," said Thane, staring over the horizon.

"Party's already divided, in a way." said Gorm. "There's those of us who know you're a part of it, and those that don't. That's a crack in the armor. Folks are already grumblin'. The past year we've all been cold, hungry, and miserable, and they're starting to question why we're even out here chasing after the Guz'Varda when there ain't a Shadowkin on Arth who doesn't hate us. The whole party's like a tinderbox next to the fire. They catch me and Burt keeping ye from them, well, it'd be a big spark, if ye catch my drift."

"I see," said the Troll.

"An introduction, though... that might go better," Gorm suggested.

"I'll think on it," Thane said.

"Good. Things can't go on as they have been forever." Gorm let out a long sigh at the admission. "And on that note, I suppose I'd best get back to the party and give them the news."

The Troll raised a curious eyebrow. "The news?"

"Aye." Gorm looked across the valley below the Glens, to the distant forest and grasslands of southern Ruskan. "We're going south."

It seemed to Poldo that his situation was quickly deteriorating.

Moments after bowling him over, his furry assailant pinned the Scribkin's arm behind his back and dragged him behind one of Boulderfolk's ornate dumpsters. Small claws pressed into his cheeks as a hand, or perhaps a paw, pressed over his mouth. He attempted to speak, but the attacker twisted his arm even further behind his back. Poldo let out a muffled whimper instead.

"Quiet!" growled a somewhat feminine voice. "Or… or else!"

Another bout of shouting rang through the alleyway. "Where are you, mongrel!" bellowed a furious voice. "If I see you or your filthy kin in my alley again, I'll call the guild! They know what to do with your kind!"

Poldo heard the muffled commotion of someone kicking boxes, and then heavy, receding footsteps. A door slammed in the distance, leaving the Scribkin alone in the dark with his assailant. After a few minutes, she loosed her grip on his face.

"Madam, I-I-I don't want any trouble." Poldo's mouth forged ahead while his brain ran in panicked circles.

"Nobody ever wants any trouble," said the attacker. "But we've both stepped in it now."

"P-perhaps, but violence is never a-an acceptable answer, and there may be benefits to releasing me—"

"I never said anything about hurting anyone," Poldo's assailant tried to interrupt. "I just need a moment to think."

She didn't get one. Poldo's speech poured out in a continuous, nearly hysterical stream. "—monetary or otherwise. I am a Gnome of some means, you see, and if you do not harm me, I am sure I can make it worth your while. My name is Duine Poldo, and I—"

"Poldo?" She started at his name.

"Uh, yes. I have an office at Boulderfolk, which may tell you what kind of money we are dealing with—"

"Mr. Poldo of Goldson Baggs?"

"—although not as much as one might expect—what? Well, formerly of Goldson Baggs Group, yes," said Poldo. "I resigned a bit over a year ago, and in the meantime I—"

His attacker's demeanor brightened at the admission. She released his arm and spun him around, revealing a Gnoll so thin that she looked almost skeletal. She wore a motley collection of old rags that covered little of her fur, and the fur that showed was covered in mange. She covered her ears and much of her face with a headscarf fashioned from an old towel, through the fox-like muzzle protruding from the head wrap was clearly smiling.

"Mr. Poldo! You used to work with my husband! My name is Feista Hrurk!"

"A Mr. Hrurk? Ah, yes, I remember," said Poldo, recalling the Gnoll attendant. "He ran the lift in Goldson Baggs' central office."

Mrs. Hrurk's eyes lit up. "Yes, and he talked about you all the time! He was always going on about kind Mr. Poldo! He thought the world of you."

"Did he?" Poldo liked Hrurk well enough, and had regretted that the Gnoll quit after the incident with the Guz'Varda Tribe. Yet the Scribkin didn't recall being especially close to the lift operator.

"Oh yes! It seems like every day he'd mention you. 'Mr. Poldo said "hello" again today!' 'Mr. Poldo gave me a copper for a tip this evening.' Or 'Why can't they all be like Mr. Poldo? He's never kicked me once.'"

"I… I… Wait, surely people never kicked Mr. Hrurk," Poldo said, his apprehension draining away in his confusion.

"Yeah," said Mrs. Hrurk sadly. "Very often. Whenever they were having bad luck, it seemed. They had an expression for it."

"What? They never said anything like that to—" A memory sparked in Poldo's mind. "Oh, you mean 'kicking the dog?'"

The Gnoll's face seemed to become a little more brittle. "That's the one," she said.

"But that was just an expression," said Poldo. "You know, when Ur'Groom or Briggs or one of the lads in sales couldn't get to their numbers, they'd say 'I just need to kick the dog!' And then they'd step out for a break and… and…"

Somewhere in Poldo's mind a wall fell, and his stomach twisted when he saw the other side. "Oh gods," he said. "They were actually kicking someone?"

"Usually not that hard," said Mrs. Hrurk kindly. "And you never did. I think that's why he was always saying how nice Mr. Poldo is. Er, you are."

"Ah, good." Poldo felt like he had ingested something greasy. It was disturbing that he was remembered for only the slightest of courtesies, and all the more so that those slight courtesies still exceeded the average. "Where is Mr. Hrurk now, anyways?"

Mrs. Hrurk's eyes fell, and her tail drooped. "Oh, he's gone."

"Surely not… dead?" gasped Poldo.

"His papers were revoked for criminal activity," sighed Mrs. Hrurk. Her tail tucked beneath her legs. "So the guild… well, they did what they do."

"But… but how?" asked Poldo.

"We were hungry, and I… I sent Mr. Hrurk to sneak out to the baker shop—"

"They voided Hrurk's papers and killed him for stealing bread for his family?" cried Poldo.

"Oh, no, Mr. Poldo!" The Gnoll was equally appalled by the notion.

The Scribkin shook his head. "Oh, well, for a moment I—"

"He bought the bread, of course. We don't steal." The last words came out in a snarl, and Mrs. Hrurk's eyes burned.

For a moment, Poldo's mind flashed back to when he was a young boy in his family workshop, when his father had sat him down and told him that if nothing else, he could take pride in being a good person. Since then, he'd discovered that being a good person was the last resort of self-esteem.

In the upper echelons of Andarun's financial industry, people prided themselves on the name of the firm they worked for, the size of the deals they closed, the title on their business card, and anything else that could be quickly boiled down to a sum of gold. With so much to take pride in beyond integrity, many bankers put little stock in it. Yet standing behind a dumpster and clad in filthy rags, Mrs. Hrurk clung to her morals like a terrier to a postman's heel.

"I meant no offense, madam. But if I may, if not stealing, why were his papers revoked?"

"Oh, he jaywalked on his way home."

"What?"

"Yes, he was hurrying back. But the law says he should have used the crosswalk. So the heroes took his papers and then—" Mrs. Hrurk's voice caught in her throat.

"I'm so sorry," whispered Poldo.

"They took the bread, and the rest of our money as well." Mrs. Hrurk took a moment to wipe her eyes. "But, we get by. I can take as much food as I need from the dumpsters up here, as long as I'm not seen. And Mr. Hrurk lost his papers, but we still have ours."

Poldo was still reeling from the story of Hrurk's demise, so it took a moment for the Gnoll's last words to register. "Excuse me, did you say 'we'?"

The dumpster next to them suddenly rattled and shook. The lid lifted up just enough to allow three tiny snouts to pop out from the gap. Behind them, three pairs of eyes sparkled in the darkness. "Mama!" the pups cried. "Did you bring the food?"

"Hush, children! That wasn't the signal," said Mrs. Hrurk. "I'm talking to Mr. Poldo."

"But we're cold, Mama," whined a young Gnoll.

"It's warmer under the trash, my dears," said Mrs. Hrurk.

"But we're hungry, too!" said another pup.

Mrs. Hrurk gave Poldo an embarrassed nod as she stepped over to address the dumpster. "I couldn't get any food today. Maybe tomorrow!" she hissed to the pups from the side of her muzzle. "But there's plenty of cans and bottles to lick in there. That will tide you over."

"Buh I cuth mah tongue, mama!" whined one of the pups.

Poldo staggered back under the weight of the guilt pressing in. His old colleague's widow and her children were starving, and Poldo hadn't even realized Hrurk had died. No, not died. Hrurk had been murdered by the industry that gave Poldo his fortune. He felt like the air was being crushed from his lungs.

Mrs. Hrurk must have noticed his wheezing. "I'm sorry," she said. "Rex, close the dumpster! The smell is bothering poor Mr. Poldo."

"No! No, it's not the smell," gasped Poldo, struggling to compose himself.

"Well, you don't look well," said Mrs. Hrurk. "Do you need to leave? If you need to leave, can you please promise to not tell anyone we're staying here? If they find out I'm trespassing, they'll take our papers—"

"You cannot live in the trash," Poldo managed to say.

"Please, Mr. Poldo!" Fear crept into Mrs. Hrurk's voice. "If not for us, do it for Mr. Hrurk!"

"You misunderstand me, madam," said Poldo. "You must come with me. We'll get you some food for a start. I believe there's a cart that sells Ten-Penny beef rolls in the park down the street."

"You're buying us beef rolls?" the Gnoll asked, clearly perplexed.

"For a start," said Poldo firmly. "Afterward, we'll see about some clothes, and then we'll discuss what comes next."

"Mr. Poldo," said Mrs. Hrurk. "Please, you don't have to do all of that."

Poldo looked up at the children peering curiously out of the dumpster, and in their faces he saw the features of a kind lift attendant who apparently thought the world of any manager who gave him as much respect as a wall fixture. "But I must, Mrs. Hrurk. I truly must."

Truth and free will were usually the domain of Arth's philosophers and priests, who liked to focus on the Big Questions. The scientists of Arth, by contrast, dedicated themselves to the Smaller-But-More-Immediately-Useful Questions, or at least the Quickly-Profitable-Especially-If-You're-Not-Too-Stodgy-About-Ethics Questions. Yet for millennia, Arth's Gnomes maintained a tradition of philosopher-scientists, high-minded individuals who sought to comprehend the essential nature of being, to answer the deepest mysteries of the universe, and to wrestle those truths into mathematical equations.

Greatest among them was the Fifth-Age philosopher-scientist Nove, best known for his work on expectations and reality. Nove's research posited that reality is partially comprised of irony in its various forms. The exact ratio of irony to matter in the universe is known as Nove's Constant, and by definition it's more than you'd expect.

It's well-established that expectations and timing shape perception, and that perception shapes reality. But it was Nove who originally inverted these ideas to posit that perception and expectations could change the timing of events. His first principle of universal irony was expressed as a long formula that involves Nove's Constant, the number of people sharing an understanding, and the amount of time in which an event disturbing that understanding would be surprising.

For the common layperson, however, it was easier to remember that the universe had a nasty sense of timing, and it was best not to voice certain thoughts out loud. People avoided statements like, "It can't be that bad," "Just one probably won't hurt," or, "Well, the native population's been drinking it for centuries, and they don't seem to mind it." While skeptics were quick to point out that a reasonable person would hardly expect a turn of phrase to alter the course of fate, proponents of Nove's work were equally quick to note that was exactly the problem.

Thus it was that Gorm's party was embroiled in controversy as they trudged through the ruined gates of the Glens.

"All I said was that things are looking up," snapped Jynn.

"Yes, and now you keep saying it," Heraldin growled. The ancient, headless skeleton pinned to the Glens' wall rattled in an unfelt wind as he stepped out of the fortress. "Have you never heard of the philosopher Nove?"

"I've heard of him, read his work, and seen it debunked. And even if it was true," Jynn spoke up to head off any argument, "The fact remains that his teachings are impractical to the point of uselessness. It's impossible to avoid saying everything that might ironically precede an event."

"You can reduce your chances," said Kaitha. "You just have to speak a little more carefully."

"Why?" demanded the wizard, stopping at the edge of the ruined gate. "It took us weeks to convince Gorm to head south! Do you think poor wording will alter our course at this point?"

"Gods!" said Kaitha. "There you go again!"

"Perhaps if you stop saying things like that, we'll have the pleasure of not finding out!" snapped Heraldin.

Gaist nodded.

"Are we all really that superstitious?" Jynn stared at the other heroes in turn. "Yes? All living in the prior age? Very well. I'll speak no more."

"Thank you," said Heraldin.

The wizard shook his head. "All I really meant to say is that anybody would be glad to be leaving these mountains and this gods-forsaken fort. I'm sure all the poor souls manning the walls would agree, if they weren't ashes at the bottom of the Orcs' pyres."

"Well, they're not ashes." Burt stuck his head out from Gorm's rucksack.

"What?" said Heraldin.

"He said they were ashes," said the Kobold with a shrug. "But the thing about Orcish pyres is that they're for Orcs. They don't burn their enemies."

Jynn scratched his beards. "Fine, the Goblin pyres—"

"Goblins and Kobolds don't burn their enemies either," said Burt. "Least, not after they're dead. I know the Stone Blood Tribe likes to use flaming arrows and burning oil traps—"

"None of ye Shadowkin burn your foes?" Gorm asked.

"Of course not," said Burt. "We leave 'em intact for their families to come back and take care of. I mean, after we nick some skulls and teeth for trophies, mind."

"You expect the widows and widowers and orphans to come back right after you killed everyone in the area and mutilated their corpses?" said Laruna.

"Well, yeah." The Kobold was getting a bit defensive. "It's not like we'd hurt them or anything while they're burying the dead!"

The solamancer shook her head. "How would they know that?"

"I don't know!" Burt's hackles were up. "We all just know, all right? It's culture. Shared experience and all that. You don't burn other peoples' dead. There are no Lightlings in those pyres!"

"Well then, where are the bodies?" wondered Heraldin.

Gorm whirled around, prompting a yelp of protest from the Kobold on his back. "Wait. Ye didn't find the remains of any defenders?"

Heraldin held his hands out. "Did you see any corpses lying around the courtyard?"

"No, but I was searching out here!" said Gorm. "I thought ye found 'em tucked away in a back room or something."

"Did you really think the Red Horde tidies up and tucks away the dead in a back room?" Jynn asked. "Maybe they swept and dusted on their way out, too?"

"Or the defenders made a desperate last stand in the keep!" snapped Gorm.

"It doesn't really matter," said Kaitha. "The problem is there aren't any bodies around."

An unpleasant silence fell over the party.

Gorm felt a chill run up his spine as he stood in the still mountain air. "Also," he said slowly, "there ain't any wind."

"Right," said Heraldin.

"If there ain't any wind, what's making them bones move?" said Gorm, pointing.

The heroes turned to the rattling skeleton hanging from the gate. The bones twitched and shook as though blown by a breeze that wasn't there, or perhaps as though trying to extricate the spear pinning it to the wall without the benefit of arms.

"It wants to get down," said Kaitha.

"But where does it want to go?" asked Jynn.

"I know one way to find out," said Gorm. He signaled to Gaist, who reached up with a thick arm and yanked the spear from the stone.

The headless skeleton dropped to the ground and crumpled into a pile of bones, then immediately set about the laborious process of righting itself. Upon regaining its footing, it hopped up and down a couple of times, as if testing its legs, and set off at a brisk march down the mountain path.

"I have a bad feeling about this," said Heraldin.

"Ye have a bad feeling about everything," Gorm replied.

"And I'm usually right," said the bard, watching the bones jaunt away.

"It might be warranted in this case," Laruna said. "We don't know where the skeleton is going."

"There's still only one way to find out." Gorm adjusted his rucksack.

"I'd actually suggest that we don't want to be wherever the walking dead go," said Heraldin.

"What I want is to know what's got a set of old bones so lively," said Gorm. "Could be a simple haunting, but it could be much worse."

"Whatever it is, if there's a serious undead threat nearby, it's best to know about it," agreed Kaitha. "Even if for no other reason than to avoid it."

The Dwarf nodded. "Or warn nearby towns."

"Now, hang on! This isn't what we discussed!" protested the bard.

"Sure it is. We said we'd help people if they need it. We're open to new paths, after all. Saving innocents is a passion, right?" Gorm set off down the path after the skeleton. "Come on. Them bones are movin' faster than they should be."

"They shouldn't be moving at all!" Heraldin called after his back. "That's the problem!"

Jynn stepped up next to the bard. "For the record, I'd like to say this was a coincidence."

"Noted," said Heraldin. "Let the record also show that you were supposed to stop talking."

The wizard's lips pulled into a thin line as he started off.

"At least it's heading south," said Laruna. "For all we know, the skeleton will take us closer to the High Coast anyway."

"Oof," said Kaitha, clutching her belly as she jogged to catch up. "I wouldn't have eaten so much if I'd known I was going to head out on a run right away."

"You didn't eat much at all," said Laruna.

"Yeah," said Kaitha. "But I'm still regretting those last couple bites of… stew."

"I regretted the first one," Jynn muttered as the party followed the skeleton away from the Glens.

"Ha! Leaves a bad taste in one's mouth, doesn't it, sire?" laughed Johan the Mighty, Champion of Tandos. The paladin's ornate golden armor shimmered in the lantern light, and one of his hands rested easily on the hilt of a massive sword. The other gauntlet held a small fluted glass filled with yellow-green liquid.

Handor set his own drink down and tried to maintain his composure as the foulness bubbled down his throat. "What was that, by the bones?" he asked once he could convince his tongue to move again.

"A Tarapin Topspin, Majesty," said the waiter. "Shall I bring you something else?"

"I should think not." Handor wiped his tongue with a napkin. "I doubt I could survive another one of your excursions to the bar."

The waiter blanched and hurried on to the other linen-lined tables in the room.

"I tell you, Johan, it's amazing what people will subject themselves to." The king's mouth twisted into an involuntary grimace as he eyed the paladin's Tarapin Topspin.

"Ha! Right you are, sire. Case in point." Johan waved out across the assembly.

Colorful sprites danced amid the lanterns hanging from the rafters of the Temple of Tandos' feasting hall. The great expanse was decorated with all the trappings of a ballroom. Andarun's elite had come out in force, wearing their finest suits and most impressive hats. Banners dangling over the affair bore the name and emblem of the Freedlands Blightworm Foundation.

"Indeed." Handor popped a trout pastry into his mouth. "Gods, the things we'll do for charity. At least this is to eradicate blightworm."

"Or save it," said the paladin. "The pamphlet's never quite clear."

"I thought blightworm was a wasting disease?"

"Yes, caused by a parasite of the same name. Perhaps it's endangered? Or maybe they want it that way." The paladin shook his head. "I'm never sure what we're supporting."

"That's how the foundations like things," grumbled the King. "A banquet here, a cocktail hour there, donations every which way. It's all a lot of chances to rub elbows and talk business, and nobody ever knows enough about the problem to tell if they're solving it."

"Ha! Well, on that note, it is a good place to talk," said Johan. "We're to meet in the vestry by the southern apse. Shall we do the rounds?"

"I suppose we must." Handor nodded and, with a deep breath, launched himself into the tide of people who were both important and self-important to varying degrees: nobles, executives, heroes, merchants, traders, guild leaders, and more. The evening became a whirlwind of shaking hands, exchanging pleasantries, expressing sympathies, and making excuses to dart on to the next guest. It was late by the time he and Johan extricated themselves from the gala and made their way down the winding stone passages of Tandos' temple to a small room.

Johan knocked three times at the door, then kicked it in. "Ha ha! Hello, fellows!"

Fenrir Goldson, Bolbi Baggs, and Weaver Ortson were seated around a small table that had several bottles and glasses scattered over it. They inclined their heads in deference and held drinks up in salute as Handor entered. "What's on the agenda tonight?" the king asked. "Aside from a real drink, I mean."

"We're to report on revenue from heroic activities around Shadowkin dens, Majesty," Fenrir Goldson poured out a finger of rum and handed the tumbler to Handor. The ancient Dwarf held up a small ledger bound in dark leather. "Shall we go over the figures?"

"They're very good, sire," chimed in Weaver Ortson, raising his glass into the air. As Grandmaster of the Heroes' Guild, Ortson's analysis of heroic activities were invariably optimistic, and all the more so while he was sampling this year's vintages.

"Let's start there," said Handor, settling back in a yew and velvet chair as Goldson read a litany of sums and percentages. Things were generally looking up, especially stock prices on the Wall, which explained the broad grins on the faces of the other occupants of the small, dimly lit room.

Long ago, before Handor graduated from prince to king, he had imagined ruling as mostly sitting on a throne and making wise-sounding proclamations. Now that Handor was old enough to possess some wisdom, he realized that wise-sounding proclamations were for pacifying the masses. The actual business of ruling was exactly that: business. Revenues and expenses, inflows and outflows, policies and addendums, and all of it done in smoke-filled rooms far from prying eyes and listening ears. Things had been done that way for generations when Handor took the throne, and the only change he'd made to the process was a partially successful effort to cut down on the smoke.

When he'd heard enough about loot appraisals and plunder fund dividends, he raised a hand to silence Goldson. "Overall, it sounds like the numbers are very good," he said. "Though I suspect you're about to tell me why they're not good enough."

The Dwarf and the Halfling glanced at each other, and then turned back to Handor with the same simpering smile plastered across their faces. "We prefer to say there's still more opportunity, sire," said Baggs.

"Oh, lots more!" agreed Ortson, whose enthusiasm was generally proportional to his intemperance.

"There's growth on the Wall, to be sure, but we've still yet to see the hiring and purchases that really move an economy," said Goldson.

"And the taxman is taking money right out of the hands of businesses who would spend it on jobs, sire," said Baggs.

"It's preventing the prosperity that the Wall has enjoyed from spreading to the common man," said Goldson.

Handor rested his cheek on his hand. "Somehow, something always is."

"Think of it this way, Majesty." Baggs set a glass in front of himself and pointed to it. "The Wall expects a certain amount of performance out of us, correct? Meeting projections and raising shareholder value and the like." He started pouring from a bottle of Whitegeld red. "We are doing well at the moment. The gold is flowing in."

"But the Wall expected that," said Goldson.

Baggs nodded. "Exactly. Until we exceed expectations, we'll have no funds to give raises or hire new workers. Now, if the giltin were to flow in a bit faster, because of a tax cut, for example…" The Halfling tipped the bottle up and poured the rest of it out, allowing some of the wine to spill over the edge. "Then we would have the funds to spare for the people. If we truly want to help the people, our cups must run over, so to speak."

"Oh? I never liked trickle-down economics," said Ortson, watching the crimson wine drip down the glass. "It implies that there's a leak somewhere."

"Get a hold of yourself, Weaver," Goldson snapped.

The king ignored the guildmaster. "It seems to me," he said to Goldson and Baggs, "that your problem is that you've too large a cup. However, proclaiming a tax hike could help investors with their unrealistic expectations."

Baggs blanched. "But… but sire! We speak only of concern for the people."

"Then hire more of them," snarled Handor. "Or donate to the temples of Fulgen and Oppo."

"If only we could, sire," simpered Goldson. "But that would hurt our profits, and thus our stock price."

"And our primary responsibility is to our shareholders," added Baggs. "As we said, the Wall has expectations."

"Well, gentlemen, it is an enviable thing to be afforded concern for the people with no responsibility to them," said Handor, settling back in his seat. He sipped at his glass of spirits. "You and your shareholders are doing better than most of my subjects."

"Perhaps, sire, but we don't know how long that will last," Goldson confessed.

"It's true that our industry has seen growth since many of the Freedlands' noncombatant paper carriers returned to the wilds," said Baggs.

"For now." Goldson raised a hand. "With all of those Shadowkin getting their papers revoked or turning them in, there's money to be made at the moment. But the Orcs and Goblins won't last more than a few years."

"If that," said Baggs. "And even in the short term, it's not enough to drive hiring. The Shadowkin leaving the NPC program may be driving good pillage-quest-loot cycles, but we can't scale that up."

"So you're saying it's not sustainable," said Handor.

"We're saying that to really grow the economy again, the professional heroics industry needs a sudden increase in revenue or a sudden drop in expenses. Such as a cut in our taxes," said Goldson.

"That cannot happen, Mr. Goldson," said Handor. "I suggest you look elsewhere for a sudden source of revenue. Perhaps your heroes could finally get around to killing the Dragon of Wynspar."

At the mention of the dragon, Weaver Ortson sprayed a mouthful of wine across the cherrywood table. "B-but sire," the fat man sputtered. "N-nobody has slain a d-dragon since the last age."

"Even if someone could slay the monster, it wouldn't do much good," said Baggs, grimacing as he cleaned the guildmaster's wine from his spectacles. "Investors consider shares of the dragon's hoard as good as gold. While it may be a boon to some firms if all that equity was suddenly liquid, it wouldn't add much to the bottom line."

"No," said Goldson, nodding. "We need a new threat. Something more dangerous than the Red Horde. Anything less won't capture enough loot to drive the heroics business forward."

"It almost sounds like you're wishing calamity on the people you're so concerned about," said Handor.

"Oh, not at all sire," said Goldson.

"We're wishing a near miss on them," said Baggs. "A threat of calamity, stopped by our fine heroes just before it harms the Freedlands."

"And just after we've cashed in," said Goldson. "Ah, but we cannot count on such a boon coming anytime soon."

"Barring another opportunity like Bloodroot, I'm afraid we must seek ways to cut expenses," said Baggs. "We were hoping by about three percent."

Handor pursed his lips. The mention of the Guz'Varda Tribe brought some unfinished business to mind. "Speaking of Bloodroot and the Red Horde, have we tied up all the loose ends after the Elven Marbles?"

Goldson and Baggs exchanged concerned looks. Johan's grin seemed somehow diminished, if only by a fraction.

"Almost, Your Majesty," said Baggs.

Handor scowled. "And by 'almost,' you mean to say that you haven't tracked down those rubes from the Heroes' Guild?"

Ortson feigned a cough. "Formerly of the Heroes' Guild," he interjected.

"Gorm Ingerson may be washed up, but he's no rube, sire," said Johan. "On the contrary, he's quite dangerous."

"Especially given what he knows," said Handor dryly.

"Yes, sire. Quite so," said the paladin.

"Nobody questions the threat Ingerson poses," agreed Baggs. "But we are in a difficult situation. As you know, the Pyrebeard and his cohorts intercepted one of our agents last year."

Goldson nodded. "They already have too much evidence of our company's involvement with the unpleasantness at Bloodroot."

"Which is why we've had to take extra precautions when hiring… problem-solving specialists," said Baggs. "We can't create another paper trail."

"What we can't have, gentlemen, is continued excuses," growled the king. "I don't want to hear about your recruiting practices. I want to hear that Gorm Ingerson and company are dead."

"You will, Majesty," said Baggs.

"Have faith, sire," said Goldson. "We're sparing no expense to see the matter resolved."

"Good," said Handor. "Once that unpleasantness is behind us, we can turn our attention back to our mutual success."

"I'll drink to that." Baggs raised his glass.

"And I'll drink, too," said Ortson, slurring the obvious.

"To what?" asked Johan.

"To just about anything, it seems," grumbled Goldson.

"Ha ha!" Johan's laughter was like a trumpet as he raised a goblet of wine.

"To success," said Handor, holding up his tumbler.

Chapter 3

"Just one sip," Kaitha murmured to herself as she rummaged through her pack. She'd been waiting for the right moment since she'd looted the tiny vial of salve from the footlocker in the Glens. The timing was a tricky matter; she needed to find an opportunity when none of the other adventurers would notice her absence, and yet she also needed to find such a moment before the burning in her wrists forced her to claw her bracers off.

Caution had won the day, but now it was the dead of night. It was time to scratch the itch. Time to let her hair down. Seriously time to find the thrice-cursed bottle of elixir.

Kaitha felt her desperation rising as her fingers probed the recesses of her pack and found them empty. She dug through her belt pouches just to be safe, and when those came up empty, she even tried overturning her Poor Man's Quiver. A steady stream of enchanted arrows fell out of the magical quiver, one by one, but there was no sign of a potion. "Bones!" she swore. "How is this possible?"

Some adventurers had problems with healing potions. Drinking elixir closed wounds and rejuvenated the dying, but careless users developed crippling addictions to the amber liquid. Kaitha knew she didn't have that problem, because unlike the average salve-head, she could stop whenever she wanted to. Her current problem was that she didn't quite want to stop yet, but she also couldn't seem to keep her hands on any healing potions.

The ranger's elixir supply had been suspiciously scarce for the past year. She procured small caches on several occasions throughout their travels, secretly buying the healing potions from the odd tinker caravan or snagging one from a cache of loot. Yet it seemed that whenever she got her hands on any salve, the potions went missing before she could use them. Equally frustrating, whenever someone else was injured or Kaitha needed a kick so bad she got the shakes, a bottle mysteriously appeared.

Kaitha was fairly sure the other heroes were oblivious to the salve management issues, mostly because she'd been searching through their packs as well. But there was nobody else around to take the potions. Except...

The ranger turned and looked into the alpine forest, dotted with the great, gray boulders that littered the base of the Highwalls. It occurred to her that perhaps the King in the Wood had expanded into pharmaceutical management.

"Is it you?" she said. "Are you... I mean, do you see it when I... I...?"

A wave of embarrassment washed over Kaitha, though she couldn't say if the shame was at the prospect of the watcher in the forest seeing her taking kicks of elixir, or just because she was standing in the woods at midnight whispering to trees. People said that salve withdrawal could addle the brain, but Kaitha knew she wasn't hooked that bad. She was fairly certain, anyway.

"Are you really out there?" she asked the woods. "Sometimes even I don't think you are."

The silence vindicated her doubts.

"I... I want you to be," Kaitha added, stepping toward a mossy stump. "I want you to be real."

She pulled the pewter figurine of Davon Royalheart from her pack and set it on the pocked and rotting wood. The toy knight seemed alone in the shadows of the trees towering over them.

"I just wanted you to know that," she said, a little louder.

For a time she stood by the figurine, waiting—hoping—for a response that never came. After a while she sat down on a nearby log. Her mind wandered to other things, such as the fact that she may not have searched the leftmost pouch in her pack as thoroughly as the others.

She had only been rummaging through her bags for a few moments when she felt something akin to the memory of a breeze, and she caught an earthy scent that brought her to the garden in the

Myrewood. She looked up, unsure of what she'd see, but sure that she'd see something.

She was wrong. The forest was empty.

Kaitha's initial disappointment faded as she leapt up and ran to the mossy stump. A quick check around its base confirmed that the figurine of Davon Royalheart hadn't merely fallen over the edge or down a crack. Someone had taken the toy. The King in the Wood was here, and he had let her know. It wasn't what she was hoping for, but somehow it was enough to sweep away some of her loneliness and take the edge off the burning need for a kick of elixir.

She scanned the woods a moment longer, searching for any sign of movement in the moonlight. Then she whispered her thanks, picked up her bag, and made her way back to camp. It was well past time to sleep.

Laruna awoke to the sound of a dropped pot. Days at the camp began before dawn's first light, when the world was still a blue-gray haze of mist and twilight. She snorted irritably and crawled from her bedroll.

A wreath of flame surrounded her as she broke down her tent. The sorcerous fire helped ward off the both the cloying chill in the air and the friendly salutations of those companions who were better adjusted to early mornings on long marches. Laruna didn't understand how Gorm and Kaitha could smile at this hour, especially given their bizarre traveling companion.

The skeletal torso was in the center of the camp, or more accurately, the camp was arranged around the spot where Gaist had staked it to the ground with the ancient spear. Despite the skeleton's best efforts at locomotion, it couldn't do more than run in place with the old weapon stuck through its ribcage and into the frozen earth. Now the undead torso sulked where it was pegged to the ground, unmoving save for the occasional half-hearted kick at anyone who got too close.

Kaitha trapped and cooked a wild hare for breakfast, and most of the party gathered around a small cookfire as the meat sizzled and popped in the skillet. Jynn, however, sat a ways away from the others, watching the first beams of sunlight leak in through the pine needles above. He might have appeared meditative or thoughtful to the other heroes, but Laruna knew better.

"What's wrong?" she asked, joining the noctomancer on the edge of camp.

Jynn's icy blue eyes flicked to the solamancer, then returned to the glowing canopy above them. "This is our third day marching with the skeleton."

"For a pile of old bones, it sets a tough pace," said Laruna. "And I've been sick of marching since the day we sold the horses."

"I'm not tired. I've gotten used to walking after all these months," said Jynn. "No, I'm worried."

Laruna nodded. "Me too. It's been too far."

Dark magics or curses could give the dead of Arth a renewed outlook on life, though one from a hostile perspective. Fortunately for the living, however, the creation of the undead was limited to a certain geographic distance around their source. Heroes often gauged the nature of undead threats by the total area afflicted with the curse; the larger the radius of walking corpses, the more powerful the threat at the center.

Laruna had never been one for geometry, but in this case, it was regrettably easy to do the math.

"If it was a simple haunting, we'd have found the site by the first day," said Jynn. "We'd have found signs of a necromancer or a wight by now. But to call the dead from this far…" Jynn shook his head. "It's a liche."

"Probably. But we still don't know that it's your father," said Laruna.

"True enough. Though I wonder if having two liches active would really be any better."

"Good point." Laruna shuddered at the idea. "But we knew all of this last night. What are you doing out here this morning?"

The noctomancer shrugged. "I'm just trying to, you know, pack some emotions."

"You mean unpack them," Laruna corrected.

"Uh, no." The wizard looked at her as if she had just channeled noctomancy. "I meant pack them."

"You're packing your emotions," the solamancer said flatly.

"Yes!" Jynn sounded a little irritated. "You take all of the things that hurt, you put them in a box, and you set the box on a shelf in the back of your mind."

Laruna was at a loss for words. "That… that is not a healthy way to deal with things."

"It's served me well enough," said Jynn. "How do you handle pain and loss?"

"I take whatever anger and sadness I've got and let it all out. Usually as fire." Laruna thought for a moment. "And preferably in the direction of the problem."

"Yes, well, some things don't burn," said Jynn.

"Maybe." Laruna raised her hand and clenched it into a fist, igniting a nearby rock. "But I haven't come across any yet."

"Yes, well, you can't set fire to the past, though." Jynn watched the stone melt to slag. "And you can't set fire to my father. I watched you try."

"Well, if at first you don't succeed…" said Laruna.

"It isn't that simple," said the wizard with a bitter laugh. "You define my father as his work, his deeds in the Agekeepers' histories. But not me. I remember him bouncing me on his knee and playing horse. I remember how long he wept when Mother died. I remember him buying me a puppy to help me feel better. I remember him comforting me when Patches ran away. I remem-remember days and days of training. And though he was harsh, I remember learning from him."

"Harsh? He was cruel to you," said Laruna.

"He… he wanted me to figure things out." The wizard's eyes glazed over. "He'd leave me clues and prod me to put them together. He was trying to make me think for myself, see the big picture."

"That doesn't excuse what he did to you."

"This is what I'm talking about." Jynn sighed. "To you and the bards, he was nothing but a villain. You see everything he did through that lens. But I lived those stories, and I know better than anyone that history is nothing but the collected lies society tells itself. To me, Detarr Ur'Mayan was a father, and I spent my entire adult life believing he and I were wronged. When the guild brought their false charges and Johan killed him, I thought the world had turned against an innocent man."

The noctomancer extinguished the flames on the stone with a gust of wind.

"But the day that we met Father in the Ashen Tower, that all fell apart," he said softly. "Wronged souls don't come back as liches, Laruna. Ghosts and wights, maybe, but to become a liche takes preparation, great expense, and dark deeds. By the time Johan stormed the tower, Father had already... well, he..."

"Detarr was already prepared to become a liche," Laruna finished for him.

Jynn nodded. "The last rite in the path to lichedom is to die," he said. "Of course, I can understand why Father was willing to postpone that step as long as possible."

"So, Johan just accelerated his plans?" asked Laruna.

"That particular plan," said Jynn. "He slowed down Father's work on the Leviathan Project and foiled the scheme to wed me to Marja for influence. But most importantly, Johan slew an evil wizard that day. The legends and songs I grew up hating were right. Johan was a hero. And what does that make me? The apprentice of a necromancer? The accomplice of a dark wizard?"

Laruna fought back an urge to throw her arms around the noctomancer, to hold him tightly and whisper what she thought he was. But those days had passed, and now all she could do was rest a hand gently on his shoulder and say, "It doesn't matter what we were. All that matters is who we are going forward."

He gave her a smile that never touched his blue eyes as he stood. "A nice thought," he said. "But to move forward, I need to set my past aside. I have to pack it away."

"You can't keep all these feelings bottled up forever," Laruna protested. "They're going to come out again, and probably in a bad way. What if that happens when we face your father?"

Jynn looked to the southeast, his eyes following the path of the skeletal torso's perpetual march. "If it is Father, he's had plenty of time to work, access to many corpses, and magic beyond even our knowing," he said. "The goal will be to not face him."

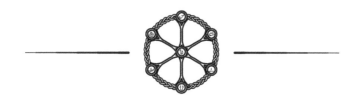

"Yes, well, circumstances change and plans are adapted," said Poldo.

"Indeed," Mr. Fitch murmured absently as he looked at the paintings that festooned the walls of Poldo's tiny office. "Well, whatever the reason, I'm glad you decided to set up this meeting."

"As am I," said Poldo, arranging the chairs around his desk. The tiny garden shed that served as his office consisted of a single room divided neatly in two; one half was filled with tools and gardening implements, and the other with a small wood stove and a desk set next to a window. Each wall sported two windows, but they afforded little light. The windows on the shed side were two feet from the Commons' brick wall, and those by Poldo's desk sat just as close to the topiary.

"I have to say, Poldo, this office isn't as bad as I'd imagined," mused Fitch. "It's warm enough, maybe even cozy. And much cleaner than I expected."

A slight smile twisted Poldo's thick mustache. "Thank you. I must confess it's much cleaner now than a couple of days ago. I brought on a new housekeeper just after I last met with you."

The Scribkin poured a pitcher of chilled milk into a fine Elven bowl. The office looked almost respectable after Mrs. Hrurk's nocturnal efforts. His apartment back on the fifth tier was spotless as well, aside from the makeshift servants' quarters he'd set up in the guest room. And they were as clean as a room housing three young children could be, which was not at all.

"Still got that Domovoy infestation though, huh?" asked Fitch.

"Hm? Oh, yes," said Poldo, setting the bowl of milk on the shelf.

"You know, I know of a rat-catcher—"

"Ha ha! What an amusing, if somewhat distasteful, joke!" said Poldo loudly, glaring at Fitch as he dashed across the room to the Halfling. "Look," he said in a hushed voice. "The Wood Gnomes are harmless provided you respect a few simple customs, and chief among those customs is to not propose massacring Wood Gnomes."

"If you say so," said Fitch, sliding into his chair. "I just don't know why you'd put up with their nonsense rules."

Poldo sighed and looked up into the open rafters of the shed, where he knew someone was probably watching from the darkness. He'd found the feeling unsettling until recently, but empathy has a way of spreading. Since the Scribkin had hired a Gnoll to work in his home, he had found himself thinking of the Wood Gnome's perspective as well.

"Oh, I suspect that if I fit neatly under a shoe, I'd be much more keen on people knocking at doors or looking around the room before tramping about. Once you get used to their laws, they do a good job of keeping rats and other pests at bay. It's not a bad arrangement, provided things stay civil," he added.

"I'll take your word for it," shrugged Fitch, pulling a gold pocket watch from his waistcoat. "Regardless, Mr. Stearn should arrive shortly. I've never known him to be—" Fitch was interrupted by a single, forceful knock at the door. The Halfling grinned. "That sounds like him now."

Poldo opened the door to greet a mountain in a black suit. Mr. Stearn, though clearly Human, was almost as large as an Ogre. His rust-colored hair was unkempt, with sideburns so long they were halfway to a beard. His heavy-lidded eyes stared down at Poldo from beneath thick eyebrows, and below his large, round nose was a smile that looked neither friendly nor sincere.

"Hello. I am Cain Stearn," he growled in a thick, northern Ruskan accent.

Poldo stood mutely in the doorway. The mere presence of the huge man triggered some ancient defense mechanism in the primordial depths of his brain, and he froze like a mouse hiding from a predator. With his higher brain functions thus impaired, Poldo reverted to his most basic instinct.

He pulled a business card from his waistcoat and extended it.

Mr. Stearn plucked the card from Poldo's hand and tucked it into his suit's pocket without so much as glancing at it. Instead, he pointed a meaty finger at the plaque on Poldo's door. "Pardon my rudeness, Mr. Poldo, but sign is saying Silver Guard Securities. Do you have much silver on the premises?"

Poldo's jaw flapped up and down for a moment as ages of civilization beat back the primeval urge to flee. "I beg your pardon?" he managed.

Mr. Stearn bent down to get closer to Poldo's eye level. "Silver. Do you have many silver things in this…" He glanced at Poldo's desk and the adjacent storage area filled with garden tools. "…Ahem, office? I must ask this because of my condition."

"Your condition?"

"Lycanthropy," said Fitch, brushing past Poldo and out the door. "Probably best if we meet on the terrace. It'd be a little cramped in here anyway."

"Yes. Is good idea," agreed Mr. Stearn, following Fitch up the dirt path.

"Wait—lycanthropy?" said Poldo, rushing to catch up with the pair.

"A mild case," said Mr. Stearn. "Not bad. Mostly not contagious."

"Surely," said Poldo, forcing a smile. "Would you excuse us for a moment?" He grabbed Fitch's shoulder and dropped back a few paces along the path.

"You arranged a meeting with a werewolf?" Poldo whispered to Fitch once Mr. Stearn was well ahead of them.

"Of course not!" said Fitch. "I'd never sully your business—or mine—by dealing with one of those monsters."

"Ah. Good," said Poldo with a relieved smile. "For a moment I thought you were serious about the lycanthropy."

"Oh, I was. Mr. Stearn is a werebear," said Fitch.

The Scribkin tripped over his own feet. "I fail to see how that's any different," he hissed at the Halfling as he righted himself. "Werebears still transform into insensate beasts every full moon, right? They both have the same fangs, the same razor-sharp claws, the same furry complexion—"

"Is very different," said Mr Stearn, turning back to Poldo.

"The same remarkable hearing," Fitch said with a pointed glare at the Scribkin.

"Oh, dear." Poldo could feel a deep blush rising in his cheeks. "Mr. Stearn, I am so sorry—"

"Werewolf is totally different from werebear," said Mr. Stearn, barreling through the conversation with no concern for the other half of it.

"Oh?" asked Poldo.

"Yes," said Mr. Stearn. "Werewolf is bad. Eats farm animals. Attacks many people. Kills for sport. Very bad. But werebear is different."

Poldo waited for Mr. Stearn's supporting arguments, but the lycanthrope just stood there with his broad, lazy smile and nodded slowly at the Gnome. "Because werebears don't do those things?" Poldo ventured.

Mr. Stearn considered the question. "Not for sport," he said.

"But—"

"Come. We will tell you of my CTOs, and we will both make many fortunes," said Mr. Stearn. He resumed his steady plodding down the path to the Boulderfolk Commons terrace, apparently satisfied that the matter was settled.

"Trust me," said Fitch. "If you want to get those numbers moving in the right direction, you need to talk to the right people. And Mr. Stearn is the right person today. It'll be fine."

Poldo wanted to turn around, but there was nothing for him back at his desk save a threatening letter from the offices of Goldson Baggs. "Very well," he said. "Lead on."

They found a private spot at the back of the Terrace Cafe, near a pond stocked with a school of golden fish and a pair of Undines. Fitch ordered a pot of exotic teas and a platter of lemon cakes for the meeting.

"Now," said Mr. Stearn as they settled in. "You are familiar with threat indexes?"

"Of course," said Poldo. Anyone in finance was intimate with threat indexes—numerical representation of how much danger the cities and nations faced from monsters, villains, and other hazards. The Heroes' Guild published threat indexes for every town, landmark, city, and nation on Arth, and they were used for everything from calculating insurance rates to issuing travel advisories.

"Good, good," said Stearn. "Then what do you know of threat obligations?"

"When I worked at Goldson Baggs, the insurance people used to mention them from time to time," Poldo recalled. "But I can't say I'm familiar."

"Is fine. I will explain." Mr. Stearn pulled a crisp, white notepad and a pencil from the pocket of his coat. He drew a few simple houses on the pad, and then a stick figure with a club next to it. "When monster attacks city, is very expensive for insurance company, yes? Many claims, many policies must be paid. So insurance company buys threat obligation from Heroes' Guild for city. Usually five-year term, with fixed payment every month." The lycanthrope wrote in thick, boxy letters next to the city: "5 YEARS—100 G PER MONTH."

"I see," said Poldo.

Mr. Stearn tapped the city with his pencil. "Now Heroes' Guild is obligated to keep the threat index for city low. So if more monsters appear…" He quickly scribbled on a couple more fanged creatures around the city. "Then Heroes' Guild must pay anyone with obligation for this city a large sum, and insurance company can pay for damage monsters cause."

"It's basically insurance for the insurance company," said Poldo.

"Oh no," said Fitch. "It's not insurance."

"Well I don't see how it's any different," said Poldo.

"Insurance is heavily regulated," said Mr. Stearn.

"Ha! What Mr. Stearn meant to say," Fitch said with enunciation sharpened to a point, "is that insurance is old. Stable. Boring. Threat obligations are ripe for financial innovation. And that's where Mr. Stearn comes in. He's a financial genius."

Poldo looked up at Mr. Stearn, who was still wearing the same ursine grin. "Insurance very restricted," said the werebear. "Only licensed companies issue it, and only for certain things, and only for what they are worth. But I discover that anyone can issue threat obligation, for any amount, for anything to do with threat index."

"Obligations can bet one town's threat index will drop next year, or double, or stay lower than another city's," listed Fitch. "So if you've got a good understanding of the heroics industry and how threat indexes—"

"You can design a financial product for almost anything," breathed Poldo. Possibilities, probabilities, and figures swam before his eyes; he could almost see the market shifting.

"Exactly," said Fitch. "It's all about blending risks, returns, and hedges. You make a product that generates a customized stream of steady income, with a measured risk of potentially needing to make a payout."

Poldo took a deep breath. In his experience, things that seemed too good to be true usually turned out to be that way. "That payout is what worries me," he said. "I don't think my finances could sustain the shock of suddenly owing large sums if threat indexes shifted. My investors wouldn't like me holding that much risk."

"Oh, you don't hold them," said Fitch. "We don't even hold them."

"That is where my CTO comes in," said Mr. Stearn. He drew a bear's head on his pad, and wrote "STEARN" in large letters next to it.

"Mr. Stearn doesn't actually issue the threat obligations," said Fitch. "He buys them and bundles them together to serve as collateral for his funds—hence, collateralized threat obligations, or CTOs."

"I sell shares of CTO to banks and large-scale investors, and get cut of sale and maintenance fees," said Mr. Stearn. He sketched a small building labeled "BANK," and then drew an arrow from himself to the bank. "And now bank has steady stream of monthly payments from people who bought threat obligations."

"Right," said Fitch. He pointed at the drawing. "Of course, the bank is taking on the risk, so they need to make sure the product is worth their investment. That's where I come in. I've developed a system for ranking threat obligations based on precious metals, from tin grade obligations that will almost certainly wind up paying out all the way to triple platinum grade obligations—the safest of the safe."

Mr. Stearn drew a small, curly-haired stick figure and labeled it "MR. FITCH," and connected it to the bear's head by a straight arrow. "He make sure I only get good threat obligations."

"Which is where you come in," said Mr. Fitch.

Stearn added a small stick figure with glasses and a bristled mustache, and wrote "MR. POLDO?" above it. "We need more threat obligations to keep business rolling," said the lycanthrope.

"Indeed? I would think everybody is looking at these," said Poldo.

"Almost everybody is," said Fitch. "But the fact that anyone can legally create a threat obligation doesn't mean everyone can cut it in the market. You need to have enough capital to cover the payout until you sell the threat obligation to Mr. Stearn, and you need enough expertise to be credible to the investors who will buy the risk. Silver Guard Securities has some capital to move around, and I don't know many people who have been investing in heroics longer than Duine Poldo. You've got a real opportunity to get in early."

Poldo combed his fingers through his thick mustache as he considered his options. "Well, it does look very positive," he said. "I'll need to do my due diligence, make sure Silver Guard is legally protected—"

"Yeah, sure, all of that." Fitch cut the Scribkin off with a wave of his hand. "I'm assuming you'll cover your bases. The question is, are you in or out? Because if you're in, I've got to say, this is the sort of thing investors like hearing about when they read my reports. But if you're out…"

Poldo got the message loud and clear. It was time to grab the brass ring, lest he be trampled by the bull. "Gentlemen," he said as he shook their hands. "This is the beginning of something great. I can feel it."

"I just felt it right in my gut," said Heraldin, breaking the adventurers' silence. "I knew this was going to be bad."

Gorm nodded. His abdomen was sending him similar signals of dread as he stared out across the grasslands that formed the porous border between Ruskan and the Wild Lands. Below the ridge that the heroes had assembled along, the headless skeleton broke into a full sprint, bounding south toward the roiling mass of smoke and shadow on the horizon.

The darkness crept across the land like a stain through linen. Gorm could barely make out the shapes of men within the black mass; some stumbled along in a stilted limp, others advanced in a stiff, jerking march, and still others glowed pale blue as they hovered among the carrion birds that swarmed around the army.

"Bones," swore Laruna.

"Obviously," said Burt, perched on Gorm's rucksack.

"So much for going south," said Heraldin.

"So much for the pirate towns," Laruna added.

"In more ways than one," added Jynn. "Father must have marched right up the High Coast."

Kaitha shaded her eyes with her hand. "They're headed north. Probably to Vetchell."

"Aye. We'll have to warn 'em," agreed Gorm. "Otherwise, a city the size of Vetchell will have plenty of 'recruits' for, uh, whatever necromancer is leadin' the undead—"

"It's my father," Jynn interrupted. He glared at the distant legion, his lips pulled into a scowl. "There's no sense in leaving it unspoken."

"We can't be sure yet," Gorm said diplomatically.

The noctomancer pointed at a spot in the middle of the black army. "See those fires?"

Gorm squinted, and amid the cloud of hovering carrion birds he could make out flickers of violet and emerald flames on the horizon. "Aye, though it's a funny color."

"It's called Shadowflame. It's an odd hue because it's not actually fire; it's elemental darkness woven in complex patterns that consume the surrounding shadows, so it seems to glow. Father used to light the bronze braziers outside of the Ashen Tower with it."

"To ward off enemies? Or focus the weaves of magic?" asked Kaitha.

"It just 'sets the right ambiance,'" said Jynn, mimicking a deep, cold voice.

"Oh," said Kaitha.

"He spent three weeks getting the right shade of green," said Jynn. "I think he even trademarked the name just before he… his death."

They watched the distant army trudge northward, a slow shambling march illuminated by bursts of the colorful sorcery.

Heraldin stroked his mustache thoughtfully. "To be fair, the Shadowflame does add a little something," he said.

Gaist nodded.

"Yeah," agreed Burt, leaning over Gorm's shoulder to get a better view. "It's got a certain *il'ne se la.*"

"A what?" said Gorm.

"You know, *il'ne se la,*" said the Kobold. "It's Elven."

"What's it mean?"

"'I don't know what.'"

"Well, if ye don't know what it means, why are ye sayin' it?" asked Gorm.

"I know what it means," said Burt. "I just said what it means!"

"Ye said—"

"'I don't know what' is what it means," Kaitha interrupted. "It's a mysterious quality that makes something special, but you can't define it."

"Well, why not say that then?" said Gorm. "Who needs a new word just to say ye ran out of words?"

"Is this really the most pressing conversation we could be having now?" asked Laruna.

"Excuse me for trying to introduce a little culture," grumbled Burt, giving Gorm a resentful glare as he clambered back into the Dwarf's rucksack. "And you Lightlings call us barbaric..."

"Ye've spent too much time in an Elf's purse," Gorm shot back. "And if ye ask me, conjuring a whole new type of sorcerous fire just for decoration seems a bit wasteful."

"It's entirely wasteful!" snapped Jynn. "Gods, who but Father would care about accessorizing an army?"

Chapter 4

More than any other Shadowkin, Orcs favor a bone motif when decorating. They place skulls on pikes, weave teeth into their bead necklaces, and stick tusks and femurs onto just about every surface. Orcish wise-ones even developed an alphabet using the hand and foot bones of their foes, though it was usually just painted on stone in bone shapes. Otherwise, it took at least three corpses to write a sentence, and the writer would still likely run out of vowels. No matter what the occasion, Orcs incorporate skeletons into the ornamentation, and the more momentous or grim the event, the more bones they bring to decorate.

Still, the funeral of an Orcish chieftain is a grim affair even by their own macabre standards.

The faces of the Shadowkin around Char Guz'Varda's pyre were painted as white death masks, so that they looked like ghosts at the edge of the firelight. Bone totems, skeletal trophies, and assorted teeth had been piled atop the pyre. Asherzu wondered if there was any wood beneath the dull, white decorations.

The only bones missing from Char's pyre were those of Char himself. The Lightlings still had them, along with the rest of Char's body. This brought shame on the Guz'Varda Tribe, who cremated their dead primarily so the fallen wouldn't become grim trophies. Whether or not the Lightlings had any propensity to decorate their homes and fortresses with Char's bones was irrelevant; the fact that they *could* cast an even darker pall over the funeral.

Asherzu stifled a sob and looked up at Darak. Tears of rage and grief ran down her younger brother's cheeks in rivulets, carving channels through his thick face paint. She placed a hand on his elbow, and he placed his forehead on her shoulder. He leaned on her long after the pyre had crumbled into coals, past the hour when the younglings were sent to bed and the workers had retired to their huts and tents.

Later, the siblings sat atop a pair of boulders painted like great skulls, watching the groups of warriors and wise-ones whisper in hushed tones around the beach. The ashes of the chieftain's pyre were not yet cool, but talk had already turned to finding a new leader for the Guz'Varda.

Orcish politics were deceptively complex. Technically, trial by combat determined the leadership of any Orcish tribe. To the outsider, that seemed to imply that the biggest, strongest Orc always led the tribe, but several nuances meant that this wasn't always the case. An Orc could have a champion stand for him or her in combat, provided there was a willing representative. There were customs and laws about how challenges were fought, but they all agreed that a chieftain could be called to defend his or her throne at almost any time.

When public opinion swayed too far against an Orcish monarch, a challenge would quickly end his career, if not his life. If a tribe had a bitter disagreement with even numbers on both sides, the tribe would split, and the fragments would settle the matter through good, honest war. The most important quality of an Orcish leader is having enough followers to stave off challenges from his or her political opponents; the second most important quality is possessing enough political skill to keep the tribe from breaking apart.

The death of a chieftain always marked the beginning of a search for such a candidate.

Asherzu only caught snippets of the conversations playing out beneath them. Gizardu the Mountain was considering a bid to become chieftain and withdraw the Guz'Varda from the Red Horde, though she was herself a follower of the old ways. Borpo Skar'Ezzod wanted to lead, though that wasn't a surprise: the Guz'Varda Tribe had been the Skar'Ezzod Tribe at various points in its history, and Borpo's family perpetually schemed to take back the throne. Of most interest to Asherzu was Kagar's bid; Kagar was a wise-one, but if he could find a warrior to stand for him, then it was possible that her father's old ally could take the throne. Asherzu craned her neck a little to hear what the old Orc was saying to Dorgun of the Great Axe, but she couldn't quite make it out.

"Go, Asherzu," said Darak, breaking his long silence.

"What do you speak of?" Asherzu feigned a stretch and turned back to her brother.

"You cannot hide yourself from me," said Darak. *"Look at how you toy with your moth necklace. Anyone can see that you long to peddle words amongst the wise-ones and would-be chieftains."*

Asherzu shook her head and touched her brother's arm. *"I would hate to see you alone on such a night, Little Warg,"* she told him.

"And I would hate to stop my favorite sister from being my favorite sister." Darak forced a smile. *"Go. Speak with them. I will be fine."*

Asherzu pursed her lips, an uncommon expression for a people with tusks jutting from their lower jaw. It didn't seem right to leave Darak by himself at such a time, but missing a chance to help steer the fate of her family's tribe seemed too great a waste to bear. She pressed her forehead to Darak's cheek before she left him, because kisses are also uncommon expressions for a people with tusks.

The young Orcess spoke briefly with Kagar, who asked for her aid in bringing Gizardu and her allies to his side. It was hard to conceal her excitement, and she couldn't stifle the wide grin on her face as she approached Gizardu and several of her followers.

"Hail Asherzu, daughter of Zurthraka," said Gizardu the Mountain. The warrior's honorific once referred to her size, for she was almost as tall as the male Orcs, but over time it had come to signify her deeds as well; the bones and skulls hanging from her armor attested to Gizardu's glorious exploits in battle. Her hair was a raven mane, long and unbraided in the way of warriors, and she gave Asherzu a lioness' stare as she approached. *"Have you come to give us your support?"*

"Truly, you would be worthy of it, mighty Gizardu," said Asherzu. *"But I come to ask for your strength instead, for Kagar the Wise."*

The warrior frowned. *"Kagar may be wise, but he follows your father's ways. I am not sure they are right for this tribe."*

"In my father's days, the children ate every day and parents came home to see them," said Asherzu. *"Can the same be said for the reign of my brother?"*

"What you say is true," said one of Gizardu's retinue. *"But our people crave conquest. We live for the thrill of battle."*

"It is so," Asherzu agreed. *"That is why I love the path of the aggressive seller. Truly, nothing is better than to crush your competition, to drive down their profit margins, to hear the lamentations of their sales representatives. It was a thrill we knew once, a conflict as glorious as any battle. And the children ate at the end of each day."*

"You speak well," said Gizardu slowly. *"And I will have younglings of my own someday, should I find a warrior worthy of siring them. In such dark times, I forget the joy we knew in the days before the Lightling's betrayal. But I cannot forget their betrayal, and I don't know that the tribe will either."*

Asherzu tried not to flinch at the mention of the betrayal. She had personally feasted and laughed with the Lightling heroes who claimed to be restoring her tribe's sacred burial stones. When Gorm Ingerson's alleged kindness turned out to be a ruse that brought the gold-hounds down upon her people, the pain cut her family deepest of all.

Steeling her resolve, she met Gizardu's piercing gaze. *"We must learn from that treachery, but that does not mean we must flee from it. That is what the Lightling dogs want,"* she said. *"They don't regret us starving in the wilderness, pillaging wealth for the gold-hounds to loot. They resented our success on the path of the aggressive seller."*

Gizardu had a thoughtful gleam in her eyes. *"Your words are wise, Asherzu, and you honor your family. But even if you speak the truth, how will you and Kagar get us back onto Zurthraka's path? None of us have our life-papers, and even our younglings are hunted by the gold-hounds."*

Asherzu had anticipated the question. *"In truth, I do not know,"* she said. *"But I am searching for a way, and we need a chieftain who will help us find the path. I have spoken to many of the Guz'Varda, and they tire of the Red Horde."*

"Was your brother one of them?" asked another of Gizardu's followers.

Asherzu followed the warrior's gaze back to Darak. Her brother was surrounded by a pack of Orcs, Goblins, and Gnolls, each wearing a red patch on the left shoulder. And at their center stood Grignot, bent over by the weight of the bones hanging from his wiry form.

Asherzu frowned. *"A thousand pardons, great Gizardu. I am needed."*

"I will think on your words," said Gizardu.

With a bow and a few more excuses, Asherzu broke away and rushed back across the beach to where Darak and Grignot spoke.

"Honor, Lady Asherzu," said Grignot. "Your brother and I were just discussing the future of the Red Horde."

"They wish me to be chieftain, Asherzu," Darak said without ceremony.

"And I am sure you would be a mighty one." Asherzu spoke with cautious diplomacy; the wrong words could dishonor Darak, but a different sort of wrong words might imply that his leadership wasn't a terrible idea. "But you have often said you had no desire to lead."

"Is it not what Char would have wanted?" asked Grignot.

"I am sure Char would want what's best for the tribe," said Asherzu carefully.

"Indeed," pressed Grignot. "Is it not good and rightful that the Guz'Varda should lead the Guz'Varda Tribe? Who would challenge mighty Darak if he chose to take up his brother's cause, to finish the work of his honored ancestors?"

"But—" Asherzu began.

"It does sound like something Brother Char would say," Darak said slowly.

A crocodilian smile spread over Grignot's face as he nodded to Asherzu. "Your brother seems a most suitable candidate to me," he said.

"Look at that smarmy grin. The snaggletoothed smile. The eyes are so small and beady—and not even pointing in the same direction!" Heraldin sputtered as he waved the wanted poster in the air. The flyer promised a ten thousand giltin reward for the bard's capture or death, a summary of his crimes, and a woodcut portrait that looked like the printer had decided to try postmodern cubism. "I'd be offended if this looked anything like me. Or if it looked anything like a Human."

"Would ye be quieter too?" asked Gorm. "Gods, ye should be thankful they hired such a terrible artist. We're across the street from the city guardhouse!"

Vetchell had several guard posts built into its stone walls, but the guards inside had insisted that Gorm and his party take their report in to the main office near the center of the city. The great stone building was the only one visible through the narrow alley that Gorm and his companions had pressed into.

"Easy for you to say," grumbled the bard, looking at the flyer listing the reward for Gorm's capture. "My poster has a mutant turnip on it."

"Gods, let it go," growled Laruna.

"Yes, and keep your cowl up," said Kaitha. "Nobody will know we're outlaws unless you do something conspicuous."

"Like rip up wanted posters," added Jynn.

"Well, listen to a bunch of marks try to teach me about stealth." Heraldin tossed the scraps of his poster into the gutter. "Trust me, if someone notices six cloaked figures huddled in a dark alley, a cheap, inaccurate poster is the least of their concerns. Gaist knows what I mean."

Gaist stood absolutely still, but the manner in which he stared at the street opposite Heraldin was reminiscent of a heavy sigh.

"All the more reason to get moving," said Gorm. "Come on. We filter in like we planned. And if it all goes to the Goblins—"

"Offensive," Burt muttered from within his pack.

"Right. Sorry. If it all goes, er, bad… we get out fast and make for the north gate."

Kaitha and Laruna left the dark alley first, then Gaist, followed by Heraldin. Finally, Gorm and Jynn set out, winding through the street shops and food carts that littered the roads surrounding the guardhouse. Kaitha and Laruna sat at a bench by the front door, pretending to have a casual conversation as they kept watch.

Vetchell's guardhouse was lit by sunlight filtered through stained-glass windows and the orange light of tarnished lamps. A heavy quiet draped over the room like an old blanket as motes of dust danced lazily in the sunbeams to the rhythm of the creaks in the wooden floors. Heraldin and Gaist sat at a guest table, making a good show of reading a few tourism pamphlets placed by the Vetchell Chamber of Commerce. A row of desks lined the back wall, each marked by small signs encouraging guests to see the next one.

The last desk was manned by a tall man with a hawk nose, a long mustache, and a fine breastplate embossed with wreaths of roses. He reclined with his heavy boots up on the blotter of his desk, idly flipping through a salacious magazine with a woodcut of a scantily-clad Ogress on the cover. He didn't look up as Gorm and Jynn approached.

"We've come with a warning for the city of Vetchell," said Gorm. "There's an undead—"

"Form 89MC." The guard pointed toward a set of shelves in the back lined with neat stacks of paperwork without looking up.

"What? There's no time for fillin' out forms!" said Gorm.

The guard licked his thumb and flipped the page. "If you need to expedite the paperwork, you'll also need to fill out form 93MM."

Gorm could feel the blood rising in his cheeks. "How does more bloody paperwork make things go faster?"

The guardsman shrugged.

"Vetchell is in dire peril!" Jynn leaned over the desk. "If you cannot take this threat seriously, then we must speak with the commanding officer at this station."

The guard finally glanced up from his book, meeting Jynn's stare with his own heavy-lidded eyes. "Go right ahead, sir."

"You're the commander of the city guard," said Jynn dryly.

"Knight-commander of the city guard, yes. Lord Tyren Ur'Thos to you."

"And you spend your days taking in the paperwork." Gorm couldn't have concealed his skepticism even if he'd tried.

"I've always believed it's important to delegate. Staying off the streets and ramparts gives me more to time to…" Tyren's hand grasped idly at nothing, as though he could pull the right words from the air. "You know… set the direction of my department. Do the big picture thinking."

"I see." Gorm glanced at the guard's magazine cover. It promised in bold, block letters that everything was bigger with Ogresses. "A man of vision, then."

"Indeed," said Knight-Commander Ur'Thos, flipping the page.

Gorm snorted, and as he did so, his nose caught a biting scent. "And you're drunk!"

"I'm hiding it well," countered the knight-commander.

"Hiding it?" said Jynn. "Who cares what you look like if you're too sauced to help us?"

"Oh no!" Tyren held up a finger with the deliberate steadiness of a man just on the edge of inebriation. "I'm not *that* drunk. I'm not helping you yet because you haven't done the paperwork."

"But this is a matter of life and death," said Gorm.

"All the more reason to do it properly," said Tyren with a tight-lipped smile. "It won't do you much good to moan about how critical this threat is if you can't be bothered to fill out a few simple forms."

"All of Arth could be in danger!" Jynn protested.

"Well then, be sure to include form 78MCA when you file your report." The knight-commander turned back to his magazine. "That's the blue one."

"Fine, thrice curse your bones!" Gorm snapped, already on his way to the shelves of papers. He located all three forms as well as a few quills and a pot of ink. On his way back to the lobby, he nodded at Heraldin and Gaist. "You two! Come help with the bloody paperwork."

They huddled around a small table in the lobby, working furiously. There were questions about the date and location that the threat was witnessed, the quantity and relative power of the foes, the immediate and long-term risks posed by the incursion, and, naturally, several pages of detailed questions about the weapons, armor, and other valuables that the enemy might have been carrying. Gorm and his companions scrawled their best guesses in most of the blanks, and progress was fast until they reached the questions about their identities.

"They want names, license numbers, addresses," muttered Jynn. "If we gave any of these to the guild, they'd be as likely to arrest us as ride out against the undead."

"And if I had to choose who to fight, it'd be us," said Heraldin. "Just use fake information."

"Can't. They cross-check the answers, and if something doesn't match up the guild will throw out the forms as fraud." Gorm shook his head.

"Do we know anyone else who can submit it?" asked Jynn.

A thought struck Gorm, and he turned back to the knight-commander. "Hey! Can we turn in these reports anonymously?"

Tyren's expression turned puzzled. "I don't think so. But I don't know why you would want to anyway. You'd forfeit any claim to the loot."

"Claim?" Gorm feigned innocence.

"To the loot, yes." Tyren spoke as though explaining wooden toys to a dull-witted child. "You submit a threat report, and if you're the first to accurately report it, you and the city get to issue a quest together. Then you get some of the gold when the Heroes' Guild comes and kills the monsters. Why else would every bit of riffraff on the street be in here trying to convince me they saw scargs in their barn or big rats in the sewer?" The last sentiment was muttered as the knight-commander returned to his lecherous periodical.

"But, we don't care about the gold," said Gorm.

Tyren put his magazine down with forceful impatience. "Don't care about gold? Why would you even—" he began, but then revelation washed over his face. "This is a real threat. You're coming to warn us because there's a real F.O.E. marching on the city."

"Finally!" said Jynn, looking relieved.

"And it's not just that you're not here for the loot. You don't want to claim the loot. So you must have some sort of problem with the law," said the knight-commander.

Jynn' s enthusiasm faded. "Uh."

"Wait for it," said Gorm. He had been around long enough to know the difference between making threats and establishing leverage.

An avaricious gleam was in the knight-commander's eye. "And that means that, perhaps, you wouldn't care if someone else put his name on the forms."

"And there it is," Gorm said, stepping forward. "And if it happened to be your name on the form?"

"Now that's a thought." Tyren put on the pretense of pondering. "The idea had never crossed my mind, of course, but since you've put it out there, I suppose I would have to personally ensure that the report was seen by the highest offices of our fine city. If my name were on the report, of course."

"And if not?" Gorm prompted.

"Why, I'd treat it with all the respect and care that I give to every other request." The knight-commander jabbed a thumb over his shoulder at a tray brimming with colorful bundles of paper. "The rank and file process forms and send them over to the Heroes' Guild on a bi-weekly basis."

"Of course," said Gorm. "A man of vision and an entrepreneur as well."

Jynn sighed. "Why is nothing ever simple?"

It was surprisingly difficult to find a venue for not having a meeting.

An enterprising individual had many options when searching for a place to meet in Andarun. There were business complexes with offices for rent, taverns with spacious back rooms, and even a few temples that would rent out their sanctuaries for a generous donation to the appropriate god or goddess.

Yet all of those options were in public spaces, and kept payment records, and were full of prying eyes, all of which were unacceptable to a person planning a meeting that would explicitly never happen. Guests who would most definitely be elsewhere demanded much more discretion from a venue that they weren't visiting.

The Moonless Night had been established for just such a lack of an occasion. The Night was never in the same place twice; officially, it was never anywhere, and why were you asking, anyway? Its clientele expected amenities such as unique and discreet locations to not hold meetings in, well-crafted fake receipts for the expenses they didn't incur, and a stylish invitation sent to everyone who would not be attending, complete with custom alibis written out on the back.

On the evening of the thirteenth of Fulgen, 7.375, somewhere in the ninth tier of Andarun, there was not a meeting at The Moonless Night. There were no servants in the alleged room; any wine and cheese would have been served by conjured sprites that dissipated as soon as they were no longer needed. Only scurrilous and totally unverifiable accounts might have implied that the most dangerous men on Arth gathered to discuss business. And that there were also some assassins present.

Fenrir Goldson and Bolbi Baggs could easily prove that they weren't anywhere near the ninth tier that night. However, anyone who might have been at the Moonless Night that evening may have recalled two similar businessmen opening the meeting by asking several pointed questions.

How hard could it really be to kill a party of six heroes? Especially if said heroes were led by a rank one warrior and the highest ranked among them was a known drunk, for Tandos' sake? Hadn't the solamancer in question spent over a decade as an apprentice? Weren't there ballads about their noctomancer's cowardice and incompetence? Why were two anonymous businessmen spending so much of their personal fortune on a gaggle of assassins who had yet to eliminate one target? How was it that the wanted posters plastered all over the Freedlands had been just as effective, when they had cost a fraction of just one assassin's fee?

On the last question, one of the two unidentifiable executives may have thrown a bundle of papers on the table for effect. Each flyer had a poorly-rendered woodcut depicting one member of Gorm Ingerson's party or another alongside the promise of a hefty reward from the Heroes' Guild.

A couple of the assassins likely protested. Someone might have pointed out that Gorm Ingerson had been rank ten at one point, and regardless of guild paperwork he remained as crafty and dangerous as ever. And had not Throden the Raven's remains been found in a mangled state, his wounds consistent with victims of either a Troll attack or an avalanche? Coupled with the final report of the Silver Talons mercenaries —

Yet if any executives were present, they wouldn't have tolerated such whining. They would remind everyone that assassins are typically paid for results, not excuses. And they would likely have added that there were only two types of assassins: successful professionals, and loose ends.

The meeting that never happened ended on that veiled threat. The anonymous businessmen pulled up the hoods of their fine capes and made for the doors. Upon their exit, fresh sprites drifted in and began packing up The Moonless Night's tableware. The assassins would have grumbled about getting the loose ends speech from civilians, but soon enough they would make for the windows and leap out onto the r͏
their dark cloaks trailing after them in a suitably dramatic ͏

One assassin, however, lingered. He picked up a wanted poster bearing a horrible woodcut of Gorm Ingerson in a hand that wasn't a hand at all. Rather, his appendage was an intricate amalgam of Scribkin engineering and noctomancy, fashioned to look like shining talons. The claws were so sharp that Gorm Ingerson's fish-eyed portrait was shredded when his mechanical hand balled into a shaking fist around it.

The tatters of Gorm's malformed image hadn't yet settled on the floor before Garold Flinn left a meeting that never happened.

Chapter 5

"It's just that your appointment isn't on the schedule, you see." The clerk pointed a damning finger at a blank spot on his parchment. "And if it's not on the schedule, it doesn't happen."

"Perhaps under normal circumstances, but this is of the utmost importance," said Knight-Commander Ur'Thos, stepping up to the podium. "I'm sure you understand."

The young clerk wore an expression that suggested otherwise, along with the dull robes of an apprentice of the Order of the Moon. "You have to have an appointment," he repeated with dim certainty.

Gorm grit his teeth, but he held his tongue. The party waited in the main chamber of Vetchell's Tower of Magi, which was far too public a place for a group of outlaws to make a scene.

There were few things that could unite the Order of the Sun and the Order of the Moon; over the ages the two great factions of mages had refined their philosophical differences into the purest contrarianism. Solamancers and noctomancers went to great lengths to be on the opposite sides of every debate, be it political, social, religious, or inane. Even amid such cultivated animosity, however, there were still forces that could push the two orders of mages to the brink of cooperation. One common example was real estate prices.

To fulfill their sacred duty of safely identifying and training Arth's magically gifted, the two great Orders needed to have bases of operations in all of Arth's major cities. Yet proper mage towers were incredibly expensive, especially those built to withstand the punishment of apprentices inexpertly fiddling with the primal energies of the universe. As such, most of Arth's small- to mid-sized cities had a single Tower of Magi shared by both the Order of the Sun and the Order of the Moon.

Within the walls, however, the orders didn't share much as far as Gorm could see. The floor was neatly bisected by an inlaid silver line, and the mages on either side of it were sorted by the colors of their robes. Unfortunately, the two Orders had come together in appointing the world's most useless apprentice to man the front desk.

"I am the knight-commander of the city guard," hissed Tyren.

"Everybody needs an appointment," repeated the apprentice. "Perhaps tomorrow morning."

As satisfying as it was to watch the knight-commander wrestle with a fellow gatekeeper to bureaucracy, Gorm was in a hurry to be away from the crowds. "Maybe we could try somewhere else, lad?" he offered.

Tyren tapped the packet of paperwork. "These forms are no good without secondary witnesses or proof. This was your wizard's idea of the fastest way to get that. So perhaps he could help," the knight-commander added pointedly.

Jynn looked at Gorm with reluctance, but they had few options and less time. The Dwarf nodded.

"Very well," said Jynn. The noctomancer stepped forward and threw back his long cloak, revealing the ornate purple robes he wore beneath them. "I know the hour is late, apprentice, but I must insist that you make an exception and take us to the Chamber of Owls."

Recognition flashed in the apprentice's eyes, burning away the disinterested patina and leaving something akin to fear in its wake. "Y-yes, high councilor. Just one moment."

"Well, I didn't expect it to go that well." Gorm watched the young mage scurry away.

"I am still a high councilor, and most noctomancers will defer to me," said Jynn softly, nodding to the young mage. "At least, when I can sneak onto the Order's premises."

"I'm surprised they let ye keep your title after… ye know," said Gorm.

"Oh, I've lost all responsibilities and much of the privilege," said Jynn. "And I'm sure that some ambitious wretch has taken my seat at the head of the Circle of the Red Hawk by now. But I still command the same spells, have the same mastery of magic, and know the same Academy secrets, and so I remain a high councilor."

"It's just that now your title is more about sizin' ye up as a threat," Gorm observed.

"It always was," said Jynn with a shrug. "Unskilled apprentices are a threat to society. Fully recognized mages are a threat to the Academy's enemies. And high councilors and archmages are a threat to each other."

"Sounds like bein' a professional hero. I just never realized ye were so high up." Gorm watched another mage give the noctomancer a low bow.

"I must admit I've missed this," conceded Jynn as the apprentice came rushing back.

The young man guided them upstairs to the Chamber of Owls, a perfect circular room at the center of the tower. The walls were black and shining near the door that Gorm stepped through, decorated with silver stars and comets. Across the room he could see a plain door marked with a golden sun surrounded by an alabaster wall. The walls on either side were a mosaic of gray stones arranged so that the room shifted seamlessly from day into night.

The floor of the room was almost entirely occupied by a wide basin as high as Gorm's waist and filled with a shimmering, silver liquid. Several noctomancers and solamancers stood around the pool, brought together by some indeterminate task and united in shock at seeing an apprentice lead a party of adventurers into the chamber.

"What is the meaning of this?" demanded the noctomancer with the fanciest robes. Her face was sharp, pale to the point of ghastliness, and framed by long locks of ebony hair, frosted white at the tips.

"We've come to use the scrying pool, Councilor of Owls," said Jynn. A collective gasp rose from the mages and a couple of the heroes at the mention of the pool. The noctomancers and solamancers from the tower erupted in immediate protest, but Jynn countered with shouted procedures. "I am declaring an emergency, with the authority of a high councilor, set forth in…"

Gorm leaned close to Laruna. "What's a scrying pool?" he muttered.

"It's an omnimancer relic. A powerful tool for divination," said the solamancer.

"Ah, thank ye." Gorm recalled that omnimancers had once worked with the Sten to build artifacts of incredible power, unreproducible with modern magic. He wasn't sure what these relics actually did, save that they usually required both halves of magic to operate properly.

Another question came to Gorm's mind. "And what's divination?"

Laruna seemed surprised at the question. "Do you know anything about magic?"

"I try not to," said Gorm. "The only thing I learned about wizards is how to beat the tar out of 'em."

"Ha," Laruna said without amusement as she rubbed her jaw. "Divination lets us see things from across space and time. A scrying pool lets you see anything within a hundred miles as clearly as if you were in the room. The omnimancers made hundreds or thousands of them, but they were all supposed to have been destroyed or sealed away years ago."

"So, why do these mages have one, then?" said Gorm.

"I don't know," Laruna admitted. "I've never been in a Chamber of Owls before."

"It may work out for us," interjected Kaitha. "Listen."

Knight-Commander Ur'Thos sauntered forward to examine the pool, eyed warily by Vetchell's mages. "I'm fairly certain this is an illegal artifact," he said, hiking up his breeches for emphasis in the manner of guardsmen everywhere.

"We have full authorization to run a scrying pool, and we take our citizens' privacy seriously." The Councilor of Owls looked like a cornered rat.

"Does that mean you aren't scrying on people in the city?" asked Tyren.

"Only when necessary," offered one of the solamancers working the chamber.

"And I suppose you're the same group who says it's necessary," pressed Tyren.

"King Klenn of Ruskan has authorized the Academy of Mages throughout the kingdom to take steps to ensure the safety of the Ruskan people," recited the Councilor of Owls.

"And he said scrying pools? He gave you permission to scry on his own subjects?" asked Tyren.

"We can't be certain that he didn't mean that," said the councilor.

"What we can be certain of is how the public and town elders might react to my report on the matter," said the knight-commander. "Unless, of course, you were to use it in defense of our city and nation."

"And there it is," said the Councilor of Owls.

"We've received word that a great threat approaches from the south," said Tyren. "And we need proof to confirm the warning and mobilize our defenses."

"And finalize your claim paperwork as well, I'd imagine," said the councilor. "I suppose if we don't help, you'll run off to tell the town about the scrying pool."

"Let's not discuss such formalities when the threat is so great." Gorm noticed that Tyren didn't specify which threat. The Councilor of Owls seemed to pick up on that as well.

"Fine," sighed the old noctomancer, signaling to the other mages. With scowls and grumbles, the noctomancers and solamancers shuffled into position. "And where is this alleged army?"

Gorm raised a hand. "Due south. It took us about four days of marchin' to get here from where we spotted them. The undead don't sleep, but they don't move fast either."

"The undead? Very well," said the councilor, now a little more serious. At her signal, the mages channeled weaves of solamancy and noctomancy into the scrying pool. Silvery light and dark shadows danced across its surface, coalescing into moving shapes. A moment later Gorm could clearly see the Chamber of Owls as though viewed from above, complete with an image of himself staring down into the pool. He could even see Burt leaning out of his rucksack to get a better vantage.

"Back in the bag before someone sees!" he whispered.

The Kobold noticed himself and ducked back into the rucksack with a muttered curse.

"Take us up," said the Councilor of Owls.

Gorm could make out light blue threads of air among the weaves as the noctomancers around the scrying table adjusted their spell casting. The image within the pool seemed to drop away, and another floor filled with wizards and mages fell over it, followed by several more, and then the tower's roof. The tower and surrounding buildings shrank as the scrying pool's vantage rose higher above Vetchell, stopping only when the city below was a mosaic of rooftops with cobblestone cracks running through it.

"South," said the Councilor of Owls.

The buildings and streets in the scrying pool began to move as the solamancers around the relic added strands of fire and water into their weaves. Gorm felt his stomach drop as his eyes told him that he was soaring over a silver city, and moving faster every moment. The walls of Vetchell flew past, and before long they were soaring over southern Ruskan. The fields and forests looked an irregular quilt with roads and rivers for seams.

As they soared along, however, the features of the landscape began to run together like eggs with their yolks popped. Bubbles started drifting to the surface of the pool, popping into small, wispy clouds of steam.

"Remember your virtues," chided the Councilor of Owls.

"Are they havin' shameful thoughts?" Gorm muttered to Laruna.

"What? No!" hissed the solamancer. "Why would they be thinking about things like that now?"

"How should I know?" said Gorm. "I can't ever think of a reason that ye tall folk are ever thinkin' shameful things, but I'll be thrice-cursed if ye ever stop!"

The solamancer sputtered. "We don't—I mean, people like Heraldin, yeah, but—why would you even bring that up?"

"The Owl Lady had to remind them about their virtue." Gorm nodded to the noctomancer guiding Vetchell's mages.

Laruna rolled her eyes. "The Councilor of Owls was reminding them of a mage's virtues. That's different."

"Like only usin' magic for good?"

"See, that's how it's different. You'll find teachings on good and evil in the temples. But a mage's virtues are power and mastery," said Laruna. "And balance, technically, when it comes to omnimancy. Most mages don't need help remembering that they want power and mastery. But when you're working with old omnimancer relics, you have to mind all three."

Gorm scratched his beard. "So… they're throwing too much solamancy or noctomancy at it?"

"Well, they were." Laruna nodded at the silvery image. "Look, they're bringing it back into balance."

The solamancers around the scrying pool were increasing the power and complexity of the weaves they sent into the edges of the silver basin, while the noctomancers were pulling their own magic back a bit. As the mages of the two Orders approached equilibrium, the picture within the pool came into focus once more.

"There," said Jynn, pointing at the pool.

Amid the roiling bubbles in the boiling pool, distant figures were moving over the plains. They looked no bigger than toy soldiers, but even from far above their shambling gaits and bloodied clothes were, for lack of a better term, dead giveaways. A collective gasp rose from the assembled mages.

"The undead," whispered the Councilor of Owls.

"Aye," said Gorm. "An army of 'em, comin' for your gates."

"Gods above," said Tyren.

There were only a handful at first, but scattered groups and then entire squads of the walking dead slid into view as the mages pushed the scrying pool ever farther. Wraiths, ghosts, and carrion birds flew over the army, looming larger than life in the silvery surface of the pool.

"It is the army of the liche Detarr Ur'Mayan," Jynn said, watching ranks of dead men lurch together in ragged formations.

The Councilor of Owls was startled at the name. "Ur'Mayan? A liche? Are you sure?"

One specter flew closer to the pool's vantage point, slipping into their view like a ghastly whale gliding beneath a ship. The ghost turned over as it flew, as if to look up at the scrying pool's invisible eye, and for a moment the boiling pool was filled with a giant, skeletal visage.

"I am regrettably certain." Jynn stared stoically down at the pool. "And with every day, he draws nearer to Vetchell."

"How… long do we have?" asked the knight-commander, his face pale to the point of translucence.

Gorm shook his head. "Three or four days. Five if the river slows their progress."

"Then we've lost too much time already," said the Councilor of Owls.

The picture in the scrying pool winked out as the mages powering it scrambled into action. Some began discussing their next steps, while others didn't wait before rushing off, already bellowing orders to apprentices. Knight-Commander Ur'Thos marked a few checks on his forms, solicited a signature from the Councilor of Owls, and made for the door with barely a wave to Gorm and his party.

"And with that," Kaitha muttered in Gorm's ear, "I think our work here is done."

"Aye," he agreed. "It's best we move on before—"

"Leaving so soon?" said the Councilor of Owls, her hand clamping down on Gorm's shoulder like a bony vise. "You and I still haven't had a chance to chat, Gorm Ingerson."

Gorm felt his stomach drop at the mention of his name. "Uh, who?"

"Don't," said the Councilor sharply. "Come. We will speak in my office."

"Come in, come in." The Councilor of Owls ushered Gorm's party into a large room near the top of the tower, windowless and drab. Old bookshelves lined the walls, each straining under the weight of ancient grimoires and stacks of parchment. A simple desk sat in the middle of the violet carpet, empty save for a quill in the inkwell, a nameplate that read "Davaya Ur'Manel," and the requisite skull set near the corner.

The councilor looked at the party standing in her chambers with condescending amusement, like a swamp drake contemplating a lost farm animal. "And now, Gorm, I think we should have a frank talk."

"Ye can start by tellin' me how ye know who I am," said Gorm.

The sorceress shrugged. "Your faces are on wanted posters from here to Silvershore."

"Drake spit," snapped Gorm. "Those posters give nothing away. The knight-commander of the city guard didn't even notice the resemblance."

The Councilor of Owls' laughter was like a subterranean pool; dark, cold, and deep. "Oh, I wouldn't hang your case on the competence of our knight-commander."

"We're hanging it on the incompetence of your woodcut artist," said Gorm. "Those portraits look nothing like us."

"They barely look like people," added Heraldin under his breath.

"Fair enough. The truth is that I recognized you because you've made a name for yourself lately by traveling with an old acquaintance of mine." The noctomancer turned and smiled at Jynn, earning him sidelong glances from the other heroes and an open scowl from Laruna.

"I'm afraid you have the advantage, madam," said Jynn, his brow furrowing. "I've had few dealings with the Ruskan branches of the Order."

"I met you well before you were in the Academy, before you walked or spoke. Perhaps this will refresh your memory." The councilor picked up a sheaf of paper and tossed it into the air with one hand, and with the other made a quick gesture. The air around the page shimmered with a faint whispering noise and the page was reduced to a flurry of scraps in seconds.

"You're Aya of Blades," said Jynn.

"Hello again, Jynn," said Aya.

Gorm started at the name. Aya of Blades was one of the five mages behind the Leviathan Project, along with Win Cinder, Teldir of Umbrax, Az'Anon the Black, and Detarr Ur'Mayan.

The wizard sputtered as he stared. "But… I thought… I mean, I assumed—"

"That I was dead?" said Aya. "A useful rumor encouraged by one Davaya Ur'Manel. I'm sure you're familiar with using an alias by now. I faked my death and left the Leviathan Project after Az'Anon found his doom. If I hadn't, I'd likely have met the same fate."

Gorm flinched at the mention of the Spider-King; he still remembered running from the quest that ended his former career. "Ye were scared the guild would send a hero like Johan to run ye through."

Aya of Blades shot him an inscrutable look. "No," she said. "That became a concern after Johan killed Detarr, but I was already re-enrolled in the Academy under a new name."

"But surely someone must have tracked ye down through all these years," said Gorm.

"They did." Aya dusted a couple of paper scraps from her sleeve. "They regretted it."

"Ah." Gorm winced as he looked at the sad pile of shredded parchment on the floor.

"An unfortunate necessity, but we do what we must. Self-preservation and all," said Aya brightly. "Speaking of which, that's why I've brought a gaggle of renegade heroes into my room and told them my little secret."

"I'm not sure I follow," said Laruna.

"I'm sure she'll be telling us about an errand she had planned for us," said Gorm.

"Close," said Aya. "I want to help you do what you're already doing. And now that you know who I am and what I worked on, you know I can help you defeat Detarr Ur'Mayan."

There was a hiss and a rustle as the assembled adventurers took a synchronized deep breath and leaned back in unison, wearing faces that ranged from alarmed shock to awkward winces.

"We... we're not going to fight a liche," said Kaitha.

"Not again, anyway," said Laruna.

Even Gaist shook his head, if ever so slightly.

Aya shrugged off their protests. "Oh, don't bother playing at this. You will."

"Why would we do that?" asked Heraldin. "It'd be suicide by dark magic!"

"Which is why you need my help," said Aya.

The senior noctomancer waved her hand and a set of drawers against the far wall suddenly shifted down the face of their filing cabinet, as though sliding into the floor. When each drawer reached the bottom, it disappeared with a gleam of sorcery. As the drawers scooted out of existence, a single drawer slid in from a similar spatial distortion at the top of the cabinet, slowing as it glided into place. Opening the single drawer, Aya produced a folio of loose documents.

"I have information on the artifacts we used for the Leviathan Project," said Aya, leafing through the folder. "Who found them, what they were used for, notes from any experiments, and most importantly, where they are today. You'll need at least one if you're to stop Detarr."

"You're presumin' too much," said Gorm. "We've already risked our necks to do as much as we have."

"Exactly," snapped Aya, looking up from her documents. "You could have left Vetchell to its fate, just as I intend to once this conversation is over. You could have fled, but instead you risked capture by the guild for the sake of a gaggle of serfs and fools. And it's because you're all… all… what's the word?" she asked, snapping her fingers.

"Good?" said Kaitha.

Aya shook her head. "I don't like to be so binary."

"Noble?" suggested Heraldin.

The Lady of Blades looked over Gorm and his muddy, road-worn armor with a critical eye. "No, that's not it," she said.

"Honorable?" said Laruna.

"Simple. Predictable. It's some combination of all of them." Aya waved away the verbal conundrum and walked over to retrieve an expensive-looking crystal from a shelf. "The point is, we all know you're going to face the liche, and we don't have time to pretend otherwise."

"I ain't pretending," said Gorm. "Now that we warned the city—"

"Do we really have to do this?" Aya rolled her eyes as she set the crystal on her desk. "Very well. I could happily live out my days on an ice floe knowing I was the last living person on Arth. Could you? I'll flee to northern Ruskan, and not care a whit for what happens to Vetchell or Parald or even Eadelmon. Will you? I won't think twice about all the young lovers and terrified parents and grubby little children fleeing for their lives, or what will happen when they finally run out of places to cower. How many of you can say the same?"

The assembled adventurers suddenly took an interest in the astral pattern on Aya's carpet, which was currently being scuffed and dirtied by the collective shuffling of several pairs of booted feet.

Heraldin cleared his throat and lifted his hand. His arm was halfway extended when he caught Gaist's expression.

The weaponsmaster stared at the bard through narrowed eyes.

"Well, I might be able to," muttered Heraldin, slowly pulling his hand back.

"I didn't think so," said Aya, giving the heroes a stern glare. "And since you all have 'consciences' or 'morals' or whatever vainglorious term you like for your suicidal tendencies, let's agree you will face the undead, sooner or later. And if you're unprepared when you do, well…" The old noctomancer pounded the crystal on her desk, shattering it.

"The guild can take care of the undead," said Gorm.

"Ha! The guild!" Aya practically spat the word as she flipped through her folder. "All of these," she added to the shards on her desk.

The air above the shattered crystal shimmered, and the page she was holding lifted from her hand. A second sheaf of parchment, this one blank, glided over as though borne by the wind, and as it did so writing and sketches burned onto its surface, mirroring the original page hovering near Aya's hand. A moment later, two identical papers settled gently on the desk.

"After all you've been through, I can't fathom why you'd trust the guild to deal with a boggart's boil." Aya tossed another bundle of papers into the air, where weaves of magic quickly swept them up for duplication. "Let me tell you a story about the thrice-cursed guild. Do you remember Tyrannax the Shadow Master?"

"The necromancer down in Daellan?" recalled Laruna. "I heard he wiped out several parties of heroes."

"Yes, he was a terror." Aya watched the paper swirling around her. "Which is why the heroes of Hawksgate petitioned the guild to let them use the Crown of Iron Thorns."

Jynn visibly started at the name, "The crown?"

"Ye know it?" asked Gorm.

"I remember Father talking about it, years ago," said Jynn.

"He possessed it, for a time," said Aya. She reached out and plucked a page from the papery maelstrom swirling around her. It bore an illustration that looked like someone had seen a pile of ship nails and thought it would make a nice hat. "Your father studied the crown for the Leviathan Project, and he kept it in the Ashen Tower until Johan took it back for the guild."

"But what does it do?" asked Gorm.

"It holds great power over the dead," said Aya. "So much so that the guild has declared it a class-one major artifact."

The assembled heroes broke out in gasps and low whistles. You could fit all the class-one artifacts ever discovered into a small room, provided the walls were thick enough and you had a very, very strong lock on the door.

"It can't be that powerful," said Heraldin. "Hawksgate was almost wiped off the map, as I recall."

The air around Aya was still a swirling storm of paper and ink. "And it wouldn't have been if the heroes defending the city had been given the Crown of Iron Thorns. But the guild just finished processing the paperwork for the request this past summer."

"What?" said Kaitha. "But Tyrannax died five years ago!"

"Six," said Aya. The last of her papers settled into place, leaving two identical piles of parchment sitting next to one another. She placed one stack into a fresh folio. "And by the time they finally went to retrieve the crown, it had gone missing."

Gorm snorted. "How do ye lose a thrice-cursed class-one artifact?"

"You don't," said Aya. "It gets stolen."

The words hit like a punch in the gut. Gorm glanced at Jynn and saw the same unpleasant thought reflected in the noctomancer's eyes.

"And that tells you where we stand," said Aya. "The guild is too slow and ponderous to do anything about a threat such as Detarr, even if they wanted to stop him. They let him steal one of the most powerful artifacts in the world from under their noses. But the right group of people—people with a specific set of skills, people who are already on the wrong side of the law—those people could steal an equally powerful artifact and stop your father."

"We're not ready to take on a liche," said Heraldin.

"And who better, master bard?" Aya smirked. "You've got the famous Pyrebeard here, a warrior without peer, except perhaps the Jade Wind. And what really matters is that you have the young Ur'Mayan with you."

All eyes turned to Jynn. "I've faced my father before. I could not best him," said the noctomancer quietly.

"You did not best him, but that doesn't mean you can't," said Aya sternly. "Arth hasn't seen many wizards as gifted as your father, and he only ever trained one apprentice. You and I both know nobody else has a better chance of stopping him, if only you'd let yourself realize your full potential."

Jynn's face scrunched up into a grimace. "You presume too much, madam," he snapped.

Aya smirked. "You presume I have other options. I don't know any other heroes nearly as qualified to fight Detarr as your party, and here you are, on my doorstep, when an hour of great need arises... well, I've never believed in destiny, but I know opportunity when I see it. You have a chance to stop your father, Jynn, provided you have the right information." She held out the folder of copied documents to the noctomancer. "And the will to do what's necessary."

The wizard reluctantly lifted the packet from Aya's hands. "You—you want us to steal artifacts from the guild?"

"I want to stay alive in a world worth staying alive in. If I have to flee to a new life, I'd rather it not to be alone on an ice floe. I even want it enough to fund your efforts." Aya pulled a heavy-looking purse from her robes and tossed it at the heroes' feet. "And I presume our interests are aligned, since I imagine you want to keep on living, and that you'd prefer that as many people as possible do the same. If you want it enough, you might have to steal from the Heroes' Guild."

"Why should we trust you?" asked Kaitha.

"You don't have to," said the old noctomancer. "Take some free gold, verify my information if you like, and just... you know." Aya waved her hand and grimaced. "Do what you were already going to do. Let your conscience be your guide. Or something."

Gorm sucked in a deep breath. Nobody wanted to fight the liche again. The prospect of robbing the guild beforehand didn't make it seem any less crazy. But rescuing innocents from evil was in his bones, and not rescuing innocents from the walking bones would be evil. Plus, Aya was right about the guild's bureaucracy; just reporting the undead had taken too long. They couldn't react with the speed needed, even if—

"Wait." Gorm looked up at the Councilor of Owls as a thought struck him. "Why wouldn't the guild want to stop a liche?"

"Oh, they'll want to eventually." Aya smirked to herself as she shook her head. "When they think the timing is right."

"Thrice-curse the speculators," Duine Poldo exclaimed, flipping through a stack of contracts. "They're the only explanation for this."

Mrs. Hrurk gave a little shrug and set the letter on Poldo's desk. "I couldn't say, Mr. Poldo. But whatever the reason, Mr. Stearn wants you to assemble five more CTOs for southern Ruskan."

"Yes, because of the undead," said Poldo, shaking his head. "Someone filed a claim on a big mob of them south of Vetchell earlier this week, and now the speculators are gambling on the threat to Ruskan. That's all these investors are buying: a bet, a risk, an idea."

"At least it's good business," said the Gnoll with a hopeful wag of her tail.

"No, it's good pay," grumbled Poldo. "It's horrible business."

Poldo prepared his threat obligations with all the math and due diligence he could muster, but he had no better idea than anyone how they would perform over their term. Mr. Stearn bought them anyway, snapping them up before the ink was dry. The werebear banker spliced and diced the obligations together into CTOs that Fitch invariably rated as triple platinum, even though Poldo wouldn't have called any of them better than tin. But Fitch's word was good enough for the banks and speculators, who seemed to have a bottomless appetite for collateralized threat obligations.

Poldo had every reason to be ecstatic, or at least enough reasons to fill a small vault. Yet he couldn't shake the notion that, despite evidence to the contrary, CTOs wouldn't work. That they *shouldn't* work. They were money from nothing, gold spun from bankers' dreams pressed through impossibly complex equations. The hairs on Poldo's neck stood up when he thought about it for too long.

"You're right," said Mrs. Hrurk, her tail tucked between her legs. "I'm sorry. I'll get back to tidying the office. I think the plow and shovels could use a good cleaning."

"No, no, I'm sorry," sighed Poldo. "I haven't been sleeping enough lately, and it's clearly making me irate. It's been helpful to have you go through the mail."

Mrs. Hrurk gave a slight smile and continued sifting through the stack of envelopes in front of her.

Poldo turned back to his own work. He needed to issue half a dozen complex threat obligations by tonight, but in the meantime, he still had a hedge fund to run. He took a small, black box from his desk drawer, and from the box he produced an azure stone inscribed with golden runes. The stone flared with magic when Poldo tapped it three times, and the light quickly coalesced into a luminescent blue figure. It glowed so brightly that it looked like a ball of light with a pair of wings.

A sprite was a sort of spectral pixie summoned for a specific task, fading away when its job was done. There were sprites for almost everything these days; sprites for sending messages, sprites for finding things, and sprites for warning of intruders. The glowing figures summoned by Poldo's rather expensive sprite-stone, however, were for trade.

Poldo consulted his pocket ledger before addressing the tiny, glowing servant. "Silver Guard Securities will place a market order to buy three thousand shares of the Dragon of Wynspar, please."

"Buy! Buy! Buy!" The sprite's inner light shifted from sky blue to a bright emerald as it chimed its order maniacally. With a flit of its wings it zipped to the window, squeezed out through a tiny crack, and ascended into the sky, where it joined the other trade sprites floating from the city's banks and financial offices. They drifted to the great dome of the Andarun Stock Exchange like luminescent moths to a giant, golden flame. Once inside, they'd execute their transactions and dutifully expire.

Poldo also sold shares of Goldson Baggs and Lamia Sisters, and bought into a civic bond fund, sending two crimson and one green sprite out his window. He was pondering his next move when someone knocked at the door, and a moment later Mrs. Hrurk told him he had a visitor.

A lanky Human stood on the doorstep in a white jumpsuit, covered in muddy smudges and what Poldo hoped were mustard stains. A small, white cap perched on his greasy mop of hair, bearing black embroidery in the shape of a dead rat. He gave a friendly wave and nod as Poldo opened the door. "Hello, Mr. Poldo, sir. I've been hired to exterminate the vermin on your premises, but I'll expect you'll want to be off before I do."

"What?" said Poldo.

"On account of the noxious cloud, sir." The exterminator pointed to a wand hanging from his tool belt. "Makes a nasty gas that'll wipe out anything in the house. Should dissipate after a few minutes, though. I could do it while you're on your lunch."

"You can't exterminate Wood Gnomes," said Poldo. "They're protected by law."

"Oh, of course, of course!" said the exterminator loudly. He gave Poldo a leering wink. "But, uh, I'm here for the mice."

Poldo's brow furrowed. "I don't have mice."

"Right, right. But your benefactor, one Mr. Stearn, was most emphatic that you do, in fact, have mice. And I can use this wand to get rid of your problem. With mice." The man spoke in the loud, slow pace of someone very stupid who believes he is being very clever. He punctuated each sentence with an exaggerated wink.

Poldo grit his teeth, and made a mental note to have a frank conversation with Mr. Stearn. "I. Don't. Have. Mice."

The exterminator looked around for help, clearly confused. "Listen, sir, I'm trying to give you a hint here. I can help you with, you know, your little nuisance."

Poldo was waiting for the word, but he still flinched when he heard it. Few knew better than Gnomes how easy it was for the big people to see the smaller ones as annoying, to define them by their convenience, or lack thereof. Most people had seen Mrs. Hrurk and her pups as nuisances too. The thought made Poldo's mustache bristle. "I am also trying to give you a hint. The only nuisance I need to be rid of is the big one standing in my doorway."

The message finally breached the exterminator's thick skull. He gave a frown and a sniff. "Well, I know where I'm not wanted."

"I suspect that makes you an expert on geography," snapped Poldo. He managed to growl, "Good day, sir!" before slamming the door in the exterminator's face.

It took a moment to find his composure again. When Poldo turned around, Mrs. Hrurk was staring at him with an odd smile. "I'm sorry you had to see that," he said, adjusting his tie.

"You're a good man, Mr. Poldo," said the Gnoll.

Poldo wasn't used to receiving compliments that didn't have hard figures attached to them, so he simply nodded as he returned to his desk. Once there, though, he noticed that Mrs. Hrurk was still watching him, though now with a face that seemed a little more pensive.

"Is something wrong, Mrs. Hrurk?" he asked.

"No, no," said Mrs. Hrurk, turning back to the stack of unopened mail. "It's nothing."

"I'm sure it isn't," Poldo said.

"I just… I don't feel right asking something of you when you've done so much for the children and I." Mrs. Hrurk knit her paws together anxiously as she spoke. "But I was talking to Barga of the Fire Hawk Tribe last night, and she and her mate were evicted from their apartment last week. I know she'll find a new job soon, but it's hard for a Goblin these days, even with a good record and clean NPC papers."

Poldo could see where this was going. "And you'd like for them to stay with us?"

"It would only be for a little while," said the Gnoll. "Just until she finds work and a new apartment. The guild will rescind her family's papers if they find them living on the streets, and there's only one other option for Shadowkin these days."

Poldo nodded. He knew where undocumented Shadowkin would wind up.

"The Red Horde!" bellowed Darak Guz'Varda, his great warhammer held high. He wore the ceremonial armor of a chieftain, with the new addition of a crimson pauldron on his left shoulder.

"The Red Horde!" the crowd roared back at him. "The Red Horde! The Red Horde!"

They were still shouting it as Darak strode off the stage built for his coronation. Asherzu barely recognized her little brother, standing taller than even Father had, draped in beads and slathered in a chieftain's ceremonial skin paint. He looked like the kind of chieftain Orcs sang ballads about; a mighty warrior striding out of legends of blood and valor. With a figure so imposing, it was no wonder that Darak had claimed the throne unopposed. Yet in his eyes, Asherzu saw only sadness and fear.

"You do not look happy, my sister," said Darak, managing a smile.

"Nor do you, honored one," she said.

"Do not call me that," he grumbled. He joined Asherzu in the shadows behind the stage, and leaned against the same fence that she did. The

wooden barrier groaned in protest. *"Not when it is just you and I. I never wanted that."*

"I did not think you wanted any of this," Asherzu said softly. She stared out at the homes of the Guz'Varda beyond the fence, a village of huts, tents, and makeshift hovels by the rocky coast. The archway holding Fulgen's Rest formed a dark silhouette against the deepening evening.

"The warriors are celebrating," said Darak. *"They wished to see me follow Brother Char's path, and I have. I will honor him."*

"And what of Father?" asked Asherzu. *"What of his ways? Or what of the people? Not all are warriors. Not all wish to join the Red Horde."*

"I… I will try the best I can," said Darak, looking about as though cornered. *"I wish to honor Father and you and Char and all of the others. But I… I don't always… I mean, how do you honor them all?"*

"You alone must choose who to listen to, and whose counsel to take," said Asherzu.

"I do not know if I can," Darak admitted.

"You can." Asherzu set her hand atop her brother's. *"You must. You are chieftain, now. And I will be with you, Little Warg. No matter what."*

He smiled down at her, but couldn't say anything.

They waited together until after the celebration had ended, staring out at the hovels of the Guz'Varda as the fire pits winked out, one by one.

Chapter 6

The fires of distant campsites flickered to life across the landscape as Vetchell's refugees made camp. From the boulder that Heraldin reclined on, they looked like earthbound stars spread across the vast expanse of the plain.

"I'm not saying that I don't feel bad for those people," Heraldin told Gaist. "I'm not heartless. But you have to admit, Vetchell's folk are doing fine, given the circumstances. They must have kept up on their evacuation drills."

The weaponsmaster, standing stoically next to Heraldin's perch, allowed a hint of a nod in agreement.

The cities of Arth had become accustomed to invasion by the forces of darkness; indeed, much of the world's economy depended on the periodic sacking of major cities by monstrous threats. Natural selection had long ago eliminated those citizens who weren't prepared to evacuate on short notice. Vacating an entire city was considered an essential skill among Arth's populace, and the people of Vetchell made retreat an art form. Within an hour of the alarm bells sounding, the streets had been lined with people methodically loading children, provisions, and supplies onto wagons and pack animals. Now that the party was three days out of the city, Heraldin was confident Vetchell was empty.

"But as they say in Daellan, sometimes life is like a sewer flood: it stinks, but it only gets worse if you go against the current. And this party is headed upstream without a paddle."

Gaist's expression might have been concerned, or perhaps taken aback. The weaponsmaster was harder to read than a blank book, but Heraldin liked to think that he had become quite adept at interpreting

Gaist's subtle cues. If the bard had overestimated the degree of insight he had into Gaist's silence, the weaponsmaster never corrected him. At least, Heraldin didn't think he had.

"Don't be so surprised, my friend," Heraldin said. "I may seem a hopeless romantic at times, but I'm a firm pragmatist at heart."

Heraldin was almost certain he saw Gaist roll his eyes as the weaponsmaster leaned down to pull a thrones board from his rucksack.

"It's a common mistake." Heraldin clambered down from the boulder as Gaist placed the board on a rock between them. "People see that I am a lover of song, of poetry, of nature, of love itself. They assume that because I have such an artful soul, I must be led by my heart. But above all, I am a lover of life. Mine, specifically. And as such, I rely on my wits and intellect to preserve it as long as possible."

Gaist's scarf rippled with a hint of a smirk as he tapped the side of the thrones board. They'd both carved a notch in the oak slab for each of their wins over the past year. Heraldin had a few scattered grooves on his side of the board, while Gaist's edge looked like it had been vigorously gnawed on by some needle-toothed animal.

"Oh, very amusing," said Heraldin, setting up his pieces. He elected to play as white this game, but as they'd resorted to scrounging improvised pieces, he was actually playing as white, light gray, brownish, sky blue, and a piece of quartz.

"I'll concede that you've a knack for thrones. And you're a sound strategist as well." Heraldin opened the game by advancing a bannerman. "But you know I lived on the streets for years. I've a knack for self-preservation. Which is why I know this plan is madness."

Gaist moved his own bannerman forward.

"You can pretend you don't see it if you like, friend." Heraldin quickly moved another bannerman, then put a knight into play when Gaist countered. "But I know you have the same questions that I do. Why did we spend a year chasing the Red Horde across the Freedlands? Why did we stroll into a city with the Heroes' Guild calling for our heads? Why are we off to rob said guild now, just so we can fight a liche? Do we gain anything, or are we just wandering in search of misery to interfere with?"

Gaist didn't look up from the board as he made a move: a bold rush with his solamancer to take a bannerman.

"Well, it may not matter to you, but I can think of a few better ways to live in exile. Most of them involve hard drink and loose women." Heraldin took the solamancer with a knight, and cursed as he realized he'd left his noctomancer exposed in his haste. "But it seems everyone else is hell-bent on diving headfirst into peril until we die."

Gaist shrugged and advanced his own noctomancer, pinning Heraldin's. With only one safe move, the bard's noctomancer flipped to Gaist's side.

"Ah, right, I forgot that you're chief among those determined to fall in combat," said Heraldin, taking the turncoat noctomancer with a bannerman. "I wonder, my friend, what could drive you to want your own end? Is it for guilt? Or grief? Or do you wish to die for honor, as you Imperials are so prone to?"

The weaponsmaster's eyes flashed with uncharacteristic emotion as they snapped up to look directly into Heraldin's. It was practically a shout by Gaist's standards.

"Easy, friend," said the bard, holding his hands up. "I meant no disrespect. Merely a musing."

Gaist stared at him for a moment, then turned back to the game. For a while they played in true silence, their faces as still as the evening air, their attacks and counters accelerating as the game intensified.

"You know," Heraldin said as he took a knight. "I'm reminded of a Tinderkin legend that a tinker's daughter once taught me."

Gaist pulled back a bannerman without looking up.

"She said that when Arth was young and the gods still roamed it, Gnome ran in the forest with Deer and Boar and Wolf and all the other animals. Gnome hunted, and he fought, and he killed. He lived with no thought for any other. Just as Deer and Boar and Wolf did." Heraldin feinted with his solamancer, then took the knight that Gaist sent after it.

Gaist's brow furrowed.

"But Gnome roamed too far, hunted too much, killed too many. This displeased Fengelde, the Lady in the Wood, and she was no longer content to have him run among her beasts. So she sent Wolf and Dog to hunt Gnome and kill him." Heraldin traded a bannerman for a knight.

"Wolf and Dog chased Gnome across all of Arth, and Gnome thought that he would die, for Wolf and Dog were mightier than he. But Erro, the Hearth Father, had pity. The god came to Gnome and gave him a mask, so that when Dog and Wolf caught Gnome, they didn't recognize him." Most of the pieces were gone now, and the action was centered around a corner of the board where Heraldin's knight was dancing with Gaist's noctomancer and king.

"Dog said, 'We've come to kill a beast called Gnome,'" said Heraldin. "But Gnome pointed to his mask and replied 'I am no beast. I am Man. I have morals, and nobility, and honor. It is much better than being a beast.' And Dog believed Gnome, and so abandoned Fengelde and went with Gnome as his companion."

Gaist narrowed his eyes at Heraldin as he pulled back his king.

"But Wolf was angry, and he told Dog, 'Gnome has not changed; Man is only a mask on a beast. If you take his mask away, he will fight and kill as much as ever. I will not be shackled by his lies.' And so Wolf ran back to Fengelde, to be free and run with the beasts forever." Heraldin pressed in with his knight and a bannerman, forcing Gaist's pieces against the edge of the board.

The weaponsmaster furrowed his brow and moved a distant knight toward the fray.

Heraldin pressed in. "People may play at morals or nobility or honor. They may believe in 'the right thing' so much that they'd even fight a liche to save a bunch of people they've never met. But in times of hardship or war or famine, times that are coming soon, the mask falls and all the honorable things slip away. They are not real. They are not worth giving your life for. Especially not when you would leave behind friends sorry to see you go."

Gaist froze for a moment, his eyes locked on the board. Then slowly, purposefully, he advanced a knight.

It was a mistake. Heraldin swiftly captured the knight and pointed it at Gaist. "I'm stuck on this so-called quest, friend, a caged animal. With the guild and Benny Hookhand after my blood, I've no chance of making it on my own. But with a fighter like you... Well, should you ever drop the mask, you and I could run free again. Think on that."

The bard advanced his last bannerman, pinning Gaist's noctomancer and turning it to his side. Gaist's king had no moves left. "I believe that's a win for me," he told the weaponsmaster, standing. "And I know enough to quit when I'm ahead. Have a good evening, my friend."

With that, Heraldin headed back to the tents and left Gaist to pick up the pieces.

"I bet that hurt!" said Ignatius Wythelm, but he stared at the shrine's eyes for another second before he allowed himself a laugh. These days, being a priest of the god of death wasn't as much fun as it used to be.

It took an odd sort to serve in the priesthood of Mordo Ogg. The Lord of the End had few followers and no treasury. He rarely afforded his clergy power and bestowed few rewards on them for their devotion. And when a priest finally arrived at their own end, all of Mordo Ogg's scant teachings were clear: there was no special treatment for his disciples.

Then again, the god of death demanded little of his followers, and people asked even less of them. And while the majority of people went all their lives ignoring most of the pantheon, all of them bowed to Mordo Ogg at least once.

Ignatius was odder than most of his brothers and sisters in service. Most of Mordo Ogg's clergy were maudlin, spending their days moping around in white makeup and black robes while they recited tragic sonnets. But Ignatius considered himself a romantic, a lover of life—most specifically the last bit. He took immense pleasure from watching people the world over pass away, their departing souls momentarily lighting the eyes of the shrine of Mordo Ogg in Sculpin Down.

"There goes another!"

The shrine was little more than a single statue carved into an alcove in Andarun's wall. It depicted a seated skeleton with steepled hands. Crimson light flashed intermittently in the skull's sockets, and with every flicker the old priest's gap-toothed grin grew.

"And another! Guess the herdsman finally bought the farm, eh? Ha ha! And—"

The old priest stopped short as the lights in the skull changed in nature, shifting in hue from crimson to a pale, sickly green that lingered even after the flare of light had faded. The worshippers of Mordo Ogg had few tenets, but they took what they had seriously.

Their chief creed said that death was a journey all mortals must make, and it should be a one-way trip.

Ignatius knew all too well the blasphemy portended by a flash of viridescent light.

"No!" the priest howled, hurling himself against the statue's dark eye sockets as though he could claw the light within them back into being. "You stay down! That isn't right!"

The red light resumed flickering, as constant and passionless as ever.

"The master hates that," he muttered, pulling himself back. He pulled his black robes around himself as though warding off a chill. "And there's too much of it these days. It isn't right for the dead to walk. It isn't right."

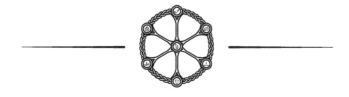

"It's all sodding drake spit!" A sweep of Tyren Ur'Thos' arm swept the clutter from his desk, including his tumbler of Dwarven whiskey. It made a sad chiming sound as it shattered.

Tyren stared at the glass shards and amber liquid pooled beneath them on the wooden floor. Part of him worried that the liquid would stain the floorboards, but then the sober part recalled that it didn't matter. Nobody would care about the floor in the morning. The guardhouse likely wouldn't be here by morning. With a shrug, Tyren poured himself another glass of Burnbristle's gold-label, aged four hundred years.

He had taken the first drink to calm his nerves and steady his hands, but by now the alcohol had pushed him long past steadiness into fluid wobbling. Yet what the burning liquor took away in stability it gave back in confidence, and by time he had drained his latest glass, the letter seemed like a good idea again. He retrieved it from the pile of papers on the floor.

At first he thought his drink must have spilled on the page, as all the writing looked blurry and smudged, but then he decided that the rest of the room looked rather blurry and smudged as well. With a shrug, he folded the missive and fetched a red candle. Wax dribbled all over the parchment as he waved the candle with the exaggerated concentration of a drunk. It took him four tries to finally hit a crimson pool with his signet ring and seal the letter.

As he shook the letter to cool the wax, his eye caught the small, framed woodcut of three smiling figures sitting in a meadow in their best dress. In the hills behind them, the Ur'Thos family castle sat on Ruskan's northern shore. The ancestral hold was usually cold and miserable, but for a few weeks each summer the snow melted, the flowers bloomed, and the hills came alive. Little Aubey had loved running in the coastal meadows.

Tyren's younger self grinned back at him from the picture, blissfully unaware that the woman at his side would be running off with a bard from Parald the next winter, taking Aubey with her. Years later, Tyren was still alone, still miserable, and living under a de facto death sentence.

The impending doom was a recent development, and one that he blamed himself for. Tyren was familiar enough with Nove's principles of universal irony to know that claiming a portion of the undead's treasure was just begging for trouble. The universe would never allow Tyren such good fortune. Nor fate, nor the gods, nor, most pointedly, the elders of Vetchell. Elder Thisel had taken particular delight in assigning the knight-commander to defend Vetchell to the last.

Tyren took a deep breath and poured himself a final drink. "To the pit with Elder Thisel," he said in a toast. "And with Nove, and with the whole thrice-cursed universe while we're at it."

Another thought struck him as he drained the glass. He made a couple of clumsy attempts to open the panel on the back of the picture. Failing that, he smashed the frame on his desk, slipped the woodcut into his belt pouch, and stood up.

Standing was a bad idea.

His office spun with such violence that he nearly fell to the floor. Between the liquor and the ceremonial armor, Tyren couldn't manage much beyond an exaggerated stagger. He fell against the door, took a few deep breaths, and threw it open.

"Knight-Commander!" Captains and sergeants charged Tyren the moment he emerged from his office. "Knight-Commander Ur'Thos, the undead are at the southern gate!"

"The bloody corpses are scaling the walls!"

"Skeletal archers are letting loose—"

"—Reported several casualties—"

"—Wards over the east wall!"

Tyren raised a hand to silence the assembled officers, but doing so threw him off-balance. It was all he could do to catch himself by leaning against the wall at a forty-five-degree angle.

"Fellows, I appreciate your troubles, but I regret to inform you that I am resigning effective immediately," he said to the floor, waving the letter in the general direction of the closest subordinates.

"What?" demanded Captain Bothwick.

"I am resigning effective—"

"We heard what you said," said Captain Ingrim. "But it cannot be so, sir. You can't abandon the men now, when they need you most."

"Well, I can't see how they need me," said Tyren. "I can't save their lives, and they'll surely manage to die without my help."

"But we're to be the town's rearguard," protested Sergeant Ur'Rastan.

"We're here to mount a facade of a defense so the citizens' insurance policies don't get voided," snarled Tyren. "If the town has no defenders, all of these houses are abandoned property. Some token soldiers have to be sacrificed. I don't intend to be among them."

"Give up your hopeless cynicism, man!" snapped Captain Bothwick. "We're buying the evacuees time to flee!"

"Maybe you are," said Tyren. "I'm here because I submitted the quest!"

The assembled officers looked aghast. "Do you care nothing for the people of our city?" demanded one of them. The fat one. Tyren couldn't think of his name.

"They got a... a good head start." Tyren walked his hands up the wall to right himself. Magda and Aubey left eleven years ago. The rest of them had, what, four days? Good enough.

"What you're proposing, Knight-Commander, is dereliction of duty," growled Captain Ingrim.

"I can't have any duty, because I'm a deserter," said Tyren, throwing the letter at the captain's feet. Slowly, trying to disguise his unsteady gait as a purposeful stride, Tyren pushed past the gathered officers and out the door.

"So that's it," Bothwick said. "We're all to die here, abandoned by our commanding officer?"

"You might be, but I'm headed north." Tyren pointed down the road in front of him.

"Should we arrest him, sirs?" asked Sergeant Ur'Rastan.

"No," said Captain Ingrim, wearing a strange smile. "No, leave him. He'll get his soon enough."

Tyren staggered on his way as fast as his legs would carry him. His progress was slow, as the street kept spinning when he moved, and nothing looked like it was in the right place. He staggered down side streets and got sidetracked in alleys as he searched for some familiar signs, but everything seemed off. Worse, the sounds of fighting were intensifying around him.

When Tyren stumbled around a corner and saw the wall, his stomach fell. Soldiers were crowded up against Vetchell's massive gate, and many more lined the ramparts. Specters clashed against magical wards that the mages had left over the city. The way the enchanted barriers shimmered and shook with every ghostly assault led Tyren to believe the magic wouldn't hold much longer.

"You there!" he shouted, stumbling up to a soldier at the rear of the mob. "Have the undead made it this far north?"

"North?" said the startled soldier. "I suppose so, yes, Lordship. They arrived at the gates this morning."

"And are you all deserters?" asked Tyren.

"Not at all, Knight-Commander!" said the soldier. He looked to be a lieutenant by the stripes above his heraldry, a middle-aged man by the gray in his hair and paunch sticking out from beneath his breastplate. "Not while I've a sword on my belt and a spear in my hand!"

"But then…" Two of Tyren's neurons finally swam close enough to make the connection. "Oh, thrice curse the gods' bones! This is the southern gate!"

"Of course, your lordship!" said the lieutenant. "The last stand of Vetchell!"

It occurred to Tyren that there was a fatal flaw in his plan: by the time he had imbibed enough courage to brazenly desert, he was too drunk to navigate to safety. He shook his head. "I can't be… I mean I've got to… I need to…" The knight-commander found it hard to form a sentence with a pickled brain and a strange piping in his ears. "Got to… do you hear something?"

"Battles are generally a noisy affair, sir," said the lieutenant. "Screams, clanging weapons, and… what is that?"

Amid the roar of battle, Tyren could make out warbling music, growing in volume and intensity.

"Is that music?" asked the lieutenant. The other soldiers looked around in bewilderment as stream of short, sharp notes overwhelmed the battle, punctuated by a longer, deeper swell of music.

At the bottom of his depths, Tyren wanted to run. Unfortunately, the rest of his depths were already running about eighty proof. Now that he had lost his momentum he doubted he could take more than a few steps without toppling over.

"It's one of them Gnomish organs," shouted another man at the barricade.

"Stop talkin' nonsense," the lieutenant hollered back. "Of course it ain't a Gnomish organ!"

A siege engine of some sort or another hit the wall, sending a cloud of stone dust into the air. Chips of masonry and ashes rained down on the resolute guards below. Sheets of paper fluttered over the wall like pale leaves among the fog. Tyren snatched one from the air and read with bleary eyes.

The page was a flyer, like the ones the General Store used to sell adventuring gear. A single skull woodcut decorated the top, and beneath it a bold message was printed in equally bold lettering of various sizes.

TREMBLE, MORTAL!

DREAD LORD

DETARR UR'MAYAN,

KING *of the* DEAD,

comes for your soul!

ETERNAL TORMENT AWAITS.

Tyren looked up from the page to see if anyone else had seen the odd advertisement. He noticed a couple of soldiers exchanging nervous glances as they read. Most of the guards were standing resolute to the last. And two of them, inexplicably, were still locked in debate.

"No, I'm certain of it, Ted!" the soldier insisted. "Listen to those staccato notes! The fugues! It's one of those Imperial toccata pieces. And Imperial toccatas were traditionally written to be played on Gnomish organs."

"Don't you lecture me on Imperial toccatas, Neddard Biggins!" snapped the lieutenant. "This ain't about music theory! It's about supply lines and efficiency!"

"This isn't really the time…" Tyren stumbled back from the gate. Whatever the instrument, the music was getting louder, and rushing toward an imposing crescendo.

"I mean, even a small Gnomish organ has got to weigh over three hundred stone, and if you shake it too hard the insides will get busted," Lieutenant Ted continued. "Who wants to haul that alongside an army? And then you'd need your regular maintenance to keep the pipes clean and the leather bits from fraying. Not to mention keeping it in tune. The logistics would be a nightmare!"

"I can't say anything about logistics, but I know a Gnomish organ playing an Imperial toccata when I hear one!" Neddard yelled back.

"Burn it, Neddard!" shouted Ted. "Why would anyone haul an extremely heavy yet very fragile instrument hundreds of miles just to play it at the dramatic climax of a siege?"

The lieutenant likely would have continued arguing, but the soldiers' debate—and their lives—were cut short by the dramatic climax of the siege. Specifically, the part where the gates of Vetchell were blown from their hinges in a great explosion of shrapnel and surprised guards.

"It's called setting the atmosphere, you troglodytes!" roared a robed figure emerging from smoke and dust. He towered above the stricken guards, in part because he was tall but mostly because he levitated a foot off the ground. A skull burned with violet flames where his head should have been, and he wore a crown wrought from iron spikes. Behind him, ranks of leering corpses shambled into the city.

Tyren didn't know much about the undead, but he knew enough to recognize a liche when he saw one. He turned to flee again, but encountering a liche was a prime example of what Heroes' Guild auditors referred to as "statistical death:" circumstances wherein a person's chances of survival were so near zero that his or her life was, for all intents and purposes, definitively over.

Tyren didn't make it two steps before the math played out.

The liche wove a plume of violet flames with a casual wave of his hand, blasting Tyren from his feet. As the knight-commander fell in agony, his belt pouch burst open, and the family woodcut fell into view. A sudden longing washed over him amidst the pain, and he tried to scream Aubey's name, but he couldn't make a sound. The picture curled and blackened to ash in moments, and then Tyren's world vanished in a flash.

Light filled Tyren's consciousness, narrowing into a circle of brilliant white, and for a moment he felt compelled to walk toward the luminous singularity. Yet longing and anger still filled him, burning hot and weighing heavily. The emotions pulled him backward, downward, and he fell into what seemed like an eternal darkness.

In time, the shadows around Tyren congealed into the charred husks of buildings and heaps of rubble. He clutched at the ground and froze when his fingers hit the cobbles with a cold *click* rather than the familiar pressure of flesh on stone. He turned his gauntlet over, and through blackened holes in his chainmail he saw that his hand was gone, replaced by a skeletal appendage.

Confusion gripped him. He turned away from the ghastly sight and immediately leapt to his feet. Not an arm's length from his face a skull bobbed in the air, surrounded by a cloud of bloodred flames. It stared at Tyren with a single, lidless eyeball.

"What is happening?" Tyren cried in a voice much like his own, but colder. More flat. Distant.

"Hello!" said the skull. It bobbed up and down in a manner reminiscent of a friendly wave. "You've been selected to be a part of a focus group!"

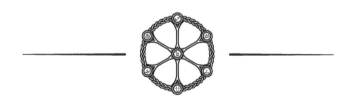

"I just never would have expected that," said Laruna, propping Kaitha up on her shoulder as they made their way toward the campsite. "I mean, not with a ranger anyway."

Kaitha grit her teeth as she limped. "Anyone can trip over a tree root and twist their leg."

"I thought it was a rock?" said Laruna.

"I feel like the key point here is my leg," said Kaitha.

Camp was still a good distance off, and the road was farther still. The campsites and cookfires of evacuees lined the main route from Vetchell to Parald. The moving city raised a constant din that could be heard from miles away.

After days with a grueling pace, Laruna's party had put enough distance between themselves and Vetchell's displaced populace to finally hear themselves think. They set up their tents shortly before the sun set, and after dinner there was still enough daylight for some sparring before bed.

At least, Laruna had presumed there was enough light, but then the Elf face-planted in the middle of the field.

"Right, accidents happen." Laruna glanced around. "So, do you need me to… heal… you?"

"No, no! That's quite all right," said Kaitha hurriedly.

"Oh, thank the gods." Spells for mending wounds, curing poisons, and cleansing disease were all part of a typical solamancer's skill set, but Laruna specialized in pyromancy. She'd never been much good for anything in the healing ward, save perhaps cauterizing wounds.

"Maybe I could borrow an elixir though?" Kaitha suggested.

"A healing potion?" Laruna looked at the Elf's limp. "I mean, I saw you fall. It didn't seem that serious."

"Right. But as a precaution."

"A precaution against what?" The mage gave the ranger a sideways glance.

"Infection? Possible breaks?" Kaitha huffed. "Look, I just thought you might have picked some salve up back in Vetchell or something."

"Gods, you sound like…" Laruna didn't consciously stop herself from saying "a salve-head." Rather, words failed her as memories from the past year hijacked her train of thought. The Elf's constant scratching of her wrists. Kaitha's frequent requests to borrow others' potions. The ranger's habit of staring into the distance, talking softly to herself.

"It might be a sprain, or worse," the Elf continued "I can't do my job if I can't walk, so I… Why are you looking at me like that?"

"Looking at you like what?" said Laruna, trying to look nonchalant.

"You're giving me the 'you have a problem,' look, Laruna," said Kaitha.

"No I'm not," said Laruna. As an afterthought, she broke into a wide grin.

Kaitha scowled. "Don't play games. Every town crier from here to the Imperial City has called me a drunk. I've had more interventions than birthdays, and I'm really old. I know the 'you have a problem' look when I see it, and you're giving me that look. Or you were. Now you're just smiling like you're guilty or kind of insane."

"I never said you had a problem."

"Good," said Kaitha. "Because I don't have a problem."

"Although that is what someone with a problem would say," the solamancer added.

They stared at each other through narrowed eyes.

"Yes," said Kaitha slowly. "But it is also what someone without a problem would say."

"I… I mean…" Laruna looked around helplessly. Like most mages, she had spent her life neglecting relationships in favor of bending reality to her will. Now that her circumstances called for diplomacy and tact, she was no more useful than a club in a wizards' duel.

There were, Laruna realized, some problems that she couldn't set on fire.

"It's just that if…" the solamancer stumbled. "If you didn't know you had a problem or you were in denial about it—"

"You know what?" Kaitha pulled away from Laruna and hopped a couple of steps away. "I don't need this right now. Life is hard enough without my so-called friends second-guessing my injuries. I'll make it back to camp on my own, thanks!"

"Kaitha!" Laruna called. "Kaitha, I'm sorry!" She started to follow the Elf, but stopped short, in part because she had no idea what to say, and in part because the ranger's limp was vanishing as she strode back toward her tent. The solamancer's hands dropped to her sides.

Laruna liked to keep things simple. It was why she loved professional heroics; there wasn't much a hero encountered that couldn't be solved with a liberal application of fireballs. Unfortunately, until recently that had been her preferred method for solving interpersonal conflict as well. She still had no idea how to peacefully resolve problems with other mages, let alone how to approach an immortal ex-celebrity about a potential drug problem.

A thought struck the solamancer. Gorm was also an ex-celebrity, and while not immortal, he was both older than Laruna and crotchety beyond his years. Plus, he and Kaitha were close friends. Perhaps he would have some insight. Laruna started walking faster toward the camp.

A quick glance around the cookfire confirmed that Gorm hadn't returned to camp yet. Just as Jynn lost himself in books, or Heraldin and Gaist ceaselessly played thrones, the Dwarf escaped the stresses of their travels nearly every night by wandering off into the woods.

If memory served, Laruna had seen the Dwarf set out for a distant copse of birch and pine. Even at a distance, the small wood looked like the perfect spot for a private conversation about how to handle a potential crisis. Gorm would know what to do.

With a nod to herself, the solamancer turned from camp and set out to find the Dwarf.

"Do you even know where you'll search?" Thane asked.

"Not sure. Aya's papers say who owns the artifacts we need, but not where they're kept." Gorm sat at the edge of the small creek running through the shallow ravine they occupied, working a whetstone over the edge of his axe. "First thing is to get to Parald. After that, we'll see if we can figure out which relic to look for."

"Just one?" Burt asked. The Kobold reclined by the shore on Gorm's rucksack, gnawing on a rabbit bone.

"Aye, and only then because we've no other good choice," said Gorm. He rinsed his stone and axe in the stream. "Artifacts are trouble, one and all. And worse, Jynn says most of these on Aya's list were made by the Sten. Ye can't trust anything the Sten touched."

"Who are the Sten?" said the Troll.

Gorm looked at the Troll. The hulking Shadowkin wore a big smile, expectant and naive.

It was hard to keep track of the boundaries of Thane's knowledge. He must have been the most eloquent and sophisticated Troll on Arth, but that wasn't a high bar to jump. Or step over. A Wood Gnome would have to work to trip over the bar. Troll culture consisted of individuals lurking in suitably ominous territories and killing anything that came too close. A Troll's upbringing would make the School of Hard Knocks look like a preparatory academy. It was the sort of education that left gaps in a student's teeth as well as in their knowledge.

"Uh, a bad sort," said Gorm, backpedaling as fast as his tongue could carry him. "At least, as far as the legends are concerned. Ain't been around for ages. Even the oldest Elves don't remember 'em."

"So, why worry about them if they're gone?" asked Thane.

"It's more about what they left behind," said Gorm.

"The artifacts?"

"That too," Burt said.

"Well, what else did they leave?" Thane said.

"Uh… look, Shadowkin are all descended from people of light, right?" The Dwarf shifted uncomfortably. "Gnolls used to be Gnomes, and Goblins came from Dwarves, and Orcs were Elves, right? Well the Trolls… they were Sten."

"Ah." Thane's smile disappeared. "So, you hate the Sten because of Trolls."

"No! Well, that's not the whole reason. Look, ye ever hear of the War of Betrayal? When Mannon led the Shadowkin to war—"

"Because he tricked and sorcerously enslaved them," interjected Burt.

"Aye, aye, not placin' blame or anythin'," said Gorm. "But when the war began, the Sten sided with the Trolls. It's one reason it's called the War of Betrayal. That and all the gods stabbin' each other in their metaphysical backs."

"So… people hate Trolls because of the Sten, then," said Thane.

Gorm and Burt winced in unison. "Well, that's not the whole reason," said the Kobold.

"There's also all the rippin' people's limbs off and eatin' them," said Gorm. "But we know ye wouldn't do that. Ye ain't like other Trolls."

"But I'm not like you either," said Thane. He reached into a pouch hanging from his bandolier and extracted something small and purple.

"What's that?" Stepping closer, Gorm saw a figurine of a knight in the Troll's palm, painted all in purple and wearing a quartz crystal on its chest. It reminded Gorm of the armor old Royalheart used to wear back in the day.

"Just something Kaitha left for… Something she gave me." Thane stared at the tiny statue for a moment, turning it over and over in his hands. "I've thought about what you said, about revealing my secret to her."

Gorm could tell where this was going. "Look, ye can't take people's feelings about the Sten personally."

"It's more the way they feel about the Trolls," said Thane.

"Well, look, just because we said —"

"It isn't just because of what you said," rumbled Thane. "It's because of how it's always been. From the first time I saved someone in the Myrewood, they always… they screamed and ran away. For years every single person I helped fled, sometimes while I was still rescuing them. It wasn't until I saved a young merchant while hidden from her that one of them spoke to me at all. But when I stepped out of the trees, she ran off as well."

Gorm started to say something, but a paw fell on his hand and stopped him. Burt looked up and shook his head.

The Troll stared into the distance, as though watching the past play out. "I tried every way to approach them. I was friendly, I was benign, I waited for them to invite me out of the shadows, I had entire conversations from the undergrowth before standing. None of it mattered. Sometimes they screamed, sometimes they went silent with fright, and sometimes they even shot arrows or threw spells to cover their escape, but all of them ran. And the worst part… the worst part was the way they looked at me right before they fled."

"It wasn't the arrows and spells?" said Gorm, earning himself a hard nudge from the Kobold.

Thane shook his head. "People make this face when they see me. Their eyes open wide and they get paler. It's all the fear and disgust they have, balled up and ready to come out as a scream. I couldn't stand to see that face, but every time… every single time. It became easier to stay hidden."

"Kaitha's different," Gorm said over Burt's pantomimed protest.

"Of course she's different." Thane laughed mirthlessly. "She's gentle, and kind, and powerful, and beautiful, all in ways I never thought anyone could be. I wouldn't have followed you from the Myrewood if she wasn't what she is. But the people I saved were as varied as the plants of the swamp. Fighters, mages, merchants, tinkers, pilgrims, and priests; I helped all sorts, Gorm. They were all different."

The Troll looked at himself in the stream. "I'm the part that doesn't change. I'm still the same. And some days you just have to wonder if they have a point. If they're right to be afraid."

Thane reached down and swiped a hand through the water, scattering his reflection. "I remained hidden for a long time, until a traveler and his wife tried to coax me out by setting a scrap of velvet on a rock as an offering. I took it when they weren't looking, and they… they knew I was there. They could see I was real, and they thanked me before they left. And I know it wasn't much of a connection, but it was still a connection, and one that didn't involve watching them run away or getting shot in the face."

"I… I'm sorry." It was hard for Gorm to argue with that logic given his own initial meeting with Thane; their first encounter had involved a lot of screaming, fleeing, and axe blows to the Troll's head.

"They must have told people what happened, because more people started setting out purple trinkets. And some began to call me the King in the Wood. I heard them tell legends about me around the cookfires." The Troll grinned at the memory, his fangs sticking out at odd angles. "And I was almost a part of their camps. Almost. The idea of me belonged, even if the rest of me didn't."

He took a deep breath before continuing. "Kaitha likes the idea of me, the legend she wants to be true. And if I can be that for her, if I can have that connection, I have to protect it. Because if she ever knew the reality, if I ever saw her make that terrified face—"

A piercing scream split the air, startling Gorm and the Shadowkin to attention. They looked up to the top of the ridge. Laruna stood at the edge of the woods, shrieking at the top of her lungs.

Thane sighed as he looked at the mage's terrified countenance. "Yeah, that's the one," he said just before the firestorm washed over him.

Garold Flinn was feeling the heat.

Not in the physical sense, of course. Spring's warmth touched the Palace of Andarun last, and at this elevation it was still cold enough to see Flinn's breath in the last of dusk's light. Rather, the pressure of his job was becoming acute in a way that was really only possible for hired killers.

The Tinderkin ran a sweaty palm through his hair as he glanced around pillars at the edge of the palace garden. His other hand, or more precisely, the silver mechanism that an artificer had replaced it with, rapped its talons on the marble of a column.

A shadow fell over the ground in front of the Tinderkin. "Good evening, Flinn," said a deep voice.

Mr. Flinn tried to suppress a shudder as he leaned back against the pillar. He didn't turn around. "Sir."

"You've heard about Vetchell."

"Indeed, sir. A pity about the undead," said Mr. Flinn.

"King Handor will find out about the attack tomorrow," said the shadow. "I think the situation presents an opportunity."

"I've bought into several promising stocks on the news," said Flinn.

"Have you now? A good move!" said the voice. "But I was asking if you had heard the rumors that Gorm Ingerson and his party reported the undead incursion."

Flinn had been expecting the subject of Gorm Ingerson to arise, but not in this manner. "Really? But... I heard it was the knight-commander of Vetchell's city guard."

"I thought you had better sources, Flinn." The voice from the shadows laughed darkly. "I certainly hoped so, given the amount of giltin we're paying you to make Ingerson and his companions disappear. After our last discussion, I assumed you would be the one providing information this time."

Flinn nodded. "Yes sir. I shall endeavor to find better sources in Ruskan."

"Do you suppose that will help?" asked the shadow. "I doubt he'll be there much longer. Ingerson does tend to pop up in random places at the most inconvenient times."

"Very unfortunate, sir."

"You have no idea, Mr. Flinn," growled the voice in the shadow. "Listen. Whether they call themselves mercenaries, heroes, or assassins, there are only two types of hired killers: useful partners and loose ends."

Mr. Flinn took a deep breath. It was the second time he'd heard the loose ends speech in less than a week. That was the problem with taking on multiple contracts for the same job: the pay may have been twice as good, but the price of failure was twice as bad. And while the Tinderkin doubted that Goldson and Baggs could find an assassin skilled enough to make good on their implicit threats, some of his clients wouldn't need to find a surrogate killer. The one in the shadows always preferred a more personal touch.

"Ingerson is a loose end. I need a useful partner to get rid of him," continued the voice.

"Yes sir." Flinn had given the loose ends speech himself to more young assassins and would-be mercenaries than he could count. Other jobs put you on notice or gave you a performance improvement plan, but professional killers got the loose ends speech. Either way, you knew you were on the path to an early termination.

"I do hope you're a useful partner, Garold."

"I am, sir."

"Good," said Johan the Mighty. "You are dismissed."

Chapter 7

"Well, I suppose that could have gone worse," grumbled Gorm, dusting the soot from his rucksack. Black dust covered the pack, and the Kobold sitting atop it had been singed, but Laruna's fireballs had otherwise left his gear unharmed.

"Maybe. But not by much." Burt produced a cigarette from his vest and lit it on a smoldering shrub. "Do you think he'll catch her before she makes it back to camp?"

There was a distant scream and the roar of a fiery blast.

"Aye," said Gorm.

They heard Thane approaching from the woods before Gorm had finished cleaning off his pack. The Troll normally moved in total silence, given his species' natural talent for lurking, but an angry mage makes a lot of noise. As they got closer, Gorm could make out Thane's attempts to negotiate amidst the screams, punctuated by periodic blasts of fire.

"This is all a misunder—" *Fwoosh!*

"What I mean to say is that once we—" *Woosh!*

"Nnnngh… the thing is that the fire is really quite painful, so if—" *Frooosh!*

By the time Thane climbed down the ravine, his head was hairless, charred, and covered in painful looking blisters. "You talk to her!" the Troll snarled as he dropped Laruna unceremoniously on the ground. With a final snort, he stamped over to the deepest part of the creek and plunged his head in. A cloud of steam bloomed around his neck.

"All right, easy Laruna. Easy," said Gorm, approaching the solamancer with his hands up. "We're safe here. There's a good lass. You're all right."

Laruna didn't look all right. Her unfocused eyes darted wildly about as she gasped for air in short, staccato gulps.

"She's in traumatic shock," Burt said, peeking out from behind a rock a safe distance away. "It's a natural physiological reaction."

Thane pulled his head from the stream. "A what?" he shouted.

"A physiological reaction," said Burt. "The body can't deal with what the eyes are seeing. That's why she's gasping like that. She needs to take some slow, deep breaths."

"If ye say as much." Gorm turned back to Laruna. "Lass, you're havin' a natural illogical reaction—uh-oh."

Laruna's breathing had already slowed considerably. Now her nostrils flared with each slow, deep breath, but it would be fatally inaccurate to describe her as "calm." She stared at Gorm with sudden intensity. "You! You're with the Troll?"

Gorm backed away. "Now, let's not jump to conclusions, lass. He's a friend."

"I don't have Trolls for friends," said the solamancer, standing.

"You might if you stopped trying to burn them alive!" Thane hollered before plunging his head back into the stream.

"Listen, Thane's been a friend to all of us for a long time," said Gorm.

"A long time?" said Laruna, her eyes narrowing. "How would you know that?"

"Just hear me out, lass," said Gorm.

"Talk," growled Laruna.

"It'd be easier to talk to ye if your hands weren't on fire like that," said Gorm.

Laruna's hair burst into flame as orange light flared from her eyes.

"But we'll make do," Gorm said hurriedly. "Listen, ain't ye ever wondered why we don't get bothered by more monsters and bandits out here? Didn't ye expect more assassins from King Handor to be on our tail? Well, it weren't for lack of threats. Thane here's been protectin' us."

"Maybe… but all of your evidence is stuff that didn't happen," Laruna said.

"What about the Headhunter thing?"

"The what?"

"The Rib-taker? The… I don't remember what it was called." Gorm waved his hand as if to brush the nomenclature aside. "The big monster that Detarr had back at the Ashen Tower. Ain't ye ever wondered what happened to it? Why a liche's big, nasty creation suddenly just went away and left us alone?"

As Gorm spoke, the flames wreathing Laruna faded away. Her skepticism did not. "Perhaps the Troll did kill the monster. But if that's when it started allegedly helping, it's been lurking in the woods and trailing us for months. Am I to believe it's just stalking us out of the goodness of its heart?"

"I wasn't stalking you," said Thane, returning from the stream. It took longer than normal for his regenerative flesh to heal from burns, but the last of his scars were smoothing away, and fresh hair was sprouting around his apelike face. "I was journeying with you."

"You can't do anything *with* someone if they don't know you're there," Laruna shot back. "We trusted you, Gorm, but it sounds like you've had a Troll following us for a year without telling anybody."

"He told me," said Burt.

"Not helping," Gorm muttered.

"Really?" demanded the solamancer. "You told the Kobold and not the rest of us."

"Oh, come now. He lives in me rucksack," Gorm protested. "It's hard to keep secrets from someone who sleeps next to your unmentionables."

"Ugh. Don't remind me." Burt shuddered.

"The point is that we all should have known about a Troll among us," said Laruna. "You should be on our side, not the Troll's."

"I ain't pickin' sides, because we're all on the same one," said Gorm.

"How can you be so sure?" said Laruna. "For all you know, the Troll is working on some cunning plot for its own dark devices."

"Okay, the language here is getting very hurtful," said Thane.

"You get used to it," Burt told him.

"Does that sound like a Troll to ye?" asked Gorm. "How many stories have ye heard about Trolls with the smarts and patience for that kind of scheme?"

"Not helping," said Thane.

"How many stories have you heard about Trolls protecting bands of professional heroes?" Laruna shot back.

"Just one," said Gorm. "Back in the Myrewood."

"What, you mean the…" The clouds of Laruna's stormy countenance broke, and realization shone through. "You're the King in the Wood."

"I was," said Thane.

"But that means… It's you." Laruna looked directly into the Troll's eyes for the first time. "You're what Kaitha's talking to. You're the one she's always saying she's connected to."

"She said that?" The Troll's face broke into a sudden grin, prompting the mage to take a step back. "What else did she say about me?"

"But… so Kaitha knows about the Troll?" Laruna looked like she was grasping for any thread of coherence that she could latch onto.

"No, she knows about the King in the Wood," said Gorm.

"It's a big difference," sighed Thane.

"She knows you're there," Laruna said. "I mean, she talks like she has feelings for you. So unless you also… oh… Oh!"

"They catch on eventually," Burt told the Troll.

"But a Troll and… and an Elf… that can't be right," sputtered the mage. "I mean, right? That's just not right."

"I understand that it's an improbable situation," said Thane.

"There's an understatement," muttered Burt. "I mean, physically it's—"

"Not helping!" the others chorused.

"But she's out there looking for you," said the solamancer. "Why not just… well, I suppose I know why—"

Thane interrupted her fumbling. "We all know why."

"But you still should be honest," pressed Laruna. "She might be… well, she might not… not…"

"Scream and run away?" said Burt.

"Shoot him in the face multiple times?" said Gorm.

"Refer to me as an 'it?'" said Thane.

"Well… right." The mage shuffled her feet awkwardly. Gorm watched warring thoughts move across her face like armies over a field. He recalled having a similar mental battle a while ago. It was hard to reconcile who Thane was with what he looked like.

But Laruna settled internal conflicts the same way she handled any other: swiftly and decisively. A moment later she gave a determined nod and held out her hand to Thane. "I'm sorry about that," she said. "I shouldn't have spoken unkindly. Or tried to light you on fire."

Thane smiled and shook her hand between his thumb and forefinger. "Don't mention it."

"No, truly, I feel terrible," said the solamancer.

"Okay, but really, don't mention it," said Thane. "Or me. Specifically, don't mention me."

"But, why keep the secret now?" said Laruna. "I could introduce you—"

"No. If she was to react as you did, if she..." Thane trailed off as he looked back into the rippling waters of the stream. His reflection stared back at him. "We've been over this. I know what you all would prefer, but I'm not ready to show myself yet."

"But—"

Gorm put a hand on Laruna's shoulder. "Lass, sometimes ye need to trust a friend to make their own choices, even if ye disagree with 'em."

Laruna gave him a strange look. "But what if it's not just a disagreement? What if what they're doing is bad for them? What if it might be actively harming... your friend? Or even the rest of the party?"

"Aye. I know it's hard. And secrets are dangerous," said Gorm. "But if you're to be a friend for someone, ye have to respect their privacy. Ye can't be there for them any other way."

"I... I guess you're right," she said.

"Good." Gorm patted her shoulder. "Now, come on. We'd best get back to camp before the others start askin' after us."

"It's just a few questions," said the flaming skull. "I know you're all eager to get back to haunting the ruins, but we really value your honest feedback."

Tyren sat at a small table in the center of what had once been a cafe, though recent events had reduced it to a broken husk. The room had more gaps than walls, and through the cracks the former knight-commander could see the undead shambling through the streets.

The walking corpses seemed distant to Tyren, but then, everything did, as though he was observing himself from across a great chasm. If he didn't maintain his focus, fond memories of little Aubey and Grandfather's castle would roll in like a fog. The whole sensation was reminiscent of being drunk, without the wobbliness or the uncontrollable impulse to say embarrassing things.

"Is everyone ready to begin?" asked the flaming skull.

The other participants seated round the tabled nodded and groaned in general agreement. The skull had gathered a motley arrangement of ex-Humans: a zombie, a skeleton, a spectral man, the creeping shadow of a woman, and a portly ghoul with a familiar face and a new set of dreadful fangs.

The toothy individual perked up when it saw Tyren. "Here now, I know that armor!" it said. "You're Knight-Commander Ur'Thos."

Tyren was about to reply, but the zombie cut him off. "Lots of knights have floral armor, Ned. That can't be the sole basis of identification."

"Well, he does have high cheekbones, Ted," said Ned.

"You're the two who were arguing about the organ," said Tyren.

"Sir!" said Ted, saluting.

Ned gave a grin that was both horrifying and horribly smug. "Although now we've seen the instrument for ourselves, so we can say with certainty—"

"Ahem," said the flaming skull, its baleful eyeball staring with disapproval at the ghoul and zombie in turn. "If everyone will give me their attention, we can get started."

"Right. Sorry," said Ned.

Several papers on the table in front of the floating skull rustled and rearranged themselves before it launched into some prepared remarks. "Hello! I'm the Head of Marketing. You've been randomly selected to participate in this focus group. I'll be asking you a series of questions, and your answers will help shape undead invasions of other cities. So be open, honest, and direct. Your opinion matters! Are we ready to begin?"

There was a generally assenting chorus of groans and moans.

"Great!" said the flaming skull. "Now, how many of you saw one of these flyers before you joined us?" One of the papers levitated into the air and flipped around. Tyren recognized the pamphlet and its promised doom at the hands of the dread lord Detarr Ur'Mayan, so he raised his skeletal hand. All of the undead around the table did the same.

"Good, good," said the Head of Marketing. It bobbled earnestly as it stared at the stack of papers in front of it, and lines of thin script burned into the parchment as if written by an invisible hand. "All right, how would you say you felt when you first read it?"

The spectral man next to Neddard let loose a long, agonizing wail, as biting and cold as frost on a grave.

"Good. That's great," said the Head of Marketing. "And what was your name again?"

The ghostly man just wailed again.

"That's our Spencer," said the shade of the woman. "He's a banshee now."

"Spencer the Malevolent," murmured the Head of Marketing. "Great! Now who else wants to talk about the flyer?"

"I agree with Spencer," offered the skeleton.

"As usual, Rudge," muttered Neddard, leaning in close to Tyren. "I'll wager you've never seen a skeleton without a spine before, sir."

"Great!" said the Head of Marketing. "Anyone else? How about you with the fancy armor? What's your name?"

Tyren looked around, and as nobody else wore armor—fancy or otherwise—he answered. "I am Knight-Commander Tyren Ur'Thos."

"We can work with that," said the skull, looking down at its notes. "Maybe Tyren the Soul Drinker. Lord Ur'Thos the Blood Guzzler. Bloodseeker the Corpse—"

"What are you doing?" Tyren interrupted.

The skull bobbed in a manner suggesting a shrug. "Just a little rebranding. It's what I do."

"I don't really want a new name," said Tyren.

"We'll work on it. I've got a few more ideas," said the Head of Marketing. "Now. How did you feel when you read the pamphlet?"

Tyren thought for a moment. "Confused," he said eventually.

"Hmm." The Head of Marketing's voice conveyed the frown that his fleshless face could not. "Care to expand on that?"

"It's just… why the paper?" said Tyren. "It wasn't any more frightening than the horde of undead trying to break down the gate. Much less so, actually."

"I'd agree with that," said the skeleton.

"Rudge, you'd agree if we said your skull was swapped with your tailbone," snapped Ned.

"You're probably right," sighed Rudge.

"And what did it want me to do?" Tyren continued. "It just told me to be afraid. I don't see what that does for anyone."

"It doesn't have a clear call to action," Ted offered. "Very important to have one of those in your advertisements."

"I'm familiar with the term," said the Head of Marketing frostily. "Anything else?" he added, in a tone that suggested there had better not be.

The focus group fell silent, but the quiet held on too long to be mere awkwardness. Tyren felt a twinge of something on the edge of his consciousness, like an itch in his peripheral vision. He looked around and saw that the other participants were sitting rigid and alert, staring straight ahead with blank expressions.

"Excuse me," said a hollow voice from behind the group.

The liche that had killed Tyren ducked through the doorway. As the skeletal wizard approached, Tyren's strange sensation became more intense, almost overpowering.

"I just wanted to have a quick talk about some of these proposed names," said Detarr Ur'Mayan. "Shouldn't take more than a moment."

"Absolutely, sir," said the Head of Marketing.

"Excellent," said Detarr. He looked at a small sheet of parchment. "I've been looking at your list, and, well… Grimblood Darkhost? Mortarion the Soul Reaver?"

"They tested well with previous focus groups," said the Head of Marketing. "Guaranteed to frighten anyone!"

"Perhaps." The liche tossed the paper into the air and it disappeared in a small burst of green flame. "They just seem so… done."

"A tried and true approach sir," offered the Head.

"One for two, at least," said Detarr. "Why all this effort to scare the living? They naturally fear us."

"Oh, our research shows that fear has a powerful effect on morale," said the Head of Marketing. "Frightened troops are more likely to flee or make fatal mistakes in battle."

Detarr was unimpressed. "They're also more likely to make valiant last stands or to rise up against all odds in unlikely moments of glorious heroism."

"Yes, aha, but not as often as the fleeing or dying," said the Head of Marketing. "You can't win them all."

"Indeed, but I want to win more of them," said Detarr. "I think we need a new angle."

"Absolutely, sir." Gobbets of flame dripped off the Head of Marketing like sweat. "That's why we're running these focus groups with our latest recruits. Why, this group was just saying they thought different messaging would be more effective."

"Is that so?" said Detarr. The liche looked around the room. "Well, what do you say? Have you been having productive discussions?"

Tyren wasn't sure what to say, and the rest of the group was still rigid and vacant.

"Sir, the Crown of Iron Thorns," the Head of Marketing said helpfully.

"What? Oh. Right." Detarr lifted the iron crown from his skull and tucked it within the recesses of his robes. Instantly, the focus group slumped in their seats, and Tyren's strange sensation drained away. "Now then," Detarr continued. "What do you make of all of these scary names and such?"

Despite the removal of the crown, however, none of the undead seemed inclined to speak. They cowered in their chairs, trembling.

"Come on, then," said the liche. "Isn't that what we're here for? To discuss our feelings and such? How are you doing since your recent transition? Anybody? Nobody feels anything? Not a twinge of emotion?"

Eventually, Neddard Biggins raised a shaking claw. "Well, Your Majesticalness, I've been hungry mostly," he offered.

"Hungry," said the liche flatly.

"Well, since you asked, yeah," said Ned. "I think it's on account of my eternal curse to crave the flesh of the living."

"Oh yes, I feel the same," said Rudge. Spencer and his shadowy wife nodded as well.

The violet flames around the liche's head glowed brighter, and a sudden chill fell over the room. "I see. That's the general consensus, then? Our big insight? We wish there was more to eat?"

"I must admit, it'd be nice if there were more brains available," said Ted the zombie.

"Well, we can all agree there," hissed Detarr. The liche whirled on the Head of Marketing. "And you've spent how much time and energy to arrive at this particular bit of perspective?"

"Er, we've had… uh… other valuable insights, Sir," the Head of Marketing said, backing away like a cornered animal. "Why… why, Sir Tyren had just been saying that he believes a call to action would have helped our last campaign."

"Is that so?" said the liche, turning his gaze on Tyren.

"Uh, yes." Tyren was suddenly grateful for his decades of experience bluffing to those in authority. "I mean, the flyer didn't ask me to do anything. It just told me I was going to die and suffer for all eternity. And honestly, so far being undead isn't that bad."

A murmuring rose up among the gathered corpses. "It's not that bad?" said Detarr.

"Not as bad as they made it sound, anyway," said Tyren with a shrug. "I mean, it was a shock when it happened, and I'm still getting used to things. But my old knee injury doesn't hurt anymore, and it's the first time in ages I've woken up without a hangover. Plus, now what do I have to be scared of or worry about? The worst is already behind me, I suppose."

"The worst is behind you," said Detarr slowly.

"What does that even mean?" hissed the Head of Marketing at Tyren.

"Yes, that's what I've always thought. Undeath only seems horrible until you've tried it," said the liche. "I think you may be on to something here, Tyren."

"I love it!" said the Head of Marketing.

"Me too!" said Rudge.

"Death is in your past, disease and injury are mere memories," Detarr said with rising excitement. "You never age, never hunger, and never die."

"Um, I do hunger quite a lot, if you'll recall," Neddard ventured.

But the idea had passed the flashpoint, and now Detarr's skeletal face was alight — even more so than usual. "You bend no knee to kings, pay no taxes, and live by no laws. All fears are behind you. You are as gods."

"What, even Rudge?" said Ted.

"This changes everything," Detarr said, excitement welling up from his infernal depths. "What if the living saw undeath as a transformation rather than an end? A boon rather than a blight! Would they join our cause?"

"It's certainly got novelty!" said the Head of Marketing.

"This could be the most innovative thing in necromancy in ages!" said the liche. "We could change the paradigm of necromancy on Arth."

The Head of Marketing nodded. "And I love the idea, but — "

"But?" said Detarr sharply. "Am I to assume you don't know how to make this work?"

"Oh, no, I definitely can see how — "

"Good," said Detarr. "I have high expectations for you and Sir Ur'Thos here. Make sure to keep him involved."

The floating skull glared at Tyren with its lone eye so fiercely that its pile of notes burst into flame. "Oh no, sir. I won't let this one out of my sight."

"Well, I don't see any sign of him." Gorm nursed a tankard as he watched the patrons mill about the tavern. The men and women in the room were dressed in extravagant bursts of bright silks and moved with the stiff precision characteristic of aristocrats and peacocks. It was the sort of establishment where a few dark figures skulking in the shadows in the back corner were sure to attract unwanted attention. "Ye sure this is the right place? Seems a bit posh for this business."

"Oh, this is the place," said Burt. The Kobold reclined in a leather purse set on the bench between Kaitha and Gorm, sipping from a tiny tankard. "Baedrun's Dream wants to be a gilded lily, but it's a copper-covered daisy at best. Maybe there's a couple of baronets in the crowd, but for the most part these are all children of merchants and tradesmen. Jalana brought me here once on an official visit to Parald, and she swore we'd never return."

"It just seems like a place where a group of mercenaries and a Shadowkin might not be welcome," said Laruna.

"Would you relax?" Burt snorted. "I'm in an Elf's purse! Nobody's going to check my papers." He gave Kaitha's arm a hearty pat for emphasis.

"Hand," said Kaitha, without looking up from her apple-rose water.

"Touchy," grumbled Burt, withdrawing the offending paw.

"Just the opposite," said the Elf.

Gorm was inclined to agree with Burt; the ranger was on edge. He attributed her short temper to her mostly-successful efforts to swear off drinking. The Elf took a glass of wine at one or two rare moments of relaxation, but for the better part of a year now she hadn't ordered anything stronger than water filled with diced fruits and flower petals. That kind of long-term sobriety might account for a lot of strange behavior.

At least, Gorm hoped it did, because Kaitha had a lot to account for as of late.

He shook off his concerns and turned back to the conversation at hand.

"Look, there's an undead army to the south. Vetchell's a pile of rubble by now," Burt growled at the mages. "Word of the threat has already made it to Parald, and yet this lot is still here trying to maneuver into favorable marriages. If they can ignore an army of the dead, they won't be bothered by a few rough-looking folk in the corner. As long as you keep your head down, stay quiet, and play commoner to a bunch of wannabe nobles, you'll be fine."

"So long as your contact shows up soon," Jynn told the Kobold. "We've lost two days waiting around Parald as is. In another two this city will be crawling with refugees."

"Reconnaissance takes time, especially when you have to go through back channels to get to your source. But look. They're here."

Burt nodded to the front door, where a gaggle of Elves in elaborate silks created a stir amongst the aspiring nobles.

"If your contact is the one in the violet gown," said Heraldin, "I'll volunteer to ply her for information."

"Don't be a skubber," Burt snapped. "Look at her purse."

Gorm squinted at the violet-clad Elf's drake-skin purse. A tiny canine face peeked over the handbag's golden rim. The Kobold's gnarled features were dusted with white and rose-colored makeup, and the uneven tufts of fur sprouting from his malformed head had been sculpted into colorful curls with a variety of greases and dyes.

"That's the strangest-looking purse Kobold I've ever seen," said Laruna.

"Yeah, yeah. Ain't he a diamond in the rough?" Burt's sneer was one that only a Kobold could achieve, a grimace impossible to perform with symmetrical features or eyeballs that pointed in the same direction. "Anyway, he's giving me the signal. Let's head out back."

"What signal?" Gorm asked. "He's just sittin' there."

"Right, acting like he doesn't see me. That's the signal," said Burt, settling into Kaitha's purse. He gave the Elf's sleeve a couple of quick tugs. "Let's go, ranger. You should know all about making tracks."

"He's just going to ignore you?" asked Laruna.

"Seems to be a lot of that going around," hissed the Kobold. "Let's move it!"

"But what kind of signal is that?" The solamancer reluctantly stood with the other heroes.

"Anything else'd be suspicious," Burt said, glaring back at the other Kobold once more. "Come on. You guys are taking forever."

"An eternity, really," muttered King Handor. "A small, agonizing eternity."

"Indeed, sire," whispered Weaver Ortson. The Grandmaster of the Heroes' Guild slumped in his chair, wearing the morose expression he always bore in the brief interlude between getting up and the day's first cocktail.

"Look at all of these people," Handor murmured under his breath. "Diplomats, finance ministers, accountants; every one of them is as dull as porridge in a gray bowl. And even they're bored to tears."

"The least they could do is serve wine," said Ortson.

"I suspect that would distract us from their meeting," said Handor.

"Exactly, sire." Ortson managed something approaching a smile.

Below them, a nervous Dwarf stood in front of a large graph, stammering about the financial distress of the Old Dwarven Kingdoms. The chart itself was a square of oak boards with a grid of holes. The Dwarves had set pegs in the grid and strung crimson twine between them, creating a red line that plotted the Kingdoms' finances. The whole graph was shaped like a mountain, but most of the Dwarf's talking points focused on the treacherous cliff near the end.

Handor sighed. The economic woes of the Old Dwarven Kingdoms were well-documented, beginning at the turn of the century when Imperial alchemists discovered a way to transform lead into gold. Within a few years, the Empire's economy was so flooded with gold that the value of gold coins plummeted across Arth. The Agekeepers said a grocer couldn't carry enough coin to buy a chicken.

The Imperial alchemists were summarily executed, and the Freedlands and Ruskan barred trade with the Empire for a decade. Shortly thereafter, Handor's grandfather, King Oven the Wise, invented the giltin and separated the value of the Freedlands' currency from the scarcity of gold. Ruskan followed suit with its own currency, and the Empire began to issue coins made from lead coated in silver.

But the Dwarves loved gold to a fault, and for ages the Old Dwarven Kingdoms had built their nation on mining and exporting precious metals. They kept an iron grip on the gold standard for over half a century too long, hoping that the markets would correct themselves and gold would come roaring back.

Yet when markets do correct themselves, the issue they most often correct is false hope. The Dwarves saw their currency drop to a fraction of its former value.

A collapsing currency is an enormous problem for a nation with more bottomless chasms than arable farmland. The rising price of imported food forced the Dwarves in the mountainous Old Kingdoms to spend away their coffers just to keep their people from starving, and the Kingdoms were now utterly destitute.

"And so, as you can see, another generous infusion of aid from the Freedlands' should allow us to remain solvent until the current economic difficulties have passed," the presenting Dwarf droned on.

Handor started to sigh again, but he felt eyes on him. He turned to see King Forder Hvarthson, the King of Khadan'Alt, watching. All the Fathers, Ancestors, and kings of the other clanhomes in the Old Dwarven Kingdoms were pledged to Khadan'Alt, making Forder the most powerful Dwarf in the world. Handor nodded to the Dwarven king and made the pretense of giving the speaker his attention.

A few agonizing minutes later, a page rushed to Handor's rescue. "Your Majesty," he whispered breathlessly. "Sir Johan has an urgent message. He requests a word with you at once."

"Praise Tandos," muttered Handor. He made his excuses to Ortson, nodded to King Forder and his attending Ancestors, and slipped out of the ballroom.

Johan waited in a nearby hall, clad in a full suit of elaborate plate mail that dwarfed the ceremonial suits of armor lining the wall.

"Johan," said Handor. "I'll never understand how you can wear that armor everywhere."

"Your Majesty," said Tandos' Champion with a small bow. "It is the fashion among professional heroes."

"You're retired," the king shot back. "And it's the most ridiculous fashion I've ever heard of to walk around girded for war every day."

"One must always be prepared."

"One must always be exhausted and chafing as well," said the king, leaning against the wall next to Johan. "Gods, that looks heavy. The pauldrons are bigger than your head."

Johan shrugged, causing the aforementioned pauldrons to eclipse his face. "They work miracles with enchantments these days, Your Majesty. They've woven enough sorcery into the steel that I don't notice the weight. And speaking of miracles, have you managed to save the Old Dwarven Kingdoms once again?"

"King Forder knows my terms," sighed Handor. "This whole meeting is just the first step of his clumsy counter. What's the sense in opening with a presentation that says the Dwarves have no money? He may as well deliver an hour-long speech to tell me that the sky is blue."

"Ha!" laughed Johan. "That would be more interesting than the Dwarves' finances."

Handor nodded. "What would impress me is if he could make a case for the Freedlands sending him more gold. We've been bailing out that foundering ship for over a decade. It's time for the Dwarves to change boats or sink for good. Plenty of clanhomes have sworn fealty to Andarun. If he wants the benefits of being in the Freedlands, he can do the same."

Johan's perennial grin widened a bit. "Well said, sire."

"If only we could say as much in those stuffy dinners," said Handor. "This one's so dull that even Marja made some excuse, and you know what it takes to keep her away from a banquet."

"Ha ha! Indeed, sire."

"She would have come if she'd known you'd be making an appearance," the king smirked.

It was no secret that Marja would have preferred to marry Johan two decades ago, after the paladin rescued her from the tower of Detarr Ur'Mayan. It was also no secret that Handor would have preferred she marry Johan as well. They each had their own way of coping with a loveless marriage; Marja took comfort in eating mountains of tea cakes and other sweets, while Handor turned his attentions to governing and the occasional chambermaid.

"I did not know I'd be coming myself, sire," said Johan, his tone more serious. "But I'm compelled to intrude by important news."

"Well, I didn't think you came just to save me from that presentation," said Handor. "Is this about the trouble in Knifevale, the dragon stirring again, or the liche near Vetchell?"

"Vetchell, I'm afraid," said Johan. "We just received word that the city has fallen to the undead."

"And the city was evacuated in time?" Handor smiled once the paladin nodded. "Good. And how are the markets reacting?"

"Up two percent, sire."

"Excellent!" said Handor. "Send my condolences and an offer of help to King Klenn. A vague offer. And have the generals ready the bannermen. I want the army ready to defend the Freedlands if Klenn can't stop this from spreading to our territory."

"I'll have them marching east within the week," said Johan. "Shall I notify Mr. Ortson that the Heroes' Guild may have a new quest coming?"

The king shook his head. "Let's meet with our associates this evening and discuss the guild's involvement with Weaver then. We need a cohesive plan to stop the undead."

"And, if I may presume, the optimal time and place to do so?" said Johan, grinning broadly.

"Of course," said Handor. "In times like this, when most men see challenges, great men see opportunities."

Chapter 8

"If your friend doesn't wanna miss his chance, he'd better get out here soon," grumbled Gorm.

"Oh, simmer down," said Burt. "I'm sure he's just seein' to business."

"I assumed we were the business he planned to see to," Jynn said.

Gorm snorted and looked around the yard. To the east, Parald was lit by manifold torches, lanterns, and braziers, and the city glimmered like an inverted chandelier set upon the grassy plain. It might have been a pretty sight at another time, but for now the city's warm glow was just a reminder how cold and damp it was behind the stables of Baedrun's Dream.

"Hey, I know we're tossing him some coin, but trips to taverns are busy for a handbag performer," Burt told him. "He's still got a day job to keep."

"Of a sort," said Heraldin. Laruna snickered.

"Yeah, go on and laugh. If I thought it was a respectable career, I wouldn't have left it." Burt looked back at the inn, and Gorm thought he saw a hint of wistfulness in the Kobold's eye. "But 'bagging is hard work. You've got to be ready to perform at any moment, always ready to babble like a pup or do a happy dance or look cute while you eat somethin'. And gods forbid your lady sees something cuter while she's out and about, 'cause if she does you'll be on the street the next day."

The Kobold shook his head and scratched his ear sheepishly, remembering himself. "So yeah, give the guy some slack. He's got a lot to do in there."

"So, would you say he's working like a dog?" quipped Heraldin.

"Not if I was tall and pink and liked breathin'," Burt growled, rolling up the sleeve of his tiny tunic.

"Someone's coming," said Kaitha, perking up.

"That's enough out of both of ye," Gorm told the bard and Kobold.

"Indeed. Half of the inn probably heard you," said a small voice. The Kobold with the strangely colored hair sauntered around the corner of the stables. "And given how problematic it would be if I were to be seen with a gaggle of wanted criminals, I must insist that you make some attempt to be discreet."

"Hello, Morty." Burt spoke in a level voice with a polite smile, but Gorm could see his friend's hackles rising.

"Burtrek," Morty acknowledged.

Burt waved an arm back at the rest of the party. "Folks, this is Morty. And this here's Gorm and—"

"Please, Burtrek, the less I know about you outlaws, the better. And if you must use my name, call me Ta'Nayde."

"What?" asked Burt.

"I prefer to go by my Elven name now," said Morty airily. *"Ja'leith Tallel Ta'Nayde."*

"Well, well. Morty's gone native," said Burt. "Look at this guy. Back in the day, we ran in the same pack. Now I have to go through three people to send you a thrice-cursed note, and he's too good for the name his mother gave him!"

Morty shrugged off Burt's comments with an amused smile and turned to Kaitha. "It's the latest trend," he confided to her. "Any Kobold worth a purse these days is fluent in Elven. Of course, those that can't keep up with fashion, well…" He looked at Burt with a mixture of mock sympathy and cruel glee.

"I see," said Kaitha diplomatically.

"I left the job on my own, and you know it." Burt was trying to hold back his temper, and clearly failing.

"Oh? What a coincidence, then, that so many of the Shadowkin in your Freedlands made the same 'choice,'" said Morty. "I always told you to come to Ruskan. Much more stable, and it's the true seat of the Elven elite."

"Psh," scoffed Burt. "If your Elf is so great, why'd she wind up in this joint with all the other would-be nobles?"

"Oh, come now, Burtrek," Morty said with a patronizing smile. "Surely you know they've come ganking."

"They've come what?" Gorm asked.

"Ganking? Slumming? You know, top-tier girl and her bottom-tier man, as they say in Andarun?" Morty looked surprised by the blank stares on the heroes' faces. "When my mistress and her companions get bored with high society," he said slowly, "they like to find some undesirable establishment and seek out someone far beneath their level for a bit of fun."

"That's disgusting," said Kaitha.

"Isn't it though?" laughed Morty. "The mistress bathes for half a day straight afterward."

Kaitha scowled. "That's not what I—"

"You must excuse me," said Heraldin, stepping away from the wall and trotting briskly toward the inn.

"Where are ye going?" Gorm demanded.

"Oh, we all know where I'm going," Heraldin called over his shoulder. "If I'm not back in an hour, I'll see you at breakfast." He disappeared around the corner of the stable with a flourish.

"Puffed up git," Gorm grumbled after him.

"Also disgusting," said Kaitha.

"Listen, Burtrek, I'm ten minutes into a twenty-minute break," said Morty, flipping a sky-blue curl with his paw. "Do you want to talk about these artifacts or not?"

"We do," Gorm interjected, with a firm stare at Burt.

"Good," said Morty. "I must say, you asked about a strange collection of items. I can't help but wonder what the connection between them is."

"We're to be discreet here, if ye recall," said Gorm.

"True enough. You're also to pay up front, if memory serves," The brightly colored Kobold waited for Gorm to toss a pouch of coins at his feet. Once he had hefted the purse onto his back, he pulled a small list from the pocket of his vest. "First of all, the Ring of Nine Faces is currently in the Emperor's personal collection at the heart of the Imperial City."

"Halfway across the world, in the vault of an emperor," muttered Gorm. He crossed it off the mental list of prospective artifacts.

"The Rod of Seven Pieces isn't around anymore," said Morty "It was in an accident when a noctomancer down in Umbrax tried to experiment on it. It's the Rod of About Three Hundred Pieces now."

Jynn scratched at his goatee. "I didn't think destroying such a relic was possible."

"You can be quite confident that my information is accurate," said Morty. "My mistress sits on the Ruskan committee overseeing the Heroes' Guild's handling of dangerous loot."

"A ceremonial position," Burt interrupted.

"A prestigious position," Morty said with a sniff. "I saw the record myself. The rod's a pile of splinters."

"Fair enough," said Gorm. "What's next?"

"The Horn of Gygaxxon is sealed away beneath the Heroes' Guild's Great Vault in Andarun."

"I'd rather try our chances with the Emperor," said Laruna.

Gorm couldn't help but agree. The Heroes' Guild had many offices scattered about the Freedlands' capital, but its treasury was located in the most secure depths of the Palace of Andarun. Given that the guild took a cut of every quest fee, hero's pay, and treasure hoard, the sums of money contained in the Great Vault were inconceivable to Gorm. He'd heard that its treasures were more magnificent than even King Handor's. Certainly it was better protected—no organization was more familiar with the varied traps that could be set for plundering intruders than the Heroes' Guild.

"Aye, best to pass over any that are with the guild," said Gorm.

Morty glanced at his page. "In that case, this is going to be a short list."

"What, they're all in Andarun's Great Vault?" asked Laruna.

"Four more are," said Morty. "And three are with the guild in Edaelmon, and two more in the guild's holdings in Knifevale."

"Is there anything that the Heroes' Guild doesn't have?" Gorm said, trying to ignore the knots his stomach was tying itself into.

"No," said Morty. "Funny thing, the Heroes' Guild is remarkably effective at acquiring powerful magical items. Although…"

"Aye?"

"Well, the Wyrmwood Staff of Geffyn is usually in the guild's Great Vault as well," said Morty. "But this year it's on loan to the Museum of Andarun for an exhibit on omnimancy."

"That's not much better," said Jynn. "It's still in the heart of Andarun, and heavily guarded."

"Less heavily guarded though," said Laruna thoughtfully. "And a lot fewer traps."

"Yeah, traps would be bad for attendance," smirked Burt.

"Well, it sounds like you've found the one for whatever it is you're going to do." Morty folded up his note and handed it to Gorm. "And the less I know about that, the happier we'll all be. So, I must bid you farewell."

"Yeah, yeah. So long, Morty," said Burt. "Good to see you and all that."

"I'm sure it was," said Morty, tossing a coiffed tuft of purple hair out of his eye. "And I'm sure you'll find a real job and get back on your feet soon. Surely some Elf from Vetchell would love a bargain for her purse."

"Shut it!" yipped Burt. "I was just tryin' to be polite!"

"Were you?" smirked Morty as he sauntered away. "Well, that's personal growth. Goodbye, Burtrek."

Burt watched him go, his tiny frame shaking with fury. "That mangy, flea-riddled—"

"Ah, don't mind him," said Gorm, giving the Kobold a pat on the shoulder.

"Yeah," said Laruna. "He's just jealous because you're free now."

"No, he ain't," said Burt, shaking his head. "He's eatin' fancy food and going to big parties and gettin' paid to do it. And if he ever wished he didn't have to perform like that, well, now he sees what's on the other side."

"Burt—" said Kaitha.

"You got it backward," Burt barked, choking back a sob. "I wish I wasn't jealous of him, but I am. Gods, I am."

"Hey, come on," said Kaitha, dropping down on one knee. "You're doing work that matters here. You're standing up for the little guys. I mean, in more ways than one."

"I know. Sorry," said Burt, wiping his eyes.

"Listen, I know what'll make ye feel better," interjected Gorm. "I took a peek in the stables, and those Elven popinjays that Morty rides with strutted in here on some of the finest Elven steeds I ever laid eyes on. What do ye say we go steal them horses, eh?"

133

A little glimmer returned to Burt's eyes, and it was hard to say if it was hope or malice. "Yeah," he said. "Yeah, I'd like that."

"Sure you would," said Kaitha, giving Burt a friendly pat.

"All right, ye heard the Kobold," Gorm announced. "Someone go pull the bard off of whatever Elf he's latched on to. We've got to get to Andarun, and there ain't no time to waste."

"There's just not enough time," Duine Poldo said, tossing a parchment back on the stack. "There aren't enough hours in the day to get all of this done."

Mrs. Hrurk said nothing in reply, and it took Poldo a moment to recall that she had gone home a few hours ago. Poldo wiped his spectacles and rubbed his eyes before having a look at the page again. The letters all seemed to run together in the candlelight.

He thought about packing the paperwork up and taking it back home, but he quickly dismissed the idea. Once he got home, he wouldn't have the energy to do anything but collapse on his bed. Besides, Mrs. Hrurk was probably helping Barga with the renovations in the new apartment by now.

Poldo hadn't expected to buy the apartment next door to his own, but then, he had only expected a pair of Goblins to show up for a few nights. It was his own fault, he reflected; Goblins never did anything in small numbers if they could help it. Shortly after Barga and her mate arrived, the entire Fire Hawk Tribe showed up on his doorstep. He didn't have enough space for them all, and the neighbor on his floor was threatening to complain about all of the Shadowkin. Yet a liberal application of money can fix most problems, and Poldo resolved both issues with a single check.

Of course, now the Fire Hawks were telling more Shadowkin about the Scribkin who was providing lodging and even hiring for odd jobs. Mrs. Hrurk was already dropping hints about a few Orcs who needed a place to stay. Poldo had even pondered buying more apartments, or even the whole building. The gods knew he could afford it now, but such a purchase just meant more paperwork, and more time.

Poldo sighed and tried to dive back into preparing yet another threat obligation. Kindness and success shared the same problem; they both set expectations. Expectations that such charity or prosperity could be easily duplicated, or that they would be constant, or that they were just milestones in an endless line of goals and objectives. He couldn't keep pace, and he didn't have time to hire help beyond Mrs. Hrurk and Vilga of the Fire Hawk, who had happily proven to be well-versed in bookkeeping.

His quill had just touched the threat obligation form when a tiny squeak hailed from the edge of his perception. Poldo might have dismissed the sound as a mouse or other pest, but something in its cadence suggested that someone was deliberately clearing a very tiny throat. He looked up.

At the far corner of his desk, a diminutive Wood Gnome crept out from behind Poldo's inbox. The tiny man was draped in the pelt of a red squirrel, with the tail dragging behind him and the skull acting as a macabre headdress. A pair of glinting eyes and a turnip-shaped nose were crammed between the squirrel mask and the Wood Gnome's bushy white beard.

"Uh. Hello there," said Poldo carefully. The Wood Gnome wearing the red squirrel was the first Domovoy to willingly show himself to Poldo. He had never heard of Wood Gnomes making any sort of contact with bigger folk, except to highlight cohabitation disputes through vandalism.

The air was still. Tense. Sacred.

The spell was broken as the tiny Gnome burst into a series of high-pitched squeaks and squeals, waving his hands emphatically.

"I beg your pardon?" said Poldo.

The Wood Gnome nodded, then piped something unintelligible over his shoulder. As silent as shadows, dozens of Domovoy slipped out from behind the piles of paper. Poldo could feel several small weights land on the back of his chair, and as he turned he could see hundreds of eyes gleaming from every nook and cranny in the shed.

It occurred to Poldo that he had grossly underestimated the population of his office. "Uh… hello to all of you as well," he gulped.

The Wood Gnomes had dark, shining eyes and silver hair, even the children. The men wore long beards, and the women long braids, and every one of them was clad in the pelt of some unfortunate rodent or another. They stared at Poldo with a stoic intensity until he shifted in his seat.

Red Squirrel chirruped something again, but it was too high and quiet for Poldo to make out more than a piping rhythm. A moment later, however, the assembled Wood Gnomes sang out in long, high notes, *"Thank you, Mr. Poldo."*

"Aha. Er, you're welcome, I suppose," said Poldo.

Red Squirrel squeaked again, and the Domovoy chorused, *"For defeating the poison giant."*

"The poison… ah, the exterminator last week? No, no need to thank me for that. Anyone would have done it. It's common decency." Poldo's nervous smile faded as he considered that idea for a moment. "Or it should be, anyway."

There was a blur of motion and a few clinking sounds. A mug of hot water, a box of herbal tea, and a tin of Redwall's Candied Nut Shortbreads appeared on Poldo's desk.

"Oh!" said Poldo, taking a shortbread to be polite. "Well, uh, this is much appreciated, especially with such a long night ahead of me."

The Wood Gnomes moved faster than Poldo's eyes could see; in an instant, the herbal tea was whisked away. A moment later, it was replaced by a jar of Poldo's favorite instant coffee, Eldrith's Black Grounds.

"Yes, that's lovely, thank you," said Poldo. "If only you could organize these orders," he quipped, nodding to one of the overflowing bins of paper on the edge of his desk.

The words weren't yet out of Poldo's mouth when the Wood Gnomes on his desk clapped three times in unison. On the third clap, the Domovoy launched themselves into the pile of paperwork, chittering and squeaking at each other so rapidly that their tiny voices blended into a high-pitched buzzing sound. The stack of papers wobbled and rocked unsteadily, pages swirling around it in a rustling storm of documents. A few moments later, the Wood Gnomes leapt from the stack, clapped three more times, and all pointed proudly at the rearranged pile.

"Ta-daaa!" they chorused.

Poldo lifted the top page of the stack with trembling hands. It was a company profile for Adventure Capital, followed by Always Gold Inc., and then Armed Conflict Unlimited. "Uh, thank you," he said carefully. "But really, I need to sort them by the opportunity each company presents, not alphabetically."

"*Buy low, sell high!*" sang the Wood Gnomes. Three claps. Another whirlwind of activity snatched the paper from Poldo's hands and rearranged the inbox. Three claps again.

Poldo looked through the documents on top of the pile. The first was a profile of Goldson Baggs, followed by Lamia Sisters, and then other large financial companies. Now he could focus on writing the most profitable threat obligations first, and leave the bottom of the pile for another night. He might even make it to bed by midnight.

A smile spread across Poldo's face as he turned to Red Squirrel. "What's your hourly rate?" he asked.

"Much better than I expected." Gorm scanned the horizon while his jaw worked over a bite of grouse. "At this rate, we'll make Andarun in just a few days."

Kaitha nodded and picked at a bone. "This sort of speed is typical when you're riding *shayd'wier*. Our legends hold that they're descended from the king of horses. The blood of unicorns flows through their veins, and they're bred in moonlight so that *Allunathaliel* will bless them and give them the gift of the wind. They're a great treasure of my people."

"Aye, they're fine mounts." Gorm watched the Elven steeds grazing in the plains a short distance from the cookfire. They looked like someone took warhorses and sanded them down to optimize aerodynamics. The mares and stallions stared back at the Dwarf with a discernible smugness.

"No, I mean, literally," said the Elf. "One of these is worth about fifty thousand giltin. We've committed grand theft here."

"That crime pales compared to the theft we're planning," said Jynn.

"For a good cause," said Gorm. "Besides, these horses were worth it."

"Yeah, all right, fine. I think we've heard enough about how rich Morty's Elf was," said Burt. He nudged Gaist's elbow. "You going to eat that drumstick?"

The weaponsmaster's eyes flicked to the Kobold.

"All right! Easy!" said Burt, paws in the air.

Gorm hurried to finish his dinner and clean his dishes. The days of late Meltwater were marked by spring's warmth driving back the snow, but the biting cold returned each evening with a vengeance. Beyond the chill, however, there were more pressing reasons to get into his tent before Burt finished eating.

"It's been a while," Gorm muttered to himself. He pulled the leather-bound tome from the parcel in his rucksack and pushed down the old pain that rose in his throat. Blinking, he opened to the third chapter of the Book of Lefil.

> Tears flow like a river
>
> The river becomes a song.
>
> The song rises from cursed stones.
>
> The stones cannot be stopped.

Gorm cross-referenced the notes that Niln had written in the book's margins.

> What does that mean?

"My sentiments exactly," said Gorm. He looked at the next note. It was written in haste, a sprawling scribble across the page.

> Destiny cannot be forced, or negotiated with, or convinced. Second Book of Epath, chapter 9, verse 7

"Heh. Ye were always trying to anyway," Gorm said to Niln. He found another note, written in Niln's more typical tight, neat script.

Once I can explain how this fits together, the others will see the path we must walk. Perhaps then they will not fight their destiny so much.

Gorm smirked. "Aye, ye always wanted us to—" He lost the words in a muffled choke as he read another thought Niln had scrawled in the far margin.

Perhaps then Gorm might not think me such a fool.

"I... I didn't think ye a fool." Gorm could manage little more than a hoarse whisper. "Well, no, I did. But ye were the good kind of fool. The kind we need more of, all ideals and courage. The kind I miss every... I..."

He couldn't find any words to say, and it struck him anew that there wasn't anyone around to hear them. The book felt heavy as he closed it and set it on his lap, resting his hands gently on the pebbled leather cover. He remained at the edge of his tent for a long time, listening to the crackle of the cookfire and watching the stars wink into sight.

"I'm sorry for being so disheveled. I just wasn't expecting this," said Jynn, struggling to pull on his robe.

"I know it's late," said Laruna. She stood outside the noctomancer's tent, pretending to take an interest in the fog of her breath. To the north, the moonlit Plains of Aberreth spread out like a sea of grass, dotted with archipelagoes of trees and rocky outcroppings.

"It's not so much the hour. I haven't had many visits from you," said Jynn, stepping from the tent.

"Yeah, well, we need to get something straight," said Laruna. "Come on."

She led him away from camp, waving to Heraldin and Gaist as they started their shift of the night's watch. It took a few minutes to reach a thicket of wild hedges, where the solamancer found a granite outcropping to sit on.

"I've been thinking about you lately," Laruna said. "A lot."

"And… and I you," Jynn confessed with a trembling voice.

"Yeah. I… I mean…" Laruna trailed off, and it took a moment for her to get back on track. "Listen, I hate secrets. I hate them more when they're between people who are supposed to be a team or in lo—you know, in a relationship… It's like they're hiding from each other. Holding back who they really are. It's like a lie without the words."

"I know," said Jynn. "And I am sorry that I kept my father's identity from you."

"Yeah," said Laruna. "But I'm starting to see, you know, that you can't tell everyone everything. You have to trust people to… to tell you what they need to. If you want to be a friend to them."

"Really?" A shadow of a smile appeared on the noctomancer's face.

"Really." Laruna rested her hand on his. "And I… what you told me about your father's schemes. About him becoming a liche. You must have suspected something, even long ago."

"I suppose so," said Jynn. "I saw some of his experiments. He had guests that frightened me, and they were frightened of him. We all were."

"You couldn't tell us that, though," said Laruna. She picked up his hand and held it in her own. "That was what you were holding back, wasn't it? When I asked if you had any secrets left, that's what you couldn't say."

Jynn's eyes flashed in the moonlight. "Laruna, I—"

"I don't care if you keep things from the party, or anyone else," the solamancer said. "I'll keep them with you. But I want more from you than everyone else, Jynn Ur'Mayan. I want no more secrets between us, no matter what they are. Just tell me now, and get them out of my way."

The wizard licked his lips before speaking slowly, carefully. "I… I knew Father was a necromancer. And I… I helped him with some of his experiments."

"It doesn't even bother me," said Laruna, grinning at the truth of it. "Anything else?"

Jynn rubbed his bald head. "Well, no, but—"

She cut him off with a long kiss and felt his surprised resistance melt away. By the time they broke apart, the wizard could only stare at her, breathless.

"Come on," she said. "I want to show you something."

The noctomancer wore a witless grin as she led him around the outcropping. "Where are we going?"

"Not far now," said Laruna. "We need to be out of sight of the camp."

"Well, I really wasn't expecting this," Jynn babbled. "And bear in mind that it's very chilly this evening—"

"We're here." Once inside the shadows of the trees, Laruna turned to the wizard and took his hands in her own. "No more secrets between us, right?"

"No more secrets. I swear it," he said, leaning in to kiss her again.

"Good," she told him. "Then there's someone I want you to meet. Come on out."

"Who are yo-hoo. Hoo. Ha. Haaa." Language failed the wizard as a nearby boulder began to move, warping and twisting into a massive Troll.

"Jynn," said Laruna. "This is Thane."

"Haa. Oooh. Oh gods." Jynn stood rigid and trembling as he stared up at the Troll with wide eyes.

"He's doing that thing," said Thane. "The physiological reaction thing."

"Listen, Jynn. Thane is a friend." Laruna spoke slowly, for emphasis. "He's my friend."

"I… It's just not what I was expecting," said Jynn vacantly. He shook his head.

"This was a bad idea," said Thane.

"No, no, this is fine," said the solamancer. "Jynn, he's been protecting us from monsters, but it's more than that. He's nothing like other Trolls."

Jynn didn't even acknowledge her. "Really, really not what I was expecting," he said.

"Actually, that's not fair," said Laruna turning to Thane. "I've never really met any other Trolls. Maybe quite a few of them are just misunderstood, you know?"

"Well, not in my experience," said Thane. "Most of the Trolls I've met are horrible. But I suppose they could become better, under the right circumstances."

"It's almost the exact opposite of what I was expecting!" said Jynn.

"Exactly. They might just be conforming to society's expectations," said Laruna. "I mean, I don't know how I would respond if everyone either screamed and ran away or tried to kill me at first sight."

"That does sound a lot like my life," said Thane.

"It defies expectations," said Jynn, lost in a parallel conversation.

"And I am sorry about that, again," Laruna told the Troll. "It is remarkable how well you've adjusted. Maybe you had a better upbringing than other Trolls?"

"Upbringing?" said Thane. "Troll mothers leave their infants on the forest floor to fend for themselves."

"Leaving babies in the—that's horrible!" exclaimed Laruna.

"Well, yes, there you are," said Thane. "That's what I was saying."

"Why would anyone expect this?" said Jynn, a hint of manic laughter creeping into his voice.

"Well, whatever other Trolls are like, it doesn't matter. The point is, you're a friend," said Laruna. "Jynn, slow breaths. He won't hurt us. Thane has been helping us since before the battle of Bloodroot. Gorm has been working with him."

"Pleased to meet you," Thane ventured, extending a meaty paw.

"Just… just never would have… who…" Jynn absently set a limp hand in the Troll's palm.

"How long do you think he'll be like this?" Thane muttered to Laruna.

"A while yet," she said, giving the noctomancer's head an affectionate rub. "But he'll come around soon enough."

Chapter 9

"But these things take time, you know?" The Head of Marketing bobbed along next to Tyren, a stack of papers bouncing in front of it. "Listen, an undead army's got a lot of things going for it, but speed isn't one of 'em. Most of the troops can't manage anything faster than an excited shamble."

"I see," said Tyren as he and the Head pushed through another rank of trudging corpses.

"And when we hit a city like Vetchell, things really slow down," the skull continued. "We've got combatants to convert, recruits to raise from the graveyards and crypts, we have to loot all of the magical items, and there always seems to be a few plucky holdouts boarded up in an abandoned house," the skull said. "Takes forever to weed 'em out. This guy knows what I'm talking about. Right, Rotgut?"

"Oh, aye, sir!" said a zombie as they passed. "We was sure we could make it until help arrived, but you got us in the end."

The flaming skull nodded toward the zombie. "Rotgut and his friends held out for almost a day and half before we overran their farmhouse," he told Tyren.

"That we did, sir!" said Rotgut. "Would have escaped too, had it not been for those skeletal archers." He turned and displayed a back so thick with protruding arrows that he resembled some sort of macabre, bipedal porcupine.

"Ha! You almost made it," said the skull as Rotgut fell behind. "Never stood a chance," he muttered to Tyren.

Tyren nodded, but he was paying more attention to the great, black carriage ahead of them. It was as large as a cottage and covered in iron spikes and bent chimneys that belched dark smoke into the air. Floating eyeballs and bat-like creatures fluttered among the billowing clouds. A team of horse skeletons dragged the ghoulish wagon along, and a hideous variety of malformed undead plodded along beside it.

"Ugh, great," said the Head of Marketing. "He's been working in the lab today. Steer clear of the experiments if you don't want to be one."

"Duly noted," said Tyren, staring at the motley vanguard. Several bony constructs with too many legs and not enough heads labored under the weight of iron braziers that spouted gouts of violet and emerald flames. A lumbering hulk of bones and skulls dragged great, scything claws fashioned from some giant's ribs. Near the head of the grim procession, a skeletal torso missing its arms was marching along on spindly legs. Part of an old sign nailed to its sternum read "ABANDON ALL HOPE" above a jagged break.

Swirling enchantments swung the carriage door open as Tyren approached, and a set of stairs unfurled in a way that reminded the knight-commander of a beetle's overcomplicated mouth parts. The stairs retracted as the knight-commander stepped onto them, and he and the Head of Marketing were quickly drawn into the laboratory of Detarr Ur'Mayan.

Every wall boasted chalkboards covered in esoteric symbols and arcane equations. Crates and cages were stacked in the dim recesses of the wagon, boxing in several tables and desks. The room was illuminated, to a degree, by disparate glowing fluids flowing through the labyrinthine tangle of glass pipes and tubes that connected the outer desks. At the center of the alchemical web, the liche sat with a few other figures.

"Ah, welcome, welcome." Detarr beckoned Tyren and the Head deeper into the lab. "Come in, join the circle. Thank you. I think that means we're all here, right? Right. Good."

Tyren sat stiffly in one of the empty seats, and the Head floated above another.

"Let's start with introductions, shall we?" said the liche. "I'm Detarr Ur'Mayan, lord of this army of the dead, formerly a wizard of some renown. I'm sure you all know me by now. Next?"

They went around the circle. Tyren recognized old Lord Hulch, a local baron who had become some sort of ghoul; he hardly looked any different after death, save the needle teeth protruding from his mouth and a few extra spots on his pale, leathery skin. Next to Lord Hulch sat a woman whose dark hair and almond eyes marked her as Umbraxian; Lady

Carabae's all-black wardrobe and excessive makeup marked her for a vampiress well before her grin revealed long fangs. A spectral lady named Genevieve went next; it was hard to tell if she was a ghost or a banshee, but Tyren had recently discovered that it was considered rude in some circles to discuss such matters. Then the Head of Marketing introduced himself, and finally Tyren stated his name and rank.

"Our knight-commander is being modest," said Detarr. "Tyren here delivered some great ideas for our marketing campaign. Speaking of which, do you have the drafts?"

Tyren nodded and looked at the Head of Marketing, who bobbed forward and floated a flyer to the liche. Detarr took it and read with interest as the Head passed more copies around the circle.

The flyers were printed with a skull and bat motif in a thick gothic font. The text surrounded a large woodcut of a terrified looking man about to be overrun by a cluster of zombies. It read:

THERE IS MUCH TO FEAR IN LIFE.
(Specifically, the horrible bit at the end.)

YOU'LL HAVE NOTHING TO FEAR
AFTER DEATH.
MAKE YOUR TRANSITION AS
PAINLESS AS POSSIBLE.
SURRENDER TODAY AND GET A
SPECIAL BONUS.

"What's the special bonus?" asked Detarr.

"Nobody will eat you," said Tyren.

"You'd be surprised how many of our focus groups wished they got a guarantee like that," added the Head of Marketing.

"Excellent!" said Detarr. "Excellent! Now, what can the rest of you tell me about this flyer?"

The gathered undead shifted in their seats. Lady Carabae gave an uncomfortable cough.

"Anyone?" asked Detarr.

"I've... never seen anything like it?" ventured Genevieve.

"Exactly," said the liche. "It's innovative!"

"It's not going to bloody work," said Lord Hulch, looking up from one of the flyers.

"Perhaps." Detarr shrugged. "But if it doesn't, we'll learn from it and try something new. After all, before I could craft the Bonereaper, I had to make Gretch."

"*Gretch!*" shrieked one of the cages.

"Why, in life I worked on the Leviathan Project. We were trying to create the perfect hero, and we failed utterly," said the liche. "But a few decades later, it turns out we created some rather useful demonic animals."

The largest cage in the back of the wagon roared to life with a sudden cacophony of vicious growling, unholy snorts and, if Tyren wasn't mistaken, malevolent squeaks. Gouts of orange fire licked at the bars, casting hulking shadows around the lab.

"I'm sure they'll be handy in a pinch," said the liche. "The point is, we can learn from mistakes. We just need to move fast and be creative. What's most important is that we're disrupting the status quo."

"Of course we're being thrice-cursed disruptive," said Lord Hulch with a chuckle. "We're trying to kill everyone!"

"Yes," said Detarr slowly, eyeing the old ghoul. "But any necromancer capable of coaxing a skeleton out of a crypt has been trying to kill everyone, and look where they wound up. Some unlikely heroes inevitably rally the living to defeat the undead. And do you know why?"

"They didn't have flyers?" Genevieve sounded doubtful.

"What? No." Detarr shook his head. "They all tried the same thing. It's always only been the one plan: dominate the undead, have them march on cities en masse, and hope to crush your enemy with sheer numbers. But do you realize how hard it is to try to magically coordinate the actions of thousands of undead on your own? By the time you've got a decent-sized army together, it's all you can do to get them to stagger in a line with their arms straight forward! Your only hope of victory with such troops is that mortals will be dumb enough to fall on their weapons."

Detarr leapt from his seat. There was a gleam in his eye—and not just from the infernal lights deep within his sockets—as he addressed each of them. "If we're going to end all life on Arth, we need a different way of looking at things. We've got to think outside the box, or the casket, as the case may be. As long as it's a brainless march forward, we're doomed to fail. We can't just dominate the undead anymore. We have to elevate them!"

"Then how will you get them to do as you want?" asked Lady Carabae.

"Does anyone have an idea?" asked Detarr.

"Leadership and delegation," said Tyren.

"That's the key!" said Detarr. "Listen, it's not hard to motivate zombies and ghouls to attack the living. It's their natural instinct. But with proper leadership, we can channel those instincts into a successful campaign."

If Tyren had lips, he wouldn't have been able to hide his smile. Leadership meant organization. Delegation meant hierarchy. And chief among the knight-commander's skills in life was a knack for traversing a bureaucracy and finding a comfortable spot.

Not everyone was as happy with the direction of the conversation.

"It just doesn't make sense," said Lord Hulch. "You can already make the undead do as you please! Why would you be looking for another way?"

Detarr steepled his fingers and stared at the ghoul. "You know, Lord Hulch," he said eventually. "This may not be the best fit for you. Not everyone is cut out for innovation."

"I should say not!" laughed Lord Hulch. Tyren recalled that the old baron always did have a hard time reading the room. "I cannot imagine how surrendering your authority is to work! Ha!"

"Don't trouble yourself," said Detarr. "I'm sure we can find another use for you. Someone needs to feed my infernal beasts, for example."

"Well, I must say, I've no mind for animal husbandry, let alone demonology," harrumphed Hulch, clueless to the last. "Why, I don't even know what a demon creature would eat!"

"I'm sure you'll figure it out." Detarr waved his hand. Lord Hulch's chair leapt into motion, flying backward across the laboratory floor into the darkness, where the door to the large cage had swung open. The liche gestured again, and the cage door slammed shut behind its newest occupant.

"Now then," said Detarr. "As for the rest of you, what do you say of my plan?"

The air was suddenly rent by Lord Hulch's screams and the unholy roaring of the beasts.

"I'm in!" said Tyren hurriedly, and the others rushed to chorus their affirmations behind him.

"Excellent!" said Detarr.

Tyren held a hand up. "And I'll also see to the infernal beasts, sir, as Lord Hulch didn't work out."

His statement was punctuated by a low burp from the shadowy cage.

"I like your initiative," said the liche. "I can see you're going to be a valuable member of my team. You all will. Each one of you has an important part to play as we work together toward our ultimate goal."

"Andarun! The greatest city in the world," proclaimed Heraldin as the city lights began to glow in earnest. Mount Wynspar thrust up from the plains before them, a black silhouette in the dusk, and the city of Andarun shone brightly from its southern crag.

"The biggest, at least." Gorm prodded the cookfire with a stick.

"And the most well guarded," added Jynn.

"Not as well guarded as usual, though." Kaitha nodded to the muddy road. Though it had been days since Handor's forces had headed east, the earth still bore the scars of the innumerable hooves and boots. "The army must be to Aberreth by now."

"All the better for us," said Laruna. "That means half the bannermen in the city will be gone."

"At least that," said Gorm, looking at the churned mud.

"Which is good," said Heraldin. "But I don't think that will make much difference when we're robbing one of Andarun's most beloved and well-guarded institutions."

Gaist nodded.

"Perhaps," said Gorm. "I've got friends who might tip the scales in our favor."

"How?" asked Kaitha.

"No idea," said Gorm. "But they're a useful sort. They have a facility up on the second tier, over in Dunedling Fens." Gorm pushed a charred log deeper into the fire, kicking up a fountain of amber sparks.

"Even with half the bannermen gone, that's far enough into the city that we could be spotted," said Jynn.

"That's a simple matter," said Heraldin. "Some charcoal in Gorm's beard, a wig on Jynn, some new clothes, a magical ward or two; nobody will recognize us. Doubly so if we pass through separate gates and meet at the edge of Dunedling Fens."

"Fair enough," said Kaitha. "But there's still a more, ah, conspicuous member of our party."

All eyes turned to Burt, who froze mid-gnaw on a soup bone. "What?" he said.

"It just might be, you know, a little telling if we brought a… you know…" said Jynn.

"No, I don't know," said Burt. "A what?"

"If we brought a Shadowkin along," Laruna finished. "Only because most of the NPCs left the city. It'd be unusual to see one with six of… er… us."

"Oh. Well, no worries there," said Burt. "I'll just stay behind."

The other adventurers stared at Burt with a mixture of relief and doubt.

Gorm raised an eyebrow. "Ye will?"

"Yeah, I'll be fine," said the Kobold. "I'll find a big rock and spend the day hiding behind it."

"And you're not offended by the suggestion?" said Kaitha.

"Oh, no." Burt said calmly. "Don't you worry about me."

"Uh, good," said Kaitha. "I guess we have a plan."

"I guess we do," said the Kobold.

Gorm stared at Burt through narrowed eyes. The Kobold never sounded this serene; not even when he was asleep. "Good," he said.

"Yeah. Great." Burt stood and hefted the soup bone over his shoulder. "I'm going to take this back to the tent."

"I thought we agreed ye'd not bring food into me rucksack," said Gorm.

"And I thought we didn't abandon each other at the drop of a hat," snapped Burt. "Live and learn, eh?"

"I knew he'd react badly," grumbled Gorm, watching the Kobold saunter off in the general direction of his tent. "He's going to get crumbs and grease in me clothes for weeks."

"He's still taking it better than I thought he would," said Laruna.

"That's not saying much," said Heraldin, standing with his plate.

The heroes set about their nightly routines. Dishes were cleaned, gear was fussed over and tended to, and the remaining food was packed away. Gaist and Heraldin broke out their ragtag thrones set and settled in for a game. The mages, Gorm noticed, went off together for some training. The Dwarf himself joined Kaitha as she tended to the horses.

"Jynn and Laruna seem to be getting along well these days," the Elf remarked, brushing her mount.

"I suppose," said Gorm, taking a brush to his own stallion.

"They're speaking to each other now, aren't arguing when they do, are training together once more, and generally seem happy to be around each other," said the Elf, watching the mages spar in the distance. "Do you suppose they're, you know, together again?"

"The only thing I know about Human courtship is it's far too frequent and open," said Gorm. "I can barely understand half of what goes on between ye tall folk, and that's too much insight for my liking."

"Oh, come now." Kaitha laughed as she stroked her horse's mane.

"I'm serious." Gorm plucked the remains of insects off the stallion's chest. "They ain't fighting and they're workin' well together. Beyond that, we've got bigger things to worry about. The undead are comin'. The bannermen are on the march. The Red Horde and the Guz'Varda Tribe are still out there, huntin' and being hunted. The world is goin' to war."

"True enough," said Kaitha. "It reminds me of how things felt when Marduk of Midnight was threatening Daellan with an army of Demons a while back."

"Aye, exactly."

"Or when Deep Thoggus was rising out of the sea near Edaelmon and threatened to wipe out Ruskan with his tide of fish people."

"Right," said Gorm. "I hear their docks are still infested with street urchins."

"And when Az'Anon was raising an army of the undead in the eastern Green Span."

"Okay, you're right," said Gorm. "But what's your point?"

"We're always between wars, Gorm," said Kaitha. "All peace is fleeting. You need to take advantage while it lasts. These are the times when you can find happiness and love."

"Hmph. Seems to me ye tall folk could find love in a dragon's gullet," Gorm grumbled. "Ye can't be convinced to stop findin' it. And then ye bicker on and on, and then ye end it, and then ye mope about what ye lost until ye either get back together or find someone else. Then the whole bunch of nonsense starts again. It's a great mummer's farce played out around those of us that are actually tryin' to get things done."

"All right, you don't have to understand it," said Kaitha. "But surely you can see that if we chase it that much, love must be wonderful. It's... it makes everything seem, I don't know, worthwhile. If you can find it." She trailed off.

Gorm peered around the flank of his mount. Kaitha was doing it again. She stared silently toward the thicket of scrub brush where Thane was spending the night.

The Dwarf shivered. Laruna had mentioned the uncanny accuracy with which Kaitha would often stare at wherever the Troll was. Gorm had once thought it a sad coincidence and later assumed it had something to do with Nove's principles. Now it was starting to give him goosebumps.

He cleared his throat. "I suppose that's true enough," he said loudly.

Kaitha shook her head as she turned back to him. "Right," she said. "Anyway, what I meant is, Jynn and Laruna may have found some small light in all this darkness. That's important, and all the more so since evil times are coming. Don't begrudge them the moment."

"Aye, I suppose you're right." Gorm sighed. "If'n they are back together, I hope they enjoy it while it lasts."

"Just so long as it's quick," snarled Handor. The king pulled his cloak closer around him as the royal carriage rattled through the dark streets of Andarun. "I should be back by my fire at this time of night."

Johan grinned. "Take my word for it, sire. This will be worth your while."

"We shall see," King Handor said as the carriage rolled to a stop. "It will be just as cold in there as it is on the streets."

"A necessary sacrifice, I'm afraid," Johan replied.

"And you're sure this scheme of yours will work?" said Handor.

"Ha! Failure is not an option, Your Majesty," said Johan.

"That's not the same thing as success being guaranteed," Handor muttered as he stepped down the gilt steps of the royal carriage.

"We've got the smartest people in Andarun working on it." Johan maneuvered slowly through the carriage doors; no small feat for a man with a suit of ornate plate and a huge broadsword.

The Dungeon Gate loomed over them in the shadows, its upper limits beyond the reach of the torchlight. The stone frame and massive doors were as big as the guard towers on either side of the entrance, which was almost as tall as the Ridge itself. Few decorations adorned the gate—there was little room for them among the rivets and braces reinforcing the doors—but a life-sized dragon head wrought in bronze occupied its center. A ring the size of a carriage wheel hung from the dragon's maw, dangling the great chains that the Heroes' Guild used to open the door whenever a group of brave or foolish adventurers was sent to challenge the perils of Mount Wynspar.

There were no oxen and pull teams today, however. A contingent of bannermen guided Handor and Johan to the dungeon's service entrance, tucked behind a guard tower. A pair of guards opened the twin doors in unison, bowing low as the king and Tandos' Champion brushed past them into the labyrinth below Wynspar.

The cavernous room beyond the door was so cold that Handor could see his breath. Nevertheless, the chamber bustled with quiet activity centered around a fantastic construct near the middle of the room. It looked like a growth of iron roots, smooth and spiraling, that splayed open at the top and grasped a gargantuan globe, green and glowing. Men in long leather coats and red goggles bustled around the pylon, working industriously.

At the end of the chamber, a large contingent of guild heroes guarded the passages that went deeper within the mountain. Johan must have noticed Handor staring at them, because the paladin leaned close and confided, "They cleared the entire level of anything larger than a rat this morning, sire. We're perfectly safe."

Handor nodded and turned his attention to the reception area, where attendants had spread a red velvet carpet and set up small black tables. Goldson and Baggs were there, along with a few other prominent members of Andarun's business community. They gave small bows as the king approached the tables.

"Ah, Your Majesty. So glad you could make it," said Baggs, offering the king a glass of Halfling brandy.

"As am I," Handor lied as he accepted the drink. "Though I should have been more glad had we done this in the palace."

"Apologies, Majesty," said Goldson. The ancient Dwarf perched on a tall chair, nursing a tumbler of amber spirits. "But the nature of tonight's demonstration requires both secrecy and safety."

"Yeah. You don't want this where any rank one newblood could see it," said a boisterous voice. Handor recognized the heavyset man it belonged to as Dannel Clubs.

Clubs Incorporated had made its fortune selling its eponymous weapon, as well as maces, morning stars, flails, and any other heavy instrument suitable for a professional hero's bludgeoning needs. Its outspoken owner held higher ambitions for the company he inherited, and so Dannel Clubs' well-known exploits included high-profile ventures into construction, security services, and real estate. Yet if business was like a sword duel, Dannel Clubs had all the subtlety and cunning of a branch with a nail through it—coincidentally, his best-selling product—and all of these side businesses had quickly folded.

"Mr. Clubs helped us broker the deal with Yutani Arm Traders Incorporated," said Baggs, a note of apology in his voice.

Handor nodded and forced a polite smile. "Ah. Well, Mr. Clubs, I'm grateful for your assistance."

"You want to deal with the undead, you gotta know how to negotiate with the Imperials," Clubs blurted. "Those guys from Umbrax are the best necromancers around. Only place necromancy is legal, Umbrax."

"Indeed," said Handor. He took a long pull from his brandy.

"Those guys from Umbrax love me," continued Clubs. "I do business with them all the time. I get great deals from all over, but especially Umbrax."

"It's true," said Goldson. "Nobody is better connected in the Umbraxian weapons market than Clubs Incorporated."

"We checked," said Baggs. "Extensively."

"I'm your only choice!" said Clubs.

"I couldn't have said it better myself," Mr. Goldson muttered into his drink.

"If we want to strike a decisive blow against the undead and end their incursion at a specific time and a very specific place," said Baggs, "we have to deal with Mr. Clubs."

Clubs smiled obliviously.

Someone behind them cleared his throat. Handor turned to see one of the workers in a long leather coat with a purple scarf pulled up over half of his face. Blue veins spiderwebbed over his pale, bald head, and his eyes were all but hidden behind the shining red glass of his goggles.

"Your Majesty, honored sirs," said the technician, bowing low. "I thank you for your understanding regarding the hour and the venue of our presentation. The, ah, sensitive nature of our demonstration necessitates a degree of secrecy."

The technician pointed across the massive chamber, and Handor felt his blood run cold. A group of three skeletons were being herded across the cavern, each restrained by chains and manacles.

"You brought the undead here?" said Handor, frowning.

"Yes, sire," said the technician. "If you wish to battle a necromancer, you must understand necromancy. A necessary evil in the most literal sense."

"It's a dire threat, that's what it is," said Handor. "And it isn't the sort of thing that happens in my kingdom without my knowing it."

"I don't see the problem," said Clubs.

"I'm sure you don't," snapped Handor. If the nobility caught wind that his court had sanctioned necromancy, there'd be riots like Andarun hadn't seen in decades.

"Apologies, Your Majesty," said the technician. "Hopefully, you will like the results."

"Just get it over with," Handor growled.

"Surely, Majesty," said the technician, bowing so low that he threatened to fold himself in half. Standing, he held a fist up in signal and gave a quick shout to the other workers.

The skeletons were moved into position by their handlers. One undead specimen stood a short walk from the great, green orb. The second stood a considerable distance beyond the first, and the third was set halfway across the cavern, almost to the edge of the red carpet where Handor and the businessmen uneasily watched the proceedings.

Handor was surprised to see technicians weaving threads of air and shadow over the great pylon; none of the Yutani Arm Traders employees wore noctomancers' robes. Violet light radiated from the base of the apparatus, creeping over the spindly structure like cracks through the ice in spring.

Then the tip of the light touched the orb itself, and the great sphere thrummed with pulses of wild, emerald energy. Jade lightning arced and spouted from the surface as more sorcery flowed into the globe. The low thrumming accelerated, warping into a high-pitched whistle that put Handor in mind of a teapot.

He tapped Johan on the shoulder and stood on tiptoe to whisper in the paladin's ear. "Is it supposed to do—"

The world went white in a sudden flash. A rush of sulfurous wind nearly took Handor from his feet, followed by the clatter of bones on the floor. When his vision returned a moment later, the orb sat inert, as did the remains of all three skeletons. Light applause broke out among the assembled businessmen.

"The orbs nullify and destroy any undead within a wide radius," said the technician. "Yutani can assemble three dozen immediately, once you say where you wish to deploy them."

"Magnificent," breathed Handor, a broad smile spreading across his face.

"I told you!" Clubs leaned back in his seat with a wide grin.

"Indeed. All that remains is to determine where and when we want to stop the undead incursion," said Goldson.

"And if we may be so bold, there's a place we'd like to suggest," said Baggs.

"Here." Grignot's claw touched a point on a crude map as Asherzu slipped into the chieftain's hut. The satchel of charts and scrolls hanging from her shoulder bumped against a pile of decorative skulls. The assembled warriors of the Guz'Varda and the Red Horde turned to stare as the bones toppled over. Asherzu smiled and tried to fade into the background.

"Why there?" asked Darak. "With the power of Fulgen's Rest, we can strike anywhere. And your target is far from any suitable site for a gate."

The wiry Orc cleared his throat and turned back to Darak. "If we use the southernmost gate in the Pinefells, we will be a half day's ride to the town; close enough for a swift strike. But there are better reasons to strike the Lightlings here."

"But why strike them at all?" Asherzu stepped forward, one hand on her scrolls. "Why attack the Human town in the first place?"

"You forget yourself, Lady Asherzu," said Grignot. "The chieftain has not called for you."

Darak looked at his sister with stern eyes, but she saw the plea behind his mask. Her impertinence dishonored him in front of the warriors of the Red Horde.

She took a deep breath. "I… I am truly sorry, great chieftain. Honor and glory to you."

Her brother's relief was evident as he nodded. "It is forgiven," he said.

"But I question the wisdom of this raid," she continued. "Why would we risk the lives of our warriors?"

"For vengeance! For the glory of bloodshed! And for the spoils of war!" said Grignot, prompting a roar of approval from the Red Horde warriors around him. Noticing Darak's stare, the wiry wise-one added, "But most of all, for the honor of our fallen leader, Char Guz'Varda."

As one, the warriors turned to a great red flag hanging in the corner of the tent. Char's likeness was smeared across the fabric in black tar, looking up and to the right with a mixture of pride, defiance, and dramatic lighting. She'd seen the same image of her brother stenciled on huts throughout the village.

"We will honor brother Char." Darak looked to Grignot for reassurance. "His death must not go unanswered."

"I miss our brother, too," said Asherzu. "But Char's death was in answer to the Lightlings he killed, and they were killed in answer to other fallen Orcs, who died for killing other Lightlings. That is the Old Ways: a never-ending argument written in blood, a cycle of death that cannot end until someone walks away or nobody is left to stand."

"Did your father's ways serve us any better?" asked Grignot. "Who else do we have to thank for our current plight?"

"They did serve us better." Asherzu pulled her scrolls and charts out, flashing numbers and graphs at the assembled warriors. "Under the reign of my father, the median income of Guz'Varda Orcs rose by sixteen and eight tenths percent! The average lifespan of a warrior increased by five years. The value of huts, the inflation rate, the whelp mortality rate; every index of prosperity went up in the years of my father's rule. And what is more, all such measures have diminished lately. There are many correlations between our raids and the misery our people suffer."

Her charts prompted thoughtful looks from several of the Red Horde warriors, but Grignot only wore his reptilian grin. "Why must the sister of the chieftain go to such great lengths to bend the will of her own flesh and blood?" the wiry Orc asked the room. "Why does she not speak from the heart?"

"I speak the truth," Asherzu said.

"The truth?" Grignot's voice danced on the edge of mocking. "The truth is that we built a wealthy city, and the gold-hounds came and murdered our people and took our treasure. The truth is that our beloved chieftains lie dead, and their blood is on the hands of Lightlings. The truth is that we have brave warriors — mighty warriors! — ready to pay the pink skins back for their crimes. And yet you come to stop them because of the numbers you have written down? You would stand with the Lightlings for the sake of math?"

Asherzu had to forcefully stop her hands from wringing Grignot's neck. "These facts—"

"The fact is that the truth is simple." Grignot waved Asherzu's charts away dismissively. "And deception must labor to be believed. I can see you have worked hard, lady, but you have lost your way amid the figures."

"What is there to be lost in knowledge?" Asherzu demanded.

"Our principles, apparently," said Grignot to the room. "But it is the chieftain's decision whose counsel to take. Will he listen to his honorable warriors, brave and ready, and stand for the true path? Or will he lose himself in the scrolls as his sister has?"

"Enough! We do not need such fighting amongst ourselves." Darak's face trembled, showing hints of the panic Asherzu knew he was feeling. But as he looked at the mass of warriors surrounding Asherzu and Grignot, the chieftain found a number he could wrap his head around. "We will go to battle for Char's honor."

The warriors cheered. Grignot grinned.

Asherzu stepped up to her brother and spoke softly in Shadowtongue. *"Brother, I cannot walk with you into this madness."*

Darak refused to meet her gaze. *"Then, perhaps... Perhaps you will stand behind me, my sister. I would appreciate that."*

"But —"

Darak glanced at the warriors watching them. *"You are dismissed, wise-one,"* he mumbled.

He may as well have hit Asherzu's chest with his great warhammer. The air rushed from her lungs, and it was all she could do to bow and rasp a farewell before rushing from the tent. The laughter of Grignot and his Red Horde warriors followed her out into the night.

"And just like that, you're on the outside," Burt muttered to himself. He watched the heroes ride away, their swift horses kicking up damp earth and dew in a cloud behind them. "They didn't even bother to leave a little breakfast for their friend."

The sun was still rising, casting the high, wispy clouds above Andarun in various hues of amber and honeysuckle. The air was crisp and cool and smelled of the new grass just starting to push through the loam of the plain. Spring was well and truly underway.

The beauty of the moment was lost on the Kobold. "Gods, I hate being up this early," he grumbled as he turned back to the woods behind him. "All right, you can come out now. They're gone."

The small clearing failed to answer, so the Kobold stamped across the campsite and into the undergrowth. After a minute or two of tramping through thick ferns and a few brambles, he found a mossy boulder that was roughly the shape of a kneeling humanoid. "Come on, come on. You know they're gone," Burt grumbled. He gave the stone a couple of light kicks for emphasis.

"What do you want?" asked a deep voice from behind him, prompting Burt to leap high into the air with a yelp.

"Don't do that!" Burt panted as he turned to face Thane. The Troll was as tall as a young tree and heavier than the boulder, but he still moved silently as he stepped out from the shadows of the forest.

"Sorry," said Thane.

"You should know I'm jumpy out here. Kobolds are supposed to travel in packs. I get the jitters when I'm alone."

"Gorm leaves you alone in his tent almost every night," said the Troll.

"Yeah, well, your visiting hours are usually well after bed time," said the Kobold. "Beauty sleep, you know?"

"He usually comes out just after dinner."

"Hey, it takes a lot of work and a lot of rest to look this good."

The Troll scratched his head. "Really?"

Burt scowled. "Look, do you want my help or not?"

"I don't recall saying I did," said Thane.

"You should have, though," said the Kobold, sidling up beside the hulking Troll. "I'm gonna help you out today, kid."

"I'm several hundred years—"

"I'm gonna take you to get your noncombatant papers," Burt continued, scrabbling up Thane's forearm. "Now help me up. I'll ride on your shoulders."

"Now, wait. Wait!" rumbled the Troll with enough force to give Burt pause.

"What's to wait for?" asked Burt. "It's perfect. Everyone else is in the city. They'll never see us. You'll be an NPC by lunch."

"Who said I even want to be an NPC?"

"I did," said Burt, still clinging to the fur on Thane's arm. "Look, having papers may not be much protection against the guild these days, but I still don't think many heroes will give a guy like you trouble. But if you want to buy anything from a shop or get anything from a restaurant or travel through any of the city-states, you'll need a little green book that says you're an NPC."

"I don't want to go to the city."

"Oh, really?" Burt's unkempt eyebrows shot up in mock surprise. "I could have sworn you were head over feet for Kaitha, the sister of an ambassador to Andarun, the daughter of a queen of one of the biggest Elven city-states, and as cosmopolitan an Elf as I ever met. And you never want to visit the city with her? Take her out for tea? Have lunch on the Pinnacle?"

"I... I don't... I may not... why would... does she..." Thane blanched and stuttered at the mention of the ranger, unable to decide how his next sentence should start, let alone end.

Burt took the opportunity to scramble up the Troll's bicep and onto his massive shoulder. "Look, I'm not gonna try to tell you when you should come out of hiding. But when you do, if you want even a Goblin's fighting chance of getting sweet with the Elf, you'll need to treat her right. And to do that, you need to be an NPC. So let's go."

The Troll's feet shuffled toward Andarun, but his mind clearly hadn't caught up yet. "I wouldn't even know what to say to her," he muttered, staring at his own hands as if he might read an answer on them.

"How about 'Hello, Kaitha. My name is Thane,'" said Burt. He gripped a handful of matted fur with each of his claws and dangled his legs over the bony ridge of the Troll's clavicle. "Now, hyah! Let's pick up the pace!"

"Hello, Kaitha. My name is Thane," said Thane slowly, carefully. He repeated it a few times, turning the phrase over in his mouth. "Yes, that could work."

"It's just telling someone your name. Of course it will work," said Burt. "The hard part is getting her to go to tea with you."

"Why do we—"

"Ergh! Why, why, why? Because it's what they do," Burt barked. "Trust me, pal. I've been in an Elf's purse for more first dates than she'd care to admit. You want to impress an Elven lady? You introduce yourself. You invite her for tea, or coffee, or even lunch if you're trying to look bold. If tea goes well, you have dinner. If dinner goes well, you do it again, and again, and eventually, if everything keeps going well, you let your handbag performer have the night off, assuming you've got any decency."

"What does that have to do with—"

"I'm not going to explain everything to you," snapped Burt. "But it all starts with telling her your name."

"Hello, Kaitha. My name is Thane…"

"Right. You're getting it."

"Hello Kaitha. My name is Thane." The Troll held a meaty hand out to an imagined lady. "Would you like to join me for some tea?"

"Oh, come on. At least offer to buy it for her," said Burt.

"Hello, Kaitha. My name is Thane. Can I buy you a cup of tea?"

"Better. Try to make it witty."

The Troll's meandering walk faltered, and he wrung his hands nervously. "I don't think I can do witty."

"I don't think any of it matters if you're not an NPC," snapped Burt. "Do you want to get your papers or not?"

Thane thought about it. "Yes," he said. "I do."

Burt smiled as they set off toward the city.

Chapter 10

Gorm didn't realize how much he'd missed Andarun until he heard the familiar clank of its cobbles beneath his iron-toed boots. The smell of the street carts roasting meats with exotic spices. The alleys and shopfronts ringing with the calls of merchants hawking their wares. Vibrantly colored posters plastered every surface at eye level, advertising anything from mummers' plays to the latest in enchanted armor. Andarun held innumerable delights for one and all, provided you could afford them.

It didn't take long, however, for Gorm to remember that he could barely afford a beef roll in the city, and so his mood had soured by the time he arrived at the meeting place. The rest of the party was doing their best to inconspicuously loiter near the gatehouse of a large compound amid the derelict homes and tiny shops of Dunedling Fens. Several large warehouses loomed beyond the black iron fence.

Heraldin jabbed a thumb over his shoulder as the Dwarf stamped up. "Are you sure this is the place?"

"Aye. This is Boomer and Buster's company."

"This place?" said Laruna. "This industrial complex?"

"That so hard to believe?" asked Gorm.

"Yes," said Jynn.

Kaitha scratched her chin. "It just looks very... legitimate."

"So?" Gorm was starting to feel defensive.

"Most of your contacts that I've encountered have had more, shall we say, legally ambiguous backgrounds," Heraldin said.

"Yourself included, given all the thievin'," Gorm countered.

"You wound me, friend." Heraldin leaned in close to whisper harshly. "And if the wrong people hear you talking that way, Benny Hookhand will do so as well. So let's keep quiet about our pasts, eh?"

"Fine by me." Gorm shrugged. "Ye were the ones who brought it up."

"I only meant to point out that these contacts defy the trend," said Heraldin.

"Aye, Boomer and Buster do that a lot," said Gorm. "Let's go."

The gate featured a large, brass plaque embossed with elaborate lettering. It read:

CREATIVE DESTRUCTION INCORPORATED
EST. 7.344

"I think ye've been expecting us," Gorm said to the gatehouse guard. "We sent word ahead."

The guard, a balding Halfling with heavy-lidded eyes, tapped an enchanted orb without ever looking up from his book. The gate swung open as though blown by an otherwise undetectable wind.

They thanked the guard, to no effect, and made their way along a brick path to the main warehouse of Creative Destruction Incorporated. A doorman ushered them into a small lobby, where a loud shout greeted them.

"Gorm Ingerson!" Boomer hollered. The old Scribkin striding toward them was almost as stocky as a Dwarf. He wore an elaborate set of goggles and a thick, white mustache so long it had to be tucked into his leather apron. Every inch of his visible skin was covered in runic tattoos. He stomped over to Gorm and shook his hand with a hearty slap to the shoulder. "Good to see you!"

"Ye as well, Boomer," said Gorm, before introducing the rest of the party.

"A pleasure, a pleasure!" Boomer shook each adventurer's hand in turn. "Oh, I could tell you stories about this Dwarf, and I guarantee they're all at least half true! Ha! Now come on! Buster will be eager to see you, but I can sneak in a quick tour on the way."

The Scribkin led them past the receptionist's desk, through a pair of oak doors, and into a jungle of steel and stone. Pipes and steel beams thrust up from every inch of the floor, towering all the way to the distant ceiling. Workers in white coveralls scurried through a thick canopy of walkways and rope bridges, congregating at workstations illuminated by floating sorcerous lights. The air hummed with the sounds of industry and magic: whistling steam, clanging tools, hissing sorcery, and an isolated scream from a careless employee.

Gorm noted a pair of Gremlins packing sword after sword into an impossibly small bag, no bigger than his rucksack. A Tinderkin in a white coat took a swig of a purple potion and faded from Gorm's vision, only to reappear a moment later to the disappointment of her colleagues. A Dwerrow blasted down a narrow track on some sort of iron sled propelled by a massive flame erupting from the contraption's rear.

"Bloody bones! What was that?" Gorm yelled, watching the stout Gnome rocket away.

"A flame-jet propelled mechanical steed. Or a jet-steed, as we say," said Boomer. "Gonna be huge. Everyone will be ridin' jet-steeds."

There was a distant crash, followed by a siren ringing.

"Once we figure out how to stop them safely," added the Scribkin.

"Seems like madness to me," said Gorm.

"Maybe so, but people were wary of firepots and grappling cannons back in the day, and now they're standard adventuring gear. That's the nature of progress, and at Creative Destruction, scientific progress is what we're all about!" Boomer declared as he led the party along a bright, yellow path painted on the floor. "We use the very latest in wizardry and advanced technology to help enterprising heroes the world over decimate their enemies."

"And your facility, apparently," said Jynn, nodding to a pile of rubble attended by a squad of Dwerrow in coveralls. The bearded Gnomes combed through the debris with strange devices, and one extracted a thin, silver rod from a pile of concrete.

"Ah, that'd be the souvenir wind chimes," said Boomer.

"Really?" asked Kaitha.

Boomer shrugged. "We made them to conjure their own wind, but then the breeze they make sets 'em off and conjures more wind. Soon enough you've got a nasty chain reaction, and they go from a gentle gust to a hurricane in seconds. But we're learning from the experience, and we'll do better next time. Or bones, maybe we can weaponize 'em!

That'd make some money! Ha! It's all progress at Creative Destruction! Why, look over here."

The Gnome pointed to a thick glass window. On the other side of it was a small room, its walls and floor painted white. The occupants of the room were presumably Gnomes of one clan or another, but they were all wrapped head to toe in baggy white linens and thick goggles. They gathered around a small stone archway with a purplish-green crystal at the top.

As the heroes watched, one of the Gnomish attendants traced a small rune on the arch with a gloved hand. The tiny portal flared with blue light, and a moment later another Gnome in white came into view through the archway, like a window to somewhere else.

"Waygates," breathed Laruna.

"Yes indeed," laughed Boomer. "That's our facility in Knifevale that they're passing fruit to. Ha! We're going to revolutionize travel and shipping!"

The attendants in white were gently nudging apples through the waygate with the sort of caution that monster handlers might use when feeding Flame Drakes. Three or four apples made it through before the crystal on top of the arch cracked. Gnomes dove for cover in all directions as the portal winked out of existence.

"Once we work out a couple of small problems," said Boomer, deflated.

"Havin' your door randomly disappear seems to be a big one." Gorm watched the Gnomes in white stand again and cautiously approach the waygate.

"Oh, it's not random," said Boomer. "Each hunk of thaumite can only pass so much matter through a portal before it starts to crack. We think we could get a lot more out of each crystal if we calibrate the thaumite's setting better, but it's an exacting science."

"Isn't thaumite really expensive?" asked Laruna.

"That's the other problem. Moving a handful of apples costs a few thousand giltin." Boomer nodded his head as they continued along the pathway. "Until we figure out those calibrations or get the price of thaumite down, we can't mass produce the waygates. But we'll get there! Progress marches on! Speaking of which, mind the path, son."

Jynn stepped back onto the yellow paint just as a crackling blue battleaxe flew through the space that his head had occupied a split-second earlier. It sailed through a large, rectangular hole in a corrugated metal wall before landing with an inexplicable splash.

"Close one! Ha! Got to stay on the yellow floor when we're in a live test zone," said Boomer. "Safety is our top priority! Or at least it's in the top five."

"What kind of test could that possibly be?" Laruna snarled as she tried to calm the trembling noctomancer.

"Oh, I'm glad you asked!" Boomer's eyes flashed as a wide grin lifted his impressive mustache. "Let me show you. Very exciting stuff."

He opened a door in the wall with the axe hole and led them into a brightly-lit, white chamber. A raised platform dominated the room, its surface a grate of tiny holes. On the far wall opposite the hole, the electrified battleaxe was embedded into a massive wooden target painted with a red bulls-eye. Beneath the raised platform a wide, shallow basin rested on short stilts, with a bottom that sloped down to a metal spigot. A Tinderkin in a white coat opened the spigot, and thick slime poured into the glass beakers she held beneath it.

The source of the slime was obvious; on top of the grate a tower of translucent jelly gently quivered. It was shaped like a large cube, albeit one that leaned sharply to one side.

Boomer gestured at the slime in the manner of a carnival barker unveiling a bearded woman or a shaved Dwarf. "That, my friends, is a Viscous Rhombohedron!"

"A what?" asked Heraldin.

"Viscous Rhombohedron. It's a type of dungeon slime," said Gorm, recalling his earliest dungeon crawls. "Slides around hallways eating anything that gets stuck in it. Same family as Spherical Jellies and Gooey Cylinders."

"Viscous Rhombo's are the worst, though," said Kaitha. "When they get hit, they spray some of their acidic slime in all directions. It's got to be one of the world's most disgusting defense mechanisms."

"Ha! Exactly!" Boomer clapped his hands. "But what we discovered is that the total volume of slime released by a Viscous Rhombohedron is directly correlated to the amount of destructive force that impacts its outer membrane!"

Jynn had recovered enough from his near miss to be impressed. "That's rather marvelous."

"It is?" asked Gorm.

"They've developed an absolute scale for the damage inflicted by weapons and spells." The noctomancer dabbed at his brow with a cloth. "They can measure which weapons are better."

"Exactly!" said Boomer. "Melis, what did you get?"

"Ten and a half pints, sir!" called the technician, dumping the last vial of slime into a large bucket.

"A good hit, then!" Boomer's grin was even wider when he turned back to Gorm's party. "Our Battleaxe of the Northern Storm always does between five and twelve pints of damage. An Axe of Lightning from those buffoons over at Vorpal Corp. only does between four and eleven."

"Can't see how that'd make much difference," asked Gorm. "An axe through the skull will kill ye either way."

"Ah, but some skulls are thicker than others," said Melis, carrying the bucket up a stepladder. When she reached the top, she poured the slime onto the Viscous Rhombohedron, which burbled happily as it reabsorbed its lost material.

"Ha! Ingerson here is living proof!" said Boomer. "And I don't just mean hacking through a Swamp Kraken's carapace. Listen, Gorm, heroes and their backers will pay sacks of giltin to know that they've got the best gear around. We can charge four times as much for a weapon that does just two pints of damage more!"

"But the system must be a little biased," mused Jynn. "I mean, slimes are immune to venom, and I'd imagine they're more vulnerable to lightning than fire."

"Ah, see, now you're sounding like Buster." Boomer waved a gloved hand dismissively. "He's trying to breed specialized slimes so he can figure out the math for different kinds of damage. It overcomplicates the system!"

"It makes it more accurate, you mean!" hollered a gulping, raspy voice. All of the heroes except Gorm started as a Gremlin stepped into the room.

The Agekeepers held that the Gremlins were once the Gnomes of Clan Remlon, known for for their rigorous science and lax ethics. Like the other lost clans of Gnomes, the corrupted god Noros warped their forms in the years before the War of Betrayal. Yet while Mannon's evil engineers had clearly made the Slaugh distinctly frog-like and the Gnolls look like canines, it was much less certain where the forces of darkness had drawn inspiration from for the Gremlins. They usually had features somewhere between feline and reptile, and often they were marked by brightly colored scales, but those weren't guaranteed traits. Gremlins often had a keen interest in biomancy, but unfortunately, their culture observed ethical standards in the way that merfolk observe hiking. As such, no two Gremlins were ever very similar. If they were, a couple of quick mutations could fix that.

Buster was bulkier than most Gremlins Gorm had encountered; half a head shorter than Boomer, but built like a barrel. He wore heavy gloves over his arms and a pair of gold-rimmed spectacles in front of amber, reptilian eyes. A thick, prehensile tail extended from behind his leather apron, gripping a large spanner that he waved for emphasis as he shouted at Boomer.

"If we don't account for natural resistances, our scale will never produce reliable results!" the Gremlin said.

"Bah! You'll just make it so confusing that customers won't pay attention!" Boomer shouted back.

Buster's hackles were up; Gorm noted that they were webbed and tipped with sharp-looking spines these days. "It's not as confusing as a system skewed by—"

"It's good to see ye, Buster," said Gorm.

The Gremlin stopped mid-shout, adjusted his spectacles, and blinked at the assembled heroes. "Gorm Ingerson! How long has it been? A dragon's age, I'd say!" He broke into a sharp-fanged grin. "Oh, I wish I'd known you'd be visiting."

"I told you he was coming this morning!" said Boomer.

"Oh, who listens to you, anyway." Buster brushed the Scribkin aside. "Come now, Gorm. You and your friends must come back to the office for tea."

"That sounds lovely," said Kaitha.

"Aye, thank ye," said Gorm.

"And after we've caught up, you can tell us about this favor you need." Buster guided Gorm back out of the test chamber.

"I didn't mention a favor," said Gorm.

"Yet," said Buster.

"When Gorm Ingerson shows up in Andarun, he needs a favor from someone," said Boomer. "Lucky for us that it's our turn! Ha! And probably unlucky for you all, as he only comes to us when he's in really big trouble."

"That, or he's attempting an insane stunt," said Buster.

"Ha! Right," laughed Boomer. "So, which is it this time, Ingerson? You in danger, or just plannin' something crazy?"

Gorm gave a grim smile. "Well, since ye lads brought it up, both."

"Both?" Buster removed his spectacles.

"I'll wait 'til you're sittin' down," said Gorm. "This is a big one."

"I think it's shock," Thane muttered.

"It's not shock," said Burt, his head in his paws.

"It looks like it." Thane's face bunched up in concern as he stared down at the clerk. "Madam, I believe you're having a physiological reaction."

"She's not. It's not shock." Burt sighed and tried to get more comfortable on the Troll's massive shoulder.

"She's got all the signs." The Troll watched the woman pensively. "Vacant stare, frozen in place, pale complexion..."

The desk clerk made a sound that might have been a disgusted grunt or the dislodging of some stubborn phlegm. It was the second such sound she made during the visit—the first uttered when Thane handed her his thick stack of forms and questionnaires. Otherwise, she had remained as silent and flavorless as a lump of Human oatmeal, decorated with excessive makeup and a wispy blond wig ill balanced on top of her malformed head. Her mouth was set in a frog-like frown as she hunched over Thane's NPC application.

"That's how they always are," hissed Burt. "If there were more clerks here, they'd be actin' exactly the same."

Yet there was only the one. The Office of NPC Relations at Tamanthan Square was otherwise empty. There were few Shadowkin, NPC or otherwise, willing to walk into any office of the Heroes' Guild these days, and management responded by cutting staff. Burt suspected that the remaining clerk kept her spot by distinguishing herself as the most dour and unhelpful of the pack.

"What is she doing?" Thane muttered through his teeth.

"She's trying to find a reason to send you to the back of the line," Burt whispered.

"What line?"

"You'd think that would matter, wouldn't you?" Burt stared down at the tiny clerk. He'd spent much of his time in the Elven Embassy helping his clan-mates get their papers, and had seen every imaginable problem that clerks could find in NPC applications. Though it had been years since those days, he'd still navigated Thane's questionnaire and its riders with the deft touch of a sailor maneuvering through familiar straits.

Form D-4, including his voucher of intent to find employment, was completed in triplicate. Form D-6 itemized his attributes, from species and height down to an inventory of applicable combat skills. Subsection D-20 catalogued all the Troll's treasures, including those carried on his person, in neat loot tables. Thane's application was flawless.

"I still think it might be a physiological reaction," said Thane, a note of panic rising in his voice. "I've been causing them all day."

Burt gritted his teeth to hold back an angry retort. He took a couple of measured breaths and said, "Those people froze up because you kept trying to skulk and lurk in the shadows instead of walking down the street like a normal person. You looked like a thrice-cursed mugger! You got to act like you belong here if you don't want people to notice you."

"I'm not sure I do belong here."

"Do you even know what you're saying?" Burt had never heard of a one-ton walking death machine being so insecure about anything. "If you don't belong here, I don't belong here! None of us Shadowkin do, let alone the monsters."

Burt's perch rose and fell as Thane shrugged, clearly uncomfortable. "It's just I've never been in a city of... you know..."

"A Lightling city?" spat Burt. "Yeah, I bet you haven't. And neither have I, 'cause Andarun ain't the Lightlings' city. It's everybody's. Kobolds and Orcs and more have been born here, grew up here, and made homes here. It's ours as much as anyone's. If we keep shuffling around the edges and apologizing for being too much trouble and all that nonsense, it won't be our city much longer. It'll just be the place we live."

"But—"

"I don't want to hear any excuses. I lived here for most of my life, Troll. You know how many hoops I jumped through to get here? Hundreds. And I mean literally. It's one of the tricks the Elves used to like a Kobold to know." Burt could feel his hackles rising as he continued. "Andarun is my city. Our city. And as long as you act like it, everyone else will too."

Thane stared at the Kobold on his shoulder long and hard. "All right," he said slowly. "I'm sorry."

"Good," said Burt. "Stop apologizing."

"Sorr—um, yes. Okay."

Silence settled back over the hall.

Eventually, the clerk lurched into motion, setting the paper down and retrieving a pair of rubber stamps from her drawer. "Never seen a Troll NPC before," she croaked in the voice of a longtime pipeweed enthusiast.

"Doesn't matter, does it?" barked Burt. "There's a manticore over in Sculpin Down that works in a foundry, and I know a boglurk that got a job in city sewer—"

"Just sayin' I ain't seen one," said the clerk without so much as looking at Burt. "Speaking of which, I ain't seen your papers either."

"Oh, don't you worry. I'm an NPC," said Burt, flashing his own booklet at her.

If the clerk had bothered to take down Burt's NPC number and look up his records, she would have found that his noncombatant papers were voided for associating with a band of violent criminals. But few people had been eager to climb up a Troll to check a Kobold's documents. Burt was counting on it.

The clerk just nodded. "So, you're the sponsor?"

Burt shook his head. Shadowkin sponsoring Shadowkin required a background check. It was much easier to procure a Lightling's help. Especially a particular sort of Lightling. "We've a friend here to sponsor him," the Kobold told the clerk. "Hey! Boggit! You're up!"

A pile of rags on a nearby bench shifted and dropped to the floor. A moment later, a mop of unkempt hair popped from the top of it, and the creature shuffled in a widely meandering path up to the desk next to Thane. A bulbous face with a red glow and glazed eyes pushed out of the hairy mess, wearing an oblivious grin. The features could have been those of a Halfling or a Scribkin, or even a Dwerrow, but there was too much beard and grime concealing them to say for certain.

"I'm'ere to vouch for this Kobold's character," said Boggit.

"Not me," whispered Burt. "The Troll."

"And the Troll," slurred Boggit. "Both stand-up gentlemen if I ever saw 'em."

The clerk's face didn't even twitch as she turned to the drunk. "You hereby certify that this Troll is of sound moral character and able to join the Freedlands as a productive member of society, and agree to sponsor him as an NPC?" croaked the clerk eventually.

"Righty-ho!" said Boggit.

"Sign here," sighed the clerk, presenting a form.

Boggit scrawled his name and birthdate on the form with the provided quill, drew an "X" through the signature line, and saluted for good measure. "A pleasure to serve. Are we done?"

"That's everything. Thanks, friend." Burt pulled a small, glass bottle of Dwarven whiskey from his pouch and tossed it down to the probable Gnome. The vial landed somewhere in Boggit's rags and disappeared from sight as the old drunk shuffled away.

"That's it?" asked Thane.

"That's it!" said Burt. "Now we just find out if your application is approved."

The clerk made the grunting noise again, stamped the application, and rang a small bell. Another clerk came and ushered Thane into a small back room where a Gnomish craftsman—a Deep Gnome, judging by the purplish hue of his skin—started working on the Troll's woodcut portrait.

"This is a good sign, right?" The Troll whispered from the corner of his mouth as the artist worked.

"Oh yeah," said Burt. "You're golden."

"I thought they'd need more time to look into my background," said Thane. "I mean, she saw who vouched for me. How do they know I won't commit a crime?"

The Deep Gnome laughed at the question.

"Buddy, if you try anything, they've got a physical description of you, a complete threat assessment, and a catalog of the loot a group of professional heroes will find on your corpse," said Burt. "You go rogue, and you'll be nothin' but a revenue stream for them to cash in."

"That's what the Heroes' Guild is supposed to do," said Boomer. "They get paid to take care of this sort of mess."

"And I'd be happy to let 'em, if they'd treat it proper," said Gorm. "But I don't see anyone else trying to muster Arth's great artifacts."

"Do they realize the liche might have the Crown of Iron Thorns?" asked Buster.

"They might," said Jynn. "They know it's missing, and there aren't too many active villains right now capable of taking it."

"The question is whether or not they'd do anything about it," said Laruna.

"Besides adjusting some numbers and upping their fees," added Gorm.

Boomer and Buster nodded, and a thoughtful silence descended once more.

Gorm looked around the conference table, which sat in one half of the office of Boomer J. Blorfindol and Buster Slyne. On the other side of the room, two desks were set opposite each other, one as neat and tidy as a grid, the other barely visible beneath an avalanche of paperwork and discarded food wrappers. Beyond the desks, a giant window overlooked the factory floor of Creative Destruction Incorporated's main workshop. Plans and diagrams were plastered across the walls so thickly that they almost concealed the certificates and commemorative plaques that lay underneath them.

"This is a big one," said Boomer, twirling his mustache.

"If we thought there was any plan with a chance of workin' that didn't involve us breakin' into the Museum of Andarun, we'd do that instead," said Gorm.

"The world hasn't faced anything like this since the Sixth Age," said Kaitha. "But the guild is treating it like a standard kill and loot quest. It may be too late by the time they realize what they're up against."

Boomer nodded. "That sounds a lot like our Heroes' Guild, unfortunately."

"But this plan…" Buster picked at his fangs with his claws.

Gorm leaned forward in his seat. "Ye help us steal the staff, and your debt to me is repaid."

"Poppycock!" snapped Boomer. "We can never repay what we owe you, Ingerson!"

The Gremlin smiled at the tattooed Scribkin. "But that won't stop us from trying. I just wish you'd given us more time," he added to Gorm.

The Dwarf snorted. "Well, we can come back tomorrow if'n ye need—"

"No, you can't," interrupted Boomer. "You need to steal the Wyrmwood Staff of Geffyn today, because the omnimancy exhibit ends tonight."

"What's that now?" said Jynn.

"You didn't know?" Buster said, somewhat surprised. "They're putting the omnimancy relics back into guild storage and opening up an exhibit on the reptilian peoples."

"The museum announced they'd be ending the omnimancy display after King Klenn of Ruskan announced the quest to slay Detarr Ur'Mayan again," said Buster. "I imagine the guild is nervous about having so many of its relics out of the vaults when so many heroes are headed far afield."

"But ye can still find a way for us to get the staff, right?" said Gorm, trying to ignore the icy fingers of panic creeping into his chest.

Boomer turned to Buster. "You thinking what I'm thinking?"

"Temporal distortion ruse?" suggested the Gremlin.

"Seems the simplest way," said the Scribkin.

"It's the only way, given the constraints," said Buster.

"We'll do it," said Gorm. "Just tell us what it is we're doing."

"Pullin' off an impossible heist, I'd say!" Boomer wore an eager grin. "But there's no time to waste sitting around here jabbering about it."

"Come," said Buster. "We'll explain down in the lab."

They led the heroes back down onto the factory floor and along the narrow, yellow path to a door with a copper plaque on the front that read "CONSUMABLES."

The door opened into a warehouse of mismatched oddities. There were racks with hundreds of vials of colorful liquids with labels like "RESIST FIRE," "BREATHE WATER," "DETECT GOLD," and every other imaginable pairing of verbs and elements. A multitude of bombs and grenades lined another set of shelves. An entire wall was dedicated to charms and cantrips, each ready to unleash a small spell once broken open.

Heraldin plucked a folded sheet of paper from a stack on the cantrip shelf, next to a sign that read "ANTI-MAGIC CHARMS." He was about to unfold it when Gaist lunged forward and grabbed the bard's wrist hard enough to elicit a surprised yelp.

"What was that for?" asked Heraldin. "I just wanted to read the pamphlet on their anti-magic charms."

"Your big friend there has the right of it," said Buster, carefully removing the paper from the bard's hand. "The rune on that paper *is* the charm. Anyone reads it, and it'll knock the sorcery off everything within fifty yards. For a couple of minutes, at least."

"Sounds handy," said Gorm.

"Handy? Those runes will take the magic out of a mage, unshift a shapeshifter's shape, and strip the bite off any magic weapons," said Boomer. "They'll change the tide of your fortunes, they will! Take a couple."

"Thank you." Heraldin slipped a few of the folded papers into one of his pouches.

"Just don't read them anywhere near our shop. Ha!" said Boomer. "But those runes won't help you get a Stennish artifact out of the Museum of Andarun."

"No?" said Laruna. "I'd think we could knock out the security wards to get into the museum at night."

"You might knock down the magical wards," said Buster, "but you'd still have to walk into a museum full of guards unnoticed if you're going to even make it to the staff."

"Let alone walk out," agreed Boomer. "If anything's out of place for a second, they'll be all over you like Slaugh on a swamp log."

"So, what's your plan?" asked Gorm.

Boomer tapped the side of his nose. "Make sure nothing's out of place for a second."

"I don't follow," said Heraldin.

The Scribkin took a key from his pocket and unlocked a glass cabinet. Carefully, he retrieved a device that looked like a copper cage built around several small, blue crystals suspended by some unseen force. "This," he said reverently, "is the chronobomb."

"You mean the time bomb," said Buster.

"That would be a bomb that goes off after a set amount of time," growled Boomer.

"You mean a delayed explosion bomb?" said the Gremlin.

"You know that's—" Boomer caught himself and, after a deep breath, told Buster, "We aren't going through the name again. It's a device that stops time."

Buster adjusted his spectacles. "More accurately, everything inside a small area around the... chronobomb will be sped up so much that—"

"So much that time stops for everyone else," said Boomer, glaring a warning at the Gremlin.

"Isn't chronomancy illegal?" asked Laruna.

"Not as illegal as robbing a museum," said Buster.

"Right! You can get permits and Academy exemptions for chronomancy," said Boomer.

"Which we did," said Buster. "Our research initially focused on developing a way to speed up production."

"Imagine it!" said Boomer, throwing one arm around Gorm and waving the other at some unseen production line. "Hundreds of golems working faster than we can even see! Why, we'd manufacture cartloads in less than a second!"

"Well, we would if the crystalline structures supporting the temporal distortion field could withstand the distortion itself," said Buster.

"Beg pardon?" said Heraldin.

"Those crystals are old, rare, and expensive enough to make thaumite look like quartz," said Boomer. "And once you set off the chronobomb, they start to weaken. There's no telling how long they'll hold out before they shatter, dissipating the time spell completely."

"But it won't be more than a few minutes," added Buster.

Gorm looked at the chronobomb and gave a snort of grudging appreciation. "It looks good, but I still don't see how this gets us the Wyrmwood Staff."

"Have some vision, Gorm!" laughed Boomer. "You're gonna buy your tickets, go into the museum, and get several minutes uninterrupted with the staff's display case. Anything you do will happen too fast for anyone to see. You'll grab the staff and nobody's going to look twice!"

Chapter 11

"They're all staring," said Thane.

"It ain't that bad," said Burt.

"It is. Nobody's sitting down. They're just staring." The Troll pointed at a pack of onlookers on the other side of the cafe's short iron gate. The growing cluster of Elves and Humans wore expressions ranging from horror to disgust to pure confusion as they gawked at the massive Troll squatting next to one of Spelljammer's relatively tiny tables. Much of the group broke off and hurried on their way when Thane looked at them.

"And what if they are? Not our problem," said the Kobold.

"I don't think our waitress is too happy we're here, either," whispered Thane, nodding to a young Tinderkin in a green uniform approaching.

"She—uh—" Burt began, but the waitress' arrival at their table ushered in an awkward silence and several forced smiles as she set out the table for tea. The Kobold waited until she retreated back under the awnings of the cafe's elaborate hut before continuing. "She's just unhappy that we're keeping away the other customers."

"Maybe we should—"

"We ain't leavin'," Burt growled. "I haven't been to Spelljammer's Cafe in ages. I used to come up here all the time when I was ridin' in an Elf's purse. We'd get jam tarts and spiced tea and watch the city go by."

He sat back in his stool and took a deep breath. "And now, after starving in a Dwarf's smelly rucksack for over a year, I'm back at Pinnacle Plaza, I have a spiced tea, and a fresh-baked jam tart is on the way. So if our waitress or any other Lightling has an issue with us being here, they can go jump off the Wall to solve it."

"All right." The Troll's voice was heavy with uncertainty.

"And quit moping. Try to enjoy this."

"I'm trying, but it's hard to," said the Troll. "I know you see the way everyone's staring at us. You must hear them whispering. Don't you get tired of pretending none of that's happening?"

Burt thought about it, then shrugged. "It beats the alternative."

Thane sighed. After a moment, he attempted to pour himself a cup of the spiced tea, but the serving set was designed for someone a fraction of the Troll's size. Half the pot sloshed onto the table, and Thane glanced around furtively as he tried to clean it up.

"Don't—" Burt began, but stopped himself when the Troll flinched. With a heavy sigh, he grabbed a napkin and started mopping up the spilled tea.

"Sorry," said Thane.

"Don't worry about it," grunted Burt. "You know, I bet Kaitha is a fan of Spelljammer's."

"Did she say that?" said Thane.

"Well, no. But I know her sister loves this place, at least. And if you didn't want to take her to Spelljammer's, then you could go to the Astral Plate. Or Sigil's. Or even the Restored Tambour, if you want something easier on the old coin purse." Burt pointed to the different cafes around Pinnacle Plaza as he named them.

"But Spelljammer's will always be my favorite. On account of the view." Burt swept his arm across the panorama beside their table. The rooftops and spires of Andarun fell away before them, streams of people and carts cascading along the streets and stairways that spider-webbed through the city. Sprites of various colors sparkled in the air, especially around the dome of the Andarun Stock Exchange, which scintillated red and green in the glow of approaching trade sprites. Beyond the city, rolling clouds cast wandering shadows that meandered over the grassland and forest.

"It is beautiful," the Troll conceded.

"You and her, sittin' up here, sipping spiced tea, talking about flowers and trees and whatever else it is you have in common."

"Maybe music." Thane rested his cheek on his hand and gazed out over the city. "She could teach me a lot about music."

"Right, whatever," said Burt. "Now imagine some stuck-up Human in velvet tights struts up with his knickers twisted and says you two have to leave."

"What?" said Thane, sitting up straight. "I don't think—"

"Doesn't matter what you think. He wants you and the Elf gone," barked Burt. "Are you going to do it?"

"No," said Thane. "No, we'd stay."

"Why?" pressed Burt.

"Because there's no reason we can't be here," said the Troll.

Burt stood up in his seat and pointed a triumphant finger at Thane. "Aha! And don't you forget it."

The Troll fell silent and turned to watch the clouds roll across the landscape. Burt took the opportunity to clean up the last of the spill and order another pot of tea.

Thane perked up when the waitress returned with the replacement tea. "Miss, I'd like a larger cup, please."

"We have a couple of beer steins in the back room," offered the Tinderkin.

"Yes, thank you," said the Troll.

The waitress nodded and headed off.

"And thank you," said Thane to the Kobold.

"Don't mention it," said Burt.

"Seriously, just stop talking about it," Laruna hissed through her teeth. "Nobody will notice."

"I noticed," muttered Gorm. "The gods alone know why you're readin' that here, and a bannerman might wonder the same!"

"This is way more complicated than I thought," Laruna murmured as she looked over the sheet of paper. It showed several woodcut diagrams of an unusually chipper wizard weaving magic at inanimate objects. The illustrated instructions were one of the hallmarks of Creative Destruction's products.

Gorm grunted and handed her a pamphlet for the Museum of Andarun's omnimancy exhibition. "If ye have to read the instructions out here, at least hide it," he said under his breath.

"Fine," said Laruna. She tucked the illustrated set of instructions into Gorm's pamphlet and feigned reading it with interest.

They sat side by side on one of the long marble benches in the museum's atrium, watching the sparse crowds make their way around suits of Imperial armor from the Fifth Age. A few bannermen patrolled the floor in polished bronze armor decorated with the teal heraldry of the Agekeepers and, by extension, the museum itself.

"I think that's the signal," said Laruna, nodding.

Gorm looked. Gaist was standing at the entrance to the omnimancy exhibit, statuesque. "You're sure?" he asked.

"I think so," said Laruna, though she sounded doubtful. "There it is again? Maybe?"

"I didn't see any—why in the seven hells did we have Gaist give the signal?"

"We didn't want someone to notice the signal. Otherwise, they might think he was acting strange," said Laruna, slipping the pamphlet back into her purse.

"But the—he just stands around, staring at walls half the time! Everybody always thinks he's acting strange," sputtered Gorm.

"Let's go," said Laruna, stepping away from the bench.

The solamancer and Dwarf took an intentionally circuitous route through the museum, moving past the giant bones and stuffed drakes of the dragon-kin room, through a chamber filled with famous documents from the history of the Heroes' Guild, and into the permanent exhibit on the Sten and the War of Betrayal. Gorm feigned interest in the glass cases filled with fragments of Stennish mortuary sculptures and sacred stones before Laruna pointed out Jynn and Kaitha.

They joined their companions standing by a large, ornate case with a single, plain-looking spear in it. Behind the case, a mural depicted an Elven hero facing off against a Stennish warrior. Kaitha stared at the mural like any interested museum-goer, but Jynn looked conspicuously like someone trying to look inconspicuous.

"What have ye got for me, lass?" Gorm asked, sidling up to Kaitha.

"It's the Spear of Issan," said Kaitha.

"That's all fine and good, but I was askin' how many bannermen you counted," said Gorm. Now that he was closer, Gorm noticed dark spots beneath the Elf's eyes. Her face looked more gaunt than slender. "Ye feeling all right, lass?"

She rubbed at the dark rings under her eyes. "Yeah, it's nothing."

"Ye've been acting strange of late," Gorm said softly. "Ye ain't… it isn't dark thoughts, right?"

Kaitha frowned at him.

"All right, all right. I just had to ask," said Gorm, hands in the air.

"I just… I thought we'd have more time in Andarun," sighed the ranger.

"Aye, we all got surprised by the museum closing the exhibit," said Gorm.

"I know. I just wanted…" Kaitha caught herself and instead gave a reproachful glare back at Laruna. "I just hoped to have some time in the city."

"Aye. I wanted to have a good, long bath," Gorm said.

Kaitha grinned. "And we all really wanted that for you."

"Hilarious," said Gorm. "But enough lookin' at old weapons and makin' wishes for the city. I counted eight bannermen on my way from the atrium."

"There are five between here and the exhibit on recent runes," said Kaitha. She nodded to the spear. "And I thought you'd be more interested in something related to Niln's prophecy."

"What's that now?"

"Yeah. If we're to kill that statue Niln was worried about, we may need Issan's spear," said the ranger. "He was the champion of Tandos who killed the last prince of the Sten at the end of the War of Betrayal."

Gorm looked at the villainous-looking Sten in the mural. "That's the Dark Prince?"

"That's what the Lightlings call him, anyway," said Burt. "I prefer 'that creepy statue that the pigeons avoid.'"

"It sounds familiar." Thane's broad brow creased as he stared at the black granite statue at the center of Pinnacle Plaza.

"Maybe you heard Gorm talkin' about it," said Burt. "The young priest that assembled the party believed all of the old prophecies about the Dark Prince. Assembled the group to fight and stop him."

"I remember Niln," said Thane. "Gorm still talks about his prophecies."

"Yeah, I wish he'd stop," said Burt. "But there's the big guy at the heart of all the legends."

"He doesn't look right. He looks…"

"Angry? Murderous?"

"Horrified, perhaps," said Thane. "Most of the statues I've seen today look more… noble. Determined. Heroic. Not… whatever that is."

Burt sat back up and took another sip of tea. "Yeah, well he ain't there for the aesthetics. The city would take him down if they could, but there's low magic and prophecy involved. Destiny or whatever."

"What do the legends say?" the Troll asked, still staring at the statue.

"Oh, you know. Standard ancient prophecy," said Burt, waving his hand dismissively. "That sculpture is supposed to be Stennish royalty, and he's still ticked about the Elf who offed him when Tandos struck down Al'Thadan. And the story goes that one day the stone will come back to life, overthrow the kingdom, take revenge for the Sten, bring back Al'Thadan and the traitor gods, and rule the world. You know, villain stuff. Heard it a thousand times."

"You don't believe it's true, then."

"Oh, I'm sure it's true. To a degree, anyway," said Burt. "Thing is, Andarun has more guild heroes than anywhere else on Arth, and if having all these thrice-cursed adventurers around is good for something, it's stopping dark prophecies."

Thane poured himself another tankard of tea, draining the pot. "I didn't know you could stop a prophecy."

"Oh yeah, if you catch it at the right time," said Burt. "Why, back when my grandsire was a pup, all the Deep Gnomes in Scoria thought the world was going to end at the hands of a great darkness from beneath the Ironbacks. They sold all their homes and bought up every can of potted meat you could find to prepare for the apocalypse. And then some hired swords running with Adventure Capital went down in some dungeon and killed a toothy demon from beyond space and time, and just like that the prophecy was finished."

"Crisis averted," said the Troll.

"Unless you were a Scorian Deep Gnome," said Burt. "They all lost their homes and were left with nothing but canned ham. I bet they're still eating it."

Thane shook his head. "It still seems dangerous to have all of this set up so close to such an ominous figure."

"Oh, to hear the Elves tell it, people worried about it a long time ago. In the Sixth Age nobody wanted to live anywhere near the Dark Prince, so the only folks you'd find near the Pinnacle were some itinerant Tinderkin, Halflings, and acolytes of various temples trying to stop his return. But at some point they decided that the statue isn't going to do anything with all these heroes running around, and hey, this view is actually pretty nice. Wasn't long before the Elves and other well-to-dos started buying up the real estate."

"Well, I suppose it's a good thing that there are so many professional heroes around here," said the Troll.

"Oh yeah. Almost makes up for all the murdering and pillaging those big, furless bastards do," Burt muttered into his tea. "Sure, they kill or steal anything within reach, but at least they're good at their jobs."

"I've no idea what I'm doing," said Gorm.

"It's got one thrice-cursed crank," Heraldin whispered over his shoulder. "You should be able to figure it out."

In one hand, Gorm held a device no bigger than a plum: a ball of swirling blue and green ribbed by bands of silver. A large key protruded from its top. In the other, he held a slip of paper with the words "CREATIVE DESTRUCTION: AUTOMATIC DISTRACTION" followed by four woodcut diagrams featuring a smiling hero in a cloaked hood and form-fitting armor.

The first illustration showed the grinning rogue winding the key on the top of the sphere. Gorm gave the key on his own device a few good cranks and checked the instructions again.

"This looks suspicious," Laruna murmured, nodding at the bannermen on patrol.

"Not as suspicious as all of you whisperin' at me!" Gorm growled. "Shut up and act natural."

The party loitered around the entrance to the omnimancy exhibit, each of them strategically positioned to block the bannermen from seeing the alcove where Gorm worked. Heraldin and Laruna stood closest, feigning a conversation about the museum's displays.

The instructions' second diagram showed the rogue whispering to the device, complete with a tiny word bubble containing a tree. The third showed the rogue tossing the ball underhand onto the ground, and the fourth showed a tree with large gouts of smoke surrounding it.

"Nothin' left but to try," muttered Gorm. He held the ball close to his mouth, whispered "dragon-kin room," and dropped it.

The silver bands whipped off the ball as it spun through the air, becoming a set of ten spindly legs that caught it before it hit the floor. Without a moment's pause it scuttled off toward the showcase of dragon-kin relics, keeping to the shadows as it did so. A moment later, Gorm lost track of it amid the bustling crowd.

The heroes quickly filtered into the omnimancy exhibit. The wing's banners showed sinister-looking wizards in gray robes, with headlines that had all the scholarly restraint of a carnival barker. "OMNIMANCERS: BETRAYERS OF THE ACADEMY" read one. "OMNIMANCY: INFERIOR BREEDING OR A DARK CURSE?" mused another.

Gorm had just stepped through the doorway when thunder roared from the dragon-kin wing. He glanced back to see plumes of black smoke billowing from beneath a wyvern skeleton, sending attendees scattering from the perceived threat. Every bannerman in sight sprinted toward the smoke, swords drawn and at the ready.

"Go get 'em, lads," Gorm muttered, stepping out of the way as attendees and guards stampeded past him. Ahead, the rest of the party gathered around a glass case. Jynn pulled the chronobomb from the recesses of his robes and twisted each end of the device, releasing the bars of copper surrounding the crystal.

"Hey!" hollered someone. Gorm turned.

A portly old bannerman had noticed the gathered heroes, and now his eyes fell on the whirling crystals levitating between Jynn's hands. "What are you doing there?" he cried, rushing forward.

"Blood and ashes," swore Gorm.

Light flared. A low *thrum* echoed through the chamber, and Gorm felt a whisper across all of his skin at once. A thin glow, a membrane of light, blazed into existence. Beyond it, the world was tinted blue and completely frozen, as demonstrated by the rotund bannerman caught mid-stride at the edge of the bubble. Beyond him, Gorm could see straight down the halls to the museum's atrium, where the fleeing attendees, rushing guards, and even billowing smoke were all locked in place.

"I think it worked," said Jynn. He set the copper pieces of the chronobomb down; the crystals powering the time bubble were dancing through the air on their own now, whirling like drunken fireflies.

"Well, all right then," said Gorm. "Laruna, you're up."

"I'm already on it." The mage held up a silver mirror about the size of her palm in one hand and the sheet of directions in the other. "This is one of those times I wish you could weave solamancy," she told Jynn. "This needs threads of light and water."

"I can still try to help." Jynn took the instructions from Laruna and held them up for her to view.

The heroes stepped up to a long display case. Beneath the glass a gray staff rested on red velvet. Its top was carved to resemble a dragon's claw clutching a polished sphere of milky-white crystal. Words were carved in tight, concentric circles around the shaft in a variety of languages, though Gorm didn't recognize any of them.

"I'd give a penny to know what that says," Gorm said.

"It just says 'rule in virtue' over and over," said Heraldin.

"I didn't know ye could read ancient languages."

"Bards know many secrets," said Heraldin. "For example, we know to always read the signs at a museum."

Gaist tapped a bronze plaque on the display case.

"Quiet," hushed Jynn. "We need to concentrate."

Wisps of light danced around the mirror in Laruna's hand for a moment, and then a silvery beam burst forth from its center onto the glass of the case. The solamancer slowly rotated the mirror, so that the light crept over the surface of the case. The beam left a pale glow as it passed, as though the case was being painted with light. It was a slow process that, judging by the expression on the solamancer's face, was going to take a while. Gorm stepped away to look at the rest of the displays.

There were a couple of omnimancer artifacts from the early centuries of the Third Age, slender devices that looked like they were spun from ivory. Nobody alive had any idea what they were intended for. They sat beneath a mural with several smart plaques that gave a neat illustrated history of the Twilight Order. It started with the heights of the Order's power in the Second Age, when, as a helpful sign explained, omnimancers had once functioned as magical enforcers that kept the other two orders of mages in line. The pigments darkened along with subject matter as the mural transitioned to the omnimancers' alliance with the Sten in the War of Betrayal, though the colors brightened again as the Twilight Order met their downfall at the hands of the Alliance of Light. The mural concluded with a few scenes depicting omnimancers as they existed today: scattered groups of transients, exiled from the Academy and living in the shadows of society.

Another large display was dedicated to the story of Antoro Ibson, an allegedly well-known Archmage of the Order of the Sun from the Fifth Age. According to the signs scattered around Archmage Ibson's personal effects, Antoro set out on a crusade to find hidden omnimancers within the ranks of the Academy.

Next to the case lurked a large, ebony wagon with bright red wheels. Gorm read that the "dusk wagon," as it had been affectionately known by compassionless men, was once used by Archmage Ibson's lackeys to transport hundreds of suspected omnimancers to the gallows before the Academy came to its collective senses and deposed the madman. After Ibson's departure, the Academy made two notable changes to its laws: first, that omnimancy was punishable by expulsion rather than death, and second, that a mage, regardless of his or her aptitudes, had to use both sides of magic to be convicted of omnimancy.

"We're just about done here," Jynn called.

Gorm broke away from the exhibit and trotted back to join the other heroes huddled around the Wyrmwood Staff. The case shimmered with silvery light from its glass top to about halfway down its four ornate legs.

The mirror in Laruna's hands thrummed with the same light, highlighting the sweat beading on the solamancer's brow. But her eyes were confident, and she gave Gorm a satisfied grin as he approached. "We've got it," she said.

"Good," he said. "How about the security?"

"There's a heavy lock and an alarm mechanism on the case for our thief to pick," said Jynn.

"Please, friend. I am a bard," said Heraldin.

"A bard who picks locks and steals things," countered the mage.

"Many bards do that. But I am a bard who does *not* pick locks and steal things, because Benny Hookhand might find out I was participating in that sort of activity."

"You're a wanted fugitive," said Laruna.

"Ah, but for guild crimes, not for thieving," Heraldin said. "It's very different."

"How so?"

"The guild would only hang me, for starters."

"Look, it's all well and good to try to avoid this Hookhand fellow, but we've all seen you pick locks," said Jynn.

"No, you haven't," said Heraldin pointedly.

"And I suppose all of those locks we've encountered together opened themselves?" The noctomancer's voice dripped sarcasm.

"Who can say? How does a flower bloom? How does the sun rise? How does a dragon-kin fly when its wings can't possibly support that much mass? More pressingly, how did this case get unlocked?" The bard rapped his knuckles on the edge of the case, and the lid popped up with a metallic *click*.

The other heroes stared at the open case. "But… how?" asked Jynn.

"It's a mystery," said Heraldin.

Gaist looked at Jynn and nodded.

"No, but… but… I didn't even see you pick the lock," protested the wizard.

"Exactly!" said the bard. "Now, you can finish stealing this staff if you like. I'll be over here minding my own business and definitely not taking part in a burglary."

"Sounds good to me." Gorm nodded to the wizard, who looked nonplussed as he slowly opened the case.

Jynn's reluctance gave way to reverence as he lifted the Wyrmwood Staff. He ran his fingers over the inscribed words for a moment before handing the artifact to Laruna.

The crystal flared with amber light the instant the solamancer touched the staff, prompting the other heroes to step back.

"Why'd it do that?" asked Gorm.

"It's... happy," said Laruna, holding the glowing staff in one hand and the magical mirror in the other.

"Careful, friend," Heraldin called from the far edge of the time bubble. "You cannot trust a weapon that thinks for itself. Soon it may start thinking for you as well."

"Perhaps," said Jynn. "But many artifacts were given rudimentary desires, like a dagger that wants to kill or a sword that seeks out a righteous warrior. As long as our goals align with the staff's, there shouldn't be a problem."

"It sounds like the stick is in charge already," said the bard.

"It just wants to be used," said Laruna, staring into the glowing crystal.

"And we ain't got no choice but to use it," said Gorm. "So let's get going."

"Agreed," said Jynn.

Laruna nodded and set the glowing mirror in her hand down in the center of the empty case. Jynn carefully closed the lid and nodded to her.

"Kalya," the solamancer muttered, weaving threads of light into the glass. A white glow flared for a moment, and then a perfect copy of the case appeared in the same space as the original, concealing the mirror. The illusion was nearly indistinguishable from the actual case, save that it contained an ethereal replica of the Wyrmwood Staff and it sat at a regrettably unorthodox orientation to the case's legs.

"Bones," swore Laruna.

"I'm guessin' it ain't supposed to be sticking out the sides like that," said Gorm.

The new, illusionary case was almost perfectly perpendicular to the old one, with half a table leg dangling from each of its four corners.

"Here, just rotate it," said Laruna, opening up the case and fumbling with the mirror inside. But the magical bauble had expended all its power, and the illusion remained immobile no matter how the solamancer twisted and turned it. With a grunt of frustration, she flung the mirror away. It flew straight until it passed through the membrane of the chronobomb's field, where it slowed to a stop mid-flight, as though trapped in the goopy mass of a Viscous Rhombohedron.

"Careful!" hissed Jynn.

"Why? It's worthless now." Laruna gestured at the illusionary case, resolutely set at a right angle to its original. "Who cares what happens to the mirror?"

"I care more about what happens to the rest of the room," said Jynn. "Everything in the chronobomb's radius is actually moving unimaginably fast. Anything leaving the bubble will keep some of its momentum. Look!"

He gestured at the mirror. The expended trinket was suspended in the air, but it was also clearly moving, creeping along like a snail among statues.

"That mirror's likely moving fast enough to embed itself in stone," said the noctomancer. "You could destroy an exhibit or kill someone."

"Ah," said Laruna.

"At the very least, that's going to alert the bannermen," said Kaitha.

"Oh? And do you suppose they might notice this freakish twelve-sided display case as well?" snarled Heraldin.

"Hey, that mirror was complicated!" Laruna waved the illustrated instruction sheet at the bard. "This doesn't make it clear that you're supposed to orient the mirror before you speak the words."

"Well, how did you think it was supposed to work?" said Heraldin.

"Like magic!" exclaimed Laruna. "It's magic! It's supposed to do what you want it to! That's what makes it magic!"

"Uh, we have bigger problems," Kaitha interrupted.

"We're wanted criminals standing in the middle of a museum full of bannermen next to a conspicuously botched illusion with a stolen relic in our hands," snapped Heraldin. "This is as big as problems get!"

It occurred to Gorm that Heraldin's words likely constituted a violation of Nove's first principle of universal irony, but events were moving too fast to dwell on it.

"Fine," said Kaitha. "We have additional problems of equal magnitude."

"Like what?" said Gorm.

The Elf pointed behind the bard. "The time bubble is shrinking."

They looked. The shimmering membrane that marked the edge of the chronobomb's area of influence was beginning to contract. It was a slow, jerking retraction, but it was accelerating.

"Bones," swore Laruna.

Gorm's mind raced through possible scenarios, searching for one that didn't involve a battle with museum bannermen and guild enforcers.

It was clear that the party wasn't going to walk out of the museum with the Wyrmwood Staff amid the confusion as originally planned. Between the old bannerman running at them, the speeding mirror on track to destroy a suit of Imperial armor from the Fourth Age, and the bizarre illusionary case set up behind them, the heroes were sure to be a point of interest for any nearby guards.

Now, the only option was to flee. He looked down the museum hall to the great doorway on the opposite side of the atrium. The fleeing crowd had shoved the doors open, and beyond it Gorm could see the streets. It was a straight shot, but it was too far to run. They'd almost certainly be caught and bogged down in a fight halfway across the Atrium.

Unless...

"Help me get the cart!" he shouted, running back to the display on Archmage Ibson.

"What?" asked Kaitha. "How will that—"

Gorm was already at the Dusk Cart. "Just help me!"

The open-topped cart's wood was old and faded, but it was solidly built, with two steel axles for its four iron-ringed wheels. Gorm's axe made short work of the cables that held it in place, and then Gaist and Heraldin helped him wheel it to the center of the chronobomb's collapsing hemisphere.

"Everybody in!" Gorm said as he and Gaist carefully lined up the front of the cart. There was a narrow path to the door through the fleeing attendees and running guards. It felt like trying to thread a needle from several hundred yards away.

"I'm still not sure how being inside a vandalized exhibit will make the museum guards any friendlier," said Heraldin.

"The trick is not bein' in the museum anymore, ain't it!" said Gorm, running around the cart. Gaist vaulted him inside before leaping into the cart himself. "We're drivin' this cart out of here just like one of them jet-sleds at Boomer and Buster's! Laruna, make a big fire."

"A what?" asked the solamancer.

"Ye know, a big stream of flame," said Gorm, waving his hands in an ill-informed facsimile of a sorcerous gesture. "A big fire to push us along like the jet-sled."

"It doesn't work that way," said Laruna. "If it did, I'd get blown off my feet every time I cast a spell."

"It could work if you had a focus," suggested Jynn. "The jet-sled must have used a latticed weave channeled through a focal nexus."

"Didn't that jet-sled crash?" Heraldin asked Gorm as the mages fell into whispered jargon.

"Aye," said Gorm, rapping his knuckles on his steel helm. "I'd try to find a helmet."

The bard paled visibly.

"Okay," said Laruna, nodding. "It's worth a shot."

"I'm not entirely sure how well it will work," Jynn told her.

"But it's bound to work better than sittin' around yammerin'," said Gorm. He stood toward the front of the cart's bed and grabbed the reins from the driver's seat. "Now, how do ye steer this thrice-cursed thing?"

"I think it has to do with how you whip the oxen," said Kaitha.

"And if ye ain't got an ox?"

The Elf shrugged. "Close your eyes and pray?"

"I figured as much," Gorm said. "A plan old Niln'd be proud of, eh?"

Kaitha found a smile for the priest, small and bittersweet. "Seems like the only plan we've ever had."

"All right, I'm ready!" Laruna had firmly wedged the shaft of the Wyrmwood Staff between two of the boards in the center of the wagon's floor, positioning the gem at the rear of the cart.

"Then go!" shouted Gorm, watching as the time bubble jerked and contracted. "Everybody hang on!"

"Here goes." Laruna wove thick, amber cords of fire into the staff's gem.

The crystal thrummed to life, emitting a red glow and, shortly thereafter, a massive gout of flame. A roar of fire immolated the empty case formerly occupied by the staff in the blink of an eye. The wagon lurched into motion, propelled by the massive blaze roaring from its rear.

Kaitha cleared her throat.

"Well, this was oversold," said Heraldin, watching the museum's exhibits crawl by as they inched forward.

"We're improvising new spells with a staff that hasn't been used for over a century!" snapped Laruna. "This isn't easy!"

"Well, I'll tell that to any bannermen that happen to stroll by," said the bard.

"It's fast enough," said Gorm as they creaked along.

"How? It'd be faster if we hooked it up to a pair of dead oxen," said Heraldin.

"It's like the mirror Kaitha threw," said Gorm. "We're really movin' faster than the speed of time or some such nonsense. So, when we come outta the chronobomb's bubble, we'll keep enough momentum to be movin' at… uh… Jynn, how fast will we be goin'?"

The noctomancer gave a slight shake of his head, lost in some mental calculations. The wizard must have reached a dire conclusion, as all of the color drained from his face. "Oh gods. Everybody hang—"

The wagon pitched forward, the chronobomb's radius contracted, and the heroes slipped through the glowing blue membrane.

Chapter 12

Sergeant Joklo Perkin's thoughts drifted to Nove's second principle of universal irony.

Nove's second principle was a straightforward equation, using Nove's Constant to show that the likelihood of an unfortunate event is directly proportional to the anticipation for whatever the misfortune would disrupt. In layman's terms, the more people looked forward to something, the more likely that tragic circumstances will prevent it. This principle was famously reinforced when Nove's experiments designed to demonstrate it failed on stage at the Academy of Essenpi, simultaneously proving and failing to prove the philosopher's point.

The second principle of universal irony was the reason that professional heroes didn't undertake quests while they were engaged to be married, or that Andarun's kings never rode out in the last days before their queen bore a child.

It was also, notably to Joklo Perkins, the reason bannermen became cautious in the last few weeks before retiring. It was a well-known fact, or at least it was well-known, that too much excitement before a bannerman's retirement was a sure way to be struck by a crossbow bolt meant for a younger, more rebellious partner; or get attacked by a horrible new villain.

Sergeant Perkins tried not to look forward to retiring, and did his best to dampen Mrs. Perkins' excitement. But Perkins' joints and wits weren't what they used to be, while his girth was significantly more than it had once been. He kept catching himself dreaming of taking the old raft down the Tarapin with a fishing pole in his hand—a hobby he'd have more time for once he finished working.

Despite his best intentions, Sgt. Perkins found himself very much anticipating the date of his retirement.

So when the old sergeant heard an explosion from the museum's dragon-kin exhibit and the younger guards sprinted toward the billowing smoke, Perkins trotted toward the site of the trouble at an unhurried pace. The other bannermen assigned to the Museum of Andarun could afford to run headlong into danger. Especially his headstrong young partner.

Then Perkins noticed a group of suspicious characters in the omnimancy exhibit, standing around the Wyrmwood Staff. The sergeant took it as a welcome excuse to remove himself from harm's way and called out to the adventurers, hoping to escort them outside for a safe and time-consuming interview. Unfortunately, that was when he noticed the strange device in the noctomancer's hands.

"What are you doing there?" Perkins demanded, as his guardsman's instincts overrode his survival ones. He took a couple of steps forward, and then the world went mad.

One moment the suspicious adventurers were looking at him in guilty surprise. The next Perkins heard a faint hiss and a small *pop* like a lemon passing through a wine bottle. The noctomancer and his device, the adventurers, and even the Dusk Cart of Archmage Ibson winked out of existence amid a sudden cacophony, replaced by a horrible conflagration that roared past the sergeant in a blur of fire and profanity. Perkins was thrown from his feet, and a red wheel passed within inches of providing a supporting argument for the second principle of universal irony.

When the old bannerman righted himself a moment later, the omnimancy exhibit was still, save for a trail of thick smoke in the air and several shards of Lord Cestil's ceremonial armor rattling on the floor.

"All right, maybe not career-ending. But close," said Burt. "The sixth tier is just about as destitute as an Elf with standing can tolerate, so it's not the sort of neighborhood I'd go looking for work in if I was you. Really, you want to work for an Elf on the ninth tier."

Thane gazed at the rooftops of the second tier down from the Pinnacle. "The ninth tier."

"Oh, yeah. Well, the Elves don't call it the ninth. They've got the place divided up into dozens of little mini-tiers. If their foundation's an inch or two higher than their neighbors', they call it a new tier and act like they're better than the folks next door. But everyone else just calls it the ninth tier."

"That sounds a little silly," said the Troll.

"Hey, if I had a silver shilling for every ridiculous thing the Elves did, well, I suppose I'd basically have my old job again. But you get used to it, and it's a good living. Provided you work for an Elf of means, of course. Which is why you don't look for jobs on the sixth tier. Otherwise you'll wind up sleeping in a cardboard box at the foot of some bed."

"I don't think that would happen to me," said Thane carefully.

"Well, not exactly, obviously," said the Kobold. "You don't have what it takes to be a handbag performer. No offense."

"None taken," said the Troll, in a way that implied some given.

Burt ignored the slight. "But the principle's the same. You want to work somewhere that gives you social status. That's how you get status yourself. And more money, of course."

"I'm not sure I want a job," said Thane.

"Well, you need one, technically, if you want those NPC papers to stay valid. But don't worry. You're not going to have any problems finding work. Anybody who wants some extra protection would pay top dollar to have a Troll for a guard."

"You think so?"

"I know it," said Burt. "I talked to a couple of security firms back in the day. Technically, they're goons, but that's not a bad thing. You could start as a goon and work your way up to thug in no time."

Thane nodded and took another sip of his tea. "You know a lot about this city," he said, staring out over the rooftops.

"Yeah, you hear a lot of things sitting in a diplomat's purse," said Burt.

"Did you hear a strange noise?" asked Thane.

"No, I meant like gossip and politics and stuff."

"Just now. I heard an explosion."

Thin plumes of smoke rose from a building down on the seventh tier.

"Isn't that where you said the museum is?" Thane stood and shielded his eyes to better see the commotion.

"Maybe," said Burt slowly. He heard screams from the tiers below, but he was hoping that Thane didn't. "I mean, we don't know—"

He was cut off by a distant shriek, a whining roar like that of something prehistoric and scaly. An amber glow flared along the Wall near the Broad Steps.

"It's them," said the Troll. "They might need us."

"It could be anybody," Burt tried.

"Then somebody's in trouble," said Thane. "Let's go."

"But the jam tarts are almost ready," protested Burt. "Look, you can see the cook setting them to cool in the window."

"Come on," rumbled the Troll.

The Kobold grabbed a few coins and a rolled note from his purse and threw them onto the table. "That'll teach me to look forward to anything too much," he snarled, scampering up Thane's arm.

"What does that have to do with it?" Thane was already running for the stairs down to the tenth tier, scattering panicked citizens as he did so.

"Ain't you ever heard of Nove's second principle of universal irony?"

"Whose principle of what?"

"Yeah, I should have figured," sighed the Kobold. He shot one last longing glance at the jam tarts as the Troll lumbered down the street, leaving a line of dazed citizens in their wake.

"It is unfair, but it is the way of things," said Dulo of the Melon, fanning himself with a large banana leaf.

Jaya stared across Andarun's Broad Steps with yearning and envy in equal measure. "Look at the lines at their carts," she grumbled. "Look how many brokers and merchants are standing there for basted meats. It's not even time for dinner."

The old man patted the round melons on his cart, one of several fruit stands clustered across the steps opposite the Wall on the eighth tier. "And perhaps, when they are full, they will come by for a slice of sugared melon. But we must be patient."

Jaya shook her head. "But if I took my cart across the steps — "

"It is not our way," said Dulo. "Remember the teachings."

"All the meat carts have crossed!"

"They are different," said the old merchant sagely.

"Yes, but only because they've crossed the street and now they're making giltin hand over fist," Jaya growled through her teeth.

"They would not have if they sold our wares." Dulo scratched at his thin beard before trying a different approach. "Consider Thulb the Wise. She has been here since your mother was a girl and never changed her spot. Thulb does not seek more sales, nor does she strive for new products. She has faith that prosperity grows from stability, and that there will always be gold in her banana stand."

An ancient Tinderkin nodded at the pair from an old shack near the steps down to the seventh tier.

"I don't care!" said Jaya. "Why should I sit waiting for traders to cross the street while my spiced oranges rot in the sun? I'm going to get in the shadow of the Wall and sell delicious fruits to those lazy bankers."

"It is not our way," Dulo repeated. "Remember the teachings of the philosopher-scientist — "

"No, this is silly," Jaya interrupted. "I'm doing it." The young woman leapt to her feet and pushed her cart forward, careful to balance the piles of oranges and spice jars atop it. Her determination faded a little as she approached the bustle of the steps. By the time she reached their edge, she had slowed to a stop.

Jaya looked up toward the Pinnacle. The odd businessperson trotted up and down the steps, but most were working in their offices at this hour. The young fruit seller turned and looked down toward the Base. A few tourists milled around the steps outside the Museum of Andarun, but the steps were otherwise clear.

With a deep breath, Jaya pushed her cart forward.

The stones of the Broad Steps were smooth, worn by the stamping of innumerable feet moving up and down the tiers. Her cart rolled easily across the way, and the pedestrians were mindful enough to keep out of her path. Halfway across the steps, Jaya allowed herself a small smile. "This is going to work," she said.

Back on the Ridgeward side of the steps, Dulo shook his head sadly.

A sudden explosion rang from the lower tiers. Jaya looked down the steps in horror as people began to pour out of the Museum of Andarun, spilling onto the Broad Steps. Her desperation swelling, she tried to pull her wares back to safety, but it was too late. A fruit cart was in the middle of the road, and universal forces were in motion.

A flaming contraption burst from the doors of Andarun's museum with a gaggle of armed heroes hanging from its shaking rails. Sparks sprayed from the screaming juggernaut's wheels as it careened onto the steps and launched itself up the stairs at an impossible velocity. Jaya barely had time to dive for cover before the burning wagon drove through her cart, sending a fountain of oranges and spices into the air. The nightmare vehicle didn't slow at all. It roared up toward the ninth tier, carrying the screaming heroes with it as pulp and chunks of fruit cart rained down on the cobbles.

Damp Otto's plate clattered on the floorboards, scattering trout pastries everywhere. It was followed by the assassin's dagger, and then a moment later by the body of Damp Otto, still convulsing in a death rattle.

Garold Flinn stared each of the remaining assassins in the eye as the sounds of Otto's feeble thrashing rang out in the dining chamber. "Now," he growled as Otto settled. "Does anyone else wish to back out of their contract?"

The assembled killers shook their heads.

"Good." Mr. Flinn holstered his handheld crossbow. "Then in that case—"

"You didn't even give him the witnesses speech," said Barty Ficer, a weathered man surrounded by a trio of war golems.

"What?" said Flinn, still fiddling with his crossbow holster.

"You know." Barty mimicked a sinister, gravelly voice. "'If you can't be a part of the team, you're just a witness. And in this business, we don't leave witnesses.' That sort of thing."

"You mean the loose ends speech?" said Mortus, who had taken the form of a finely-dressed old Dwerrow today.

Barty scratched at the stubble on his chin. "I suppose," he said slowly. "But back in Scoria, we used to call it the witnesses speech."

"On the Daellish coast, it's the 'dead men tell no tales' speech," offered Captain Jones.

"My people call it the 'circle of trust speech,'" said Deathbloom, a dark-skinned Imperial woman in violet silks.

"What?" asked Mortus. "How does that go?"

"You know. 'We are all in a circle of trust, and once you're out of it, you can't get back in,'" said Deathbloom. "You see where it goes?"

"Well, I guess," said Udina the Raven, a dark haired noctomancer in robes more black than purple. "But I hope nobody here thinks we trust each other."

"It's just an expression," Deathbloom snarled over the other assassins' laughter.

Mr. Flinn sighed as he rapped his silver fork against his crystal goblet. "Ladies and gentlemen, please. Whatever the protocol, I think Damp Otto's fate makes it clear what will happen to anyone who tries to abandon their obligations." He nodded to the remains of Damp Otto, which were already being rolled into an extravagant carpet by a pair of servants dressed in gray and white.

Andarun boasted plenty of discreet establishments where an unsavory clientele could eat, meet, and kill each other away from the prying eyes of the bannermen. Most of those businesses, however, had a dim and dank ambiance, the only saving grace of which was that it made it harder to see the food. For a more well-to-do and discerning criminal, the White Hand offered top-tier dining with first-rate secrecy. The food was excellent, the wine cellar featured an enviable collection of vintages, and the staff offered a number of useful services including, happily, body disposal.

The two servants hefted the rolled-up corpse and hurried from the room.

"Can we all agree on that point?" asked Mr. Flinn.

"Yeah, sure," said Barty over the affirmative muttering of the other assassins.

"Good. Now, who has information about where Gorm Ingerson might be?"

The muttering from the collected assassins was distinctly less affirmative.

"Nobody?" Mr. Flinn felt another surge of rage and panic flushing his face. He stepped over to the window, trying without much success to hide his consternation. "Nobody has any leads on where Ingerson is, despite all the information I provided?"

"I've got clues clogging all my bilges," said Captain Jones, whose dedication to maintaining pirate branding often wore thin. "It's four Humans, an Elf, and a Dwarf. That's pretty much every other party of professional heroes workin' between Silvershore and Edaelmon. Everybody and their mother has leads for me; it's sortin' through 'em that's impossible."

"They've a noctomancer and a solamancer among them," snapped Mr. Flinn. The window overlooked a small plaza with a fountain and a few benches in between a couple of office buildings. A cluster of fruit stands sat at the far corner of the plaza. Beyond them, Flinn could see the Broad Steps, where traders milled about in the shadow of the Wall. "Surely two mages from opposing Orders make for a distinctive combination."

"It's uncommon, but not so much as you'd think," said Udina.

"And it poses another problem," added Barty. "They're clearly puttin' up concealing wards and anti-divination charms on themselves now and again. All my gazers gave up. The bloody search sprites are totally baffled. They just flutter around pointing out interesting shrubs."

Barty's mechanical golems nodded in agreement, as they were enchanted to do.

Mortus shrugged. "I've tips in Edaelmon, I've tips in Parald, I've tips in Scoria—"

A high-pitched note cut Mortus off as Mr. Flinn traced a silver claw along the window, etching a thin line into the glass. "You'll pardon me, but I did not assemble the world's foremost assassins for the sake of hearing excuses. I need results, and I need them soon."

There was a loud bang in the distance, like a cart losing a wheel. Flinn ignored it.

"Exhaust your networks, contact every source, try every spell, and use any other tool you have at your disposal," the Tinderkin continued.

"It is essential that we find Gorm Ingerson and his party, and they're not going to just pass us in the street."

The other assassins protested, but Flinn wasn't paying attention to them. The high note still hung in the air, although he had removed his claw from the glass. The people on the Broad Steps were starting to scatter, shouting and pointing at something downhill. The reason for the sound and the panic quickly became apparent as an old wooden wagon flew up the Broad Steps, a great gout of flame blasting behind it. The wagon rammed through a fruit cart, hit the steps to the ninth tier, and flew from view in the span of a second, leaving the windows of the White Hand and the surrounding buildings shaking in its wake.

Flinn was shaking as well, but with excitement. "Go!" he cried numbly. "We've got to go! Come on!"

"What was that?" asked Barty.

Flinn could barely speak. He'd only seen the wagon for a moment, but there was no mistaking the figures clinging to the rails. "It's them!" he gasped. "They're here, and leaving fast!"

"Too fa—aa—st!" Gorm screamed into the rushing wind as the jet-cart roared out of the Museum of Andarun's front doors, sailing through the air over the museum's front steps in a cloud of smoke and detritus. Panicked citizens and bannermen scattered before them, trying to get out of the cart-turned-projectile's path. His beard whipped back over his shoulder, tugging at his face with such sudden force he was sure it would rip off. Tears welled in his eyes and his knuckles whitened as he gripped the edge of the cart.

Kaitha screamed something, and Heraldin and Gaist pointed. Gorm's stomach dropped as the smooth, stone face of the Wall loomed in front of them across the Broad Steps, promising a swift and terminal end to their flight.

He felt something shift behind him and turned to see Jynn throwing his entire body into an overarm weave of air magic. A split-second later, a gust of wind spun the wagon to the left, sparks flying from its wheels as it careened up the Broad Steps.

"What are ye—" Gorm began, but he was interrupted when a loud crack and a burst of citrus assailed his senses. Fruit spattered on his armor and a rind crammed itself into his mouth.

"I'm trying to steer!" Jynn yelled back through a cloud of oranges and spice.

"Do it again! Do it again!" shrieked Heraldin, pointing.

Ahead of the speeding cart, a caravan of Imperial merchants was trying to coax a trio of quasi-domesticated Mud Drakes down the Broad Steps from the Pinnacle. The three stout dragon-kin plodding down the stairs in parallel formed a stone wall of sorts; one that was considerably toothier and more irritable than most.

"Bones!" swore Jynn, and once more he threw his whole body into weaving.

The wagon veered so fast that it was all Gorm could do to grip the rail as another gust of wind wrenched them off the Broad Steps and onto a short plaza. Traders and brokers scattered at the sight of the flaming cart. Beyond them, Gorm could see a stone wall as wide as a street but no higher than a short hedge. Beyond the wall, the plaza ended, and there was nothing but open sky and a final descent. Ice ran up Gorm's spine as he deduced that they were on the tenth tier.

"Wall!" shrieked Laruna.

"It's *the* Wall!" Gorm shouted.

"Jump!" shouted Kaitha, but it was already too late.

The Dusk Cart of Archmage Ibson slammed into the Wall and, still propelled by the power of the Wyrmwood Staff, flipped over the edge. Gorm and his companions were launched into the air, over the Wall, high above the jagged rocks of Mount Wynspar. The harsh cliffs of the mountain slipped into view far below him, and he plummeted, screaming, toward them.

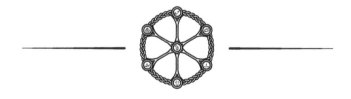

"Well, 'plummeted' is a strong word," said Mr. Fitch.

"Rapidly descended? Fell in an alarming manner? Cratered?" Duine Poldo set down his coffee on the lacquered iron table and gestured at a sheet of figures. "Take your pick, but the Stearn Southwestern Ruskan Continued Prosperity Index dropped to almost nothing when the undead took Vetchell. Thank the gods Silver Guard wasn't holding much of it."

Fitch shrugged and selected a tea cake from the platter. "That sort of rise in the threat indexes is going to trigger a lot of threat obligations. At least you're not Lamia Sisters; they're the ones who had to pay out most of the obligations in that CTO."

"They must be reeling," said Poldo. He looked out over the expanses of Boulderfolk Commons' lush gardens from his seat at the Terrace Cafe.

"Hey, I'd be lying if I said it wasn't going to hurt their profits this year," said Fitch. "But you have to look at the big picture! Lamia Sisters has lots of CTOs they're still collecting payments on—they're raking in giltin hand over fist. And now that investors have seen that you can make money buying threat obligations, they're more in demand than ever."

"But who will take on the obligation?" asked Poldo. "Are the banks really so eager to take that sort of risk?"

"You leave that to Mr. Stearn. He's finding plenty of buyers."

"Really?" Poldo shook his head. "Well, I wouldn't hold these things, and I'm the one writing the threat obligations."

"And top-notch ones, at that," said Fitch. "Yours are the best obligations I'm rating these days."

"Thank you, but how can you tell? How could you distinguish one from another?" Poldo asked. "The payout is all based on events we can't control, and the investors are all betting on a future they can't foresee. Anyone holding CTOs is little more than a casino at this point."

Fitch smiled. "Hey, the house always wins, right?"

"The house usually rigs the system more effectively," said Poldo. "What if the undead take Parald?"

"Then too bad for Parald," said Fitch. "The northwestern Ruskan CTOs will take a big hit, and everyone will start buying threat obligations for the rest of Arth. The Heroes' Guild will stop the undead eventually. And when they do, any bank that wasn't riding the CTO wave is going to be left out at sea."

Poldo looked the Halfling in the eye. "You seem confident that the undead won't make it beyond Parald."

Fitch's brown curls bobbed as he nodded. "Not far past, anyway. Word on the Wall is that King Handor's waiting to see if the undead will cross into the Freedlands before he sets the guild on them. It's likely Detarr Ur'Mayan's coming for vengeance, and if he gets on our soil, the king can issue a new quest for the same monster. That way, all that Ruskan loot comes to Andarun."

"And you think the Ruskan people will stand for that?"

"The Ruskan government seems to be planning for it," Fitch said with a shrug. "Their army and Heroes' Guild hasn't been the same since Deep Thoggus, and word is King Klenn's pulling all his defenses back into Edaelmon. I'm sure he'd like it if the liche gets killed on Ruskan soil, but the important part is that the liche gets killed before it wrecks his entire country."

"Assuming the liche is slain at all."

"Hey, come on! How many times has the Heroes' Guild wiped out huge armies of the undead? Why should this one be any different?" The Halfling leaned in close and whispered. "Besides, people are saying Clubs Incorporated has brokered a deal to sell the kingdom some secret Umbraxian weapon."

"I've heard as much," said Poldo. "Everyone seems to have ideas about what's going to happen next."

"Better still, they're willing to bet on it." Fitch grinned as he set a briefcase on the table. "We've got work to do."

Poldo left the cafe with a fresh stack of requests for more threat obligations. Old habit took him toward the small shed in the hedge maze, but he quickly stopped himself and made for Boulderfolk's main gate instead. He'd been working from his home office for the past few days, primarily because the other inhabitants of the Boulderfolk garden shed had recently taken up residence underneath the floorboards of his apartment.

A familiar weight dropped onto Poldo's shoulder as he passed a sculpture. He glanced down to see a Wood Gnome wearing an old squirrel skin and a new tie. A moment later, three Wood Gnomes clambered onto the briefcase in the Scribkin's hand. Poldo could sense a company of tiny men and women in the skins of various rodents running and ducking through the shadows in his wake.

"Good afternoon," he said to Red Squirrel. "What's the latest?"

The Wood Gnomes chittered something high and unintelligible, and a moment later a Domovoy blurred from the shadows, scampered up Poldo's leg and torso, and deposited a slip of paper in his hand before leaping back into a shrub.

Poldo glanced over the list. He recognized Mrs. Hrurk's neat handwriting. "Lamia Sisters is down three percent," he muttered as he read. "But our funds are still up by a few basis points despite the business in Vetchell. Well, that's a spot of good news. And now it seems Mrs. Hrurk has found a family of Slaugh that need a home... Will we have enough room even with the new apartments we're purchasing?"

Red Squirrel shook his head.

"No, I suppose not." Poldo stepped through the gates of Boulderfolk Commons and hailed a carriage.

He thought for a few moments as the carriage rolled up. His briefcase was heavy with paperwork for even more CTOs, though he couldn't imagine what new equations he could tease into existence to satisfy the market. Above him, emerald and crimson trade sprites danced on their journey toward the Andarun Stock Exchange.

"Reach out to Entreri Property Management," he told Red Squirrel as he climbed into the carriage. "I'd like to inquire about purchasing our building and buying out the other lodgers."

Red Squirrel chirruped something like a question.

"Oh, yes, I meant it," Poldo told the Wood Gnome. "There's no shortage of people who need our help, and Mrs. Hrurk seems to be determined to find them all, Wust bless her." He peered out the carriage window, where he could still see a sliver of sky crowded with green trade sprites. "Besides, it seems a good time to invest in real estate."

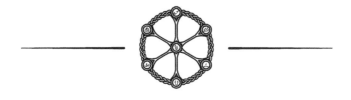

High-end condominiums and luxury offices at the Wallward edge of Andarun's topmost tiers blurred through Gorm's vision. Then the vast, stone expanse of the Wall sped by, before his tumbling brought the hovels and shanty towns down by the Tarapin River into view. A moment later, he was looking down at rock formations that might have seemed picturesque—majestic, even—had they not been pointed straight at him and approaching so quickly.

"Hang on!" shouted Jynn.

Gorm's stomach heaved anew as he lurched to a stop. He hung upside down in the sky over the crags of Mount Wynspar. A cold wind spun him slowly in place, and as the Wall came into view he could see a crowd of confused and startled onlookers staring down.

"What the blazes is going on?" Gorm roared.

"Jynn used the staff," yelled Laruna from where she was similarly suspended. "It's a slow-fall spell!"

Gorm looked toward his feet, trying to keep his lunch down—or rather up—as the clouds and sun spun into view. The other heroes drifted above him.

"Where's the cart?" he asked.

A faint crash from below answered his question.

"Apparently it was too heavy," said Kaitha.

"How long can the wizard keep us up here?" Gorm called.

"Not as long as we'd like," said Laruna.

"Not... exactly... easy!" Jynn growled through gritted teeth, gripping the Wyrmwood Staff with both hands.

"Is he all right?" Kaitha asked.

"Maintaining a slow-fall spell on six people is a lot of magic," said Laruna.

"I've seen noctomancers fly with less effort," said Heraldin.

"Well, it's a lot for Jynn," conceded Laruna.

"Not... helping!" the wizard snarled.

"It's the staff," the solamancer continued. "It doesn't really want him to use it."

"It's... fighting!" groaned Jynn. "Wants... Laruna!"

"See?" said Heraldin, slowly tumbling through the air. "This is the problem with using weapons with a mind of their own."

"And the problem with not usin' this one is that we'd all be purply stains on those rocks without it," snapped Gorm. "Jynn, can ye steer us?"

"Nnngh!" groaned the noctomancer.

"Good. Take us toward the trees at Andarun's base." Gorm waved his hand in what he hoped was the right direction.

Kaitha stared at the noctomancer with concern. "I don't think he said yes."

"I don't think 'no' is an option," said Gorm, looking up at the Wall. Bannermen were already arriving at the scene of the crash, and it wouldn't be long before they broke out the crossbows.

Jynn grunted and groaned and went more than a little violet in the face, but a moment later a wind blew down from the mountain top. The heroes drifted south as they descended.

"Ha ha! Good on ye, lad!" hollered Gorm.

They rode the current of air swiftly down the mountainside, headed toward a small village on the Tarapin River by the base of the Wall.

"We're making good time," Kaitha remarked to the Dwarf as they floated along.

"Aye." Gorm watched the distant cluster of huts and fishing boats grow larger. "Faster than any bannermen can get down the Broad Steps, I'd imagine."

"Ha!" said Laruna. "Faster than a quicksilver imp could get down the broad steps!"

"Yeah," said Heraldin, more thoughtfully.

The adventurers took a moment to consider the rapidly approaching village.

"A little too fast, actually," said Kaitha.

"Can we slow down, Jynn?" Laruna asked.

"Or move up," suggested Heraldin, arms and legs flailing as an ominous tower loomed in front of them.

"Nnnnerrrggg," growled Jynn, and the look in his eyes said that it was a definitive "nerg."

"Fine then, steer for the trees!" shouted Gorm.

"Or the river!" said Laruna.

"Or anything that's not a tower with a barbed iron fence!" hollered Heraldin.

With significant effort and even more notable groaning, Jynn managed to accommodate all three requests, conjuring a final shift in the wind that took the heroes around the tower, through the branches of a thorny tree, and into the middle of the Tarapin River. They landed in a burst of splashes and cursing.

After a frigid interlude, Gorm pulled himself from the river downstream, the others not far behind him. They coughed and sputtered on the muddy banks for a few moments. Then, grumbling and wringing out their clothes as best they could, they made their way toward the public stables near the Riverdowns.

"We don't have much time to get the horses," Gorm told them as they squelched down the street at a quick trot. "The alarm's been raised by now, and someone'll tell the bannermen they saw us floatin' down the mountain."

"Not to mention Benny Hookhand," moaned Heraldin.

"I can hear the bells going off up in the city," said Kaitha.

"Then we'd best move quickly," said Gorm. "Come on."

The common stables sat amid the hovels and farm plots between the Great South Gate of Andarun and the Tarapin River. It was close enough to the water to bear the architectural hallmarks of the Riverdowns—namely pervasive graffiti and other signs of drunken vandalism—but close enough to the Great South Gate to have the decency to be ashamed of it. A pair of stable hands were whitewashing the front gate when Gorm and his party arrived.

"Foblerson. Here for our horses." Gorm gave the stable boy a wooden chit along with the false name he'd used to stable the mounts.

"Why are you all wet?" asked the other stable boy, a pimply adolescent whose teeth appeared to be outgrowing the rest of him.

"Swimming practice," said Laruna.

"Surely, miss." The stable boy stopped painting and carefully set his brush down atop the bucket of whitewash. "It's just that the alarm is sounding, and people along the road are saying some robbers flew down the mountain and fell into the river."

"You're awfully curious for a stable boy," said Heraldin with narrowed eyes.

"It's just that we're a reputable establishment, sir. I don't want to be known for associating with the criminal type."

"Would ye rather be remembered for making a stand against them?" asked Gorm, his hand resting on his axe.

"Um, that was six horses, then?" The boy's voice cracked as he spoke.

"Good lads," said Gorm. The stable boys were already scurrying out back.

A short time later, the heroes rode out of the common stables and away from Andarun. The wind was frigid in his soaking armor, and Gorm would swear his horse had seemed disappointed to see him, but nothing could dampen his mood.

"We did it!" The Dwarf raised a fist in the air as they past the last hovel on the eastern edge of the Riverdowns.

"And in such short time!" said Laruna.

"I really thought we'd be in Andarun longer," said Kaitha. Emotion must have overwhelmed the ranger; her voice cracked when she spoke, and it sounded more like crying than laughter.

"It's about time somethin' went better than expected," said Gorm, spurring his horse back toward last night's camp. "We need to make up all the time we can."

"Definitely," said Jynn. "But where are we going next?"

"Back to a warm fire and dry clothes," said Heraldin. "It's freezing out here."

"Right," said Laruna. "But I meant after that."

"The guild heroes are going to fight the liche's army at some point," said Gorm. "We want to be there with the Wyrmwood Staff to help."

"So, we just head east?" asked the solamancer. "How will we know where to find them?"

"I've seen enough of how Handor and his cronies work to know how they think," said Gorm. "I'm fairly certain of where they're going."

Chapter 13

"To Highwatch?" King Handor sat forward in his velvet lined chair in a private corner of his study.

"Indeed, sire. It's perfect," said Bolbi Baggs. "The fortress has never fallen, no doubt due to its position in the cruel Highwalls."

"Better still, it's just on our side of the Ruskan border," added Fenrir Goldson. "Yet not so close that King Klenn could reasonably accuse you of baiting the undead into the Freedlands for the loot."

"So it's defensible in two ways," added Baggs.

"Yes, I've already agreed on as much," said Handor. "I'm just not sure why we would go there."

"We'll only make the journey if you wish, sire." Baggs poured himself a finger of Halfling sour rum and dropped in two ice cubes.

"And we'd fly, of course," said Goldson, sipping his own drink from a spot near the fire. "Fastest way to travel."

"But why go at all?" said Handor.

"To protect our investments, sire." Baggs settled into a comfortable armchair. "To ensure that the plan is executed properly."

"They want to make sure those giant orbs get used before guild heroes finish the liche off," grumbled Weaver Ortson. The Master of the Heroes' Guild was unusually sober for this time of evening. "Otherwise they won't get their finder's fee for bringing Clubs and his Umbraxians in."

"Indeed," said Baggs, with a withering look at Ortson. "We also wish to ensure the heroes from our subsidiaries have the first rights to fight the liche itself."

"And it does promise some entertainment," said Goldson.

"Always a factor," said Baggs. "Regardless, we heard Your Majesty might also be interested in providing inspiration and leadership for the troops."

"And more importantly, that you might be interested in being seen providing inspiration and leadership for the troops," said Goldson.

Handor nodded; he wouldn't mind hearing tales of his bravery from the town criers. "But is it safe?" he asked.

"Ha! Highwatch is the greatest fortress on Arth, outside of Andarun," said Johan the Mighty. "It hasn't been successfully assaulted in a thousand years."

"We wouldn't take such a trip ourselves, let alone suggest Your Majesty take it, if we weren't confident that the bannermen could protect us all," said Baggs.

"The bannermen can't keep a simple staff safe in the middle of a fortified museum at the heart of our city," snapped Ortson. "I shouldn't trust them with Your Majesty's safety."

"We're all unhappy about the museum robbery, Ortson," Handor said, staring into the crackling fire. "I'm especially concerned that I heard a rumor that it might have been Gorm Ingerson's band of outlaws who perpetrated it."

The room fell silent. Johan's perpetual smile faded, just a little. "It's possible, sire, but I don't want to jump to that conclusion."

"No, I shouldn't if I were you," Handor said. "Especially as you've given me your word Ingerson would be dead by now."

"Ingerson will meet his end very shortly," said Johan stiffly. "As will whoever stole the Wyrmwood Staff."

"See that it's so," said Handor. He turned back to Goldson and Baggs. "And you remain confident that this trip is safe?"

"We watch heroes at work on a regular basis, Your Majesty," said Baggs. "Why, just last month Mr. Goldson and I flew out to watch a team from Adventure Capital clear a warren of scargs outside of Fenrose Heath."

"An excellent show," said Goldson. "And we stopped for supper in the Haerthwards on the way home."

"The undead are more dangerous than scargs," said Handor pensively.

"Yes, but Highwatch is safer than the tents we had set up outside the scarg nests," said Baggs.

"The journey isn't without risks," conceded Goldson. "But we've taken every precaution to mitigate the danger. We'll have a vantage point set up atop the inner keep, bodyguards from the Heroes' Guild, and flights waiting nearby to evacuate us in the unlikely event that the battle goes the wrong way."

"We doubt it would come to such measures, naturally," said Baggs. "When you've observed as many quests as Fenrir and I, you get a sense of how these things tend to go."

"Yeah, this is typical," said Burt. "Everyone always forgets about the little guy."

"They didn't forget you," said Thane, plucking the note off the tree at the edge of the former campsite. "They told you where they're going and how to follow them."

"Yeah, leaving a Kobold on his own in the wilderness," snarled Burt. "My people don't do anything alone, let alone travel. I might get eaten by a wild boar, for all they know!"

"They know I'm here with you." Thane glanced over the note again.

The Kobold kicked at a stone in the damp earth. "Half of them do. The other half may as well have left me to die."

The Troll squinted at the paper in his hands. "Where is Highwatch?"

"East," sighed the Kobold, scrabbling up the Troll's arm. "Bones, how are we going to catch them on those fancy horses of theirs?" Keeping pace with the Elven steeds on the journey to Andarun had stretched the Troll to his considerable limits.

"They only have a few hours head start," said Thane. "If we camp late, we can catch up over the course of a day or two."

"You really think we can make up the lost ground?"

"We have to." Thane slipped the note into a pouch he wore on his bandolier. Burt heard glass vials clinking together within it.

"Maybe we have to go, maybe we don't," said Burt. "We could just send a letter."

"Burt, they need us." The Troll gave a fanged grin to his passenger. "Did they really write anything that offensive?"

"It ain't what's in the note!" fumed Burt. "It's the fact that they left a note at all! It just says something, you know?"

"It sends a message," said Heraldin grimly.

Gaist looked down at the brightly colored cork that the bard pressed into his hand. It was narrower at one end, with a red stick driven through its center. A tiny hole was drilled through each end of the stick, and a length of string wound through them.

"You don't leave a fishing buoy in a man's saddlebags unless you want him to know he's dead." Heraldin pointed at the cork. "This says I'll be taking a trip down the river. Or sleeping with the fishes. Or on the hook. You choose whatever metaphor you like, so long as it implies that I'm not long for this world."

Gaist raised an eyebrow, though almost imperceptibly.

"It's from Benny Hookhand!" snapped the bard. "He knows! He knows I robbed the museum!"

Gaist stared into the simmering coals in the center of the camp, all that remained of the evening's cookfire.

"It was the stable boy," fumed the bard, stalking around the fire. "That little knock-kneed, pimply, scum-sucking slug! He must be in the Hookhand's pockets. That's why he was asking so many questions. I bet he got a tip about me from someone in Benny's organization, and then the bloody stupid Dwarf all but confirmed we robbed the museum to him."

Gaist shrugged.

"You do not understand, my friend," sighed the bard, gripping his forehead in his hand. "I tricked the Hookhand into a truce long ago, and for years he has been waiting for me to slip up and break the peace. Now he knows I've been thieving, and he's free to take his revenge. Who knows what terrible death he has in store for me?"

Gaist looked at the bard, ferocity blazing in his dark eyes.

"True. I am traveling with a weaponsmaster of remarkable talents. And I trust in you, my friend." Heraldin's smile held no joy. "You may keep me out of trouble for a time."

The bard sighed and looked at the buoy in his hand. "But Benny Hookhand is relentless. He will not rest until he has me, and once he does it will be my end. To get a fishing buoy in your backpack means that someday, sooner rather than later, death comes for you."

"I mean, we're all going to die eventually, right?" said the guard.

Hana shook her head. "This is madness, Chovek."

"It's not. We all pass on one day or another, and today seems to be ours." Chovek waved a hand toward the grassland beyond Parald's shining walls. The fields were black in the waning sunlight, every yard of them crammed with stinking corpses that stared up at the city's last defenders with hollow, hungry eyes.

"Our duty is to protect our city," said Hana, though she couldn't sound as certain as she wanted to. She glanced at Fiora for back up, but the portly guard was busy reading a paper flyer. Similar brochures drifted down over the ramparts all around the cluster of soldiers.

"And what are we defending?" said Chovek. "The families and elders have fled toward Edaelmon and Aberreth. The heroes aren't coming. The city will fall with or without us."

"—With or without you." Fiora read along, her finger holding her place on the flyer. "Yeah, that's what this ad says."

Chovek held up his own paper as a cleric wields a holy symbol. "It also says nobody will eat me if I take advantage of this special offer."

"You mean joining the undead," said Hana, her hand on her hilt.

"We're all going to join them one way or another! That's the point!" Chovek pointed out at the waiting army. "Do you think any of them had a choice? We're no better off than they were, except we can avoid getting mauled and eaten alive!"

Fiora gasped and held her hands to her cheeks. "But how?"

"Just show up outside the walls with a copy of the flyer in hand," Chovek read. "But we have to act now! This offer ends at sunset."

"Oh, yeah. They've got this little box that tells you everything you need to do!" Fiora marveled, looking down at the flyer.

"Well, it's important to have a clear call to action," said Chovek.

"But we don't have time," said Fiora. "The sun's almost down, and we'd never make it out of the gates in time."

"Well, that's only because of all the sods clogging the stairs." Chovek pointed to the base of the wall, where a steady flow of deserters trickled out from the guard houses, waving flyers in the air above their heads. "There's got to be a faster way down."

Hana's sword rang as she pulled it from her scabbard. "Enough!" she growled. "You can't betray our nation. Our people!"

Chovek and Fiora glanced down at the lieutenant's sword, and then at each other, and finally at the sun dropping behind the horizon. Chovek sneered. Fiora licked her lips.

"Now," said Hana slowly. "You will take up your spears, hold the—"

Fiora broke away. Two steps took the stout woman to the edge of the wall, and her third launched her over the edge, a flyer gripped firmly in her hand. A moment later, Hana heard a wet thump from below.

Hana's mouth opened and shut as she turned back to Chovek. The wiry man was already shifting toward the edge of the wall.

"Don't," Hana said, raising her sword. "I'll… I'll…"

"Don't blame yourself," he said. "It wouldn't have made a difference, anyway." With that, Chovek gave her his typical smirk and stepped back over the edge.

218

"And bam! Just like that, they're on our side!" said the Head of Marketing. "It's brilliant! We're converting the enemy without firing a single arrow!"

Tyren Ur'Thos looked at the walls of Parald. Beneath the city's flickering dome of magical wards and protective spells, he could see the thinning ranks of soldiers lining the ramparts. The sun had just set on Parald, and now the undead were waiting for moonrise to let the metaphor follow through.

"Impressive," said Tyren. He sat on a large rock in the middle of a clearing marked off with red rope attached to several posts. A gap in the left rope marked an entrance to his makeshift office, within which were several undead lined up to meet with him. Another gap to the right was marked with an exit sign. In between the signs, the corrupted earth was bare save for an old table that served as Tyren's desk.

"Impressive doesn't cover it!" said the floating skull. "Seven percent of Parald's defenders self-converted. Seven percent! Do you know how many of the living have defected to our side before now? Ever? In all of history? I'll give you a hint: I could count 'em on my fingers, and I don't have any fingers!"

"It's an excellent conversion rate," agreed the knight-commander, flipping through the pages in the marketing report. At first he was surprised to see all the red ink in the Head's numbers, but he quickly realized that it probably wasn't red ink. "Excellent work. Anything else?"

"We've been doing some brand work for Lady Carabae, given her recent promotion. That's on page six," said the Head of Marketing.

"Lady Carabae, Mistress of a Thousand Thralls," the knight-commander read.

"Is she beguiling? Or deadly? Why choose?" The Head bobbed excitedly as it spoke.

"She doesn't have a thousand thralls," said Tyren.

The Head of Marketing rolled its eye. "It's creative exaggeration. You've got to allow for a bit of hyperbole if you want to build a memorable brand."

"A bit?" Tyren looked up from the sheet. "She can't have more than a dozen or so vampire thralls. I mean, best case scenario is that you're off by a factor of fifty. Right?"

"Well, 'the Mistress of a Dozen or So Thralls' doesn't exactly rattle the bones, does it, sir? But I'll change it if you want. You're the boss, after all." The Head couldn't stop the flames around his head from flaring a little higher when he noted Tyren's relatively recent rank increase. Jealousy and resentment radiated from the skull along with infernal heat.

Tyren sighed. "Listen, the master may have put me in charge of a number of functions recently—"

"To say the least," grumbled the skull.

"But I believe leadership is all about empowering people to do their work. Trust me, I don't want to do your job." Tyren's favorite management line was disarming because it was absolutely true; the knight-commander didn't want to do anyone's job, including his own. "You're still the Head of Marketing. I'm here to help you be the best Head of Marketing you can."

"I... I know." The skull nodded reluctantly.

"Listen, if you think that's the right brand for Lady Carabae, you run with it." The knight-commander held up his hands. "I'm not here to get in your way. You've been delivering. Keep it up."

"All right, yeah." The Head of Marketing gave Tyren an inscrutable stare. "Yeah. Thanks."

"No, thank you," Tyren pointed at the skull and tried to wink a couple of times before he remembered that his eyelids were gone. He opted to snap his finger bones together instead. "I really appreciate all your great progress. I just wish I had more time to talk about it."

"Oh, uh, right. Right." The Head of Marketing bobbed off toward the exit. "Thanks, Knight-Commander."

"Any time." Tyren leaned back in the old chair. He still had his natural talent for delegation; only a master of middle management could give away all of the work for a project, stay in a place to get much of the credit, and still get thanked for it. The knack must have been in his bones, as evidenced by the fact that there wasn't anywhere else for it to be. Perhaps undeath hadn't taken that much away from him after all.

His next meeting, Ned and Ted, shambled in through the rope, while Rudge and his group of skeletons shuffled to take their place in the line. Tyren looked up at the stars winking into view across the sky;

the moon would rise soon. "Let's try to get through these last two meetings quickly," he said. "The attack is about to start."

"Ah, eager to get on the front lines, eh sir?" said Ted, stepping up to Tyren's desk.

"Something like that." Tyren was actually eager to be at the front of the middle ranks: far enough back that he wouldn't get his hands dirty, but close enough to the fore to keep up appearances. "How is the demonic animal husbandry team coming along?"

"Could be better," said Ned, the newly appointed stable master of the damned. "We've lost one, I'm afraid."

Tyren sat up. "You let one of those demon animals get away?"

"Oh, no sir!" said Ted. "We lost a stable hand. Turns out the infernal beasts can fly when sufficiently motivated, and apparently seeing a zombie too close to the training pit was sufficient motivation for Boris."

"That's what we call the boar," said Ned.

"Really?" Tyren steepled his hands.

"Yes, sir," said the ghoul. "We've named all the beasts. They're right vicious bastards, but you know how it is. You work with anything long enough and you start to get attached."

"I meant that I was surprised they ate another stable hand," said Tyren. "I thought you said you were making progress with the animals."

"Oh, we are sir!" said Ted. "Why, we've gotten to the point where old Boris doesn't try to kill Ned and I."

"Provided he's eating someone else at the time," added Ned.

"And Scruffles—that's our hellhound—why, I don't think he's aggressive at all," said Ted. "He's trying to be affectionate."

"Not that it makes much difference. He'll melt your face off either way," said Ned. "And nobody is taming that weasel."

Ghoul and zombie paused for a moment to shudder in unison at the mention of the mustelid.

"So, progress then?" said Tyren.

"I'd say as much," said Ned. "It's still rough going, but we're much better off than when we started."

"Good, good," said the knight-commander. "Well, let me say that those demonic beasts are very important to the master, as is everything related to that kraken mission."

"The Leviathan Project, sir," said Ted.

"Right," said Tyren. "Anything related to that project is top priority. Rudge and his relic recovery team will be searching the city for connected items and documents."

"Yes, sir!" Rudge and all of his skeletons saluted, save for the odd one with no arms, no head, and a sign nailed to its chest.

"You've made some great gains on a top project in just a week," Tyren told Ned and Ted. "Keep this up, and who knows how high you'll go in this organization."

To the knight-commander's surprise, the promise of a reward didn't have much of an effect. Ned and Ted exchanged a knowing look.

"Very good, sir," said Ned, without enthusiasm.

"No, wait," Tyren said, pointing a bony finger at the ghoul. "I'm telling you, you've got a great career here with the undead. You should be excited."

"It sounds nice," said Ned. "We just don't believe we're going to get promoted."

"You know how that flyer on your desk says that rich or poor, noble or low-born, all are equal in death?" asked Ted.

"Yes," said Tyren, glancing at the page.

"It's rubbish," Ned pronounced.

"What we've actually got is a rigid caste system, based on which sorcerous curse brought you to undeath," said Ted. "Your rank among the dead is entirely determined by the nature of the magic that binds you. Which, in turn, often depends on your character in life."

Ned nodded. "The master made himself a liche, the highest of the high, and beneath him we're all arrayed down to the lowest of the lows: the skeletons."

"What, really?" asked Tyren.

"Oh, yes," said Ned. "Nobody wants to be a skeleton."

"It's true," said Rudge.

"I meant about the caste system," said Tyren.

"Very much so, sir," said Ted. "All we are is magic and force of will made manifest, and higher ranks of undead have both of those in spades. So much so that they can take control over the rest of us. The lower your caste, the less you can control yourself when some necromancer or higher undead is telling you what to do."

"Not to mention the less chance you stand against the armies of the living," said Ned.

"Oh yes, that's a given," said Ted. "The point is, we've got an inherent hierarchy that favors the powerful. Undeath is much easier for a ghost than for a zombie such as myself."

"And vampires have it pretty thrice-cursed good as well." Ned added. "Lyin' around on red silk and seducin' young virgins willy nilly, while us ghouls can't find a decent meal."

"Just look at Ned and me," said Ted. "I outranked Neddard in the service of the city of Vetchell, in part because he was always a bit of a glutton."

"I'd prefer to say I had a taste for the finer things," said Ned.

"I'm sure you would," said Ted. "But the point is, when the master cursed us, Ned's appetites transformed him into a ghoul. Whereas myself, not having any character-defining flaws —"

"Nor any personality whatsoever," Ned muttered.

"I just became your basic zombie." Ted shook his head sadly. "And now he outranks me, just like all the people with unfinished business who became ghosts or the spiteful murderers who became wraiths and the like."

"But we're running an undead invasion like Arth has never seen before. This time is different." Tyren held up a bony hand. "I mean, look, I'm a skeleton, and I've come far."

Ned scoffed. "Please, sir, you may be skeletal, but you're not a skeleton."

"Definitely not. I saw him looking around when the master had his crown on," Ted told the ghoul. "He could move his head and everything."

"I saw it too," said Ned. "I can barely keep my wits about me when the master is within a hundred yards, to say nothing of when he's wearing the crown, but Knight-Commander Ur'Thos here was making suggestions about the advertising and volunteering for a leadership post."

"I was showing initiative," said Tyren.

"I'll bet he's a wight," opined Ted. "Maybe even an arch-wight. On account of his high stature in life and desire to protect his territory."

"Ah, but you're forgetting that wights come from opulent tombs, Ted," said Neddard. "My money is on a revenant."

Ted shook his head. "Can't be. Revenants look as they did in life so they can stalk their prey among the living, and our knight-commander definitely looks... uh..."

Zombie and ghoul looked at Tyren, and then at each other.

"Well, let's say he's lost weight," Ted finished carefully.

"So? It's not all appearances, is it?" said Ned.

"Listen, revenants are the spirits of evil men who die dishonorable deaths, right?" said Ted. "Remember Carl?"

Ned's face screwed up at the name. "Ugh. Total rubbish, Carl was. A bully and a fool."

"And a deserter. So now he's a revenant," said Ted. "Our knight-commander here was a man of the highest character to the very end. He died defending the gate with us, if you'll recall."

"Uh, right," said Tyren.

"I don't know," said Ned. "I think that sort of creation myth might just be another example of folklore using a simple moral duality to whitewash what is in reality a complex series of factors."

"A ghoul would say that, yes," said Ted.

Tyren covered his eye sockets with a bony hand. "Enough. Does it really matter if I'm a revenant or not?"

"Begging you're pardon, sir, but you'd have to be a wight to say as much," said Ned.

"At least," agreed Ted. "The whole caste thing may not seem that important when you're sitting up top, but those of us down near the bottom of the sorcerous economic ladder think about it constantly."

"It doesn't matter." The knight-commander shook his head. "Maybe it used to, but not anymore. We're changing the way things are done. The living have never volunteered to join the undead before, remember? And the master's plan is never going to work if people don't have an incentive to succeed." Nor would Tyren's designs, but he kept that point to himself.

"Do you really think so, sir?" asked Ned.

"I know so," said Tyren. "Listen, we're doing big things here. We can change the model, break down old barriers."

"Yeah!" Ted bubbled with growing enthusiasm. "We can do this!"

"There's no question in my mind," said Tyren. A shuffling sound caught his attention. "Well, perhaps one question. Do you think we're ready to deploy the infernal beasts?"

"Now?" The excitement drained back out of the zombie.

Tyren looked around. The ghoulish brigades around Tyren's office had lurched into motion—literally, in most cases. The front ranks of the undead army were already moving toward the doomed city of Parald. "Yes, now would be good."

"It ain't like we've got much time left, ye know?" Gorm spread his hands out. "That gnurg's almost lost us, and once one o' them scaly bastards goes to ground, there's no telling how long it'll take to find it again."

"That's what I hate most about gnurgs," said Laruna. "Something that big shouldn't be able to hide that well."

"Or move that fast," said Heraldin. "Gods, gnurgs are the worst."

Laughter rang out around the remnants of the cookfire. With the Wyrmwood Staff in their possession, the museum guards at their backs, and the horses making a great pace, the heroes had been in high spirits in the days since leaving Andarun. They'd even found time to buy a bundle of rations and a skin of wine from an inn just outside of Haertswood, and now they were enjoying one of the best meals Gorm could remember.

"Exactly," said Gorm, pointing at the solamancer with his spoon. "So our rogue yells, 'We're fallin' behind!' But I stands up on my horse, and I says, 'No, I'm getting a head!' Ha! So I jump—"

"Wait," Laruna interrupted. "You said what?"

"He's getting a head," Heraldin snickered.

Gorm nodded "Aye! So I jumped—"

"You made a joke?" said Laruna. "In the middle of the fight?"

"Yeah, 'cause I was gonna... ye know." Gorm used his spoon to pantomime a few axe blows. "I was gonna chop off its head."

The mage was incredulous. "It was a struggle for life and death with a giant, monstrous worm. Why were you making a pun?"

"And a really bad one at that," said Jynn.

Gorm gave an exasperated shrug. "It was just a quip."

"A quip? Do heroes often engage in wordplay when killing things?" the wizard asked with a smirk. "Do palindromes or anagrams count, or is it more about observational humor?"

"When I'm fighting, I'm not running around making jokes," said Laruna.

"Not jokes," said Heraldin. "A quip. You're allowed to make one. Only one, though."

"Oh, aye. Any more than that would be in poor taste." Gorm spoke through a mouthful of chicken and potatoes.

"One is in bad taste!" said Laruna. "Why would anyone say it's all right to make a joke in the middle of a life-and-death fight?"

Gorm shrugged. "I dunno. It's one of them unspoken rules."

"Yes, I thought everybody knew that," agreed Heraldin. "Gaist knows."

Gaist sat motionless on the edge of the firelight.

The bard nodded at the weaponsmaster. "See?"

"No," laughed Jynn.

"And I'm fairly certain he isn't making jokes in the heat of battle," said Laruna.

"Maybe he is." Heraldin grinned. "Maybe you just don't get them."

"I…" The solamancer stopped herself and looked at the weaponsmaster, who suddenly seemed a bit more aloof. "Well, I think it's silly."

"Maybe, but it can keep your mind off the stress a bit," said Gorm. "And it looks great in a quest report. My publicist used to love it when I had a good quip. The town criers go nuts for 'em. Kaitha, your publicist must have… have…"

Gorm trailed off as the heroes turned to the Elf.

She looked back at them with sullen, hollow eyes. "What?" she said softly.

"We was just talkin' about quips," said Gorm.

"Oh. Yeah, you're allowed to make one," said Kaitha dully.

"Lass, are ye feeling well?" asked Gorm.

Kaitha looked around at the concerned faces. "Ah, no. No, it must be… something I ate. I need to lie down." She stood slowly, unfolding like a rusted training golem before making some half-hearted goodbyes. A sudden shaking came over her, and she pulled her cloak close to ward off the night's chill before she headed for the copse of trees where her tent was set up.

"I have concerns about our ranger," Jynn murmured once the Elf was out of sight.

"Aye," said Gorm. Kaitha hadn't been herself for a while, but over the past day whatever condition she was in had deteriorated. "Do ye suppose she's sick?"

"I didn't think Elves got sick," said Heraldin.

Laruna opened her mouth to say something, but then shook her head. "Maybe it's the wine," she muttered.

"She didn't have any," Jynn countered.

"Maybe that's the problem," said Gorm. "Let's talk to her about it in the morning. Perhaps a good night's sleep will improve things."

"It's getting worse," murmured Kaitha. "I can't sleep."

"What is it?"

"Nothing." Kaitha sat up in her bedroll. The moonlight outside shone through the fabric of her tent, casting her pack and gear in sapphire hues. The camp outside the tent was silent.

And then there was…

Kaitha shook her head. "It's nothing."

"Oh, come on. It isn't nothing. You can tell me."

"Well, there's a turtle in my tent," said Kaitha.

"Tortoise," said the tortoise.

"Right, sorry," said Kaitha. "There's a tortoise in my tent. And most tortoises I've encountered didn't glow blue or float in the air. Or talk."

"Maybe I'm your spirit animal," suggested the tortoise.

"Like the ones that guided the old Elves on their… things?" Kaitha blinked a few times. It was hard to find the things. Words.

"Spirit journeys?"

"Yeah. Those. Are you here to guide me on a spirit journey?"

"Why not?" said the tortoise. "Come on. Let's go."

"I'll… wait, no, I can't." Kaitha shook her head. "We're on a mission. We've got to stop Jynn's father from… being a liche? Doing something bad. And then help the Orcs after that, I think. Something."

"Well, all the more reason to go on a spirit journey," said the tortoise. "Taking time for self-discovery can lead you to an epiphany that unlocks your true potential."

Kaitha rubbed her eyes. "What?"

"Come on," said the tortoise, already floating toward the tent flap.

"Yeah, all right," said Kaitha. "Just let me get… I need my stuff… gear. Let me put on my armor."

"Kaitha," said the tortoise. "Do you really think weapons and armor will help you on a spirit journey?"

The ranger thought about it. "No, I suppose not," she said. "That'd be ridiculous."

"Exactly. Come on." The tortoise slipped through the tent door.

Kaitha grabbed a cloak and slipped from her tent into the cold evening. The stars were still winking into sight across the deep blue sky. To the southwest, she could see the orange glow of the fading cookfire through the trees. She turned and walked north, relishing the cool mud on her bare feet.

"We need to hurry," she told the tortoise. "We're only a day away from… from Highwatch." She gestured southeast, where the mountains blotted out the stars on the horizon.

"Don't worry about that," the tortoise reassured her as it floated north. "Focus on reaching your full potential. On finding that epiphany that leads to inner peace."

"Okay." Kaitha took a deep breath. "Epiphany."

They wandered across the moonlit countryside for what seemed like hours. Her cloak offered a little protection from the cold, and she clutched it tightly around herself. The small tortoise hovered by her shoulder, rambling on about the finer points of spiritual awakening.

As they journeyed onward, though, her thoughts cleared. The crisp air felt good in her nostrils and lungs, and the more she breathed it in, the less she noticed the chill. Her limbs filled with warmth and energy, giving her steps a renewed vigor. By the time she saw the first hint of dawn's light on the eastern horizon, she was practically dancing over the grassland.

"Feeling good?" asked the tortoise.

"I feel great," said Kaitha. "Though, you know, I thought a spirit journey would be different."

"I'm glad," said the tortoise, beaming. "But what were you expecting?"

"Well, in all the stories about spirit journeys that I've heard, the Elves encounter different animal spirits that ask insightful questions. And that's what drives the Elf toward introspection and then enlightenment. So I just assumed, you know, that we'd meet a bear or a fox or something out here."

"So far, I'm it," said the tortoise. "I could try asking you personal questions?"

"Sounds good," said Kaitha, leaping over a small stream.

"All right," said the tortoise. "Have you been thinking about healing potions much lately?"

"Oh, that's what this is about?" Kaitha's mood curdled. "You dragged me all the way out here to have a talk about salve?"

"Haven't you been pulling away from your friends lately?" asked the tortoise. "Haven't you been sore and hurting for days, only thinking about getting more potions?"

"I like potions," said Kaitha. "I want them because they're fun, not because I need them. I could stop if I wanted to."

"Remember the salve-heads you saw when Leiry sent you to Lady Fjord's Gardens of Recovery for your drinking?" asked the tortoise. "Didn't they say the same thing?"

"I am not like the salve-heads!" snarled Kaitha. "Listen, these questions aren't very insightful. I'm going to go talk to that spirit falcon instead."

"No, no," said the glowing green falcon, alighting on a nearby stump. "I think the tortoise has a point."

"It's time to admit you have a problem," said the tortoise. "That's the first step to recovery."

Kaitha sighed. "Fine," she hissed through her teeth. "I have a little problem with salve. And it's bothering me because I haven't gone this long without a kick in… in a long time. I was supposed to get some in Andarun, but now I just need to get a potion so I can make it through this battle at Highwatch and save the world. Then I'll check into Lady Fjord's and take care of my… little issue."

"Did I say 'little'?" said the tortoise.

"You didn't say 'little,'" said the falcon.

"Because I heard her say 'little,'" The tortoise floated over to hover beside his avian counterpart.

"She said 'little' twice," said the falcon.

"I didn't think I came here to talk about a 'little' problem," said the tortoise.

"You didn't say little," reiterated the falcon.

"Let me be clear," said the tortoise, turning back to Kaitha. "You have a huge problem with healing potions. A healing potion crisis, really. And you know you do, because you saw what the elixir addicts went through at Lady Fjord's when they stopped getting kicks."

"Reduced social interactions," said the falcon. "Trouble concentrating. Sallow complexion."

"Sound familiar?" said the tortoise.

"I... there are... it's..."

"The worst part comes after the shakes," the falcon said to the tortoise.

"Oh, it's awful," agreed the tortoise. He looked to Kaitha. "You remember the final stage of elixir withdrawal?"

"Hallucinations," said Kaitha. Icy fear hit her in the gut.

"And delusions," said the falcon.

"Like talking spirit animals," said the tortoise.

"I'm hallucinating," said Kaitha. "And now I've wandered off... and all my weapons and armor, and oh gods. I... I..."

"Yes?" said the tortoise.

"I have a huge problem with salve," sobbed Kaitha.

The tortoise nodded sagely. "Good. Good. Now remember that on the other side of withdrawal. Admitting your problem is the first step to recovery."

The falcon spread its wings as the tortoise started slowly ascending.

"Wait!" cried Kaitha. "Don't just leave me out here!"

"Sorry, but you've had your epiphany!" said the tortoise. "I've helped you all I can. Now it's up to you to follow your path and reach your true potential. Besides, I don't want to be here for what comes next."

"Oh yeah," said the falcon. "Things are about to get weird."

"Really weird," agreed the luminous tortoise. "Hey, where are you headed anyway?"

"There's a shaman up in House Galantia that just ate a bowl of night mushrooms," said the falcon. "I'm going to go have a talk with him about his relationship with his father."

"Sounds fun. Mind if I come with?" The tortoise was ascending rapidly now, keeping pace with the falcon as it flapped away into the sky.

"Not at all. I'd welcome the company," said the falcon.

"Wait!" Kaitha shouted after the retreating spirit animals. "I need help!"

"And now that you've recognized that, you're ready to move forward!" the tortoise called back to her. "Good work!"

"No, I mean your help!" cried Kaitha. "Help getting back to camp!"

"Some journeys you must walk alone," yelled the tortoise, now merely a blue dot among the fading stars. "Or something like that."

"Close enough," said the falcon.

Then they were gone, disappearing into a sky that was starting to melt and run down over the plains. The moon opened its great eye, and its laughter summoned spider-squids with tongues of flame from the earth and water. Sobbing and screaming, Kaitha turned and fled into a nightmare.

Chapter 14

Gorm awoke with a cold sweat on his brow and a scream in his throat. His fists were clenched and his knuckles white as he thrashed into a sitting position. Blood pounded in his ears so hard it sounded like a roaring beast.

"Keep it down," said a voice beside him, prompting another yell from Gorm. Burt was standing atop his rucksack.

"Oh," said Gorm. "It's ye."

"'Oh, welcome back, Burt,'" the Kobold pantomimed. "'Haven't seen you in a week, Burt. Sorry I abandoned you in the wilderness, Burt.'"

Gorm rubbed his temple, as if to dislodge the last of his memories. Inky black tentacles still swam in his mind's eye, and he could almost hear the echoes of Az'Anon's laughter. "Aye, sorry... Sorry. I just had the most terrible dream."

"Yeah, things aren't too much better out there, either," said the Kobold, jabbing a thumb over his shoulder at the tent flap. "They could use your help."

Gorm paused to listen. His heart's pounding had slowed a bit, but the roaring sound remained. And now it was punctuated by the shouts of his party. "Bones," he swore, scrambling for the tent flap.

The wan light of an oncoming dawn filtered into the campsite. Heraldin and Gaist stood stiffly by the dying remnants of the cookfire, weapons drawn, while the mages tried to calm them with outstretched hands and presumably reassuring words. It was difficult to make out what they were saying, however, as there was a Troll storming around the camp.

"Gone!" bellowed Thane, running in panicked circles. "She's gone!"

"Gorm!" shouted Heraldin, wearing a forced grin as he turned to the Dwarf. "Jynn and Laruna say you might offer some explanation for this."

"In a minute," said Gorm, marching past the other heroes. "Thane!"

The Troll stopped in his tracks, wild eyes focusing on the Dwarf. Something primal in Gorm shoved his heart into his throat. Friend or not, staring down a furious Troll was enough to freeze the blood. He took a deep breath. "Thane, it's me, Gorm."

"She's gone," said Thane. "Gorm, she's gone."

"Kaitha's left?" Gorm turned to the other heroes.

"That seems to be the matter at hand, yes," said Jynn.

"One of them," said Heraldin, eyes never leaving the Troll.

"And she left her weapons and armor behind," said Laruna, holding up a bow and quiver.

"Why would she do that?" Gorm shook his head. "But we'll find her. We will."

The Troll nodded. He was still breathing heavily as he sat back on his haunches.

Heraldin seized Gorm's arm. "You knew about this?" he hissed.

"Aye. Thane's been protecting us for a long time now. But we got bigger problems to deal with." Gorm brushed the bard's hand aside, along with his comments.

"Bigger? This one's twice as tall as a man and just destroyed our campsite!" said the bard. "I thought we trusted each other!"

Gorm raised his eyebrows in reply.

"Okay, fair enough," conceded the bard. "But I thought we weren't keeping these sorts of secrets, at least! Right?" The bard looked back at the weaponsmaster.

Gaist shrugged.

"We'll talk about it later. Our ranger's gone missing in the wilderness, unarmed," Gorm told the bard.

"We have to find her!" fretted the Troll.

"This isn't something you just shrug off," snarled the bard.

"It sure as fire ain't something you'll make me talk about while the lass is missing," snapped Gorm.

"She needs her potions!" said Thane.

"Aye." Gorm gestured to the Troll. "She needs her — wait, what now?"

"These," said Thane, reaching into his pouch. He pulled out a couple of vials of elixir and handed them to Gorm. "I hate it when she takes them—she has to cut her arms, and then it's like she's not herself. But if I don't let her have any for too long, she shakes and acts strange."

"So ye bought her healing potions?" asked Gorm.

"No! Of course not," insisted the Troll. "She finds them on her own, gods know how. I've... I've just been keeping the potions from her unless she really needs one."

"How?" demanded Jynn.

"Ah, well, I am sorry about this part," said Thane, scratching the fur on the back of his head. He pulled another fistful of vials from his pouch, and then a third. Soon a mound of bottles of elixir lay at Gorm's feet. "I've been... managing the party supply. I make sure the only potions available are what's needed. And I keep the rest safe."

"Okay, I didn't know anything about that," Gorm told Heraldin.

"Do you think that makes it any better?" said the bard.

"I think I knew," said Laruna quietly. "Well, not that Thane was hoarding salve. But I've suspected Kaitha had a problem with healing potions since we left Vetchell."

"Why didn't ye say something?" asked Gorm.

"Well, if that isn't the Orc calling the Goblin green," said the bard. "Her addiction might have come to light earlier if your Troll here wasn't keeping her in supply."

Thane turned away as though struck in the face. "I'm... I'm sorry."

Jynn took Laruna's hand in his own. "Listen, I'm sure we all realize that it's best not to keep secrets from the party," said Jynn. "I learned that lesson myself a year ago. But we need to focus on what's important now. Kaitha is likely suffering from withdrawal from elixir. She could be hallucinating, or delusional, or..." He trailed off, and the silence spoke volumes.

"Aye," said Gorm grimly. "We all know what it could be."

"So we go after her," said Heraldin.

"Just like that?" Burt's hackles rose. "You couldn't wait an hour for the Kobold and Troll to get back to camp, but you're just going to drop everything to charge after the Elf?"

"Burt has a point," said Gorm.

"Thank you!" said the Kobold.

Gorm shook his head. "Much as I hate to say it, the undead could reach the fortress gates any day now, and if Laruna ain't there with that fancy staff, the whole world's at risk."

"That wasn't the point!" Burt barked.

"We can't just leave Kaitha," said the solamancer firmly.

"I know, but we can't just abandon our quest," said Jynn.

"So, what?" said Heraldin. "We split the party?"

"We can't split the party. Not any more than it has been," said Gorm. "But without our ranger, there's only one of us with any chance of trackin' Kaitha through the wilderness."

The adventurers looked as one to the Troll, who looked uncomfortable with the sudden attention. "I... I don't know if I can do it—"

"Ye found us, didn't ye?" said Gorm. "You're the only one who can bring her back safe."

The Troll hesitated. "But when she sees me, she might... what if she—"

"And what if you don't go?" asked Laruna, pressing Kaitha's bow and quiver into the Troll's hands.

Thane stared at the ground and took a deep breath. When he looked back up, any traces of indecision on his gnarled face had melted away, leaving only stony resolution. "I'll do it," he said.

Gorm looked east, where the glow of dawn had set the edge of the mountains ablaze. "Good," he said. "Ye best get moving. We all should, for that matter. We've got to make for Highwatch."

"I know they're making for Highwatch," said Garold Flinn. "The question is, how are they moving so fast?"

The mechanical gazer chittered softly—a sibilant chatter produced by the muffled prattling of the sprites encased within Barty's hideous creation. The construct had seven tentacles made from interlocking plates, each terminating in a glass orb that contained an enchanted sprite of some variety—search sprites, sentry sprites, pathfinder sprites. The seven arms connected to a brass orb, featureless save for a pair of whirling propellers and a large porthole, luminous with the glow of additional sprites fluttering among the gears within.

A hatch approximating a mouth swiveled downward. The tiny shouts of trapped sprites strung together in a high-pitched cacophony, but Flinn could catch a few words above the din. "Don't know!... Teleportation?... It's probably magic!... Elven horses?... Giant eagles!"

"Enough," said Flinn, waving a hand.

The little flying construct shut its hatch obediently and hovered over to the unit of combat golems. The twelve sorcerous constructs kept pace with the assassins' horses, striding along in their odd, four-legged gait. Flinn wished he could send the rest of Barty's golems ahead to scout, but Mr. Ficer had a certain *modus remotus operandi* that mandated the engineer remain safely in Andarun and left his combat golems unable to do much beyond their basic murder protocols.

"The liche might do our work for us," said Deathbloom.

"Do our contracts have an undeath clause?" asked Udina.

Flinn pursed his lips. "No, I have it on good authority that the undead will fall swiftly. And even if they got to Mr. Ingerson beforehand, the Dwarf has a habit of surviving circumstances that he shouldn't. We'll need proof that he and his companions are dead."

Captain Jones pulled up beside the Tinderkin. "Yarr, that may be, but if'n we, uh, sail too close to the reefs of the damned—"

"Just say it like a normal person," sighed Flinn.

"If we get too close to the thrice-cursed undead, they may do Ingerson's work for him," said Captain Jones.

"I've no desire to face Detarr Ur'Mayan," said Mortus.

Neither did Mr. Flinn. Then again, he'd seen what Johan the Mighty was capable of, and he'd set himself against anything living or dead before he'd get on the wrong side of the paladin. He gave the other assassins a tight smile. "All the more reason to make haste."

"That's right. You'd best get moving, fast," said the bannerman. "You won't get in here. Nobody gets into Highwatch."

"Ye've said as much," said Gorm. "But ye need to listen!"

"We can stop the liche," Jynn said.

The guard's face wasn't discernible through the slot in the ironbound door, but he managed to effectively convey a smirk nonetheless. "Oh, so the five of you have the key to stopping the undead? I suppose the fate of the whole world depends on you right now?"

"Um, yes," said Laruna.

"Yeah, same as every one of the thousand heroes up on the walls," said the bannerman. "You know how many times I've heard this spiel in the past three days?"

Heraldin raised a hand. "But—"

"Listen, everybody wants a shot at the loot and the points that are gonna flow when the undead finally fall. And everybody thinks they're the chosen ones who finally found the secret to bringing down the liche," said the bannerman wearily. "But everybody else has a corporate sponsor, and a contract to fulfill the quest, and arrived with His Majesty's army as requested by the Heroes' Guild. So if you want me to open this door, you had better have a remarkably good reason."

Gorm hesitated. Talking about the Wyrmwood Staff would be tantamount to confessing to robbing the Museum of Andarun. He couldn't imagine many worse places for the crime to come to light than in a massive fortress full of bannermen and guild heroes. "Er, it's… our destiny?" he tried.

"Right. Look, the undead will arrive by nightfall. You could be nearly a day's ride away from Highwatch by then. And that's exactly what I would do in your shoes. But if you want to stick yourself between the liche and the walls, that's your problem. So long as you sod off!" said the bannerman. The slot in the door snapped shut.

"And so here we are, locked out in the middle of nowhere with the undead bearing down on us," said Heraldin, throwing his arms in the air.

"Don't be so dramatic," said Jynn.

"First of all, being dramatic is my job. I am a bard."

"It's easy to forget, given the way you play the lute," said Laruna.

"Hurtful. And second," continued Heraldin, "this is exactly where I expected to wind up."

"Don't matter now. We need a new plan," said Gorm.

"We could break down the gate," suggested Laruna. "Force our way in and then try to sneak up to the ramparts in the confusion."

Gorm looked up at the wall in front of them, as tall and unassailable as the mountain cliffs around it. The banners on the fortress' towers looked like ship sails on a vertical horizon. He shook his head. "Nobody's ever forced their way into Highwatch, lass, and plenty of armies have tried. This is just the door to the gatehouse. There's a bigger gate behind it, and a hundred more in the tunnels beneath the fortress. We'd get nowhere."

"Well, we can't take the undead on from down here," said Laruna. "We'll be trapped with our backs to the wall."

"I think I know a way," said Burt, poking his head out of Gorm's rucksack. "Or at least, I know about a way."

"A way into Highwatch?" asked Laruna.

"Well, no. But almost as good," said Burt. "See, our legends say that Kobolds used to live in the mountains south of Highwatch. Back when heroics was still more of a hobby than a profession, Humans and Dwarves used to run quests to drive out the Highwall tribes and loot their lairs. So this one Kobold, Ratrup, decides he's sick of his people getting murdered and robbed. He and his warriors make a path up the mountain next to Highwatch and set up their own fort there. From there he could keep an eye on Highwatch and warn the other Kobolds when any adventurers were riding out to quest."

"I'm not familiar with that story," said Heraldin.

Burt snorted. "And how many Kobold legends do you know?"

"Fair enough," said Heraldin.

"Still, I'm not sure we should go chasing after it," said Laruna. "Even if the legends are true and Ratrup did build a fort, there's no way to know if it's still around."

"Of course there ain't," said Burt. "It's not like anyone's been there since back in the Sixth Age. The Highwall tribes got driven out long ago, and nobody's left to care what the Lightlings are doing in Highwatch. But Ratrup's path might still be there, and if it can get you to a good, defensible point with line of sight to the battle, maybe you can, I don't know. Do whatever it is that staff does."

"It's a chance, at least," said Gorm.

"A slim one," said Jynn.

"That's as good as we ever get these days." Gorm set off. "Let's go."

The adventurers led their horses down the winding path away from Highwatch's western gate toward the scrublands at the base of the mountains. They mounted and rode south once they reached the foot of the mountain, making their way around the rocks and crevasses along the edge of the Highwalls.

Burt gave up his spot in Gorm's rucksack to ride in the saddle in front of the Dwarf. The Kobold's misshapen ears were perked up and alert. His long tongue flapped in the wind as the horse raced through the low brush.

It was nearly noon when the Kobold leapt up, his tail wagging furiously. "There! Right there!"

"Hold up!" hollered Gorm, raising a hand.

Burt led them a short way up the side of the mountain to a large boulder with several smooth stones piled atop it. At its foot, they found a stake in the ground with a rusted chain dangling from it.

"This marker probably used to have a bunch of bones and skulls around it," said Burt. He scratched at the ground and sniffed. "And Kobolds have been here since Ratrup's day. A group came through a few years back. The path to Ratrup's watch must be nearby."

"There," said Laruna, pointing to a cleft in the rocks a few dozen yards up the mountains. Looking at the crack from a specific angle, the heroes could see a small, gravelly path winding up the mountainside before it disappeared around a bend.

"That's it! We've found it!" said Burt. He sidled up to the small marker by the boulder and started to untie the drawstring of his trousers. "Now, hang on a second. I gotta do a thing."

"What are ye—ah, bones, Burt!" Gorm turned away and shut his eyes tightly. The other adventurers groaned and shook their heads as they headed for the trail.

"Oh, grow up!" Burt called over his shoulder. "I'm letting future Kobolds know I was here."

"So carve a note into a tree trunk," said Laruna, already stepping through the cleft in the rock.

"Hey! Wait up! I'm almost finished!" Burt yelled.

The stream of heroes pouring into Haertswood had dried up in the first days of Dawngreen.

The city was, by all accounts, little more than a support system for the massive Heroes' Guild office that dominated the center of town. Yet despite being the Freedlands' easternmost bastion of professional heroics, Haertswood usually had remarkably few heroes in residence.

Adventurers were financially motivated to spend more time dungeon spelunking or ranging in the field than doing paperwork. When a particularly important quest was launched from the Haertswood guildhall, the city's population swelled to the bursting point. When fame and fortune were better sought elsewhere, Haertswood shrank back down to a ghost town, populated by clerks, shopkeepers, and the odd hero popping in for an eye exam.

Once soldiers and adventurers sent to fight the undead moved on to Highwatch, the guildhall was largely silent. Clerks and laborers quietly prepared the ledgers and loading bays for a sudden influx of ectoplasm-soaked loot. Calm and quiet had returned to the sleepy town.

And then the Red Horde came.

It was a host out of the Agekeepers' histories, the sort of giant warband that Mannon once set out against the great Elven cities. The Shadowkin aptly referred to such an army as *zabbarundar,* or a "Great Storm;" the army of raiders spread out over the plains of Aberreth like a thunderhead, and their arrows and slingstones fell like rain. Orcs, Goblins, Gnolls, Kobolds, Slaugh, Gremlins, Ogres, and even a few Naga scaled the walls and flooded into the city streets. The defenders, such as they were, barely had time to ring the warning bells before they were overwhelmed, and the fight, such as it was, ended before most of the invaders had seen a foe.

Shortly thereafter a smaller, yet equally intense, fight broke out in a back office of Haertswood's former guildhall.

"You always do this!" growled Darak, trying to contain his growing fury. *"You have done such since we were whelps!"*

"I am truly sorry, my chieftain." Asherzu put a sardonic spin on the honorific, turning her brother's title into a metaphorical tweak in the ear.

There is a particular rage that only a sibling can inspire, and it bloomed across Darak's deep green features. *"Why must you dishonor me so? And do not feign ignorance like some simpering Gnome!"*

There is also a particular delight that can only be attained by irking a sibling, and it took all of Asherzu's will to hide it. *"I do not know what you speak of, honored chieftain."*

"You know exactly what I speak of!" snarled Darak. *"I brought you on this raid to show the Guz'Varda that we remain unified, and yet you have done nothing but sow discontent among the ranks!"*

Now Asherzu felt her own blood rising in her cheeks. *"I did nothing of the sort!"* she hissed. *"The Guz'Varda came to me with their own concerns, as did many other warriors. They wondered where the honor is in attacking an empty town, or why we would risk ourselves for so little plunder. I did not tell our people what to think! I warned you of their thoughts!"*

"In view of my generals! In the presence of Grignot and his warriors!" Darak shook his head. *"You are supposed to be a wise-one now! Do you know nothing of command and power? Your words make me look weak!"*

"You make yourself look weak when you fawn over that snake!" Asherzu snapped back. *"Your people are frightened and unhappy, and all you care about are the thoughts of Grignot and his fools!"*

"Enough!" hissed the chieftain. *"All I care about is family. Father's people, Char's legacy, the memories of Challu, Derdod'zu, and Frak. And always your well-being! Everything I do is for us! Everything! And you still dishonor me and treat me as a child!"*

Asherzu glimpsed the brother she helped raise in the lord of the Red Horde's rage. *"I... I am sorry —"*

"No!" Darak hissed. *"No more! There is much to do, and we must be away soon. I cannot have you making more trouble for me. Seek me out when you can speak without shaming our family!"* With that, the chieftain kicked the door open and stalked out into the hallway.

Asherzu exhaled through her fangs and kicked idly at an overturned filing cabinet. There was nothing to be done when Darak had set his mind to something. Her brother's stubbornness had earned the pet name "Little Warg" when he was but a whelp, and just as with warg pups, his tenacity had become less endearing with time.

She shook her head and reminded herself that this wasn't all her brother's fault, especially when it was apparent that Grignot was taking over the tribe.

Jorruk once told a young Asherzu that a weak mind is a malleable one. Once it is convinced it has been lied to, it begins to lie to itself. Once persuaded that it is hated, it becomes hateful. Once made to fear violence, it becomes violent.

Now the Orcess saw the unfortunate truth of Jorruk's wisdom all too well. Grignot's constant raving about the Lightlings' evils was twisting the Red Horde into the murderous caricatures that they claimed to stand against. And while most Shadowkin she knew saw his warped fantasies for what they were, they had something more tangible to fear: the Horde was becoming less tolerant of dissent by the day. Asherzu's station as the chieftain's sister had inoculated her against recrimination thus far, but there was no telling how long Darak could protect her. Or if he even wanted to…

Asherzu shook the foul thought from her head. Darak was comprised entirely of muscle and loyalty, and for all her brother's flaws, she knew she could depend on him.

A horn in the distance snapped her from her reflections. Like the great storms the *zabbarundar* was named for, the warband never stayed in one place for long. It arrived like thunder, it struck like lightning, and it was away like the wind, ideally with heaps of plunder in its collective arms.

Darak would be happier if she returned with at least a little loot; Asherzu had refused to take part in any killing, but she could pillage a bit for show. She was scanning the room for something of apparent value when a familiar face caught her eye.

The poster on the far wall clearly bore a portrait of Gorm Ingerson, and it was labeled with his name, but the text below it promised a huge sum of money for his capture. It was surrounded by several other portraits, most of which were recognizable as Gorm's treacherous band, save the horrifying woodcut on the poster labeled Heraldin Strummons. More shocking than the bard's hideous features, however, were the descriptions of the party's crimes. All of the posters accused the guild heroes of colluding with the Orcs of Bloodroot to murder Niln of the Al'Matrans.

Asherzu pulled the posters from the wall and read them again. These were clearly the heroes she remembered from her father's last days, but they had never spoken an ill word of Niln. The Orcs had thought of Gorm, Niln, and their party as friends when they'd parted, and that opinion hadn't changed until the guild heroes came and made Gorm's betrayal apparent.

Had Gorm betrayed Niln and the Heroes' Guild? But if so, why would the posters implicate the Orcs as well? Why would the guild invent a crime for a band of criminals?

A second blast of the horn reminded Asherzu that she needed to hurry. Any reflections on Gorm's betrayal would have to wait. She tucked the posters into her satchel, grabbed a valuable-looking urn from the top of a desk, and ran out to join the rest of the *zabbarundar*.

"The what?" shouted Handor.

"I said a great storm, Your Majesty." Johan reached over the king's shoulder to point at looming thunderclouds on the eastern horizon.

"Perfect," grumbled Handor, looking at the dark clouds. He gripped his pommel tightly as the Great Eagle veered in the wind.

Handor hated flying. He hated seeing the ground whisk by below his mount, and he really hated the deadly space between him and that ground. He'd thought flying at night might be better, but as it turned out, blurring the world into a black and blue smear speeding beneath him did little for his nerves. Icy wind burned across his face, and the straps of his flight goggles whipped at his skin.

"We'll beat it. Look!" Johan hollered from the back of the double saddle. The paladin pointed again, this time to a flicker of lights in the mountain. Highwatch.

The Highwalls were aptly named, as their craggy peaks were marked by sheer cliffs that rose to dizzying heights above the plains and forests. At their northernmost tip sat Highwatch, a mountain fortress that was more like a fortified mountain.

Handor nodded, trying to wiggle the numbness out of his extremities and willing the eagle to descend faster.

Eventually, he could make out the shape of Highwatch's inner courtyard, outlined in torches and flaming braziers. Much of the fortress was separated from the surrounding mountains by a black chasm. According to Johan, the only way to the keep was through the tunnels and hallways beneath the fortress, all controlled by a complex series of interlocking gates.

"We'll be landing soon, sire!" Johan yelled.

Those riding the other Great Eagles in the flock couldn't be heard at all; Handor could only just see them in the gloom of the moonlight. Dannel Clubs appeared to be talking incessantly to Weaver Ortson atop the eagle to his left. On his other side, Goldson and Baggs sat in stoic silence; Handor started when he realized that they were both reading small ledgers propped up on their saddles.

"The orbs!" Johan called, pointing.

Handor wiped his goggles and looked again. Now he could see the great, green orbs set up along the stone ramparts of the outer wall. Bannermen and Umbraxian workers scurried around them, finalizing preparations. He spotted a couple orbs set up in the courtyard, likely a precaution against the unthinkable.

"Seems to be coming along nicely," the paladin yelled.

Handor nodded.

The Great Eagles carrying the king's guard were already touching down on the top of the inner keep. Handor watched the bannermen and heroes fan out and form a perimeter as his own eagle finally swooped in to land.

"I trust Your Majesty's flight was a good one," said Fenrir Goldson as Johan helped the king dismount.

"Yes, fine, wonderful," grumbled Handor. It perturbed the king that everyone else seemed to enjoy flying so much; they focused on the sensation of being in the air, the speed at which you traveled, the majesty of the eagles. Handor didn't think any of that justified the terror of the ground beneath him, the nausea of rising and falling so suddenly, and the frozen snot that encrusted his whiskers after a ride in the icy air.

"We shall have to invite you to fly out of the city with us more often," said Bolbi Baggs, stepping down beside Goldson.

"And under happier circumstances," said Goldson.

"Certainly, certainly." Handor tried to discreetly clean his facial hair. He found a handy distraction in Weaver Ortson plodding up to them. "Ortson, I'm surprised your heroes don't use these all the time."

"Sire?" The loose straps of Ortson's goggles slapped his face as he looked around in confusion.

"The eagles, Ortson. One can imagine uses for Great Eagles on just about any quest the Heroes' Guild could undertake." Handor nodded to his eagle. It eyed him dispassionately before preening its neck. "Why, how many strange and dangerous journeys could heroes skip if Great Eagles were on hand to carry them to any destination? And what danger could they not escape if the eagles were waiting to sweep them away? I should think you'd want to employ the birds all the time."

"And we would, sire, believe me," said Ortson. "But the accursed creatures have unionized."

"Unionized?" Handor stopped brushing his mustache.

Handor's eagle made a satisfied clicking noise.

"Oh, yes, sire. The United Avian Workers dictates all the terms when it comes to hiring Great Eagles for any job. Giant Falcons and Dire Hawks as well. And once you factor in overtime and hazard pay, there's no way we could afford to have them on anything but a fraction of our quests."

"A pity," said Goldson.

The eagle gave a high-pitched cry.

"Yes, you can go on your thrice-cursed break!" snapped Ortson. "Twenty minutes, and not a moment longer."

The eagles snapped their beaks at the grandmaster, but collectively shuffled off toward the far corner of the keep.

"This way, Your Majesty," said Johan. "The heralds are announcing you now."

"Very well." Handor headed across the flat roof to a small, raised platform. Aides and attendants helped him remove his goggles and flight helmet as he walked, and a circlet was placed on his head as he stepped onto the dais. Below and all around him, bannermen looked up from their duties expectantly. He hadn't prepared a speech, and he didn't understand the tactics, but he was more than familiar with appeals to blind patriotism.

"For Andarun!" he hollered, thrusting a bony fist into the air. "For the Freedlands!"

"For Andarun!" the bannermen echoed, raising their weapons in reply. "For the King!" Yet the cry faded as quickly as it was raised.

"Well said, sire," said Johan.

"Perhaps," said Handor. "That sort of thing usually gets them cheering and singing for at least a few minutes."

General Gurgen, high commander of the bannermen, stepped forward. She was an ex-hero, with one gray eye and a nose that still looked broken in a few places. Her hair was cropped short and her suit of silver armor was scratched and dented. "You must pardon them, Majesty," she said in a low, crackling voice. "They have other things on their mind." She nodded to the horizon.

Handor turned, and his insides turned to jelly. At first it looked like the storm clouds were casting black shadows over the Ruskan landscape, but then he saw the glowing specters twisting above the black tide. A vast army crept over the land like a foul mold overtaking a carcass.

"Bones," he swore.

"Indeed, sire," said the general. "The liche's force is at least three times the size of our own, though there's no way to know if we've yet seen the end of their numbers. It is a threat unlike anything we've seen in our lifetime."

"When will they attack?" Handor's lips were dry and his belly had turned to soup.

"They should reach the walls by midnight, if our scouts are correct. I doubt they'll wait for dawn to attack. You can be certain that some of those soldiers are going to die tonight." She thought for a moment, and added, "More than once, in some cases."

"I see," said Handor, mustering his courage. "And... and do you think we'll carry the day?"

The general considered the question carefully before nodding. "I do," she said.

"We have the orbs, after all," said Baggs.

"They're very, very good orbs," said Clubs. "The best! And they're going to—"

Ortson mercifully cut the blathering businessman off. "And we have the best of the guild's heroes assembled here."

"Plus, we have a greater power on our side," added Johan.

Goldson and Baggs rolled their eyes, and Handor could understand why. The king often surmised that Tandos must truly be a god of the people, because his champion always seemed to find religion in public places.

"Those are all well and good," said General Gurgen. "But we'll carry the day because we're in Highwatch. In war after war, for ages upon ages, this fortress has never fallen."

King Handor watched the coming darkness on the horizon. "Let us hope that you are right, general. Gods help us if it falls now."

Chapter 15

Gorm seldom invoked the gods. It wasn't that he didn't believe that the pantheon could or would involve themselves in the affairs of Man; it was that, historically speaking, everything always got much more convoluted and dangerous when they did. As a general rule, he tried not to bother any deities in the hope that they would return the favor.

Heights, however, inspired a bit of piety in the Dwarf, if not propriety. He muttered prayers and curses in equal measure as he pressed his body against the stone of the cliff. Below him, the narrow path dropped away into a craggy abyss.

"Come on, Gorm," urged Laruna from the other side of the chasm.

"You can do this," added Jynn.

The problem with Burt's plan was that Ratrup's pathway up the Highwalls was intended for Kobolds, and therefore was engineered for someone less than a quarter of Gorm's size. The trail led into passages so narrow that the heroes had to crawl on their bellies. It brought them through ravines so tight they had to walk sideways. But worst of all were the narrow pathways that ran along the cliffs, barely as wide as Gorm's boots.

"Thrice… cursed… bloody… fire," the Dwarf grunted, inching his way along the path. With a final push, he leapt and landed belly first on the wider ridge beyond the gulf. For a brief moment he scrabbled at loose rocks, but Gaist grabbed him by the collar and hauled him to relative safety.

Just around the next crag, the trail widened into a large, flat ridge, painted blue and black by long shadows cast in the evening's last light. The fortress of Highwatch dominated the view from the ledge, looming above the heroes even across the mountainous gulf.

"Is this it?" asked Heraldin.

"There doesn't seem to be any more of the path," said Jynn, looking up the mountain.

"What did you expect?" asked Burt. "We're high in the mountains, and we can see Highwatch."

"Ye said there'd be a fort," said Gorm.

"There is. Sort of." Laruna pulled aside some scrub brush to reveal a motley heap of stones, no higher than Gorm's waist, arrayed in a semicircle against the fortress of Highwatch.

"There it is!" said Burt, his tail wagging madly as he ran around the tiny fortification. "Ratrup's Fort! Legends walked where we are now!"

"It's a pile of rocks," said Gorm.

"It ain't—" Burt growled and shook his head. "That ain't just a pile of rocks. It's disguised to look like one, so the Lightlings looking out of Highwatch would think it's harmless."

"Well, it's workin' a little too well then," said Gorm. "'Cause I ain't that far away and even I think it's just a pile—"

"It isn't a pile of rocks!" Burt's hackles were up far enough to give the impression of a ruffled collar.

"When you're through discussing the scenery, we have more pressing matters to attend to," Heraldin said from the easternmost edge of Ratrup's ledge. The bard and Gaist stood on the edge of the cliff, staring out over the Ruskan landscape.

The eastern foothills of the Highwalls teemed with shambling ranks of the walking dead. Beyond that, the blighted grasslands were covered with a seething, black mass of undead illuminated by the occasional glow of erupting Shadowflame.

Gorm turned to Laruna. "Ye ready with that staff?"

The solamancer nodded, her mouth pulled into a tight line. She walked to the edge of the cliff and set the bottom of the Wyrmwood Staff into a small notch in the stone, releasing it with an arcane gesture and a murmured incantation. The staff remained upright, an amber glow emanating from the crystal at its top.

"What does this thing do, anyway?" asked Heraldin.

"Lots of things," said Laruna. "It amplifies power, aids in weaving, provides meta-magical benefits—"

"Yes, yes, that's fine," said the bard. "But I meant here. Now. Specifically, what can it do against that many undead?"

"We don't know, exactly. We're going to use it as a focus for sigils of light and life and find out." Jynn took Laruna's hand in his own as they stared out at the grim army. "Together."

"Whatever happens," the solamancer whispered with a brave smile.

"Whatever happens," said Jynn.

"Whatever happens should happen quick," said Gorm.

"Right." Laruna released Jynn's hand and began to weave.

Wisps of flame flickered into existence around the solamancer's arms, spiraling around her wrists toward her palms, where her fingers deftly twisted them into the beginnings of a spell. Her hair rose up as though carried by the wind, and soon the mage herself lifted off the ground, borne aloft by the currents of magic.

Gorm shivered and adjusted his furs and cloak; a deeper chill settled over the plateau as Laruna's gathering power drew out the last of the warmth in the air. He noticed Burt creeping back away from the mages.

"Off to hide?" he asked Burt.

"Hey, do you know the average life span of a Kobold soldier?" said Burt. "It's one battle."

"I'd heard as much," Gorm said.

"That's why I make a point of attending zero battles. So if you need anything afterward, give me a shout. Otherwise, I'm gonna duck down behind those shrubs and have a smoke."

"Fair enough," said Gorm, turning back to the mages.

Now Laruna wove thick cords of flame into strange sigils, and her eyes glowed with power. She spoke otherworldly litanies in an echoing voice, and Gorm could see that Jynn was mouthing the words along with the solamancer as he looked up at her. When the chant reached its zenith, the solamancer thrust both hands toward the Wyrmwood Staff. Her flaming symbols flew into the staff's crystal, followed by the errant threads whirling around her. The glow in the solamancer's eyes faded and she dropped back to the ground as all the magic nearby was drawn into the sorcerous focus.

They stood and watched the staff for a breathless moment. The glow in its crystal faltered, then faded altogether.

"Did it fail?" said Heraldin.

Gorm scratched his beard. "It must need to—"

The Wyrmwood Staff flared with searing golden light, bright enough to send the heroes stumbling backward. Gorm shut his eyes and dove for cover, but he could still see the blinding, all-consuming luminance.

Tyren surveyed the battlefield from a raised platform. Before him, endless ranks of the dead rolled like a black wave toward the mountain fortress. Beyond the marching ranks, he could see the soldiers and warriors on the walls of Highwatch, staring with grim determination at the approaching force. Some of the figures on the ramparts scuttled around what looked like massive glass spheres, glowing with a wan green light.

"Is everything in order, Knight-Commander?" asked Detarr.

"We launched an hour ago, lord." Tyren turned back to the liche.

"Excellent," said Detarr. "And how goes the campaign?"

The knight-commander glanced down at the clipboard. A grid of figures was scrawled out in the Head of Marketing's handwriting, for lack of a better term. "A disappointing conversion rate, sir."

Detarr looked at Tyren. "And by that you mean…"

Tyren was prepared for the line of inquiry. The key to managing failure was to make it sound like success. "Our forecasts predicted this particular demographic, especially given their geographic location and particular needs, would be very reluctant to embrace our message. So I'm happy to report that we've confirmed our forecasting model to be accurate." It also helped to make everything sound as complicated and technical as possible.

"Well… good," said Detarr without enthusiasm.

Tyren moved on to future successes quickly. "The Head of Marketing is working on the next campaign. We think the fall of Highwatch will give us a powerful message to—"

"Yes, yes, I'm sure it will be grand. It seems the task of taking Highwatch shall fall to… other methods. Are the troops ready, Lady Genevieve?"

"Ready and willing, lord," said Genevieve, hovering in the air above them.

"Great. And your arrangements are ready, Lady Carabae?"

The vampire materialized from the shadows. "Indeed, master."

"Excellent!" The liche nodded happily. "The moment is at hand, yes? Bachopel's Tocatta and Fugue in D-Minor should do nicely."

From behind them, the Gnomish organ roared to life. High, piping notes filled the air.

"Ah, now there we are." Detarr paused for a moment, humming along with the music and counting out the notes. At the height of the piece's exposition, the liche pointed to a brazier on the ground borne by a skeletal construct. A flare of viridian Shadowflame separated from the blaze and rose high into the air, bursting on a high note. Across the battlefield, the undead shambled forward at the signal.

Flashes of light erupted from the ramparts of Highwatch as its defenders sent arrows and spells raining down on the encroaching monsters. Lady Carabae gestured toward the spells. "Master, perhaps it is time to—"

"Almost. Timing is everything." The liche swept his hand back and forth with the deep swells of the music. "And you may give the signal in five… four… three… two—"

A boom like the gods' own cannon rang out, and a wave of searing light washed over the undead legion. The southern half of the front ranks were vaporized in an instant. Ghosts and banshees caught in the blast were reduced to nothing more than traces of ectoplasm and faint wails on the rushing wind.

The blazing light remained even after the shock wave faded, shining like a beacon in the Highwalls south of the fortress. Something about the light held Tyren's gaze as a flame binds a moth's attention, and as he stared he felt a deep terror welling up within him. He could sense the Master's commands in the back of his mind, the Crown of Iron Thorns compelling him to stand firm, but to no avail. The knight-commander took a step back. On the edge of his vision he could see the ranks of the undead breaking apart in open flight, and he heard the banshees and ghosts screeching around him as they retreated.

"Why is it always at the worst possible time?" sighed Detarr.

"What is it?" Tyren backed away from the horrible light.

"A distraction. How fortunate that I have countermeasures," said the liche, rising into the air. "Release the infernal beasts! Lady Carabae, I leave the fortress to you. Knight-Commander! The beasts!"

The last order snapped Tyren from his stupor. He turned and pushed his way through the fleeing mob of undead. Zombies, ghouls, and skeletons all ran from the sight of the agonizing light, and the knight-commander had to fight the tide to reach the large cage.

"Open the cage!" Tyren yelled, staggering toward the door. "Loose the infernal beasts!"

Nobody responded. Ned and Ted had fled with the rest of the dead.

With an unholy growl, Tyren shoved aside a panicked skeleton and fumbled with the latch. Dark shapes stirred in the depths of the cage, lurking shadows that the magical light never seemed to touch.

Then the latch released, and within a split-second the cage door burst open in a sudden wave of fire and heat. The knight-commander fell to the ground as three blazing shapes erupted from the cage and launched into the air. They trailed after the distant liche like fiery comets arcing across the sky.

Lights swam in front of Kaitha's eyes as she ran through waves of glowing grasses, psychedelic colors rolling through the field with every gust of wind. Strange faces leered up at her from the logs and rocks littering her path, and a gibbous moon laughed at her as she fled.

She wasn't sure what was pursuing her. It often sounded like more than one thing, and it certainly had more legs and eyes than any one creature should rightfully possess. At times it looked like a massive, bat-winged scarg, at others a sort of fleshy drake with faces leering from every inch of its skin, and sometimes it seemed just a bubbling

Her pursuer's amorphous nature had initially led Kaitha to believe that it was merely a hallucination of her elixir-deprived mind. But then the first swipe of its arm, or perhaps its tentacle, had connected with enough force to knock her off course. Pain has a way of connecting you to reality, or at least something approximating it. The threat was clear enough.

The ground beneath her swam, catching her leg. With a choked cry she stumbled and rolled through yellow and blue wisps. By the time she righted herself, her pursuer had surrounded her. Or rather, her pursuers.

Their faces were blue and scaled, each with long fangs and no fewer than three eyes. Their bodies ran together like too many slimes pressed into a barrel, but their faces were distinct and grinning with undisguised malice. They pressed in around her, and amid their laughter and gibbering she heard the whispers of steel being drawn from scabbards.

"Go away!" she screamed, closing her eyes and putting her hands over her ears. She could hear her own blood roaring in her veins. "Just go away!"

The first blow came from behind, a hard knock to the back of her head that sent her staggering. A knee caught her in the stomach, knocking the breath from her, and another strike hit her in the shoulder. She lashed back with a right hook that flowed into a high kick, both of which connected firmly. A hard punch slammed into her side, and the uppercut that followed took her off her feet. She landed hard on a field of teeth and bone, the taste of copper and dirt filling her mouth. A scaled hand grabbed her wrist, and another seized her ankles. Kaitha let out a long scream.

To her surprise, the hands let go. She curled into a small ball, still shrieking, and braced herself for an attack that never came. After a while, it occurred to her that she wasn't the only one screaming.

She opened one eye and caught a brief glimpse of one of the blue scaled creatures sailing through the air, its face a mask of terror. A couple of her assailants lay twitching on the ground, bent in places that seemed unnatural even for their strange anatomy. Another attacker ran across her field of vision, but something grabbed the creature mid-stride and pulled it into the air. A moment later its shrieks cut off with a sudden crack.

Kaitha shut her eyes and held her breath. The screams of her remaining pursuers faded in the distance. She heard the ragged breathing of a huge creature and could sense its presence inches from her. Her whole body trembled no matter how she tried to keep still.

She was startled as great hands slipped under her, but they were gentle and soft. Strong arms lifted her slowly, cradling her to a massive, furry chest. She felt the wind in her hair, but the great creature sheltered her body from the chill. She opened one eye, and this time saw a shaggy blue and gray coat of fur and hands the color of stone.

When her eyelid drifted closed again, though, she could see wildflowers and green mosses and an ancient maple tree. For the first time in a long while, she felt safe. "Just like the garden," she murmured.

As hallucinations went, it was as pleasant as she could hope for. She held onto the thought until finally, mercifully, sleep found her.

"No time for lyin' around." Gorm gave the bard's leg a kick. "Get up."

"Did it work?" asked Heraldin, pushing himself to his feet.

"Had an effect, that's for sure." Gorm squinted as he tried to survey the battlefield beyond the brilliant light. "Seems like there's a lot less of the undead out there."

"But did we kill Detarr?" asked Laruna.

"No," said Jynn. The noctomancer pointed to the sky, where four glowing comets were hurtling toward the heroes. "We just made him angry."

The foremost plume of light accelerated. Gorm barked a few orders, but his party was still scrambling to get into formation when Detarr Ur'Mayan arrived in a burst of violet flames. He hovered in the air above the heroes, arms outstretched and shadows dancing from his fingers. "Who dares to stand against—you again?" The liche's grandiose speech slumped into paternal exasperation. "What are you doing here?"

"W-we've come to… t-to… w-we've c-c-c-ome—!" Jynn choked back a stammer.

"It doesn't even matter!" snarled Detarr. "The gods alone know how anyone could blunder into so many of my plans, let alone my son. You're a veritable avatar of Novian philosophy."

Jynn pointed at his father. "You—you can't—"

"You can't possibly have intended to cause all of this chaos, I know. That would require careful preparations, and, well, you see where I'm going with this." Detarr was calm as he descended to the plateau. "I'm more inclined to believe your talent for disrupting my schemes is nothing more than a novice's luck. And as you don't seem to have a serendipitous Troll to rescue you this time, we can surmise that luck has run—"

A sudden blast of golden flame melted through the liche's magical defenses, cutting off his speech and very nearly doing the same to his arm. Detarr recoiled with a hiss.

"Gods, do you ever stop talking?" growled Laruna. She leveled the Wyrmwood Staff at the liche as she advanced on him. The brilliant light had faded from its crystal, but the gem still thrummed with latent power.

"The Wyrmwood Staff of Geffyn?" said Detarr, eyeing Laruna warily. "How did you—well, I suppose it doesn't matter how you found it. It does change things, though."

Laruna fired another volley of sorcery. The liche dodged and returned a blast of violet flames, but she brushed away his attack with a wave of the staff. Detarr followed up with a spell when Laruna was off-balance, but a bolt of noctomancy from Jynn threw the liche off guard again.

Gorm stalked around the edge of the magical battle, looking for an opening to strike. He spotted an opportunity, signaled to Gaist, and made it two steps into his charge when a flaming comet crashed into the stone in front of him. As Gorm leapt back, the black ball at the projectile's blazing center unfolded itself into a hulking form with tusks of iron and bone and a single, baleful eye that glowed like magma.

"I wouldn't say one against five is unfair under these circumstances," Detarr called, dodging a blast of solamancy. "But it does seem inefficient. My infernal beasts will help speed things up."

Gorm took a step back and found himself next to Gaist, who was facing off against what appeared to be a crossbreed of a pit dog and a

Gnomish furnace. "Infernal beasts? Ye ever seen the likes o' these before?"

Gaist shook his head grimly.

"I think the brute force of my netherboar and the fury of my hellhound will be more than a match for the likes of you," said the liche.

"And this one?" said Heraldin, pointing his rapier at some sort of flaming rodent in front of him. "What do you call this little fellow?"

"Ahem, yes. That's, uh, that's the fiendish weasel," said Detarr, with notably less enthusiasm.

"The fiendish weasel?" laughed Heraldin. "Look at his tiny, angry eyes! He's more adorable than—aurarablaugh!"

The fiendish weasel, while indisputably cute, was also remarkably ferocious. It whipped around the bard in an orange blur, a tiny firestorm that left bite marks and burns in its wake.

"I didn't exactly set out to make one," said the liche smugly. "But you know how it is when you're experimenting. Every so often you get one of those happy accidents."

Gorm kept a wary eye on the one-eyed boar. The demonic creature pawed at the stone with an iron hoof, snorting with obvious menace.

"Easy, lad. Easy," said Gorm slowly.

The netherboar loosed a horrible squeal and launched itself toward the Dwarf. Red flames bloomed around the creature as it lifted its hooves from the ground and flew forward, gobbets of magma trailing from its fangs. Gorm feinted, then dove to the left once the boar was too close to correct itself. The beast rushed by in a storm of fire and smoke, sparks flying from its hooves as it attempted to stop. A classic straight-line charge from a creature with no depth perception.

"Easy," Gorm muttered with a small smile. Many low-ranked heroes had been felled by monsters of sufficient speed and size effectively employing a good, old-fashioned trampling, but any experienced hero knew how to deal with such tactics. He sprinted across the battlefield.

As he ran, Gorm caught glimpses of the mages battling Detarr. The noctomancer and solamancer sent coordinated lances of light and shadow at the liche, but Detarr dodged their spells as he flitted through the air. The flame around the elder Ur'Mayan's skull surged in intensity as he wove his own dazzling counterattack—a great web of shadow and lightning that spread across the sky with a crack of thunder. Laruna only just managed to deflect the assault with a burst of light from the Wyrmwood Staff.

Gorm stopped when he was within a few feet of where the stony plateau met the jagged wall of the mountain. As he turned to ready himself, he nearly stepped on the prone figure of Burt crouched behind a gnarled mountain shrub.

"What are you doing?" hissed the Kobold. "Go fight!"

"Ye go and hide!"

"What do you think I'm doing behind this thrice-cursed bush?" snapped Burt.

"Somewhere else!" Gorm roared.

The Kobold scurried away, likely due to the unholy roar of the charging netherboar.

Gorm waited until he saw the red of the boar's eye, and then dove to the side again. He was already up and running as he heard the squeal of fear and the screeching of the iron hooves trying to stop on weatherworn granite. A moment later, however, the netherboar loosed a triumphant bellow as it managed to stop a few inches from ramming into the wall.

"That's right," Gorm muttered as he ran. "Get confident."

Heraldin stumbled into view. The infernal weasel raced around the bard's body like a dancing flame. "The teeth!" the bard cried, wildly swinging his rapier at the tiny figure darting around him. "The tiny, fiery teeth!"

"Out of the way!" Gorm shouted, shouldering the hapless bard out of his path. He could hear the netherboar flying up behind him. Straight ahead, Gaist was locked in combat with the hellhound, his dancing blades flashing amber and crimson in the glow of the infernal beast. "Incoming!"

Gaist caught the Dwarf's eye and gave a hint of a nod.

It was the only signal Gorm needed. He stayed on a collision course until the last possible moment, when he dove to the right with a full-throated scream. "Now!"

The weaponsmaster leapt aside with a flourish of his cloak. On the other side of the garment, the netherboar was doubtlessly surprised to see the hellhound, which itself gave a desperate yip at the sight of the oncoming avalanche of demonic pigflesh.

The squeal of the netherboar and the shriek of its hooves on the stone both cut off with a *hork* as the hellhound lodged headfirst in the pig's wide maw. Thus entangled, the infernal beasts tumbled end over end, choking and yelping until they crashed into the pile of rocks that had previously been known as Ratrup's Fort.

"Hey, watch it!" shouted Burt from wherever he was hiding. "That's a historic site!"

The infernal weasel ceased its assault when it saw the feebly twitching forms of its two companions, and a spark of comprehension appeared within its cute little eyes. With a peal of high-pitched, sinister laughter, the last of the infernal beasts leapt from the stricken bard, launched into the air, and flew away.

"Ye think that did it?" Gorm asked Gaist, staring at the netherboar and hellhound.

The weaponsmaster shrugged and watched Heraldin try to pat out his smoldering clothes.

The prone beasts erupted in a mushroom cloud of flame and dust. Gorm ducked under a flying piece of shrapnel, and when he looked up there was nothing left of the beasts—or Ratrup's Fort—save a scorch mark on the stone.

"Aw, come on!" hollered Burt.

A low rumble, dark and sinister, was audible amidst the sound of the mages' battle. The charred stone began to bubble and bunch, and the smoke coagulated into two small forms, each no bigger than a cook's pot. Gorm saw hints of red eyes and yellowed teeth before the pair flew off into the sky on leathery black wings, still rumbling with horrible laughter.

"What are demons doing here?" asked Gorm, watching the retreating fiends.

"And what is that?" said Heraldin, pointing.

A brown and gray blur was streaking toward where the mages were still locked in sorcerous combat.

"Whatever it is," said Heraldin. "It's headed straight for—"

"Jynn!" Gorm shouted, already running.

Yet his warning was too late. The creature leapt upon the noctomancer, tackling the wizard to the ground. Jynn waved his arms in futile panic as his assailant dove for his face.

"Hang on, lad!" Gorm shouted, readying his axe. "It's a—"

"Dog?" said Laruna.

The magical battle momentarily subsided as Jynn sat back up, a brown and gray mongrel licking his goatee.

"Is… Is that… Patches?" Jynn tried to study the dog's features in between vigorous slurps.

Patches paused his slobbery assault and barked twice, his tail wagging furiously.

"But, how? You were a puppy, and that was over twenty…" Insight flashed in Jynn's eyes, preceding a dark storm cloud that rolled over his face. "You!" he snarled at the liche hovering in the air above him.

"Well, this is… unexpected," Detarr scratched the back of his skull with a bony hand. "And a bit awkward."

"This has something to do with the hellhound, doesn't it?" The noctomancer pushed Patches aside and stood to confront the liche.

"Yes, well, the demise of any soul-bound subject seems to give nearby matter the potential to reconstitute—"

"Yes or no!" snapped Jynn. "Did you turn my dog into a hellhound?"

"I knew you wouldn't handle this well." Detarr sighed. "Technically, I soul-bound Patches to a demon, and then a hellhound was born at some point decades later."

"Y-you killed my p-p-puppy. The pet that you gave me when M-M-Mother died."

The liche avoided the noctomancer's eyes. "Well, I'm not proud of it. The Leviathan Project had run out of funding, you see, and I hadn't any other test subjects, but we really felt we were near a breakthrough…"

"You told me Patches ran away!"

"In my defense, once the experiment began, he did try to—"

"Y-y-you m-monster!" shouted Jynn, hurling a bolt of lightning at his father.

"This reaction? This is why I had to hide things from you," said the liche, dodging easily.

"You a-always s-say I-I ruined this plan or that p-plan—"

"It's not about any one plan," interrupted the liche. "It's that it's all part of a larger pattern."

"B-but you stole from me, k-k-killed my d-dog, and l-lied about it. T-to your own s-son!" Jynn snarled. "You're evil! You always were!"

"Oh, evil? Now you're throwing around those outmoded labels as well?" said the liche, clearly offended. "Did you read any of my work since I was killed? Have you even been to Kesh? No?"

"I-I d-don't need to—"

"That's the problem!" yelled the liche. "You don't listen! You don't even know what you're dealing with, but you still blunder in like any other ignoramus spouting off about old ideas without thinking them through! And that's how you ruin my plans, over and over again!"

Jynn was about to holler a reply when a bang sounded behind Detarr, not unlike the fireworks that Scribkin often peddled at big celebrations. In the distance, a pinpoint of violet light was ascending from the ranks of the dead into the sky.

"Case in point!" said Detarr, waving a hand at the rising spark. "Now they've had to start without me! Do you know how long I've been planning this moment? And now I'm going to miss it!"

"Y-y-you d-don't... y-you c-can't... y-you—argh!" Jynn couldn't manage more than an unintelligible snarl as he loosed another spell at his father. The liche dodged the weave of black shadows and blue lightning, but Jynn corrected the blast's trajectory with a twist of his wrist. The searing spell raked across his father's robes.

Detarr shrieked in pain and floated to a higher altitude, clutching his side. The fires in the sockets of his eyes blazed as he glared down at his son. "Well, boy, it seems you've managed to learn some skill after all."

Jynn sputtered in fury, trying to answer. "Y-y-your f-fight is h-h-here, with m-me!"

"No, you fool," snarled the liche. "There is no fight. I've already won."

Chapter 16

Ferra of House Lleweryn lobbed a fireball over the edge of Highwatch's ramparts. It fell until it was nothing but a glowing speck. A moment later its descent was punctuated with a distant flash and rumble. The solamancer nodded in satisfaction.

"Ye are not to attack yet," said Jedik. The burly Dwarf glared up at the Elf.

Ferra snorted. "Tell that to whoever cast the massive light spell," she said. "They took at least a quarter of the kills in one shot. And they weren't even the first to fire."

"They won't get points for the kills," said Jedik. "The guild shan't reward those who ignore the contracts."

"Oh, look around you. Everyone's ignoring the contracts." Ferra waved her arm across the fortress. Along the eastern ramparts, professional heroes wove spells, tossed exploding vials of phosphorescent liquid, slung enchanted stones, loosed arrows, and in one instance, fired blasts of glittering dust from an elaborate Gnomish steam cannon.

"Even the Silverfire Six are attacking," Ferra pointed to the famous crew, already weaving another fireball in her off-hand. "Besides, it's only a matter of time before they fire up those big orbs and annihilate the whole undead army." She nodded at the luminous sphere a short way up the rampart. Strange Umbraxian workers scuttled around its base, clad in their body-length coats and crimson goggles. "And nobody gets the points for all those kills."

"T'isn't right," said Jedik. "The contracts say we're to go in order."

"The contracts are for the lawyers to sort out," Ferra said, hurling the fireball over the rampart. "At the end of the day, there are going to be two groups of heroes walking out of Highwatch. Those who got enough kills to earn some points or a spot of loot, and those who forgot to bring a ranged weapon."

Jedik only snorted and turned back to the battlefield, his warhammer slung impotently over his shoulder. "T'isn't right."

"A travesty," Ferra murmured, looking over the ramparts. "How many do you suppose I hit with that last fireball?"

"What's that dancin' light?" Jedik asked.

"A flaming zombie, I think," said Ferra, squinting down at the crater left by her spell. "Must have been close to the blast."

"T'isn't a zombie," said Jedik.

"A ghoul, maybe? But look at the way it staggers—well, who can say from this distance? It looks like a drunken firefly from up here."

"I'm talkin' about the glow in the sky," said Jedik, pointing.

Ferra looked up and saw a faint purple spark rising toward the clouds. Just short of its zenith, the spark burst into a starburst of amethyst light. The heroes on the ramparts ducked behind the wall, but the expected blast of sorcerous nastiness never reached them. When Ferra peeked over the edge of the fortification, she saw strange writing emblazoned in glowing violet trails across the sky. They read:

'YUTANI ARM TRADERS'

"Is that some kind of advertisement?" asked Jedik.

Ferra felt a sinking feeling in her gut. She turned to stare at the great glowing orbs being set up across the ramparts. "Isn't that the Umbraxian company that built the—"

"Look, they're movin'," Jedik interrupted.

The letters slid around in the sky like tiles from a Gnomish printing press. The blood froze in Ferra's veins as they found their final place.

IT'S DETARR UR'MAYAN

"Bones," swore Jedik. It looked like he was saying something else, but his voice was drowned out by the screams erupting around the ramparts.

The Umbraxian attendants around the great orbs had thrown aside their long coats, revealing rotten, pitted torsos. Azure flames sprang from their hands, setting the bannermen about them alight.

"Revenants," gasped Ferra.

Jedik brushed past her, charging toward the cackling undead. Ferra followed him, already readying a spell. Ahead of them, other heroes rushed toward the orbs to mount a counter-offensive against the revenants. A golden spear impaled one abomination, and a noctomancer's lightning reduced another to a twitching mass of charred flesh. Ferra wondered if there would be any left to kill by the time she reached the base of the glowing, green orb.

Then she heard the crack.

The wretched sound rent the air, leaving a high-pitched whine at the corner of hearing. Then there was another crack, and then a snap, and she could see deep fissures winding up the side of the great emerald orb.

"Run!" Ferra yelled amid a chorus of similar warnings, but they were all too late. The orb exploded in a tide of vile, viscous fluid. The cries of the heroes and bannermen closest to the epicenter cut off as the green wave rolled over them. Ferra watched the entire Silverfire Six fall under the noxious wave in an instant. Moments later, their oozing remains stood back up and shambled toward the survivors.

Ferra turned and fled. Behind her, the ooze was creeping along with sinister purpose, winding its way along the ramparts in a grim river. Any bannermen or hero caught in the viscous mass was sucked under the surface, only to emerge as another undead soldier trying to pull the living into the slime. The remaining defenders pushed each other out of the way to flee.

Ferra turned her attention to retreat and then stopped short. Ahead of her, another orb had already completed its grim task. Her path was blocked by a horde of shambling corpses and a chartreuse pool of bubbling death. There was no escape.

The solamancer grit her teeth and began to weave a fireball. "I'll just have to fight my way—"

The words were knocked from her, along with the rest of her breath, as something heavy slammed into her ribcage. She stumbled and turned to see Jedik looming over her. The remnants of the Dwarf's black beard barely clung to his green and shriveled flesh, but his gaunt frame was imbued with a supernatural strength. The second swing of his warhammer swept her over the edge of the ramparts and into oblivion.

"An anagram." Jynn was stone-faced as he stared at the glowing letters in the sky over the battlefield. "The big r-reveal of your m-master plan was an anagram."

Gorm and the other combatants stared at the message in the air above Highwatch. Screams rang out along the ramparts.

"Perhaps the wordplay was a little indulgent," conceded Detarr. "But I needed a good line to ensure the living will grasp the full scope of my plans."

"It's just… It's just so v-vulgar!" spat Jynn. "People are dying, and you're worried about how it looks!"

"I take pride in my work!" said the liche. "And there's nothing wrong with a good quip. They say you're allowed to make one."

"Are you s-serious?" Jynn hurled a spell at his father. "It's a m-maladroit, tacky joke punctuating a tr-travesty!"

"Tacky?" The liche made a rapid series of precise gestures, and an intricate web of darkness and stone sprang up from the plateau to intercept the spell. "How dare you?"

"Y-you have the subtlety of a-a-a warhammer!" shouted the noctomancer. "You always d-do everything so g-garishly over-the-top! E-even those oh-ov-overcomplicated wards you're w-weaving are just meant t-to im-im-impress us!"

"As usual, you are mistaken, boy." Detarr shrugged and flexed his fingers, sending the glowing wards around him into an intricate dance. "I might have strong aesthetic sensibilities, but there's always a purpose to my work. These weaves are a perfect example. They weren't for your benefit."

Jynn shook his head. "Then who?"

"Why not ask the solamancer?" The skeletal wizard nodded to Laruna.

Gorm and the other heroes turned to look at the mage. The solamancer leaned back as though wrestling an invisible opponent. Her face and knuckles blanched as she gripped the Wyrmwood Staff. "I can't!" she wheezed, her voice strained to the breaking point. "Jynn, I can't…"

"You can't what, girl?" mused Detarr as his son rushed to the mage. "Fight? Weave? Or even hang on? It looks like that staff you're holding is proving uncooperative."

Gorm swore under his breath, but then he realized that all eyes were on the solamancer. It was as close to a chance as the berserker would ever have. He charged, rapidly closing the distance between himself and the distracted liche.

A shard of stone erupted from the rock in front of him, catching his shoulder. Another ripped through the spot where he landed, forcing him to pivot awkwardly into the path of a third lance of stone. Cursing, the Dwarf scrambled back in retreat.

The liche turned and caught his eye, and Gorm felt his stomach drop. The window of opportunity to attack the liche was gone. It had never really been an opportunity at all.

"Come on," Jynn said, rushing to Laruna's side. "You can do this."

"Can't hold… it," gasped Laruna. "It… doesn't… want to be used."

"Close!" Glee was evident in Detarr's voice. "It doesn't want you to use it."

"And this is why you never trust a sentient weapon," said Heraldin.

"Not… helping!" hissed Laruna.

"I'll concede that you have power, solamancer," Detarr rose higher, weaves of noctomancy spiraling around him in complex patterns. He thrust his arms out, and the lightning and stone coalesced around him into a pair of sinister wings, bat-like spindles of bone webbed with crackling green lightning. "But I have power as well, and beyond that, I have mastery!"

"No!" shrieked Laruna, stumbling as the relic lurched in her hands.

"Come, staff!" called Detarr, raising a skeletal hand into the air. "I am the master of the Crown of Iron Thorns, the commander of the host of the dead! No living mage is as worthy of your service as I!"

Jynn gripped the weapon with Laruna, and Gaist leaped into the fray to grab hold of the shaft. It wasn't enough. The Wyrmwood Staff wrenched itself free of the heroes' collective grasp and floated through the air into Detarr's waiting hand. The crystal at its top flared with violet light as the liche's bony fingers wrapped around the grip.

Swirling winds suddenly rushed around the plateau. Blinding viridian and amethyst light surrounded the liche, and lighting spiderwebbed across the black sky. Beyond the undead wizard, Gorm could see an unholy green glow rising from the ramparts of Highwatch. Sporadic explosions of incandescent ooze sent plumes of foul vapor into the sky above the fortress.

Heraldin rapped the Dwarf on his shoulder as he sprinted past. "Run, you fools!" the bard shouted. "Live to run another day!"

Jynn and Gaist turned to flee, carrying Laruna between them. Patches whimpered and bolted away. Gorm didn't bother moving as the liche wove a final spell. "Too late," he muttered to himself.

"Thank you all for the staff!" called Detarr from the center of the maelstrom. "I must be off to cement my victory at Highwatch! But don't think of it as goodbye. It's more of a 'see you soon.'"

The liche dipped the Wyrmwood Staff and a red light fell from the crystal at its tip. The glow trailed downward in a slow, meandering descent, like an autumn leaf.

"Because I'll be bringing you all back as the undead after the battle, in case that wasn't clear," added Detarr.

"Oh by the g-gods, Father!" Jynn stopped at the edge of the plateau. "It isn't witty if you have to explain—"

A thunderclap loosed as the crimson light touched the mountain, sending a blast of dust and molten stone flying in a wide radius. Gorm was blown into the air like debris in a hurricane. The edge of the cliff passed beneath him, and he and his companions fell screaming down the mountain.

General Gurgen screamed something at the bannermen, but the chaos below drowned out her words. King Handor gazed down with dull eyes into the swirling nightmare, watching the tide of ooze rise over the remnants of his army. Highwatch was a sea of glowing green, punctuated by flashes of orange and red flames.

"All of our greatest heroes," the king muttered to ashes blowing in the wind. "The army of the greatest nation on Arth. Gone. All gone."

With the defenders of Highwatch in shambles, the undead outside the wall were free to advance at will. Spectral ghosts, dark wraiths in flowing robes, and keening banshees flew over the fortifications to attack the survivors in the inner courtyard. The dead heroes and bannermen from the ramparts turned their bows and slings upon the living.

An arrow bounced off the stone at Handor's feet. He stared at it impassively.

"My kingdom... everything," he said, staring bleary-eyed at the scene below him. "Doomed."

A mailed hand grabbed the king's shoulder and pulled him back from the edge of the keep. "To the eagles, Majesty!" General Gurgen roared in his ear as she shoved him toward the waiting birds. "The eagles!"

Handor stumbled toward the massive raptor dancing nervously at the center of the keep. It occurred to him that Goldson, Baggs, and their eagle had already departed. Weaver Ortson and Dannel Clubs rose into the sky on their own bird, gliding in lazy circles above the burning fortress. The king watched them ascend as he allowed a bannerman to help him mount. A moment later, he felt his seat shift as Johan leapt into the saddle behind him.

"Ho! Upward!" cried the paladin. The eagle hopped to the edge of the keep and launched into the sky, rising into the dark sky on currents of hot air.

"Gone," the king moaned, tears beading at the edges of his eyes. Now ghouls and skeletons were clambering over Highwatch's walls. Pockets of resisting heroes and soldiers fled for the tunnels beneath Highwatch. The banners of the army of the Freedlands lay scattered through the courtyard. "It's all gone. The races of Man will join the kingdom of death. All is hopeless."

"It is a setback, sire," yelled Johan. "But where most men see challenges, great men see opportunities, right? Ha!"

"Opportunity?" Confusion catalyzed Handor's grief into rage. "How could there be any thrice-cursed opportunity in this? The army is gone. Our heroes are gone. My kingdom is defenseless. And I was party to the thrice-cursed scheme that led to this disaster!"

"A major setback, sire," said the Champion of Tandos. "But surely you can come back—"

"It is more than a setback," moaned Handor, looking down at the carnage as the eagle's circuitous ascent brought them over Highwatch once more. "It is the beginning of the end. There's nothing left for me now but to confess my sins and abdicate the throne."

Johan was silent for a moment. Then Handor felt a mailed hand rest on his shoulder. "You haven't failed entirely, sire. On the contrary, you've been most useful," said the paladin.

Something in the champion's voice stirred Handor from his stupor. "What do you mean by that?"

"And there is still a way for you to serve the kingdom." Johan ignored the king. The warrior's grip was getting firmer.

Handor tried to pull away. "Johan? What are you—"

The paladin's left arm wrapped around Handor, and sudden pain flared in the king's chest. He looked down to see an arrow, still clasped in Johan's fist, protruding from a dark stain that was spreading across his royal robes.

"Martyrdom," the paladin said in Handor's ear.

The king tried to speak, but there was no air in his lungs.

"Ha! Goodbye, old friend." The Champion of Tandos began to loosen the dying man's straps.

Questions filled the king's mind as his assailant worked, but they all fled his consciousness as Johan gave him a shove. Handor tumbled through the air, looking back at his murderer. Johan was leaning over the edge of the saddle, screaming something he couldn't make out. The paladin's arm was reaching in a pantomimed effort to save the king, but behind the outstretched hand Johan was still smiling. It was all an act, of course.

It had always been an act.

The wind flipped him over, and the king could see the sea of ooze and flame rushing toward him. Silently screaming, Handor plummeted into a storm of fire and death.

"Didn't see that coming! Heh!" Ignatius allowed himself a small giggle as he watched the lights flash in the eyes of the shrine of Mordo Ogg. One particular glow lingered longer than normal before fading away. "Must have been a big one. Always interesting when the important ones go."

The light quickly resumed its rapid flickering, blinking on and off at a pace indicative of huge battles, natural disasters, or large cults attempting to reach the gods by sharing a barrel of fermented hemlock. In a way, such cultists succeeded; everyone involved encountered Ignatius' god, at the minimum.

Normally such deadly events were an amusing interlude for a servant of Mordo Ogg, but Ignatius' glee was muted. At the end of every crimson pulse of light came an equally emphatic green pulse. The old priest grimaced.

"They're gettin' up. All the dead are gettin' up again." Ignatius scowled and drew his cloak around himself as if to ward off a chill. "Dark times are ahead."

Gorm's world was darkness and agony. Every part of him felt like it was on fire, and given the charred smell in his nostrils, he very well might have been. Somewhere on the edge of searing pain, he felt something wet.

The wetness was new. His brow knotted as he concentrated on the sensation. It wasn't like the persistent dampness around his shredded, broken limbs, or the warmth of the blood leaking from the slash across his chest. Instead, it was a moist, rhythmic slathering, gently pulsing up his cheek toward his—

Gorm sputtered and choked as a dog tongue slid into his open mouth.

"Good find, Patches," said Burt's voice, approaching from a distance. "Now, down. Stop kissing the Dwarf. No! Stop kissin—augh, don't kiss me neither! No! Down!"

There was a brief scuffle in the gravel, and then tiny paws stepped up next to his head. Gorm heard the glassy pop of a cork being removed from a vial, and a moment later he felt the bottle pressed to his lips. A familiar, coppery taste filled his mouth and seared down his throat, a comforting warmth spreading through him in its wake. He felt ribs mending, wounds closing, broken bones stitching themselves back together. He grunted as his shoulder popped back into place and muscle spasms dragged his shattered legs back into the proper alignment. They fused back together with a sudden *snap*.

Gorm choked on a gulp of air and opened his eyes.

"Morning, sunshine," said Burt, leaning over him. A high cliff loomed behind the Kobold, and above the mountain the sky was warming with the dawn's first light. "Feeling better?"

"The others?" Gorm croaked.

"Same as you," said Burt. "Scattered across the mountainside and banged up, but Patches sniffed them all out, and none of them had wounds a vial or two of salve wouldn't fix. Good thing old Burt had the sense to grab your rucksack and make a break for it."

"Aye, thank ye—" A thought struck Gorm. "Wait, ye can carry me rucksack?"

"Well, I had to dump a few non-essentials. To maintain speed, you know?"

Gorm eyed the Kobold warily. "Non-essentials such as?"

"Everything that wasn't either salve, edible, or mine."

"What of Niln's book?"

"Yes, I brought your precious book, heavy as it was. Look, the point is, the Kobold saved you all," said Burt.

"Aye. Thank ye, Burt." Gorm sat up and tried to make sense of the world. The liche's victory. The fate of Highwatch. Where to go from here. And then there was another question. "What's with the pig?"

Burt glanced back at the dead hog sitting in the branches of a gnarled tree. "It was there when we found you."

"Strange," said Gorm.

"That's par for the course, I'd say," said the Kobold. "Weird things show up all the time around you. At least this one's edible."

Gorm stared at the pig. It had one eye. "Assuming we can get it down from there."

"I'm sure you'll find a way." The Kobold gave him a pat on the knee. "Come on. Laruna's found the horses, and the others are waiting."

"What's keeping them?" Duine Poldo asked, sitting at the small conference table he kept in his new home office.

"Well, the permits, for one," said Mrs. Hrurk, glancing at her clipboard. "You've owned the building for less than a week, and the city already granted us several exceptions. The clerk said things don't usually move this fast."

"It's hardly fast enough. No, let me," he added, lifting the teapot before Mrs. Hrurk could take it from him. He filled his own mug, and then topped off the Gnoll's as well. "We can't keep up with demand. How many tenants do we have now?"

"Oh, well over four dozen," said Mrs. Hrurk, reluctantly accepting her tea. "And that's just the Shadowkin. We also have an Ogre, a family of Tinderkin, and a Human."

"A Human?" said Poldo.

"Oh, yes. Aubren is a young girl. She fled Parald when Vetchell fell. I found her wandering the streets a couple of days ago, poor dear. She's helping out around the house and watching the pups while I work."

Poldo nodded. "Fair enough, but is there room for her to sleep? For any of them?"

"We've shifted some furniture around, and Graz'gub Bloodroar has put together three sets of bunks so far." Mrs. Hrurk dropped a sugar cube into her tea, and then put one in Poldo's. "Did I mention that Mr. Bloodroar has a knack for carpentry? No? Well as it turns out, he does. Anyway, we can probably take in another three or four before the bunk rooms are complete. Six if they're Goblins or Kobolds."

"And when will the bunk rooms be done?" asked Poldo.

"Not until we get the permits. They can't come soon enough." Mrs. Hrurk sighed and looked out the window. "We expect more refugees from Parald and Vetchell soon."

Poldo nodded and watched the Gnoll. Mrs. Hrurk's mange had cleared up in recent weeks, and now her coat had an orange hue to it. Coupled with her fox-like features and her large ears, she looked like she was at least part Fennekin, though Poldo wouldn't dream of asking her. It was usually considered rude to inquire which clan a Gnome belonged to, and he assumed that asking Gnolls if they had Demi-gnoll heritage violated similar social mores.

Mrs. Hrurk glanced back at him, and he quickly looked out the window and cleared his throat. Trade sprites were darting through the air, bright spots of crimson and emerald against the dark and brooding sky.

"Well, let me know if you need help getting the permits," Poldo said. "In the meantime, we'll do what we can. There will always be more people to help."

Mrs. Hrurk smiled at him. "You're a good man, Mr. Poldo."

The Scribkin chuckled without humor and looked to the sprites fluttering across the skyline.

"I mean it."

Poldo shook his head. "Mrs. Hrurk, do you know how much gold I made because Vetchell fell? And how much more I took in from investors speculating about the sacking of Parald? Everything I give those refugees is a cut of the profits I made off their misery."

"Mr. Poldo—"

"And the Shadowkin... I've done far worse to all of you." Poldo stared at the window, but he saw old quests swimming before his eyes, every one of them a death warrant for some monster or Shadowkin. "I made my fortune plying in loot taken from your people. And now they're my tenants. I try to be social in the hallways, but I… I can't even look them in the eye."

"You give them a place to stay, Mr. Poldo. You give them hope in a dark time," Mrs. Hrurk countered.

"They only need what I gave them because of how much I took from them," said Poldo wearily. "I wonder if I can ever lift them up to the heights I pushed them from."

He started as Mrs. Hrurk placed a paw on his hand, leaning over the table. "Mr. Poldo, I believe you are a good man," she said with an air of finality.

Poldo knew that people only prefixed a statement with "I believe" when there wasn't sufficient evidence to prove it, but he also knew when Mrs. Hrurk would brook no argument. He managed a small smile.

A tiny bell rang, signaling that Poldo's next meeting was set to begin. Mrs. Hrurk took the tea set and left Poldo with his thoughts. He took a moment to collect them, then carried his mug of tea over to his desk.

A pack of Wood Gnomes led by Red Squirrel waited on his blotter next to a small silver bell. Several more were already hard at work, rapidly transcribing a message onto a sheet of paper on Poldo's desk. They used a set of tiny rubber stamps that Poldo commissioned expressly for that purpose, each with a single letter or number and a grip sized for a Domovoy's hands. Working in concert, the Wood Gnomes could create a reasonably legible document almost as soon as it was dictated.

"Is it time for the afternoon report?" asked Poldo, sipping his tea. Then he read the message and promptly sprayed the beverage over his desk.

LICHE DETARR UR'MAYAN DEFEATS
BANNERMEN AT HIGHWATCH. KING
HANDOR SLAIN. WORLD'S TOP HEROES
(UN)DEAD. HAERTSWOOD RUMORED SACKED
BY RED HORDE OR OTHER SHADOWKIN.

"By the gods." Poldo stumbled as he fell into his chair, suddenly dizzy.

Red Squirrel nodded gravely as he wrung out a corner of his pelt. The Wood Gnomes kept stamping out their report.

HEROES GUILD RAISES THREAT INDEX
ACROSS ARTH. THREAT INDEX FOR
HAERTSWOOD UP BY OVER 2,000%. THREAT
INDEX FOR ABERRETH AND SURROUNDING
REGIONS UP BY 347%.

A deep chill ran up Poldo's spine. "The threat obligations."

NEW AGE'S TOTAL THREAT OBLIGATIONS
PAYOUTS EXCEED ESTIMATED CASH ON
HAND BY OVER 10BILLION G. DAELLAN ELVEN
ASSEMBLAGE'S TOTAL PAYOUTS EXCEED
ESTIMATED CASH ON HAND BY OVER 3BILLION
G. LAMIA SISTERS TOTAL PAYOUTS EXCEED
ESTIMATED CASH ON HAND BY 19BILLION G.

"They can't pay all of their threat obligations," said Poldo weakly.

Figures and amounts swam before his mind's eye, a grim litany of financial ruin. If banks missed payments to the holders of their threat obligations, then the holders of the obligations would stop paying for the obligations they held, and the banks would have less cash to pay their obligations. It was a more than a vicious cycle; it was the quick, terminal spiral of an ant caught in a drain, and it could drag the whole market down with it.

"S-sell! Sell! Sell!" Poldo stumbled over the word as he scrambled for his summoning stone. The Gnomes on his desk scattered, quickly fetching his ledger and various reports.

Immediately he issued orders to sell the rest of any CTOs he still held, then he dumped all of his shares in the major banks. A line of scarlet sprites bobbed across his office as fast as he could summon them, casting the room in ruby light. Yet at some point after he had issued a sale order for Goldson Baggs, he noticed that the red hue was also pouring in through his windows. The Wood Gnomes crowded on the sill of the largest pane, staring out with upturned faces.

Poldo stood and approached the window with a sinking feeling in his stomach. The sky was painted blood red by a multitude of crimson sprites swarming through the air toward the Andarun Stock Exchange. Every single one was a stock for sale, a company abandoned, another dip in prices that were already tumbling. They drifted along errant paths up the mountain like embers in the wind.

Chapter 17

The wind and rain raked across Gorm's face, stinging his red, raw skin. Spring on the Plains of Aberreth brought a uniquely damp variety of misery. Bitter cold and biting rains swept down from the eastern Ironbreakers. The weather chilled travelers to the bone, but still allowed enough of a thaw for the roads to become a soggy, dismal bog.

The mud was thick enough to slow even the Elven steeds. It sucked at their hooves as they plodded along through the rain, and their riders wore the vacant grimaces of a funeral procession.

"Are we going to set up camp soon?" Burt shouted from the vicinity of Gorm's boots.

The Dwarf glanced down. The Kobold was clinging to Patches' back, a thick clump of fur in each of his paws. Both rider and mount were dripping water, and they looked skeletal with their fur clinging to their wiry frames.

"I'd not camp in this muck," said Jynn.

"The bannermen and refugees found a way," said the Kobold, jabbing a thumb over his shoulder. Behind them, the camps of heroes, soldiers, and civilians fleeing toward Andarun were marked by the sputtering cookfires.

"All the better to make for Haertswood," said Gorm. "I don't want to cross paths with any of Handor's men."

"I don't think any of these soldiers care about trying to arrest us at this point," said Laruna.

"Aye, but I'm sure they'd like to have six horses," said Gorm. "Last thing we need is a bunch of bannermen decidin' to kick off a career in banditry by robbin' us."

"Not everyone on this road is going to turn to banditry," said Laruna.

"And not everybody on the road will return to Andarun, either," said Heraldin.

"Us included," said Gorm. "We'll figure out where to go next once we find Thane and Kaitha. But tonight, we'll take shelter in Haertswood."

"Haertswood, a field, a forest, whatever!" barked Burt. "I don't care where we stop, as long as we get there soon. It's more cold and damp than an ice hag's armpit out here."

"Ye could have ridden in me rucksack," Gorm told the Kobold.

"I thought I'd like the independence of making my own way and carrying my weight." Burt shook some of the water from his head, leaving his ears jutting out at odd angles. "Turns out, I was wrong."

"Fair enough," said Gorm. "But it was your choice, and ye ain't getting in and soaking me bags now."

"It's not my fault!" whined the Kobold. "We never had a mount for me before. Now that the wizard got me one —"

"We found a dog," said Gorm.

"What'd you think Kobolds ride? Tiny ponies?" asked Burt. "My ancestors have been riding wolves for countless generations. And Patches here is practically a wolf."

Patches barked and wagged his tail at the mention of his name.

"He's a dog," said Gorm.

"He's a wonder of sorcery," said Jynn. "By all rights, he should be dead."

"The same could be said of most of your father's associates," said Heraldin.

"True," said the wizard. "But Patches isn't undead. He's in the prime of his life. It warrants further study."

"So long as you do it somewhere dry," grumbled the Kobold.

"We'll be in Haertswood soon enough," Gorm said. "We should see the lights of the town any minute."

That seemed to satisfy Burt, or at least quiet him, and Gorm surmised that was as close as anyone ever got to pleasing the Kobold. They rode on for another half hour, willing their horses to trudge through the muck as the gloom darkened.

"Any minute now," Gorm said, peering into the murk. "We'll see those lights."

"We should have seen them by now," said Laruna, squinting into the darkness.

"Look," said Heraldin, pointing.

A patch of blackness was barely visible against the surrounding gloom, a dim skyline rising through the mist and rain. As the heroes drew closer, the buildings of Haertswood took shape. It was quickly apparent the town gates were nothing more than a tangle of twisted iron and burnt timbers. Dark banners dangled from the ruined walls, painted with a strange shape. When they reached the walls, Laruna conjured flames to illuminate the strange heraldry.

Gorm peered up at a recognizable silhouette emblazoned against the crimson fabric. "Char Guz'Varda?"

"It looks like him." Laruna maneuvered her conjured light along the contours of the portrait.

"Especially since they wrote 'Char' beneath it," said Burt, pointing to Shadowkin glyphs beneath Char's face.

"But what would the Guz'Varda be doin' here?" Gorm asked.

"I'd say that's fairly obvious." Heraldin peered through the gate as he dismounted.

Gorm felt a pain in his chest. "No, they wouldn't... I mean, the Red Horde would, but not the Guz'Varda Tribe."

"We can't be certain there's a difference anymore," Jynn said softly.

"We'll ask the locals what happened," said Gorm. "There's got to be somebody left in town."

Heraldin peered down the street. "There's some bodies left in there, but that's a bit different." The bard grunted as Gaist nudged him in the ribs.

"Come on, then," Gorm said.

Cautiously, the heroes made their way into the desolation. The streets were vacant, save for the crows feeding on the remains of a few bannermen. The buildings that still stood had broken doors and shattered windows. The entire city felt like a mausoleum for the ruined Heroes' Guild office at its center.

"I just can't imagine the Guz'Varda attacking the guild like this," said Laruna.

"I can't imagine anyone successfully overrunning a guildhall," said Jynn.

Gorm's stomach knotted at the idea. "Come on," he sighed. "Let's get out of the rain. We can find somewhere safe and dry to sleep."

"They're making camp in the guildhall." Mortus clambered down the side of a ruined building to join the other assassins.

"Uh, good." Garold Flinn was glad for the darkness as he tried to maintain eye contact with the doppelganger.

Mortus dropped to the ground. "I counted five, but the ranger could be scouting, and… what?"

"Yarr, nothing," said Captain Jones, looking away.

"No, seriously, what?" demanded Mortus. He put his hands on his hips, prompting groans and winces from the other assassins. The doppelganger wore the form of a middle-aged Halfling, and little else.

"Can't you put on some clothes?" Deathbloom asked, staring at a patch of sky above their heads.

"I didn't bring any outfits this size," snapped the doppelganger. "Nobody said I'd be scouting ahead. I assumed that floating golem thing would do it."

"The mechanical gazer?" said Udina the Raven. A nearby barrel jolted at the mention of the device, humming and chittering as iridescent light shone through its boards.

"We can't be usin' that flyin' bilge rat if we don't want them to hear us comin'," said Captain Jones.

Udina gave the barrel a kick, and it fell silent. "All the sprites can't keep quiet with their targets this close," she said.

"Which brings us to the matter at hand," said Mr. Flinn. "Fortune continues to smile upon us. We have stumbled upon a city with no witnesses. And given that Ingerson's party has arrived alone, tonight presents an unparalleled opportunity to complete our mission."

The assassins looked at each other with bloodthirsty grins. Weapons were drawn. "Arr, let's get to it, then," said Captain Jones.

"Ah, but first, if I may, let's run through the plan again." Mr. Flinn set his satchel on the ground. "Mortus, watch where you're pointing that thing."

The doppelganger put away his spear with a muted, "Sorry."

Flinn handed Mortus a bound parcel from his pack. "Now, if you'll go get changed, and also dressed, we'll start with Udina. What is your role?"

The noctomancer sighed. "I'll use a shadow step spell to get close fast and eliminate the party's bard. Which seems a waste of my talents, frankly. I mean, just about anybody could assassinate a bard."

"And yet, nobody has managed to yet," said Mr. Flinn. "Don't underestimate Heraldin Strummons. Next, Deathbloom?"

"Once the battle is joined, I'll set four of the war golems on the mages." The Imperial assassin flashed a handful of throwing daggers. "I'll strike once they're distracted."

"Good," said Flinn. "And Captain Jones?"

"Yarr, once we board them scurvy dogs, I'll—"

"Perhaps without the seafaring metaphors," interrupted Mr. Flinn.

"I spent many a coin and many an hour working with my publicist on this personal brand, and I'll not throw it overboard for the likes of you," said Captain Jones.

Flinn rubbed his temples. "Very well. Just make it fast."

"I'm to find the ranger and run her through," said the assassin. "Or at least duel the scurvy wench until Udina comes to help."

"Be sure to check the outskirts of the camp," said a deep voice from behind them. A tall, dark-skinned Imperial stepped into the alley, clad in dark leathers and wearing a crimson scarf over his face. "She's not with them now, and we don't need her sniping from the surrounding buildings."

"Indeed not, Mortus," said Mr. Flinn, smiling up at the likeness of Gaist. "And your role?"

"I'll try to kill the bard before Udina. The weaponsmaster will stop me. I'll keep him busy until Deathbloom can come and help me finish him off."

"And do not forget to stay silent," said Mr. Flinn. "One word will give you away, and if any two heroes gang up on any one of us, this will not end well. And speaking of endings, what do we all do once the rest of our job is done?"

"Converge on Gorm Ingerson." The assassins chorused the well-rehearsed command.

"Exactly. It will take all of us to end him," said Flinn.

"Arr, but we save the final blow for you, right?" offered Captain Jones.

"What?" said Flinn.

"You know, we all kind of weaken him bit by bit, and then you get to finish him off," said Udina.

"We assumed that's what you wanted," added Mortus.

"Now you see, this is why clear communication is so important," said Mr. Flinn. "If you have a chance to kill Gorm Ingerson, you take it. Don't hold back anything for anyone, least of all me. With any luck, the Dwarf won't see me at all."

"What, really?" said Deathbloom.

"I thought you'd be fighting him once the battle joined," said Mortus.

"And risk provoking a berserker into a battle rage? Of course not!" said Flinn. "Why do you think we brought the other eight combat golems?"

"So, what will ye be doin'?" asked Captain Jones.

"Don't worry, captain." Flinn drew his crossbow and cocked it for effect. "I'm sure I'll be of some use."

The other assassins didn't seem convinced.

"If you say as much." Deathbloom sounded reluctant.

"I mean, I suppose that would work," said Mortus. "But you and the Dwarf having a big rematch after he took your hand…"

"I guess I just assumed you'd be going for, you know, the poetic justice," said Udina.

"Ah, no," said Mr. Flinn. "We are paid killers, not storytellers. Our job is to be fast, efficient, and lethal. Justice is irrelevant, and there's nothing poetic about it."

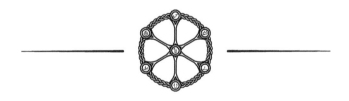

Hand-scrawled verses and related notes flashed by Gorm's eyes as he flipped through the Second Book of Niln. The words on the pages blurred together, perhaps because of the dim light cast by the old lantern sitting next to him in the abandoned office, or perhaps because of the dampness gathering at the edges of his eyes.

"Give me something," he whispered to any god listening, mad or otherwise.

Inger had raised young Gorm in a world of absolutes. Something in the Dwarven soul values certainty above anything else. When Gorm left the clanhome so many years ago, he had done so with a bag full of provisions, a purse full of gold, and a head full of convictions so deep they might as well have been engraved on the inside of his skull. Most of those beliefs dealt with who was good and who was bad.

Time, knowledge, and experience had eroded most of Gorm's ideas and opinions. His interactions with the Guz'Varda Tribe had washed away the last vestiges of his old prejudices. After working with Zurthraka Guz'Varda, Gorm had reached the happy conclusion that there were no inherently bad people, no monolithic group that could be described as uniformly evil.

Now, staring at the ruins of Haertswood through the windows of an abandoned guildhall, Gorm was confronted by the other side of that revelation.

There were no good people, no innocent townsfolk to save. Today's victims were tomorrow's monsters. His heart ached for the people of Haertswood, yet his head knew that by now the survivors of the raid were already filing quest paperwork in Aberreth. The next atrocity was already in motion, and it would prompt another, and another, and another.

If there was a way out of the mad cycle of violence, Gorm couldn't see it. In desperation, he'd turned to Niln's scriptures for direction.

They were uniformly unhelpful.

He found himself reading the prophet Epath's second book. Even among the Al'Matran prophets, a famously ill-adjusted and inscrutable group, Epath managed to stand out as particularly obtuse. His second book somehow managed to be even more nonsensical than his first.

She will not know what she still knows

She will not see what she can see

She speaks in riddles that we may

Dwell in the same darkness as she

In the margin next to the verse, Niln had scrawled a note with a fast, loose hand.

Destiny cannot be known. And so I cannot find my answers. Asepth, chapter 4, verse 8

"I need answers." Gorm's voice was a hoarse whisper. "I need help."

On a whim, he flipped to the passage of Asepth's first book that Niln referenced in his note.

The Seventh Hero descends and rises

With a blade ancient and unbloodied.

His wrath will smite the smoke and shadow

Yet he shall lament the lack of hot beverages.

There was another of Niln's rushed notes next to the passage.

I have nothing but the All Mother's prophecies. Sehick, chapter 3, verse 17

"Useless," said Gorm. He switched tactics, and tried reading through the Book of Gerd. Gerd's writings were the most understandable to Gorm, mostly because Niln had left out vast swathes of the book when transcribing them. Entire passages were omitted, with a small footnote like "The next fourteen verses describe the common features of spider anatomy. —N" or "Herein Gerd discusses the politics of bakeries. —N" Chapter six was omitted in its entirety, paraphrased with a concise remark: "Olives again. Entire chapter. — N"

Unfortunately, even removing the most incomprehensible parts of Gerd's text didn't render the rest of his scriptures useful. Much of his remaining work consisted of commandments for the handling of ceremonial incense; a common theme was that acolytes shouldn't sneak behind the sacred altar to smoke it. Even Niln had apparently steered clear of Gerd's writing; beyond the descriptions of his omissions, the high scribe had left just one note in the prophet's book.

It was next to a passage in the seventh chapter that shifted suddenly from commandments on observing holy days into several depressing verses.

> In darkness all the people dwell.
>
> In endless night, all light has flown.
>
> Blindly they toil and rest, buy and sell.
>
> Darkness is all they've ever known.

Near the edge of the text, Niln had scrawled a hurried, insipid note.

> That is why you must carry a torch.

The tome bounced off the far wall with a deep *thud*. Gorm waved a frustrated hand at the prone book; as far as he could see, Niln's scriptures were only useful for projectile therapy. He rested his head against the wall, breathing heavily.

He hadn't fully caught his breath before remorse overcame him. The scriptures may have been unhelpful and full of nonsense, but that just reminded Gorm of the inept priest who wrote them. "I'm sorry Niln," he muttered as he gathered the pages back up. "It's just... the whole world's fallin' apart, and the party feels on the edge of the same."

He wrapped the book in a neat parcel and tucked it into his rucksack. "I hoped there would be something in there... some teaching, or anything..." he muttered. "I... I don't know how much more we can take. One more setback may be the end of it all."

Unfortunately, while the Second Book of Niln was woefully short on words of encouragement, the mathematical proofs of the philosopher-scientist Nove had much to say about the universe and its timing.

Gorm, like many residents of the northern Freedlands, held on to an old folk belief that the manner in which an individual wakes up holds omens of what sort of day he or she could expect. Rising to the scent of baking bread was a sign someone dear was due to visit, while waking with a crick in the back meant that you were sure to meet an enemy, and a bobbinjay's song first thing in the morning was a sign that a good fortune would find you.

Over Gorm's career, he had discovered several other varieties of such omens. Ravens cawing in the morning signaled that death was near. Regaining consciousness in a dungeon usually meant that some villain or another would soon divulge their nefarious plans. In later years, he'd found that waking up with a hangover was a sure sign that he'd be drinking that day and passing out that night. And then there were all the smaller horrors that only a professional hero endured in the morning: monstrous slime dripping on the head, tentacles gripping at one's bedroll, a frantic Goblin to the face, and so on.

Yet in all his years, he'd never encountered an ill omen as certain or forceful as a mechanical warrior smashing through the wall of his chambers.

Dust and rubble fell around Gorm as he scrambled to his feet. Amid the smoke above him, he could see a single, glowing orb searching the abandoned office. The golem's eye shifted from golden to red when it fell upon Gorm, and a series of chimes sounded from somewhere within its metal chest.

"This is going to a bad day," Gorm said to himself as he grabbed his axe. With a heavy sigh, he darted left just as a huge blade cleaved his bedroll in two.

The combat golem lurched through the wall in pursuit. It looked like a giant's suit of armor supported on four sturdy legs. One of the centaurian centurion's arms ended in a massive sword, the other bore a thick shield crackling with enchantments. Worst of all, it was followed by at least five duplicate golems, their cyclopean eyes glowing red as they spotted Gorm through the dust.

"A really, really bad day," Gorm growled. The craftsmanship and ingenuity of the golems were recognizable as Barty Ficer's work, and that meant that this was no random encounter. If Barty was sending golems, there was a lot of gold involved.

"Assassins!" Gorm shouted a warning as he ran down the narrow passage to the main chamber of the guildhall. "We've got assassins!"

"What tipped you off?" screamed Heraldin from somewhere ahead.

Gorm dove through the door to the main hall moments before the pursuing golems smashed through it in a cloud of splinters. The great hall was a battlefield, illuminated by spreading flames and occasional gouts of sorcery. Jynn and Laruna fought back to back, surrounded by four of Barty's constructs. A lithe Imperial woman in dark silks leapt among the feet of the golems, throwing daggers at the mages.

Heraldin was locked in combat with a woman in dark purple robes. The bard threw down a glass grenade that exploded in a cloud of amber smoke, but the enemy noctomancer conjured a gust of wind to send the choking smoke screen back in Heraldin's face, and followed it with a bolt of lightning.

Gaist darted by, pursued by Gaist. The weaponsmaster and his double were locked in a deadly dance, wielding blades, maces, and handy pieces of furniture. One of the Gaists was clearly winning, but it was impossible to be sure which one it was.

"They've got a thrice-cursed doppelganger!" Gorm yelled. He started to charge forward, but a sweep from a golem's blade forced him to dodge, and he quickly found himself cornered by a squad of Barty's soldiers. The warrior braced himself.

Deep breaths. That was the key.

For a berserker, the secret to successfully losing control was controlling when you lost it. Battle rage wouldn't intimidate a golem, but it would inhibit Gorm's pattern recognition, and pattern recognition was everything when fighting constructs.

The lead golem's head snapped forward. There was a flicker in its single eye-orb. Its elbow wound back with a ratcheting sound, and then the pistons in its arms and torso gasped as it swung its blade.

Gorm leapt out of the way. He could already hear the next golem's arm clicking into position for a strike. A couple more quick dodges, and he had the sequence.

Snap. Flicker. Click-click-click. Jump.

Gorm was in mid-air by the time the next golem's blade embedded itself in the guildhall's ancient floorboards. His legs were already pumping by the time his heavy boots clanked against the golem's armored forearm. Before the mechanical warrior could react, Gorm launched himself onto its shoulder and put his axe through the glass orb in the center of its mechanical head. There was a flash of light as the sprites within the orb winked out of existence.

Gorm didn't pause. He dropped and slid down to hang from the reeling golem's shoulders just as the next construct's swing came. The blade passed through the air where Gorm had been a moment earlier, and then it passed through the distressed golem's head with a shriek of steel on iron. Sparks flashed in the darkness, a few of which fell near a bright red bladder prominently placed between the mechanical giant's shoulders.

"Bones!" Gorm swore as he launched himself from the stricken golem. He danced off the head of the next centurion in line, but a swing of a third golem's shield knocked him off course and sent him flying across the room. His landing was a tumbling, skidding affair that nearly crushed a diminutive figure.

"Watch it!" barked Burt from the safety of an overturned desk.

"Burt! What are ye doing, lad?" Gorm hollered, righting himself.

Burt ducked as an errant spell seared the wall overhead. "Hey, what did I tell you about the average life expectancy of a Kobold in battle?"

"Fine! Make yourself useful then." Gorm watched the remaining combat golems realign on him. There were still more than half a dozen standing. "Go find help!"

"Oh, right. I'll just fetch someone, right?" Burt's hackles rose. "You Lightlings all sound the same. 'Oh, laddie, someone's fallen and hurt themselves! Go find help, boy!'"

"Get going!" Gorm roared, bracing himself as the golems charged.

Whether it was the tone of the Dwarf's voice or the onrushing wall of steel and death, Burt leapt out the window with a yip just before the lead golem brought its giant blade slamming down onto the floor.

Gorm leapt atop the golem again. A quick blow from his axe shattered the golem's glass eye before he vaulted off its shoulder, kicked off the next one's head, and leapt over the next two. He landed on the pauldron of the last golem in his path and let the momentum of his flight carry his axe through its eye.

"Ha!" Gorm barked, launching himself into the air once more. Any satisfaction he took in the successful maneuver faded when he noticed that his trajectory was on a collision course with Heraldin. Just beyond the bard, the assassins' noctomancer was weaving crackling strands of lightning and shadow. Sudden inspiration struck. "Heraldin, get down!"

Adventuring in the wilds of Arth had a few hard and fast rules: Always bring a rope. Never split the party. Don't trust dark pools in remote locations with suspiciously still water and a dearth of wildlife nearby. And when your companion yells "get down," drop as fast as gravity will take you.

A year on the road had conditioned Heraldin well. He flopped onto the floor without hesitation, much to the surprise of the noctomancer attempting to assassinate him. She was likely even more surprised to see a flying Dwarf sailing toward her, though it couldn't be said for certain, as she didn't even have time to scream.

"Fancy meeting you here," the bard quipped, dusting himself off.

"This ain't the time for being clever," Gorm growled, shaking bits of mage off his boots. He nodded at the pack of metal assassins trying to sort out how to maneuver around their blinded squad mates.

"Right. I've got it," said Heraldin, drawing a throwing dagger.

"No!" Gorm reached out, but it was too late to stop the flick of Heraldin's wrist.

The dagger shot through the air, through the gap in the closest golem's shoulder blades, through the red membrane of bulbous bladder hanging out of its back. The golem was instantly engulfed in noxious, olive-colored gas.

"Get back!" Gorm roared, dragging the bard away from the billowing cloud. "Don't breathe it in!"

"What is it?" choked Heraldin, his arm over his face.

"It's thrice-cursed poison ye released with your bloody dagger," snapped Gorm.

"Why would it have poison gas in its weak spot?" Heraldin asked incredulously.

"It ain't a weak spot!" snapped Gorm. "It was a trap!"

"Well, how was I to know?" Heraldin jerked his arm away from Gorm's grip.

"By using your bloody head!" snapped Gorm. "When an artificer finds a weak spot on a golem, they fix it or cover it in armor! They don't paint the bloody thing red unless it's a trap for thrice-cursed fools!"

"Seriously?" hollered Laruna. One of the golems surrounding the mages had been reduced to molten slag, but the remaining three pressed in menacingly. "Are you seriously having this conversation right now?"

"It seemed relevant!" Gorm shot back.

"It's not a matter of relevance!" Jynn unleashed a ball of conjured lightning that narrowly missed the assassin darting through the golems. "It's about prioritization!"

"Help us!" shouted Laruna. "Or Gaist!"

Sudden inspiration lit up the bard's face. "Or both!"

"What are ye gettin' at? We still haven't escaped your last idea." Gorm eyed the rolling green fog and the golems looming behind it.

"Trust me." Heraldin drew a small, folded slip of paper from one of his belt pouches. "Just get ready to help the mages."

Gorm exhaled through his teeth and trained his sights on the darting assassin dancing atop the golems facing Jynn and Laruna. "Fine. Just do it quick—them golems have almost sorted themselves out."

Heraldin nodded and readied himself. "Just say when."

"Now!" barked Gorm.

The bard flipped the slip open and looked at the rune inside.

The Creative Destruction Anti-Magic Rune flashed briefly. A gentle explosion emanated from the symbol like faint whispers in the fabric of reality. Gorm watched the world ripple behind the shockwave, leaving everything but the magic intact.

Jynn and Laruna's spells died in their hands. The light in the golems' eyes flickered out, and they froze in place. The constructs' sudden stop was doubly unfortunate for the Imperial woman leaping between them. She sailed through the spot where a golem's shoulder should have been and, finding it empty, dropped to the floor.

Gorm was waiting for her.

There was a common adage that a successful assassin strikes first, strikes fast, and strikes hard. Perhaps it was professional pride, but it was left unspoken that assassins should avoid being struck back at all costs. Gorm had often found that those who carried a poison dagger often had a glass jaw as well.

It only took one punch. The Imperial woman squealed as she flew through the air with much more force and considerably less grace than usual. Her head cracked against a stationary golem's leg, and she dropped twitching to the floor

"Ha! That worked, lad!" beamed Gorm, turning back to his companions.

They didn't respond. Instead, they were all agape as they stared at the far corner of the room.

"What are ye lookin'…" Gorm dropped the sentence as his jaw fell open.

The rune had forced the doppelganger fighting Gaist to revert to its natural form: a lithe figure with ashen skin and a face that was featureless save a pair of bulbous, dusk-colored eyes. It stood in bewilderment with Gaist's signature black leather armor and crimson scarf dangling from its thin frame.

Across from it, looking equally bewildered, stood another doppelganger, also draped in Gaist's armor.

Burt scuttled through the ruined town of Haertswood, sticking to the back streets and alleys. The rain had subsided, and now the full moon peered from between the remnants of the clouds. This far from the battle in the guildhall, the town was eerily quiet.

"Hello? Can anybody help us?" Burt's shout was more of a throaty whisper or a hushed yell. It was enough to give the pretense of searching for help without actually being heard.

"Help. We need help."

It wasn't that the Kobold didn't want to send aid to his companions. He did, but he also wanted to live to see the sun rise. Burt doubted anyone within earshot could help, but he was certain that a gang of bloodthirsty assassins had recently infiltrated the city. There was only so much one Kobold could do. At least, that was what he kept reminding himself.

"Nobody? Nobody wants to help?" he said, ducking into a small alley filled with the debris of battle.

There was no response. Given the circumstances, he had mixed feelings about this. There was a disproportionate amount of guilt in the mix no matter how determinedly he convinced himself that he was doing all he could.

"Yeah, I didn't think so." The Kobold produced a cigarette from his vest and struck a match on a nearby stone wall. He leaned against the wall, took a long drag, and nearly choked to death as the entrance to the alleyway was suddenly eclipsed by a hairy figure.

"Burt?" Thane stepped into the alley. In his arms, he cradled Kaitha, still in her filthy nightclothes, holding her bow and quiver as a sleeping child clings to a doll. "What's wrong?"

The Kobold dropped to his knees. He could only manage a barking cough as he tried to dislodge a lit cigarette from his throat. "Argh! Arph!"

"Is it Gorm and the others?" asked Thane.

"Ark! Ack!" Burt waved a paw toward the guildhall.

The Troll looked back over his shoulder, worried. "Are they in trouble?" asked Thane.

"Arf! Aargh!"

"Is there danger? Do they need help?" The Troll squatted down next to the Kobold. "Is that what you're trying to tell me?"

With a final cough, Burt spat the cigarette onto the cobblestones. "Bleah! Gods, yes, they need help! Of course that's what I was trying to say! They've run into a team of assassins and murder golems. And also, I couldn't breathe, if anyone cares!"

Thane looked to the guildhall. "All right," he said. "I'll go and help them. You watch over Kaitha."

"What?" Burt danced out of the way as the Troll gingerly laid the Elf down amid the debris. "What am I supposed to do?"

"Just keep her safe." Thane smiled as the Elf scowled and shifted at the touch of cool stone. "I think she'll finally wake soon."

"She's been asleep this whole time?" said Burt.

"Since I found her, yes," said Thane. "I've been worried, but she's stirred more lately. Watch over her until she wakes up."

"Well, yeah, but… I mean, there's assassins out there," said Burt. "I'm a handbag performer by trade, right? And the average lifespan of a Kobold soldier is one… one…" The Kobold fell silent as Thane leaned down.

Burt stared into the Troll's giant, weary eyes. Eyes that said their owner hadn't had enough sleep lately. Eyes that didn't have time for excuses. A meaty finger pressed against the Kobold's chest. "Keep. Her. Safe," said Thane.

"Yeah," said Burt. "Yeah, okay."

Thane snorted and stood. "I'll be back as soon as I can."

The Kobold nodded, but as the Troll turned, he called out. "Hey, Thane."

"Yes?"

"You ever, you know, get tired of saving them? Of being the one that has to fix everything from the background, and still get none of the credit?"

The Troll bared his fangs in a weary grin. "It beats the alternative," he said.

"Yeah," said Burt. "I guess it does."

With that, Thane was away. Burt turned his attention to searching the debris around where the sleeping Elf lay. He found an old kitchen knife amid the rubble that fit his paws like an oversized sword. With his new weapon resting easily on his shoulder, he clambered up to a perch on an overturned barrel and took up his watch.

.

Chapter 18

Gorm watched the two doppelgangers circle each other warily, blades still in hand. "Still can't tell 'em apart," he muttered.

"They're both imposters!" sputtered Heraldin.

"I guess that depends on how long our Gaist has been the Gaist traveling with us," said Jynn, running to join them from beneath the frozen golems.

"This is another one of those discussions that needs to wait for a better time," Laruna growled as she stalked over to them.

"We need to figure out which one's the doppelganger," said Gorm.

"The new doppelganger," added Jynn.

"I mean, this whole time?" said Heraldin, who was participating in a tangential conversation.

"Later," said the solamancer. "Look!"

The pair of doppelgangers, still facing off in a wide circle, charged one another. Their skin shifted back to a rich brown. Noses pulled away from their blank faces. Their frames expanded, bulging with new muscles.

"They're turning back to their true forms... I mean, the ones we're used to," said Gorm.

"Right." Laruna conjured flames in her palm. "The magic's coming back."

Iron and steel groaned behind them, like the creaking of a frozen lake under a boot.

"Thrice-cursed bones." Gorm turned back to the remaining golems. The lights in their glass orbs winked back on as the constructs looked around. Gorm imagined they were suffering from the mechanical equivalent of a hangover.

"Jynn and Laruna, ye take the ones to my left. I'll—" His instructions cut off at the familiar *pop* of a crossbow bolt embedding itself in the floorboards behind him. "Down! Get to cover!" he shouted, diving for an overturned desk.

The rest of the party followed him, but whoever fired the shot had a repeater crossbow. Another bolt *pocked* into the floor, followed by a cry from the solamancer.

"Laruna!" cried Jynn, pulling the mage behind the desk with Gorm.

"I'm fine! I'm fine," she growled, clutching at her arm. "It just grazed me."

Cursing himself for forgetting his shield, Gorm looked around him. The best he could find was a small, silver spoon amidst the shards of a crushed teacup. Maneuvering the spoon into position at the edge of the desk, he could make out a crouching, black-clad form in the reflection of the third window on the far wall.

Gorm turned to Heraldin, who had sheltered behind a large cabinet a short distance away. "Smoke bombs," Gorm mouthed, holding up three fingers.

"The golems," Heraldin mouthed, pointing to the main room. Gorm could hear the clicks and clanks of the golems restarting their protocols.

"Smoke bombs!" Gorm pantomimed with extra emphasis, and the bard relented with a shrug. Heraldin produced three glass orbs from his belt pouches.

"What are we going to do?" Jynn asked as he tied a makeshift bandage around Laruna's arm.

"Well, there's a trick to fightin' archers," Gorm growled, hefting his axe.

"What's that?" said Laruna through gritted teeth.

"Shoot first," said Gorm, signaling Heraldin. "Cover me."

The bard's arm jerked. Three clouds of smoke burst from the floor, billows of emerald and sapphire that wound together in turquoise swirls. Gorm launched himself over the desk, axe in hand. He couldn't see the crossbowman through the smokescreen, but he could see the top of the window that the assassin was crouched in. After some quick triangulation, he sent his axe flying through the dust clouds in an arc that terminated with a *thunk* and panicked scrabbling. A bolt embedded itself into a nearby floorboard.

The Dwarf launched through the smokescreen with a manic grin and a fist cocked for a skull-cracking punch. As he emerged from the colorful vapors, he finally glimpsed the face of the crossbowman. Gorm recognized the assassin's features instantly, which likely contributed to the panic spreading over them.

"Flinn!" Red mist was already closing in around Gorm's vision as he charged, mixing with the last wisps of Heraldin's seafoam-colored smoke.

The Tinderkin paused to do some quick calculations. Without a word in reply, he dropped from the windowsill and ran.

"Get back here, ye bloody bastard!" Gorm roared, launching himself after the fleeing assassin. His pursuit was interrupted, however, by a massive iron blade slamming into the floor in front of him. The golem it belonged to stepped into his path, its eye glowing crimson.

"Ye mindless hunk of metal," Gorm snarled. "If'n Barty'd given ye a brain, ye'd know how stupid that was."

In reply, the golem snapped its head forward as it locked on again. Its eye flickered as its arm ratcheted back into position.

Gorm was ready. When the golem's predictable swing came, he leapt on the arm and launched himself at its face. It briefly occurred to Gorm that, given his axe was still embedded in the windowsill, he probably should have improvised a weapon. Unfortunately that thought, along with most of his other cogent ones, was quickly being drowned out by a rising tide of crimson.

Instead of searching for an alternative to his axe, he attacked the problem, and the golem itself, as a berserker did: directly and with excessive force. With one hand he grabbed the golem's head; with the other he punched the glass eye repeatedly, slamming his bare fist into it until his bloody hand crashed through the orb and smashed the mechanisms behind it.

Bellowing in triumph, Gorm leapt from the staggering golem onto the next construct in line, trying to make for the window. A third golem intervened, swinging its blade and shield to block the Dwarf's path. Gorm hollered again as he landed on the floor, this time in frustration.

Another, louder roar answered him. All eyes turned to the opposite end of the hall.

The guildhall's wall collapsed inward as Thane made a door out of a window, bellowing in fury. The closest golem turned to look at the new combatant and chirruped quizzically as it searched for the right combat protocol. Its query ended in a metallic squeal as the construct's head was torn from its body and shoved down its neck hole. The Troll tore off its arm as he passed, and wielded the steel appendage like a club against next golem.

Gorm's attention was pulled back to the nearest golems by the telltale ratcheting of an incoming strike. He leapt to the right, but his dodge proved to be unnecessary. A combined storm of fire and lightning from the mages washed over the golem, blasting it from its feet and melting it into a glowing, red lump.

That left just one golem facing Gorm. It brandished its weapon and stared with mindless malice at the Dwarf, ignoring the chaos around it. It didn't even falter as another golem's blade erupted from its chest, or as its own sword arm was seized by a Troll and torn off. The angry light in its ocular orb only faded when Thane decapitated it with its own blade.

"Is that the last of them?" Laruna asked.

"Almost," said Heraldin.

The heroes turned to where Gaist and his double were battling. The doppelgangers, in turn, paused in their duel to look at the approaching heroes and the Troll rumbling up behind them.

"Don't worry," Gorm told the shapeshifters. "We got time to figure this out. Thane here's got a good sense of smell."

One Gaist stared at the Troll impassively. The other wavered and bolted for the door with a cry of "Sod this!" That turned out to be an unfortunate choice of last words. The doppelganger didn't make it two steps before the Troll was upon it.

"Now is that the last of them?" said Laruna.

"I count twelve golems down," said Jynn.

"We've still got to go after Flinn," growled Gorm, his fury still burning.

"We need to find Burt and Patches as well," said Jynn.

Heraldin looked around the empty room. "And what about the pirate guy?"

"The who?" asked Gorm.

"The guy in a long coat and a pirate hat," said Heraldin. "Shouted in nautical terms? Carried a saber? Said 'yar' a couple of times?"

"You're sure it was a pirate?" Gorm's raised a skeptical eyebrow.

"It's not the sort of thing you can mistake for something else." Laruna spoke through gritted teeth as she clutched her wounded arm. "Right down to the big hoop earring."

"I saw him leap out the window at one point," said Jynn.

"I didn't see him." Thane dropped the deflated remains of the doppelganger as he stalked back toward the party.

"It was well before you arrived," the noctomancer said. "I think it might have even been before Gorm showed up."

Gorm shook his head. "Why would he run away then? They were winnin' for a bit there."

"He didn't look like he was running." Heraldin scratched at his whiskers. "More like… searching for his target."

Jynn nodded. "They knew our group, and came after each of us individually."

A ball of ice ran down Gorm's spine and dropped into his stomach. "That means he was probably searchin' for—"

"Kaitha!" bellowed Thane.

"Now, she's a beauteous sight if'n I ever seen one," said the pirate, or rather the assassin dressed as a pirate. The important bit, Burt felt, was the saber the man held as he sauntered into the alley.

"You stay back." Burt brandished his knife in a manner that even he knew was ridiculous.

"Yar, I don't think I will," said the assassin, advancing. "See, Old Captain Jones here was sent to kill a particular wench, and 'tis my good fortune to find her sleepin'. Makes the killin' all the easier."

"Yeah? You'll have to get by me first." Burt had heard about people saying such things in ballads and epics. Now that he said the words, they sounded a lot more foolish.

"Aye, that be the idea," said Captain Jones. "If'n I want to kill her, I gotta kill you."

"Well, I didn't mean that, exactly," said Burt.

"Oh? No matter. I'll be doin' it anyhow." The assassin leapt forward. His saber flashed in the moonlight.

Burt ducked and slashed out blindly with his own knife. He felt his blade bite into the pirate's flesh as a searing agony raked across his ear. The Kobold leapt back with a yelp of pain.

The assassin withdrew as well, clutching a bloodied wrist. "Yarr, that was a lucky blow," Captain Jones hissed through gritted teeth.

"You sure about that?" the Kobold growled, waving the knife and trying to ignore the blood dribbling into his eye.

"Burt? Is that you?"

Burt and the assassin both froze at the Elf's murmur. Glancing back, he could see that she was stirring as though from a dream, her eyes shut and her brow furrowed. Her hand had found her bow, however, and she clutched it close.

"Yar, I clearly don't have the time for this bilge," snarled Captan Jones. "So I suggest ye run your flea bitten arse out of here and leave me to my work 'afore I run ye through!"

"Yeah right, sailor," Burt's hackles were up. "You've got no idea what I'd be up against if I let you touch her."

The pirate assassin took a step forward. "Arrr, let me assure you that I—"

Any promise that the assassin might have made was cut off by a thunderous shout, a sound somewhere between an avalanche and a dragon's roar.

"Well, now you've got some idea," said Burt.

Captain Jones didn't have time to respond. He glanced down the street intersecting the alley just as a Troll hit him like a catapult stone.

"Yeah, now you get it." Burt grimaced and looked away. A man wasn't supposed to make the noises that Captain Jones was making. Then again, a man wasn't supposed to bend like Captain Jones was bending either. "All right, Thane, enough. I mean, ugh, c'mon. He's done."

Thane didn't seem to notice the Kobold. It would have been hard to hear anything over the final screams of the assassin and the Troll's own enraged roaring. There was a fury in the Troll's eyes that Burt had never seen before, and it didn't seem like anything could snap Thane from his frenzy.

Then the arrow struck.

The shaft protruding from the back of the Troll's head didn't seem to hurt him as much as surprise him. He turned around, only for another shot to strike him in the throat, snowy fletching sprouting from his jugular like a wildflower. A heartbeat later, yet another arrow bloomed in his right eye, prompting a grunt of pain.

"Troll!" Kaitha screamed.

Burt turned to find Kaitha standing, her hair wild, her nightclothes filthy, and her face a mask of terror. She was already notching another arrow while her eyes searched for some way out of the alley. "Kaitha! No!" Burt hollered.

It was too late. Kaitha loosed the arrow, striking Thane in the vicinity of his heart. In one fluid motion she grabbed Burt and threw him through a nearby window. "Run! Get away, Burt!" she screamed before taking off down the alley. By the time Burt righted himself and got back to the window, the Elf was already scaling a fence at the end of the alley. She hit the ground running on the other side and sprinted down the streets of Haertswood.

"Well, ain't that a fine way to treat a guy who saved your life," grumbled Burt, clambering through the window. "I took a saber to the ear, but a Troll shows up and it's everyone for themselves. Just chuck a guy through the window and hope he doesn't get eaten."

Burt hopped down into the alleyway and dusted himself off. "I tell you, the Kobolds always get the worst of it. Uh, I mean, I suppose you got the worst of this one, right? Thane?"

He looked up at the Troll. Thane still watched the fence the Elf had disappeared over. His throat made little gurgling noises as he breathed, and black blood seeped from his eye down the side of his face like a trail of dark tears.

"You all right?" said Burt. "Thane? I mean, I know that didn't go well, exactly, but... you know. It'll be fine. Probably."

Thane pulled the arrow from his eye with a horrible *shlucking* sound. By the time he blinked twice, his eyeball had regenerated enough to stare in shock at the enchanted arrow that Kaitha had shot him with.

"Look, she'll be back, and we'll explain what happened. It was a misunderstanding, right?"

If the Troll noticed the Kobold at all, he didn't show it. He absently plucked the arrow from his neck as he stared down the alley. The closing gap in his throat made little whistling noises with every breath. They were coming shallow and fast now.

"I mean, that looked bad, right? Killing a guy like that, you know, all messy? Just as she's waking up? And you all covered in…" Burt struggled to find the words. "Human? It'd be easy to get the wrong idea, you know? But it's not you. It's just how it looks."

The Troll pulled the last arrow from his chest. It had punctured one of the pouches on the bandolier he wore, so that a few trinkets fell amid the blood gushing from his wound. He opened his mouth as if to say something, but he only made a small choking noise, like stones grinding together.

"She will come back," Burt said. "And we'll talk to her, all right? She'll see… Thane? Thane. Take a deep breath, buddy."

Thane took a deep breath, and then another, and soon his whole body was shaking with the force of the ragged, sobbing breaths that he gulped in. He shut his eyes, dropped to all fours, and let loose a long and mournful roar, halfway between a bellow and a groan.

"No, no," said Burt. "Listen, it's gonna be—"

Thane was beyond listening. He set off at a full run, fleeing toward the north gate in a blind sprint.

Burt threw his paws in the air helplessly as the Troll retreated. "And there we go," he grumbled, fishing another cigarette out of his vest. "It's all down the gutter now."

Water splashed over the muddy street as Garold Flinn dropped into the gutter and took off running. The sounds of battle had faded behind the Tinderkin, and that meant the sounds of pursuit would start soon enough. He dove down a side street, making tracks in the mud, and then quickly doubled back through the gutter again.

Flinn grimaced as he ran. Weeks of planning and a small mountain of gold had gone down the drain in a few minutes, and he wasn't any closer to killing Ingerson. No, worse. He was farther behind; now, finding assassins willing to take the job on would be much harder, and those brave enough to take on the job were likely to raise their rates and demand hazard pay. It would be hard to find the gold for that, especially now that had he forfeited his deposit on Barty's golems. And gold was the least of his problems; all the giltin in the Freedlands wouldn't buy him a day of Johan's patience.

His silver claws, he noticed, were reflexively clenching and unclenching, making soft scissor sounds as they did so. The assassin ducked into a ruined house, braced himself against a wall, and took a moment to collect himself. He recalled that all assassins were eventually stoic, either by maintaining a calculating demeanor or by letting their emotions get them terminally ensnared by one of the many perils of the profession.

The key was to look on the bright side. The mission may have failed, but Flinn had gathered valuable information about the nature of the weaponsmaster. It was also possible, if unlikely, that Captain Jones had successfully taken out the ranger. And even if the pirate had failed, there was a good chance that Flinn had taken down one of the ex-heroes. The Tinderkin smiled at the thought.

Flinn's breathing had slowed some, and his blood no longer pounded in his ears. Given the circumstances, he figured this was about as calm as he could muster. He was about to set back out when a mournful howl rang out in the distance. The note had a deep and stony timbre, and while Flinn was no expert on supernatural fauna, he was inclined to think that it sounded like a Troll.

The only other Troll that Flinn had ever encountered had been hunting Gorm Ingerson in the ruins of Bloodroot. Reports of Troll sightings were extremely rare, but that was largely because people who encounter Trolls usually didn't survive long enough to make reports.

Although, now that Flinn thought of it, neither did any of the assassins sent after Ingerson's party.

The Tinderkin stared to the east. It couldn't be more than a coincidence. But if it was... Flinn tried to wrap his head around the possibilities.

"What does that mean?" Gorm growled.

Burt took a long drag on a short cigarette without looking up at the Dwarf. "Well, *spug's* a Shadowtongue swear, and so when I say it's all gone to *spug*—"

"I know what *spug* means!" Gorm barked as the rest of the party approached. "But what do ye mean, 'they're gone now'?"

"They're not here?" said Burt. "I thought that part was obvious."

"Aye, but Kaitha and Thane were gone before!" said Gorm. "What do ye mean they're gone now? Did ye see them? Did they see each other? What happened!"

Burt exhaled a cloud of blue-gray smoke that joined the evening mist. "Yeah, they saw each other. They ran off."

"What? Together?" asked Jynn.

"No." The Kobold shook his head and took another drag.

"The pirate was here, as well," said Heraldin, retrieving a crumpled hat from the remains of the late assassin.

"Here too." Laruna made a face and held her stomach as she stepped over something glistening.

"Yeah, he really got around at the end there." Burt gestured at the carnage with his cigarette.

"Would ye just tell us what bloody happened?" asked Gorm.

"Thane came back with Kaitha, but she was blacked out. Told me to keep her safe, so when that pirate guy showed up and wanted to kill the Elf, he took a good chunk out of my ear." The Kobold pointed to the dirty bandage that he wore like a lopsided hat. "Thanks for asking, by the way."

"I been askin'—" Gorm sputtered.

"Yeah, no, don't worry. So then Thane finally comes back, and he's mad enough to… well… to do all this." The Kobold nodded at the remains of the assassin. "'Course, it ain't quiet, so that's when the Elf came to. And of course she assumed the Shadowkin was on the wrong side of it. So she shot him in the face and ran off screaming."

Gorm's stomach lurched. "Thrice-cursed bones," he swore under his breath.

"Yeah." Burt took another drag.

"Gods," said Jynn. "So he…"

"He left, yeah," said Burt.

"I feel sick to my stomach." Laruna looked pale as she shook her head slowly.

"We'll go after him," said Gorm determinedly.

The Kobold laughed bitterly. "Really? That Troll runs faster than even your fancy horses. And have you ever found him when he didn't want you to?"

"Really, really sick," said Laruna.

"It's easy to get fooled by shapeshifters," said Heraldin, staring daggers at Gaist. The weaponsmaster parried with a sidelong glance, then looked away.

"We've got to try to find him, though," said Gorm. "I mean, after all he's done for us, we owe him that."

"Do we?" asked Heraldin. "Do we really have to charge off to chase a Troll? Because I'd like to point out that you made us follow the Orcs, and then we ran after a liche, and neither of those chases worked out well for us."

Gorm whirled on the bard. "He'd do it for us! He already has!"

"And look how it turned out for him!" Heraldin shot back.

"No, really…" Laruna mumbled.

"Laruna?" said Jynn.

The solamancer made a little gasping noise as she collapsed in the street.

"Poison." Jynn's voice was muffled and distant somehow. "The thrice-cursed Tinderkin poisoned his bolts."

Laruna felt icy fingers of terror creeping over her, or perhaps that was the toxin. She watched Jynn as if through a mist, standing above her. He looked regal and frail all at once. She tried to reach out a hand for his, but the ice in her flesh kept her from moving. It took effort just to draw in labored breaths.

"A cure potion," Jynn leaned down, and she saw worry painted across his face in deep lines. "We need a cure potion!"

"We ain't had any for months." Gorm's voice drifted to her from the fog.

"Thrice-cursed bones of the Sten! Are you sure? Check again!" Jynn barked orders as he worked his arms under Laruna and lifted her. His classical wizard's physique, however, was ill-suited to bearing her weight, and after a moment's staggering he shouted, "Help me get her into shelter!"

She felt more arms beneath her, and her head was gently lifted to a place where she could better see Heraldin and Gaist holding her. She rolled her eyes toward Jynn, and the fear and anger welling up within her subsided a little at the sight of him. Gods, she wanted to hold his hand.

They carried her through a door, and possibly another. It was harder to see in the room. At Jynn's direction, they laid her on a bed and propped her head up on an old pillow.

"No potions on me," she heard Gorm say, and she could hear sorrow in his voice. "I don't think we got any cures back at the camp, either."

"Why, by the bones, wouldn't we have cure potions?" Jynn clutched his head with both hands.

"We ain't exactly well provisioned here," Gorm said. "And elixir's been in short supply, so we always bought that instead. Besides, curin' poison is a simple spell."

"For a solamancer or a cleric!" snapped Jynn. "Didn't you think about what would happen if our healer got poisoned?"

"I'm sorry, lad," said Gorm. "I... I'll go check the guildhall. Maybe the Red Horde left potions behind in the vaults."

Jynn looked back at Laruna, and she could see the fear and sadness on his face. "There's no time."

It was terrifying and infuriating to hear, but Laruna couldn't react. It was all she could do to breathe and focus on Jynn. Gorm said something to the noctomancer, but Laruna couldn't make out what.

"No. Leave us," said Jynn.

Gorm must have replied, because a moment later the noctomancer turned to the entrance and shouted, "I said leave us!"

When he turned back to her, Jynn took Laruna's hand in his own and looked into her eyes. She wanted to tell him the things that she'd never said aloud, that she felt things for him she had never thought herself capable of feeling. She saw all the same sentiments staring back at her from his glassy blue irises, and a moment of peace came upon her even as a tear ran down her cheek.

Then he let go of her hand. Her arm fell limply on her belly as he turned away from her. Laruna was confused, and all the more so for the clinical way he spoke to her next. "I wonder, is a secret really a secret if you intend to take it to your grave? If nobody knows a fact, is it really a fact at all?"

Dark mists were closing in around Laruna's vision. She wondered why he'd stopped holding her hand, and what she had done to drain the warmth from his voice, and, perhaps most pressingly, why he had chosen such an inappropriate moment to wax philosophical on the nature of truth.

"I suppose I know the answer," he said, rummaging around somewhere she couldn't see. When he stepped back into her field of vision he carried a long riding glove made from smooth, black leather. "I suppose I've always known. I just wanted it to be different."

Laruna tried to silence him, to get him to just hold her in her last moments, but all she could manage was a burbling gasp.

He looked at her again. His blue eyes looked cold and distant in the dim light, as though all the warmth and affection from moments ago had been packed up and set aside. "I would die, Laruna. I would let the world burn. I would give almost anything to keep the truth from coming to light. But not you. I couldn't live with myself, and no afterlife could hold peace for me, if I let you die so I could keep this secret."

Confusion and fear threatened to overwhelm what thoughts Laruna could manage, but she couldn't form a coherent question when it took so much concentration just to breathe.

"This is going to hurt me far more than it does you," said Jynn. With his right hand, he wove threads of noctomancy, pale green strands of wan light. The spell slipped in serpentine spirals from his hand to coil around his left arm, from the elbow to the tip of his fingers. As he finished the incantation, the weave melted into his flesh and vanished.

"Remember that when you think of me." Jynn flexed his left hand experimentally, as if doing so for the first time.

The dark mists continued to close in around Laruna. She tried to focus on the wizard as he repositioned her arms. She felt the weight of his hand on her chest, just above her heart. It made it even harder to draw in air.

"Remember," said Jynn again, and then he gasped. Laruna felt his hand jolt, saw his face shift between alarming shades of purple as the veins in his forehead surged into stark relief. She heard something wet and heavy drop onto the floor. Then she gasped too, and not just for the sensation of the cool energy flowing into her. Because now that the mists had stopped advancing and her breaths were coming a little easier, she could recognize the cure spell being cast upon her.

Jynn was channeling solamancy.

"Dawn's coming," Gorm said, tightening a strap on Jynn's horse.

Nobody responded. Gaist stood a short distance away with the solemn silence of a funeral attendee. Heraldin sat near the back of the alley, plucking at a lute. Burt sat near the door, leaning against Patches. The Kobold had found the dog cowering behind a nearby dumpster, and now they watched the sun rise in silence.

"We should leave," Gorm continued. "The guild's sure to come soon, and we'll want to be elsewhere."

A sour note rang out, and the bard cut off the tone abruptly. Heraldin gave the Dwarf a sidelong glance, shook his head, and resumed picking at his lute.

"I meant after... ye know." The Dwarf shrugged. "We'll give Jynn time to make peace with things."

He looked up at the ruined house. The mages had been inside for over an hour. If it wasn't over by now, it would be soon.

Losing comrades was the worst part of a professional hero's job. Some laypeople thought that honor would belong to dying at work, a fate that most professional heroes eventually meet. But death only happened on the last day of a hero's career, while burying friends was something an adventurer would deal with over and over again.

Gorm could imagine what Jynn was feeling; the Dwarf had lost many colleagues over his career, and only three to retirement. But what he'd learned over the years was that there was no time for mourning in the field. Whatever killed your friend might still be around and hungry. You had to tuck your grief away until there was time to drown it in a tankard or three of ale.

As he thought about the fallen, one particular face stood out. With a heavy sigh, the Dwarf stamped over to lean against the wall next to Gaist. The weaponsmaster didn't acknowledge his presence.

"Back when we first met, in the Temple of Al'Matra, I always called ye Iheen," Gorm said eventually. "And even when I started using your name, I thought it was just Iheen rebrandin' or some marketing thing. I still thought... I thought ye were him. That I'd seen it wrong back in the dungeon of Az'Anon. That I didn't watch him die."

Gaist's eyes flicked to Gorm, and then back to the red glow on the horizon.

"I wanted that to be true. And it was possible. We always were surprised at how many quests he got done. Ataya once swore he could be in three places at once, ye know. I suppose lookin' back it... makes sense..."

Gorm trailed off as the weaponsmaster strode away to lean against a different wall. The conversation was over.

"Awkward," Heraldin sang, without looking at either of them.

"Sorry," Gorm kicked at a couple of stones in the alley. One of them caught his eye. He bent down.

A few odds and ends lay in a small pile amid the debris and bits of assassin. There were semi-precious stones, buttons, charms, and other bits that would have been unremarkable, save for the fact that they were uniformly one shade of purple or another. A few had shattered, and most seemed worthless, but among them he recognized a small figure welding a bent sword.

Gorm plucked the toy knight from the dirt. "This was Thane's," he said. "I think Kaitha gave it to him."

"Oh?" Burt said. "He dropped that stuff just before —"

The Kobold was both interrupted and upended as Patches leapt to his feet in a flurry of excited barking. Gorm peered into the darkness where the dog was looking and saw a figure darting toward them.

"Is that…?" Heraldin squinted.

"Aye," said Gorm, feeling the first twinge of relief in a long while. "Ho! Kaitha!"

"Gorm!" hissed Kaitha, running toward them with her head down. "Gorm! Is that really you?"

"Aye, lass. And glad to see ye, but—"

"We have to get out of here right now and go and run!" Words tumbled out of Kaitha in one long breath. "We have to run! I think there's a Troll! I saw it!"

"She's still stuck on that, huh?" said Burt, dusting himself off.

"Why are you all just staring at me!" Kaitha hissed, drawing close now. "I saw a Troll attacking a man and—"

"That man over there?" asked Burt, pointing to the broken figure lying in the street.

"Yes!" The Elf clutched her forehead. "Why is everyone acting so calm about this? What is happening? Did I really wake up here? Or is this another vision?"

"Deep breath." Gorm held a hand out to her. "This ain't a vision."

"That's just what a vision would say," said Kaitha. "Although the tortoise was pretty up-front about things."

Gorm brushed the comment aside. "Look, there's a lot to tell, but, all in all, ye blacked out because of your salve addiction and wandered off. A friend brought ye back to us, but not before we lost our battle against Detarr Ur'Mayan."

The Elf shook her head. "That doesn't… who said anything about me and salve? And who would bring me back? And… and where did you get that?"

Gorm followed the Elf's gaze to the toy knight in his hand.

"Awkward," Heraldin sang again.

"Not helpin'," Gorm growled from the side of his mouth.

"Not trying to," the bard shot back.

"Where did you get that figurine?" said Kaitha. "I gave that to the King in the Wood."

"I know, but I—"

Kaitha's eyes narrowed to slits. "How did you know? Was he the friend who brought me back?"

"Aye, but—"

"So, you did see the King in the Wood? Or how else would you know?" the Elf pressed, stalking closer to Gorm. "Where is he now? Why would he leave? And it still doesn't make any sense. If he brought me back to you, why did I wake up next to a Troll mauling a… a…pirate?" She stared at the corpse of Captain Jones. "I thought the outfit was part of the hallucinations."

"Which is understandable," said Gorm, hands out. "But that pirate was an assassin. They ambushed us while ye were still away."

The ranger's brow furrowed. "And what? A Troll just happened to walk by and maul him?"

"No," said Gorm gently. He handed her the toy paladin.

"But then…" Realization spread over the Elf's face at a glacial pace as the revelations crystalized. "So then he was… and a Troll made that garden… and then he… but I didn't… and that's why…"

"Easy, lass," Gorm said.

"And then I… oh, gods, he was helping… he saved… but then I… and I…" Notes of despair crept into the ranger's voice.

"Deep breaths. His name is Thane," said Gorm. "He found ye in the Myrewood, but I didn't meet him until we were back in Ebenmyre."

"You knew that long ago?" Thunder roared in Kaitha's voice as she turned back to Gorm. "How many times did I tell you about him? How many times did I set off to search for him? And you knew who he was—you knew him!"

"I know," stammered Gorm. "But he didn't want us to tell ye—"

"Us?" screamed Kaitha. "How many of you knew? Why would he hide from only me? Why would all of you help him?"

"And this is where it all blows up," said Heraldin to nobody in particular.

At that point, the universe took a cue from Nove's principles. The ruined house next to the heroes blew up.

A massive fireball sent the roof skyward and scattered flaming debris through the muddy streets. Embers rained down over the remains of the building, which was little more than a pair of walls propping each other up. As the dumbstruck adventurers stared, the door in one of the walls opened and Jynn stepped through. A magical barrier around the wizard winked out of existence as he pulled a black riding glove over his left hand. Behind him, wreathed in wind and flames, stood Laruna.

"You said there were no more secrets!" the solamancer bellowed at Jynn's back. "You said I knew everything!"

"Laruna!" Gorm cried. "You're alive!"

"That's not the point!" growled the solamancer. "I could have been cured well before if he had been honest about being an... an..."

"A what?" Gorm glanced at the wizard, and then did a double take so hard he nearly got whiplash.

Jynn's robes were changing.

A wizard's garments always reflected his status within the Academy of Mages. Young mages were given enchanted robes, attuned to the network of magical ledgers that constantly recorded spellcasters' ranks and titles within their respective orders. Jynn's solamancy had radically altered his status within the Academy, and now his robes were following suit, so to speak.

The gemstone linings and elaborate gold trim had already been absorbed by the fabric of Jynn's robes. Intricate designs faded and were replaced by ragged edges and tattered holes as his high councilorship was rescinded, his titles stripped away, and his membership within the Order of the Moon revoked. The iridescent purple dye drained from the garment. By the time Jynn was halfway to the horses, he was wearing the dusty, tattered gray robes of an omnimancer.

"Try not to stare," Jynn said to the Dwarf tersely. "Surely you didn't think you were the only one hiding things."

"Why didn't you tell me!" Laruna ran after the omnimancer. "It wouldn't have mattered!"

Jynn stopped and turned to level a withering glare at the solamancer, skepticism pushing his eyebrows to new heights of condescension.

The fire around Laruna wavered a bit. "Well, I still would have... we could have..."

"As I thought," said Jynn. He turned and walked away again.

"You should have told me!" Laruna sobbed.

"Did you know about the King... about Thane?" Kaitha interjected.

The flames around Laruna winked out as she noticed the Elf. "Kaitha? You're back?"

"Did you know about the King in the Wood?" The ranger's voice was as cold and hard as iron. "Did you meet him as well?"

"I... He..." The solamancer was overwhelmed by the conflict and her conflicted emotions. She turned away and disappeared from view in a pillar of crimson fire.

"Bones!" swore Kaitha, and Gorm could see tears in the corners of her eyes. She followed Jynn toward the rail where the horses were tied.

"Awkward!" sang Heraldin.

"If'n you're not helping anything, shut up!" Gorm snarled at him.

The bard laughed bitterly. "We're far beyond help, my friend."

"Is all of my gear here?" Kaitha asked, rummaging through the satchels on her horse.

"Don't do anything rash," Gorm began.

"I have to go after him," Kaitha said, slipping her jade bracers over scarred wrists. "I have to find him and... I have to meet him."

"We'll all go," said Gorm. "We'll make it right."

"I won't," said Heraldin.

Gorm fought the overwhelming urge to wring the bard's neck. "Lad, if ye open your mouth one more time—"

"I won't be going either," Jynn announced, climbing atop his own horse.

"But Jynn—"

"It's fine," said Kaitha, saddling her own horse. "You've all done enough already."

"No, Kaitha. Jynn. Ye can't split the party."

"Gorm, there is no party," said Kaitha, not unkindly. "A party is a team of heroes that works together. We aren't heroes anymore, and can you honestly say this is working?"

"Could we ever trust each other again?" Jynn asked, staring at Laruna.

The flames around the solamancer subsided once more. The woman they left behind shook her head silently and made for her own horse.

"Did we ever really know each other at all?" Heraldin said, staring at Gaist.

The doppelganger turned away, eyes shut tight.

"Come on now. Don't do this." Gorm felt despair rising in his throat as he watched the other heroes pack their bags and mount their horses. "What about the Guz'Varda Tribe? What about stopping Detarr? We can get past all this."

"I intend to," said Jynn. "It starts by leaving it behind."

"But ye can't—!"

"It's already done, Gorm," interrupted Kaitha. She gave him a final, curt nod and spurred her horse north.

"Come, Patches," said Jynn, turning his own mount west.

"You headed by Andarun?" Burt scrambled after them and climbed up to ride the dog. "You can drop me off in the city."

"Very well," said the wizard, snapping his reins.

Gorm stared after them. "You, too, Burt? Eh?"

The Kobold turned back to wave to the Dwarf. "It was a good try. But these things don't always work out for guys like us. In fact, they usually don't."

"But—"

"Take care, Gorm."

Burt kicked at Patches' sides, an unnecessary gesture as the dog was happily bounding after his master's horse. One by one, the remaining heroes followed suit, their eyes downcast as they rode away. Gorm stood alone in the street long after they were gone, flaming wreckage smoldering all around him.

Chapter 19

Panic is like a fire. It starts with a spark, and if it's not snuffed out, it spreads quickly. Fear is driven by winds of gossip wherever nervous minds and an uncertain future provide fuel. Terror is as swift and damaging as any blaze.

And all of these things, as real and present as they are, exist only within the confines of peoples' minds. Just like markets. And value. And security.

The panic started in Andarun's financial sector, lit up by the fall of Highwatch. Thousands of bankers, brokers, and financial clerks simultaneously realized that their balance sheets were anything but balanced. Stocks plunged. Bonds flew up, and then dropped precipitously as investors took a closer look at the kingdom's coffers. The entirety of the Freedlands banking system seemed to be going mad.

The market had its tumble when Andarun was deep in mourning for its heroes and its king, and for a time the city's dampened spirits were inoculated against the turmoil on the Wall. But the economic fallout was bad enough to call the financial world out of the back corners of the public consciousness and onto the lips of every newsboy and town crier within a week of Handor's fall. One by one, every citizen of the Freedlands felt that precipitous drop in the stomach that heralds a new status quo worse than anything anyone could have imagined.

Commerce ground to a halt. Credit dried up, and without funds to pay employees, companies began to shed jobs. Temples and government offices were overrun by the people who had been just barely clinging to financial solvency before the crash; the sudden drop in the markets had given them a firm shove over the edge and into poverty.

People were frightened. Many were panicked. Many more were starting to become angry. And while some blamed the bankers, and others the government, and others still the Heroes' Guild, there was one point that virtually everyone could agree on.

The future looked a lot darker.

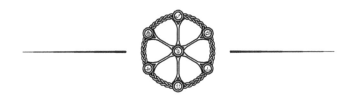

"It only gets worse from here!" said Gorm Ingerson, hoisting a tankard of grog into the air. His dire proclamation was incongruent with the wobbly grin he wore on his face, but he had long passed the point of drunkenness where his circumstances and his emotions had completely separated from one another.

Grunts and slurred sentiments of agreement rose up from the figures hunkered around the bar at The Black Swan, Aberreth's premier tavern for professional heroes. The bar sat just inside the city's northern gates, the last night in civilization for many a party headed for adventure in the Pinefells.

"Here's what happens. Firs'," Gorm slurred to the blurry woman next to him. "Firs' step is to drink all your money away. Then... then ye have to get some money, so ye take it from some poncy heroes. But they won't let ye drink where ye been lootin', so ye gotta move on. Drink, fight, loot, move... fight, loot, drink, move, drink, fight, drink... drink... and then... then ye start again."

"What... point?" rumbled a voice above his companion.

Through his inebriated haze, it occurred to Gorm that the woman next to him was not, in fact, a woman, but instead a tattoo of a comely young Ogress inked on the side of a massive arm. He looked slowly up the appendage to see an Ogre staring vacantly across the bar. He seemed familiar.

The Dwarf shook his head. "Ah, there ain't a point beyond the drinking," he said. "What else is there?"

He took another pull of his grog, and the Ogre drank from a keg with the top torn off.

Something still tugged at the back of Gorm's mind, a niggling sense of loss that refused to let go and be washed away on a tide of alcohol.

"Thing is…" he started, and lost the thought in a belch. "Thing is, I thought there might be somethin'… ye know, a reason to… do things."

The Ogre drank from his keg. Gorm drank from his tankard. For a time he sat and let his brain pickle pleasantly, but unpleasant ideas and memories kept bubbling up in the sloshing haze at the edge of his eyes. He saw heroes from his old career, from the days when he'd been Pyrebeard. He still missed Ataya Trueheart, and he still felt a sting deep within when the image of Garriel swam past his mind's eye. And Iheen the Red, of course…

Iheen's countenance and Gaist's were one and the same. That reminded Gorm of Kaitha, who reminded him of Thane, and that brought the mages to mind. He even missed the bard, a little. And beneath those new wounds, old ones still festered… He saw Tib'rin and Niln in the foam atop his mug, staring up from the suds with apparent disappointment.

"It was the priest… priest and the Goblin…" Gorm said. "They had me fightin' and… believin'. Thinking I could do some good, like a fool."

"Good…" said the Ogre.

"Aye, be a hero. Save the world. Fight for truth and justice," said Gorm. "Tha's… Tha's what they wanted. But ye can't…. Ye can't…" Gorm fell into silence. Fighting for loot and gold had its downsides, he'd learned, but at end of the day you could hold loot and gold in your purse, and maybe swap them for a cold ale. High concepts like truth and justice couldn't fatten your coin purse or fill your tankard.

Or save a friend…

He took a swig from his drink.

The Ogre, oddly enough, abstained. "Fight… for justice…" The huge patron sounded reflective, or at least shiny.

"I tried," Gorm said. "I tried to be a… a hero. Save the thing. The world. Be better…" He shook his head. "It doesn't work. Or maybe it's just me. Either way, I always wind up back here."

"Be… better…" The Ogre slowly, deliberately set his keg down behind the bar.

"I just said I can't!" snapped Gorm, looking irritably up at the Ogre. There was something familiar about that empty stare.

"Justice!" the Ogre erupted, independent of any external stimulus.

Gorm's face screwed up. "Are we havin' the same—?"

"Justice… Brunt style!" Mr. Brunt finished, standing.

"Mr. Brunt! That's how I knew ye!" Gorm slapped his knee and knocked over his tankard in the process. "You're that weasel Flinn's old lackey! I thought I did ye in back in Bloodroot? How ye been?"

Mr. Brunt, however, was clearly participating in a different conversation. He raised a massive fist in the air. "Be hero!" he said. "Be good!"

Some of the closer patrons scooted their barstools farther away.

"Ye ain't… ye didn't listen!" barked Gorm. "There's no point! Remember?"

But Mr. Brunt was, in so many ways, a blunt instrument, and he didn't need a point to be destructive. With a final roar of "Justice!" bellowed to the entire room and yet nobody in particular, the Ogre rushed out through the front door, sending cracking shudders through the tavern's old timbers.

"Could have at least said he remembered me," Gorm grumbled.

"Could have at least opened the door," said the barkeep, staring at the trampled wood and mangled hinges.

"Doesn't matter." Gorm stood in his stool and refilled his grog from Mr. Brunt's abandoned keg while the barkeep was preoccupied. "Nothing matters," he added, surreptitiously spiking his drink with a flask of Dwarven rum from his belt pouch. He took another long drink and let the burning liquor pull him closer to the edge of nothingness.

"Sweet oblivion!" Queen Marja gasped, dabbing tears from her eyes. "The end of my lonely suffering. A time when I can join my true love… in death."

One of the newest ladies-in-waiting moved as if to step forward, perhaps to comfort the queen, but the royal baker stopped her with a wave of her hand and a shake of her head.

Preya Havenbrook had been the royal baker since she was twenty—still a girl by Halfling standards—and now she was well into middle age. She'd been baking treats for Queen Marja for more years than many of the ladies-in-waiting had been walking, and none could read the queen's moods and thoughts better than she.

You didn't need Preya's decades in service to the crown, however, to see that the queen's latest emotional outburst had nothing to do with grief for her late husband. Firstly, because Handor and Marja had never held more than a mild disdain for one another, and secondly, because the queen was clearly caught up in one of her books again.

The queen gripped a copy of *Trotbury Tales* by Tayelle Adamentine. Preya was familiar with the author; all of Adamentine's books featured swarthy men, swooning damsels, notoriously predictable plotlines, and a few scenes that made the royal baker blush to think about. Given that Marja was near the end of the book, she had likely reached the point wherein some young and gorgeous person was at the point of lovelorn suicide, either the victim of a tragic misunderstanding or about to create one.

"So beautiful," gasped Marja, dabbing at her eyes. "I'll take my tea, now."

The queen's appearance reminded the baker of a great Daellish house cat, with tiny features in the middle of too much face, and bright eyes that were at once vibrant and clueless. She was perched with the grace of a fat tabby on an intricately carved chair that strained and warped under the weight of her royal bulk. Linen-lined tables were set in front and on either side of her, covered with platters of tiny, brightly frosted tea cakes.

"Majesty, the court is waiting," said the most senior of the ladies-in-waiting. As the eldest in that position, it was her duty to remind the queen of her duties, an unfortunate fact that meant everyone knew she would sooner or later fall into disfavor and be sent to work in the kitchens. Then the next girl would step up to take the burden on for a season. It was said that what the ladies-in-waiting were waiting for was a different job.

Judging by the flash in Queen Marja's eyes, the current girl wasn't long for the position. "I know, Clarista. But I'm busy."

"Yes, Majesty," said the lady-in-waiting, who was not named Clarista but who knew better than to correct the queen.

"I don't see why I should go anyway." The queen's painted face set into a petulant pout. "It's going to be a gaggle of stiff-necked geese in suits, gabbling and squawking for hours about petty matters."

"The city is in peril, Majesty," said not-Clarista. "The undead are on our doorstep, and the markets continue their free fall. Courtiers whisper about riots brewing, or even rebellion—"

"Yes, yes, all of that. That's what I was talking about." Marja waved away the lady-in-waiting's concern and pointed a meaty finger at a tray of round cakes with sunburst yellow frosting. "What are these?"

"Lemon with raspberry mint filling," said Preya.

The queen daintily lifted a cake from the platter and popped it into her mouth. After a prolonged session of thoughtful mastication, she began plucking the cakes off the tray with both hands and shoveling them into her mouth in a sort of delicate frenzy. In a few seconds the entire platter was gone.

Marja dabbed at her face with a linen napkin, then clapped her hands together. "Wonderful!"

The royal baker brushed some errant crumbs from her face and apron. "Thank you, Majesty."

"And what are these?" asked the queen, pointing at another tray.

"Those are chocolate crumble with—"

"News!" shouted a lady-in-waiting, bursting through the door of Marja's private quarters.

"What is it?" asked the queen, scowling as she popped a chocolate crumble tea cake with strawberry jam into her mouth.

"A thousand pardons, Majesty," panted the lady-in-waiting. "It's just that you told us to come immediately if Johan—"

"Johah!" chirped the queen through a mouthful of cake. She clapped her hands quickly. "Ish 'e 'ere?"

The young maid nodded. "He says he needs an audience with—"

"He's here! Ooh, he's here! Hurry hurry hurry! Help me! Ooh, I need to get ready!" Marja bounced up with such sudden force that she nearly upended her table.

The ladies-in-waiting rushed to assist the queen, adding powder, neatening the lipstick, wiping frosting and stray tea cake crumbs from the royal gown. After a few moments of hurried preparations, Marja had arranged herself to her satisfaction on another couch, a velvet pillow beneath her voluminous arm and holding her book in one hand. "Come in!" she sang.

"Ha-haa!" laughed a voice like a trumpet, and an armored foot kicked the door open. Johan the Mighty strode into the room, a vision in shining armor, his red cape and golden hair streaming behind him. The royal baker felt her heart flutter at the sight of him.

"Oh, Johan," said the queen with what could only be described as desperate casualness. "I was just doing some light reading, as I often do."

"Majesty, I am sorry to visit you in your time of grief." Johan's flashed a conciliatory smile, his teeth sparkling.

"What?"

"I know it is hard still, for it has not yet been three weeks since good King Handor's fall," Johan gently prompted.

"Right," said the queen. "Him."

"But the kingdom needs you," said the champion. "In dire times such as this, our land needs a strong leader to guide us against encroaching threats."

"I know." Marja seemed to deflate a little as she looked away.

"Perhaps..." Johan strode further into the room, prompting the royal baker to press herself back against the wall. "Perhaps grief has sapped your strength."

Marja shrugged and nodded half-heartedly.

"Perhaps you need a shoulder to lean on, to support you," suggested the paladin.

Marja nodded again and dabbed her eyes with a handkerchief.

"Perhaps something beautiful can come from tragedy," said Johan.

Marja's eyes lit up and her jaw went slack as she turned back to the champion standing at her feet.

"Something that we've held back for an eternity." Johan was leaning over the couch now, his voice low and breathy as he stared into Marja's eyes.

The queen's lip quivered as if to speak, but all she could manage in her excitement was to rapidly clap her hands.

"Oh, my queen," rasped Johan. He wrapped a gauntleted hand around her and, with a grunt of exertion, lifted her to his lips. Marja threw her arms around him.

It took a few moments for the queen to remember herself enough to dismiss the servants with a wave of her hand, though by then it was an entirely unnecessary gesture. The royal baker and the ladies-in-waiting were already making for the door as fast as decorum would allow.

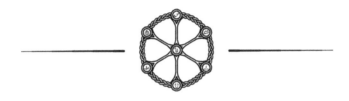

"*Have they no shame?*" Asherzu muttered to Jorruk. "*Nobody should have to see this.*"

"*Patience, Asherzu,*" said the ancient wise-one. "*They are trying.*"

"*They should have known better,*" she retorted, watching the pair of Orcs setting up a crude easel and charts. "*This should have been complete when we entered the room. The key to a successful presentation is preparation.*"

"*And an audience with an open mind,*" said Jorruk.

Asherzu was about to reply when the portly Orc giving the presentation cleared his throat. His topknot was peppered with gray, as was the finger-length chinstrap beard he wore. "*Thank you for coming, great lady. I'm sure our presentation will bring you great joy.*"

"*It had better, to warrant calling on me at this hour,*" said Asherzu, bundling her furs around her. The meeting was in a tiny hut on the outskirts of the Red Horde's encampment, far from any bonfires or braziers, and the damp chill of a late spring night still hung in the air.

Jorruk's elbow gently pressed into her side. He managed to give her a stern look and a sidelong smile in the same expression.

Asherzu sighed and slumped back in her seat. "*But I will hear you, Oggor daz'Nabbug,*" she said. "*You may proceed.*"

"*Thank you, honored one,*" said the Orc. "*Now, imagine this: You are going about your life, trying to feed your whelps, keep your hut clean, and perform feats of might and excellence for the glory of your people. Valra, the visual aid!*"

The only other occupant of the hut, a young Orcess in a simple red shawl, placed a frame with stretched lambskin on the easel. A happy-looking Orcess was painted in thick, fast strokes on the canvas.

"When all of a sudden, you are told your great tribe is no more!" Oggor continued, gesturing at the painting. *"And you must fight for a new tribe, one that does not honor your ways or see your great deeds. One that will lead your people to ruin! Valra!"*

Valra replaced the lambskin canvas with another painting, this one depicting an unhappy looking Orcess dressed in crimson robes. *"Oh no,"* she intoned, as stiff and well-rehearsed as a military drill.

"It is so enraging, is it not? Has this ever happened to yo-ah!" Oggor's question ended in a small cry as he finally turned back to his audience.

"Get. To. Your. Point." Asherzu pushed each word through gritted fangs.

"Aha, yes, it will be so. A thousand pardons, great lady." The Orc dabbed sweat from his brow with a small handkerchief. *"Valra! Put up the fourth image. No, the one with the chart. The other chart! Here!"*

Asherzu closed her eyes, rubbed her temples, and tried to ignore the sounds of a small scuffle up by the easel. Eventually, the pair seemed to get their presentation back in some facsimile of order.

"Your pardons again, great lady." Oggor pointed to a new lambskin, this one adorned with several graphs. *"Now, did you know that, according to recent surveys, over half of the Shadowkin in the Red Horde wish to return to their original tribes? And seven in ten said they do not support the Red Horde's violent ways?"*

"Yes," said Asherzu.

"Truly? Uh, good." Sweat ran down Oggor's olive skin in rivulets, unhindered by the constant dabbing of his soaked handkerchief. Nevertheless, he thrust a moist palm toward Asherzu and put on a smile that made up for its lack of confidence with face-contorting scale. *"So, when will you be talking to Chief Darak about the Red Horde?"*

"You presume too much," said Asherzu, fighting to retain her composure.

Oggor withdrew his hand as if from a fire. *"I am sorry, lady. I was merely attempting to be closing at all times."*

"That was your closing pitch?" growled Asherzu. *"That was how you close a sale?"*

"My Lady —" Jorruk put a hand on her shoulder, but it was too late to stop her now.

"You muddied your pitch with a poor analogy, you failed to define your proposition, you buried your lead, and when you finally got around to it, you added no value to your ask!" The young wise-one leapt to her feet and stalked toward the shrinking Orc. *"You called me forth in the middle of the night with this poorly strategized presentation?"*

"I… I was merely…" Oggor stumbled, literally and figuratively, as he backed away from Asherzu. *"I thought… the path of the aggressive seller says that —"*

"You would tell me of the path of the aggressive seller?" Asherzu hollered. *"I am the daughter of Zurthraka daz'Guz'Varda! I have sold to Goblins and to the largest of Lightling corporations. I wrote a pitch that impressed officers of the Vorpal Corporation! I walk the path of aggressive sales as nobody else, and I will not be sold by the fumblings of a novice!"*

"Forgive me!" Oggor groveled. *"We are desperate, Lady Asherzu! Someone must stop your brother before we are all killed. The people whisper it in secret, but fear for their lives if they should speak. You must talk to the chieftain! He will listen to you, the daughter of his sire!"*

"If the chieftain cared for me and my thoughts, would he have moved my hut so far from his own?" Asherzu snorted.

"Honored one, if the chieftain did not care for you, you would be dead," said Oggor. *"Those who speak against the Red Horde are slain, taken in the night."*

The words hit Asherzu in the gut. *"Taken at night… no, my brother would never dishonor himself with such trickery."*

"Perhaps that is so," Jorruk interjected, measuring his words carefully as he spoke. *"But others would. Perhaps there is more to this pitch than the presentation it was wrapped in, honored one."*

"It seems as much." Asherzu took a deep breath. *"I am sorry I did not hear you, Oggor daz'Nabbug da'Guz'Varda."*

"So, you will talk with the chieftain?" Hope filled Oggor's eyes.

"I will think on it," Asherzu said. *"Your words ring true, as does Jorruk's wisdom. But what would the tribe do if I convinced Darak to leave the ways of the Red Horde? We have raided a Lightling town, and they do not forgive such offenses. If we are to return to the path of the aggressive seller, I must have a plan to bring before the chieftain, an alternative to the Red Horde's ways."*

"May you have all speed then, lady. I fear our opportunity to act will not last long," Oggor said, inadvertently straying back too close to the script. On cue, his assistant stepped forward and thrust out a woven satchel.

"Plus, you shall receive this attractive bag when you act now!" said Valra automatically, just before Oggor managed to wrestle her back toward the door.

"We will wait on your wisdom," the would-be sales Orc called over his shoulder. *"Thank you for hearing us."*

Asherzu and Jorruk hurried out of the hut and made their way through the maze of tents and shanty huts, past the warg kennels and the pig farms, to the small hovel that Asherzu and her attendants had been banished to. She bid her mentor goodnight before entering her room, a solemn space of rough-hewn pine and sparse decoration.

Her bedroll brought her no peace, and she tossed and turned for much of the night. Possibilities and consequences drifted before her sleepless eyes, each less desirable than the last. It felt like the Gnomish puzzle boxes that the Vorpal Corporation managers had kept on their desks in Bloodroot, except now she was trapped in the center of one.

And one piece just didn't fit.

Dawn found Asherzu seated on the dirt floor of her hut, staring at a wrinkled parchment. A grizzled face stared back at her from above a promise of a very large sum.

"What have you done, Gorm Ingerson?" she muttered. *"They say you were on our side, but we assumed you were with the guild. Why do they want to arrest you?"*

Dev Strongarm wasn't sure what Gorm Ingerson had done to merit such a large bounty. He was mostly focused on the bounty itself, which was printed in bold letters across the poster in the young hero's hands.

"And you're sure you're Gorm Ingerson?" he said again, doubtful. "The criminal?"

"The worst," groaned the pile of furs and armor in the hallway outside of Dev's room. "Everyone… dead or miserable… it's all my fault. I'm turnin' myself in."

Dev looked at the poster again, trying to compare the inebriated face below him to the crude woodcut portrait. It was hard to concentrate with all of those zeroes looking up at him.

"And you want me to turn you in to face justice."

"You're with the Heroes' Guild, right?"

"Yes." Dev answered with some reluctance.

"Aress' me, sir!"

The young warrior thought about it for a moment. In his short career as a professional hero, he'd found that chances for success didn't come his way very often. Now, opportunity was literally banging on his door in the small hours of the morning, and if Dev didn't hurry, opportunity was going to wake up every other hero in the tavern. Most of the higher-ranked heroes would be happy for a shot at so much gold, and equally happy to shove Dev aside for it.

"All right, come in." He ushered Gorm into his room and stepped across the hall to wake Matina.

A few moments later, Dev and the young cleric stood just inside the door to Dev's room, weighing their options.

"What if it's not him?" said Matina.

"It looks like him," said Dev. "And if it is…" He held up the poster.

"It's me!" said the Dwarf, who had settled onto Dev's bed and was nursing a large flask.

"Wow," said Matina, still looking at the zeroes.

"All we do is take him down the road to the guildhall, turn him in to—"

"The Aberreth guildhall?" hissed the cleric. "Are you crazy?"

It was an unspoken truth that Aberreth's local branch of the Heroes' Guild was completely corrupt. It remained unspoken because the arbiters and masters of the Aberreth branch had spies everywhere, and the only way to get any questing done in the city was to work within their complex blend of patronage, bureaucracy, and graft. Most upstanding heroes preferred to run out of Haertswood if they had the ranks and reputation to get work there.

Dev and Matina didn't.

"No, you're right," said Dev. "If we bring him there, all of the reward and credit will go to one of the arbiters' bootlickers."

Matina sniffed. "We'd be lucky to see a copper piece."

"Tragic that Haertswood's been sacked," said Dev. "We'll have to take him all the way to Andarun."

"That's a long way to go," said Matina.

Dev shrugged. "So? If the undead are coming here like everyone says, evacuations will begin in a couple of weeks. And we've been between quests for days now."

"I'm still not sure it's him." The cleric glowered at the Dwarf.

"Well, it's worth the chance," said Dev. "I'm taking him to Andarun. Do you want to help me or not?"

"Of course! You're not cutting me out of the deal!" snapped Matina. "We just have to figure out how to get him there."

"I've a horse!" said the Dwarf.

"Well, that's a start," Matina said.

"But then he could just ride away when he sobers up," said Dev.

"We'll chain him." The cleric turned to Gorm. "We'll chain you, all right?"

"'Course," slurred the Dwarf. "Ye'd have to!"

Dev nodded. "Now all we need are some—"

"I've got a pair of manacles in my room," said Matina.

"Perfect. So we… hang on, you've got manacles in your room?"

The cleric rolled her eyes. "Oh, don't try to make it sound weird."

"I'm not making it sound anything," said Dev. "It sounds weird. I'm just observing that it sounds weird."

"You've got fifty feet of rope in your pack," Matina shot back.

"I… well, yes, but… I mean, everyone knows you need a fifty-foot length of rope for an adventure," sputtered Dev. "What if you fell down a pit?"

"What if you needed to take a prisoner?"

"How often does that happen?"

"Well, we're not in a pit, are we?" hissed Matina.

"Ha! She's got ye there!" laughed the Dwarf.

Dev exhaled through his teeth. "Just… just go get the manacles."

Within the hour, they had packed their belongings and, at Gorm's earnest insistence, retrieved the Dwarf's pack and axe. Their gear secure, Dev and Matina tried to inconspicuously guide the Dwarf out through the inn's common room.

Unfortunately, there are few things more conspicuous than a drunken Dwarf in chains.

"You guys are great," Gorm leered at Dev. "So great. 'M...'M so happy we're travelin' together."

"Shut up," breathed Dev. He was doubled over so the Dwarf could sling a heavy arm across his shoulders, but with Gorm's hands manacled together, it felt more like he was in a headlock. He noticed several posters around the room identical to the one Gorm had brought him, and hoped that nobody else did.

"Just keep moving," hissed Matina from next to him. She nodded to a pair of burly warriors in enchanted armor watching from a dark table.

They stumbled out the inn's back door into the stables and sent a stable boy to fetch their mounts. The lad returned with their pair of gray mares, as well as a handsome Elven steed for the Dwarf. They saddled the horses and loaded their gear quickly before confronting another problem.

"How do we get him on to the horse?" Matina asked.

"Can't he just... you know?" Dev looked at the Dwarf.

Gorm burped and toppled over sideways.

"I don't think he can," said Matina.

"I told you not to chain his hands yet," sighed Dev. "If we hadn't manacled him, he could have climbed up."

"I wouldn't worry about it," said a gruff voice.

A pair of shadows fell over the young heroes. Dev turned to see the pair of burly warriors stepping into the stables, blocking the main exit.

"What'd you find there, newblood?" said the larger of the two. "Looks like a Dwarf lost his way."

"Looks like the sort the guild would want to hear about," said the slightly-less-massive warrior, holding up a copy of Gorm's wanted poster. "We'll take it from here."

Dev's mind raced and his heart sank. The warriors had at least fifty pounds and five ranks on him, each. "Uh—"

"No, no!" said the Dwarf, heaving himself to his feet. "These guys... these are me friends! I'm goin' wit' them. They're takin' me to Andarun."

"Nobody asked you!" The larger of the two warriors loomed over the Dwarf and grabbed him by the shoulder, which was his last mistake.

Dev wasn't quite sure what happened in the next few seconds, even though he saw it all; he couldn't unsee it no matter how hard he shut his eyes. Flashes of violence were burned into his retinas: breaking jaws, swords sparking as they carved through their owners' armor, a warrior's face contorting as he was strangled by a pair of manacles.

The assault was over just as suddenly as it began. Gorm dropped to the ground amidst the remnants of the warriors, looking at Dev and Matina with black, dead eyes, a snarl or a grin on his face. They stood staring at each other. Dev didn't dare to breathe.

Then the Dwarf's smile relaxed and looked more genuine, or at least more genuinely inebriated, and a warm haze spread over his irises. He gave a happy burp.

Dev's eyes flicked to Matina, who had gone pale as a ghost. She glanced back at him, and he could see that she'd had the same thoughts. It was becoming apparent why the Dwarf warranted such a large bounty. What wasn't clear was what Gorm would be capable of when he sobered up.

Or how he would feel about his new friends...

"We ready?" slurred Gorm.

"Almost," said Dev slowly. He nodded deliberately to Matina. "I'll help our friend—our good friend—get in the saddle. You go buy as much rum as the horses can carry."

Chapter 20

"And keep the spirits flowing," Weaver Ortson told the waiter pouring his drink. "I don't want to see the bottom of this cup all night."

"I doubt you'll be able to see anything if you keep drinking at this rate," commented Bolbi Baggs.

"Or at least, you won't remember it," Fenrir Goldson looked more dour than usual.

"Who'd want to remember today?" Ortson drank his wine in a few long gulps and held out his glass again. The waiter, to his discredit, had already wafted away, taking the drinks cart with him.

"It's a historic occasion," said Baggs.

"It's a macabre fiasco. The ashes are still warm in the pyre," Ortson murmured into his wine. "It hasn't yet been three weeks since Handor's death."

"We're all aware of the date, Ortson," muttered Goldson, glancing around uncomfortably. "Not least because this month has been cursed."

"And it isn't over. That's the point." Ortson said. The death of Handor had been the start of a series of calamities, and even the least suspicious of Andarun's citizens hoped that the end of Dawngreen would bring some relief from misfortune. "The timing warrants comment."

"On the contrary, it warrants keeping quiet," snapped Baggs.

The great hall of Andarun's palace inspired some of the Halfling's unease. White funeral lilies were set at the doorways. Black banners of mourning still hung from the rafters and draped over the furniture. Handor's ceremonial crown sat wreathed in white and crimson roses atop a black silk pillow on the vacant throne. Yet amidst the dreary decor, tables had been set up and decorated with white silks and overflowing bouquets. Half of the room had been cleared out for a dance floor. Nobles, dignitaries, and captains of industry sat around the tables, contorting their faces as they tried to look happy for the new couple while maintaining an appropriate somberness.

"I think we should just agree that it warrants another drink." Ortson raised his empty glass at a passing servant.

"Always a safe proposition with you," said Goldson.

"An especially good one today," added Baggs.

"Hold on." Ortson squinted and peered into the crowd. "Is that Dannel Clubs?"

"Where?" asked Baggs.

"Over there. The one in the ridiculous pompadour wig." Ortson pointed.

"I don't believe that's the case," said Baggs.

"Oh, it's unmistakably Clubs," said Ortson. "Listen, you can hear the lout boasting across the hall!"

"Quite so. But I don't believe that's a wig," said Baggs. "Clubs is a Gnome of my clan, you see, and that hairstyle is quite popular among some of my kin."

"A Halfling?" said Goldson. "But he's almost as tall as an Elf!"

"A glandular disorder, I'm told," said Baggs.

"Well, that explains the tiny hands." Goldson held out his glass and a servant filled it with a Daellan white.

"Who cares about how he bloody looks?" Ortson bristled as he stared at the businessman laughing across the room. "That buffoon is the one who vouched for the liche's shell company! He's the reason those thrice-cursed orbs were on the wall. Do you know how many good men and women we lost in that fight?"

"It was most likely unintentional," said Goldson.

"He lacks the competence for subterfuge." Baggs smirked into his own glass.

"Burn what he meant," barked Ortson. "He's personally responsible for this travesty!"

"Preposterous," Baggs snorted. "It's business!"

"You can't go about holding business leaders accountable for everything that goes wrong," added Goldson.

"Indeed," said Baggs. "People of a certain level are running small empires. We can't be expected to monitor every little detail."

"Little?" Ortson's jowls quivered as he shook with rage. "Thousands of bannermen and heroes died! Uncountable civilians are at risk! The whole world may be in danger because of his dealings!"

Goldson and Baggs looked unaffected. "Well, I'm fairly certain someone was fired over it," said Goldson.

"That's hardly enough for me. His negligence was criminal," harrumphed Ortson. "Nobody is above the law!"

Baggs shrugged and sipped his wine. "Perhaps, but with enough money you can usually get out from under it."

"We have other concerns for the moment," said Goldson. "The groom is coming."

Weaver looked. Through his agitated, inebrious haze, he could see Johan the Mighty making his way toward their table. The paladin's ivory teeth sparkled like the candelabras above, and he must have purchased a glamour for the evening, for his golden hair seemed to wave in a breeze that wasn't there. He was, as always, clad in enchanted armor, though today he wore a white cape and, perched atop the gorget of his chest plate, a small bow tie.

"Ha ha! Weaver! Baggs! Fenrir! So glad you could make it," Johan trumpeted. He gave Ortson a slap on the back for good measure. "Are you having fun? Quite the ceremony, eh? But nobody's dancing yet."

"Perhaps it is the timing of the event, sire," said Goldson. "The… difficulties throughout the city are dampening many spirits, ours included."

Ortson took a deep breath and nodded. "And it's not been a month since the tragedy at Highwatch," he said, trying not to stare at Clubs.

"The kingdom is still in mourning," Baggs added.

"Ah yes. We all miss good King Handor, Tandos hold him. Some people say Marja and I courted too fast." Johan grabbed a fluted champagne glass and took a swig. "But I don't believe in such an idea. The heart wants what it wants."

"Does it?" asked Ortson, shooting a sidelong glance at Queen Marja.

"Indeed, we've all noted what high spirits Her Majesty has been in of late," said Baggs.

"Yes, it must be a powerful love to pull her from her grief, or the unrest on the Wall, or the coming undead threat," said Goldson.

"Or her tea cakes," added Ortson.

"Exactly! Ha! With a bond as strong as ours, we couldn't possibly wait," said Johan. "Besides, my lady knows I saved her from Detarr Ur'Mayan before. I shall do it again."

"Naturally, sire," said Baggs. "Good show."

"But on that note, I must discuss affairs of our security with my most trusted advisors away from prying eyes." Johan winked and pointed at a gaggle of waving nobles. "Care to join me on the terrace?"

Guests hurried out of their way as Johan and his retinue crossed the ballroom. The paladin blew a kiss to Marja, and she stopped eating tea cakes for just long enough to return it. Then a pair of servants opened the great doorway to the balcony, and Ortson found himself standing with Goldson, Baggs, and Johan in the cold night.

The stars glittering above them seemed almost a faint reflection of the lights of Andarun shining below. Goldson took an imperial cigar from a case in his front pocket. Baggs retrieved a long pipe and began stuffing it with dried leaves from a pouch. Ortson stuck with his trusted vice and poured himself a finger of Dwarven whiskey from a small cart that had been wheeled out onto the balcony.

"Ah, smell that fresh air!" Johan took a deep breath, sauntering up to the balcony railing. "It's the sort of night that makes you glad to be alive! Ha! And if we want to stay that way, we need a plan to take down Detarr Ur'Mayan."

"Of course," said Baggs. "Though naturally, we believe responsibility for defense lies with the kingdom."

"And not the business community," added Goldson.

"True enough," said Johan. "But the chaos on the Wall hasn't been good for the kingdom's coffers. The royal treasurer keeps mentioning combined lateral threats in the market, or something like that."

"Collateralized threat obligations." Goldson's scowl was even more pronounced as he spat the words, as though the term itself was bitter.

"Sounds right." Johan shrugged and poured himself a drink. "The point is that Andarun will need gold to train more bannermen and recruit heroes."

"Much more gold for the heroes. They'll be demanding big premiums to face a threat that… that took the lives of so many." Ortson felt a lump rising in his throat and tried to wash it back down with a splash of whiskey.

"Just give them an expanded share of the loot," said Baggs.

"Well, that's a given," agreed Ortson. "But you can't kill a monster with a weapon you haven't looted yet. Guild heroes will want to equip themselves with top quality gear and consumables, and that will require up-front payments."

"I'm certain that when the undead come calling, merchants and heroes alike will answer the call of duty," said Johan. "Their kingdom needs them!"

"Then their kingdom will very likely need vast sums of gold," said Ortson.

"I'm sure you'll find some way to make it work, Ortson. Ha! And let us worry about the finances. Right, gentlemen?"

"Quite," said Baggs, with the uneasy caution of an explorer who has spotted a suspicious log drifting toward him in a tropical swamp.

"Though I'm unsure of what, precisely, we could do," added Goldson.

Johan took a sip of his drink and stared out over the balcony. "Your firm could purchase Thacovia Bank, for a start."

"I beg your pardon?" said Goldson.

"Thacovia," said Johan. "Scoria's biggest bank. Or it was, before this horrible business on the Wall. Now their stock is plummeting."

"That sounds precisely like the sort of firm that Goldson Baggs would not like to buy," said Baggs.

"Why would we?" asked Goldson.

"To stabilize the market? To shore up the tax base? Or perhaps to satisfy a royal edict?" laughed Johan. "Though I hoped there was no need for such a formality among friends."

Goldson and Baggs glanced at each other with narrowed eyes. "My apologies for any insult, sire," said Baggs. "We didn't realize you had already been coronated."

"Given that the wedding was but an hour ago," said Goldson.

"Think nothing of it," said Johan with something between magnanimity and indifference. "I certainly won't. Ha ha! Anyway, cake is in five minutes, and then we'll do the first dance, and then the coronation."

"How… expedient," said Baggs carefully.

"What can I say?" Johan grinned as he opened the door to the ballroom. "The heart wants what it wants. Ha! I'll leave you three to work out the details. I'm sure I'll see you by the buffet. Try the griffin. It's phenomenal."

The paladin pointed at the businessmen, made a clicking noise with his tongue, and strutted back into the reception.

"Well, this is an interesting development," said Baggs as the door to the balcony shut.

"Only if you have a fascination with tragedy," snorted Goldson.

"Do you think purchasing Thacovia will stabilize the market?" Ortson asked.

"Stabilize the market?" Baggs said incredulously. "Good gods, man. Have you been listening to the town criers? Or watching the figures from the Wall? Or listening to your own guild's proclamations?"

"I've been focused on other things," Ortson said. It was technically true, although all of those things had been poured from bottles and taken neat.

"I'm sure you have," said Baggs. "But what about the quests you signed this morning?"

Ortson thought back over the day. Mostly he remembered trying to get into formal wear without spilling his cocktail, but somewhere in there were hazy visions of putting his seal on several sheaves of paperwork. "I vaguely recall them," he said truthfully.

Mr. Goldson rolled his eyes. "Well, Mr. Ortson, let it suffice to say that I don't believe our impending purchase of Thacovia will help matters. Things are too far gone for such a simple solution."

"Is it truly that bad?" asked the guildmaster.

Baggs leaned against the railing of the balcony and took a long puff of his pipe. "Mr. Ortson, consider that since the fall of Highwatch, the threat index for the Freedlands and Ruskan has skyrocketed. Almost every threat obligation written in the last decade has been triggered."

"I'm well aware. The rising indexes have done no small damage to the guild coffers," said Ortson.

"True enough, but at least you know what you owe," said Goldson, taking a drink. "Now, consider that almost every financial institution out there has discovered, and continues to discover, that through their investments they are responsible for billions of giltin in threat obligations due to their direct and indirect investments in CTOs."

"Perhaps trillions," said Baggs. "Those CTO funds are worse than worthless now. Nobody will pay into them until they pay out. They're all debt."

"The Royal Bank of Scoria announced last week that half of their assets were actually liabilities." Goldson shuddered.

"Now, look at the lights of the city," Baggs said, pointing at the tiers below with his pipe. "You can be sure that next to each tiny glow, there's a person who watched their retirement savings, their pension, their bank account, all of it evaporate faster than the melting snow. And rest assured that they are all beyond anger."

"They'll be out for blood." Ortson paled.

"They already are," said Goldson. "Especially given those quests you signed."

"Exactly," said Baggs. "Finally, consider how many of those lights are moving."

The glow of the torchlight crept through the windows of Duine Poldo's Boulderfolk office. Unseen crowds marched in the streets outside, their shouts punctuated by the occasional crash of windows shattering.

"It was a mistake coming here," the Scribkin muttered.

The Wood Gnome on his shoulder chirruped sharply.

"Yes, I know you told me!" Poldo had decided that it was vital to retrieve several documents and shutter the old office before the Wall was engulfed in complete chaos. Nobody else knew the combination to the safe, nor which papers were important, so he had made the trip personally.

Now, however, the flaws in his plan were becoming apparent. It wasn't that the reasoning was bad, but the timing certainly was. Poldo's miscalculation had brought him to Boulderfolk moments before the arrival of an angry mob. "How do we get out of here?" he muttered.

Several Wood Gnomes chittered from a pile of gardening equipment.

"Good idea," said Poldo.

After some rummaging and a bit of a struggle, Poldo emerged from the shed wearing overalls and a wide-brimmed garden hat. One of Boulderfolk's gardeners was a Halfling, so the overalls were a bit long in the leg and spacious around the middle, but with the cuffs tucked into rubber boots and the midsection stuffed with paperwork and nervous Wood Gnomes, Poldo looked like he wore the gardening clothes every day. At least, he hoped he did.

With a deep breath, he grabbed a pitchfork and pushed through the hedge. The north gate was already twisted off its hinges, and it was easy enough to join the mob milling throughout the courtyard. The Scribkin stabbed the air with his pitchfork and marched with pantomimed outrage into the street.

It was like leaping into a river of anger. The dizzying press of bodies around him, the smell of sweat and smoke, and the blurring lights threatened to overwhelm Poldo. A current of shouting, furious people carried him through the streets of the eighth tier until an eddy finally deposited him in a small alleyway near the Broad Steps.

The Scribkin cowered away from the shouting crowds, watching them rage by as he caught his breath. He was in such a state that it took several minutes before he realized that he wasn't alone in the alley. Turning slowly, he found a pile of rags that stared back with a familiar face.

"Fitch?"

"Poldo?" gasped Fitch. "Oh, thank the gods. Poldo, we have to get out of here."

"Hush! I know!" Poldo snapped, ushering the Halfling behind a dumpster. "What are you doing anyway?"

"I was holed up in Mr. Stearn's office when the riots broke out," Fitch said. "But pretty soon the mob broke down the door, and we had to make a run for it. I-I got myself separated from him."

"You lost Mr. Stearn?"

"Eventually, yeah. It took no small effort." A hint of relief flashed over the Halfling's grimy face.

"Good gods, man! You just left him at the mercy of the rioters?" demanded Poldo.

"I'm just trying to keep all my guts where they belong," Fitch insisted. "It's life and death out there, Poldo. You know how many bankers fell off the Wall today?"

"I heard several professionals jumped," said Poldo.

Fitch gave him an odd look. "Jumped? Maybe. I mean, I would, too, if there was a pack of heroes chasing me."

"Guild heroes?" Poldo gasped.

"Is there another kind? Lamia Sisters got declared a F.O.E. this morning."

"Surely not Pradessa and Maliss!" Poldo had met Andarun's most powerful Naga on several occasions. "They were two of the first NPCs! They're patrons of the arts! Pillars of society!"

"All the guild cares about is that they were a perceived threat sitting on top of a lot of wealth. A quest with their name on it got signed this morning, and now they're handbags." Fitch shook as he spoke. "But I was talking about their bank, Poldo! The guild didn't just declare the sisters foes. They made the Lamia Sisters corporate office a dungeon, and everyone working there a henchman."

Poldo shook his head slowly. "I just can't believe it."

"The public's lost a lot of their money, Poldo, and watching a rich man bleed feels like justice to an angry pauper," said Fitch. "If Goldson and Baggs were a Goblin and a Gnoll, they'd be dead already. Heck, if the markets get much worse, I'm not sure even their skin will save them. But for now, the guild is mostly targeting Shadowkin and Darkforged."

"The Shadowkin!" Poldo's mind leapt to the tenants that Mrs. Hrurk had brought into his home, and his stomach leapt into his throat. He took a deep breath. "We have to get out of here."

"That's what I've been saying!" said Fitch.

They deposited Fitch's coat, suspenders, and footwear in the dumpster, and found a colorful rag that could serve as a foul bandana. With his shirt untucked and Poldo's pitchfork in hand, the Halfling looked like another angry gardener, albeit one with suspiciously well-tailored pants. Disguise in place, the pair leapt back into the tide of people rushing down the street.

The mob proceeded to the Broad Steps in disorderly fashion, breaking windows and shouting at nearby bannermen. The stairs to the ninth and tenth tiers were blocked by Elven bannermen and a contingent of heroes, prompting most of the rioters to turn around and march back down another street of the eighth. Many stopped to watch a commotion up on the Wall. A few, however, broke off and made their way down the steps to the lower tiers. Poldo and Fitch joined them, trying to blend in with the thinning crowd without getting too close to any of them.

They were halfway down the steps to the seventh tier when Fitch elbowed Poldo in the arm and jabbed a thumb over his shoulder. Poldo turned back and saw the spectacle that had transfixed so many of the other rioters on the steps.

The eighth tier was near the top of the Wall, and the activity on the tier was visible to anyone on the Broad Steps. It made for a sort of raised stage, and on it a group of professional heroes performed a deadly dance. They darted around a shadowy foe and loosed colorful, pyrotechnic attacks. From their center came a low growl, and then a roar as a hulking, ursine form reared up among them.

Poldo gasped. "Is that—"

"Shut up!" Fitch hissed.

Mr. Stearn, or at least the giant bear that Mr. Stearn periodically turned into, loosed a furious roar and swiped at his assailants with massive claws. But the party assaulting him was prepared to deal with his transformation, and the bursts of magic around him were suddenly punctuated by flashes of silver weapons. A shining arrow caught the werebear in the throat, and with a final roar the lycanthrope toppled backward off the Wall.

"Good gods," breathed Poldo.

Fitch grabbed the Scribkin by the arm and hurried him down the steps. "Just keep moving!"

They hurried down the steps while trying to look unhurried, quickly sidling along with desperate nonchalance. They made their way down to the fifth tier, where they splintered off from the other drifting rioters, then ducked into a side street before breaking into full sprints.

Sprinting to any degree, however, is not an activity that Gnomish bankers engage in very often. Poldo made a mental note that he needed to exercise more as he staggered up to the gated yard in front of his home. A couple of Wood Gnomes crawled from his overalls to pat him on the back as he doubled over, hands on his knees. He still hadn't caught his breath when Fitch flopped down on the cobblestones next to him. "Wha... Whe... where?"

Poldo just shook his head and pointed to the sign that Mrs. Hrurk had recently erected over the doorway. Thin, brass letters read "MR. POLDO'S HOME FOR THE DISPLACED."

Fitch just shook his head and stared up at the sign with a perplexed expression.

"I... I have some matters I must attend to," Poldo breathed.

"Is it collecting your money?" Fitch managed eventually.

"No, I—"

"Then forget it!" the Halfling pleaded. "Come on, Poldo. The guild may not declare us foes, but soon investors are going to come asking questions. And gods, the undead aren't going to stay holed up in Highwatch forever. They might even make it here. Andarun isn't safe for us!"

"I just have to see to—"

"It doesn't matter, whatever it is!" Fitch insisted. "Any business you had here is over. Learn to fail well! I suggest buying a bar on some island in the Teagem Sea and serving fruity drinks for the rest of your life."

Poldo stiffened. "Failing well is exactly what I intend to do, Mr. Fitch. It seems we just have different definitions of the term."

"Well, mine involves sandy beaches and Tinderkin in grass skirts." Fitch pointed Baseward. "I've arranged a secure carriage down by the river, and I'm headed there once I fetch my gold. This is your last chance to join me."

Poldo nodded and extended his hand. "Good luck, Mr. Fitch."

Fitch stared at the offered hand for a moment, then shook it uncertainly. "Yeah. Yeah, good luck to you too, Poldo." And then the Halfling was away.

A Wood Gnome scrambled up Poldo's arm and chittered a question.

Poldo looked up at his eponymous home for the displaced. He could see Mrs. Hrurk's silhouette peering down from a window above. "Yes, I'm staying because… It's for our residents," he told the Gnome on his shoulder. "Come, we have much to do."

"Now the hard work begins," said Johan, the crown of the Freedlands resting amidst his golden locks. The paladin's eyes swept over the crowd standing beneath the dais. "We've been through hard times, and harder times are coming. But now is a time for all of us to come together!"

"Together," echoed Queen Marja, still in her white wedding dress.

The assembled nobles, businesspeople, and town criers gave the king a light smattering of applause.

"Only together can we rally our defenses against the evils of Detarr Ur'Mayan." Johan strutted about the stage, flashing his impeccable grin at the attendees. "Only together can we rebuild what we've lost. Only together can we keep our families safe. Which is why I hope this kingdom can do as my lovely bride and I have and unite despite our losses."

"Unity!" said Marja, clapping.

"And on that note, my lovely bride has prepared a few remarks." Johan turned and gestured to the queen.

This announcement raised eyebrows around the throne room. It was widely known that in her previous marriage, Queen Marja had preferred to let King Handor see to the public speaking, along with all matters of diplomacy, policy, and ceremony. A popular joke within the halls of the castle was if you wanted Marja's attention on a matter, the best course of action was to write it in frosting on a tea cake.

The queen shuffled a pack of notecards as she stepped to the front of the dais. "Ahem. The undead are invading the Freedlands. We face a danger that… um…" Marja briefly stopped reading to flip to the next card. "That is unlike anything we have faced. I must ask that… that…" Flip. "That we put aside our differences and divisions, and unite behind our new —" Flip. "King."

Marja looked up from her notes with evident relief. Perhaps her relative success had given the queen a sudden rush of confidence, because she added some commentary of her own. "Now, I know you must have questions…"

It was a rookie mistake. Most public figures with any experience in speeches avoided mentioning questions, or discussion, or anything that would give the town criers an excuse to begin shouting inquiries.

Hands sprouted from the crowd like an impromptu forest, accompanied by a chorus of shouted questions.

"Why marry so soon?"

"Did you and Johan court before Handor's death?"

"Why was King Handor on the front lines at Highwatch?"

"What's become of the eagle that carried Handor and Johan?"

"Ha ha!" King Johan's laughter was booming as he stepped in front of Marja, but his grin seemed more brittle. "Friends, I hear your concerns, but we don't have time to waste on these little details. We need to work together to save our nation. After all, isn't that what King Handor would have wanted?"

Chapter 21

"I don't care what Handor would have wanted!" snarled Detarr Ur'Mayan. "What I want is to ply him for information on Andarun's defenses, to watch his face as he realizes what has befallen his kingdom, to laugh as he… he…"

The liche seemed to remember himself and, more crucially, the audience of undead gathered around him in the ruined hall of Highwatch's keep. He unclenched his fist and stood up straighter. "Well, it's no matter. The point is, Handor's wishes for his afterlife are irrelevant. He should be raised as a zombie for my army."

Tyren Ur'Thos watched Genevieve squirm under the liche's steely glare.

"Well, uh, right. Right." The spectral woman fumbled over the words, trying to find the right way to say the wrong thing. "The thing is, we have our best vampires and wights looking at the king's body. Good people. Great at necromancy. Really smart."

Detarr waved impatiently. "Yes, yes, out with it."

"He's been thoroughly consecrated," blurted Genevieve. "It's like he was blessed by a high priest in death, or slain by a paladin. The ghouls wouldn't even try taking a bite out of him. The vampires want to drop him down a deep pit, and even then, the hole will probably turn into a sacred site within a few years."

"Enough." Detarr paused in a manner that suggested he would have taken a deep breath, were it possible. "Very well. It seems all of our effort to raise the old king has been a waste of time. I hope someone else has been more productive this week."

Tyren took his cue to step forward. "Lord Ur'Mayan," he said, holding aloft a rune-encrusted shard of stone, about twice as long as his own hand.

The liche's face lit up at the sight of the stone. "The Dark Spire of Nephan!"

"Yes, lord. I personally retrieved it," said Tyren. This was true, although technically he'd retrieved it from the charred remains of several members of Rudge's relic recovery team. Relatively few of the skeletons had survived the deep, trap-laden vaults beneath Highwatch.

Detarr waved the Wyrmwood Staff, and the stone lifted from Tyren's grasp. It floated through the air and into Detarr's skeletal hand. "Excellent," said the liche, staring at the Dark Spire. "Once again, Knight-Commander, you've proven yourself most useful. I must say that it's a pleasant novelty to have such competent help. Which brings to mind, where is my son?"

Tyren took his cue to step back and, thinking ahead, sidled behind a pillar.

"Well?" demanded the liche. "I want my son seated here at my side, where he can't ruin anything."

"We've had... less success there," said Genevieve, floating forward with a curtsy.

"More bad news?" Detarr's eyes glowed with a red-hot light. "Surely your troops have had enough time to locate six dead heroes. I was very clear about where I killed him and his companions, was I not?"

"Yeees." The spectral woman drew out her concession. "We found the site of the battle, lord. But your son wasn't there. Nobody was."

"And you're sure that he hasn't, you know, joined the ranks of the zombies and just neglected to let me know?" pressed the liche. "Skulking with the ghouls out in the courtyard without thinking to tell anyone? That's just the sort of thing my son would do."

Genevieve shook her head. "We've searched everywhere. We think that... we think your son survived."

Detarr Ur'Mayan sat back as though struck. "It can't be," he said. "I would have thought... I mean, I just assumed..."

"I'm so sorry, lord."

"No. Perhaps this is my fault for being careless," said Detarr.

"Nobody has to be at fault," offered Lady Carabae. "Sometimes these things just happen."

"I know. You just always assume they'll happen to somebody else." The liche rapped bony fingers against his jawbone. "I wonder what has become of my son and his companions?"

The undead minions around Detarr were silent. It was best not to interfere when the master's mood seemed to be improving on its own.

"Well, I'm sure we'll figure it out sooner or later. My son does pop up at inconvenient moments," said Detarr. "For now, we must press on toward our goal."

"Andarun."

The name of the city loosed Gorm from the depths of blackness, and he slowly drifted up toward consciousness.

"Greatest city on Arth, they say," said the same voice, masculine and familiar, though only vaguely so on both counts.

"Have they been here?" asked another, more feminine voice. It also seemed familiar. "Gods, the smell alone is enough to make you long for a dungeon. I can already get a whiff of it out here."

Gorm inhaled and the acrid, earthy smells of Andarun's Base wafted over him, though mostly he smelled horse. That explained the furry shoulder his face was pressed against, and the gentle rocking beneath him.

"Well, you won't have to endure it long," said the man. "Once we get our gold, I'm leaving town. We've tarried too long as it is."

"We didn't tarry. Our cargo slowed us down."

"Of course, but that doesn't do us much good now, does it?"

"It's not like we could have done better! He kept falling off the horse!" the woman complained. "And you're the one who let him slip off to that tavern in East Upshore."

"You tell that to the undead when they catch us, and see if they treat you any better for it."

"Assuming they're coming this way," said the woman.

"They are," the man replied. "Everyone said Ur'Mayan must be out for revenge on Johan the Mighty for killing him in the first place, and that was before they made Johan king. Why would the liche take Highwatch unless he's coming into the Freedlands?"

Gorm's brow furrowed under the weight of pressing questions. Johan was king now? What happened to Handor? He tried to remember and came up blank.

The man continued. "He wants to settle the score after Johan chopped off his head all those years ago. You know, closure."

"Closure." The woman's voice dripped skepticism.

"Closure! Mark my words: before spring is out, the undead will be on Johan's doorstep."

"Well, undead threatening a city sounds like a job to me," said the woman. "Not that we'll need it after this."

"I wouldn't take that quest if I didn't have a copper to my name," said the man. "The kingdom isn't offering any premiums."

Even through the haze of a descending hangover, that sounded wrong to Gorm.

It must have sounded equally appalling to the woman. "No premiums? To face a liche? Are they mad?"

"That or broke," said the man. "That ranger from the tavern last night was telling me all about it. Whatever's gone wrong with the quest, they won't see many heroes take it. I'm making for the coast and buying passage down to the Empire, myself."

Gorm shifted his arms, with mixed results. On the downside, he discovered that they were chained together with some cheap manacles. On the upside, there was a flask already clutched in his hands. With some effort, he pulled the bottle to his lips and found it empty.

The Dwarf sighed. It was going to be *that* sort of day.

He opened one eye and immediately squinted at the harsh sunlight beating down on him. He recognized some of the hovels and farms near the road. They were just outside the city, headed through the hamlets and farmsteads that would eventually thicken into the Riverdowns.

The people riding with him were still locked in conversation.

"They'll need a massive army to take on the undead without heroes, and they lost half of the bannermen at Highwatch," the man opined. "I hear the remainder can hardly keep the peace in their cities."

"Maybe the Old Dwarven Kingdoms will send troops," suggested the woman.

"The Dwarves won't leave their clanhomes undefended if there's no profit in it. Especially as the Old Kingdoms are even more destitute than the Freedlands these days. You'd need a lot of gold to tempt them to face a liche."

Gorm had to acknowledge that the man's characterization of his people was harsh but true. He patted at his pouches and pockets in search of another flask, but came up empty.

"Well how about Daellan or Ruskan?"

"After Handor abandoned Parald to bait the liche to Highwatch? I doubt Ruskan will send a sympathy card. And Knifevale doesn't think much better of Andarun. Even if either of 'em could send an army in time, I doubt they would."

"So, there's no sizable army left in the Freedlands?" the woman asked.

"Maybe the Red Horde," chortled the man.

Regret washed over Gorm like a wave at the mention of the Red Horde. He thought of the Guz'Varda, and Zurthraka's death, and Tib'rin, and soon all of the memories that he'd tried to drown bobbed to the surface. They swirled around his skull freely now that his recent sobriety had unleashed them.

"Well, if the gods are kind perhaps we are wrong and the liche will spare Andarun," said the woman.

The man just chuckled darkly. "Closure," he said ominously. "Trust me. Nobody likes to leave things unresolved."

Closure. Amid the roiling memories, Gorm suddenly found purchase on the idea. He couldn't make things right, but at least he wouldn't leave them unresolved.

He opened his eyes again, and he could see his rucksack swinging from his horse's side. Niln's life's work was swaying inside it. He could return the scriptures to the Al'Matrans and make sure the young high scribe and his work were remembered by the Temple. It wasn't much, but it was something.

"Right," said Gorm, heaving to a seated position and nearly startling the riders ahead of him out of their saddles.

"Oh! Oh, you're awake!" said a young Human with sandy hair and a broad nose. He wore mismatched armor and a cheap sword on his belt. A low-rank warrior if Gorm ever saw one.

Gorm sniffed and looked around. His shield was tied to the other side of his saddlebags, but he couldn't see his weapon on his own horse. "Where's me axe?"

"Ahaha. He… he wants his axe, Matina! Probably because his bottle is empty." The warrior growled the last statement at another Human, a slight cleric in the raiments of Musana's clergy. She looked even greener than the warrior; Gorm would have shaved his beard if they had five ranks between them.

"So strange." The cleric twisted round in her saddle and spoke through a forced smile. "Because I filled the bottle just this morning."

As the woman turned, Gorm caught a glimpse of his axe hanging by her saddle. "Ah, there it is. Give it here," he said, scratching himself. "I need to be off."

"No!" the young heroes shouted in unison.

"I… I mean, we should travel together," added the warrior.

"Don't see why," said Gorm. "I don't know ye from a hole in the ground, and while I appreciate any drinks ye may have treated me to, it also looks like ye tried to chain me." He held up his hands and inspected the manacles.

The cleric cleared her throat. "Well, we may have—"

"I'd have taken it personally," Gorm added loudly, "if ye used real chains. Like a Durham Brothers or Steel Golems. But a pair of old Hickmans? These things are as flimsy as they are cheap. Never knew why the tall folk buy 'em." He flexed and twisted, and the shoddy manacles cracked open.

"You don't say," said the warrior, giving the cleric a dark look.

Gorm tossed the broken manacles away. "Ye gave me drinks, but ye brought me to Andarun. Ye chained me hands, but ye made it easy to get out. Ye brought along me horse and gear, but ye still haven't handed me my axe. I can't tell if'n you're trying to help me or turn me in for a reward, but it doesn't matter, because either way you're really bad at it. And either way, I've a matter to attend to elsewhere. The only question is how I'm going to leave things here."

He held out his hand. "I'd prefer 'still alive,' but it's up to ye."

The two young heroes had gone as pale as ghosts. They stared at him in mute terror for a moment before the cleric reached back and retrieved Gorm's axe. After some fumbling with the straps, she handed it to the Dwarf.

"A wise choice," said Gorm with a wink. He patted his rucksack to make sure it was still full, then set off for Andarun with a wave to the pale newbloods. Up on the fourth tier of the city, at the Temple of Al'Matra, he could return the works of Niln to their rightful place. He could leave things where they'd started.

He could find closure.

"And that's why you came here? To bring Niln's books back?" High Scribe Pathalan tried to hide a smirk as he dropped into his chair. The office of Al'Matra's high scribe was small but well-furnished. The walls were lined with long shelves, all of them brimming with rolls of parchment—some blank, some full.

Gorm's brow furrowed as he stepped into the high scribe's office. "Aye. It's the work of your old high scribe, ain't it?"

"Well, yeah, sure." The high scribe gestured for Gorm to sit in one of the chairs on the other side of his ancient oak desk.

Gorm remained standing.

Pathalan shrugged and put his feet up. "But, look, this is all unexpected. I mean, when the acolytes told me there was a Dwarf here for me, I assumed it was someone from the Old Dwarven Kingdom begging for gold. King Forder's been asking everyone in the city for a handout for the Old Kingdoms. They'd do almost anything for some gold at this point. More than usual for a Dwarf. Uh, no offense."

Gorm shrugged.

The scribe grinned. "Still, I never would have dreamed it was you. And not just because of the wanted criminal thing, you know."

"The city watch is already short on bannermen," said Gorm. "Most of 'em ain't got time for a washed-up hero drinkin' in peace, and those that do don't want the headache of dealin' with me."

"I'd think it'd be more of a prestigious honor to bring you in than a headache," said the high scribe.

"Pretty much everything's a headache when ye've taken an axe to the skull," said Gorm. "But it doesn't matter. None of 'em have cared or been foolish enough to try me, and I won't be in the city long, anyway. Just long enough to give ye Niln's book."

"Right. That." The Elf scratched at his long, silver hair. "Thing is, we already have the Book of Niln in the library."

"Aye. But this here's the Second Book of Niln." Gorm pulled the leather-bound tome from his rucksack and dropped it on the desk. "Plus select scriptures from the other prophets and all his notes on them."

"An anthology then. Wonderful," sighed Pathalan. "Well, thank you. I'll... I'll take care of this."

"Ain't ye going to read it?"

"Oh, gods no," laughed the high scribe. "The last thing I need is more scripture to read. Especially not Niln's. He always took this stuff so seriously."

"But... why wouldn't ye take it seriously? Ain't readin' scriptures your job?"

"Okay, yes, technically," said the high scribe. "But look, nobody joins the Temple of Al'Matra looking for deep insights into the meaning of the universe, right? I mean, her latest scriptures are a rambling manifesto about the weasel and the marmot. Not the species, mind you. A very specific weasel and a very specific marmot."

"Which ones?"

"I haven't a clue. But she was two chapters' worth of specific." The high scribe grinned and shook his head. "They call her the Mad Queen for a reason."

"Then why bother bein' an Al'Matran?"

"Oh, the other temples are always sending their people on quests. Even Fulgen's people are always getting divine tasks somehow, and their god doesn't speak. The All Mother's kind of lost in her own world up there. She doesn't bother anyone much unless you stir her up, you see?"

Gorm rubbed his bleary eyes. "Ye wanted an easy job."

"Not an easy job. The easiest job," laughed the high scribe. "It's mostly state banquets and relaxing in gardens, with a bit of writing here and there. And nobody even cares what you write because everybody knows the All Mother isn't going to say anything of use. At least, that's how it usually goes. Back when Scribe Niln was getting the goddess all excited, it was a real headache. Minus the axe, of course. Ha."

The Elf leaned back in his seat and stared up at the ceiling. "Niln almost knocked me out of the high scribe position, and at that point it was so busy I was almost ready to let him have the job. In a way, you did me a favor when you and your party... you know."

"No. I don't know," said Gorm flatly.

"Oh, you know." Pathalan drew his finger across his throat and made a choking sound.

Gorm knew that he should feel angry at the implication, but any emotion and most of his coherent thoughts had spent the past few weeks pickling in despondent sorrow and cheap grog. He couldn't muster so much as a growl when he said, "We didn't kill Niln."

"No, of course not," said Pathalan with a leering wink. "But if you did, it might have been a favor to, you know. Some people."

"We didn't."

"Hey, nobody blames you," said Pathalan. "Well, I suppose the palace and the bannermen do, but not the Al'Matrans. Don't get me wrong; we loved Niln—great little guy. The high priestess even had a statue of him put in the sanctuary downstairs. But that was a suicide mission, and professional heroes kill to survive. You did what you had to do."

"We didn't kill him," said Gorm.

"Right." Pathalan tapped the side of his nose knowingly.

"Ye know what? I'm just goin' to keep this." Gorm picked the book back up.

"Oh? All right, yeah, why don't you take it down to the 'archives' for me?" The high scribe pointed at his wastebasket with a wide grin. "Sound good?"

Gorm only snorted in reply and stamped out of the room.

He pulled the hood of his cloak up as he made his way through the Al'Matran temple. Most of Andarun's citizens and bannermen were preoccupied with the coming undead horde and the turmoil in the markets, but he still tried to take some precautions when walking the city. It wasn't wise to tempt fate, especially not when fate had seemed so prone to indulgence lately.

He glanced into the All Mother's sanctuary as he passed, and his breath caught in his throat. Near the edge of the room, amidst the murals depicting Al'Matra's descent into madness, Gorm saw a familiar face cast in bronze. With quiet trepidation, Gorm stepped into the inner sanctum and approached the statue of Niln.

The former high scribe was depicted in a long robe, holding a book in one hand, the other outstretched in greeting. He wore a small smile that was likely intended to look serene, but seemed sad and wistful.

Something in the air felt sacred, holy. Gorm had been in the sanctuary a few times before, and experienced nothing beyond a morbid curiosity about the strange artwork on the walls. But now he could sense something else in the room, a quiet power much bigger than the architecture it occupied.

It made Gorm shift uncomfortably. In the distant past, he'd been a devout follower of the Dwarven gods, but as his career progressed, he found it difficult to muster devotion to the governing powers of a universe that often seemed designed to kill adventurers in creatively horrible ways. After the dungeon of Az'Anon, the gods seemed to turn their backs on Gorm entirely, and he returned the favor.

Ill at ease as he was, Gorm couldn't pull himself away from the sculpture of his old friend. Trapped in his uncertainty, he sat down at the foot of the statue.

"Hello, Niln," he said, if only to fill the expectant silence. "I came to bring your books back to… to where they belong. Ye know. Wrappin' things up."

The statue stared back at him with its sad, lifeless eyes.

"I know ye gave them to me, but I ain't… I ain't the one in your prophecy. I know. I read it all, just as ye asked, and it ain't talkin' about me. I ain't the sort."

Gorm shook his head. "Not that I didn't want to be, mind ye. I've been tryin' for a year to make things right. I need to… to atone for what happened to ye, and to poor Tib'rin, and all them Orcs of the Guz'Varda. But I only made a bigger mess of things."

Gorm had to look away from the statue's silent stare. "Gods, this is like talkin' to Gaist," he muttered. "I guess I wasn't so different from ye in the end. We both wanted to do more than we could. And, thrice curse it all, ye had me believing it was possible. Not that I was the Seventh Hero or anything, but... just that we were destined for somethin'. Believin' we could save the world."

He glanced to the base of the statue, where Niln's epitaph was engraved in the granite. Beneath the scribe's name was a citation from Al'Matran scripture — the Book of Thyrus, chapter twelve, verse two. It could have been Niln's favorite passage, or perhaps a common invocation for the Al'Matran dead. He looked up at the statue, and from where he sat Niln's frozen gesture looked much like an invitation. With a resigned sigh, Gorm opened Niln's leather tome to the notes on other prophets and flipped to the Book of Thyrus.

> *As the sun cannot comforte thee in the dead of night,*
>
> *Knowledge cannot be thy only comforte, for there will always be questions.*

"Illuminatin' as ever," Gorm muttered with a deep scowl. He searched the margin for notes, and found one written in a small, tight script.

> *It has been here all along. I see it now... Rahballa chapter 6, verse 3*

"What's been here?" Gorm wondered. He flipped to the Book of Rahbella and found the cited verse. Next to it was another note, though it was written in a looser hand.

> *For too long I sought to know my destiny. Epham, chapter 19, verse 22*

The thought sounded incomplete, so Gorm found the Book of Epham and looked for another note in the margins.

> *I wished to take holde of the prophecy of the Seventh Hero. Pathlil, chapter 7, verse 1*

Now Niln's handwriting was hurried and scrawling, and little gobbets of ink were hastily splattered below the note.

"It's one thought," Gorm realized. "They're all connected." He could almost see the high scribe caught in the throes of epiphany, hastily scribbling notes and related verses down as he flipped back and forth through the scriptures, his handwriting getting faster and looser with every page. Gorm wondered what had excited the priest so.

"Only one way to find out," Gorm muttered as he pulled a stub of charcoal pencil from his pack and a loose sheaf of parchment from Niln's notes. Sitting with his back to the statue, he diligently hunted down the fragments of Niln's revelation and transcribed them in his own rigid, angular script, omitting the scriptural references.

> It has been here all along. I see it now.
>
> For too long I sought to know my destiny.
>
> I wished to take holde of the prophecy of the Seventh Hero.
>
> To wield fate as Man holds up his sword.
>
> It was all folly, and I a fool.
>
> Destiny is not wielded as a weapon.
>
> Destiny cannot be forced, or negotiated with, or convinced.
>
> Destiny cannot be known. And so I cannot find my answers.
>
> I have nothing but the All Mother's prophecies.
>
> But is that not enough?

"Don't seem like much to me," Gorm murmured.

> The Falcon Lady has said that her words will come to pass.
>
> The Dark Prince will rise, the Seventh Hero will appear,
>
> the world will be saved.
>
> This cannot be accomplished by mortal hands, least of all by mine.

Her holy words are not a map that leads to a destination.

They are signs, to show that we are in the right place.

As we walk our own paths.

They remind us that all will be as it should.

Even when we cannot see how.

Gorm thought that a novel idea. Most of the heroes he knew approached prophecy as a formula, a set of detailed instructions along the lines of "Place object of legend A into slot B on sacred altar C, and wait for the path to treasure D to appear."

I will not pretend at fighting. That path is for Gorm and his fellows.

I will not pursue a destiny that is not mine to command.

I will play my own part.

It struck Gorm that Niln must have scrawled this manifesto in the final days, or even hours, before he left the party and was murdered. It could have been the last thing he ever wrote. He bit back the sorrow rising in his throat and turned to the next verse.

I will help the downtrodden in my way.

I will remember the virtues.

I will give strength to the weary. I will lift up the broken.

I will be a hope in the darkness, because I know better than any

There is not always a light at the end of the tunnel.

That is why you must carry a torch.

Gorm's hands shook as he stared at the parchment. The only sound was the pounding of his heart and the low rumble of his universe quietly rearranging itself around the words on the page.

There is not always a light at the end of the tunnel. That is why you must carry a torch.

He'd almost let the darkness around him snuff him out completely, just because he couldn't see a way out of his current predicament. But encroaching gloom was more of a reason to keep burning, to shine brighter, and a berserker didn't need a torch to do it. A berserker was one with the fire.

Deep in the cold void within Gorm, something sparked.

He looked up at Niln, and now the statue's permanent gesture seemed to extend a helping hand. Gorm took hold of the outstretched palm and hauled himself to his feet. "Thank ye," he said. "I needed a reminder."

A plan was forming, forged in the bright and furious blaze of Gorm's rekindled spirit. A wide grin spread over his face. Or perhaps he bared his teeth.

Sometimes even he couldn't tell which it was.

Scribe Pathalan had just settled into his chair with a cup of honeyed tea when he heard a low *thump* from behind him. When he turned to find the source of the noise, he noticed that the window to his left was wide open, its curtains flapping in a spring breeze. The Elf paused to ponder that for a moment, then turned back to his tea just in time for a fist to slam into the right side of his jaw and send him sprawling to the floor.

"Ye scream for the guards and they're only gonna find your corpse. Nod if ye understand," said Gorm Ingerson, pushing the high scribe's chair out of the way as he advanced.

Pathalan nodded as he propped himself up on his elbows, his eyes wide and watery.

"I'm here to set the record straight." The Dwarf stomped up to the prone scribe and pointed his axe at his face. "I don't give a ratman's arse what ye believe about your goddess and her writin', but I'll be thrice-cursed before I let ye go around spewin' lies about me. So if ye like having a spine without any right angles, there's two things ye better well understand."

Pathalan stared cross-eyed at the shining blade and whimpered something unintelligible.

"First off, I've never killed a high scribe. And second, just because I ain't killed one doesn't mean I won't. Ye understand?"

"Esh," said the high scribe, nodding vigorously.

"Good," said the Dwarf with a toothy smile. "Now, this here's the Second Book of Niln, includin' his collected notes and commentary on the other prophets. I'm lendin' it to ye so ye can get it properly copied and archived and whatever else ye'd do for an important book. And ye can bet it's important, because I'll be back for it as soon as I've visited some old friends."

Barty Ficer stepped up to a small door in a side street of Lowly Heights. It was a simple oak door in a brick building, notable only for a few small, metal plates fixed to various parts of its surface. One of the plates, specifically the one in the middle of the door at eye level, was engraved with the words "BARTY FICER, ASSASSIN."

The plaque, Barty often remarked, was to keep away any wandering thieves or curious kids who might sneak into the workshop. Threats and deterrents were a crucial part of being an assassin. Of course, another important part of being an assassin was backing those threats up, which accounted for how cautiously Barty approached the door, even in his hurry.

The old man carefully inserted a large, brass key into the lock, rotated it counterclockwise, counted to three under his ragged breath, and then twisted it again by half a turn. He withdrew his hand a second before a tiny blade snapped out above the keyhole, jabbing the air where his thumb had been a moment earlier. Then he pulled the key from the lock and hooked it over the exposed blade, which ratcheted down like a switch. Gears clanked into life within the door.

"Come on, come on," Barty muttered impatiently.

The other metal panes in the door slid open, each revealing a unique mechanism. Barty attacked them with tempered impatience. He rotated the left dial to the number sixteen, pulled three levers in precise succession, tapped out a specific sequence on three glowing stones, and rotated the right dial to four. He took a step back as another mechanical blade stabbed out of the door, this one at eye level, and then flicked a switch that retracted both of the weapons. Finally, he set the dials back to zero, tapped the central glowing stone, waited for the lock to click open, and slammed his face into the door three times.

The last step was involuntary, and entirely due to the meaty hand that gripped the back of Barty's head as though trying to crush a ripening melon. The assassin choked back a sob.

"Hello, Barty," said his assailant.

"Gorm Ingerson," Barty fumbled, feebly struggling against the Dwarf's grip. "I didn't know you were in town."

"Oh? I'd assumed ye heard." Gorm spoke in a casual, almost friendly tone, but he didn't loosen his grip. "Why else would ye be tryin' to scamper off like a rat down a hole?"

"Well, you know," said Barty limply. "The new king says we should do everything we can to keep the city safe. In my line of work, that's easiest done by vacating it."

"Speaking of your line of work, what do ye know about this?" Gorm held up a flat piece of metal that he immediately recognized as a small armor plate from a mechanical assassin.

"Wouldn't know anything about that," said Barty, avoiding looking directly at the plate.

"Really? I would if I was ye." The Dwarf pushed the door open with the assassin's face. "Let's have a chat inside."

Barty renewed his struggles with frantic desperation. "No! Stop! There's more—" He was cut off, nearly literally, by a massive blade that swung in a wide arc in front of them. A few of Barty's silver whiskers drifted down to the dusty floor.

"Bones, that was a big one," laughed Gorm. "What's next? Well, I suppose there's only one way to find out."

"Stop!" shrieked Barty. "You don't understand what will happen if I don't disarm the system!"

"True enough," growled the Dwarf. "But I'm fairly certain whatever it is will happen to ye first."

"All right, all right! I did it! The pay was good, and you don't say no to Mr. Flinn!" Barty cried, his hands flailing feebly. "Just let me get to that panel over there, and I swear I'll confess. I'll do anything!"

"It's good of ye to say as much, Barty," said Gorm. "As it happens, I'm in need of a favor."

Chapter 22

The mechanical gazer vibrated with excitement as it bobbed down the hall, its steel tentacles weaving intricate patterns. A soft chattering emanated from within its metallic shell, the constant, muffled conversations of the various sprites that animated Barty Ficer's creation.

Gorm stamped along behind it. The floorboards of the Red Sow creaked beneath his heavy boots. His limbs were stiff and aching, the price of prolonged riding on an Elven steed. Everybody knew they moved half again as fast as a normal horse, but nobody talked about how doing so made you twice as saddle sore in a third of the time.

The mechanical gazer seemed enamored with one room near the back of the hall. It hovered back and forth around the door, squeaking softly to itself. As Gorm approached, the construct swiveled around, opened its jaw with a mechanical snap, and loosed a chorus of erratic, excited jibbering. *"She's in there! ... In there! ... Behind the door! ... Open the door!"*

"Fine, fine, I heard ye. Shut your trap." Gorm grumbled, flipping the gazer's jaw closed as he stepped up to the door. He paused for a deep breath before knocking three times.

"Come in," said a tired voice.

Gorm pushed the door open and stepped into the modest room, helm in his hands. "Hello, lass."

"I didn't expect to see you again." Kaitha was curled up on an old mattress, her left arm and both legs wrapped in long bandages. She looked frail, a weak shade of herself. A withered blossom.

"Well, I ain't the sort for quittin'," said Gorm as he approached the bed.

"Oh, I know." The Elf wouldn't look him in the eye; instead, she stared out a grimy window at the gray, drizzly sky. "But I know myself as well. I drive people away. My old adventuring parties. My agent. Even the King in the Wood."

"And I hang on to things once I've made up my mind." Gorm sat in a simple oak chair near the bed. "And on that subject, I'm gettin' the party back together. I want ye to help me track 'em down."

Kaitha gave a small, joyless laugh. "You don't need me. You've got that flying contraption with the sprites."

"Aye, but the bastard that built it tells me it has trouble tracking mages, which is nearly half the job. Besides, I want a tracker that I don't perpetually want to punch."

They both looked at the mechanical gazer, which erupted into a tiny, inquisitive cacophony. *"Why are they looking here? ... What's she doing? ... What'd he say?"*

"I said shut it!" growled Gorm. The mechanical gazer snapped its jaw shut.

"I still don't know, Gorm," said Kaitha. "Honestly, I don't know if I'd be helping or hurting your cause. I'm a disaster these days."

"Aye. That's why ye fit right in with us," said Gorm.

Kaitha laughed again, genuinely this time, but she only shook her head and continued staring out the window.

"What happened to ye, lass?" Gorm asked eventually.

The Elf watched dark clouds sweeping over the hamlet of Ebenmyre. "I've been asking myself that for a long time."

"I meant to your arms and legs." He nodded to the bandages.

"Oh." Kaitha shrugged. "The Myrewood."

"And ye don't want a healing potion?"

"Oh, I want one," she said, looking at Gorm with a sudden intensity. "I've been lying in bed for weeks just thinking about how badly I want a healing potion. I want one so bad it burns. It just doesn't burn as much as the memory of withdrawal. The shame of what I've done for a kick. Never again, Gorm. Never again."

"Feels good to hear ye say as much."

"Well, I'm happy for you. It feels thrice-cursed awful from this side." She waved a hand at her bloodied leg. "A bogling got me in the thigh, and their venom stings like dragonfire. I swear, the Myrewood is one of the hells."

Gorm nodded. "Honestly, I thought I'd have to go in myself to find ye when that little flying golem led me this way. I assumed ye'd gone after Thane."

"I did. He isn't there." Kaitha shook her head. "The innkeeper told me the swamp's been more dangerous without the King in the Wood around, but I went in anyway."

"No sign of him?"

Kaitha sighed and looked back out the window. "I found the garden he used to keep, but it's dead. Choked with swamp vines. A blighted crocotrice is nesting in the middle of it now. He's gone, and I have no idea where else to look."

Gorm cursed inwardly. If Thane hadn't returned to the Myrewood, there was no telling where the Troll was. "I'm sorry, Kaitha," he said. "For everything. I should have told ye—"

"I wasn't angry at you," the ranger interrupted. "Well, I was, but I shouldn't have been. I was mostly angry at myself. I've been traveling with a Kobold for more than a year, and Tib'rin before him. I've been working hard to convince the Guz'Varda we were friends. And still, I see a Troll and I... I just assume he's a monster."

She shook her head. "And I'm angry with him as well, honestly. Why would he hide from me? I was *talking* to him, Gorm. If he had found almost any other way to introduce himself..."

"He was scared, lass." Gorm sighed. "Of what ye'd do if ye found out he was a Troll."

"But not everyone else?" the Elf asked bitterly. "I mean, what was so wrong with me that he assumed the worst? Or then again, what's so wrong with me that I would prove him right?"

"Nothing's wrong with you."

Kaitha turned back to Gorm, her eyebrows raised in profound skepticism. "Let's not pay lip service."

"Fine. But whatever's wrong with ye can't hold a candle to all that's good in ye," said Gorm. "You're the Jade bloody Wind, one of the finest heroes ever to walk Arth."

"If that was true, I don't think I would have wound up here." Kaitha gestured at her bandages.

Gorm put a hand on her shoulder. "If it wasn't true, I wouldn't have come here after ye."

The Elf shook her head. "You're different."

"You're thrice-cursed right we are," said Gorm. "Now, are ye coming?"

Kaitha laughed despite herself. "Why are you doing this? Handor's dead, Gorm. Who will you hold a grudge against now? The Orcs still hate us. We can't best Detarr. We failed."

"First of all, never tell a Dwarf he can't hold a grudge," Gorm held up his index finger. "We can always find someone worthy of a good grudge. Johan is still out there plottin', and nobody's touched Goldson or Baggs."

"True enough."

"Second," said Gorm, counting on his fingers. "I've an idea that may get us back into the good graces of the Guz'Varda, and more importantly, get them into the good graces of the Freedlands. And third, we couldn't beat Detarr. That doesn't mean we can't. This time's different."

"How so?"

"I've got a plan for getting the staff back."

"You had the staff before. You'd need an army."

Gorm grinned. "I'm pretty sure I can get one of those as well."

The Elf shook her head with a smirk. "Well, what your plan lacks in specifics it makes up for in absurdity."

"We find the party. We get 'em back together. We save the world. Everything else is just details," the Dwarf said. "Point is, the undead are threatenin' everything, and whatever comes of it, there's only going to be two kinds of people in the end. Those that gave it everything, and those that quit."

He stood. "We both know which group I belong to. Which one will ye be in?"

"Oh, don't make a mummers' play of it," the Elf chided him as she shifted her legs over the edge of the bed. "You already know my answer."

"Wouldn't have come all this way if I didn't." Gorm extended a hand to the ranger. "But it's good to see I was right."

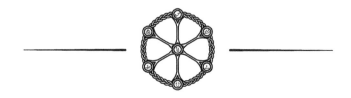

"Turn left!"

"I ain't turnin' left!" Gorm twisted around in his saddle to shout at the mechanical gazer. "There isn't even a bloody intersection here! Where is there even a left to turn on?"

"I think it means that game trail," said Kaitha, pointing to a small gap in the undergrowth. "It's just confused."

"There's an understatement," grumbled the Dwarf. "At least we must be getting close to them wizards if their magics are scrambling the sprites this much."

"Turn around!" pleaded the mechanical gazer as it bobbed along behind them. The construct had brought Gorm and Kaitha to the northeastern edge of the Green Span after they left Ebenmyre, but over the past day it had grown increasingly disoriented. Now it seemed convinced that its target was somewhere in the middle of Drakehead Lake. *"Make a u-turn! … Take the next available left!"*

"Is there a way to turn it off?" Kaitha asked.

"I don't think so, short of taking an axe to it," said Gorm.

"Let's not rule out any options," said Kaitha. "But for now, I think we're getting close. Look. There isn't supposed to be anything but an old ruin out this way, but a lot of carts and horses have been through here as of late."

"Could be trouble," said Gorm.

"It could be a conclave of omnimancers," said Kaitha.

"Same thing."

"Turn around at the next intersection!" screamed the gazer.

Gorm sighed and spurred his mount on.

The ruins of an old granite fort came into view just before noon. Ramshackle wooden structures were haphazardly perched atop the crumbling ramparts and fallen towers, and long black banners with a strange gray symbol hung from the windows, gently flapping in a spring breeze. Gorm and Kaitha dismounted and tethered the mechanical gazer to a tree before approaching the fort's gate.

A thin slot in the door opened before Kaitha could knock. "And what exactly is it that you want?" said a muffled voice.

"We're looking for a friend," said Gorm.

"You won't find any here. Try taking up a hobby or talking to people in pubs." The tiny peephole slammed shut.

"Clever git," Gorm growled, and hammered on the door three times.

The slot opened once more. "We don't take visitors."

"And I don't take 'no' for an answer," Gorm barked. "We've come to see a specific friend. Jynn's his name."

"How do you even know he's in here?" said the hidden guard.

"There's two ways to find out," said Gorm. "But only one of them involves a battleaxe."

"Ha! This gate is made from solid oak with steel bracers and is enchanted with the secret wards of the Fane Amada!" the guard crowed. "Your axe won't do much against it."

"Perhaps," said Kaitha. "But the wall over there is patched up with some pine boards and a broken barrel."

There was a thoughtful silence.

"Um, those have wards too?" the guard suggested.

"I could check for ye," said Gorm, brandishing his axe.

"No, no!" said the guard. "We're... uh.... We can make an exception for you. But you'll have to leave your weapons in the gatehouse."

Gorm shrugged. "If ye really think that'll make us less dangerous."

The door clanked as it was unlocked, then creaked open to reveal a young, knock-kneed man in an omnimancer's ragged gray robes. He scuttled back to a relatively safe distance and then pointed to a wooden bin, where Gorm and Kaitha deposited axe and bow, respectively. Once they were disarmed, the wizard pushed open the inner door, or more accurately, he began a laborious attempt to push open the inner door. The entryway had been built to withstand a siege and the omnimancer had been built for a life of reading in the corner, so the way was opened with more struggling than ceremony.

Kaitha leaned close to Gorm as they watched the frail man labor. "I'm glad the guard could be intimidated, but if we're going to get Jynn on our side, it can't all be about threats and violence."

"Oh, come now. We made our careers on threats and violence." Gorm snorted. "We got paid because sometimes threats and violence are the only way anything gets done."

"Sometimes," conceded Kaitha. "But if we want to convince him to fight for us, we need to stay calm and make a compelling case."

"If ye say so," said Gorm, unable to conceal his doubt.

The panting wizard finally finished opening the door and ushered them into the courtyard. The grounds beyond were teeming with omnimancers. Young men and women in gray robes stared at them from every corner of the courtyard, looked down from the ramparts, and peeked out from the windows of the inner keep.

"They might be dangerous," Kaitha whispered in his ear.

Gorm glanced over to a makeshift training ground, where a group of omnimancers were practicing their weaving. One of the older mages attempted to hurl a spell at a burlap target. Nothing came of it except a few pathetic sparks of sorcery.

"I'm pretty sure we'll be fine," he said to Kaitha.

They hadn't made it halfway across the courtyard before an omnimancer in a tall, plumed hat burst from the keep and stormed toward them. He was decidedly plump for a man living in the middle of some overgrown ruins, and his gray robes were decorated with a multitude of feathers and other trinkets. His beard was thin and curled, and put Gorm in mind of moss clinging to a stone. "What is the meaning of this?" he screeched. "Rob, you were to drive off all who dare approached our fortress!"

Rob muttered an apology and kicked at the gravel.

"And you!" The omnimancer in the ridiculous hat turned to Gorm and Kaitha in turn. "You would dare to trespass in the lair of the Fane Amada?"

The discussion was momentarily interrupted by a commotion from the communal gardens on the east wall, where a young omnimancer was waving her arms to avoid falling off a stack of barrels. Her wild gesticulations sprayed twisting threads of elemental magic in every direction, scattering the omnimancers around her. An errant bolt of sorcery flew into the henhouse, and after a moment of ominous clucking, something hideous, scaled, and vaguely resembling poultry lurched from the coop and began chasing screaming mages around the courtyard.

"…Yes," said Kaitha.

"Oh, for the love of Musana — Wilt, just hit it with a shovel! The shovel! The one in your hand!" The omnimancer in the hat was crimson-faced when he turned back to the adventurers. "Ugh, very well. What do you want, anyway? I'm very busy."

"Clearly." Kaitha tried to hide a smirk and failed.

"We're looking for our friend," said Gorm. "Thin, Human, always looks like he's sick, black goatee. Know where he is?"

"Do I know?" laughed the omnimancer. "Why, you stand before Rathwyne, High Amada of the Fane! I am the master of night and day, of ice and fire, of enigma and paradox! I alone have seen the *tet ahua* rise above the Emerald Infinity! All secrets of the gloaming are at my command."

"So you're the head wizard here?" said Kaitha.

"We are not wizards!" snapped Rathwyne.

Gorm watched an omnimancer throw a spell at the rampaging ex-chicken. The magical missile missed its target, ricocheted off a wall, and struck the caster's face hard enough to knock him to the ground. "Well, I'll grant ye that," he said.

Rathwyne sniffed and waved a dismissive hand. "We have moved beyond your petty concepts of mages and wizards and heroes! We are the Fane Amada, the secret-keepers! We know the names of the four—"

"Right, right," said Gorm. "But ye know where Jynn is?"

"Yes. Fine. Brother Jynn chooses to regard the mysteries of many things in the Chamber of Silence," said Rathwyne.

"He what now?"

The High Amada sighed. "He's studying in the library, if you must speak of things in the old ways."

"And where's the library?" asked Gorm.

"You will have found it when you come upon the third portal on the weaveward side."

Kaitha thought for a moment. "So that's the third door on the…"

"The left, fine. The third door on the left," conceded Rathwyne, pointing to the keep. The courtyard rang out with renewed screams as the fowl abomination cornered a cluster of Fane Amada. "Excuse me, I've got to deal with this."

"Don't let us keep you," said Kaitha.

Rathwyne set off across the courtyard without so much as a nod. "I said to use the shovel, Wilt!"

"Omnimancers," muttered Kaitha under her breath.

"Aye. Barmy to the last," said Gorm. "Come on, let's go find ours."

They found Jynn seated at a large table in the center of the library in the Fane Amada's keep. The walls were lined with glass cases. Papers and notes blanketed the furniture and floor around the recent omnimancer, including several pages carefully balanced atop Patches. The dog lay dutifully next to his old master, motionless except for the thumping of his tail on the floor as Gorm and Kaitha approached.

Jynn didn't look up from the page. "I didn't expect to see you again."

"Didn't expect to have to come all the way out here to find ye," said Gorm. "What are ye doing with this lot?"

Jynn gestured at the papers surrounding him. "Researching my father's work. Trying to figure out what he was planning."

"I'm fairly certain he's marchin' for Andarun," Gorm said.

"The bannermen are evacuating Aberreth," Kaitha added.

Jynn glanced up at them just long enough to be condescending. "Yes, I'm well aware of his current plans. I'm researching the Leviathan Project."

"The one you and your father were working on before he died?" asked Kaitha.

"The one that he and some other mages were working on," Jynn corrected her. "Father may have let me see an experiment from time to time, but he didn't trust me with his plans. I knew that it was a secret project and that it involved live test subjects, but I didn't put it all together until Father unleashed the hellhound and the... uh... fire pig?"

"Demon boar?" suggested Gorm. "No, I think it was a netherboar."

"Ah, yes. Gods, it's like he has an involuntary reflex for the grandiose." Jynn reached down to scratch Patches behind the ears. "Regardless, it was no coincidence that Patches and the dead pig appeared after we killed the infernal beasts. I realized that it must have something to do with the Leviathan Project. And so I came here to research it."

"Here?" Kaitha's doubt was punctuated by a final-sounding squawk from the chicken-beast outside.

Jynn gave an apologetic shrug. "The Fane Amada are... misguided, but if they're good for anything—"

"Doubtful," Gorm muttered.

"It's collecting hidden knowledge," continued Jynn, ignoring the interruption. "Forgotten tomes, runic glossaries, compiled notes; exactly what I need for my investigation."

"I can believe that," said Kaitha, looking over at the glass cases lining the wall. "Just look at all of these old books."

"They've assembled an impressive collection of forbidden grimoires," said Jynn. "*Encyclopedia Daemonica*, the *Seven Cryptical Books of Solumn*, a translation of the *Al'Thadac Shards*, the *Psalms Mannocolai*; the list goes on."

"What's this one?" asked Gorm, picking up the only tome not locked within a glass case.

"That's perhaps the most powerful book never written," said Jynn.

"It's all blank." Gorm flipped through the empty pages. "No, wait, there's a line at the front."

Gorm read the small, neat script on the page aloud.

Imbalanced. Too powerful. Breaks mechanics.

He lowered the book and looked about in consternation. "What the bloody bones is that supposed to mean?"

"That's the *Retconomicon*," said Jynn. "A book of forbidden chronomancy. Or it would have been, if it hadn't written itself out of reality."

"A book that unwrote itself?" Gorm gave a small chuckle. "That don't sound so powerful."

The omnimancer shrugged. "It changed the fabric of the universe. It could have unmade and remade lives, brought the dead back en masse, or destroyed Arth outright. It might have done all of those things multiple times before redacting itself, and nobody on Arth, now or ever before, would know it."

Gorm carefully set the book down.

"What do they keep in this one?" asked Kaitha, pointing to a wooden case near the back of the room. It was covered in glowing runes, chalk circles, and other arcane symbols that were individually indecipherable, but collectively conveyed a clear warning.

"That's the *Ordo Diluculum.* An ancient book outlining the functions and teachings of the Twilight Order before it fell. It was written by omnimancers in the Third Age."

"That one must be fairly tempting for ye," said Gorm.

"Not in the least," said Jynn. "I came here to study the same runes and rituals my father did, and to do that I need... darker texts. The notes Aya of Blades gave me indicate that Father and his colleagues were combining demonology and low magic."

"Bones," gasped Kaitha.

Gorm felt his blood run cold. Demonology was among the darkest of dark sorceries, considered worse than necromancy in many circles. After all, everything summoned by the necromantic arts had at least had business on Arth at one point, but demons were never meant to be in the mortal realms. Low magic might have been even worse. It was the magic of the Sten, the rituals and rites that changed fate and bound the gods.

"What could drive a wizard to that?" Gorm wondered aloud. "No, wait, never mind. It's—"

"Immortality," said Jynn and Kaitha at the same time.

"Aye, of course it's bloody wizards and their thrice-cursed immortality," said Gorm. "Whenever there's some terrible darkness anywhere on Arth, it's a good bet an old mage decided that he shouldn't have to shuffle off this mortal coil—even if it means shovin' everyone else off it instead."

"We're all familiar with the lengths my father would go to for the sake of avoiding death," said Jynn. "But you'll recall that the Leviathan Project was commissioned by the Freedlands and Ruskan."

"Fair enough," said Gorm. "I don't see how any of this relates to demonic pigs and dogs."

"It's the story of the Leviathan," said Jynn. "When the gods vanquished the great darkness Mannon, he bound himself to a fish. In time, the fish became the Leviathan."

"And you believe that the ultimate evil possessed a fish?" said Kaitha.

"Not possessed," said Jynn. "Possession is when a supernatural entity forces a mortal to act against its own will."

"So it was more like an incarnation," said Kaitha.

"No, that's when a supernatural being is born into a mortal form," said Jynn. "There's no original mortal bound up in that process."

"I thought that was an avatar," said Gorm.

The mage shook his head. "An avatar is a supernatural being lending its power to a mortal to achieve a mutual purpose."

"I think I fought some cultists like that back when I was running with Crimson Justice," said Kaitha. "When we killed the strongest of them, Ysether-soth the Frog Demon burst out and attacked."

"That sounds more like a dark pact," said Jynn. "That's when an evil force inhabits a willing mortal to gain access to our reality. It's set free on Arth when the mortal dies."

"I thought that's what happened with Mannon and the Leviathan," said Kaitha.

"And it all sounds like possession to me," said Gorm.

"There are similarities, but there are important differences," Jynn explained. "My father and his colleagues believed Mannon and the great fish were tied together in death by prophecy and fate. Aya of Blades called the resulting creature 'soul-bound' in her notes, which is the term Father used for Patches and the pig. I believe soul-binding requires both the mortal and the supernatural to occupy parallel threads in the weave's matrix with a concurrent termination point."

"Beg pardon?" said Gorm.

"For lack of better terms, they have to 'die' at the 'same time.'" Jynn made little quotation marks with his fingers as he spoke. Gorm noticed that he still wore the long, black glove over his left hand. "Though it's inaccurate to apply words like 'die' or 'time' to demons and the greater powers. But if you think of it that way, the story of the Leviathan makes more sense. If the lord of darkness could escape judgment by binding himself to any soul, why choose a fish? But if you narrow the candidates for soul-binding to mortals that died in a particular instant, a fish may have been the best choice available."

"Well, desperate times, I suppose," Gorm said.

Jynn nodded. "Regardless, my father's associates never saw any soul-bound come from their experiments and assumed they had failed. But based on the writings in the *Saura'Parymo* and the *Shadar Khaz Manuscript*, I believe the type of low magic used in soul-binding creates meta-distortions in the weave. The resulting variable shift chronologically displaces the subjects at terminal events."

"Ye might as well skip the gibberish and just do the quote thing again," said Gorm.

"When a soul-bound is created, it's shifted forward in time," said Jynn. "It appears minutes, months, years, or centuries after the death of the bound souls."

"This is sounding less and less like immortality," Kaitha said.

"Agreed, but the bound souls may not be lost forever," said Jynn. "There's a shorter chronolateral move when a soul-bound is killed. Death restores both the mortal and the supernatural to... to their 'rightful' state. The legends say that within a day of the death of the Leviathan, Mannon reemerged in the heavens. Theoretically, a fish could have rematerialized back in the sea as well, though that detail failed to make history."

"Just like a demon and Patches came back after we killed the hellhound," said Gorm.

Jynn scratched the dog behind the ear. "Exactly."

"And ye solved all this in a few weeks?"

"Oh, nothing's been solved," said Jynn. "It's just a theory, and one with more questions than answers. Patches was a puppy when Father... performed his experiments. I don't know why he's a full-grown dog now. And why was he alive after the death of the soul-bound when the pig didn't survive the same transition? What brought the dog back? How long did it take the hellhound to appear on Arth, and why was it less than a few decades? I could spend a lifetime studying this."

"I've a different proposition," said Gorm.

"I didn't think this was a simple friendly visit," sighed Jynn. "I'm guessing you're attempting to reunite the party and stop my father."

"Aye," said Gorm.

"It's a fool's errand," said Jynn. "Leave the liche to the guild and the bannermen. They're better suited to the task."

"You don't sound convinced," said Kaitha.

The wizard sighed. "Perhaps not, but I believe that if they can't defeat him, we can't either. What would we bring to the fight that the guild cannot?"

"An omnimancer," said Gorm.

Jynn's scowl drew deep trenches across his face. "Do not call me that. I may wear gray robes and reside with the Fane Amada, but I am still a noctomancer at heart."

"You wove solamancy," said Kaitha.

"Only once," said Jynn. "And under what can only be described as extreme duress."

"But ye wove it," said Gorm. "Ye saved Laruna with a cure spell — could a noctomancer do that? Could one of them Fadin' Tomatahs do it?"

Jynn narrowed his eyes. "The principles of magics have enough similarities —"

"And ye know them," said Gorm. "Because you're a thrice-cursed brilliant wizard, Jynn, trained by the Academy. Ye were the big poobah of the blue bird —"

"High Councilor of the Circle of the Red Hawk," Jynn interjected.

"Even better," said Gorm. "Your Faint Armada don't have any of that. They ain't wizards!"

A wayward spell flew in through the window, bounced off the ceiling, and set one of Jynn's papers alight. "Sorry!" someone shouted from the courtyard.

"I'll grant you that." Jynn extinguished the smoldering note with a gust of wind.

"Arth ain't seen a wizard such as ye for ages," said Gorm. "The sort of mage the Wyrmwood Staff was made for. The kind who can master all a wizard's virtues."

"No!" snapped Jynn, slamming his hands down on the table. "I can see what you're getting at, Gorm, and even if I thought your mad errand might be possible, I wouldn't go along with it. I will not be an omnimancer!"

"But ye can cast both —"

"I have been able to touch both sides of the weave since I was a boy, yet I have always been — and am still today — a noctomancer!" Jynn took a deep breath and composed himself. "If I focus on casting only noctomancy, my robes will eventually return to their true color. And once they do, I can take a new name and rejoin the Order of the Moon —"

"Assuming your father hasn't wiped 'em out," said Gorm. "Ye'd risk 'em all for the sake of fancy robes and silly titles."

"For the sake of having a life worth living," hissed Jynn. "I'd rather Father burn me to ashes than spend my years in the gutter as an omnimancer."

"It can't be that bad," said Gorm.

"It's worse. The common man mistrusts wizards and magic users, and wizards and magic users mistrust omnimancers. They are exiles among exiles." Jynn shook his head and stared out the window. "The Twilight Order is nothing more than a stain left on history. So long as I wear these robes, all I can do is live like some sort of sorcerous leper among these untrained fools and hope I don't die in one of their experiments."

A loud explosion and a flash of violet light somewhere outside the windows punctuated the last sentiment.

"So don't wear robes," said Gorm. "Change your thrice-cursed clothes."

"Shave your beard off," the wizard retorted.

Gorm and Kaitha gasped in unison. "How dare ye?"

"Exactly," said Jynn. "I will not take off my robes, nor will I weave omnimancy. It isn't who I am."

"You don't know who you are," said Kaitha softly.

Jynn glared at her. "What?"

"You don't know who you are. You only know what will happen if you aren't the person everyone expects." The Elf ran a finger along the edge of her jade bracers. "Trust me, wizard, I've been more rich and famous than you've dreamt of, and all it ever made me feel was pain and fear of losing it. Success and status are a gilded cage. But when you let go of those things, or life takes them from you, the expectations don't matter anymore. Strip it all away, and nothing can hurt you. You lose the fear."

She shook her head and looked at the wizard. "Except you haven't. Your old status means nothing now, but you're still hanging on to the idea of what you should be, hiding from what you could be. You're still scared."

The wizard shook his head. "Y-y-you don't k-know me," he managed.

"Then that makes two of us," said Kaitha, turning to leave. "Come on, Gorm. You can't help someone who won't help himself."

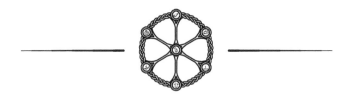

Jynn Ur'Mayan watched the Elf and Dwarf leave the library with bleary eyes. He doubted he could have kept his voice level had he spoken to them again, and the gods knew he was embarrassed enough without his vocal cords cracking like a scared apprentice.

Patches whimpered.

"Don't worry. I'm fine," Jynn lied. For a time, he sat staring at the black glove on his left hand. He flexed it once or twice, wincing at the numbness of the appendage. He couldn't feel his fingers moving, or the leather of the glove against their tips.

Then again, he couldn't feel any pain either. He could hear Kaitha's words in his head. *Strip it all away, and nothing can hurt you.*

He shoved away from the table, scattering papers and prompting Patches to leap up excitedly. The dog danced around his heels as he paced the length of the library.

"No, Patches. It's not time for walkies," muttered the wizard. "I need to think. I need to clear my head. I need…" He trailed off as he realized that he had stopped in front of the rune-encrusted case containing the *Ordo Diluculum,* the book of the Twilight Order.

He stood still, staring down at the case. In his mind's eye, he could see the rows and rows of boxes where he had tucked away a lifetime of memories and emotions. One in particular drew his attention; a small spot in the back where he had tucked away his memories of experimenting with omnimancy. The knowledge that it was there, that he could touch both sides of magic, had haunted him for most of his life, but he hadn't let himself touch the box or recall the memories within for years…

With a deep breath, Jynn opened the box.

Memories swirled into his mind. He recalled a child, barely older than a toddler, pulling fire from the air as easily as he pulled shadow. He remembered the bruise that formed on his tiny hand as his attunement fell out of balance. He could still hear the way Mother screamed when she saw it; feel his relief when she told him that she differently; he remembered Detarr correcting him, not harshly—he was never cold until after Mother died—but still firmly speaking to his son.

Jynn, you must never cast solamancy, Detarr had said. *When omnimancy tempts you, remember who you are. If you give in, you'll shame our Order. You'll shame the name of Ur'Mayan.*

"I'm not sure how that name could be shamed much more at this point," the omnimancer muttered. He shut the mental box of memories and heard Kaitha's voice again.

Strip it all away, and nothing can hurt you.

He waved his right hand, and the amateurish enchantments of the Fane Amada blew away like dust in the wind. Another gesture popped the glass lid open, exposing the *Ordo Diluculum*. It had a pebbled gray leather cover, with inlaid precious metals and stones weaving complex patterns across its ancient surface.

You lose the fear.

His father's voice echoed from the depths of Jynn's memory, refusing to be shut away entirely. *When omnimancy tempts you, remember who you are.*

"How could I remember who I am?" he said to himself, picking up the tome. "I'm still finding out."

The text was in Pre-Imperial Daellish, but the Fane Amada kept a few translation glasses handy. The thick lens cast the book below in various shades of green and showed the ancient script in modern Imperial. Holding the glass over the book's first page, he could see that it opened with a bold salutation.

Welcome, Initiate, to the Greatest Order of Wizardry on Arth.

"History might say otherwise," the wizard murmured as he turned the page.

He scanned through the pages of the book. The opening chapters were devoted to a lengthy treatise on the Order's history at the point of writing, some mundane notes on the layout and living arrangements in the Tower of Dusk, an outline of the heraldry and functions of the various circles within the Order, and near the end of the opening section, a closing letter to new apprentices by the Archmage Livella. A paragraph near the bottom caught his attention.

It has been my experience that some initiates are unhappy to discover that they will be counted among the omnimancers. They wish to join the larger Orders, where they believe there is more power to be gained. Such thinking is folly. You cannot reach your full potential using only half of your magic. If you reject who you are, you will never become the person you could be.

Jynn's hands began to tremble. He turned the page as if to escape from the words, but that only brought him into the chapters on advanced spellweaving. The tremors in his limbs graduated into violent shaking.

"Permanent illusions…" he muttered, flipping through page after page of complex spell diagrams. "Teleportation!… Short ranged displacements without a focal component… conjured metal… permanent conjurations… scrying at will… counterspells… counter weaving!"

Jynn recalled old legends of omnimancers performing impossible feats with sorcery, spells that couldn't be woven by collaborating solamancers and noctomancers. Those spells had been lost to time with the fall of the Order of Twilight. It was only now dawning on him that such secrets could be rediscovered. Power that no mage had dreamed of for ages was, quite literally, at his fingertips.

He read for hours. Each page opened up entirely new disciplines of magic to him, spelling out techniques and secrets that he'd always presumed were legends. Diagrams of arcane devices and artifacts were littered among the spells and runes. He recognized a few types of attunement orbs, including a useful-looking variant set in a ring or amulet. There were scrying pools, reservoir gems, waygates with great crystals set atop their arches, and more than a few devices that Jynn couldn't even identify. Near the back was a drawing of a long stave, inscribed with ancient languages, with a dragon's claw clutching a glowing orb at one end. The Wyrmwood Staff.

Jynn shook his head and turned the page again. He flipped past the technical diagrams and sections on advanced theory to a thin chapter on philosophy at the end of the book. These pages were more worn and fragile, likely because they were the only parts of the book that the untrained mages of the Fane Amada could comprehend. One passage in particular stood out.

> We do not police the other Orders; that is, we do not use our magic to impose our laws or will upon them. But the pursuit of balance often drives us to rebuke the noctomancer whose quest for mastery has gone too far, or to restrain the solamancer who lusts after too much power. Not necessarily because they are wrong, but because omnimancers can only thrive when we are in balance, and one cannot be in balance when the world has gone askew.
>
> Thus, our path to the wizard's virtues is also the path to common good. In serving others, we advance ourselves. In serving ourselves, we better the world for others. We are not selfish, nor selfless, for either way would lead us to the same destination. The omnimancer's path is always clear.

Jynn set the book down. His path was clear.

Patches wagged his tail and danced in circles as the wizard tucked the *Ordo Diluculum* and the translation glass into his satchel.

"Yes, Patches. We're going out," Jynn murmured as he closed the book's case and rewove the protective enchantments over it. Then he left the library, collected his possessions from the Fane Amada's sleeping quarters, and hurried out the door of the keep.

The dog ran at his heels as he trotted down the steps. The sun was setting over the forest, but if he could ride through the night, he could still catch them. It might take some scrying to locate the Dwarf, but those spells were available to Jynn for the first time. A smile spread over the wizard's face as he hurried toward the stables, already planning spells of divination to locate his friends.

"Where ye goin'?" said Gorm.

Jynn skidded to a halt in the loose earth of the courtyard. Gorm and Kaitha were sitting on a pair of crates, sharing a platter of meat.

"You're still here," said the wizard.

"We figured it'd take ye a while. Besides, there was free chicken for dinner," said Gorm.

"Of a sort," added Kaitha, brushing a scale from her drumstick.

"It's good enough," said Gorm, feeding a scrap to Patches. "Sit and have a bite with us. We've a long ride ahead of us tonight if we're to make good time."

"Uh, yeah. Sure. I just…" Jynn shook his head as he pulled up a crate. "I was getting ready to follow you. I assumed you'd have given up and left without me."

"I guess we knew you better than that," said Kaitha.

"I suppose you did," said the omnimancer with a smile.

Chapter 23

Laruna's face contorted into a warped frown as the punch slammed into her jaw; it hit with enough force to turn her around in a spiral of flames. As she spun through the air, she glimpsed a familiar figure standing in the crowd. Confusion and pain washed over her, sending her reeling toward the line. By the time she stopped herself, she had nearly stumbled over the glowing, azure boundary.

"Kaitha?" she said, wiping blood and sweat from her eye.

The Elf waved and said something, but Laruna couldn't hear her over the roar of the crowd.

"Hang on," Laruna slurred, wiping the blood from her face. "I've got to finish a thing."

She took a deep breath and turned back to the fight. Across the illuminated ring, a meaty-looking barbarian encased in iron and furs glowered at her from the other side of the enchanted flag. He tossed a glowing hunk of metal toward her. It hissed and sputtered as it landed in the dirt.

"You melted it!" bellowed the barbarian.

Laruna nodded absently, checking her teeth with her tongue. She'd assumed that reducing his blade to molten slag would end the duel, but Hogarth the Wolf had proved remarkably tenacious. Her lips ached as they broke into a bloody smile.

"You know how much that sword cost me?" Hogarth shouted.

"About half my purse, I'd wager," Laruna retorted.

The barbarian bellowed and charged across the ring. Laruna sent out a blast of flame that forced him to dodge, and followed it with a pillar of fire that erupted from the earth beneath the startled warrior. Hogarth soared through the air with a despairing wail and landed on the far side of the ring once more, rolling about in the dirt to extinguish the flames. A sudden hush fell over the crowd.

Laruna gave a short nod and turned back to Kaitha. "What are you doing here?"

"Recruiting you," said Kaitha.

"You've got a gig with a new party?" asked Laruna, working out a cramp in her neck. Hogarth punched harder than she would have thought.

"No," said Kaitha.

"Not interested," said Laruna.

"Hey! Get back to the fight!" called a spectator.

Laruna leveled a glare in the direction of the comment, and the crowd shrank back from her in terrified silence.

"You're interested," said the ranger.

"What makes you so sure?"

Kaitha nodded at the dueling flag. "You're in for the same reason that you're pit-dueling in a shanty town along the Tarapin."

"Because I can make a lot of gold where the bannermen won't bother me?" said Laruna.

"Because you're looking for a fight." The Elf smirked at the smoking barbarian.

Laruna spat and shook her head. "I've found plenty of them."

"Not the kind that can prove what sort of mage you are. Not the kind that shows the world you're one of the best of our age. Not a fight as big as Detarr Ur'Mayan. It's the job of the century, Laruna. Maybe the age. Heroes lined up for days for a chance to take him on."

"And they're all dead now," said Laruna.

"But you and I both know we're stronger than they were," said Kaitha. "Nobody else has faced him and lived. You've done it twice."

"We still lost," said Laruna.

"Maybe. But I'd bet you've been thinking about what you would have done differently," Kaitha said. "About whether or not we could have won."

"We could have!" exclaimed Laruna before she caught herself. "But the point is that we didn't."

"No, the point is that we still can," Kaitha said. "Come on. Let's go."

"You know I didn't agree to that," growled the solamancer.

The Elf shrugged. "What I know is that you'd never hold back for the sake of a man."

Laruna's eyes narrowed to bloodshot slits. "What?"

"Because we both know there's only one thing that would hold you back from this."

"No, he wouldn't," snarled Laruna.

"Good. Let's go," said Kaitha.

"That's not… Look, it's really complicated." Laruna struggled to find the right words. "Jynn saved my life, and he gave up a lot to do it. I'll always, you know, have feelings for him. About him. In his vicinity. But he was never honest, and you don't lie about being an… you know, an omnimancer. What if we had stayed together and had kids? I mean, think about the children—"

"Let me stop you there," said Kaitha. "It's not complicated. You want to fight the liche again. It would be good for your career, and you know we can do this. Everything else is irrelevant."

"I just think it'd be hard to work with… I mean, it's not just because… Rrrgh!" In her frustration, Laruna sent a streak of flame burning across the ring. Regrettably for Hogarth, the barbarian's efforts to right himself put him directly in the line of fire, as it were. He screamed as the spell blasted him back to the ground.

Kaitha leaned forward. "We're taking on the job you want, doing the quest you want, and if we pull it off, we'll get the glory you want. It's exactly what you're looking for, and you're not the type to give that up because you might encounter one man or another."

Laruna grit her teeth. "Don't think I can't see how you're trying to manipulate me."

"I assumed you'd see right through it." Kaitha grinned. "And I knew it wouldn't matter. Let's go."

The solamancer grinned and shook her head. "Fine. Give me a few minutes to finish up here," said Laruna. She turned back to the ring, where a charred barbarian was desperately crawling for the safety of the glowing boundary.

"Oh, come on Hogarth," the solamancer shouted across the ring, cracking her knuckles. "Try to make this last a little while! I've got some anger to work through!"

"This is going to be painful," said Jynn.

"Ye think so?" Gorm leaned against the side of an all-night soup shack on the edge of the Tarapin River, nursing a bowl of fish and noodle soup. The people bustling about the surrounding docks reminded Gorm of river crabs; nocturnal, prickly, and usually sideways.

"Finding a doppelganger on the streets of Andarun?" The omnimancer stared at the towering shape of Mount Wynspar silhouetted against the starry sky. Innumerable lanterns illuminated Andarun's streets, a glowing amber waterfall running down the southern slopes of the mountain. "Yes, I'd say that's going to be about as fun as doing dental work on a Flame Drake."

"I've tracked doppelgangers before—" Gorm was cut off by the roar of the crowd from the fighting pits. He took the chance to slurp a mouthful of noodles.

"Yes, but those doppelgangers talked to people. We can safely say nobody in the city has heard anything from Gaist. Although, that assumes he's even in the city. And that Gaist is even what he calls himself now." Jynn groaned and clutched his forehead. "It's too bad we don't have the mechanical gazer anymore," he added pointedly.

Gorm shrugged. "Why? The blasted thing wasn't working any more. I don't know if all your protective spells and wards were scrambling the sprites, or if Barty just gave us a defective one, but either way it wasn't doing us any good."

The mechanical gazer's descent into malfunction had begun shortly after Gorm and his companions left the lair of the Fane Amada. It started out with nonsensical directions, but by the second day on the road the construct had begun to move erratically and ask existential questions whenever it was addressed. By the time they camped on the third night, the gazer could only fly in small circles, and it responded to any question by saying, "It looks like this item doesn't work here."

"You still didn't have to smash it," said Jynn. "It might have started working again."

Gorm smiled at the memory. "Worth it."

"Was it? Now we don't have any idea where Gaist is, what he's doing, or even who he looks like."

"My gold says he still looks like Gaist, er, Iheen the Red."

"Even after he's been exposed?" asked Jynn, taking a bite from his own bowl.

"If he wanted to look like anyone else, he could have done so long ago," said Gorm, gesturing at his face with his spoon. "No, I'm thinkin' back to the days when I ran with Iheen. He and I went on more than a few quests together, ran in the same circles, even had to… well, we knew the same people. But even I always wondered how he got so many jobs done. We used to say it was like he could be in two places at once."

Jynn nodded. "It seems he was."

"Aye," grunted Gorm. "Iheen must have partnered with a doppelganger, and together they made quite a name for… well, for both of them, I suppose. But then the original Iheen died in the dungeon of Az'Anon."

"And so the doppelganger took the name of an Orcish mask," said Jynn.

"The face ye wear when you're about to die." Gorm nodded as he poked around his wooden bowl with a spoon. "The face that you want to be remembered by. That's what Zurthraka said a *gaist* is. And then Gaist starts tryin' to commit suicide by foe, get a noble death and all. But his problem was that he's too good at fightin'."

"The theory makes sense, I suppose."

For a few moments they ate their soup in thoughtful silence, watching the city in the distance.

"I still don't understand why he never speaks," Jynn said after a while.

"Mmph." Gorm waggled his spoon at the wizard as he finished off a mouthful of noodles. "I been thinkin' about that one. See, it's been so many years, I can't remember what Iheen sounded like. Could picture his face like he was sitting there, but the memory of a voice? That fades away. I'd imagine somewhere along the line, Gaist lost track of Iheen's voice and decided he'd rather stop speaking than get it wrong."

"Perhaps," said Jynn.

"Or maybe not," said Gorm with a shrug. "Not like he's going to tell us."

"Hey!"

Jynn and Gorm turned, noodles dangling from their mouths, to see Laruna storming up the gravel street toward them. Behind the mage, Kaitha waved.

"Listen," the solamancer snarled at Jynn. "I want you know that you aren't the reason I'm here. But I'm not going to let you be the reason I'm not here. I go where I want, even if that means traveling with you. But I'm not traveling *with* you. You're not the reason I travel, or that I don't. Am I clear?"

"I feel I can safely say 'no,'" said Jynn.

The solamancer jabbed a finger at the omnimancer. "Just remember that my business decisions don't take you into account."

"Of course," he said. "I'm sure we can keep things professional."

"Good." Laruna nodded with a snort.

"Glad to have ye back on board," said Gorm.

Laruna rubbed her jaw as she pulled up a stool. "Well, Kaitha says you've a thrice-cursed impressive plan, and I'm not about to miss out on it."

"Aye," said Gorm. "If it works, we'll be on the other side of this mess soon enough. And if it doesn't, well, we'll be able to say we didn't go down without one sire of a fight."

Laruna grinned. "Where do we start?"

"We were just discussing how to find Gaist," said Jynn.

"It won't be easy." Kaitha shook her head. "We've never heard the man speak, let alone talk about his plans. Who knows what he was thinking when he left?"

Gorm turned to look up at the city of Andarun. "I've a feelin' we know who might."

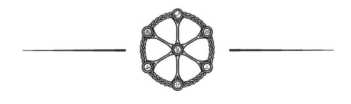

Heraldin Strummons nursed a lukewarm grog in the back corner of a moldering tavern. The Missing Serpent was a miserable hovel masquerading as a bar in the shadows of the Underdim, but it was also the third establishment that the bard had visited in as many hours, and he was too drunk to care about the accommodations. He was too drunk to care about much of anything, which meant that it was the ideal time to find a diversion for the night.

There were three barmaids working the commons. The first had introduced herself by threatening to stab Heraldin if he looked at her cross-eyed, and given that he was too inebriated to look at anything any other way, he ruled her out. The second server was an Ogress, and Heraldin was still a couple of grogs short of sinking that low, or perhaps climbing that high, as it were.

That left the third barmaid, a Human who looked like she must have been pretty before the years carved weary furrows beneath her eyes and above her brows. She was the best he'd do in this bar, and as he couldn't walk in a straight line long enough to find another, Heraldin drained his grog and beckoned her over.

He flashed a winning grin at the barmaid as she approached. "What are you serving tonight, my lovely?"

"Smitty's Grog and Mondo's Legal Ale," the barmaid said automatically.

Heraldin's brow furrowed. "Why's it called a legal ale?"

"They couldn't prove it wasn't ale in court," she replied.

"Well, that gives it a leg up on Smitty's, then." The bard made a face as he pushed his tankard away. "I'll take a pint of Mondo's. And what have you got for dessert?" he added, looking her up and down.

The barmaid started to scowl, but then recognition flashed in her eyes. "That's how I remember you! You used to come into the tavern I worked at back when I lived up in Dunningham Hollows."

"Did I?" asked Heraldin, thinking back. There were a lot of taverns and even more barmaids in his past.

"Oh, yeah!" The server nodded. "You'd pretend to be the young Duke of Waerth, sneaking away from his royal life."

"Ah!" That narrowed her identity to one of a half-dozen or so young women from a decade ago. Heraldin leaned closer and waggled his eyebrows in his most alluring manner. "And how do you know I'm not really the Duke of Waerth?"

The barmaid brought her face in close to Heraldin's and breathily whispered, "Because the Duke of Waerth was assassinated over a trade dispute back in sixty-eight."

"Aha, yes," said Heraldin.

"So, one Mondo's Legal, then?" The barmaid straightened up and stared down her nose at Heraldin.

"Well..."

"Cantrelle."

"Well, Cantrelle, as you guessed, I am no duke. I am Locuerdo, a humble troubadour." Heraldin gave a new false name to conceal the current one.

"Fine, Locuerdo. Just the drink?"

"I'd take two if you'd join me," said the bard, patting the stool next to him.

"Pfft. I've better things to do than watch an old liar try to convince himself that he's still got a knack with the gals," said Cantrelle. "The only fun I get these days is dumping a mug of swill on handsy patrons. So unless you're up for that..."

"Just the ale, please." Heraldin grimaced as he watched another missed opportunity stalk off.

With a new name, a fresh outfit, and a recent dearth of known associates around him, the bard was making a fresh start in Andarun. He hadn't intended to; originally, he'd planned to busk enough gold for a ferry down the Tarapin, and start fresh in Embleden or Chrate. But he'd earned enough on his first day that he could spare enough giltin to enjoy a pint. The pint became a half-gallon or so, which led to a night of pleasant adventures with a barmaid, which left him so broke he had to head back out with his lute the next morning.

For well over a month, the bard had been pursuing lost liberties around a circular track. He busked in the city square under the name of Sanderson by day, and spent his nights drinking away his take and looking for someone to warm his bed. Nobody knew his name, or his past, or ever spared him a thought after the pillows were cool. It was the sort of carefree existence he'd been longing for since the day the Al'Matrans recruited him.

It was inexplicably miserable.

As it turned out, a life could be free of cares and yet also devoid of fun. Busking earned a pittance, barely enough to buy cheap beer.

Cheap beer didn't taste as good as it used to, especially on an empty stomach. The women were nowhere near as agreeable as Heraldin remembered, nor were tavern keepers as patient for payment. He never slept in the same bed twice, and not in the good way.

A sudden squeal roused Heraldin from his thoughts. He glanced across the common room to see Cantrelle struggling to pull her wrist away from a man in red and black armor. The thug was big and ugly enough to qualify as an honorary Ogre, and he grinned at the barmaid with malicious amusement. Apparently, not everyone appreciated jokes about grog down the back.

The other maids and the tavern keeper ignored the assault, which meant that either it was a common occurrence or an uncommonly dangerous perpetrator. Either way, it wasn't the sort of situation to get mixed up in when you wanted to keep a low profile, or even a profile with a straight nose. Heraldin turned back to his drink.

Something else was bothering him. It wasn't just that fun was less fun these days, nor was it the added difficulty of trying to live a carefree life without being careless about his real identity or the very real threats to it. The problem was something else entirely, a yearning that he hadn't felt before.

All he could think of as he pondered that feeling was Gorm's face on the day the party delivered the Elven marbles to the Guz'Varda Tribe. The Orcs threw a celebration beyond anything the bard had ever experienced, and Gorm Ingerson sat in the middle of it, beaming like a drunken idiot as Orcs paraded by to offer him thanks in a language that he couldn't understand. There was something in the way Gorm smiled, a quality that Heraldin couldn't name and yet longed to —

Cantrelle shrieked, setting Heraldin's teeth on edge. To his surprise, he found that his hand had involuntarily slipped to the hilt of his rapier. "Do not be a fool," he whispered quietly. The bard reminded himself that the Underdim had a distinctive set of social norms, most notably the one that said it was perfectly acceptable to stab anyone that didn't follow the Underdim's distinctive social norms. He took a deep breath. He counted to three. He released his blade.

Heraldin became a professional hero by accident; 'recruited' by the Al'Matrans to avoid being sold out to Benny Hookhand. He took it as a given that it was the wrong job for him. But when he thought about the celebration at Bloodroot, he wondered if he didn't miss something about the career after all. Perhaps there was a small part of him that—

Cantrelle was screaming again, and Heraldin thought that someone else was hollering as well. It was difficult to tell, however, as the next few moments were a blur.

When he regained his senses, he found himself standing with one foot atop a barstool. Cantrelle was behind him, staring in shock at Heraldin's right hand. He followed her gaze to see his own rapier. It was pointed at the throat of the Ogre-sized hooligan, who stared at the blade with bloodshot eyes.

"What did you say?" growled Cantrelle's assailant.

Heraldin had no idea what he'd said in the haze of bravado. It didn't much matter at this point; there'd be no mercy if he backed down. "I said the lady would appreciate some space," he improvised.

"Do you know what you're doing?" The huge man's breath was fetid. "Do you know who you're tangling with, little man?"

"I can't say for certain. Still, I think it's best that you leave," said Heraldin with absolute honesty.

"You're a dead man," said the thug. "You're going to die for the sake of a tavern wench."

"I'll regret nothing done for the sake of a lady's honor." The key to any performance was commitment.

A chorus of snickers rang out from every corner of the bar. "Her what?" someone shouted.

"Her honor. Her dignity." The words felt right, like lines of a song sung to him in childhood. Heraldin started to grin despite himself.

"I would say any honor she had—" The hooligan cut off mid-snarl, a drop of crimson blooming where the point of the rapier had grazed his skin.

"I wouldn't," said Heraldin.

The brute didn't waste a moment. He leaned backward and grabbed the blade of the rapier in one fast motion. A maniacal grin split his face as he jerked the rapier from the bard's grasp with a bloody hand.

Yet, though the man was faster than he looked, he was still slower than Heraldin. The bard hadn't let go of the rapier before his off hand was fishing a couple of glass bulbs from his belt pouch. He hurled them at the brute's eyes, and they burst against the gnarled face in clouds of blue and yellow smoke. The heavy man screamed and doubled over, putting his face in line with Heraldin's boot. A solid kick sent him reeling back into a table, his face still trailing brightly colored smoke like fireworks at a Mordo Ogg's Day festival.

"I wouldn't do that, either," said Heraldin, retrieving his rapier from the floor near the prone man.

His opponent tried to scream something, but he couldn't manage coherent words as he clawed at his smoking face. He was still shrieking unintelligibly as he sprinted for the door, ran into a support beam instead, and staggered out through the front window.

"Well, at least he knew how to make an exit," said Heraldin as he turned back to Cantrelle. "Oh."

The look in the barmaid's eyes ripped the air from his lungs: breathless, caught between admiration and adoration, ringed by teardrops like diamonds. In her eyes he saw hope restored. He saw belief, absolute, bedrock belief in him. He saw that she would never forget him. It was the same look that the Orcs of Bloodroot had given Gorm, and Heraldin finally knew why the Dwarf had looked so overjoyed at the celebration.

He felt like a hero.

"Thank you," said the barmaid, straightening her dress. "I mean, you probably shouldn't have done that. Rek isn't one to mess with, but... Thank you, Locuerdo."

"Ah," said Heraldin, his sense of heroism deflating a little. "Well, my lady, I must confess that I'm not who you think I am."

"Oh, come on," smirked Cantrelle. "I always knew you wasn't a duke."

"Ah, yes. As it turns out, I'm not really Locuerdo, either," confessed the bard.

The barmaid was unfazed. "I don't care what you call yourself or who you're pretending to be. It's what you did that matters."

Her words were like a lance of ice through Heraldin's heart, draining away the warmth of a moment earlier. "What?" he whispered.

"I said it doesn't matter who you're pretending to be," said Cantrelle. "Actions speak louder than words, you know? You're a good guy."

Heraldin could barely hear her. His mind whirled back to the celebration at Bloodroot, where he'd sat at the table next to Gaist. He remembered the weaponsmaster drinking in the surrounding joy stoically, the subtlest hints of happiness creeping around the edges of his dark face. More memories poured in, of daily lopsided talks with Gaist, of the weaponsmaster saving his life time and time again, of countless games of thrones played by firelight. Of the man who'd become a brother to Heraldin. Of the rejection Heraldin gave him in return.

"I've been a fool," the bard said in barely more than a whisper.

"Well, yeah. I mean, Rek works for Benny Hookhand, after all," said Cantrelle. "Still, I really appreciate it."

Heraldin looked at the barmaid as though seeing her for the first time. There were a lot of things that he could see more clearly now. "Cantrelle, I've more regrets than a man has any right to, but defending you will never be one of them."

"It will be if you don't make tracks soon," the bartender interjected, still idly wiping the bar glasses with a rag.

Heraldin heard shouts coming from the dimly lit streets outside. By the sound of it, Rek was returning with a small army. He pressed a few giltin into the barmaid's hand. "I must go now. To find old friends and right old wrongs," he told Cantrelle, though he was forced to shout it to her as he ran for the back. He made it through the rear window just as Rek and his cronies burst through the front door.

"It's a very noble gesture, but not a wise one." Mrs. Hrurk's paw hesitated, her quill pen hovering above the parchment.

"Mrs. Hrurk, please," said Poldo, trying to hide the desperation in his voice. "It is essential."

"It's just that I don't know how to manage all of this money." The Gnoll looked overwhelmed as she stared at the sheaves of papers scattered around her.

"You'll have Vilma of the Fire Hawk Tribe to manage the books. And I will still be overseeing the finances as well," said Poldo. "All you need to do is continue to run the home, and you've been doing that admirably for some time."

Mrs. Hrurk shook her head. "Well, I've had help, but this will mean I have to take on more. I'm not sure Aubren is ready to run the kitchen for herself. And young Graknar has been very handy, but without oversight he—"

"I have every confidence in you and your staff, Mrs. Hrurk." Poldo tapped the paperwork again.

"I... I've never had so much money." The Gnoll sighed. "And I don't even know if I'm allowed to hold a deed on a property."

"You still won't own the property," Poldo said gently. "Neither of us will own any of it. The house, the gold, and the stocks will all be held in trust for the incorporated charity that we have set up. That's the key."

"But—"

"Mrs. Hrurk... Feista, please," Poldo pushed the papers closer. "Trust me. This is the best way to preserve everything we've built here."

The Gnoll looked at him, and then glanced out the window. Poldo followed her gaze to the cobbled street below, where the residents of Poldo's Home for the Displaced were enjoying one of the year's first warm evenings. Orcs and Humans sat together, sharing cool tea and watching the last of the sun's light retreat across the tiers. The children had found an old wand somewhere, one with enough magic to shoot out a few sparks of sorcery when shaken with sufficient vigor. They laughed and whooped and flung tiny spells across the street until a young Goblin's antics conjured a lightning bolt that incinerated a trash bin. A nearby adult hurried over to take the wand away.

"You're a good man, Mr. Poldo." Mrs. Hrurk's tail thumped on her chair as she signed the papers.

Poldo kept looking out the window. He recognized more than a few of the figures in the street below. Hurg was an old Orc of the Merga'Lerdak Tribe. Poldo recalled the tribe's name; he once received a big promotion at Goldson Baggs after negotiating a buyout of the Merga'Lerdak quest days before the tribe was obliterated. He still had a gold coin from the loot in the desk drawer upstairs. Kitrik was a

Goblin without a tribe; she was left in swaddling rags at a Shadowkin orphanage twenty years ago. Poldo recalled working the paperwork to wipe out several Goblin tribes back in 7.355, right around the time when Kitrik was born. The young Orcs from the Daellans, Mogta the Gnoll, Joren the Kobold, even the strange Slaugh that liked to lurk in the rainwater barrel; the more Poldo learned about his guests, the better he could connect them to the quests and contracts and funds that he once traded in.

"Perhaps, Mrs. Hrurk." It was all he could bring himself to say.

"Look at all you've done for them. For all of us." The Gnoll smiled, misreading the way he stared out the window. "You've given them hope. You gave me hope."

Poldo managed a wan smile. "Thank you."

Mrs. Hrurk squinted at him as she slid the paperwork back to Poldo. "No, really, Mr. Poldo. You are too hard on yourself. The gods will reward you for what you've done."

Poldo wasn't sure that would be a desirable outcome. He was even less sure of how to reply, but a squelchy knock at the door saved him the trouble.

Poldo bade the knocker enter, and a young Slaugh hopped into the kitchen and up to Poldo. "Mr. Poldo, sir!" he croaked. "There's men come to see you at the door. Said they had an appointment, sir."

Poldo scowled and checked his pocket watch. "My first appointment isn't until ten o'clock," he said. "Did they say what it was about?"

"No, sir. Just that it's important."

Poldo thanked the lad and sent him on his way with a copper coin. He begged Mrs. Hrurk's pardon, instructed a pair of Wood Gnomes to take the newly inked papers to his lawyer, and made his way down to the front hall.

Two man-shaped slabs of muscle and ire eclipsed the door. "You Duine Poldo?" rumbled the larger of the two.

"I am," said Poldo.

"Of Silver Guard Securities?"

"Yes. And where did you say you were from?" Poldo asked.

The larger man pulled a business card from the inner pocket of his fine black coat and handed it to Poldo.

Merle D. Knucker, Lcnd. Goon
Department of Personal Business
Imports, Exports & Stuff of Andarun

"And what exactly is the 'stuff' that I.E.S.A. deals with?" asked Poldo as he examined the card.

"Stuff. Things. Miscellaneous," said Mr. Knucker. "One example is investing. We hold stock in Goldson Baggs, J.P. Gorgon, and until recently, Lamia Sisters."

"Ah," Poldo read the card again. "What does the Department of Personal Business do?"

Mr. Knucker ignored the question. "Although recently, I.E.S.A.'s portfolio has lost over thirty-seven percent of its value due to the fallout from CTOs originated at Silver Guard Securities."

"Ah. Well, unfortunately, gentlemen, any investment comes with risks," said Poldo.

"Yes," said Mr. Knucker. "Mr. Plank and I are two of them."

The other goon tipped his cap.

"I'm not sure I like your tone." Poldo took a step back.

"The board of I.E.S.A. is very upset about the CTOs," said Mr. Knucker.

"And I'm sorry for it," said Poldo. "But many board members across Andarun share their sentiments, and —"

"None of the others are B. H. Ur'Kend," said Mr. Knucker.

"More commonly known as Benny Hookhand," added Mr. Plank.

Poldo felt the blood drain from his face and drop into the void opening up in the pit of his stomach. "The Hookhand…"

"Now, don't make a fuss," said Mr. Knucker. "It never goes well when people scream."

"That's when bystanders become witnesses, if you get my drift." Mr. Plank nodded at the residents sitting and watching with some interest from the yard.

"You wouldn't want anything to happen to all these nice people living in your big house, right?" said Mr. Knucker.

Even amidst his rising panic, Poldo had enough sense to nod. "What… what does Mr. Hookhand want with m-me?"

"A meeting," said Mr. Knucker.

"We've arranged for your transportation," said Mr. Plank, gesturing back at an ominous black carriage at the edge of the walk.

"Ah, but gentlemen, I've other meetings to—"

"Consider your schedule cleared."

"But—"

"Mr. Poldo," said Mr. Knucker pointedly. "You're going to be on that carriage in the next three minutes. The only choice you've got is how pleasant your trip is."

"And what kind of mess we leave behind," added Mr. Plank.

A sudden peal of laughter rang out in the street. By the sound of it, Mrs. Hrurk's pups were playing with some of the Halfling children. Poldo took a deep breath. "Very well, gentlemen. Lead the way."

"Oh, after you," said Mr. Knucker, stepping to one side.

"We insist," chuckled Mr. Plank.

Poldo stood up straight and walked down the cobblestone path to the street. Mr. Knucker stepped up to the carriage and opened the door. Poldo peered into a bleak and windowless interior, with long benches along the sides. The seats already had two occupants: a plump Tinderkin woman with a lazy eye, and a slender bard wearing a red and yellow suit and a broad, floppy hat. Judging by the bard's bruised and bloody face, he had opted for the unpleasant trip.

"I didn't realize there would be other passengers," said Mr. Poldo, scanning the street.

"Mr. Hookhand keeps a busy schedule," said Mr. Knucker. "But don't worry about Lemba. She's harmless."

"And Heraldin's not going to be any trouble for a while," Mr. Plank said.

"Aha, of course," said Poldo. But he'd bought enough time to see a few tiny figures staring at him from amidst the flowers in the window boxes. "Send help," he mouthed to the Wood Gnomes, just before Mr. Knucker ushered him up the stairs and into the black carriage.

"Not much hope now, right?" said the old bannerman. His purple and silver tabard matched the banners hanging from Aberreth's walls. "I mean, I says to myself, 'it's join them rotters, fight 'em and join 'em anyway, or get myself hung for a deserter and then join 'em later. Might as well make it easy.' And here I am."

"Seems like sound logic," said Tyren, flipping through the pages of an old magazine. He lounged by an old desk that was occupied by a few stacks of papers and his own feet, still clad in the unholy armor that had become a part of him. On the other side of the desk a long queue of potential recruits stood next to a skeletal torso with a sign nailed to its sternum. Tyren had covered the original message with a sign that read "FORM LINE HERE."

"Uh, so how do they… you know… do it?" asked the bannerman.

"I beg your pardon?" Tyren sat up straight and closed his periodical, though he dog-eared the page with a particularly salacious woodcut of an Orcess.

"How are they going to make me… one of you guys?" The bannerman shifted nervously from side to side.

"Ah, right." Tyren leaned back and set his feet on the desk once more as he launched into a rote speech. "You'll have three options. You can imbibe a potion of hemlock and blue shadeleaf. We have several bladed weapons that you can use—swords to fall on, daggers and such. Assistance is available. And finally, you can throw yourself to a pack of ravenous ghouls."

"I see." The bannerman's face screwed up in thought for a few moments before he asked, "Why would I want that last one?"

"Some soldiers are concerned about meeting old colleagues after their initiation," said Tyren, flipping open his magazine. "A little battle damage might help it look like they didn't defect."

"Makes sense, in a way." The old bannerman thought some more. "Still, I suspect that I can do a number on myself with a good blade, if it's all the same to you."

"I've been hearing as much a lot today. Be sure to mark your preference on your entrance form," said Tyren. A bell rang from one of the tables beyond the front of the line. "And on that note, it looks like Millicent is ready to assist you at table three. Don't look her right in the eye, or you won't get a chance to use a sword." The last warning was called out as the bannerman shuffled off toward a table with a dark-robed wraith.

Another bannerman shuffled up to the desk and mumbled a nervous greeting.

"Welcome. You've made the right choice. If you've brought an advertisement, please put it on the corresponding pile." Tyren flipped to the next page, and when he pulled his hand away, several strings of green goo hung from his bony fingers. He reflected on the downside of asking zombies to fetch your reading materials as he shook the gunk from his hand.

The knight-commander was so preoccupied with the goop that he didn't notice the Head of Marketing bobbing up, flanked by Ned and Ted. "How are we doing, sir?" asked the flaming skull, hovering eagerly around the piles of flyers on the desk.

"Quite well, I'd say," Tyren replied. A bell rang. "Table sixteen," he said to the bannerman.

"Good, good," said the Head. "We're estimating that over twenty percent of the garrison is joining us! We're going to shave days off the siege."

Tyren nodded absently, still halfway through his welcome to the next bannerman in line. "You've made the right choice. If you've brought an advertisement—"

"I'll take it," said Ned, snatching the paper from the young bannerman's hands. The ghoul added it to the corresponding pile of flyers, which he and Ted were counting fastidiously. The ex-members of the demonic animal husbandry team had been eager to prove themselves after their wards were killed or driven off at the battle for Highwatch, and there was plenty of opportunity in marketing.

"Which promotions are performing?" the Head of Marketing asked them.

"'All things perish. Not all do it well,' seems to be doing quite well among the lesser nobility," said Ted, shuffling through one of the larger stacks on the table.

"A luxury play to an elitist market. Interesting!" The Head made a note on the clipboard bobbing near him.

Ned rapped on another stack. "'Quick and painless' remains popular. Although I wonder, sir, if we've had any takers on the option for us ghouls to—"

"Not a one," said Tyren, looking back to his magazine.

"Ah, a pity," said the ghoul. "Some of the lads were thinking we might just take the other choices off the table for the stragglers, then? A sort of last-come-first-served arrangement?"

"I don't know that anybody is going to eat anyone else today," Tyren muttered. "Still, a rousing success overall. Good work."

"Right..." The Head floated awkwardly nearby. "Uh, sir, not to question your judgment, but I thought you might be heading up the military action."

"Commander Genevieve is seeing to it," said the knight-commander.

"Of course, but I thought you might want her to have some oversight," said the Head.

"That's why we established the committee for oversight," said Tyren. "And the subcommittee for oversight review."

"But—"

The knight-commander flipped the page. "Now, it's important to make sure I don't lose touch with the common corpse. Show that I'm not above any task." A bell rang. "Table seven."

"Uh, very well, sir," said the floating skull.

Tyren settled back into his seat, savoring every moment.

There was a point of equilibrium in any organization's middle management, a fulcrum of responsibility that remained still while the upper and lower ranks of the bureaucracy moved around it. Tyren knew from experience that a shrewd official could find this pivot-point within the org chart and, once entrenched, enjoy near-complete autonomy with almost no responsibility. After nearly two months with the undead, he had once again managed to precisely calibrate his career for an optimal effort-to-authority ratio.

Marketing was getting results. The army had been restructured and was well positioned. Operations were running smoothly. Everyone oversaw and reported to each other in an inscrutable web of accountability that left Tyren blameless for failure and ready to share any success. He'd been planning for this position, working toward it since his untimely death removed him from his last job. Now that he'd reached it, there was nothing to do but sit back, wait for accolades, and pass the time ostensibly reading articles.

Something nagged at the back of Tyren's mind, an uneasy notion that perhaps he had anticipated this moment too much. His thoughts drifted to Nove's second principle of universal irony, and he was still ill at ease and distracted when the next in line stepped up to his table.

"Welcome. You've made the right choice," the knight-commander said automatically. "If you've brought an advertisement—"

A pamphlet was shoved into Tyren's face. "Hi. I'm here to become a vampire," said a young voice.

Tyren started and looked up. Instead of a bannerman or adventurer, a teenage girl stood at the table. The black dress that she'd draped over herself threatened to fall off her bony frame. Her skin was undoubtedly pale even before she applied copious amounts of powder, contrasting with the colorful makeup she'd liberally applied.

"Excuse me?" he asked.

"My name is Betelle Ur'Parde, and I'm here to become a vampire," the young woman said, pointing to the flyer.

Tyren looked down at the paper. It was printed in thick, blocky letters and had woodcuts of smiling skulls set around the border.

YOUNG MEN AND WOMEN
Is your life **UNFAIR?**
Do the authorities **NOT UNDERSTAND YOU?**
Are you tired of doing as **THEY** tell you?
Because **SOCIETY** says **THEY** are **IN CHARGE?**

ALL ARE EQUAL IN DEATH.
Rich and poor, young and old, all must die.
And then the **UNDEAD** enjoy **IMMORTALITY**.

YOU can **JOIN THE UNDEAD.**
Together, we will **REMAKE SOCIETY** and enjoy
worldly pleasures **FOREVER.**

Bring this pamphlet to an Undead Officer before
sundown on the 15th of Bloomtide.
Join early for **PREFERRED TREATMENT.**
Elves need not apply.

"Ah, right, but... er..." Tyren fumbled for the right words.

"Wait. Vampires are the ones that dress in tight lace and sneak into people's bedrooms late at night, right?" said the young woman.

"That sounds like vampires," Ted said.

"That's for me, then," said Betelle.

"But... but you're so young," Tyren said. The girl couldn't have reached her eighteenth year yet. Perhaps it was her proud posture as she stood, and the way her makeup obscured most of her features, but something about her put him in mind of little Aubey.

"Oh, don't you start with me, too. You sound just like my father!" The young woman launched into an unflattering impression of an older man. "'Betelle, don't go running around the stables after dark.' 'Betelle, you're too young for making off with squires!' 'Betelle, don't go making an unholy pact with the dead!'"

Something ancient and paternal welled up from Tyren's depths. "Now, listen for just a moment—"

"I don't have to! That's the point, isn't it?" Betelle thrust the flyer in her hand forward again. "I get to choose, right? And I choose to die, and to help make a society where we're all equal!"

"Some creative license there," said Ted, looking back at the Head of Marketing.

"And you, and mum, and dad, and the headmaster won't tell me what to do!" said the teenager. "Nobody will get to boss me around!"

"Some exceptions may apply," chimed the Head of Marketing.

It was becoming clearer to Tyren why the young woman might bring back memories of his five-year-old daughter. He tried a different approach. "Listen, I appreciate your independence, but you could do so much more than join our army. You could finish up at an Academy, take up a trade, join a guild or industry—so many of the things I used to want to do. You have your whole life ahead of you."

"Well, not really." Betelle smirked back at Aberreth, surrounded by a thick and rotting siege line. "I mean, you are going to kill us all, right?"

"Well, er, technically," Tyren said. "But you could flee and join the refugees in Andarun."

Betelle's face was the blend of exasperation and contempt typical of an adolescent educating a parental figure. She plucked another flyer off the table and held it up in reply. Its headline proclaimed in bold block letters:

EVEN ANDARUN WILL FALL.

Tyren nodded and waved in reluctant assent. "All right, yes, fine. Not Andarun. You could flee somewhere else."

The young woman grabbed up another flyer from the table. It read:

THERE IS NOWHERE SAFE FROM THE UNDEAD.

"I see your point," Tyren conceded, "but I'm sure there's something you could—"

Exuding triumph—so much so that it almost warranted a smile— Betelle picked up yet another flyer.

THERE IS NOTHING YOU CAN DO
TO SAVE YOURSELF.

Tyren shot an incredulous look at the Head of Marketing, who bobbed and tilted to one side in an approximation of a shrug. "Targeted messaging," said the floating skull.

A bell rang behind them.

"The point is that it's my choice!" snapped Betelle. "And I choose to be a dark seductress of the night."

"And we're glad you made it," interjected the Head of Marketing, swooping down to the front of the table. "Now, if you're ready, it looks like Millicent is ready at table three. Ha! She's a fast one. Good luck, Betelle, and welcome aboard!"

Betelle shot Tyren one last smirk before sauntering off toward the line of tables.

She wasn't out of earshot before the Head of Marketing spun around and shot a baleful glare at Tyren. "Sir, if I may, advertising generally works better when you don't try to talk people out of your product."

Tyren, however, was just as angry. He grabbed the flyer that Betelle had brought and shook it at the floating skull. "You were marketing to children?" he snarled.

"Well, teenagers," said the Head. "Any younger and you really have to target the parents — "

"Why would you advertise death to children?" demanded the knight-commander.

"Why?" The Head pivoted back, surprised by the question. "Why wouldn't I? I told you that I'd be hitting every demographic, and you said that'd be great!"

"I... I didn't... I didn't think..." Tyren's vocabulary failed him again. She was so young. So much life ahead of her.

"I'm selling the geriatric on reanimation as a cure for joint pain! I'm reminding unhappy wives that their wedding vows don't extend past death!" said the Head of Marketing. "What do you think is going to happen to the kids, anyway? That we'll just orphan all the little wretches and then leave them alone?"

"I... I don't..." Tyren's vocabulary failed him again as an image of little Aubey flashed in his mind. He could still hear Betelle's voice in his mind. A moment later, the flashing was much more external, and Betelle's voice rose into a high-pitched scream.

The undead turned to look at a small, sad pile of ashes in front of table three.

"Ahh, you forgot to mention the bit about not looking Millicent in the eye," said Ted.

"Wraiths are tricky that way," said Ned.

"Ohhh, right. Right," said the Head of Marketing.

"She's gone?" asked Tyren.

"Well, for a bit," said the ghoul. "Should be back along any moment."

"Here she comes now." Ted pointed to a wisp of darkness forming over the ashes, smoke and shadow running together.

"I don't see what the problem is anyway, sir," said the Head, turning back to the knight-commander. "She was going to be dead soon enough."

A low moan was rising, growing louder and more intense as the darkness coalesced into the form of a young woman draped in shadow. As the shade of Betelle took shape, her groaning turned into an angry roar. "The problem?" she snarled. "The problem is that I was supposed to be a vampire!"

A sudden sense of loss overwhelmed the knight-commander when he looked at the dead girl. He clutched his forehead with a skeletal hand. "If we could all quiet down for a moment," he said.

"Oh, we'd all like to be vampires," Ted told the approaching shade of the young woman. "But I'm afraid there are no special requests accommodated, miss."

"Yeah," chuckled Ned. "Don't suppose old Rudge would've turned out the way he did if he could've asked to be different."

From somewhere in the crowd, Rudge called out, "It's true!"

Bells were ringing from the empty tables. The bannermen closest to the front of the line muttered nervously to one another.

"As I was saying, if we want to get the numbers up, we can't ignore any markets," said the Head of Marketing.

"Quiet," said Tyren. He could see little Aubey running to him through the fields, curls bouncing around her big smile, laughter in those big brown eyes. He felt he could have heard her laugh, were it not for the commotion around him.

"I was going to sneak through Dustin Ur'Fronen's window and make him my thrall," wailed the spirit of Betelle. "We were going to have an eternity of dark pleasures together! And now look at me! How am I supposed to seduce anyone without a body?"

"I can see that being difficult," said Ned.

"Oh, I'm not so sure," offered Ted. "The art of seduction is really more about attitude and perception than—"

"Silence!" roared Tyren.

Absolute stillness fell over the undead in an instant. Jaws snapped shut, words died in rotting throats, hands dropped to the sides of rigid torsos, and all eyes, corporeal or otherwise, turned to the knight-commander.

"I… I'm sorry," said Tyren, looking around at the frozen undead. "I just… I just need time to think. Uh, as you were."

The other undead began moving once more, although now it was to simultaneously take a cautious step back from the knight-commander.

"All right, yeah," said the Head of Marketing. His one eye looked around fearfully, and the flames around his skull had died down a bit. "Yeah. We're going to go around to the other tables before the invasion gets going. Come on, guys."

Ned and Ted shuffled after the skull, glancing back at Tyren with reproachful eyes. Betelle floated off as well, guided by a helpful ghost toward orientation. Even the skeletal torso bearing the sign to start the line slunk away.

Eventually, the other undead at the recruiting center resumed work, and the skittish bannermen nervously approached Tyren's table once more, dropping off their flyers before stepping up to open booths. The knight-commander didn't notice any of the activity. His magazine lay in the mud at his feet. He was held fast by the sounds of Betelle's final screams, by the face that could have been what his daughter looked like now, by the laughter of a child he knew he'd never hear again.

Ghastly horns and trumpets sounded, followed by the swelling notes of a Gnomish pipe organ. The undead army assembled and advanced. The city's defenders fell and, after a brief interlude, got back up again. Tyren sat in silence through all of it, as motionless as a more typical corpse, haunted by his memories.

Chapter 24

Many people go to the tavern to forget their troubles. Lidda's Pipe was a tavern where troubles went to be forgotten. The common room had plenty of hidden nooks and crannies, poor lighting, and a clientele that largely kept to themselves—at least until the heat died down. It was a good place to find people who had secrets they were willing to part with—for a modest price.

At least, it usually was. "It's a seller's market," Gorm grumbled, slumping onto the bench next to Laruna. "Barely anybody here, and everyone's lookin' for information."

"Well, some are also interested in procuring services," said the solamancer. "I've had two people offer me gold to do assassin work."

"Better than the proposition I got," said Kaitha, nodding to a table set in a dark alcove in the wall.

"That'd explain the crashing a while back then." Gorm peered back at the nook and the wreckage contained therein. "Did ye have to break two chairs?"

"I told the server he'd pay for the damages." Kaitha shrugged. "When he's conscious again."

"I'd say that's more of an 'if' than a 'when.'" Jynn winced at the mess.

"Anyway, we're no closer to finding either Heraldin or Gaist," said Laruna.

"Or Thane," added Kaitha.

"Aye." Gorm turned back to his ale. "We need to—oh." A small, folded slip of paper sat in front of him, leaning conspicuously against his tankard.

Laruna cast him a sidelong glance as she took a long pull from her tankard of ale. "Where'd that come from?"

"That's what I'd like to know." Gorm opened the paper and found a message stamped out in the blocky lettering that one might expect from a Gnomish printing press. All the letters were slightly askew, as though the words had been vigorously shaken. He read:

> YOU HAVE BEENE ASKING FOR HERALDIN STRUMMONS. WE CAN HELPE EACH OTHER. MEET IN THE ALLEY BEHIND LIDDA'S PIPE. COME ALONE.

"What is it?" asked Kaitha.

"A sign from the gods," said Gorm, standing. "They've decided to start being useful."

"Is it one of those pamphlets from the Temple of Oppo?" asked Jynn. "Honestly, I never understood why they do that."

"It's a tip about the bard," said Gorm. "I'm to check it out in the back alley. If I'm not back in ten minutes, ye know what to do."

"Drink your ale," said Laruna.

"And order me a cold one." Gorm headed for the back door.

The alley behind Lidda's was dark, lit only by the last of the twilight leaking through the crowded rooftops of Darkridge, the cluster of slums and derelict factories on the Ridgemost end of the second tier. Stacks of crates and piles of rags littered the alley, casting strange shadows across the broken cobbles.

"*Gorm Ingerson?*" buzzed a strange voice from the darkness.

He turned. In the deepest shadows of the alley, a strange figure slumped against a stack of boxes. He wore a long coat with sleeves that totally covered his hands. A scarf and a wide brimmed hat obscured the man's face; Gorm could only determine it was a man at all from the mismatched tufts of hair sticking out from the scarf at odd angles.

"Aye," said Gorm. "This your note?"

"*Heraldin Strummons is in danger.*" The figure's voice sounded like the chorus of rats, or perhaps like the wings of a swarm of insects.

"Can't say I'm too surprised," Gorm muttered. "Well, how bad is it this time?"

The figure rustled like leaves in the wind, and Gorm heard tiny squeaking sounds at the edge of his hearing. *"Benny Hookhand has taken him."*

"That's pretty thrice-cursed bad," swore Gorm.

"We know where he's being held," said the figure. *"You need to go tonight."*

"If we're not already too late," agreed Gorm. "But I'll wager there's a price for this information."

"Save Poldo!" exclaimed the figure, its voice high and warping with sudden enthusiasm.

"Save what now?"

The figure trembled and chittered again. *"Duine Poldo is being held along with Mr. Strummons. You will set him free as well."*

"Enemy of my enemy is my friend, eh?" Gorm scratched at his beard. "And how do I know this ain't some sort of elaborate trap?"

The figure squeaked and chittered to itself. Its belly warped and wiggled for a moment, and then a bulge emerged between the buttons of its heavy coat. The mass unfurled itself as it flopped out onto the cobbles in front of Gorm. The Dwarf picked up the brightly colored hat.

"Don't know many who'd wear a hat like this," said Gorm. "All right. We'll think on it."

"Yes. Go soon." The figure leaned forward precariously, its arms swinging as though on pendulums. A slip of paper slid out of the end of one of its sleeves and fluttered down on the cobbles. "Here."

Gorm picked it up and read.

"This address is in the Riverdowns," said Gorm. When there was no response, he looked up. The odd figure had already shambled back into the shadows.

"Strangest thing was, he left all his clothes behind in a big heap," Gorm later said as he recounted the meeting to the party.

"It could be a trap," said Jynn. "That hat has clearly been recently purchased, and anyone who knows the bard will be familiar with his sense of fashion."

"Or lack thereof," said Laruna.

"Could be a trap," conceded Gorm. "Then again, anyone who wanted to get us somewhere could find better bait than a fight with Benny Hookhand."

"True enough," said Kaitha. "Honestly, even if it's a real tip we need to think twice about—"

The ranger was interrupted by the sharp *thunk* of a dagger embedding itself in the table beside her. A neatly folded piece of paper was pinned down by the blade.

"What is it?" Gorm asked as Kaitha read the note.

Kaitha smirked as she read aloud: "You have been asking around after Heraldin Strummons. I can show you to him. Meet me in the back alley."

"Intrigue begets intrigue," said Jynn, passing a scrap of food to Patches under the table.

"Intrigue's startin' to beget nausea at this point." Gorm tossed a few giltin on the table and stood again. "Come on. Let's go see what this is about."

The alley was slightly darker but otherwise unchanged when Gorm led the other heroes through Lidda's back door. There was even another man in a long coat and wide-brimmed hat lurking in the shadows. "Are you Gorm Ingerson?" he asked in a gravelly voice.

"Ye know I am. What's this all about?" Gorm peered into the darkness. There was a familiar quality in the timbre of the informant's voice.

The mysterious figure held up a gloved hand. "I can tell you where Heraldin Strummons is."

"We already know where he is," said Laruna.

"He's—wait, what?" The informant stumbled over his words.

"We know where the bard is," said Gorm. "So your information ain't worth much to us."

"Well, that's a little hurtful." The indignant informant lost the gravel in his voice, and the other heroes recognized it at once.

"Wait. Heraldin?" said Gorm.

"Of course it's me," grumbled the bard, throwing off the long coat as he stepped out of the shadows. "But you already knew that, didn't you? Not that you wouldn't take the chance to ruin the moment."

"So, you were following us the whole time?" asked Jynn.

"Once I found out you were looking for me I searched for all of you, yes," said the bard. "And I spent half the day planning this reunion. The surprise reveal, the heartfelt apology, the long embraces—"

"Don't push your luck," warned Kaitha.

"The respectful handshakes." Heraldin didn't skip a beat. "But, in typical fashion, you brushed it all off and ruined the moment. 'Not worth much,' indeed!"

"Sorry. We were misinformed," said Jynn.

"We got a tip that ye were taken by Benny Hookhand," said Gorm, holding out the hat given to him by the previous informant.

"What?" The bard snatched the hat out of Gorm's hand, his resentment forgotten.

"Aye, must have been a trap. They said ye was taken to an address in the Riverdowns—"

"We have to go to Benny's lair!" said Heraldin, taking off his ratty old hat and replacing it with the newer, less damaged one. "There's no time to waste!"

"But why pick a fight with Andarun's most dangerous gangster?" asked Gorm. "Benny Hookhand obviously didn't get ye."

"Exactly," hissed Heraldin. "But he likely thinks he did."

"Don't talk as much as you used to, do you, Heraldin?" asked Mr. Plank, prodding at the prisoner with the tip of a wooden club.

The bard leveled a burning glare, but said nothing.

This was an unsurprising response. The thin man hadn't said a word since Poldo had met him. For the most part, the Human just sat up straight on the prisoners' bench, staring at the walls of the rickety dock house they were held in.

Something in Heraldin's eyes must have unsettled the goon. Poldo winced and leaned away as Mr. Plank gave the captive a couple of solid whacks to the shoulder with his club. "Don't you look at me like that," barked their captor.

The bard didn't so much as flinch, let alone cry out. He stared at the goon a moment longer and then turned away with a slight shrug.

Unnerved, Mr. Plank turned his attentions back to Lemba, who, by contrast, hadn't stopped talking since Poldo met her.

"Oh, gods, this is bad. I knew I shouldn't have done business with the Hookhand's goons," the Tinderkin muttered to herself, rocking back and forth on her stool. "I mean, yeah, I cut the potions a bit, maybe they make you a little sick, yeah, but what did they expect at those prices? People need low-cost potions. I was just meeting market demand, is all."

"Shut it!" The floor of the old dock house creaked and cracked as Mr. Plank stalked across the small room they occupied. "I told you to be quiet."

Lemba fell silent, but only for as long as the goon loomed over her. As soon as he stepped away, she resumed her vacant litany of regrets and excuses.

Poldo was actually glad for the Tinderkin's muttering. Her murmurs and those of the river bubbling along beneath the floor masked the conversation he was having.

"Did the paperwork for the trust make it to the lawyers?" he whispered softly.

The Wood Gnome hiding in his collar chirruped once. Yes.

"Excellent." Poldo allowed himself a small smile of relief. Benny Hookhand had kept them waiting for the entire day, but that had provided Poldo and his diminutive staff time to make arrangements. "And is the real estate agent set to come yet?"

Two chirrups. No.

"Send another missive, then. It has to be tomorrow," Poldo said. "If these heroes you've arranged for show up and rescue me, the home won't be safe for the residents. We need to find a new location within the week."

Two chirrups.

"I know it's unreasonable, but—"

A scream rang out from beyond the ominous red door at the back of the room, followed by a final-sounding splash. A moment later, the red door opened and Mr. Knucker stepped into the room followed, improbably enough, by an even larger goon. "Mr. Hookhand is ready to see you now, Lemba."

The Tinderkin protested and pleaded, but Mr. Knucker took her by the arm and led her back into the recesses of Benny Hookhand's lair. The red door slammed behind them with an air of finality.

"Stepping out for a smoke," the massive goon told Mr. Plank, pulling a silver cigar case from the inner pocket of his jacket.

Poldo waited for the goon to make his way across the small antechamber and step out the front door before resuming his conversation with the Wood Gnome perched on his shoulder.

"Look, I appreciate the difficulty involved, but consider the consequences of failure," he exhorted. "Mrs. Hrurk's Home for the Underprivileged must open as soon as possible. The only way to protect the guests is to make it seem as if they never stayed with me."

The Wood Gnome reluctantly conceded a single chirrup.

"Good," Poldo said. "I know you can make it happen. And give my regards to Mrs. Hrurk and the pups." He felt a tickle down his spine as the Gnome clambered down the back of his shirt, and then the tiny employee was away, leaving Poldo alone with his thoughts. They were, by and large, unpleasant, but much less so than the scream that interrupted them a few minutes later.

"That was quick," said Mr. Plank as Mr. Knucker stepped through the red door.

"The Hookhand was eager to get to these two." The senior goon leered at the prisoners. "He likes to save the fun ones for last."

"So, which one does he want first?" asked Mr. Plank.

"Mr. Strummons here, of course." Mr. Knucker prodded at the bard, who stood and walked solemnly through the red door. "Gods, you know how much money that little Scribkin cost Benny? He's gonna want to take his time on that one." He shot Poldo a menacing grin before the red door slammed behind him.

"Too bad for you." Mr. Plank laughed at Poldo.

The Scribkin felt the sweat beading on his brow, blurring his vision. Nausea settled in the pit of his stomach. He put his head down by his knees and breathed deeply until he heard a sound like someone choking. Or screaming. Or choking while screaming.

Poldo lifted his head. "Is that—"

The front door ripped from its hinges as the massive goon crashed through it. A cigar dangled from his lips and two arrows protruded from his throat, constricting his death rattle to a struggling whine. Poldo recoiled as the dying man crashed to the floor at his feet.

"What the—" Mr. Plank began, but he never finished. A whirling ball of fury and beard launched though the hole in the wall where the front door used to be and slammed into Mr. Plank with horrifying ferocity. Poldo looked away and squeezed his eyes shut, though he didn't cover his ears in time to block out the sickening sounds of a live dissection via axe. Something splattered on his shoes.

The carnage only lasted a few seconds. A gruff voice rang out. "Ye Duine Poldo?"

Poldo opened one eye. A Dwarf-shaped demon loomed over him, speckled with the mortal remains of Mr. Plank. He stared down at the Scribkin with burning, intense eyes.

"I said, are ye Duine Poldo?" the Dwarf repeated.

Shock threatened to overwhelm Poldo, and his terror precluded forming coherent sentences. His brain fell back to the businessman's most basic instinct. With a subconscious spasm of his arm, he pulled a business card from his coat pocket and extended it to the Dwarf.

Other armed heroes were running into the room as the Dwarf took the card and looked at it. "Is this the secondary?" asked a tall Elven woman.

"Aye," said the Dwarf, reading the card. "Well, Mr. Poldo, you're free to go wherever ye please."

"Though I'd suggest you be somewhere else for a while," said a man in the gray robes of an omnimancer.

As shocking as it was to see a brazen gray mage, it wasn't nearly as surprising as the man who bounded in on the wizard's heels. "But where is Gaist?" asked the spitting image of Heraldin. "Er, the bard. Someone who looks like me."

Poldo pointed mutely to the red door.

"Then there's not a moment to lose!" shouted the new Heraldin.

"Aye," said the Dwarf, hefting his axe. After a couple of swings, the red door exploded in a cloud of crimson shrapnel. The adventurers streamed through the antechambers, leaping over the various bits of Mr. Plank as they rushed into Benny Hookhand's inner sanctum.

Poldo stared after them, violently shaking, until a chorus of chirps and tweets brought him back to his senses. He turned to a crowd of Wood Gnomes at the front door, jumping and pointing emphatically.

"Oh, yes. Yes! We must make our escape," said Poldo, hopping off the bench and trying not to think of whatever had just squelched beneath his foot.

"A lot of guts," the woman snarled at Gorm. She stood near the far corner of the back room of the dock house, surrounded by a phalanx of overmuscled men in dark suits. Heraldin's double was held in place next to an open trapdoor, and beneath him the Tarapin River rushed and bubbled with quiet menace.

"It takes a lot of guts to break into one of my dens." The woman spoke in a low growl as she brandished an ornate sailor's hook at the adventurers. A lithe figure in dark leather armor, she had raven hair pulled into a single ponytail and a Daellish face marked by a myriad of long, thin scars crisscrossing each other from every angle. "Who do you think you are?"

Heraldin stepped around Gorm before the Dwarf could offer an answer. "Hello, Benny," said the bard.

"Heraldin Strummons?" exclaimed Benny Hookhand. The woman turned back to the figure held in place by her goons. "But then who—"

"That glorious bastard is an imposter." Heraldin smiled and nodded to his double. "A fool who thought he could clear my name by dying in my stead."

The doppelganger, for its part, stared at Heraldin in bewildered shock.

"Or you might be the fake," snarled Benny.

"Perhaps, but when have I ever been that quiet before?" asked Heraldin.

Benny thought for a moment, then shoved the doppelganger away from the trapdoor with a curse.

"Wait," Gorm interjected. "Benny Hookhand is a woman?"

"You always said he was a man," said Laruna.

There was a chorus of low groans, snorts, and general derision from the assembled goons. Even Heraldin turned back to the party with a look of incredulous scorn. "What are you talking about?" hissed the bard.

"You mean this old thing?" laughed Benny, strutting closer. The woman brought the point of the hook to within a finger's length of her eyeball. "I couldn't care less about this meatbag."

Gorm felt his stomach turn as she stepped into the light. Though the woman's mouth was smiling, her eyes were wide with terror. "Benny's the hook," he said.

"Obviously," sneered Benny Hookhand.

"The name is quite clear," agreed Heraldin.

Gorm never knew what possessed ancient wizards to make them create sentient weapons, but once they did so, much of the possessing was done by the weapons rather than the wizards. A sword or an axe that thought for itself was bad enough, but nothing was worse than a blade that thought for its wielder.

"The woman that Benny is currently, ah, attached to was once an assassin sent to dispatch him," said Heraldin.

"Well, I wouldn't say I'm attached to her." The hook withdrew from her eye, only to drag itself down the right side of her cheek, carving a thin, crimson line amid the innumerable scars on her face. "Not like when I was with you."

"Wait, what?" exclaimed Kaitha.

"Oh yeah," said Benny. "Heraldin here was one of the best bonesacks I ever got hooked on. But when this one showed up," the hook swung perilously close to the woman's face again, "Strummons fought back long enough to get himself disarmed."

"And I never looked back," said Heraldin. "Until now."

"Oh?" said Benny.

"The doppelganger is a friend of mine. No, a brother," said Heraldin, smiling at his double. "And there's no way I'll let him throw away his life for the sake of my freedom. He's got too much to live for."

The doppelganger stared at Heraldin, confused.

"So you planned to, what, storm in here and take him back?" laughed Benny. "You know how many goons and thugs I've got around this place?"

"By my count, I'd say six less than ye did ten minutes ago," said Gorm.

Benny's vessel narrowed her eyes. "Good to know there's some fight in you, but that doesn't make this any less of a fool's errand. What's to stop me from having Gritty over there slit your friend's throat?"

"Things could get pretty violent if that happened," growled Laruna.

"I still like my odds," said Benny. "If everybody dies, it's only a matter of time before someone comes along scavenging for weapons. You fleshies come and go, but I keep sticking around."

"But why let it come to that?" interjected Heraldin, stepping forward. "Why not make a deal?"

"A deal?" said Benny.

"What's he doing?" Kaitha hissed in Gorm's ear.

"Improvisin'," Gorm whispered.

"You're not in on this?" Jynn looked at the Dwarf in alarm.

"My life for the doppelganger's." Heraldin extended his arms. "Or more accurately, my body."

"What?" Gorm and his party chorused in disbelief.

The doppelganger lurched forward against the goons' grasp, as if to yell out in protest.

"Your friends don't seem to like the idea," laughed Benny Hookhand. "Besides, I had an agreement with you before, and look how that turned out for me."

"This would be different," said Heraldin. "There's no contract this time, and that means no escape clause. Even if I could get disarmed again, you could just have your goons make me pick you back up."

Benny shook his vessel's head. "No. I don't make deals. There's always catch. You're planning something."

"What could I be planning?" The bard unbuckled his belt, letting his rapier and supply pouches drop to the floor. "Benny, you said yourself that this whole building could burn and you'd come out on top. I have no other chance to save a friend."

"So you say, but I wouldn't be stuck in this two-bit body if you weren't such a conniving snake." Benny gestured at his host body with a derisive scowl.

"I've no weapons, no more tools, and my hands are empty." The bard displayed his bare palms with an elaborate flourish, ending with his arms straight up above his head like a prisoner's. "You've got the upper hand, Benny, and I'm offering you what we both know you really want."

Benny Hookhand thoughtfully scratched at his host's chin, carving another bloody line down it. "You always were my favorite flesh puppet... But you're still not the sort to be trusted."

Heraldin glanced at the doppelganger. "Sometimes you have to trust people who don't really deserve it."

Heraldin's double stared at the bard with an inscrutable expression on his face, but he stopped fighting the goon behind him.

"All right," said Benny. "We'll give it a shot. You wield me again, and I let your doppelganger go. But keep those hands up in the air, or my boys there are going to start slitting throats."

"Of course." Heraldin stepped forward, holding his hands above his head.

"Shouldn't we stop him?" Laruna whispered.

"We do, and they'll kill Gaist for sure," murmured Gorm. "And Heraldin won't fare much better, given that the fool left his blade behind."

The former assassin holding Benny Hookhand was extending the enchanted weapon to Heraldin now. Its handle was a t-grip formed from great spikes of iron woven together. "You better not try anything funny," said Benny.

"There's nothing left to try," said Heraldin. He looked at the other adventurers with a final smile for the doppelganger. "Goodbye, my fellows." With that, he grabbed the handle of the hook.

Immediately, the Daellish assassin dropped to the floor as though cut down from a hangman's noose. She gave a choking sob as she scrambled away, but it was overshadowed by the hideous, warped laughter rumbling up from the bard's throat. "Finally!" shouted Benny Hookhand with Heraldin's mouth. "Finally, a little closer to my old self!"

"So ye'll honor the deal, then?" said Gorm.

Benny Hookhand cracked his neck and shook out his legs. "Give me a second, here. It takes a moment to—ergh—get used to a new body, you know? But yeah, the doppelganger's fine to go."

The goons gave Heraldin's impersonator a forceful shove, sending the doppelganger crashing into a pile of crates and crab traps.

"As for the rest of you, well, you weren't really part of the bargain," laughed Benny. "And now the cavalry has arrived."

Gorm turned to see a long line of well-armored men and women creeping into the room behind him, brandishing an assortment of wicked looking weapons. Unlike the goons that Gorm and company had already dispatched, these licensed thugs had the right experience and certifications to combat professional heroes.

"Bones," swore the Dwarf.

"Yeah, we'll get to those eventually," said Benny, stretching Heraldin's legs. "But we're going to start with your skin, fingernails, that sort of thing. It's going to be slow and... eh?" The crime lord stopped and looked at his left hand with a confused scowl. He was holding a small slip of paper.

"Thought his hands were empty," Benny Hookhand said, flipping the paper over.

The blast from the anti-magic rune sent ripples across reality with a low *thrum*. The flames around Laruna's fists winked out. Jynn staggered back, clutching the glove that covered his left hand. Magical weapons wielded by the encroaching thugs flickered and went inert. And Heraldin began to laugh again, though now in his own voice.

"It's called sleight of hand you worthless hunk of sharpened scrap!" the bard hollered. Before any of the nearby goons could stop him, he hurled the enchanted hook through the trapdoor in the floor.

Gritty dove to catch the flying weapon, but he was too late. Benny Hookhand disappeared beneath the burbling Tarapin River with an unceremonious *plunk.*

"Ha! Right on ye, lad!" shouted Gorm.

"Oh, you're going to regret that," snarled Gritty, climbing to his knees.

"I don't believe so, my friend," said Heraldin with a confident smirk. "You see, this is the signal."

"What are you—" The goon froze mid-sentence, cut off by a series of ominous tearing sounds.

All eyes turned to the pile of crab traps and fishing gear, where a dark figure was rising like some ancient horror from the grave. He had the ebony skin of an Imperial, and much of it was visible as his muscles had recently burst through the tattered bard's costume hanging from his chiseled frame. In one hand he held a broken oar, and with the other Gaist wrapped a torn piece of red fabric around his face in place of a red scarf.

"Oh *spug*—" Gritty's swear wasn't an inspired choice for last words, but the goon didn't have long to regret them before he was stabbed in the throat with an oar handle and flipped through a window into the rushing river, the oar still protruding from his throat.

Many within the Heroes' Guild consider the term "weaponsmaster" to be something of a misnomer. While all agree that anyone worthy of the title must show considerable mastery of a wide arsenal of bladed and blunt implements of death, the defining characteristic of the profession is that its members do not need an actual weapon to kill. Anything is deadly in the hands of a weaponsmaster.

Gaist charged into the nearest pack of surprised goons with a length of knotted rope in one hand and a small anchor in the other, and put both to work with gruesome effectiveness.

"I didn't know that could be done with a rope," said Gorm.

"Even if it can, I'm pretty sure it shouldn't," said Jynn.

"We've got bigger problems!" shouted Kaitha, loosing an arrow. It ricocheted off the shield of an advancing thug, a massive woman with dark hide armor and a frost-encrusted mace.

Gorm grinned. "Aye, but they're the right kind of problems to have," he said.

"How so?" hollered Laruna. Magical flames sputtered back to life in her hands.

"They're the kind with a straightforward solution!" Gorm launched himself at the nearest foe. His target parried deftly with a wicked falchion, but Gorm slammed his shield into the thug's side and put the man off-balance. The Dwarf's next swing cut into his opponent's side, and the one after that put a definitive end to the thug's career. Gorm barely had time to pull his axe from the twitching body before the next foe was upon him.

"My friends, I don't like to be dramatic—" Heraldin danced out of the path of a thug's hammer.

"Could have fooled us!" shouted Jynn, throwing a spell at an approaching pair of bola-wielding thugs.

"Hilarious, I'm sure." The bard bent backward to dodge a goon's iron flail. "You may recall that I dropped my gear, and some assistance would be most appreciated."

A strangled scream rang out amidst the chaos as Gaist put a fishing net to creative and deadly use. The goon's corpse hadn't yet slumped to the floor before the doppelganger was at Heraldin's side. Without irony, he offered the bard a riverman's gaff.

Heraldin sneered down at the gaff. "And what am I supposed to do with that?" he demanded.

By way of demonstration, Gaist reached out to snag the face of the flail-wielding thug with the thin hook, snapped the struggling man's neck, and flipped him through the trapdoor and into the river in one fluid motion.

"Well, we can't all do that!" snapped Heraldin.

Gaist wore a hint of a smile as he shrugged. He turned back to face the thug with the hammer just as the man was immolated by an arcing bolt of strange energy.

"What the blazes was that?" hollered Laruna, hurling a blast of fire at her own opponent, a gnarled woman with one eye and an ensorcelled tower shield.

"Sinusoidal weaves of fire and lightning." Jynn pursed his lips as he watched the thug stagger for the trapdoor and hurl himself into the river. "Somewhat effective, but I didn't expect the fractal helix pattern."

"Stop your silly experiments and fight!" The solamancer dodged back to avoid a quick series of sword thrusts, then countered with another ball of flame. The tower shield deflected it easily.

"I'd say I'm effectively doing both!" snapped Jynn. He hurled another blended weave at the tower shield just as the solamancer loosed her own spell. Jynn's tiny weave bounced off the shield and into Laruna's onrushing mass of flames. Surprisingly enough, the omnimancer's spell split the fireball as a stone splits a river. Half of Laruna's weave splashed harmlessly against the gnarled thug's tower shield, but the rest skipped up into a tight arc and rained down on the unfortunate woman's head. She was blown through the rickety floor in a torrent of raging flames.

"What did you just do?" yelled Laruna, staring at the charred hole in the floor.

The omnimancer looked just as surprised. "I think the helix weaves formed a polarized lattice that—!"

"You messed up my spell," said Laruna, more shocked than angry.

"No, I re-wove your spell!" Jynn sounded much happier about it. "Let's try it again!"

"That's going to be difficult," said Kaitha, loosing an arrow. It caught a goon in the back, and he fell screaming through a window.

"No, it's quite simple," said Jynn. "I think I could rework the lattice to—"

"She means ye've run out of targets." Gorm pulled his axe from the remains of one of the thugs.

Jynn and Laruna looked around the wreckage of the room, covered in splintered wood and the mortal remains of Benny's henchmen. "Ah, so we have," sighed the omnimancer.

"But not for long," added Heraldin. "Listen."

Gorm could hear angry shouts in the distance. "More thugs?"

"Or the bannermen," said Kaitha. "So, either way…"

"We should get going." Gorm turned to Gaist, who—in the fashion of a true professional—had looted a long, black cloak from a fallen thug. With the cape concealing his shredded garments, the weaponsmaster looked almost like his old self again. "Welcome back," said Gorm. "It's good to see ye."

Gaist set a huge hand on the Dwarf's shoulder, looked him in the eye, and nodded once.

"Oh, don't get all emotional on us now," Heraldin told the weaponsmaster. "Look, there will be plenty of time for talking and-or stoically glaring later. For now, we need to get out of here."

"Soon as we collect our fee." Gorm bent down and grabbed a coin purse off the corpse of the thug.

"You want to loot Benny's henchmen now?" asked Heraldin.

"Well, we won't get to do it later," said Kaitha as she deftly relieved an ex-goon of his Arthly possessions.

"And it's been a long while since our last bit of income," agreed Laruna, pulling a steaming coin bag from some charred remains.

"Plus, stopping my father will be incredibly difficult," said Jynn. "There's bound to be significant expenses."

"Yeah, probably more than you can afford!" shouted Burt.

The Elf snickered as she walked away, the heels of her shoes clicking on the brick streets of Stonewood Summit.

"Gutter scarg anyway," Burt muttered, running painted claws through a recently-dyed coif of fur.

"Hey, now," said Ginner, a gap-toothed Kobold in a garish pink vest. He lit a cigarette. "No need for that. There's plenty more here."

"Yeah, plenty more gutter scargs," grumbled Burt. Despite its lofty name, Stonewood Summit was firmly set on the Ridgeward side of Andarun's sixth tier. The bricks on the streets and in the houses were cheap and crumbling. Most of the street torches were broken or burnt out. Unsavory characters lurked in the few pools of light along the damp road, including the pair of Kobolds.

Any Elf forced to live down here was scraping at the bottom of Elven society, the kind of immortal that Burt used to turn his nose up at back when he lived at the embassy. Times had changed.

"Heads up." Ginner stamped out his cigarette and nodded at a pair of Elven women making their way down the street.

Burt was already up and dancing. "Hey, miss! Nice purse, miss!" he shouted to the pair.

"That purse looks a little light!" yelled Ginner.

"Might look nicer with a little accessory, eh?" said Burt.

The Elves rolled their eyes, but otherwise ignored the Kobolds.

"What's wrong, Miss?" barked Ginner. "We know some good tricks!"

The flap on the closest Elf's purse opened, and a Kobold with long rows of brass earrings poked his head out. "Hey, I got a trick for ya!" he growled, and raised a paw in a rude gesture.

"That the best you can do?" Ginner snarled back. "Why not get a real Kobold, miss?"

"Your friend has a Kobold, miss!" Burt hollered to the other Elf. "Why not get a matching one?"

"Hey, maybe there's a Halfling down in Tenderfoot Lane that needs a way to get rid of table scraps," yipped the purse Kobold. "You guys could probably do that!"

The Elf carrying him clucked her tongue and tapped the Kobold on the nose. He gave a placating whine and dove back into her handbag. The Elves continued on their way, quietly talking as though the exchange had never happened.

"Yeah, all right, keep walking!" Ginner shouted after her.

Burt couldn't even muster the enthusiasm for a parting insult. He dropped to sit on the curb. "Did you see those earrings? Are those in now?"

"They did look fantastic," Ginner conceded.

"I can't wear earrings like that." Burt shook his head and stared at the brick pavers. "What's left of my ear is too floppy."

"I couldn't afford earrings like that," said Ginner.

"What am I gonna do?" asked Burt. "I mean, I can't even keep up with mid-tier fashion. And I'm not getting any younger. Plus, look at my ear! It might never heal right! How am I gonna get back to the upper tiers? Bones, how am I gonna eat?"

Ginner sat down next to him. "We'll get by," he said. "It will be tough, but you and me, we can—"

"Hey!"

The Kobolds turned to see that the pair of Elves had returned. The woman without a Kobold presented her empty purse. "You in the pink. You want a job or not?"

"Best of luck, buddy." Ginner gave Burt a pat on the shoulder before scampering off and jumping into the Elf's purse.

"Thanks," muttered Burt. It was hard to bear Ginner too much ill-will for abandoning him; Burt would have done the same in that position. Bones, he had *planned* on being in that position; Burt had paired up with the older Kobold because he thought he'd look good by comparison. It had been a poor assumption, he reflected as he watched the Elves walk off into the gloom. For a while he sat watching the darkness where they had been, letting the weight of the world press in on him.

"What am I gonna do?" he wondered aloud, dropping his head into his paws.

"Well, hopefully wash that dye out of your fur, for starters. Ye look ridiculous."

"Gorm?" Burt looked up as the Dwarf stepped into the torchlight, flanked by the old party. "But… But what are all of you doing here?"

"Searching for you," said Kaitha.

"Which took all day, by the way," said Laruna.

Burt felt a lump in his throat. "You… you all came back for me?"

"'Course we did," said Gorm.

"I wouldn't make Patches wear this otherwise," added Jynn.

428

The wizard stepped aside, and behind him Burt could see Patches padding into the torchlight. Thin leather straps traced dark lines across the dog's fur, connected to a small saddle on his back.

"We assumed it would be more comfortable, yes?" said Heraldin.

Burt leapt up and threw his arms around Patches' neck. He couldn't have spoken anyway, and burying his face in the dog's fur conveniently hid the tears streaming down the Kobold's muzzle.

"All right," said Gorm, giving Burt an uncomfortable pat on the shoulder. "All right, lad. It's only a saddle."

"Yeah." Burt sniffed as he tried to compose himself. "It just says something, you know?"

Chapter 25

"Sometimes I wish you'd say something," said Heraldin, advancing a bannerman.

Gaist's only reply was to advance a knight. Suddenly Heraldin found his last piece under a dual threat.

"I suppose I should count my blessings," said the bard with a grimace. He knocked over his king, conceding the match. "If you spoke right now, I'm sure you'd be intolerably smug."

The weaponsmaster's eyes conveyed sufficient smugness without the benefit of spoken words.

"Yes, fine. You win again," said Heraldin, moving the thrones pieces back into place.

The weaponsmaster tapped the table and nodded at the surrounding space. The tavern's common room had emptied by this hour, and even the barkeep had shuffled off to bed. The only other occupant of the room was a wrinkled Slaugh, pushing a mop along with short hops.

"I know the hour is late," said the bard. "But stay for one more game, my friend. I want to show you something."

Gaist shrugged and set up his own pieces.

Heraldin started the game with the Northerner's Gambit, a well-known opener from the Edaelmon school. Gaist countered with the Lion's Ruse, regarded as one of the best counters to any number of openers. The game of thrones continued in a familiar way, following patterns they'd played through many times.

Then Heraldin moved his king into the path of Gaist's queen. The stoic man smirked a little as he took the bard's piece.

Heraldin shrugged as he swapped the fallen king with one of his paladins still on the board. The bard had often surmised that the mechanic of allowing a king to be "succeeded" by another piece of sufficient rank was why the game was called "thrones" and not "throne."

With his new king in place, Heraldin immediately moved it into range of Gaist's knight.

Gaist scowled at the board. His eyes darted back and forth over the pieces, clearly searching for a ruse. Seeing none, he cautiously took the bard's king again.

Heraldin promoted his last paladin and immediately charged it into danger.

Now Gaist was glaring at him, annoyance flashing in his dark eyes.

"Is something wrong?" the bard asked innocently.

The huge man pointed a finger at the king.

"Yes? What?"

The weaponsmaster narrowed his eyes at the bard.

"Are you implying that I've given up?" said Heraldin with mock indignation.

Gaist nodded once.

"That I'm throwing everything away too early? That I've abandoned the good possibilities in exchange for a foolish sacrifice?" Heraldin pressed.

Gaist was still staring at the bard through slits.

"Yes, now you see my point," said the bard. "But will you remember it this time? I don't want you to die for me. And if this Iheen the Red was worth half the loyalty you've shown him, he wouldn't want for you to die for him, either. We want you to live, my friend. And if you want to honor him, or to help me, you must want to live as well."

Gaist sat motionless, but Heraldin had learned to look closer. There was a barely perceptible tightening around the mouth beneath the weaponsmaster's crimson scarf. A tensing of the muscles around the eyes that brought the doppelganger's harsh stare closer to an introspective squint. A faint motion, more of a hint of a nod than an actual affirmation.

It wasn't much, but Heraldin smiled anyway as he picked up the pieces. It was the answer he had expected.

"No response?" Gorm trundled down the path on the gravelly slopes.

Kaitha turned to him as he approached, a small and weary smile on her face. The patchwork farmlands west of Andarun spread out behind her for as far as the eye could see. Dawn's light was creeping around the edges of the landscape, but Mount Wynspar still shadowed much of the view.

"None," Kaitha said, turning back to look out over the farmland.

"How long have ye been out here?" he asked, sitting down beside her.

The Elf rubbed at the bags beneath her eyes. "A few hours before dawn. I thought he might come when it's dark."

"I see ye've set out the customary offering for the King in the Wood." Gorm pointed at a rock a short distance away, topped with purple trinkets piled on a lavender handkerchief.

Kaitha shrugged. "I just wanted him to know… to see why I'm out here."

"Makes sense," said Gorm.

For a time, they sat and watched the sunlight draw long shadows over the land.

Gorm scratched his beard thoughtfully. "Ye know that if we had any idea where he is…"

"We don't," said Kaitha in a small voice.

"All I'm sayin' is if we did —"

"I've searched everywhere. We've asked everyone." The Elf shook her head. "I can't find any sign of him. And if we're going to stop Detarr, we can't wait for him."

"I know," said Gorm.

They continued to watch the amber sunlight creep over the gold and green fields of early spring.

"We're bound to find signs of Thane at some point, and ye can be sure that when we do, we'll go after him as fast as we can. And when we find him, ye can… er, can… uh, ye know…"

"I really don't know." The Elf shook her head with a bitter laugh. "I mean, I had all these dreams of what it would be like when I met the King in the Wood, but they were… I mean, he was different in them, obviously. A Troll? I don't know what you would… I mean, how can you relate? How would that work?"

Gorm just shook his head and tried very hard not to think about it.

"But I don't know that it couldn't, either," Kaitha added. "We had a real connection. I could feel it, Gorm. I could feel him."

"I know. We all saw it." Gorm suppressed a shudder.

"Besides, most men I've encountered buy you a drink and some cheap food and they expect you to… you know."

"Say no more," said Gorm, and meant it.

"But Thane… I mean, he left his home for me. He saved us more times than I can count. And he's never asked for anything. You look your whole life for someone that devoted, and that's saying something for my people. So when the chance at… whatever this could be comes along, I have to take it. But instead, I shot him in the face. Now I just… I can't…"

"Not exactly how ye want to leave things with him," said Gorm.

"Yeah." Kaitha's hands balled into fists. "Or start things with him."

"I put my axe in his face a couple of times when we first met, and we still became fast friends," he said.

"That's nothing," said Kaitha. "Thane followed me from the shadows for months, and I was a fool who fancied him some sort of ancient king. And then he saved me from wandering in the wilderness while in withdrawal, brought me back to the party, and killed an assassin who wanted to slit my throat. And to thank him, I put an arrow through his eye."

"It is quite a bit of history to get past, when you put it like that," Gorm acknowledged.

Kaitha smirked and wiped her eyes. "It's hard to imagine a more dysfunctional relationship."

Gorm looked back over his shoulder at the tiny inn sitting in Mount Wynspar's shadow by the side of the Tarapin River. "Oh, not too hard," he said.

Laruna wasn't glaring at Jynn.

He knew that she wasn't, because she had been avoiding looking at him for three days now. She looked past him, spoke over him, undermined him, and found myriad other ways to circumnavigate their relationship without crossing his path. Her frosty silence reminded him of when they first met, he noted wistfully.

Yet, Laruna's demeanor was a bit different now. She was definitely not glaring at him, per se, but she was leveling a burning stare at the air just over his left shoulder, as though menacing the rafters behind him. "There isn't another table," she remarked to no one in particular, and gestured at the tiny common room of the tavern.

The River Otter was an unusual establishment, set on the edge of a small hamlet just outside the Riverdowns. By most standards it wasn't an inn at all—the bedrooms were scattered throughout the working farm behind the tavern. For a fee, heroes and mercenaries could bed down in an old barn, find a quiet corner of the loft, roost with the chickens, or rent a private tool shed. It was far from luxurious, but for a certain patronage, secrecy was the only important amenity, and the Otter offered that in spades. The differences between a night at the Otter and a night sneaking into a farmer's loft were discretion and a surprisingly hefty bill slipped under the doorway.

"I'm aware." Jynn set his breakfast of bread and cheese down at the edge of the table, next to Burt. "That's why I'm sitting at this one."

"I think it would be polite to let others finish eating before disrupting their meal," Laruna insisted to the ceiling.

"And I think it ridiculous," said Jynn, "that you cannot eat with an omnimancer. But that is your own concern. I won't be bothered by it."

"It isn't that!" she hissed. The solamancer's flash of anger melted her resolve not to make eye contact, and she stared at him with eyes like embers. "I just have a problem eating with liars!"

"You're eating with Heraldin," Jynn said.

"Leave the bard out of this," Laruna snapped.

"No, no," said Heraldin through a mouthful of eggs. "That's a fair point."

"I meant bigger lies than that," said Laruna. She shifted her eyes back to the rafters. "Lies about who you truly are."

"We're here with a doppelganger," said Jynn. "No offense."

Gaist shrugged.

"I don't want to be near your kind of sniveling mongrel!" Laruna sputtered at the ceiling.

Burt pointed a claw at Jynn. "Let me stop you before you go there."

"I wasn't going there." The omnimancer put his hands in the air.

"You're thrice-cursed right you weren't." Burt snorted and turned back to his breakfast.

"Didn't the wizard save your life?" Heraldin asked the mage.

"And I… appreciate that," said Laruna carefully. "But the fact remains that he wouldn't have needed to if he had been honest about what he was. How much different could the fight with Detarr have been with an omnimancer wielding the staff?"

Jynn shrugged off the accusation. "My entire life is a series of events that could have been great if they went another way. What if Mother didn't die? What if Father's research had been successful? What if my marriage to Marja had kept Father alive? What if the Al'Matrans never recruited me? What if you and I had done things differently?"

He dismissed these alternative realities with a wave of his hand. "We could spend an age wondering about the things that could have been. None of them will be. It's best to set such feelings aside and focus on the work at hand."

The solamancer finally looked at him again, albeit with the same face she might have used if he had grown a tentacle from his ear. "You really can dismiss your feelings that easily, can't you?"

"I already have," said Jynn. "There is a job to be done."

"Then you and I are just, what? Colleagues?"

"Professional acquaintances, if you prefer."

The heat and fury seemed to drain out of the solamancer's face, leaving a small, tight smile. "As you'd have it," she said coldly. "I'll take my breakfast outside, if none of you mind."

Jynn watched her go for a moment before he realized that the other occupants of the table were staring at him. "What?" he asked.

Heraldin and Gaist shared a sidelong glance. "Nothing," said the bard.

"The bard may be dressed like a fool, but you play the part better," said Burt.

Gaist nodded.

"Don't encourage him," the bard told the weaponsmaster.

"I thought Laruna and I resolved things rather well," Jynn said.

"Yeah, like lantern oil resolves a fire," grumbled Burt.

"It could have been worse," said Jynn.

"Not without getting violent," the Kobold shot back.

"And there's still plenty of time for that before we ride out," said Heraldin. "I don't want to be here if she comes back."

"Yeah, come on," said Burt, hopping to his feet. "Gorm and Kaitha should be back soon."

Jynn mulled over his encounter with the solamancer as the other adventurers filed out of the tavern. In retrospect, he surmised that Laruna had likely ended the conversation more upset than she started. A part of him wished that he had said things differently. Better.

The wizard set those dreams aside in the box in his mind where he stored all such regrets. It was, he reflected, a very large box. Then he tossed his most recent speck of remorse in as well, closed the mental lid, and turned his thoughts to the day ahead of them. There was much work to do.

"For starters, they should tear this place down," Gorm glowered.

"That's harsh," said Kaitha.

Gorm nodded at the crumbling exterior of the Dwarven Embassy. "It's just hard to see the ancestral kingdoms reduced to... to this."

The Old Kingdoms' delegation had set up their embassy in the remnants of a Dwarven jeweler's shop, moldering in the shadow of the Ridge on the fifth tier. Bleached and weathered wood was nailed over the display windows, and tattered banners hung from the second story windows. There was little indication that it was the embassy at all, save for a small sign and a pair of Dwarven guards standing stoically at the door.

"It does look, ah, a bit modest," said Kaitha.

"More like it has low self-esteem," said Laruna.

"It's a thrice-cursed disgrace is what it is," said Gorm as the three heroes walked toward the decrepit building.

The well-armed Dwarves eyed Gorm and his two companions as they approached. The older of the pair, a warrior with a snowy beard spilling from beneath his full helm, pointed at Gorm and made a sound like he was struggling to swallow an enraged owlverine.

"Was that Dwarven?" Laruna whispered.

"Far as I can tell. He's got quite an accent," said Gorm. He waved a hand to hail the guards. "Ho, there!"

The younger guard was a stout lad with thick braids in his beard and a thicker brogue in his speech. "What business do ye have wid' der seat of Khadan'Alt?"

Gorm stepped squarely in front of the two guards. "I'm seekin' an audience with His Majesty to discuss matters of import."

"Ye have a writ of royal invite, do ye?" said the guard.

"Not as much, no," said Gorm.

"Na' see Forder Hvarthson widdout He Majesty's writ!" The older guard was only marginally easier to understand when he used the Imperial tongue.

"And how do we get a royal invite?" asked Kaitha.

"Not bringin' a leaden Elf and a she-mage wid' ye would be a good start," chuckled the younger guard.

His elder snorted at the jest. "Only He Majerster or der court can giff a royal invite, 'curse."

"But if the king doesn't know we want an invite, how would he send one?" said Laruna.

"Ye'd have to talk to him or his court," said the younger guard.

"But we can't without an invite," said the solamancer.

The guards looked at each other and shrugged. "It's a very secure system," said the younger of the two.

Long careers in the Heroes' Guild had prepared Gorm and Kaitha for such bureaucracy. "Well, that's a shame," Gorm said loudly.

"We're old friends of King Johan, hoping to help King Forder with his financial troubles. But if'n he's too busy, we'd best be on our way."

The old guard nodded. "A wise course o' action."

"The only one available, it seems." Despite his proclamation of surrender, Gorm didn't step away. The bait was set, and now all someone needed to do was bend the rules enough to take it.

The embassy door cracked open and there was a harsh whisper in Dwarven. Someone yanked the guards to the door and into an animated, if muted, debate.

"How'd you know that would work?" asked Kaitha.

Gorm shrugged. "To hear the town criers tell it, King Forder is the only one in the Freedlands in a worse state than us."

The two guards slunk back to their posts, staring askance at the ground. "It seems His Majesty's court wishes to extend ye a verbal writ of invitation," said the younger Dwarf.

"Well, let's not keep His Majesty waitin'," said Gorm.

They were ushered into a musty antechamber, still save for thick motes of dust wafting through the air. A Dwarven clerk in a worn suit greeted the adventurers with a stoic nod. He ushered them into a barren conference room at the back of the embassy featuring a round table and a poster with a woodcut of a saber-toothed dire cat dangling from a rope over a spiked pit. The caption below the picture read "HANG IN THERE."

Gorm went to take a seat at the table, but found that there weren't any.

"It's a bit sparse," said Kaitha as she and Laruna filed into the room behind him.

"Certainly not what I expected," agreed Laruna.

"I'm going to stick with 'a disgrace,' if'n it's all the same to ye," said Gorm.

"I'm afraid it is all we can afford at the moment," said a voice from the doorway.

Gorm turned to see a graying Dwarf in silver chainmail robes standing in the doorway, a gaggle of dour advisors huddled behind him. A thin circlet set atop his head marked him as Forder Hvarthson, King of Khadan'Alt, eldest elder and most revered Ancestor of the Old Dwarven Kingdoms.

Gorm and the women immediately dropped to their knee. "Your Majes—"

"Enough of that. We've already dispensed with too many formalities for ceremony to matter now." The king waved them to stand as he stamped over to the head of the conference table. "A bow means little when it follows an insult to our embassy."

"I was just remarkin' that it ain't worthy of our people, Majesty," said Gorm, feeling a bit of sweat pool on his brow.

"Of course it isn't," said the king over the rumbles of the Ancestors and Fathers tromping into the room behind him. "We used to have a fine palace up by the Pinnacle, but we had to liquidate it. It's a sun-blasted luxury hotel now!"

"You sold the embassy?" exclaimed Laruna, forgetting herself. Gorm shot her a dark glance.

"I've sold just about every bloody thing my people can't eat by now, and they're still starving," snapped the king. "If it were any other way, I'd be in the blessed depths instead of taking audience with whatever gangue drifts in off the street. And in that vein, what do you know of King Johan's plans?"

King Forder's face said the audience would be short, so Gorm spoke as fast as he could. "We're just a trio of old heroes, Majesty. My name is Gorm, and I quested with King Johan back before he was 'the Mighty.' He and I have enough history for me to know how he operates."

"I know who ye are, Pyrebeard. There ain't many Dwarves who've adventured with Johan, and the rest of them ain't driftin' around Arth like slag in a smeltin' pot." Forder grimaced. "If'n times weren't so dire, I'd have your clanless hide hauled off to Johan for the reward. As it is, I'm willing to listen to ye first."

Gorm had expected the reaction, and he pressed on quickly. "Your Majesty knows as well as I that Johan wouldn't pay ye a penny for me or any other reason when there's so much benefit in leaving the Old Kingdoms broke. He'll keep Your Majesty and his delegation dangling here until ye agree to his demands. Based on what I've heard, I'm guessin' he wants to annex the Old Dwarven Kingdoms into the Freedlands."

The king looked unmoved. "And ye can guess whatever ye like. You're here to provide information, not garner it. I'd suggest ye get to it soon."

"What ye need is a way to gain leverage over Johan. And I know how ye can get that, if the Heroes' Guild of the Old Dwarven Kingdoms is still intact."

"It still exists," said King Forder. "Though I wouldn't say much beyond that for it."

"Many of our heroes have abandoned us to sign on with the Freedlands," said one of the Ancestors seated near Forder. A pin on the lapel of his suit bore the crest of sword and sorcery. Gorm surmised that he was the guildmaster of the Old Dwarven Kingdom's branch of the guild. "Better work, they say, and a more favorable tax situation."

The king rolled his eyes. "Korgen, I've heard all I can stomach about the taxes."

"Apologies, Majesty. To answer the question, the guild stands, but 'tis weak in numbers."

"All it needs to do is stand," said Gorm. "What ye need is heroes from the Old Dwarven Kingdom to take down the army of Detarr Ur'Mayan."

"Are ye mad, boy?" barked Korgen. "We just told ye—"

"Let him speak." The king silenced the guildmaster with a gesture, his eyes never leaving Gorm's. "Most tales of the Pyrebeard involve mad plans, and a surprising number of them actually worked. But beyond the obvious difficulty with slayin' a liche, I don't see what leverage it gives me."

"Pardon me for bringing them up again, Majesty, but it's the taxes," said Gorm. "If'n Old Kingdom heroes kill Detarr and his minions, it's the Old Kingdom that gets the lion's share of the taxes off the loot."

"Especially if you're fulfilling the Ruskan quest, and not the new one the Freedlands spun up when Detarr marched on Highwatch," said Laruna.

"That would cut Andarun's share of the loot down to zero," said Kaitha.

"And you can bet Johan's countin' on the revenue from Detarr's hoard to rebuild what the liche has already destroyed."

The king shook his head. "I thought ye said ye'd worked with Johan before. He would never let our heroes leave the Freedlands with all that treasure."

Gorm tapped the side of his nose. "Aye, but he wouldn't be too keen on startin' a war with the Old Kingdoms either. All the clanhomes in the Freedlands would revolt, and there'd be Dwarves riotin' in every city-state."

"It'd be much better for him to come to the table with you and negotiate a solution," said Kaitha.

"Where you'd have some leverage," said Laruna.

King Forder nodded, staring at the wall. Eventually he gave one curt nod. "It's a fine idea and a happy thought, but as Korgen said, we've not a party of heroes qualified to do it."

"I ain't sure any party could do it," said Korgen. "Ye'd need an army of heroes."

"Exactly," said Gorm. "If ye conscript an army into the guild, all as rank one heroes, ye might have enough."

"And where am I to find such conscripts, both soldiers and heroes?" chimed in another of the king's advisors. The bars and medals on his chainmail robes marked him as the High Commander of Khadan'Alt.

Korgen scowled at his colleague. "Anyone who can swing a stick at a rat can be a rank one warrior, Harak."

Harak snorted. "Anyone who can swing a stick at a rat is already in my rosters, and I'd still want three times as many Dwarves as I have to take on the armies of the liche."

"So, it could work?" asked the king.

The guildmaster and the commander shuffled and harrumphed noncommittally, but eventually the Ancestors conceded the point. "Ye'd need high rankin' heroes to take down yon liche, but they might be able to with an army takin' down the zombies and skeletons," said Korgen.

Forder turned back to Gorm. "It is an interesting plan, but do ye know where I can triple the size of my armies?" The king was leaning forward over the table, an eager gleam in his eyes.

Gorm took a deep breath. "I can, Majesty, but it'd involve ye takin' on some new citizens for conscripts. And they wouldn't be Dwarves, in the strictest sense."

The assembled Ancestors and Fathers harrumphed and shouted protests, but Forder Hvarthson raised a hand to silence them. "There are Humans and Gnomes living in the Old Kingdoms now, though not many. There's even a handful of Elves. Better they join our Kingdom than us being forced to join theirs."

"But sire—" Korgen began.

"I will not hear protest on this," said Hvarthson. "If it means a way to save both our Kingdom and the Freedlands, it must be done. If ye can bring us an army, we will take your Humans, Gnomes, and Elves as citizens."

Gorm bowed his head, if only to hide the sweat beading on his forehead. "Generous and wise, Majesty. But the army we can bring ain't of Humans, Gnomes, or Elves."

The Dwarves murmured to one another in confusion. "Then who do ye propose to bring to us?" said Hvarthson.

"The Red Horde." Gorm's words were nearly drowned out by a collective gasp rising from the Dwarves.

The king stared at his guests with something between wonder and horror. "Ye *are* mad," he whispered.

"*Completely crazy. A monster.*" Burt clambered up to the Orc's shoulder and grabbed his face for emphasis. "*Beneath these cold eyes is an endless sea of bloodlust. Gorst of the Broketooth puts down a Lightling village before he breaks fast every morning. And that is just for exercise.*"

The Gnoll and the Orc on the opposite side of the table glanced at each other. They wore mismatched armor of dark leather and tarnished metal, and both had crimson patches stitched on their left shoulders—the mark of the Red Horde.

"*I don't know.*" The Orcish recruiter spoke Shadowtongue with the guttural accent of the Pinefells. "*Why would we only hear of his deeds now?*"

"*Maybe you should pay better attention,*" said Burt. "*Down in Daellan there isn't a Lightling that doesn't fear Gorst. Right, Gorst?*"

The large Orc nodded. Gorst was clad in black leather armor, with a hooded cape and a bright red scarf around his neck.

"*Why does he not talk?*" yipped the Gnoll.

"*He can barely hold back all his murderous rage,*" said Burt. "*Even now, it's all he can do to sit in this stinking pink-skin tavern without killing all the*

Lightlings. If he even let one word out, it might all start coming to a head and then he's on a killing spree in the Riverdowns."

"If you say as much," said the Gnoll, with obvious doubt. *"And who are you again?"*

"Me? I'm his agent." Burt jabbed a thumb at his chest.

"We specifically said that recruiters need not apply on the poster," snarled the Gnoll.

Burt felt his hackles rise. *"Did I say recruiter? I am representing top talent here. And if you want top talent, you go through me."*

"He sits very still and is very quiet for top talent," smirked the Orc. He poked Gorst in the chest, or rather, he reached out to poke Gorst in the chest.

"Mistake," muttered Burt. Regardless of his shape, Gorst or Gaist or whatever he went by, was still a weaponsmaster.

The doppelganger grabbed the Orc's wrist and wrenched his arm around with a sickening crunch. The Orc screamed, but Gorst silenced him with a series of quick jabs to the face before he heaved the stunned warrior across the room into a pile of barrels. The patrons sitting closest to the barrels scooted their seats away from the destruction, but otherwise the tavern's few occupants remained unmoved. One didn't drink in the Riverdowns without expecting a bar brawl or three.

Burt turned back to the Gnoll. *"See? Murderous rage,"* he said.

The Gnoll nodded quickly. *"It is so. He has my vote. Ghabrang?"*

The wreckage of the barrels shifted. A shaking green fist emerged and extended its thumb upward.

"Aha, then it is settled." The Gnoll recruiter extended a small clipboard to Gorst. *"Welcome to the Red Horde, warrior. Fill this out and come with us."*

"You're not going to regret this," Burt's eyes were on a pair of figures huddled by a table across the bar. One wore a wide brimmed hat, and the other a set of tattered gray robes.

Jynn caught his eye and gave him a small nod. The spell was set.

"And are you ready to depart now?" asked the Gnoll.

Burt grinned. *"No time like the present."*

"Because tomorrow I'll be gone," said Poldo.

Red Squirrel perched on the edge of the bar, nursing a thimble of grog. The beverage splashed a little as the Wood Gnome waved his hands in the air and chittered at the Scribkin. Poldo couldn't make out his words, but he knew his assistant well enough to guess the sentiment.

"I don't like it either, but I must leave the city." Poldo used the tip of his finger to pat the despondent employee on the back.

The tiny man chirruped a single syllable.

"Because soon the liche will arrive, and then there will be no leaving the city. It's going to be hard enough with all these refugees pressing in." Red Squirrel looked like he was going to say something else, but Poldo cut him off. "And I know that if Andarun falls, nowhere on Arth is safe from the undead. But that's not the point."

The Wood Gnome shook a hand in the air and loosed a frustrated squeak.

"The point is that Benny Hookhand is in this city. Or at least, his organization is, and from what I've learned of them, I'd have a better chance with the undead." Poldo drained the last of his Halfling brandy. He slapped two giltin onto the bar next to his empty glass. "Now, I need to rely on you to keep track of my movements and keep me connected to the businesses. It'll be hazard pay and a travel stipend for anyone making the journey. Can you do that?"

The Wood Gnome chirruped.

"Overtime on weekends only."

A sly squeak.

"In this economy? Come now. Things are tight," Poldo protested.

A more insistent chitter.

"It is that bad!" said Poldo. "I'd be surprised if we haven't lost another bank by the end of the week."

Someone further down the bar must have overheard Poldo, as a sob rang out in the quiet of the tavern. Most of the other traders and brokers crowded into the common room were too traumatized to react. They stared at nothing and sipped their drinks in silent misery.

Red Squirrel shook his head and looked back to his grog, chittering a presumably unflattering remark. But Poldo could see that he had won.

"Thank you, my friend," said Poldo. "I'll rendezvous with the team later tonight at the city gate."

The Domovoy squeaked a question and pantomimed a hook for one of his hands. He drew the other hand across his throat, stuck his tiny tongue out, and went cross-eyed.

Poldo shook his head sadly as he hopped off the stool. "Oh, I heard that rumor as well. And I hope it's true," he said. "But you don't stay in the business as long as I have by taking bad risks, and I know better than to bet against Benny Hookhand."

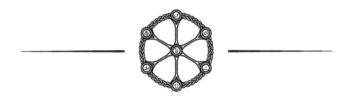

"Well, well. What are the odds?" Garold Flinn muttered to himself as he examined the broken arrow protruding from the river house's weatherworn wall. The shaft was perfectly cylindrical and smooth, the fletching precisely spaced. Either it was the work of a master fletcher, or it was made by magic such as that held in the Poor Man's Quiver. And now that he looked closer, he could see silver wisps trailing from the shaft as the magical arrow slowly dissipated. It would completely dissolve within a few days.

He knew that Kaitha of House Tyrieth wasn't the only hero to have a Poor Man's Quiver. Then again, how many adventurers who could afford such distinctive ammunition were also traveling with a solamancer capable of blasting half of a wall to charred rubble and someone wielding an axe to brutal effect on the inner doorway? Flinn rubbed the stub beneath his metallic claw as he thought about the axe that took his own hand.

This was Gorm Ingerson's work. He could feel it in his bones.

The Dwarven outcast's return to Andarun was a boon to Mr. Flinn. The assassin's job wasn't finished, a point his employer had been emphasizing lately by having gift baskets of fruits and baked goods delivered to Flinn's residence. There was nothing malicious amongst the baskets' contents, save perhaps for cookies with raisins in them, and the attached notes from the king were always cordial and pleasant.

The message wasn't about the actual contents of the baskets. It was the manner in which they showed up just inside Flinn's doorway once every few days with a note personally penned by King Johan. No matter where the Tinderkin was hiding, no matter how carefully he covered his tracks, he'd inevitably find a fruit basket sitting on the border of his defenses, broadcasting a threat loud and clear.

Johan was taking a personal interest in his work. Johan could find him. Johan's people could reach him. And, oh, by the way, how is that job with Gorm Ingerson coming?

Flinn flexed his claws. The job was going a little better now that there were clear signs the Dwarf was back in the city. Word on the street was that Barty Ficer had skipped town a couple of weeks back with a new name and new face, and the latter was involuntary. More recently, an informant had seen the Dwarf and some of his party down at the River Otter. And now there were rumors that the berserker had taken on Benny Hookhand in the Riverdowns.

Yet knowing where your enemy has been, however, is not nearly as valuable as knowing where he will go next. Flinn turned his attention to searching the rubble for signs of Ingerson's plans.

He was disappointed. Between the bannermen and the Hookhand's thugs, the crime scene had been cleared of any valuable evidence. More specifically, it had been cleared of any evidence that would be worth more than a few coppers at the local pawn shop. Aside from the damage to the building and a splintered arrow here and there, there were few clues to go on.

It struck Flinn that he should check the riverbanks below the ruined shack. This was a new sensation, the Tinderkin reflected as he climbed down the overgrown stone steps to the shore—he'd been struck by thoughts before, but never with the strange force that had just planted the idea in his skull. It was like a slap that bypassed the face to strike the brain directly.

He ducked down and surveyed the muddy banks obscured in the shadows beneath the creaking ruin. There wasn't anything but river grass and muck.

Check by the third pylon.

A chill ran down Flinn's spine. The last thought had definitely not been his own. But a quick glance at the rotting support closest to the water revealed the glint of dark metal. He crept closer.

A metal hook was half-submerged in the mud and river grass.

Pick it up.

"I think not." Flinn smiled at the flash of displeasure that flared in his mind. "I'm quite familiar with the dangers of touching enchanted weapons, let alone the famous Benny Hookhand."

Pick me up! Benny snarled in Flinn's mind.

"Oh, I'm not going to wield you," said Flinn. "But I might be able to help you in exchange for information."

What information? Flinn could feel the blade's suspicion.

"Just some questions about the party that attacked your building here," said Flinn. "You answer them, and I'll return you to your thugs."

Pick me up! It was less a suggestion now, and more of an attempt to force Flinn to bend to the weapon's will.

"I could spend a considerable amount of time detailing the rigorous training that I've endured to protect my mind from such invasion," said Flinn. "Alas, I'm in a hurry, as is my client, so if you're not interested in my proposal…"

Wait.

Flinn grinned. "Yes?"

How can you take me anywhere if you won't pick me up?

"Oh, I'll lift you from the muck. Just with the necessary precautions." Slowly, carefully, Flinn reached down with his enchanted prosthetic. With Benny Hookhand's iron handle clutched in the metallic talons, the weapon was safely held a few inches away from Flinn's skin. He regarded the muddy hook at arm's length. "So, do we have a deal?"

In place of a response, the iron bands that comprised Benny's handle suddenly unwound themselves with the swift fluidity of serpents. They flexed as they wove between the mechanical fingers of Flinn's prosthetic, dismantling the silver claw as they wound down to drive their spikes into the stub at the end of the Gnome's arm. The scream died in Garold Flinn's mouth as the part of him that was Garold Flinn was pulled down, back and away from his own eyes, until he was a passenger in his own body.

Benny Hookhand cracked his new neck and worked his jaw experimentally. "Yeah, I don't make deals," he said.

Chapter 26

"Come now, everybody has a price," said King Johan. "Surely the brave men and women of the Heroes' Guild stand ready to take up their swords and staves when the clarion call goes out!"

"As I've said multiple times, sire, I cannot deploy heroes without paying them." Weaver Ortson pointed at the offending pieces. "These assumptions move beyond optimism into folly."

Below the guildmaster's accusing finger, Mount Wynspar's dramatic topology was cast in ink and watercolor. The huge map covered the oak table that occupied the majority of Johan's war room. Hundreds of tiny, painted blocks were arrayed along the thin blue lines that marked Andarun's walls and ramparts. Each block was painted with the livery of the bannermen that it represented, save for those gold- or silver-plated pieces that stood for parties of professional heroes. Arrayed against the cubical forces were myriad cylinders set in purple, green, and white: the undead.

"Unless we find sufficient gold in the kingdom's coffers, we won't have nearly as many heroes as you presume." Weaver plucked a few gold cubes from the front lines and set them off to the side.

"Those bannermen can't hold the gates without heroes backing them up, Majesty," said General Gurgen. "We'll need professionals of at least the fourth rank, and that's not even talking about those that are to face the liche."

"I don't disagree, but you won't have such heroes unless you pull them from another rampart." Ortson avoided looking directly at the general; dark lesions spread from her throat and up across her face. The wounds bore grim testament to the horrors of Gurgen's escape

449

from Highwatch. "The kingdom doesn't have the coin to hire that many heroes."

"They'll work for loot, of course," snorted Johan, placing the pieces back in place on the map. "Ha! That's how professional heroics works!"

"Loot is where they make their fortune, sire. But there's no guarantees in plunder these days, and most heroes aren't willing to risk their lives and their estates in the same go." Ortson reached for the pieces again, but paused when he caught the king's eye. The guildmaster cleared his throat and tried to explain. "Loot alone can't attract top talent. Modern quests pay an up-front wage, plus a stipend for housing, equipment, and other expenses."

"Ha! Are you serious? Aberreth has fallen, for Tandos' sake! The liche will be on our doorstep soon," Johan insisted. "Surely they must understand our current circumstances!"

"Indeed, sire," said Ortson, dabbing his brow. "They're demanding hazard pay."

"You're joking!" The king's laughter faded as he noticed the somber faces around the table. "You're not joking."

"After the... incident at Highwatch, good heroes are in short supply, sire. Other cities are luring the remaining ones away by paying for their defense up front," said Ortson. "Knifevale is offering exorbitant rates, and our adventurers have taken notice. If we want heroes to defend Andarun, we must pay them a premium."

"We wouldn't with proper leadership in the guild." Johan's grin was somewhere between a smile and a snarl. "The bannermen have missed their last paycheck, and they're still planning a vigorous defense of the city!"

"Actually, I've been wanting to ask you about that, sire," interjected General Gurgen.

"The point is, there are more ways to motivate people than money," snapped the king. "There had better be. Ha! You all know the kingdom's coffers are empty! We've spent just about every last giltin propping up the thrice-cursed banks after their fiasco with the threat indexes. Perhaps the Heroes' Guild should front the bill for our city's defense."

"Our coffers are just as empty, sire," said Ortson miserably. "We've had to pay out on many of our own threat obligations. The banks bought too many for our accounts to keep up."

All eyes turned to Goldson, Baggs, and several other bankers standing at the far end of the table. Bolbi Baggs choked on his pipe at the sudden attention, sending dark clouds billowing over the miniature city.

"I think you may be forgetting the dire straits the financial institutions of Arth find themselves in, Majesty," said Fenrir Goldson.

"All that money had to have gone somewhere," said Ortson.

"Not at all, Mr. Ortson," Goldson growled through gritted teeth. "Not every giltin is a coin. Most of them are numbers in ledgers."

"But they're still there," said Ortson.

Goldson shook his head. "If we built a house that fell into the sea, where would the money go? If we bought fertilizers for a crop of grain that burned away, which of us would have the gold? We all invested in security, ladies and gentlemen, every one of us. And as the sea can wash away a building or the flames scour a crop, the undead have destroyed our investment."

"You took the money, though," pressed General Gurgen.

"And what do you think we did with it?" snapped Baggs. "We bought CTOs as well! We hedged our obligations with other banks' obligations, and they with us. Now that your guild has failed to control the threat indexes, all of the gold is wrapped up in broken promises and meaningless assurances."

"And salaries. And bonus funds," said Johan. The paladin was smiling, but the grin put Ortson in mind of a Swamp Drake: predatory and dangerous.

Goldson's gaze was steely and unflinching as he stared back at the king and his advisors. With a deep breath and shaking hands, the ancient Dwarf picked up a few silver and gold pieces from the side of the table and tossed them onto the map. "I suppose our senior teams could forego their annual bonuses this year," he rasped.

"Given the circumstances," said Baggs.

"That's the spirit!" laughed Johan. "Everybody pulling together under a common threat."

Ortson saw Goldson and Baggs exchange a dark glance, and he knew their sentiment. Threats were becoming increasingly common for anyone in charge of Andarun's institutions, especially veiled ones delivered by the king himself.

"This many heroes will help, but our defenses are still full of holes," muttered General Gurgen, arranging the new pieces on the city map. "It's still not enough to guarantee the walls will hold."

"It will be enough," said Johan. He pulled a small block from his belt pouch and placed it at the fore of the army. It was a small cube wrought in gold and red velvet, with a star embossed on its surface.

"Sire?" asked the general.

"I alone will fight the liche," said Johan.

General Gurgen shook her head. "Sire, after what happened to King Handor —"

"General, I'm the only man who's ever defeated Detarr Ur'Mayan," Johan shot her a confident smile, pausing for a moment to let the light gleam on his perfect teeth. "I'm the only one who can take his head again. Ha!"

The king's advisors looked at each other, making no effort to hide their obvious concern. Weaver Ortson wondered what would possess any man to fight a liche alone. Then his eyes caught Johan's, and he saw it lurking behind the king's persistent smile.

"It's madness," said Heraldin. "This whole plan is crazier than an Al'Matran hymnal."

"Shush," hissed Gorm, peering out through the thick brush.

Down the embankment he could see Gaist in the role of Gorst, standing with a small group of recruits for the Red Horde. The recruiters had led the assorted Shadowkin to a small pond north of Dunhelm, where they stopped by a ruined stone wall with an odd gap in the middle.

"I'm not going to say this was a bad idea," whispered Heraldin.

"The less ye say, the better," said Gorm.

"And I'm not going to remind you that I told you this wouldn't work."

"I'm pretty sure ye just did," Gorm grumbled. The bard had been voicing similar concerns since they'd used Jynn's tracking spell to follow the Red Horde's newest recruits from Andarun. Now that they had crept to within fifty yards of the Shadowkin, the bard was in the middle of a hushed panic attack.

"It's just that we did recently risk life and limb to save Gaist. Not half a week ago, you'll recall. And now we've sent him and Burt to act as bait for a murderous army of invaders."

"They're fine," sighed Kaitha, peering toward the idle Shadowkin. "They're just sitting by the pond."

"As they have been for quite some time," said Jynn.

Gorm could see Burt sitting on Gorst's shoulder, idly kicking his feet. "Aye, this is awfully long for a water break."

"Maybe they're planning to meet the Red Horde here?" suggested Laruna.

"Gods, I hope not," said Gorm. "If the Red Horde's base ain't close, we won't have enough time to make it back to Andarun."

"Does the Red Horde even have a base?" said Heraldin. "There are splinter groups all over the Freedlands."

"Aye, but the biggest group of them by far is said to be traveling with the Guz'Varda. That's why they had Char's picture up," said Gorm. "And one of the recruiters Burt found was Ghabrang, our old friend from the Guz'Varda Tribe. With any luck, we'll find a big cluster of the Red Horde and at least a couple of friendly faces in the bunch."

"You're counting on a lot of good fortune," said Heraldin.

"Not to mention the goodwill of the Shadowkin," added Jynn.

"Which is unfortunate, as they hate us," said Heraldin.

"We ain't got the luxury of anything better," said Gorm.

"Hush!" hissed Kaitha. "Look."

The stones bordering the gap in the ruined wall sputtered and sparked. Azure flames flared in old runes, engulfing ancient mosses and lichens as they blazed up the sides of the stones. The magical energy raced beyond the last stones in the wall as they traced an archway that must have stood there in ages past. They met at the top, and a shimmering doorway blinked into existence.

"Bones! It's one of them waygates," said Gorm.

"How could they create one of that size?" asked Laruna.

"They didn't," said Jynn. "It was made by whomever was on the other side." He pointed to the faint, blurry figures moving beyond the static sheen of the waygate.

"The Orcs are moving through," said Heraldin, pointing. Below, the recruiters and their charges had formed a line, and one by one they stepped into the portal. Burt was glancing around nervously as he rode toward the waygate on the doppelganger's shoulder.

"Bones again!" swore Gorm, hopping to his feet. "Come on!"

"But we don't know where they're going!" protested the bard as the other heroes followed.

"We had better find out, 'cause we can't afford to lose 'em!" Gorm leapt through the bushes and slid down the embankment. The other heroes fell in behind him, cursing as they slipped in the loose gravel.

Ahead of him, Gaist and Burt winked away. Only the two recruiters remained. "Hurry!" Gorm shouted.

Kaitha passed him, sprinting across the field. The Orc and Gnoll, alerted by Gorm's shout, stared in wide-eyed surprise at the adventurers sprinting toward them. The Elf was almost upon them before they scrambled through the waygate, and she leapt through after them.

"Wait!" Gorm sprinted for the waygate, but the Dwarven physique is built for holding ground, not covering it quickly. His arms and legs pumped like pistons in a Gnomish engine, but he was still a ways away as the glowing line around the doorway began to waver and close.

"No! Not again!" Gorm's muscles burned and his lungs heaved, but with a final jump he managed to fling himself through the shimmering portal.

Passing through the waygate gave Gorm the sensation of stepping through a summer breeze, followed closely by the sensation of slamming into a surprised Elf's back. He and Kaitha tumbled into the loose, smooth gravel of a rocky beach. The scent of salt and pungent seaweed assaulted his nostrils as he righted himself.

The perplexed recruits stood in a ring around the waygate, but beyond them were ranks of veteran Red Horde soldiers. Shadowkin of every race and size stared in surprise at the Dwarf and Elf untangling themselves on the shore. A moment later, the mages and the bard spilled through the portal just before it winked out of existence.

"Uh, hello," Gorm said, raising an empty hand into the air. "I suppose this doesn't look too good."

The only reply was the steely whisper of hundreds of swords and axes being unsheathed.

"Kill them!"

Asherzu was startled from her charts by a cry on the edge of her hearing. If she strained her ears, she could just make out a commotion coming from down by the beach. The raucous sounds were growing in volume and intensity, and she could see a few whelps and Gnoll pups running into the camp. Hurriedly, she packed her research away.

There was already a mob in the center of camp by the time Asherzu donned her beads and rushed from her hut. Red Horde warriors shouted with jubilation and wrath in equal measure, and they hurled insults and the occasional rock at someone in the middle of the throng. Orcs, Goblins, and Gnolls hollered and howled threats.

Amid the fighters' cries for blood and justice, the shouts of a familiar voice rang out in the tongue of the Lightlings. "Don't fight back! Raise a weapon and we're done for!"

The Dwarven brogue had burned itself into Asherzu's memory. "Gorm Ingerson?" she gasped.

She glimpsed him through the masses, a bruised and bloodied face amid the screaming Shadowkin. The other Lightlings from his party were there as well, bearing their punishment with determined stoicism.

The Dwarf's face lit up as his eye caught hers. "Lady Asherzu!" he shouted. "I've come in peace! I've a way to save your tribe and restore them to—oomph!" An armored elbow to the ribs cut Gorm off. The Orc closest to him growled something that was lost in the screams of the mob.

"Let him speak!" Asherzu screamed. Some of the warriors in the mob fell silent, but now shouting Shadowkin from all throughout the village were surrounding the throng. "Let him speak!" she called again in the tongue of the Lightlings.

Asherzu turned to see Grignot practically dancing his way to the front of the crowd. Darak loomed behind him, looking over the crowd's heads at the Lightlings.

"Your honor!" Gorm Ingerson had found his lungs again. "We come in peace! We've a way—"

"Peace?" Grignot shrieked, a cruel grin flashing amid his straggly beard. "You dogs who betrayed the Guz'Varda for blood gold, and now you mewl for peace? Ha! The great Chieftain Darak daz'Guz'Varda laughs at your feeble words!"

Darak was not laughing. His face was completely devoid of mirth, or warmth, or anything but the murder that flashed in his dark eyes.

The Dwarf kept shouting, hints of desperation creeping into his voice. "It was all a misunderstanding! The guild tricked us as well! We never meant any of that to happen, but now—"

But now the rest of the Shadowkin were shouting as well, and any point the Dwarf might have made was washed away in a tide of jeers.

Asherzu's mind was racing. Any message the Dwarf brought could be another trap by the Heroes' Guild, but then why would Gorm and the others be wanted as criminals? Besides, the guild didn't need a pretext for killing the Orcs anymore; if they had sent Ingerson here, they could have and would have sent more powerful heroes to wipe out the tribe.

Not that they'd need to. Asherzu had heard about how Gorm Ingerson and his party had battled a liche to retrieve the burial stones of Ogh Magerd, and she had believed it. And any Shadowkin in the Freedlands had heard of the Jade Wind and the Pyrebeard; their deadly reputations had been one of the hardest things for Zurthraka to overcome when convincing her tribe to trust them the first time. The heroes in the throng were more than capable of defending themselves, yet they were clearly opting not to.

There was a chance the Dwarf was telling the truth, a chance that the only heroes wily enough to recover the burial stones were still the heroes who had listened to and befriended the Shadowkin. And with that chance came the slim hope that Gorm Ingerson had found a way to restore her tribe to her father's path, if the Shadowkin would only listen to him.

Darak shouted for his warhammer, a roar that rang out over the Red Horde's bloodthirsty calls.

"*No!*" Asherzu ran to place herself between the chieftain and the prisoners. "*No, my brother. Let the Dwarf speak!*" she pleaded in Shadowtongue.

Darak reared back as though from a venomous snake. "*What are you doing?*" he growled under his breath. His eyes darted back and forth among the mob of Shadowkin, like a cornered animal. "*Do you not see where we are?*"

"*I have seen posters, brother. Back in the guildhall of the Lightling town we raided,*" Asherzu blurted. "*I saw posters about Gorm Ingerson and his warband! They were wanted by the gold-hounds as well! They may not have betrayed us!*"

"The people grow impatient," said Grignot, tapping his foot.

"*These are the dogs that befriended you only to try to kill you!*" hissed Darak. "*The tribe is calling for their blood. If ever there was a simple decision for a chieftain, here it is! And yet you still see fit to try to complicate everything! And in doing so, you shame me in front of the entire tribe!*"

"*This is not about you and I, Darak!*" said Asherzu. "*This is about our peoples' survival! This is about the life our tribe longs for!*"

Pain flashed in the huge Orc's eyes, and it left grim determination behind. "*If it isn't about family or honor, I have no time for it.*" The chieftain extended his hand, and his massive warhammer was placed in it by a pair of young warriors. Without another word, he stepped around Asherzu and strode toward the Dwarf and his companions with dark purpose.

"*Darak!*" Asherzu called after her brother's back, but he would not turn from his task. Fear and anger and desperation welled up within her, and it all burst out in a sentence that surprised even her. "*I challenge you!*"

A hush fell over the Shadowkin who could speak the old tongue. Darak froze.

"I challenge you!" Asherzu said again, this time in the tongue of Lightings. Her mind was racing and her pulse was keeping pace, but she squared her shoulders. "I challenge you for the throne of our tribe."

Darak said nothing. He just turned to stare at her with the eyes of a man run through, his jaw clenched to hide its quivering. "The beach," he rasped, pointing his warhammer.

Grignot's lips twisted into a wicked grin. "To the beach!" he shrieked. "The great chieftain will defend his throne before he takes the heads of the *barg'hegga spi'nix'hest!*"

Asherzu nodded, her eyes never leaving her brother's. "So be it," she said.

"So, what happens now?" Kaitha muttered to Burt.

"They fight it out," said the Kobold from Gorm's shoulder. He shifted and swayed to keep balance as the Dwarf negotiated the loose stones of the beach. "The winner gets to decide what happens to us."

"Of course it's trial by combat," said Kaitha. "It's always trial by combat!"

"And I suppose the Elves do it better?" The ember of Burt's thin cigarette glowed brighter as he puffed at it. "Teach us savage Shadowkin the right way to settle a matter?"

"I'm just saying there has to be better qualifications for leadership than a talent for killing people."

"Yeah? Like maybe whoever's parents are a bigger deal? Or maybe whoever has the most money? Oh wait—those are almost always the same thing." The Kobold clapped his paws to his cheeks in mock surprise.

"Let's just focus on surviving to our execution," said Heraldin. The Red Horde soldiers around them leered and snarled.

Orcs and Goblins were arranging a circle of barrels and logs down by the icy sea. Uncounted Orcs, Slaugh, Gnolls, and other Shadowkin gathered where the rocky beach's slopes formed a natural amphitheater. The gnarled, sea-bleached trees that dotted the shore brimmed with Goblins, Kobolds, and Orcish children perched in neat rows like buzzards.

From their vantage point near the front of the crowd, Gorm watched the Orc chieftain step over a log into the combat circle. The massive Orc carried a warhammer with a thick, rune-covered shaft and a head like a boulder. The crimson beads and painted skulls hanging from his long chinstrap beard swayed as he stalked into the ring. He screamed something in Shadowtongue over the crowd as Asherzu stepped forward.

"What's he saying?" Gorm whispered to Burt.

"He's angry she's challenging him," Burt hollered into Gorm's ear. "He says she's bringing dishonor to him and their name by standing against her brother."

Asherzu wore a flowing dress of lilac and golden yellow. Against her emerald skin, the silks reminded Gorm of a bouquet of spring lilies. Her braids were topped with yellow and orange beads, and her hands toyed with a holy symbol that she wore around her neck.

"Is that an icon of Fulgen?" asked Laruna.

"As much as I can tell." Jynn shielded his eyes as he peered across the beach. "What do we know about Asherzu?"

"She's Zurthraka's daughter. We met her back in Bloodroot," said Gorm. "And now she's standing up for us. That's all that matters right now."

"That and the fact that she's clearly outmatched," said Heraldin.

The slight Orcess was dwarfed by the massive warrior facing her. She raised her hand and spoke. Gorm couldn't understand the Shadowtongue, but he could see that whatever she said was calm, level, and presumably upsetting—given her brother's reaction.

"What was that?" Gorm said to the Kobold.

"She's saying she doesn't wish him dishonor, but the Guz'Varda Tribe and all the Red Horde need a new direction." Burt's ears perked up and twitched as he listened. "And that's made him pretty angry because he's saying—oh!"

Darak launched into a spittle-streaked litany of guttural shouts as he gestured angrily at Gorm and his fellows.

"Now he's saying it's your fault for turning her against him, and that when this foolishness is over he's going to—wait, what?" Burt bounced to his feet and waved a fist at the Orc chieftain. "Yeah, come over here and say that, you overgrown lump of—"

"Hush!" hissed Gorm. Kaitha and Jynn leapt to pull the agitated Kobold down from the Dwarf's shoulder. "What do ye think you're doing?"

"He was talking about me!" snarled Burt. "Oh, I knew the doppelganger should have stayed disguised as an Orc! Now they think I'm one of you!"

"That may be, but there's too much at stake to go shooting off your mouth at every insult," snapped Gorm, helping the Kobold step back up to his perch. "Wait a minute."

"I thought you were one of us!" demanded Laruna, giving voice to the revelation that was striking the other adventurers in turn.

"Well, yeah, but to you," said the Kobold, scrambling to gain purchase on Gorm's pauldron again. "Not to them."

"That doesn't make any sense," said Kaitha.

"Trust me, it does," said Burt. "Now be quiet. They're starting."

Asherzu planted her feet, and the crowd of Shadowkin fell silent. "I am Asherzu, sister to Char Guz'Varda, second daughter and fourth child of Zurthraka Guz'Varda…"

"Why's she talkin' like that?" Gorm asked Burt.

"She's using her lineage to establish her right to lead — "

"No, I mean why's she talking in the Imperial tongue?"

"Oh. The whole Red Horde's watching the challenge. Most of them grew up as NPCs." Burt waved a hand at the assembled Shadowkin. "The Guz'Varda Orcs may have kept their traditions well, but I'd bet half of the Horde doesn't speak three words of Shadowtongue. Not to mention all the Goblin dialects and such."

"I challenge you for the right to wield the Guz'Varda Tribe," Asherzu finished.

Darak listened sullenly, his eyes avoiding her for the entire speech. Asherzu had barely finished speaking when he shouted, "I am Darak daz'Guz'Varda, son of Zurthraka, brother to Char. I am Chieftain of the Guz'Varda Tribe and leader of the Red Horde. All that wear crimson, in this camp or scattered across the land, bend their knee to me. No champion will stand for me!"

Only then did the chieftain turn to his sister, staring her down with bloodshot eyes. "Now let your champion come forward, that we may end this farce."

"No champion will stand for me," Asherzu shouted.

There was a sound like a rushing wind as the assembled crowd gasped in unison.

"Wait, what?" said Laruna.

"What is she doing?" said Gorm.

Nobody looked more surprised or dismayed by Asherzu's announcement than her opponent. Darak's face contorted in confusion and despair. "You must name a champion!" he shouted. "I will not fight you unarmed."

Asherzu deliberately drew a small knife, held it up for the crowd, and dropped her arm to hold the weapon at her hip. "It is done. I am your opponent. May honor choose the victor."

"No," said Darak, shaking his head. He held his warhammer up like a shield, backing away from his sister as she approached. "No. I do not want to fight you. Do not make me do this."

"You do not have to fight me, Darak," Asherzu said. "You never wished to grow the chieftain's beard. You wanted to fight for Father, and then for Char."

"Do not make me do this," groaned Darak.

"Set aside your pride. Do what you know is best, and lay down your weapon," Asherzu continued, striding toward him. "Remember the teachings of our father. Would Zurthraka Guz'Varda have wished this for his tribe?"

"Ah, she's doing the old 'we don't really have to fight' routine," said Laruna. "Appealing to his better side."

"She's doing the old 'get all of us killed' routine, that's what she's doing," said Burt.

"The legends and histories are filled with tales of people talking down a foe in an arena, or ending a trial-by-combat by throwing down their arms," said Kaitha.

"Yes, but if it worked that often, we wouldn't have trials by combat at all, would we?" said Jynn.

"Aye, there's a reason the old 'we're better than this' routine makes history when it works," said Gorm.

"Stop!" Darak lashed out with his warhammer, a side blow that caught Asherzu in the arm. The impact sent her sailing through the air, trailing long silks that rippled like flames after a comet. She crashed into a barrel at the edge of the ring. A cloud of dust and splinters bloomed at the point of impact.

"Because we usually ain't, and it usually doesn't," Gorm finished sadly.

"*Spug,*" said Burt.

A great cacophony of voices rose from the crowd, though it was impossible to sort the despairing screams from the cheers. But as Asherzu stirred, the crowd fell silent once more.

"Ra tazo rug! Tazo rug!" Notes of desperation rang in Darak's screams. *"Da go'bola rarbargfeeba ra gi'tazo rug!"*

"He's telling her to stay down. Says he'll show mercy if she does," Burt said.

"Well, that's a relief," said Heraldin.

"Just to be clear, he's talkin' about Asherzu," the Kobold said. "He's still going to murder us."

"Should we help her then?" asked Jynn.

"You can't help her now," said Burt. "Getting aid would only make her look weak."

"Then what do we do?" said Heraldin. "Because if this goes bad for her, we're all going to be decorating someone's beard."

Gorm took a deep breath. "Hold fast," he said. "It's all we can do."

The shattered timbers of the barrel twitched. Splintered planks shifted and fell as Asherzu pushed herself to her knees. Dark red stains spread slowly across her dress from several points of impact, and she clutched her side as she pushed herself to her feet.

"Tazo rug!" Darak shrieked.

"I will not stay down." Asherzu trembled with every step, but her voice still reverberated with power and certainty. "I will be Chieftain of the Guz'Varda. I will lead the Red Horde."

"Why do you stand against me?" said Darak, backing away slowly. "How could you dishonor me so?"

"I do not stand against you!" Asherzu yelled, and now there was pleading in her voice as well. She walked toward the chief, her arms held out in supplication. "I stand for our tribe, for our people. If you had taken any other path, I would have followed you to the ends of Arth. If you truly wished to lead, I would have fought for you 'til my last breath. But a chieftain's beard weighs heavy on you, and you have lent your ear to dogs and snakes—"

"Be silent!" shouted Darak, lashing out with his warhammer. It was clearly a half-hearted swing, a slow arc to keep a foe back, but if Asherzu had the instincts to dodge, she didn't have the energy. The massive hammer caught her leg, spinning her around and bending her knee in the opposite direction. She collapsed with a small cry.

Darak looked in horror at his bloodied hammer and backed away. *"Da... da go'bola rarbargfeeba,"* he said, his voice cracking and choked. *"Tazo rug!"*

462

"I will not!" Asherzu snarled. Slowly, laboriously, the young Orcess pushed herself to her feet. Despite the blood dampening her dress and the useless, broken leg she dragged behind her, Asherzu's voice was as strong and clear as ever. "I will take this tribe on Father's path, or I will die. You cannot take that from me."

"Do not make me do this!" Darak cried.

"I cannot make you do anything, my brother, my chieftain. You have a choice! Let me free you from your burden, let me lead the tribe in the way of Zurthraka Guz'Varda. Or kill me, and lead the Red Horde in the way of violence and death." Asherzu delivered the ultimatum gently, kindly. "But you must choose."

The Orc chieftain's face twisted with rage, flushing to a deep brown as he stepped up to her. "Then you bring this upon yourself!" he bellowed, raising his hammer high.

"The choice is yours alone." Asherzu stood unwavering in the shadow of Darak's weapon. "Whatever you decide, you are my brother, *Kib'hestzuggo.*"

They stood frozen there for a moment, the towering Orc holding a hammer high above his sister. The assembled Shadowkin waited silently, breathlessly. Gorm couldn't hear anything but the pounding of his own heart.

Darak's eyes were the first to change, softening like melting ice, squinting as they welled up with tears. His snarl broke as a ragged sob ripped from his throat. A moment later, the chieftain crumbled like a toppling colossus, his warhammer falling uselessly to the grass as he dropped to his knees. *"Da nubgra,"* he gasped. *"Da nubgra.* Make it swift, my sister. End my shame."

Asherzu stumbled forward wordlessly, hunting knife in hand. She reached under Darak's chin with both hands and made a quick motion. Then she kissed her brother's forehead and whispered something in his ear. He slumped forward, face down in the grass as she stepped back.

"I can't believe that worked," said Burt.

"I can't believe she just cut his throat," said Laruna.

"She didn't." Kaitha shook her head. "Look!"

Darak had fallen, but he wasn't still. His shoulders shook and his whole body heaved as he was wracked by long, silent sobs.

Gorm could see the knife Asherzu held glittering in the sunlight, still stainless. In her other hand, she held a long tuft of Darak's beard. The severed hairs whipped in a cold wind as she lifted her trophy above her head. She found the strength to raise her voice above the crashing waves once more. "I am Asherzu daz'Guz'Varda, daughter of Zurthraka, sister to Char and to Darak, Chieftain of the Guz'Varda Tribe, leader of the Red Horde!"

Gorm and his companions' shouts were lost in the roaring of the crowd. Cheers and jeers crashed over Asherzu as she stood in front of the sea, fist still in the air.

"She did it!" Gorm cried.

"It ain't over yet," said Burt.

Among the cries and shouts, one voice rang higher than the others, shrill to the point of madness. "What is this nonsense!" screeched an Orc, vaulting over the makeshift fence to enter the ring. Gorm recognized the pale wise-one in red war paint as former advisor to Darak.

"Grignot Gabuk'mug." Asherzu's voice was shaking as the blood from her wounded side ran down her leg, but she didn't waver as she stared at her new adversary.

"Does the blood of the Guz'Varda flow so thin?" snarled Grignot. "Do you really think the Red Horde will follow the likes of you, traitor queen? You are weak, and your path is weaker. I am Grignot Gabuk'mug, son of Hurdak Gabuk'mug, and I challenge you for the right to wield your tribe, and with it, the Red Horde!"

Asherzu starred at him dispassionately. "So be it. I accept your challenge, Grignot Gabuk'mug." She turned to the stunned crowd. "Who will stand for me?"

"Should we offer to fight?" Gorm muttered to Burt.

"The tribes would never accept a leader who needed a Lightling to fight for 'em." Burt pointed at the crowd around them. "Besides, doesn't look like she'll need us."

A huge Orcess shouldered her way to the front of the ring. "I am Gizardu, called the Mountain. I would stand for you, Chieftain Asherzu."

"As would I, Nibbrok of the Gut'lab!" shouted a menacing looking Gnoll.

Another cry rang out, and then another, and Shadowkin across the beach raised their weapons as they called out pledges of loyalty.

Asherzu smiled at the outpouring of support, but she didn't accept any of the offers. She wobbled on her one good leg, waiting until the shouts faded away and her would-be champions lowered their weapons.

A silence fell over the crowd as a shadow fell over Grignot.

Darak Guz'Varda cracked his neck as he drew himself to his full height. "I will stand for you," he said levelly.

"May you find victory, Darak of the Guz'Varda," said Asherzu. She touched her brother on the arm as she limped back to the edge of the ring.

"And who will stand for me?" asked Grignot, notes of fear cracking his voice.

The crowd was silent as Darak retrieved his warhammer.

"Who will stand for our old ways? Who will help me lead us to glory?" said Grignot.

The warriors of the Red Horde watched as Darak approached the center of the ring with the ominous certainty of a storm cloud. The former chieftain was a giant among Orcs, the sort that you would follow into any battle solely for the sake of not being in front of him. There's a fine line between martyrdom and suicide, and public opinion clearly held that Grignot was on the wrong side of it.

"Is there no one? Nobody?" Desperation crept into Grignot's pleas as his warriors studied the beach and the sky with sudden, acute interest.

"It appears not," Asherzu said to Grignot. "May honor choose the victor."

"Come on," said Burt, nudging Gorm. "Now it's over, and everyone's going to want to talk with the new chieftain. Let's beat the crowd."

"But the duel's just startin'," said Gorm.

"Maybe, but it's just ending too," said Burt. "And we've got a lot to talk about with Her Majesticness."

As if to prove the Kobold's point, Grignot let out a piercing squeal. The cry was cut off with a sickening crunch followed by a collective "oooh" as the assembled Shadowkin winced in unison.

Chapter 27

A broken skull cracked and clattered as it fell to the stone floor of the crypt. Tyren didn't look up from a small, bronze plaque on the wall above a dusty alcove. "Go away," he said to whatever intruder had disturbed the ancient bones.

"Um, right, well I would, sir, but some of the lads were asking after you," Ned offered. The ghoul shuffled farther into the crypt, wearing a toadying smile that looked more desperate than ingratiating.

Tyren said nothing. According to the thin and tarnished engraving, the young woman whose grave preoccupied him had died during the Sixth Age. The exact date was impossible to read, as time had corroded away the year. Her mortal remains had long decayed; there was nothing left of her but dust and chunks of brittle bone. Yet most of her sad epitaph was still legible, noting that she had died at sixteen years of age. Tyren recalled that Little Aubey would be almost sixteen by now, assuming she was still alive.

"You see, sir, it's just that you were going to personally lead the sacking of East Upshore, and while I don't want to suggest that it isn't going well—"

He was interrupted by the cry of a bannerman outside being violently conscripted into the undead army.

"Because it is going very well," Ned continued. "But we couldn't help notice that you've ah, recused yourself from the battle. And you know Ted and I respect that there are many styles of leadership, and we didn't expect you on the front lines, but it was suggested that you might want some say, as to, ah, what we're doing out here."

"And what are we doing out here?" Tyren asked, touching the plaque with a skeletal finger. The young woman's name had faded away, lost to the ages.

"Well, I figured you'd come looking for a snack, which didn't seem too bad an idea to me, of course." The ghoul shrugged his shoulders. "But anyone worth eating has already clawed their way to the surface and joined the ranks. Nothing down here but broken bones and grave dust."

Tyren had stopped listening. "What did she dream of?" he wondered aloud. "Did she want to take up a trade? To travel the world? Would she have had children of her own? What did her death deny her?"

The ghoul's jaw flapped open and shut like a fish gasping for breath. "I... I... I suppose I couldn't say, sir."

"There's a first time for everything," murmured Tyren.

Ned's face lit up as he made a sudden connection. "Ah, but sir! That's why we're marching on Andarun, isn't it? All these poor sods died and that was it. No more hopes and dreams for them. But we came back after we died. It isn't the end for us."

"Oh?" asked Tyren. "And what hopes and dreams are you currently pursuing, Ned?"

"Well, I..." Ned stopped and thought for a moment. "I suppose there's always immortality. Continued existence is always a fundamental drive of any biological organism. Not that we're strictly biological these days, of course. But beyond that I... I've..." the ghoul trailed off with his fangs set in a troubled grimace.

"Is this what you always dreamed of?" Tyren's voice was bitter and hollow, even for a walking skeleton. "Did you always want to raze Parald, or march on the Freedlands?"

"Not specifically." Neddard Biggins always ceded as little ground as possible in any debate.

Tyren's hand curled into a bony fist. "We can do nothing that isn't the master's will, and all the liche wills us to do is shackle other people with the same curse that we bear."

"Whoa, whoa, easy there, sir," said the ghoul, waving his hands in the air. "These are dangerous thoughts."

The knight-commander shook his head and stared at the plaque. So young.

For a creature who allegedly spent his existence skulking about crypts, Ned couldn't endure silence very long. "Besides, sir, there are worse fates than undeath. Remember? You said yourself it isn't so bad."

Tyren whirled on the ghoul, arcs of crimson energy crackling across his hands. The plaques on the walls darkened, and shadows like black flames licked stones by his feet. "It isn't so bad for me!" he snarled. "It isn't so bad for a drunken, washed up soldier who threw everything away. But not for her! It's not enough for her!"

Ned's face screwed up in confusion. "But you aren't... I mean, sir, you're a noble hero. You were with us at the walls of Vetchell."

"Not on purpose," said Tyren. "I was drunk. I lost my way, and wound up dying. This wasn't my fight then, and it's not my fight today."

"I... I don't know what to make of that." Ned's voice was more of a whisper to himself. "But still, given the—"

"I do not care," said Tyren, straightening himself. "I want no part of it. Leave me."

"But sir—"

"I said leave me!" Tyren said it with more force than he intended, but the message was received better than expected. The ghoul went rigid as though affected by the sudden onset of rigor mortis. Without another word, Ned turned and goose-stepped out of the crypt.

Tyren turned back to the grave. A miasma of dark magic emanating from him was corroding away the plaque on the wall, and jagged scorch marks had crept up the stones of the mausoleum and over the grave dust. For a time, he stared at the remains, haunted by his own memories. He saw the many men and women he'd sent to their deaths at the recruitment tables. He saw himself drinking alone in his offices, blithely ignoring the soldiers asking him for help. He saw the fights with his wife, scaring the little girl hiding in the corner. And he saw little Aubey playing on his knee, her tawny curls bouncing around her smile. An ache roiled in the dark cavern where his heart used to be.

Tyren's mood was as foul as the sludge dripping from his armor by the time another figure cast a shadow through the door of the mausoleum. "Leave me," he said.

"I think not," said Detarr Ur'Mayan. "You and I will have a word."

A piercing chill ran through Tyren, cutting through even the veil of undeath. He remained defiantly silent as the liche floated into the chamber.

"I must admit, I'm surprised that you would be one for treason," mused Detarr. "I mean, I've learned that you can't trust anyone with all of your secrets. And I certainly suspected Lady Carabae would eventually try to overthrow me. She's a vampire, after all, and the gods know how much they love their schemes and intrigue.

"But you?" The liche shook his head as he paced in a wide circle around Tyren. "You've been instrumental in shaping the movement. You're a founding figure of the revolution. Our revolution! You've been given boundless authority, limitless opportunity. No master of undeath before me has offered any of his subjects such freedom. And you repay me with this defiance?"

In truth, keeping his silence was about as much defiance as Tyren could muster. The same foul sorceries that bound his soul to his remains shackled him in Detarr's service, and a part of him wanted to bow his head in deference and get back to work.

"I suppose that I should have learned by now to expect this sort of disappointment." The liche paced around the knight-commander. "I had so much planned for you. For us."

"More... power and... subjects," growled Tyren.

"Oh, you have no idea what sorts of power I'm dealing with," said Detarr. "Nor do you need to. It is enough for you to know that you are making a better world. A world without pain, without struggle, without ending."

"Without movement... Without achievement. Without joy." The words were coming easier to Tyren now, his will gaining strength as he exercised it. "You may take away life's hardships, but you also take away everything that makes it worth living."

"It's worth it," said Detarr.

"Maybe for you or I," said Tyren. "But is it really what you'd want for your children?"

"Obedience? Conformity? An unshakable constitution?" said Detarr. "Gods, you don't know how many times I've wanted that for my son. And now I'm bringing all that and immortality to him. To all of Arth."

"Believe what suits you," said Tyren. "I want no part of it."

"So that's where we stand." From within his flaming skull, Detarr leveled an icy stare at the knight-commander. "You must understand that this would be a very inconvenient time to modify the organizational chart with our upcoming march on Andarun. Plus, you play a pivotal role in our invasion. Most of my troops report to you, and delegating rather than subjugating is the key to my success."

"I said I'll have no part in it," said Tyren.

"No, you said you wanted no part of it. There's a difference," said the liche. "Fortunately, I don't have to use my energies to directly control the entire army. All I need to do is control the one in charge, the one who has put himself at the center of my operations, and the rest of my subjects can still enjoy the benefits of their freedom."

Fear welled up in Tyren, but he raised his chin and looked the liche in the eye sockets. "If dissent is insubordination, if I'm to be shackled for not taking part, are we really free?"

The flames around Detarr's head boiled and flared. "I suppose not," he said, pulling the Crown of Iron Thorns from within his robes. "But as it turns out, I can make peace with that."

Tyren braced himself for the moment the crown touched the liche's skull, but it was futile. Some deep shred of the knight-commander's soul screamed, trying to fight the onslaught of the crown's power. The majority of him, however, felt any such notion washed away in a tide of dark magic. Inwardly writhing in silent torment, Tyren marched out of the mausoleum, through the flaming remains of the town of East Upshore, and to the head of the ranks of skeletons, zombies, ghouls, and ghosts on the road to Andarun.

"It's to be a siege then. No later than the end of the month."

Bolbi Baggs made the ominous pronouncement as he stared out the window. His back was to the rest of the ebony and marble office at the top of Goldson Baggs Group's headquarters on the tenth tier of Andarun. With one hand, he idly signed a document presented to him by some office acolyte or another. In the other, he held an ornate gold spyglass.

"It's been a siege for days," barked Fenrir Goldson, without looking up from the paperwork on his desk. "It's about to be a bloodbath."

Weaver Ortson stood between the titans of industry with a beleaguered scowl on his face. "You're talking about different things again," he sighed with waning patience.

"Not at all, Mr. Ortson. I was just commenting to Mr. Goldson that I can see the smoke from the undead incursion in the southeast." Mr. Baggs shrugged. "Their arrival will send the stock tumbling."

"Which is what I was talking about," said Mr. Goldson. "We've been propping our share price up with a few rapid acquisitions, but with the attack on Andarun the threat indexes have gone mad. The investors will be out for blood."

"So you see, we're on the same page," said Baggs. "Although you do worry too much, Mr. Goldson. We have plenty of liquidity."

"Which is what brings me to your office, gentlemen," said Ortson.

"This had better not be about paying more for the city's defense," said Goldson.

"You'll recall that our firm already made a generous donation," added Baggs.

"Oh no! I mean, yes. I mean..." Ortson took a deep breath. "I'm not asking you to directly pay for the heroes. But the Heroes' Guild would appreciate an up-front payment from your firm. An advance of sorts."

"An advance on what?" snorted Fenrir.

"Well, on the death of the liche, and... and... and on the value your CTOs are sure to gain once he's finally dead. Er, again."

"The value—you think—the CTOs..." Goldson was indignant and mystified in equal measure. "Do you even know how collateralized threat obligations work, sir?"

Ortson felt a bead of sweat on his brow. "Uh, do you?"

Mr. Goldson and Mr. Baggs shared an awkward glance. "Well, I... uh... generally. I'm not intimately familiar with the details," said Goldson.

"The math is very complicated," added Mr. Baggs.

"Still, it's apparent that we understand them better than you," asserted Goldson. "Once a threat obligation has been triggered, it pays out. After that, it's worthless paper. They don't gain value again. And if our CTO was using such threat obligations for collateral, it's no better off."

"Besides, even if they gained value, we wouldn't owe the Heroes' Guild a cent," said Baggs. "We're not obligated to pay you a portion of our profits."

"Just like you're not obligated to pay us for the massive losses your guild's ineptitude has cost us." The ancient Dwarf gave Ortson a withering glare.

"Well, aha ha, in a very real way, we have." Ortson forced an uncomfortable smile. "You see, the Heroes' Guild was the original issuer of threat obligations. We've been selling them for quite some time, as a way to generate immediate revenue. The guild has paid out huge sums for our threat obligations."

"We're aware of the obligations you've paid," said Goldson coldly.

"And we're much more concerned with the ones you haven't," added Baggs.

"The king—no, the entire kingdom—is depending on the guild to rally heroes to the defense of the city. And those heroes aren't rallying without funds," said Ortson. "Surely you must see my problem."

"Yes, but we also see that it is exactly that," said Goldson.

"Your problem," Baggs added, noting Ortson's confusion.

"It's going to be everybody's problem soon," said Ortson. "If I can't get more heroes to the city, we're all doomed."

"Ortson, you're so melodramatic when you're sober," sighed Baggs. "Help yourself to a drink."

"I don't want a drink!" snarled Ortson.

"There's a first time for everything," smirked Goldson.

"We're running out of time. It may already be too late!"

"Poor odds and bad timing don't sound like a good investment, Mr. Ortson," chided Baggs, pouring himself a tumbler of whiskey.

"Investment?" said Ortson. "You could die!"

"Or we could take the pair of Great Eagles on our roof down to the Knifevale office." Goldson opened a small, black case on his desk to reveal a sprite-stone. "Buy forty thousand of Andarun Insurance at five giltin," he commanded with a tap on the stone.

A small, green sprite leapt into existence and flew for an open window.

"But… gentlemen, please! Andarun is your home," protested Ortson.

"Home is where the heart is," said Baggs.

"Or at least where it stays beating," added Goldson mirthlessly. "Buy five hundred thousand shares of Vorpal Corporation at two giltin."

Ortson was flabbergasted. "And what of the people in the streets? What about your workers and colleagues? Where are your principles?"

A hint of a scowl creased Baggs' face. "We are standing on our principles."

"Buy low, sell high," Goldson said, just before he unleashed another green sprite with a muttered order.

"Keep to the investment strategy, no matter what the markets do," said Baggs.

"Watch fundamentals, not sentiment," Goldson barked.

"Those, Mr. Ortson, are key among our principles," said Mr. Baggs. "Although we also hold it true and dear that private companies should not be pressed upon to fund public institutions beyond the exorbitant tax rates we already pay. We hope that Andarun can rally and defeat this threat—"

"We'll make a killing if they do," Goldson muttered to himself as he made a note in his ledger.

Baggs didn't skip a beat. "But if they cannot, if darkness triumphs, then our duty will still be to our investors. And the responsibility for the tragedy will fall upon the city-state and its institutions."

"It's time to hold government accountable," said Goldson.

"And what of the business community's part in this mess?" Ortson demanded. "Need I remind you of the role your firm has played in this calamity?"

"There's already been much done to hold business responsible," said Baggs. "Surely you'll recall that Lamia Sisters took a tumble last month."

"And they were thrown over the Wall, too," added Goldson.

"Were they really?" asked Baggs.

"M'hmm, yes. And a number of other bankers with them. James Sapphire, that Mr. Stearn fellow, half the board of J.P. Gorgon…"

"Ghastly. I thought people were just talking about their share price." Baggs shrugged. "But there. Several bankers paid the ultimate price, and many more have been shut down."

Goldson perked up for a moment. "Which reminds me, we're to sign for buying out Silver Guard Securities from Mr. Poldo in a half hour."

"And there it is!" snapped Weaver. "Others may be suffering, but you're still buying up companies. How have you two been brought to account for your role in this disaster?"

"Oh, we take full responsibility for our actions," said Mr. Baggs.

"We had to say as much in front of the Royal Court," added Goldson.

"That's it, then?" said the guildmaster. "Full responsibility and no consequences?"

"Now we're playing semantics," said Baggs with a reptilian smile.

"And we're better at it than you," said Goldson.

Weaver was about to press the point further, but a tiny ball of pink light wafted in through the window, working against the line of Goldson's green sprites that dutifully streamed out the window. It fluttered over to hover a few inches from Ortson's face.

"I have a message for Weaver Ortson!" chirruped the sprite.

"Yes, I can see that," said Ortson, shielding his eyes from the intensely pink luminescence. "Pardon me, gentlemen. Play the message."

"Hello? Hello? Is this… how do I start this?" said the sprite in its high, tweeting voice. "Just tap the stone, sire. Like this? Yes, sire. Oh. I thought I did that."

Weaver rolled his eyes.

The sprite was filled with sudden bravado, "Ha! Weaver! The forces of evil are massing at our doorstep, and we shall meet them in glorious battle! I look forward to riding with your heroes into the heart of the darkness and ridding this land of the undead scourge once and for all! Ha ha! Come join us as soon as you can to finalize the plans for the defense of the city!"

Weaver felt the blood drain out of his face at the sprite's laughter, like a blast from a minuscule trumpet. He'd have to face Johan with a woefully small cadre of heroes to offer, and there was no time left to recruit more.

The sprite was still buzzing inanely in Ortson's face. "How do you stop it? Has it stopped? Tell it you are done, sire. What? I thought it would have made a sprite by now. Just tell it you are done, Majesty. Oh, I just say—" With a little sigh, the glowing ball winked out of existence.

"It seems you are in high demand, Mr. Ortson," said Baggs. "Well, we do wish you luck with your plans. We have a lot invested in your success."

"Indirectly," added Goldson. "Please, don't let us keep you from your duty."

"Ah, but gentlemen..." Ortson began in a quivering voice.

Two of the most powerful men on Arth swiveled to face him, eyebrows raised, wielding expectant smiles as a phalanx raises shields. It was answer enough. There were no funds coming, and it was too late to spend them even if they did.

Ortson dabbed sweat away from his forehead. "I think I will have that drink before I depart."

"And make this one on the rocks, please." Duine Poldo looked around the empty common room of The Stranded Sailor. The inn sat on the road between Andarun and Dunhelm, close enough to the capital that it still fell in Mount Wynspar's shadow in the early morning. The road should have been bustling with carts and caravans, but Poldo hadn't seen a fellow traveler in days.

The bartender returned and set a gold-colored cocktail in front of Poldo. "I'm afraid that's the last of them, sir. I've run out of grundant juice. And brandy, for that matter. If you're still thirsty afterward, we have good Dwarven whiskeys left."

"This will do, thank you." Poldo was too fond of his internal organs to inflict Dwarven whiskey on them. He turned back to the papers in front of him. "I should get back to work while I still can."

"As it suits you, sir." The barkeep turned his attention back to his own task, which involved an unusual amount of shoving things into a satchel.

Poldo took a stamp from his briefcase and pressed it firmly down on the contract in front of him, leaving "OFFICIAL DOCUMENT" branded in scarlet letters across the top. He initialed the first page, and then the fourteen others after that, and finally signed and dated the last sheet in the bundle. Then he slipped the documents into a brown paper envelope and handed it to a quartet of Wood Gnomes waiting patiently at the end of the bar. "I suppose it's time to take this to the headquarters of Goldson Baggs," he said with a sigh.

The Wood Gnomes chittered a question.

"Yes, well, Silver Guard may not be worth much anymore, but it was mine," said Poldo. He drummed his fingers on the old oak bar that was serving as a makeshift desk. "I planned to grow the business into the talk of Andarun, a firm successful enough to show Goldson and Baggs what they'd lost in Duine Poldo. And now, they've made a light snack of it."

The Wood Gnome closest to Poldo chirruped sympathetically.

"Ah, well. The gods weave what they will," Poldo said. "Safe travels." The words hadn't left his lips before the Wood Gnomes vanished, taking his document, and his business, with them. Then he drained his Imperial Pepperup on the rocks.

Two small glasses were set on the bar in front of him. He looked up to see the bartender pouring two Dwarven whiskeys.

"A toast," the barkeep explained. "To losing our businesses."

"You as well?" asked Poldo.

"Aye, I'm leaving it all behind and sailing for Knifevale. Even when the thrice-cursed liche is finally sent back to Mordo Ogg, the Freedlands won't be a place fit for running a business." The barkeep glared out the window, sending a long-distance evil eye toward Mount Wynspar. "The big banks are all dying off, and the merchants and carters can't get notes of credit to cover the goods they're shipping. Not that there's anyone to ship 'em to, mind you. The markets in Andarun have all but shut down. It'll take years to recover from this. More years than I've got in these old bones."

"That assumes the undead will fail," said Poldo.

The innkeeper shrugged. "Oh, I'm sure the forces of light will find a way to rally and save the day. They've done as much against dragons, the Sten, Slaugh, Orcs, undead, the Red Horde, the Dark Ones, Gremlins… Seems to me if the forces of good weren't adept at that sort of dramatic, last-minute victory over the forces of darkness, a place as volatile as Arth would have burned itself out long ago."

"Who's to say it hasn't?" Poldo stared out the window at the distant mountain. "The Sten were considered paragons of the light's forces until they were wiped out in the War of Betrayal. And Andarun was part of the Empire of Man in the Fifth Age. The Imperials must have thought their world was crumbling when the rebels seized it. How many times has the world ended before? Perhaps we are just toiling among its ashes."

"A good point, but it stands to reason that if the forces of Mannon or their ilk triumphed, none of us would be here," said the barkeep. "Evil's never really won."

"Perhaps," said Poldo grimly. "But there's a first time for everything."

The innkeeper held up his glass in toast. "Well then, to the status quo, and gettin' by among the ashes," he said.

"As best we can," said Poldo, holding up his own glass. They drained their glasses in unison, and then endured synchronized facial spasms as the Dwarven whiskey lived up to its reputation.

"And on that note, I've a few matters to attend to," said Poldo. A trio of Wood Gnomes carried a folio of papers to him. The first page was a letter from Mrs. Hrurk, letting him know that more tenants were arriving daily and requesting that he move some funds around. Vilma of the Fire Hawk Tribe had attached the necessary documents.

"You've got to keep fighting the good fight, eh?" The barkeep resumed packing up his bar.

"Indeed," Poldo muttered, dipping his quill in ink. "And there will always be more paperwork."

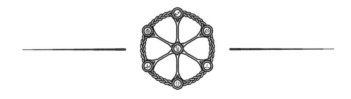

"It always comes down to paperwork," muttered Laruna. "Though to be fair, it usually doesn't involve this much effort."

"Not to mention this much sorcery." Jynn nodded at the structure erected by the Orcish wise-ones and a few Goblin shamans.

It was a timber archway, built on the sea-smoothed foundations of some long-forgotten building and propped up by barnacle-encrusted rocks. Runes were carved into the bark of the trees and filled in with red paint, apparently for emphasis, but they could do little to attract attention in light—literally—of the huge, luminous crystal set at the top of the arch. It rested in a cradle of hewn logs, where Gremlins and Goblins in shaman's garb fawned over it incessantly.

"Extraordinary times call for extraordinary measures," said Gorm. "That thermal crystal is the key to gettin' back to Andarun in time."

"Thaumite crystal," Jynn corrected him.

"Whatever ye call it," said Gorm.

A voice spoke up behind the four heroes. "My people call it *Worbo Zaberb'farast,* the Path of the Stars."

"Chieftain," said Gorm, leading the other heroes in a bow as Asherzu strode up to them, accompanied by a retinue of wise-ones. The chieftain wore a fresh set of gold and violet silks, and any sign of her wounds had been washed away by her shamans' healing magic. Darak loomed behind her, studying his knuckles in the idle manner of someone prepared to put them to good use.

Asherzu acknowledged them with a nod, and then pointed at the great hunk of thaumite atop the ramshackle arch. "The crystal came from the Gremlins of the Shadespear. They gave it to the Guz'Varda when Char saved them from a Lightling band soon after… after Father's death. And before Char gave it a new name, the Gremlins called it 'Fulgen's Rest.'"

"So, they followed Fulgen as well?" asked Laruna.

The chieftain watched the Gremlins and shamans work over the great crystal. "I think they mostly thought it a good joke. Father Tinderhope is the light at the end of the tunnel, and these… waygates, as you call them, are the tunnels at the end of the light. But I suppose they wouldn't have known to make the joke if there weren't so many followers of the Underglow among our peoples."

"Including yourself," said Gorm

Asherzu gave a small, private smile. "My father always said that silent gods are the easiest kind to follow. Beyond that, Fulgen teaches us to strive onward and take hope when all seems lost. It is a message my people need."

"We all need it, sometimes," said Gorm.

"You speak truth." The chieftain turned her attention back to the archway. "Let us begin."

The waygate attendants nodded and began weaving threads of magic over the runes. The glyphs flared with light, and a moment later a shimmering portal winked into existence beneath the arch. Through the waygate, Gorm could see a cadre of Dwarves clad in the blue and white heraldry of the Old Kingdom. A familiar figure led them.

"This way, this way!" Heraldin ushered several Dwarves lugging heavy-looking chests through the shimmering gateway. "Mind your step! Loose gravel ahead."

"I see ye managed to convince King Forder to send a delegation through a magic portal," Gorm said, ambling up to the bard.

"Was there ever any doubt?" asked Heraldin. "I can talk my way through just about any situation."

"Aye, but they say half of diplomacy is listenin'," said Gorm. "And you're rubbish at that."

"Right. That would be Gaist's half." The bard nodded to the weaponsmaster, who was carrying a large crate through the waygate.

Gaist rolled his eyes.

Within an hour, a long line of Shadowkin shuffled toward rows of Dwarven clerks sitting at desks made from repurposed chests and crates. A sibilant whispering filled the air as a multitude of pens scribbled furiously on reams of forms. A swarm of Dwarves worked behind the line, fetching paper and ink, reviewing and stamping applications, and trying to fight the growing pile of paperwork to be filed away. It was a losing battle.

Gorm walked along the line with Asherzu and several of the leaders of the Old Dwarven Kingdom, surveying the progress. "How long do ye think this'll take us?" he asked.

Guildmaster Korgen pursed his lips. "If we work hard and Khazen is with us, we might be mobilized in five days."

"Five days!" exclaimed Gorm. "The liche is bearin' down on Andarun. We don't have a week for thrice-cursed paperwork! How do we get this goin' faster?"

"Faster?" Korgen waved toward the crowd of Shadowkin "Do y'know how many steps we're skipping to get these Shadowkin sworn in as citizens and conscripted into the guild? The clerks are going to be sorting this out for weeks. Maybe months! You can't just hand them a bit of paper and call them a hero! Or a Dwarf, for that matter."

"Congratulations. You're a Dwarven hero." A nearby clerk handed a small red booklet and a bundle of loose pages to an Orc across the table.

"Da gub Zed'farast!" The Orc held his new papers over his head as he shouted back to the lines of Shadowkin behind him. Several cheers and whoops rang out in reply.

"Yes, well, it takes a lot of steps to get there," said Korgen airily.

"Of course, honored guildmaster, but I wonder if there is not a way to save time," suggested Asherzu. "Many tribe-mates share the same homeland, for example."

"Hrmm. Much of the same family history too." Korgen stroked his beard absently as he watched the clerks work. "And they share a dialect, of course."

"Dialect?" asked Gorm.

"Language," Korgen snapped, waving the question away. "The form assumes it's a dialect of the Dwarven tongue, naturally, but it works well enough."

"It is so," said Asherzu. "With so much common information, is there not a way to fill out the pages faster?"

The Dwarf scratched at his beard. "Aye, since it's going to be the same for so many, perhaps we could make a cover sheet for a docket of applications. And that would mean they don't need to fill out Guild Form 1974...."

"Then let it be said that we have found many opportunities for efficiency," Asherzu said.

"Looks as much," Korgen acknowledged grudgingly. "I'll see what I can do."

Gorm watched the guildmaster trudge off to confer with his clerks. "I thought it'd take a team o' minotaurs to get Korgen to take a step he didn't think of. And ye've got him toddling off like a forge-lad fetching water."

"People move mountains, but words move people," said Asherzu. "Such is the way of persuasive selling. My father showed me its power, and now I shall sell the world a vision."

"Heh. It's a nice thought, chieftain, and I wish ye luck with it." Gorm watched Korgen and his clerks working furiously to alter a running process. It put him in mind of trying to build a dam while the river was flooded. "But the dream won't be worth much if we can't get these fighters to Andarun fast enough."

"Or if we don't have enough of them," said Kaitha, walking up behind them.

"That too." Gorm looked over on the neat rows of troops, softly chatting with one another as they waited in queue. Many Shadowkin had declared that they would never follow Asherzu, and several tribes and factions splintered away from the Red Horde. Or perhaps they left to be the new Red Horde. It was hard to follow the politics, but any way you looked at it, the Old Dwarven Kingdoms lost a third of their new army before a blade was drawn against the undead.

"How goes the strategy session?" he asked.

Kaitha shrugged. "It's looks to be a long, hard fight. Nobody knows which way it will go."

"Aye, but the point of having a strategy is to improve your odds," said Gorm.

"I was talking about the strategy session."

Gorm squeezed his eyes shut and let out a heavy breath as he rubbed his eyebrows. "Trouble cooperating?"

The Elf nodded. "There's more than a little tension between High Commander Harak and the Shadowkin generals. Orcs and Dwarves were often in fights together, but never on the same side."

"Well, there's a first time for everything, ain't there?" Gorm bowed to Asherzu. "Pardon, chieftain, but I've got to go settle a matter if we're to ride out anytime soon."

Asherzu smiled and inclined her head. "May your words be persuasive and your dealings be successful, Gorm Ingerson."

Gorm answered through his teeth before he stamped down the muddy path. "I'll leave that to better speakers in better times. If ye want to get anything done, there comes a point when ye have to crack a few skulls."

Chapter 28

"And don't think I won't dock pay, either," Feista Hrurk snarled, stalking through the kitchen of Mrs. Hrurk's Home for the Underprivileged. "I ordered five barrels of salted riverfin! Five! Who accepted a delivery of three?"

"Sorry, ma'am." Aubren trailed after the Gnoll, clipboard in hand. The Human girl was still locked in the gangly phase of adolescence, and her face looked perpetually uneasy with her circumstances. The effect was appropriate for the moment. "Um… I think everybody's really distracted. They say the undead are gathering outside the city."

"Exactly! The undead are here!" Mrs. Hrurk glared up at Aubren. "And when you're about to be under siege, getting the right amount of food is important!"

"Um, ok. I'll let Mr. Blackgum know you're unhappy," said Aubren, making a note in her clipboard.

"I'll do it myself. Mr. Poldo paid for two more barrels of fish, and that Orc is going to see them delivered!" Mrs. Hrurk stopped at the door, her hackles up.

"Let me get that for you," mumbled Aubren, opening the door.

"Thank you," growled Mrs. Hrurk. Mr. Poldo had bought the new home in a hurry, and in his haste he had neglected to account for the fact that it had been built for Elves back in the Fifth Age. All of the doors and fixtures were designed for someone taller than a Human, when Feista barely reached a Scribkin's height.

The Gnoll made her way through the hallway quickly, her thoughts lost in inventories, schedules, and the rising prices for salted fish. She stopped short when she passed the common room.

Much has been made of the power of a mother's intuition, but a share of the credit for maternal insight belongs with a child's inability to keep a secret. Two of the Hrurk pups were sitting in the common room, conspicuously not destroying it. When Mrs. Hrurk cleared her throat their heads snapped around, their faces filled with terror, guilt, and feigned indifference.

"What's going on?" said Mrs. Hrurk. "Where's Rex?"

The remaining pups responded with unconvincing shrugs.

"Where is Rex?" Mrs. Hrurk repeated, leveling her most effective glare at the younglings.

Little Terrie broke first. "He wanted to protect you from the zombies," she said, her tiny jowls quivering. "He said he was going to the first tier."

"We tried to stop him—" Dogo added, but Feista wasn't listening. Her insides had turned to ice.

"Go! Go tell Mr. Zug'Gath what happened, and do everything he says. I'm going to find your brother!" Mrs. Hurk was bolting for the front door before she finished barking the order.

"Mrs. Hrurk!" called Aubren, following closely. "Wait—!"

Feista was nearly frenzied. "Open the door before I tear it down!"

"I know, Mrs. Hrurk." Aubren took a couple of garments down from a coat hook and extended one to the Gnoll. "I just wanted to grab our cloaks."

"T-thank you. But we have to hurry," said Feista, throwing the cloak around her shoulders. "They've already begun evacuating the first and second tiers. If Rex… if he's made it down there somehow…" She couldn't finish the sentence.

"I know," said Aubren, opening the door. "You don't need to say it."

"Doom," whispered Ignatius, staring at a menacing spiral of clouds circling above Andarun. A deep shadow crept over the city as the ominous weather blotted out the afternoon sun.

The priest of Mordo Ogg looked at his master's shrine. The lights set within the eyes of the stone skull were flashing green as much as red. The old man set his jaw in snaggletoothed determination and marched up to the sculpture.

Mordo Ogg didn't demand much of his followers. Usually, priests of the Lord of the End had few duties beyond observing their god's endless task and reminding people of their ultimate fate. It was easy work, though the pay was atrocious and being a death priest could really kill your social life. That was the joke among the priests and priestesses, anyway.

It took a certain sort.

When need arose, however, the priesthood of Mordo Ogg did have one supreme duty: to make sure the dead stayed that way.

Ignatius knelt prostrate before the statue, arms outstretched, until his searching fingers found the two buttons located in the skeleton's feet. Pressing both of them opened a small alcove in the god of death's throne. With considerable effort, the old man drew out a suit of ancient chainmail, a cudgel with a head of black iron, and a dark helmet with its faceplate fashioned into the likeness of a skull.

He could barely lift the cudgel. His head wobbled under the weight of the helmet, and he struggled to move with the armor on. Still, ritual demanded that he wear the uniform when the time came to take up arms. He glared up at the blackening sky.

"Soon," he rasped.

"Very soon." Jynn shielded his eyes in the noonday sun, staring at the distant profile of Mount Wynspar. "Probably tonight, if not before."

"Bones!" Gorm's curse was loud enough to startle the Shadowkin behind him. Several Goblins instinctively fell to the ground before an all clear was sounded. The Dwarf gave an apologetic wave as the Shadowkin resumed preparing the heroes' mounts.

The Elven steeds had been startled when Gorm and Heraldin showed up with a pack of Orcs to retrieve them from the fields north of Dunhelm; they'd been downright terrified as they were ushered back through the magical portal to the northern coast. The horses were none too happy with the second waygate journey either, despite their clear relief at returning to the central Freelands. Now they stamped and snorted as Goblins and Kobolds fastened nets filled with stones, small logs, and bundles of exotic ingredients to their saddles.

"How can you even tell when the undead will strike at this distance?" Heraldin squinted as he stared. "You can't see Andarun from this side of the mountain."

"Look at them storm clouds," said Gorm, pointing to the ominous cyclone developing in the dark skies above the southern slope of the mountain. "Spiraling, too. Clouds like that only arrive about the time a really big fight's about to start."

"I thought the sky looked portentous today," said Kaitha.

"You can tell what's happening by the weather?" asked Heraldin.

"Oh yeah," said Laruna. "You always check the clouds before a big job."

"It's the influence of low magic," said Jynn. "When enough fates intersect at a given point in time and space, it can warp the weave enough to distort weather patterns."

"Why did ye think all the bard's tales have thunderstorms at the big, climactic fight?" Gorm asked.

Heraldin shrugged. "I suppose I thought it was creative license."

"You thought the bards were all ending their stories in similar fashion for creativity's sake?" said Burt.

"You give the people what they want," said Heraldin. "The ballads all end with the heroes overcoming evil as well. That's not terribly original either."

"Then let us hope against novelty," said a portly Goblin shaman walking up from the horses. Hibbirp was commissioned by Asherzu to lead the Shadowkin on their mission.

"Aye, that's a good word," said the Dwarf. "Everything ready?"

The shaman assured them that the horses were loaded and asked that the adventurers prepare to ride shortly. Gorm agreed, but held the others back for a moment.

"This is it," he told them, standing in a tight circle. "We're a day's ride from Andarun, and we've half a day to make it. If this plan don't work—"

"It'll be like all of the others?" said Heraldin.

"If it don't work," Gorm repeated loudly. "I just want ye to know it's been an honor. And I wouldn't change a thing."

"I'd change the parts where the plans didn't work," said Heraldin.

"I'd make the bard a mute," said Laruna.

Gaist nodded.

"I wouldn't be risking my whiskers to save Johan. Or the Heroes' Guild, or Goldson and Baggs," said Burt. "I'd avoid propping up the whole corrupt system."

"We're saving the good folk of the city," said Jynn. "Johan and his ilk are just collateral beneficiaries."

"Yeah, I know," grumbled Burt. "But I'd still find a way we could kick the king in his big, shiny teeth."

"I guess there's a lot we'd change." Kaitha smiled. "But we're here anyway."

"Only thing I'd change is we'd wrap this up faster," snapped Gorm. "Let's ride out! We ain't got much time."

"We have minutes, not hours, Majesty," said General Gurgen. The wind tousled her closely cropped hair as she looked over the ramparts. Grim ranks of corpses and specters stared back at her. "They could launch their assault any moment now."

Weaver Ortson shifted his gaze to the king with some effort. It took additional exertion to focus on Johan, and more effort to hold his flask, and still more to do it all while standing upright. All in all, the guildmaster was straining himself just to stay atop Malcolm's Gate, a grand stone gatehouse separating the third tier from the second.

"Excellent! Ha!" laughed Johan, the light gleaming off his grin. The champion-cum-king stood with one leg atop the ramparts, chest out, eyes forward, smile confident, cape and hair billowing majestically in the wind.

The king's eagerness stood in stark contrast to everyone else on the wall of the second tier. Most of the bannermen hunched over in nervous huddles, whispering to each other as the army of the dead approached from the southeast. Gurgen looked troubled as she stood and wavered on the edge of desperation. Ortson had opted to drink himself right over the boundary.

"Here we are, staring death in the face!" said Johan. "There's naught but a ragtag band of weary soldiers and a few bold heroes standing between the Freedlands and total annihilation."

"A very few bold heroes," said General Gurgen, casting a dark glance at Ortson.

"As many as we'd pay for!" Ortson slurred the retort.

"It's enough." Johan's smile was broad enough to nearly bisect his face, and he breathed the words with rapturous certainty.

The king swept his gaze over the edge of the ramparts. Below him, the city streets were empty and deserted. Most of the lower tiers' citizens had fled to cram the upper tiers, but the wretched faces of those unable or unwilling to evacuate peered from many windows. Soldiers lined the tops of the walls between the tiers, their company banners flapping in the ever-strengthening wind. The city was silent, save for the cries of frightened children and the distant, dissonant rumble of the dead marching.

"People of the Freedlands!" Johan's voice rang out over the whispering streets. Bannermen turned to look at him. Windows creaked open. Clusters of curious faces bloomed in the doorways, turned up toward Johan as flowers twist to face the sun. Behind Ortson, the bannermen and citizens occupying the upper tiers stared down at the king like spectators at the opera.

"I know you are frightened," boomed Johan. "I see the fear in your eyes. And I will not lie; the danger we face is great. But we, we are greater still, my friends. Ha! Did we not build this city atop dungeons full of foul creatures? Have we not tamed the Wild Lands and hauled treasure from every dungeon in the kingdom? Some fear the darkness, but we have made careers of driving it back! And while we have a lot of work to do, I know that you, my people, are up to the task!"

The crowd burst into resonant cheers. Johan drew his enruned sword and held it high in the air, basking in the adoration of the masses.

"The gods are with us! Tandos is with us!" Johan's blade shone like a beacon, sending rays of golden light to pierce the gathering darkness.

Weaver Ortson stared through a haze of liquor at the divine beams dancing around the king's sword. They shone out into the darkness beyond the city, where another glow caught the guildmaster's attention. He rubbed his eyes and checked again to make sure he was seeing things correctly. "Uh, sire?" he said.

Johan was caught up in ecstatic glory. The light gleamed off his polished armor, his raised blade, his perfect teeth. "And I, my good people! I am with you! I have already slain the foul Detarr Ur'Mayan once! It is no different this time!"

"Sire!" hissed Ortson.

A hint of a scowl crossed Johan's face as he glanced back at the guildmaster. "What is it, Ortson?"

Ortson pointed to the rising mass amid the undead. "There is, ah, at least one difference."

"Everything has changed!" Detarr Ur'Mayan had to shout to be heard over the moans of the dead army, the piping of his unholy Gnomish organ, and the ear-shattering roar of the earth behind him.

The liche drove the Dark Spire of Nephan into the ground. Then, with Detarr's magic flowing through it, the shard of rune-encrusted stone slowly pulled itself out of the dirt, and behind the liche, the artifact's giant twin did the same. The land trembled and groaned as a tower of stone began to rip itself from the earth.

"There's never been an invasion like this!" Detarr gestured out to the gruesome crowd as the Gnomish organ's music swelled to a climax. "Every necromancer or liche before me believed that power lay within dominating the dead. But what you've all shown me is that dead people are people too, and the power lies in you!"

The liche's officials nodded and clapped, standing in a wide semicircle that gave Detarr plenty of room to manipulate the Dark Spire. The undead gathered behind them broke into a cacophony of groans and shrieks that could be taken as the loose equivalent of cheering. Despite himself, Tyren Ur'Thos was compelled to join in the applause. His hands moved of their own accord, his head bobbing up and down like a marionette's.

"Thank you," yelled the liche. "Thank you for making all this possible. And listen, we're going with a more traditional image for this invasion—"

"All terror, all the time!" interjected the Head of Marketing.

"Yes, thank you," Detarr said without gratitude. "But there are reasons to avoid an extended siege here, and I remain confident that you all have the power to triumph! I'd like to extend my most sincere thanks to Knight-Commander Ur'Thos for making this possible."

The liche turned his cruel, skeletal grin on Tyren, and the knight-commander's right hand raised itself.

"After all, he's the one who found the Dark Spire of Nephan!" said Detarr, thrusting the Wyrmwood Staff toward the sky. The Dark Spire of Nephan finally loosed itself from the loam and rose into the air. Behind the liche, the shard's giant simulacrum freed itself from the earth with a final rumble and heaved skyward.

The undead cheered and waved their appendages at the airborne monolith, carved from the deepest strata of the fields outside of Andarun. Loose stones and sprays of dirt cascaded from it as it hovered in the night sky, a jagged scar in the canopy of emerging stars.

"It does have a certain *il'ne se la,* doesn't it?" Detarr remarked to his assembled generals. He gestured at the smaller spire with the Wyrmwood Staff, and both stones swiveled upward in unison. More earth shifted and fell as the spires aligned themselves horizontally.

"It's stupendous! Amazing! Earth shattering! Literally!" bubbled the Head of Marketing. "People are going to be talking about this for the rest of their lives! And long afterward, I suppose."

"Magnificent." Lady Carabae's jaw hung open, her long fangs shining in the glow of passing specters.

"But what does it actually do?" asked Genevieve. The banshee flew up for a better view.

"What does it do?" said the Head of Marketing, bobbing in an agitated hop after the banshee. "This is the Dark Spire of Nephan! The flying fortress of the Dark Lord of Nagarok! The soaring citadel of the bloody-handed necromancer!"

Genevieve squinted her blank eyes at the spire, which was now parallel to the muddy plain. "So, does it shoot a death beam or something?" she asked.

The Head of Marketing rolled its eye. "Sure. Fine. Probably." It tried to share a knowing look with Tyren.

The black crown compelled the knight-commander to give a curt nod.

"There's no death beam." Detarr stood perpendicular to the smaller of the spires, clasping the base of the Wyrmwood Staff so the tip pointed down at the artifact.

Genevieve looked disappointed. "Does it amplify magic?" She asked.

"Or empower the dead?" suggested Lady Carabae.

"It's really not that kind of artifact." Satisfied with the alignment of the staff, the liche swiveled his arms to bring the staff behind his head—almost as though wielding a club to smash a tiny trespasser.

"But what does it do?" insisted the banshee.

"It's thousands of tons of flying stone," snapped Detarr. "Try to have some imagination."

The undead wizard swung his staff in a wide arc, bringing its head within a hair of striking the ground. There was a flash of light and a loud crack as the head of the staff collided with the enruned shard of stone, and the smaller Dark Spire flew through the air like an arrow.

"What—" said Genevieve, but even her supernatural voice was lost in the rushing wind as the giant spire launched as though fired from a great ballista. The pillar of earth soared over the army of the dead, over the clusters of buildings outside of Andarun, over the great stables and bazaars on the main road to the gates. The massive projectile sprayed loose rocks and soil as it spiraled along its deadly trajectory toward the Great South Gate of Andarun.

"Get back!" shrieked Weaver Ortson, stumbling away from the onrushing stone projectile.

"Bloody bones," swore General Gurgen, a moment before the Great South Gate exploded in a spray of white dust and surprised bannermen. The Dark Spire barreled through Andarun's outer wall and continued up the empty street, sending cobblestones and debris flying. A moment later, it crashed into Fafnir's Gate, the great portcullis that could seal the gates of the second tier.

Ortson felt the stone beneath him heave at the impact. The buildings on the tier below shuddered violently, breaking many of their windows. Screams rang out as Fafnir's Gate began to buckle and topple, ripping a gash in the city's second line of defense.

General Gurgen barked orders. A flight of messenger sprites took to the air as the officers behind her relayed commands to their soldiers. Chaos broke out in the streets below. Bannermen and a handful of professional heroes rushed toward the breaches while terrified citizens and refugees abandoned their hiding places and fled madly toward the barricades blocking the gates to the upper tiers. Beyond them, skeletal warriors were already pushing through the wreckage of the main gate.

"Ortson!" Johan's eyes were fixed on a point in the distance, somewhere amid the sinister glow of the unliving throng beyond the shattered gates. "Are there any bards among the heroes you've managed to hire?"

"Uh, yes, sire." Ortson knew the answer, but he didn't understand the question. "By necessity, you see. There's always a bigger supply of bards than demand for them, so on a low-wage, high risk quest—"

"Good." Johan cut the guildmaster off without looking back. "Make sure they're watching. I want to hear details in the ballads."

"Sire?" said Ortson.

"Ha haaa!" With a trumpeting laugh, the paladin leapt off the ramparts of Malcolm's Gate. The king's crimson cape trailed him like a shooting star until he hit the cobbled streets with the stone-shattering impact of a meteor. With a flourish of his glowing sword, the king righted himself and cracked his neck.

"For my kingdom! For my people! For all that I stand for!" the king shouted. He turned a pointed glance back to the guildmaster wobbling atop the ramparts. "Are you writing this down?"

"U-uh, yes sire!" Ortson fumbled at his robes for a parchment and charcoal nib.

"Ha haaa!" Johan launched into a subsonic charge that left no trace of him save a plume of dust leading toward the ruins of Fafnir's Gate. Moments later, a glowing path scythed through the undead pouring into the Great South Gate, a slash of light against the encroaching darkness.

Ortson dabbed the sweat from his brow. "Remarkable," he breathed.

"Predictable," Detarr told his generals. They watched the distant golden comet carve through a cluster of zombies and ghouls. "It's the narrative, you see. He can't resist the glory of a climactic duel."

Tyren could sense the power at the gates. The light it cast sent a searing sensation through his skeleton, and it brought with it memories of his death. He would have taken a step back had he been in command of what remained of his body. As it was, he mustered enough will to shift his eyes away from the horrible brightness burning a path through the streets outside of Andarun.

"Shouldn't we, uh, move out of his way, then?" asked the Head of Marketing, glancing back and forth between the liche and the obliterating light.

"I imagine you should," said Detarr, setting the Wyrmwood Staff before him. "We're going to need some space."

It was enough of an order to compel Tyren. He struggled against his own body as he walked away from the liche, and was surprised to find that he had a small degree of control over his motion. It wasn't enough to do as he wished, but he could pull or push on individual joints at certain moments. Tyren surmised that it was because the liche's attention was on the approaching foe.

The other generals stared at the knight-commander's awkward, hobbled gait as he joined them a safe distance from Detarr. "Are you quite all right?" asked Lady Carabae, a smirk twisting her ruby lips.

Tyren stared at her for as long as he could hold out before the will of the Crown of Iron Thorns forced him to nod.

"Really? Because you—" Genevieve began, but then something behind Tyren caught her attention. "Look!"

Tyren stepped into position next to her and turned mechanically. Viridian swirls of sorcery wreathed Detarr as he chanted in a forgotten tongue. The Wyrmwood Staff hovered in the air in front of him, the gem clutched in its carved claws glowing violet and red in turn. His hands worked furiously, weaving spells as a maestro directs an orchestra. The haunted Gnomish organ had noticed as well, and now the music was reaching its crescendo as Detarr's unholy magic swirled to its zenith.

That was when the closest ranks of undead exploded.

The ghouls and zombies were blasted into to the air as a red and gold comet shot through them. A moment later, a supersonic laugh drowned out the wails of the re-dying soldiers.

"Ha-HAAAAAA!"

Tyren's eyes flicked to Detarr. An armored paladin, shining with a golden light, seemed to materialize behind the liche. The man wore a manic grin as he raised a glowing sword for a definitive blow.

"You," said the liche drolly.

"Me!" laughed the champion, swinging his blade. The enchanted sword cut a blazing trail through the liche. Or at least, through the place where Detarr should have been.

But the dead wizard had darted away with a sudden speed that matched the paladin's own unnatural velocity, and re-materialized in the air behind the confused paladin. With a wave of his staff, Detarr sent a blast of darkness into the warrior's back. The hero screamed as hooks of shadow raked across him, knocking him down into the mud.

The paladin wiped a clod of damp earth from his eye as he whirled to face the liche. "You!" he snarled.

"Oh, come now, Johan." Detarr floated back down to the field as lazily as a lord might descend a staircase. "This moment has been decades in the making. I think we can muster some polysyllabic banter for it, hm?"

The king opted for an enraged snarl instead. He swept his sword in a wide arc, sending a luminous crescent blazing toward Detarr. The liche dodged easily and sent another blast of dark tendrils at Johan.

"Did you think I wouldn't be prepared for you?" Detarr watched calmly as the king danced through the shadowy projectiles slamming into the ground around him. "Did you think I don't know what you're capable of? You may have caught me off guard at our first meeting, but I can assure you that it won't happen again."

Johan leapt away from the last strike of the spell and brandished his blade. "Ha! I'll not be so quickly dispatched either, foul wizard!"

"Oh, no, of course not," said Detarr. He pointed at a small gash in the paladin's cheek.

Johan raised an uneasy hand to the cut and winced. A dark barb was embedded just above his jaw, and the flesh around it was already becoming discolored.

"Slow and painful was always the plan," said Detarr. "You will be exposed and broken before the end comes, and that is going to take a while."

Johan roared again and leapt, sword blazing. Detarr dodged the king's shining counterattack by flying into the sky, then forced the paladin to leap away with another spell. The two darted, dodged, thrust, and parried their way over the battlefield. Eventually they looked like distant will-o-the-wisps—one green and violet, the other golden—dancing across the night sky.

"Whoa," said Genevieve, gawking with the Head of Marketing and Lady Carabae. "That was intense."

Tyren wasn't paying attention any more. The Crown of Iron Thorns compelled him forward in a lurching, laborious march. He was so focused on not walking that he didn't notice his hand involuntarily drawing his sword and raising it above his head.

"The knight-commander is right! We've got a job to do while the master's fighting!" said the Head of Marketing, floating up beside the knight-commander. The undead around him fell in step. "Now's when the magic happens! Specifically, the necromancy. Am I right?"

It took all of Tyren's effort not to nod. "Right! We need to concentrate on the job!" said Genevieve, floating above them. "I can lead the spectral forces and fly over the eastern fortifications on the lower tiers. But they have wizards raising wards on the upper city." As if for emphasis, blue light flared above the city as a distant ghost floated too close to the domes of protection shimmering over the ramparts.

"Leave the wards to me," said Lady Carabae. She pulled her cape up around herself and disappeared in a cloud of shadow. A moment later, Genevieve soared off, a flight of ghosts and wraiths behind her.

"I heard they raised up these strange corpses down by the bottom of that huge wall," said the Head of Marketing. "I'm betting I can make something terrifying out of that bunch. You'll handle the troops, right?"

Tyren's inner monologue was laden with profanity, but his mostly-corporeal form marched forward wordlessly, weapon outstretched.

The Head of Marketing, unsurprisingly, took silence for assent. "Yeah, you've got this!" he said to Tyren as he bobbed away toward the walls of Andarun.

Chapter 29

"What I've got is about half the materials I need, a crew that's been riding hard all night, an army of walking corpses that's uncomfortably close to my work site, and two thrice-cursed trees that I'm supposed to turn into a stone arch. In the dark!" snapped Hibbirp. The rotund Goblin's headdress shook as he jabbed a meaty finger toward Gorm. "So how about I go back to trying to calibrate an ancient artifact across time and space, and you stop bothering the workers with your questions?"

"It's just one question," Gorm countered. "When are ye gonna be done?"

"Wouldn't we all like to know?" The shaman jabbed a thumb over his shoulder at the small crew of Goblins and Gremlins working to lash two large trees together at the top. "But that's the thing about tinkering with the fabric of the universe: it's hard to plan for. Also, it takes concentration."

"How easy do ye suppose it'll be to focus with a pack of ghouls and zombies tryin' to pick your brains? 'Cause they do that bit more literally," snapped Gorm. "It's only a matter of time afore some of 'em take notice of us."

"Well, who decided to set up an extra-planar gateway this close to the undead, huh?" said the Goblin. "Because it certainly wasn't my crew!"

"Do ye want to explain to Asherzu why her troops had to ford the Tarapin River to get to a fight?" Gorm shot back. "Because if not, this is the farthest we could get from the undead."

"Well then, it's a good thing we've got professionals protecting us, ain't it?" said Hibbirp. "How about you do your job and let me do mine?"

Gorm watched the Goblin stalk off.

"How much longer?" Burt stuck his head out of Gorm's rucksack, a cigarette dangling from his muzzle.

"He doesn't know," said Gorm, turning to join the others. "And some help ye were. I thought ye came along to help me negotiate with the Goblins."

The Kobold shrugged. "Not much to negotiate. You both want to get that waygate running as fast as possible. Follow my lead and keep quiet, and he just might do it."

Gorm snorted. "And didn't I ask ye not to smoke in my bag?"

"Probably," said Burt. "But you're also the one who said I had to leave Patches back with the Orcs."

"Ye know a dog would have a hard time keepin' up with the horses all night," said Gorm.

"Yeah, a pity." The Kobold tapped the loose ash from the end of his cigarette.

Laruna stood as they approached the edge of the worksite. "How much longer until —"

"He doesn't know," Gorm interrupted. "But judgin' from what I see, they're hours away."

"We don't have hours," said Kaitha. She pointed toward the mountain, where Andarun was falling.

The great gates of the city had been rent apart by some unimaginable force, and undead of every foul variety pressed through the hole in the walls. Fires were burning throughout the Base, and some had even moved up to the second tier. Ghosts and specters wove through the plumes of black smoke that rose up to join the spiraling, thundering clouds that loomed over Mount Wynspar.

"The wards won't hold much longer," said Jynn. "The Academy's mages can't keep them up."

The shimmering domes of azure magic that hung over the upper tiers were beginning to flicker and fade, save for the point closest to the Wallward side of the third tier. There, the sorcerous shields flashed and crackled as a cluster of dark figures attacked them.

"Looks like vampires," said Kaitha. "They're weakening the shields."

"I should be on those ramparts," said Laruna, shaking her head. "I could keep the wards up."

"It won't matter much if the ground troops take Malcolm's Gate," said Burt. "They'll just go under the shields. And we don't have a way to stop them."

"Not until the thrice-cursed waygate is ready, anyway," Gorm grumbled.

"No, but we might have a way to slow them down." Heraldin looked at Gaist.

Gaist nodded.

"We'll do a reconnaissance mission," said Heraldin. "A tiny group, deployed to just the right point, can have an outsized impact."

Gorm shook his head. "I see where you're going, but we can't leave Hibbirp and his workers undefended."

"We won't," said Heraldin. "You stay behind to protect the waygate while Gaist and I go to the tiers by the Ridge."

"And Kaitha and I head for the walls to bolster the wards near the Wall," Laruna added. She turned to the Elf. "Right?"

"Right," said the ranger, unslinging her bow.

"Wrong," said Gorm. "We have to stick together."

"We have to buy the army of the Old Dwarven Kingdoms time to get here," said Jynn. "And their plan might work."

"It might not! It might get us all killed!" said Gorm. "After all we've been through, ye should know ye can't split the party!"

"Exactly!" said Heraldin. "No matter what happens or what distance separates us, you can't split this party."

Kaitha grinned. "We might tactically reconfigure our proximity, but we can never be split."

"We should know," said Laruna. "We tried. Multiple times."

"It never works," added Jynn.

"But—" Gorm cut off as a heavy hand dropped on his shoulder. He looked up at Gaist.

The weaponsmaster nodded.

"Aye." Gorm's shoulders fell. "You're right. No matter what happens, we're in this together." Gorm stuck his fist into the center of the group.

"Always." Kaitha stepped up to press her fist against Gorm's. One by one, the other heroes did the same, shaping their huddle into a six-spoked wagon wheel.

Burt scampered up Gorm's arm. "What... what are you doing? What is this?" he muttered in Gorm's ear.

"We're doing the hands in the circle thing," Gorm murmured.

"Yeah, but why do you do it?" asked Burt. "Why's everybody looking at each other like that? This is weird, right? Is this not weird for Lightlings?"

"We're just... it's just a thing we do," Gorm whispered harshly. "We're... we're part of the team. We're in this together."

"Well, why don't you just say it? I mean, you just did say it!" said Burt.

"We all know what it means. It's culture," said Laruna.

"Shared experience and all that," added Jynn.

"Oh. Yeah, I guess." After a moment's thought, the Kobold scampered along the Dwarf's arm to extend his own paw into the center. "Still weird, though."

"You've really stuck your paw in it now, Rex," Mrs. Hrurk muttered to her missing son. All her thoughts were on him. She couldn't tell if she wanted to hold him close or wring his furry neck for bringing her down to the second tier in the middle of a siege, but either way she ached to have him in her arms. The only thing that helped was talking to him under her breath.

"Just look at it out here," she murmured. "This is no place for a child."

It was no place for anyone. Whatever calamity had shaken the city occasionally brought debris raining down around her and Aubren, and Mrs. Hrurk's shoulder had been battered by a falling shingle. Every scream of Rex's name brought ash and stone dust into her burning lungs. Each corner, each side street, brought a new vision of flames and death.

"Now what are we to do, Rex? It doesn't get much worse than this," she mumbled, giving the cosmos an invitation to demonstrate Nove's second principle of universal irony.

Aubren screamed for Mrs. Hrurk, and everything got worse.

Little Rex was folded up amid the rubble of a burning storefront like a broken toy. One of his paws was wrapped around the wooden sword he'd brought to fight the zombies; the other had been crushed and mangled by falling stones. He didn't move when Feista lifted him, didn't hug her back as she clutched his tiny frame to her heaving chest.

She couldn't hear anything but her own howling, could barely feel anything but the void in her heart. All other sensations were distant, like they were happening to someone else. Someone was grabbing her shoulders. Someone was screaming her name. Someone was yelling that he was still breathing.

"What?" Mrs. Hrurk started and looked down at the bundle of fur in her arms. Rex's eyes were firmly shut, but now she could see his tiny ribs rising and falling slowly, too slowly. She looked up into Aubren's eyes. "We have to get out of here!" she gasped.

"Yes! Exactly! We have to get out of here!" The girl pointed down the street, where ghoulish creatures were battling a squad of bannermen. "The undead are in the second tier!"

Andarun's second tier was the highest point on Andarun accessible from the Ridgeward side of the city. The treacherous drops and sharp edges of Mount Wynspar's western slope deterred all but the most determined climber. Near the higher tiers, the mountainside was pocked with caves and chasms that could send an unwitting climber to the depths of the dungeons beneath the mountain. If the fall didn't finish off such a foolish climber, the darkness below was filled with horrors eager to do so.

Yet a climber with enough skill and dexterity could brave the lower slopes to bypass the southern walls and reach the Base or the second tier. It was difficult, and the bannermen on the southern wall would quickly notice anyone scaling the mountain, but the biggest deterrent from entering the city by this surreptitious route was the destination: the climb was a lot of trouble just to wind up a two-story drop from the Underdim or Darkridge.

"As far as I'm concerned, the only difference between dropping into the Darkridge and falling into Mount Wynspar's dungeon is the color of the cobblestones," Heraldin muttered to Gaist as they crept down ramshackle roofs to the ash-choked streets. "And that was before the zombies and walking skeletons."

Gaist nodded and pointed a sword at a wandering band of ghouls and zombies shambling up the street.

"I see them, my friend. This calls for a stealthy approach." Heraldin scanned the street. "If we wait a moment, we should be able to sneak past them to that alleyway, hide behind the trash bins, and then climb the gutter to the rooftops. From there we… Gaist?"

Heraldin was surprised to see that the weaponsmaster was already in the thick of the dead. The doppelganger moved with an alien fluidity; his limbs almost seemed to stretch and snap as he wove through his foes. Every swing of his blade sent another limb or head flying into the air, like grim popped corn in a circus vending cart.

A moment later, it was done. Gaist glided back to the bard, his face characteristically stoic and yet somehow intolerably self-satisfied.

"Yes, well, impressive as that was, perhaps we should prioritize not getting noticed," Heraldin said. "We need to get across the tier as quickly as possible."

Gaist shrugged as he sheathed his weapons.

They made their way through the ruined neighborhoods of Andarun's second tier, sneaking, lurking, and occasionally butchering small packs of the dead. They passed by the projectile that had destroyed the Great South Gate, a pillar of stone and earth that had torn the streets and leveled buildings in its path. Eventually, they came to a familiar warehouse.

"You'll recall that there are all sorts of useful tools and devices inside," Heraldin explained to Gaist as they approached the main doors of Creative Destruction Incorporated. He tested the doorway and practically giggled when he found it locked. The bard's hands trembled with anticipation as he produced a set of intricate lock picks from his belt pouch. "All that remains is to get inside."

He selected the first pick and moved to insert it into the keyhole, but before he touched the lock it clicked and unlatched. A moment later, the door swung open.

"Heraldin? Gaist?" said Boomer. "Well, if you aren't a sight for sore eyes!"

"Come in, come in!" added Buster. The Gremlin ushered them inside hurriedly, where Heraldin could see several workers armed with crossbows stationed in the windows. "What are you two doing here?"

"I could ask the same." The bard hid his disappointment as he discreetly put away his lock picks. "It looked like they evacuated the lower tiers."

"They did, of course!" said Boomer. The stout Scribkin pushed the doors shut behind them. "But there's no way we're abandoning all our gear and equipment to these rotters! We've got some brave men on hazard pay, a warehouse full of supplies, and enough potions, runes, and gadgets to make those walking stiffs pay for every inch they take."

"If we're going to go out, we'll go out fighting," said Buster.

"And preferably several days from now," laughed Boomer.

Heraldin raised a finger. "A noble approach, to be sure," he said with a grin. "But may I suggest an alternative?"

"There must be a better way," gasped Laruna, doubled over and holding the edge of the rampart. "There's a huge hole in the Great South Gate. It would have been an easier spot to climb up than here."

"It's also an easier way to get into the city, which is why most of the undead are crowded around it." Kaitha nocked an enchanted arrow in her bow. "We're trying to avoid being seen, for the moment."

A ghostly old sailor flew overhead. His blank eyes opened wider as he recognized the living women beneath him, but an arrow of silver light blasted him back to the afterlife before he could cry out.

Kaitha readied another arrow as she watched the last traces of the spirit evaporate. "Are we almost ready?"

"Hang on," panted the mage. "We're not all accustomed to scaling sheer surfaces."

Kaitha held her tongue as she shot another curious specter.

The Wall had stood as the defining feature of Andarun's eastern border since it was built by the Sten, and modern architects had been unwilling or unable to alter the great edifice's stonework when adding a new, shorter wall to the southern limits of the Base. As such, the corner between the Wall and Andarun's southern fortifications was marked by regular gaps and crannies. They made for a notoriously easy climb to the southern ramparts. Kaitha had scaled it one night on a dare while drunk.

The Elf peered into the city. Hordes of zombies and skeletons rampaged through the lower tiers. Above the ruined streets she could see tiny, dark shapes attacking the sorcerous wards cast over the upper tiers. The crackling shields faded a little with each assault.

"We need to hurry." Kaitha obliterated a nearby banshee with another arrow. "The wards won't last long."

"I know," the mage said, bracing herself against the ramparts. "How many vampires are there?"

"Two dozen or so." The ranger squinted at the distant figures. "Thirty on the high side. It's hard to tell with them moving through that light."

Laruna nodded. The solamancer's fingers danced in complex patterns, wisps of flame and light dancing between them. Nearby torches flickered and leaned toward the mage. Embers and flames from the burning city danced toward the fiery nexus between her palms. The threads whirled and wove themselves tighter and tighter, bundling into a white-hot singularity.

A nearby ghost noticed the light, but Kaitha eliminated it with a quick shot. "Any time now," she told the mage.

Laruna shifted her feet, and tendrils of light extended from the glowing ball between her palms. The strands of silvery luminescence drifted over the city as though blown by a billowing wind, finally snapping into place as their tips reached the shield. White light suddenly spread up the lower part of the ward, casting the Broad Steps in baroque shadows.

"Are they coming?" the mage growled.

"They're starting to." Kaitha readied her bow as several shadows detached themselves from the pack and drifted toward them. She took aim as they flew into range. "Keep weaving."

The ranger's first shot downed the lead vampire in a cloud of shadow and ash. Her second silver bolt only grazed the next shadow in the pack, and it took another arrow to slay it. By the time she sighted on the third vampire, she could make out the bat-like creature flying toward her.

"Time for some improvised dental work," Kaitha muttered, then loosed the shot. Her enchanted arrow struck home, slamming the onrushing shadow between the gleam of its fangs. Kaitha felt a flash of pleasure at a perfect shot finding its mark, but her satisfaction faded when the vampire failed to react.

The ranger grimaced and fired another bolt, and then another. The silvery lances slammed into the oncoming vampire again and again, but with no effect. Kaitha heard the hint of a laugh as the shadowy figure alighted on the edge of the ramparts, wrapped in leathery wings. When it stood, it had taken the form of shapely woman with jet-black hair, ruby lips, and a pair of pearly fangs peeking out from beneath her smile. "What was that about my teeth?" the vampire said in a voice like wind on silk.

"I… Nothing. It was nothing," said Kaitha, taking a step back.

"It sounded like something about dental work?" said the vampire, tapping her chin. "Or perhaps you were making jokes?"

"You know. It was a quip." Kaitha shrugged.

"A what?"

"A quip. A joke," the Elf mumbled. "You know. Everybody's allowed to make just one."

"You're allowed to make one joke in the middle of a fight to the death?" The vampire's smile turned disdainful. "Do you have any idea how ridiculous that sounds?"

"I do!" Laruna growled, still sending strands of magic into the distant wards.

"Just get the wards reinforced," Kaitha snapped back. In one fluid movement, she drew another arrow, nocked it, and fired at the vampire. "I can handle this!"

The arrow flew straight and true for the vampire's heart, until the undead woman's hand snapped up and plucked it from the air. She held the sizzling bolt in a pale fist, her cruel smile unwavering. "Oh no, my dear," she said. "I am Lady Devalla Carabae the Third, Mistress of a Thousand Thralls. I do not make jokes. I do not engage in idle banter. I do not show mercy. And you most certainly cannot 'handle this.'"

"All right, so it's bad. Ye've made your point," said Gorm. "We don't know if all the army is gonna get through the waygate. I get it."

"I don't think you do. We're absolutely sure some of the army won't make it across before the waygate closes." Hibbirp watched Dwarves and Shadowkin marching through the crackling passage. "You do your best to calibrate things just so, but no matter how well you do it, sending stuff through the gate puts strain on the thaumite. At some point, that big crystal back at camp is going to have one heck of a fragmenting event. And sooner rather than later."

"Your workers should be able to reweave the sorcery matrix around the fissure," Jynn told the Goblin. "Or even recalibrate the waygate attuned to a chunk of the shattered thaumite."

"Well, yeah, of course." Hibbirp spoke with the wary condescension of a craftsman whose expertise has been challenged. "But reweaving or recalibrating is going to take hours. Maybe half a day."

"We do not have half a day," said Asherzu, grimacing at the makeshift archway.

"We ain't got an hour," said Gorm, looking at the smoke rising above Andarun. The warding spells shielding the inner tiers were glowing a worrying hue of white. "We'll just have to hope that the waygate stays open long enough."

His statement was punctuated by a sound like a wine glass breaking, followed by a low twang akin to a bowstring. The Dwarves and Kobolds currently stepping through the gate were thrown forward as the waygate's magic faded and the laws of physics reasserted themselves.

Gorm found himself the target of damning stares from almost everyone within earshot. "Well, I mean, that's..." His excuses withered and died in the heat of the collective gazes on him. "All right, I should have chosen my words better."

"It's like you've never even heard of Nove's principles of universal irony," grumbled Burt.

Gorm shook his head. "I know about Nove's principles. I just—"

"I mean, it's right there," said Burt. "First principle. Some things you just don't say out loud."

"We call them the Teachings of Phrek," offered Asherzu.

"I know what I'm not supposed to say," barked Gorm. "Can we just go see how many fighters made it through?"

The troop count provided another opportunity for reality to deal a blow to expectations.

"We already had less troops than we'd want to take on a horde of that size," said Guildmaster Korgen, surveying the ranks. "And now half of them are stuck on the other side of the Ironbreakers."

"What do we do now?" asked Darak.

"Get in formation anyway," said Gorm. "Whatever we got has to be enough."

Korgen and Darak began bellowing orders, and the troops launched into motion. The Dwarves and Shadowkin began to form ranks quickly. Squads of Orcs and larger Demi-gnolls were supported by smaller teams of Goblins, Gnolls, and Dwarves. A few Ogres and Naga attached themselves to squadrons, weapons at the ready.

Burt hopped down from Gorm's shoulder "So, uh, where should I go?" he asked. "I... I can fight. If I need to."

Gorm smiled at his friend. "Don't ye know the average lifespan of a Kobold soldier? Ye've already survived your one battle." He pointed to Burt's mangled ear.

The Kobold smiled. "Yeah, I suppose."

"Come on," said Gorm. "Let's connect ye with Lady Asherzu. Ye can work with the chieftain and her wise-ones in the healers' tent."

Across the muddied road, they found Asherzu and her advisors in discussions with Commander Harak of the Dwarves and several Fathers.

Asherzu shook her head. "I know this isn't ideal—"

"Not ideal?" the old Dwarf sputtered. "This thrice-cursed plan is fallin' apart!"

"Perhaps, but we must press on anyway." Asherzu's hand unconsciously played with the icon of Fulgen around her neck. "It's our only chance at success."

"Ye know she's right, sir," Gorm added.

Harak looked at the resolve in the faces around him, and his shoulders fell. "Aye, you're right. But burn the ashes, the gods have led us down a dark shaft on this one."

Asherzu nodded. "The gods do as they will."

"The bastards," Burt muttered under his breath.

"And we do as we must," the chieftain finished, looking back at the burning city of Andarun.

"Well, looks like we're all done for," said the elderly bannerman. "Them walking bones got us trapped, and the king don't seem to be doin' too well neither."

General Gurgen allowed herself to glance across the second tier to the ruins of Fafnir's Gate, now little more than a pile of rubble. Atop the fallen stones, King Johan and the liche remained locked in a fierce duel. Yet in the mounting twilight, the general could see that the golden aura surrounding the paladin was fading, and the king's breaths were visibly labored.

"Focus on what we can do, Guine," she told the leathery old soldier.

"Ain't much," said Guine, scratching at his snowy beard. "Men been fightin' hard all night, and the second tier's all but overrun. The Base never had a chance. Captain Federan ain't sure how much longer he can hold Malcolm's Gate, and the wards look like they'll come down any minute."

"Take heart, friends," said Cedric. The young bannerman was starry-eyed as he stared out over the carnage. "I've heard it said that it is always darkest just before the dawn."

"That's the spirit, Cedric." General Gurgen nocked an arrow in her Bow of Unrelenting Flames, sighted, and set a distant ghoul alight.

"That's daft," said Guine. "It's always darkest in the middle of the night."

"Yes, but—"

"I mean, you can see all them skeletons and ghosts pressing in on us now, can't you? It's light enough to shoot them, ain't it?" The old soldier pointed at a pack of encroaching undead below them.

"It certainly is," said General Gurgen pointedly. She immolated another zombie with a well-aimed shot.

"Three, four hours ago it was darker than a River Hag's breeches out there," said Guine with certainty. "Definitely darker than now."

"It's an expression," said Cedric, finally notching an arrow. "But look!"

He pointed. The clouds broke beyond the Wall, and the first warm light of dawn spilled over the plains. Celestial rays of golden sun blazed across the sky and fell impotently on the empty horizon.

"Yep, that's a sunrise," said Guine, clearly unimpressed.

Cedric's shoulders fell. "I just thought, you know, maybe the gods would have some miraculous way to save us with the coming of the dawn."

Guine snorted and spit over the edge of the ramparts. "Don't seem as much."

"You know, the noble heroes, or a big army, or a powerful wizard of light... They always come with the dawn to save the beleaguered defenders." Cedric peered into the distance, still hopeful.

"Well, clearly not always," said Guine.

"It just seems like a thematically appropriate moment to—"

"We're all there is now, Cedric," barked General Gurgen. "Stop making burning wishes and start shooting thrice-cursed arrows!"

"But—"

"No arguments, soldier!"

"But General, look closer!"

General Gurgen squinted at the horizon and then shifted her gaze closer to the ruined walls of Andarun. A small army had arrived from nowhere, as if it had materialized somewhere near the Riverdowns. They weren't many, but they were forming ranks and preparing a charge.

"Is that... the Dwarves?" Cedric wondered aloud, looking at the banners carried by the army. "It's the banner of the Old Kingdoms."

"They look too tall for that. Or short. And green," puzzled Guine, scratching his chin. "If'n I didn't know better, I'd say they was Orcs and Goblins."

"It doesn't matter," breathed General Gurgen. "They're reinforcements."

Chapter 30

The air vibrated around Gorm as he rode across the muddy field toward the ruins of the Great South Gate. There was a rhythm to the sounds of the battlefield, a familiar drumming in harmony with the pounding of his own heart. He swung his axe in time to the song. It hummed through the air and rang out as he decapitated an unfortunate skeletal archer. A moment later, his horse smashed into the rearmost ranks of the undead army near the ruined gates of the city.

Every stench that death had to offer assailed Gorm's nostrils in waves: the dry mustiness of a crypt; the nauseating odor of decaying flesh; the faint, burnt fragrance of spectral essence. Undead troops pressed in close behind their own stink, surrounding the horses and clawing for the heroes atop them.

Gorm chopped off reaching limbs and careless heads as he tried to maneuver his mount around the leering dead and Jynn's indiscriminate blasts of sorcery. "Push on!" he hollered to the wizard. "Keep pushin' until—"

The first wave of the Old Dwarven Kingdoms' new army crashed into the undead, sending up a spray of ichor and spare parts. Dwarves pounded skeletons into dust with massive warhammers. Orcs and Gnolls hacked at zombies with axes and cleavers. Goblins and Gremlins scuttled underfoot, jabbing at rotting flesh with short spears, while Slaugh launched stones from their slings at a safe distance.

Gorm was in the heart of the violence, and he reveled at the violence in his heart. At some point early on, he decided that fighting on horseback was too cumbersome and had dismounted. So unsaddled, he was a tempest of axe and shield, chopping and battering any undead that couldn't scramble out of his way. "Press on," he shouted, in tune with the rhythm. "Keep pushin' 'em!"

Caught off guard by the sudden assault, the undead ranks were beginning to fall apart, often in more than one sense of the word. The army of the Old Kingdom carved a path to the ruined gates. The undead on the other side of the outer wall weren't any more prepared for a sudden assault on their flanks, and the Dwarves and Shadowkin ground them down as they pressed into the streets of the city.

Gorm and Jynn regrouped just inside the ruined wall, falling back from the front lines for a moment. "Any sign of the others?" Gorm asked the wizard.

"No." Jynn tried to calm his horse amid the rush of troops pouring into the city. "But they're expecting us to go after my father."

The wizard pointed toward the upper tiers. Some massive chunk of stone had carved a deep scar across Andarun's base, a channel of torn-up streets and knocked-down buildings. At the end of the trail of destruction, the great stone projectile protruded from the wreckage of Fafnir's Gate. And atop the ruined gatehouse, Gorm saw a tiny figure wreathed in purple flame.

"Well, it'd be a shame to let 'em down." Gorm's lips pulled back from his teeth. "Come on!"

The various neighborhoods and markets crowded up against Andarun's main gate had been a warren of winding streets and hidden alleys, but the channel cut by the undead's siege weapon made for a convenient thoroughfare up the middle of the Base. Gorm and Jynn made their way north, flanked by a couple squadrons of Dwarves and Shadowkin. They encountered little resistance at first, but after a few blocks Gorm could see ranks of zombies and skeletons forming up in the channel ahead.

"They're going to make a stand!" shouted Jynn.

"If'n they want a second funeral, who are we to deny 'em?" said Gorm.

The vanguard of Dwarves and Orcs slammed into the zombies at the front of the undead formation, and at first the heroes of the Old Kingdom pressed forward with typical ferocity. Their progress slowed to a halt, however, as the crowd of skeletons behind the zombies began to rise up like a wave ready to crash over the fight.

"I think this is one of them Skull-taker things!" Gorm shouted at Jynn.

Now it was clear that the bones weren't a crowd of skeletons at all, but instead one sinister construct. It rose to its full height with the jerking, stilted movements of a golem, but instead of wood or metal, it had been constructed entirely from an intricate lattice of bones and ribs. Each of its four arms ended in a long, scythe-like blade of fused bone. Its head was fashioned from a cluster of Human and animal skulls, all of which chattered menacingly as the abomination stared down at the fighters below it.

"A what?" shouted Jynn.

"A Skull-taker!" shouted Gorm. "Remember? Your father had one at the Tower of Ashes. I told ye Thane killed it."

Jynn's brow furrowed. "I thought he called it a Rib-taker. Fleshmonger. Corpsethresher? Something garish like that."

A bestial roar chorused from the monstrosity's collection of grotesque faces.

"Who cares what it's bloody called?" snorted Gorm.

Jynn snapped his fingers. "I'm sorry, it's going to drive me crazy."

"It's going to eat ye, that's what it'll do!" roared the Dwarf. "What is it with ye wizards naming everything?"

The great construct took a scything swing at the heroes' front lines, sending Orcs and Dwarves crashing back. The zombies and more traditionally-sized skeletons around its feet swarmed forward, pressing their newfound advantage. Slavering ghouls and howling specters emerged from the ruined buildings around them, springing the trap.

"I know, I know. Corpse-taker?" Jynn tried to calm his panicking horse while rattling off possible names for the bony giant. "Fleshreaper. No, that's it! A Bonereaper! He called it a—oh."

Gorm had given up on the taxonomy of the dead, instead opting to launch a pre-emptive strike on the Bonereaper's knee. Years of professional monster slaying had taught the Dwarf that the trick to fighting any giant creature was to get underfoot without getting caught under its feet. The berserker ducked under one of the abomination's giant claws and deflected another with the back of his shield in a quick maneuver that brought him to a point that was both beneath the great construct's rib cage and out of its reach.

The Bonereaper howled and tried to back up quickly, but Gorm was on the offensive now. He hacked at legs and ribs with reckless abandon, cracking joints and protruding bones with rapid punches from his shield. With a roar and a heave, Gorm launched himself through its weakening frame and into its torso.

Tiny fingers of bone and old teeth clawed at his skin as he bounced around the inner chamber of the construct, but they only spurred him to lash out with more fury. With a final cry of triumph, Gorm chopped off an arm near its unnatural connection to the hellish torso, severed a piece of internal scaffolding, and used the creature's spine as a point of leverage to launch out of the Bonereaper's chest cavity.

A moment later he landed next to Jynn, covered in bone dust and wearing a grin that spread from ear to ear. Behind him, the Bonereaper groaned and stumbled. "And that's how ye do it!"

"I wish that was true," said Jynn, nodding at something behind them.

Gorm turned and watched as the stricken Bonereaper scooped three wailing skeletons into the Dwarf-sized hole in its chest. The joint bones and fingers that made up its innards quickly dismantled the undead troops and passed their various components throughout its wounded body. Broken bones were replaced, skeletal scaffolding was reinforced, and gaps were closed with cadaverous replacements. Moments later, the Bonereaper stood back up again, three new skulls emerging amongst the chittering mass at the construct's center.

"It just took their bones," said Gorm as Dwarves and Shadowkin fell back into formation around them.

"The name may lack subtlety, but it does convey the right idea." Jynn took a step back as the creature gave an unholy howl, only to be drowned out moments later by another cry echoing through the burning city.

There was a buzzing shriek, almost like the air itself was screaming, as a fusion of flame and metal roared through Gorm's field of vision. The bizarre contraption sent a scintillating stream of glass and metal into the ranks of the dead.

An explosion of pale green smoke enveloped the Bonereaper, followed by a more typically fiery explosion. A few skeletal soldiers near the front lines froze solid. A zombie transformed into an undead frog. A pair of undead bannermen were overcome by a suffusion of yellow.

Despite all that, Gorm was more focused on the strange vehicle skidding to a halt on the far side of the makeshift thoroughfare. "Heraldin?" he shouted.

The bard flashed Gorm a grin from astride the back of the iron sleigh he rode, but kept his hands on the mouth of a small velvet satchel. The bag vomited forth a steady shower of glass vials and small charms that exploded, ignited, froze, transformed, shrank, or otherwise afflicted whatever they broke on. Heraldin sprayed the magical knickknacks across the ranks of the undead with devastating effect.

Gorm caught a glimpse of Gaist leaping from behind the bard, a blade in each hand. The doppelganger hit the flanks of the panicked undead and quickly set about a weaponsmaster's work with grim stoicism.

"Ho there, Ingerson!" shouted Boomer, waving from the pilot's seat of the contraption. "We got our jet-steed working, and we thought you might need some Creative Destruction brand consumables!"

"All of them!" added Buster, who clung to the back of the jet-steed.

"I'm out!" yelled Heraldin, holding the bag back. Buster darted forward, tapped two silvery objects together, and dropped them in. The bard closed the bag quickly, aimed again, and loosed another blast of wind and consumables.

"What is that thing?" Gorm shouted as the bard reloaded.

"An extra-dimensional satchel, a set of wind chimes, and every other offensive consumable in our warehouse," said Buster.

"Most expensive weapon you'll ever see!" laughed Boomer.

A chorus of screams rang out from the cloud of emerald and flame that had engulfed the Bonereaper. The massive construct loomed up from the flames, its faces pocked and charred by the corrosive gas. Yet it still raised its scything arms and staggered forward for another attack. Its scythes made short work of the unfortunate Dwarven soldier in front of Gorm.

This renewed assault of the undead monstrosity was the final straw for Jynn's horse. The Elven steed reared to its full height as it turned to bolt, throwing the unfortunate wizard. The omnimancer kicked up clouds of dust as he tumbled across the ground, coming to rest directly in front of the rather incensed Bonereaper. It raised its monstrous arms and leapt for a final strike before Jynn could right himself.

And then Gaist was there, a blur of shadow and steel. The weaponsmaster caught the Bonereaper's foremost arm and sliced it neatly in twain, his enchanted blade leaving a burning nub where a scythe had been. Whirling and striking, the doppelganger then leapt onto the monstrosity. Its many skulls squealed and shrieked as it reared back.

"Incoming!" yelled Heraldin, swiveling the extra-dimensional bag at the cluster of skulls that served as the monster's head.

Gaist kicked away from the Bonereaper just as a spray of glass vials caught it in all of its faces. It gave a horrible, garbled scream as its heads shrunk and grew, petrified and melted, froze and caught fire. Waving its remaining limbs in agony, the construct lost its balance and pitched over backward into the pooled remnants and byproducts of the magical oils and potions.

Cheers erupted from the army of the Old Kingdoms when the abomination fell, and they charged forward once more as the Bonereaper's horrible screaming faded. Swirling clouds of colorful gas rose from the putrid pool as the magical byproduct dissolved, burned, transmuted, and otherwise broke down the pile of inert bones.

"Ye all right, lad?" Gorm asked, helping Jynn to his feet.

Jynn nodded impatiently. "Yes, but you should be worried about—"

"Gaist!" cried Heraldin. The bard leapt from the jet-steed and dashed to the spot where the weaponsmaster crouched, still clutching his side. Gorm and Jynn arrived just as Gaist slumped over, a dark dampness spreading from his wounds.

"Salve!" Heraldin yelled, propping the doppelganger up. "We need elixir! Now!"

"Pull up his armor," said Jynn, skidding into the dirt beside the stricken weaponsmaster. Faint threads of solamancy danced around the fingers of his black-gloved hand. "I need to see the wound if I'm to treat it."

The wizard reached over the stricken fighter's wound as Heraldin moved to unbuckle the armor, but Gaist reached up with sudden determination and grabbed the wizard's gauntleted hand in his own fist.

"What are you doing?" Heraldin demanded. "Let the man weave a spell."

"I need this hand to heal you," Jynn said, looking the weaponsmaster in the eye. "I cannot weave water from my other arm."

Gaist only returned the stare, squeezing Jynn's gauntlet so hard the leather crumpled and buckled around his fist. Gorm thought it a marvel that the wizard didn't cry out.

After a moment, the weaponsmaster broke the gaze and stared up at Heraldin, laboring to take each breath.

"No, my friend," said Heraldin. "I see what you are thinking, and I'm saying no."

Gaist stared at him, unblinking.

"I won't!" shouted the bard. "It's senseless! I don't care how perfect the moment is!"

"What are they arguing about?" Gorm asked Jynn.

"Are they arguing?" the wizard asked. "Is that what this is?"

"Fine," the bard hissed through clenched teeth. He turned to Jynn and Gorm and spoke in the measured cadence of a messenger who loathes the message. "You two need to go on."

Jynn shook his head. "But I can—"

"You can't waste magic and time healing." Heraldin's face was set in determination. "We came and fought and bled so that you could confront your father. All that matters is that you reach Detarr, Jynn. That is what is most important."

Gaist nodded.

Gorm shook his head. "But—"

"All that matters," Heraldin repeated loudly, "is that you reach the liche. But if you and Gorm can make it on your own, if you can go the rest of the way without me, then I can get our friend here back to the healers' tent and see to his wounds. Can you reach the liche without me?"

Gaist reached up with his bloody gauntlet and grabbed weakly at the bard's wrist.

Heraldin ignored the doppelganger's protest. "Can you make it?" he said again.

Gorm took a deep breath. Amid the chaos of the battlefield, a tiny fire flickered a little brighter at his core. "Aye," he said. "I can get him there."

"Good." The bard grabbed the weaponsmaster's arm and slung it over his shoulder. "You see, my friend? They will be fine. Let's get you back to the healers' tent."

Gaist didn't look happy with the decision, but he didn't look strong enough to offer much in the way of protest either.

"Stop pouting," said the bard. "It was a valiant stand! It doesn't have to be your last one."

"Come on, Jynn." Gorm put his hand on the wizard's shoulder. "Let's go."

"Yes, hurry," said Heraldin, helping Gaist to his feet. "And kill a few extra of those ugly rotters for us, will you?"

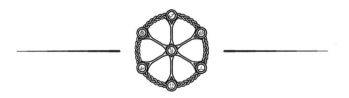

"Well, that's hurtful," said the skeleton with a club.

"We prefer the term 'differently-existing,'" said the skeleton with a spear, with more than a little reproach in her hollow voice.

Feista Hrurk tried to back farther up, but a wall was behind her, and the pair of skeletons in front of her blocked the only exit from the small alleyway. She clutched little Rex closer and bared her fangs. "I don't see much difference, undead monsters," she snarled.

"You'll get it soon enough," said the spear-wielder.

Her partner raised his club. "Once you've walked a mile in our shoes. Metaphorically."

The ill-fitting metaphor, however, was the last sentence the skeleton ever spoke. The undead stopped in place, weapons raised, frozen like the bizarre experiment of a mad taxidermist. Aubren and Mrs. Hrurk exchanged a quizzical glance before violent tremors overtook the bony assailants, flinging ribs and bones in all directions. Within moments, whatever dark force animated the corpses had left them, and they collapsed into a pile.

As Mrs. Hrurk watched, two orbs of crimson light rose from the inert skulls and retreated back into the waiting hand of a dark figure hobbling down the alley. He was doubled over from the weight of the chainmail he wore over his midnight robes, and a silver beard spilled out from the base of his dark, skull-faced helmet. In one hand he dragged a brutal-looking cudgel, and the two red lights swirled about his other like drunken fireflies.

"Two more!" the dark warrior laughed, watching intently as the wisps in his hand winked out. "Two more for the master. And here, three more..." He turned his horrible gaze on Mrs. Hrurk and Aubren. Feista held little Rex closer and cowered back against Aubren's legs.

The warrior's scrutiny lasted only for a moment. "Nope! Not time. Yet." The dark warrior added the last word with a small laugh and retreated out of the alleyway.

"Was that a... priest?" Aubren asked.

"It was a lucky break, that's what it was," said Mrs. Hrurk, checking on her son.

Aubren stared after the armored figure. "It's just that he had robes and a holy symbol, but I've never seen a priest of Mordo Ogg do that sort of thing."

"And we likely won't see it again, so let's get out of here before more undead come. Let's go!" barked Feista.

They dodged packs of zombies and the odd ghoul as they ran, taking shelter under awnings to avoid the notice of low-flying ghosts. They finally found their way to Mycen Avenue, then made it to the edge of Sculpin Down, moving toward the old gate that led to the third tier.

They were halfway across the tier when they saw a group of Humans and Gnomes running toward them, back toward the Base. "No! Hey! Make for the upper tier!" hollered Feista, pointing back over the approaching mobs' heads.

"Run!" shouted an oncoming Human.

"Zombie bankers!" screamed a Gnome.

Feista's heart leapt. Behind the oncoming mob, a grotesque, ursine form rose up and let out a gurgling roar. She recognized the risen corpse of Mr. Stearn, frozen forever in his werebear form. On either side of him, a pair of undead Naga moved in a strange, shambling slither—the Lamia sisters, no doubt. They were surrounded by a pack of zombies in fine suits; the broken remains of the clerks and accountants who had gone over the Wall.

"That's right! Zombie bankers!" A flaming skull floated along beside the ghastly businessmen, howling like a hellish carnival barker. "Which is more terrifying: their eternal hunger for the flesh of the living? Or their reckless fiscal irresponsibility? No, seriously. Your input is valuable!"

"Go!" Mrs. Hrurk yelled to Aubren, joining the fleeing crowd. Rex shifted and moaned in her arms. They ran back toward the gate down to the Base, where they stopped short.

Another mob of zombies and ghouls shambled toward them on the second tier, led by a skeletal warrior in black, warped armor.

"Go back!" shrieked Aubren.

"We can't!" shouted a desperate Tinderkin from the rear. Behind them, Feista could see the crowd of zombie bankers lurching down the road. She felt panic rising as she searched for some escape, but the nearby alleys and side streets were blocked by rubble and debris. Between the two groups of approaching undead there was nothing but stone walls and a cluster of terrified civilians.

"Mrs. Hrurk," said Aubren, taking her paw.

"I know, child." The Gnoll gave the girl's hand a long squeeze.

"They're right behind us." Jynn looked over his shoulder as he and Gorm ran up the dirt path recently plowed up the Base. He couldn't see much in the ash-choked streets, but he didn't like what he saw. There were too many bodies in his field of vision, and too many of them were ambulatory, and way too many had broken away from fighting with the Shadowkin and Dwarves to give chase.

"All that matters is that ye reach the liche," breathed Gorm, pumping his stout legs to keep pace. The Dwarf banged his axe on his shield as if to emphasize the point.

"Well, yes," breathed Jynn. "That's why I'm concerned about the—argh!"

A Halfling-turned-ghoul leapt from the gutters of a ruined building, claws outstretched and maw dripping green ooze. Jynn didn't have time to weave a spell. Yet he didn't need to.

Calmly, almost lazily, Gorm dismembered the airborne undead with a few strokes of his axe. The Dwarf didn't even seem to break stride; one moment he was on Jynn's left, and the next he was on the right, banging his axe on his shield as ghastly bits rained down around them.

"Thanks," said Jynn.

"All that matters is that ye reach the liche."

"So you've said." Jynn cast a sidelong glance at the Dwarf. "Look, we're almost there."

Now that they were approaching Fafnir's Gate, Jynn could begin to grasp the magnitude of the stone that had shattered Andarun's gates.

Even lying on its side, the pillar was taller than the gatehouse of Fafnir's Gate had been before it was reduced to the scattered rubble before him. Great grooves were carved into the stone, a huge design that covered the entirety of the projectile. The wizard recognized several runes of noctomancy amid the patterns, though they were on a much larger scale than he had ever encountered before.

A groan from behind them drew Jynn's attention away from the massive runes. Dark figures were shambling from the haze around them.

"The undead are almost upon us. Why are you laughing?" Jynn looked irritably at the Dwarf.

"All... all that matters... all that matters," cackled Gorm, his eyes wide and his teeth flashing amidst the tangle of his beard.

It occurred to Jynn that the banging of the Dwarf's axe on his shield had adopted a particular rhythm, while the tenor of his voice had lost a certain presence. Veins stood out on Gorm's arms and forehead, and his skin had become almost as red as the fiery beard from which he had once derived his professional name.

"This is that berserk, Pyrebeard thing you do, isn't it?" said Jynn.

Yet Gorm was only listening to a singular refrain from somewhere deep within. "All that matters is that ye reach the liche!" he shouted, and then he was gone.

Jynn blinked at the cloud of dust where the berserker had stood. The screams of nearby zombies snapped his attention back to the present, but by the time he looked up, the nearest undead were already re-dead. Somewhere in the gloom beyond the slumping corpses, more zombies and ghouls shrieked in terror amidst the horrible, rattling laugh of Gorm unleashed.

"Yes, well it also matters that we defeat the liche!" Jynn shouted after the Dwarf.

The mad cackling was growing more distant. Ghosts and specters floated high overhead.

"I'll just... I'll get s-started m-m-myself then," said Jynn. Fear and self-loathing welled up inside him as he looked at the heights above, where his father flew in the height of his power. Staring at the flashes of necromantic magic crackling through the purple haze, all of his planning and preparation seemed woefully inadequate. It took the entirety of his will to cram the swirling terror and doubt into a tiny box and stuff it in the back corner of his mind.

With a deep breath and trembling hands, Jynn began to climb.

Kaitha exhaled and steadied her hands. She kept her eyes on the blaze in front of her, burning like a pyre in the middle of the ruined outer wall.

Laruna grunted from the ramparts behind the Elf. "Do you think we got—"

Lady Carabae burst from the flames with an inhuman wail, flying toward the two heroes with claws outstretched. Kaitha caught the flash of her eye and fired; there wasn't time for another chance. The vampire veered to dodge the incoming projectile, and a subsequent blast of fire from Laruna drove the creature below the ramparts.

"Do you think we got her?" Laruna asked again, stepping back to back with the ranger.

"No." Kaitha nocked another arrow, watching the ghastly forms circling above them. Ghosts and specters had swarmed to the fight, and vampires lurked among the glowing souls like sharks amid a school of fish. "The thralls are still alive. Or... moving. Whatever."

"I get it," muttered Laruna. "So, they'll all die when we kill her?"

"Yeah, but it'll work faster if we do it the other way around," said Kaitha softly. She loosed the arrow, but it fell well short of the vampire she'd aimed at. "Every one we kill makes her a little weaker. If we kill enough, she can't keep those defenses up."

"We have to kill them all?" Laruna whispered incredulously.

"No, just enough to get her guard down." Kaitha fired another arrow. It fell out of the air long before it reached a thrall. "If we can get her to make a mistake when she's weakened, I can land a shot."

"But she has a thousand of them!" hissed the solamancer. "We've taken out, what, ten? Maybe a dozen? We could have hundreds to go."

"She doesn't have a thousand thralls," said Kaitha dismissively.

One of the vampires, lulled into overconfidence by the short shots, drifted a little closer to the pair of heroes. Kaitha blasted it to oblivion with a bolt of silver.

"And now she's got one less," added the ranger.

Laruna shook her head. "A thousand. That's what she said."

"That's creative exaggeration," said Kaitha. "You know, building a brand. Remember Lorgrim the Devourer of Skulls? A nasty old warlord, no doubt, but he started every morning with a bowl of oat bran and went the whole of every day without having a single bone in his diet. It was just image."

"Yeah, but that's a title," countered Laruna. She loosed a ball of fire that incinerated a ghost swooping in for an attack. "A thousand thralls is a specific claim. You have to back those up."

"She's a villain! She's not going to go to court for false advertising." Kaitha watched as the remaining thralls scattered and dropped down into the shadows. "Besides, 'Mistress of a Couple Dozen Thralls' doesn't exactly sound impressive."

"Well, however many there are, they're plotting something." Laruna shifted her weight.

"Yeah," agreed Kaitha. She scanned the ramparts, watching for the next attack.

They didn't have to wait long. At the far end of the ramparts, several dark figures swirled into a cloudy mass and rushed toward the heroes in a sudden charge.

"They're protecting her!" Kaitha said, picking off a thrall. She downed another quickly, and a third, but the shadowy ball was approaching faster than she could fire.

Laruna added her own flames to the assault. The vampires slowed and wavered under the women's onslaught.

"It's working!" Laruna shouted.

"Careful!" Kaitha warned her. "Vampires are really—"

The Elf was mid-sentence when Lady Carabae leapt up from beneath the ramparts directly next to the Elf and mage.

"Clever," Kaitha gasped.

The moment lasted a tiny eternity. Kaitha watched the vampire's fangs flash in a triumphant grin as her ruse brought her to the heroes' flank. The Elf swiveled her bow, but it was slow—far too slow to hit the mark. Laruna was turning too, but she couldn't weave fast enough, and Lady Carabae was already diving forward, claws ready for the kill.

Then a rock hit her.

It was the sort of large block of rough granite used in laying foundations, unremarkable save for its trajectory. It caught the vampire in the side, snapping bones and twisting wings. Lady Carabae gave a pained squeal and took a moment to find her bearings.

A moment was all Kaitha and Laruna needed. Three arrows and an incinerating beam of fire and light slammed into the dazed vampiress in quick succession. As her ashes drifted down toward the street, the surrounding thralls began to disintegrate with horrid wails.

Kaitha wasn't paying them any mind. She ran to the edge of the ramparts, staring at the muddy, trampled earth outside the outer walls. Her eyes scanned every pile of stones, searching for some sign of life.

"Hello?" she yelled, straining to raise her voice above the death cries of the fading thralls. "Thane? Are you there?"

But now another scream was drowning the ranger out, a high-pitched whine cutting through the air. On the edge of her hearing she could make out Heraldin shouting and Laruna hollering back. Kaitha remained focused on the stones just on the other side of the outer wall.

A hand gripped her shoulder. "Kaitha!" Laruna said. "Come on! We need to go!"

"It was him!" The Elf shook her head. "Thane's out there! He threw the rock."

"Kaitha, look!" The solamancer pointed up. High above them, a specter flew over the edge of the Wall, dislodging one of the stones from its ramparts. The brick soared out across the road and demolished, with fated accuracy, an abandoned fruit cart.

"No." Kaitha shook her head. "No. The rock that hit the vampire wasn't falling. It… I thought it came from… I don't think it was falling."

"Maybe," said Laruna. "I don't know. I was looking at the vampire. But I do know that Heraldin is down below, and Gaist is wounded. And Jynn has gone on to fight his father."

"But Gorm's with him," said Kaitha.

"Heraldin thinks he's gone berserk," said Laruna. "So, he may be with the wizard."

Somewhere in the distance, a mad cackling echoed above the fray.

"But maybe not," said Laruna.

Kaitha's breath caught in her throat. "So Jynn is fighting the liche alone?"

"You cannot be serious." Detarr Ur'Mayan sighed as he held his flaming face in the palm of his skeletal hand.

"I... I am, F-Father," Jynn said to the liche's back. The wizard struggled to clamber from the ruins of Fafnir's Gate onto the top of the huge stone that had ruined it. "I-I've come to stop you."

"Of course you have," said Detarr, looking at the sky. "It's practically a guarantee that you'll show up to interfere with any plan I have. Why should my greatest triumph be any different?" The liche waved a hand at the crumpled form of Johan the Mighty on the corner of the spire.

The King of Andarun was unrecognizable save for the bits and pieces of his distinctive armor still hanging from his battered frame. Barbed hooks of shadow protruded from every inch of his skin, drawing up great, swollen, purplish-black welts and pustules wherever they touched. He used his sword like a crutch as he kneeled, breathing heavily. Two bloodshot eyes watched Detarr warily from the mass of black boils that had once been his face.

Jynn struggled to find his voice. "Y-you've committed cr-crimes against all the people of A-arth."

"You have no idea what I've done, what you're interfering with. You're just cluelessly — *what are you doing?*" The liche finally turned to face his son, and his snarl became a surprised shriek. "How dare you sully the Ur'Mayan name with an... an omnimancer's robes?"

Jynn's heart fell into his stomach. The inner defenses he'd spent decades fostering melted at the sound of his father's voice. Embarrassment and fear welled up within him.

His mouth was dry and wouldn't form words. "I... I..."

"You what?" said the liche, his voice laden with exasperation. "You've managed to somehow find your way back to Andarun, make your way past my army, climb atop the Dark Spire of Nephan, and now you can't even form a simple sentence to explain… this?" Detarr waved at the offending robes again.

"I… Y-y-you…"

Detarr made a sighing noise again. "Why is it that the only thing you're good at is ruining—"

The liche was interrupted by a scraping, clanging noise. Father and son turned to see Johan drop from the spire and scuttle off into the shadows.

"Oh, for the gods' sake!" Detarr turned back to Jynn. "Now look what you've done! It will take hours to track him down! Longer still to get him in that state again."

Jynn grit his teeth and shook his head. It was like every box had fallen from the shelves in his mind, and the swirling memories and emotions threatened to overwhelm him. Visions of his childhood kept bubbling into consciousness whenever he tried to speak.

"First you ruin my plans at the Ashen Tower, then I have to miss my victory at Highwatch dealing with you, and now you've ruined my plans here, and that's not even the worst of it. An omnimancer! Honestly!" the liche fumed to himself. "It usually goes without saying, but I am very disappointed in you, Jynn!"

Some part of Jynn screamed that he should be weaving, but the rest of him was sliding down well-worn grooves in the depths of his mind, slumping back into old habits and patterns at rock bottom. "I… I-I know."

"Still, I blame myself. I've probably done something to deserve you." The flames surrounding Detarr's skull flared a little brighter. "One way or another, son, I'll get you back in line."

The liche waved the Wyrmwood Staff, sending crackling bolts of black lightning at his son. Jynn's drive for self-preservation momentarily seized control, and he instinctively raised a ward against the incoming spell. A spell woven in haste, however, was no match for the full power of a master of undeath. The dark magic forced its way through Jynn's defenses and found its mark.

Chapter 31

"Good kill, sir!" exclaimed Ted.

Ned pointed a talon down at the twitching body. "I don't suppose you're going to eat that?"

Knight-Commander Tyren Ur'Thos ignored the zombie and ghoul as he stepped over the prone man. The rest of the civilians fled from him, and dark magics compelled him to pursue.

"He's not going to even dignify that with a response, Ned," said Ted. "Our knight-commander is focused on the mission at hand, as we should all be."

"Which is odd, given his recent hesitance to take part in the siege," Ned said, shuffling along to join the pack of walking dead.

"A momentary lapse," said the zombie. "Clearly. The knight-commander has been nothing if not motivated of late."

"Quiet as well," said the ghoul.

In the confines of his own mind, Tyren screamed a litany of curses at the pair of idiots.

The civilians ahead had stopped, cornered by another squadron of the undead. Tyren pressed in. He felt his blade raise for the kill. His eyes fell upon his victim, a tiny Gnollish woman holding a young pup. His arm was at its zenith when a Human girl pushed the Gnoll away and stepped in the path of the blade, staring up at the knight-commander with bravery and defiance on her face—

Her face!

From the haunted corners of his memory, Tyren saw the same rebellion in the brown eyes of a toddler claiming she'd not go to bed for the night. He heard her laugh as she bounced on his knee, helped her wipe away tears as he cleaned the scrape on her elbow, marveled at the radiance of her smile as she bit into her first tea cake, held her close as they watched fireflies dance in the garden at Vetchell. Her cheeks were thinner now, her features those of a woman rather than a babe, but there was no mistaking his daughter's face.

Somewhere beyond consciousness, something snapped. Power surged through Tyren, flooding into him from unknown depths and melting away bonds and barriers alike. It broke from his throat in a singular, anguished scream. "Stop!" he roared in a voice like that of death itself.

To his surprise, he did. His blade halted inches from little Aubey's face. The other undead froze as well, locked in place. Black scorch marks spread from beneath the knight-commander's feet, creeping over the pavers and up the walls like a rapid mold.

For a long moment, father and daughter stared at each other from opposite sides of Tyren's unholy sword.

"Au... Aubey," Tyren managed to croak. Wherever his newfound strength came from, it wasn't sufficient to give him complete control of his own body. He was caught between his own will and that of the Crown of Iron Thorns, unwilling to strike and unable to sheathe his blade.

"How... How do you know my name?" The girl's face was a mask of horror. "What are you?"

Tyren couldn't answer.

"Perhaps I can help, miss," said Ted, prompting alarmed stares from the assembled civilians. "The knight-commander's exact nature has been a matter of some debate among us, you see. But with his newfound ability to control the rest of us, the black flames he's throwing off, and the new glow in his eyes—"

"Not to mention the foul magic oozing from his armor," added Ned.

"I tried not to mention that, yes," said Ted. "Embarrassing. Regardless, I think it's safe to say now that Knight-Commander Ur'Thos is a death knight."

"Ur'Thos?" breathed Aubey. Tyren saw recognition and pain in her eyes, and it felt like a stab in the heart he didn't have anymore.

"We probably should have known as much," said Ted. "All the classic signs of a death knight origination story are there. He had all those family issues a few years back when Lady Ur'Thos left him for that bard."

"Certainly some unresolved grievances there," agreed Ned. "And then the public fall from grace when he was demoted to head of the guardhouse."

"Right. And again when he was put in charge of Vetchell's defense," said Ted. "Which brings us to the dereliction of duty leading to an untimely death."

"Oh, that's the key bit," said Ned.

"You're my father," breathed Aubey, looking into the flaming sockets where Tyren's eyes used to be.

Slowly, laboriously, the knight-commander nodded.

"Another important detail," said Ted.

"And... and now you're saving us?" asked Aubey.

"Well, let's not be hasty," said Ned. "The knight-commander's sudden burst of willpower might delay the inevitable, but the curse of undeath still drives us all to eat you."

"I don't want to eat anyone," offered Rudge from somewhere in the back.

"Nobody cares, Rudge!" snapped the ghoul.

"I know..." said Rudge.

"No, no," said the Gnoll. "I like where the skeleton is going with this."

"What we want is beside the point, really," said Ted. "It's only a matter of time before the liche re-exerts his will, and then Commander Ur'Thos won't have any more choice in the matter than the rest of us. We'll be compelled to kill you all. "

"But we won't be allowed to eat anyone, if that's a consolation." Ned sighed. "So nobody wins, really."

"Well, some of us lose by a much bigger margin!" snapped the Gnoll.

Tyren could already feel his grip slipping. The blade inched closer to Aubey.

"Still, it's impressive that our knight-commander has held out against a liche's will this long," said Ted.

"Perhaps the master is distracted," suggested Ned.

"I just can't concentrate when you slouch like that." Detarr paused his weaving, wisps of Shadowflame and noctomancy still suspended around his fingers and staff. "You know how bothersome I find it."

Jynn Ur'Mayan could barely lift his head to look at the liche. His vision was blurring, and he clutched his side with his gloved hand to staunch the flow of blood. "W-what?"

"It makes you look like a feeble street urchin," the liche said. "Stand up straight."

Jynn stared at the specks of light where his father's eyes had once been, drawing deep and ragged breaths. "I-I'm dying and you want me to think about my posture," he said levelly.

Detarr nodded. "It's a major milestone in your existence."

"I… I can't even die well en-enough for you." The omnimancer shook his head. Memories sloshed around in his mind, recollections of his father telling him to stand up in classes, at events, during dinner, at Mother's funeral. An echoing chorus of a father reminding a son how stupid, how foolish, how weak, how poor he looked whenever he didn't sit the right way. A thousand voices chorusing about his posture, fusing into a single line that ran through the chaos in his mind. And at the end of it, a feeling that had always been there, locked away.

"You could if you stood up straight! There, like that, yes," said Detarr. "Appearances matter at times like this."

"You are literally in the process of killing me, and you're giving me a lecture on my bearing." Jynn's voice was as flat and even as a frozen lake. The emotions went farther down than the memories, to depths he didn't know he had. Reserves he never knew existed.

"I'm not lecturing you. I'm just saying that I stood up straight when I died," said Detarr. "You could have asked Johan if you hadn't helped him escape."

In that moment, however, Jynn didn't really hear his father. "How?" he said, channeling water through his gloved hand. The wounds on his side closed as he straightened up. "How can this be the most important thing right now? How has it ever been the most important thing?"

Detarr rolled the pinpoints of light in his eye sockets. "Look, I only said that appearances matter—"

"No! They don't!" Jynn was shouting, solamancy and noctomancy wreathing his hands. "If you cared how we look, you wouldn't be trying to raze the biggest city on Arth right now! This isn't about how you look! This is about you holding me back!"

The liche's lower jaw swiveled down, his skull agape. "How dare you?" he hissed, weaving his dark spell once more. A blast of black tentacles burst from Detarr's skeletal fingers, reaching toward Jynn. "After all I've done for you?"

"Done for me?" snapped Jynn. He attempted to catch the spell in a web of omnimancy, but his father's weaves were stronger than anything the wizard could manage, and he was forced to dodge away from the blast. He grunted in pain as the spell raked across his back. "You pushed me beyond my limits and then punished me for failure! You locked me away from the world and then degraded me for not having social skills! You ridiculed me as weak when it was you keeping me from my true power!"

"Your true power? Omnimancy? Yes, I kept you from shaming yourself out of a career." The violet flames around Detarr's skull grew into a towering inferno roiling over his black crown. "Gods, I make one remark on your stature and you lose your mind, boy!"

"It wasn't one comment! It's everything you've ever said! It's all part of a larger pattern." Jynn's screams dropped to an awed whisper as he saw the truth of his own words. "It's part of a larger pattern," he said again, glancing down.

The interlocking grooves etched into the stone beneath his feet didn't just have a few noctomancer's runes; every line was part of runes drawn into the strata of stone and earth. The spaces between the great sigils of noctomancy were runes of solamancy. When arranged together in interlocking tessellation, they formed a third type of rune that Jynn had only encountered in the libraries of the Fane Amada: runes of the Twilight Order.

The Dark Spire of Nephan was an omnimancer's artifact.

"Oh, and I suppose I'm the bad guy in all of this?" said the liche.

"Yes! How is that even a question?" Jynn twisted threads of light and shadow around himself. There wouldn't be a second chance. "You could have supported me! You could have helped me instead of punishing me. Mother never cared that I was an omnimancer, but once she was gone, you kept me from weaving solamancy! You knew that was all I had of her!"

"You leave your mother out of this! You—" Detarr shook his head and leveled the Wyrmwood Staff at Jynn. "You never appreciated what I gave you. You'll understand soon enough."

There was a noise like a bumblebee shattering the sound barrier, and then the crystal on the end of the staff flared with pale green light. A shockwave rippled through the air, and behind it a wave of emerald sorcery rolled from the tip of the staff. The noxious plasma flowed toward Jynn like an elemental battering ram; ponderous and unstoppable.

The omnimancer feigned as though he would raise a ward, but at the last moment he slammed his weave into the runes of the Dark Spire of Nephan. Scintillating colors ran over the stones, running through ancient runes like water through canals. Light and shadow flickered as the air above the runes began to distort the view of the burning city around them.

Jynn could feel the matrix of omnimancy rising up, could sense it responding to the weaves. He twisted his fingers, tugging at the web as a puppeteer might maneuver a marionette. The threads of noctomancy and solamancy tugged and pushed on each other, pulling and repelling and reshaping magic in their proximity. Detarr's oncoming spell was refracted through the fractal lenses of omnimancy. Threads of noxious energy flowed in every direction, spilling through the Dark Spire's magical field like water through a sieve before bending back around themselves.

"And what exactly is that supposed to be doing?" snarled Detarr.

Jynn wasn't entirely sure there was a term for it, but his hands moved with a certainty brought by years of spellcasting. Deftly twisting his fingers, he conjured weaves in helix patterns to adjust the polarity of the magical network. With some simple adjustments, he re-wove the liche's spell into something new, a crude lance of lightning that the omnimancer fired back at his father.

Detarr raised a ward of shadow that easily deflected the bolt. "Was that supposed to impress me?" he snarled.

"No," said Jynn. "It's not all about you." He extended his hand and held it open expectantly.

"What do you—gah!" Detarr shrieked as the Wyrmwood Staff lurched from his grasp and floated across the gulf toward his son. "No! For once, stop flailing about in ignorance and listen to me! You still don't comprehend what you're tampering with, you fool! Why must you always meddle and never think things through?"

"That's not who I am," said Jynn, reaching out. The staff landed lightly in his palm, pulsing with unexpected warmth as he gripped it. A tingling sensation washed over him, and as it did so his magically attuned robes shifted again.

Layered silks and fine embroidery sprouted among the ratty folds of his omnimancer's robes. Tattered edges mended and grew emerald buttons. A long, white mantle grew from the shoulders, cascading down over the intricate pattern surging through the fabrics. Power and light wreathed Jynn as his robes acknowledged what no wizard could deny; with the Wyrmwood Staff in hand, Jynn was an Archmage of the Order of Twilight.

The liche stopped to study his son's new attire. "Perhaps," he said. "You may have come farther than I expected of you, but let's be honest. That's not difficult." He punctuated the declaration with a burst of dark magic as wings of shadow and malice erupted from his back. The liche's foul sorcery crashed onto the Dark Spire of Nephan, overwhelming and collapsing the magical matrix as the dark spell rushed toward the omnimancer.

Jynn studied the incoming spell without concern. With the power of the Wyrmwood Staff thrumming through his veins, the tide of sorcery seemed to drift lazily toward him, like leaves on the breeze. "Basic," he said, erecting a shield.

His polarized ward absorbed Detarr's spell and sent it back at the liche in a ball of lightning. The liche dodged and fired off another volley. Father and son darted and ran, wove spells and erected wards, spiraling around each other in deadly sport.

Jynn loosed a particularly powerful bolt of fire and lightning when something passed within inches of his face, forcing him to duck. He got a protective spell up just as the banshee's wail washed over him. The world went wobbly as the ear-splitting keen rattled Jynn's head. A moment later, a violet comet slammed into his back, sending him sprawling.

"I tried to make this easy for you," said Detarr, floating a little closer to his son. "I would have raised you as something nice, something powerful. We could have ruled Arth together as father and son."

Jynn pushed himself to his knees and took a deep breath. Gripping the Wyrmwood Staff in both hands, he drew fully from its power. Thick cords of light and shadow whipped around him, vaporizing the banshee and several other specters. Electricity buzzed in his teeth. A great wind rushed up from the ground beneath him, blowing away the smoke and ash in the air. The black leather glove he wore on his left hand burned away.

"I never wanted that." Jynn stood, or rather, rose to a more vertical position, carried by the wind and magic that wreathed him. "I never wanted any of that."

"Nobody wanted it!" snarled the liche. "Nobody said this was ideal! But if we want to continue on, sacrifices must be made for power. You know it's true!"

"I wouldn't make the sacrifices you have!" Jynn said. "Necromancy? Demonology? I'd never stoop to the evils you have, Father. I'm nothing like you."

"Oh? And what have you done to yourself there?" The liche pointed at Jynn's left hand. Or rather, what was left of it.

Jynn glanced down at the appendage. Using solamancy after decades of attunement to noctomancy had stripped the flesh from his frame. The bones of his forearm protruded from a blackened stump, and they ended in a skeletal hand animated by Jynn's noctomancy alone.

The omnimancer flexed his dead fingers, sending threads of fire dancing around the staff they gripped. "I guess I am like you in some ways," he said, pointing the staff at his father. "Just not the ones that matter."

A white beam of fire and lightning erupted from the tip of the staff. Detarr erected a quick ward, but Jynn's spell punched through it as though it had never existed. The liche's right arm disintegrated the instant the spell touched it. Half of his pelvis and one of his legs were sheared off as he tried to jerk away from the fiery light. The ray of brilliant energy continued through the second tier, punching through walls and carving holes in rooftops until it eventually seared into the laboratory of Creative Destruction Inc., where it completely vaporized an unfortunate Viscous Rhombohedron.

Detarr stumbled back and lifted into the air. What remained of his skeletal body was wracked with spasms as wisps of scintillating light strobed across his dark robes. The black crown on his head was hanging askew, and he gripped it with his remaining hand as he rose. "To me!" he cried.

Spectral figures swirled around the stricken liche. Skeletal and rotting soldiers clambered up the ruined gatehouse. Jynn incinerated the nearest zombies with a simple weave, but more were already flanking him and Detarr was floating away toward the outer gates. A wall of corpses and spirits pressed in toward the omnimancer, obscuring his father.

"This isn't over, Father!" Jynn hollered at the retreating liche, though he wasn't entirely sure that was the case. The Wyrmwood Staff's energies were reaching their limit, and the omnimancer was as close to running out of magic as his father seemed to be. Yet Detarr didn't have a swarm of enemies bearing down on him.

The lead specter in the mob of spirits broke away and swooped at the wizard, arms outstretched. Its face contorted into a leering scream, and then contorted farther still as a silver arrow bored through its translucent body. By the time the ghostly fighter had evaporated, a cloud of green smoke had enveloped the zombies and skeletons behind it.

Jynn grinned. "It took you long enough," he said to Kaitha as she leapt spryly to the top of Fafnir's Gate.

"Hey, blame the weaponsmaster," said Kaitha, loosing another arrow. "He's the one who got mortally wounded."

"Is he well enough to fight?" Jynn watched Heraldin and Gaist whirl amidst the emerald clouds, lopping heads and limbs off the confused undead within. The weaponsmaster still clutched his side with his off hand.

"Laruna healed him!" shouted Heraldin.

"So… should he be fighting?" Jynn asked.

"He was actually worse before she did," Kaitha added. "That's progress."

A storm of flames surged up from the opposite side of the ruined gatehouse, sending charred corpses flying out over the second tier. A moment later, Laruna climbed into view. "Would you just get going?"

With a nod to the solamancer, Jynn ran to the edge of the Dark Spire. It was a long drop down to the Base below, but Detarr was floating level with the top of the second tier's walls. The one-legged liche wriggled through the smoke and ash like a leech swimming through a murky pond.

"I wasn't at my full power!" Detarr tried to look back at his son, but his awkward flight sent his head twisting and bobbing in odd directions. "If I hadn't been fighting all night, your little tricks wouldn't have been enough to save you!"

Jynn raised the Wyrmwood Staff. "I'm sorry, Father. I really am."

"I don't need your pity!" shrieked the liche. "Stop laughing at me!"

The omnimancer's brow furrowed. "I'm not laughing," he said.

Detarr cocked his head. "Well, someone is—"

The wall of the closest building erupted in a cloud of splinters and bricks as a mad ball of fury burst through it. Most of Detarr Ur'Mayan's physical form exploded in similar fashion as Gorm Ingerson slammed into his side, and what was left of it was dragged away by the trajectory of the airborne Dwarf. The liche's ribcage crunched as Gorm landed atop it. A second later, the Crown of Iron Thorns bounced off the dirt next to him.

Heraldin shook his head in admiration. "He really does know how to make an entrance."

"And an exit as well, I suppose." Kaitha watched Gorm's retreating figure. A fading cackle followed the Dwarf as he rampaged onward to parts unknown.

Jynn ignored the fate of his father's body. The important part was Detarr's head, still hovering in the air with stubborn purple flames flickering around it. With the liche's protective spells all but obliterated and his skeleton removed, a glittering crystal was clearly visible at the base of the floating skull. Thin tendrils of necromancy wove outward from it like searching tentacles.

Detarr noticed his son's attentions. "Jynn... No... You don't understand," he gasped.

"I doubt I ever will," said Jynn, already weaving.

The air shimmered briefly as the omnimancer extended his right hand. Strands of air flowed from him as he reached out to the bottom of Detarr's skull. His skeletal digits wound threads of fire and light around the wind, pushing aside the last wards protecting the liche. Closing his fist, Jynn pulled a long, violet crystal from his father's head.

"No—!" moaned Detarr Ur'Mayan, and then his voice died with the flames surrounding his head. The inert skull hung in the air for a moment, the lights in its sockets flickering out. Then it dropped to the earth below and shattered.

The spell broke like melting snow.

When Tyren first felt the liche's grip weaken, he could move his blade away from Aubey. A short while later, he dropped his weapon to his side and managed to say her name again. Soon the power of the liche faded entirely, but Tyren remained staring at his daughter. Everything around her seemed to fall away.

"You're in control, aren't you?" said Aubey, looking at his black and blasted armor. "Father?"

"Little Aubey," said Tyren.

"Aubren," she corrected. "I mean, nobody's called me Aubey since you passed... well, I thought you were dead."

"Technically correct," offered Ted. He backed away with a rueful shrug as Tyren's gaze fell upon him.

The young woman was clearly trying to avoid looking directly at the zombie. "Right, but... I meant, Mom and Chadwick said—"

"Let's not talk about your mother and Chadwick. We don't have much time," said Tyren. Without the influence of the Crown of Iron Thorns, he could feel the undead all around. Hungry. Fearful. Furious. Barely restrained.

"But... you're saving us, right?" Aubren said.

"Oh, yes, of course. Yes!" Tyren's last affirmation was made with extra force.

Ned closed his mouth and slowly backed away from a panicked man in a cobbler's apron.

"But I cannot stop the other undead for long," the death knight continued. "I need to leave soon if you're to be safe. And I... I just want you to know that... I know now I wasn't the father I should have been. The man I should have been. But I love you, Aubey — Aubren. There wasn't much good in me, but you had the best of it. Always."

Aubren nodded. "Okay."

An awkward silence hung in the air between the skeletal knight and his teenage daughter. "Okay?" he said. "Just okay?"

"I'm sorry. It's just a lot to take in." Aubren gave an apologetic shrug. "I mean, I barely remember you. Up until a few minutes ago, I thought you drank yourself to death."

"Also not entirely inaccurate," suggested Ned, earning a withering glare from the death knight.

"And now you're here, but you know... you're a skeleton in evil-looking armor. And you're with a pack of zombies and a bear monster —"

"A bear monster?" Tyren asked.

"Mr. Stearn, if it pleases you." The crowd parted to reveal the speaker: an undead, ursine creature wearing a predatory grin and the tattered remains of a business suit. "Is nice to meet you."

"This guy's great!" said the Head of Marketing, bobbing into view next to Mr. Stearn. "He's got big ideas, Knight-Commander. Big ideas!"

"Right. And the flying skull that's on fire," said Aubren, giving the Head of Marketing a sideways glance. "And then you show up and you save us and say you always loved me... This sort of thing takes time to, you know, process."

"Right." Tyren tried to take a deep breath with his missing lungs. "Right."

The assembled townsfolk and unliving abominations glanced around and cleared their throats nervously.

"Well, we should probably... you know..." Tyren left the pause hanging in the air, watching Aubren for any sign of interjecting.

"Eat them all?" suggested Ned.

"Leave," growled the death knight. "We should probably leave."

"Sir, this is the largest city on the continent," protested Ted. "You'll not find a better place to invade."

"I don't want to invade anywhere. I don't want to kill anyone. I wish to let people make whatever they want of their lives."

Ned snorted derisively, "Well, that might work for you, sir, but the rest of us are under curses that—"

"We're all cursed," snapped the death knight. "We all suffer. We all still must make our own decisions, and let other people make theirs."

The ghoul scratched his chin thoughtfully. "But if I choose to not let other people make decisions, vis-Ã -vis eating them, how would—"

"You will come with me." Tyren said it with an air of finality, but the speed and coordination with which the surrounding undead all stopped and mechanically turned to follow still surprised him.

"There's that magically-enforced social hierarchy again," muttered Ted.

"But where will we go?" asked Ned.

Tyren thought for a moment. His mind drifted back to summers spent by the freezing, stinking salt bogs, wandering a dusty fortress. Castle Ur'Thos was leagues away from anyone, and his memories from the old family estate were mostly pleasant. "To my ancestral home. On the coastal marshes of the Icegale Sea."

"I like it!" said the Head of Marketing. "Needs some rebranding, but there's a lot to work with! How do you feel about the Dead Tundra? Or the Frozen Wastes? Frostweep Castle? The Icemire of Death?"

Tyren nodded absently, ignoring the proposed trademarks, and turned once more to his daughter. "Farewell, Aubren Ur'Thos. Remember me a little more fondly." Nodding to her, he started to lead the pack of shambling undead down the road.

"Father?"

Tyren turned back to his daughter. She wore a conflicted wince.

"Maybe… maybe I could write you a letter?"

"I'd like that," said Tyren, his skeletal grin more sincere than ever before. Unable to hold back his surging paternal enthusiasm, he added, "You could even visit Castle Ur'Thos!"

Aubren wrung her crimson kerchief as she looked at the slavering, rotting dead surrounding them. "Or write a letter."

"Yes. Right. Of course. A letter would be great." With a final wave to his daughter, Tyren set off down the street.

He could feel the walking dead gathering around him now, could sense them bending to his will as he made his way back toward the main gate. Skeletons and zombies broke away from confused defenders to hobble after him. Ghouls clambered from the shadows to fall in line with the marching throng. Genevieve and a few ghosts drifted down from the sky. In the distance, the Gnomish organ began playing a sad song of retreat of its own accord.

Genevieve flew up beside Tyren. "Where are we going?" she asked.

"To Castle Chillmourne on the Iceblood Coast!" said the Head of Marketing.

"Why? What are we going to do there?" asked Genevieve.

The flaming skull bobbed in a shoulderless shrug. "Beats me. We can figure that out once we have a good name."

"I have some thoughts on the matter," chimed in Mr. Stearn. "What do you know about mortgage backed securities?"

"I have always considered myself a bit of an expert on real estate," said Ted, straightening up a bit. "And finance."

"And everything else," grumbled Ned, rubbing his empty stomach.

"Say what you will, Ned, but I think us undead could make excellent investors." The zombie tapped his rotting skull. "No more emotions, see? Nothing but cold, rational logic."

"Oh yes, absolutely!" said Rudge, eager to be part of the discussion.

"But do you really think we can open a bank?" Genevieve asked Tyren. "I mean, don't we need money?"

"Leave capitalization to Mr. Stearn," said the zombified werebear. His grin somehow looked more menacing than when he was trying to eat the townsfolk.

"Sure, we can do it," said the Head of Marketing. "I'll run marketing, of course, and Genevieve can handle customer service. And the knight-commander can be chairman of the board."

"Does he know much about the business?" asked Ned.

"Probably not, but we still have to do everything he says anyway," said the Head of Marketing.

"Sounds like chairman to me," said Mr. Stearn.

Tyren paid the others' plans no mind. He strode quietly through the ruined streets of Andarun, drawing the undead to him as a lantern brings evening moths. A familiar skeletal torso emerged from a ruined building, and the armless, headless body bobbed along with enthusiasm, rattling the sign nailed to its sternum.

The knight-commander considered the sign for a moment before delivering a couple of swift strokes with his sword. Wooden blocks bearing the words "ABANDON" and "ALL" clattered on the cobblestones, leaving the shaken skeleton with the word "HOPE" nailed to its chest.

"Hardly the time for playing with signs, what with us retreating," grumbled Ned.

"The knight-commander's setting a tone, Ned," said Ted. "It's symbolic."

"It's indulgent and tacky, that's what it is," said the ghoul. "This isn't the time for wordplay."

"Well, they say everybody's allowed just one," said the zombie.

Tyren remained silent. His eyes were to the east, where the rising sun marked his path back to Ruskan, but his thoughts were with the young woman on the second tier and the future that lay ahead of her.

Chapter 32

"So, what happens next?"

Jynn looked up from the violet crystal in his skeletal hand. Laruna leaned against a ruined wall, arms crossed.

"I think we're going to try to find Gorm before the meeting," said the omnimancer.

"They're as much trying to find you," said the solamancer. "Half the city watched you fight your father alone. And the Archmagi of the Academy just saw the return of the Twilight Order. People are already talking, whether you're there or not."

Jynn shrugged. "I needed time to think."

"Fair enough," said Laruna. She walked into the charred ruins where Jynn had found refuge and sat down next to him on the steps. "But I'm most curious about what you'll do with your father's phylactery."

Jynn looked back to the crystal. He could feel the power and heat radiating from it even in his fleshless hand.

It was a matter of some debate whether a liche's crystalline phylactery was created during the transition to undeath, or if it was an ingredient of the dark ritual that prepared a mage for their dark transformation. Presumably liches themselves knew, but they were both naturally reticent to talk about their sole weakness and eager to convert curious researchers into abominable, unliving servants, and so the secret remained hidden from the living.

"I don't know," he said truthfully.

"They'll want you to destroy it," said Laruna.

Jynn nodded. "That makes sense, I suppose." He watched the tiny, muted threads of necromancy curling from the crystal, probing the enchantments and wards that Jynn had woven around it. As long as the phylactery remained whole, it would try to regrow the liche.

"But you don't want to?"

"I don't know if I do," said Jynn. "He was a horrible father, no doubt. But... but I remember he was different with Mother around. And for years after she died, for most of my early memories, it was just me and him against... against the world, really. It'd be one thing to kill him in battle, but now he's helpless. And through the phylactery, I... I can sense his feelings. Sorrow. Anger. Fear. A bit of paternal pride, much to my surprise. And even remorse."

Laruna shook her head and gestured toward the hole in the wall in the ruined square. "None of that changes what he's done here."

"No," agreed Jynn. "Which is why I don't know what I'll do."

"And you'll just keep the soul of a liche in your pocket until you decide?"

"I've plenty of experience handling dangerous and forbidden relics." Jynn smirked. "Father's phylactery would be the third most deadly relic in my study in the Chambers of the Red Hawk. At worst."

"I suppose." Laruna tried to hide the subconscious glance at Jynn's left hand. He flexed the dead appendage and held it up for her to inspect.

"So, you did that when you saved my life," said Laruna.

"Yes."

"And then you hid it from all of us."

Jynn shrugged. "It's my hand, and my business."

Laruna shook her head. "I just don't understand why you would conceal something like that."

"Because I know you, Laruna."

"Me?" The solamancer's brow furrowed. "Did you just assume I'd accuse you of necromancy?"

Jynn sighed. "I knew you'd be angry about my omnimancy, and all the more so that I kept it from you. But I also know that the only thing you hate more than being lied to is being indebted to anyone. If you knew that curing you cost me my hand, you'd feel guilty. And then you'd try to make it up to me by..." He shifted uncomfortably. "By taking me back, I suspect. I didn't want you to be with me, or anyone, because you feel like you have to be. And I won't be anybody's obligation."

The solamancer glared at him. "You don't know everything."

"True enough," said Jynn, looking back to Detarr's phylactery. "But I know that."

"It might have been different," said Laruna.

"Maybe. But probably not."

"I'd still rather you let me decide for myself."

"I knew that, too."

Laruna laughed bitterly to herself as she stood. "Well, be that as it may, thank you for saving me. I owe you my life, and I'm grateful for it. All things considered, you've been a good friend."

"I'd say we were more than friends."

"Yeah, but it doesn't matter what we were. All that matters is what we're trying to be going forward." The solamancer smiled at Jynn, but he could see the sparkle of tears at the corner of her eyes.

Jynn set the pain in his chest into an imaginary box, placed the lump in his throat on top of it, and closed the top. "Agreed," he said with a joyless smile. "You're a good friend as well."

"Yeah," said Laruna. "Come on. Let's go help the others find Gorm."

The first thing that Gorm Ingerson was aware of was the stench of decaying meat wafting over his face in noxious waves. His shut his eyes tighter and covered his nostrils with his hand. A moment later something wet and slimy dragged across his face.

"Gerrofff!" he growled through a mouthful of tongue, pushing a muzzle out of his face.

"Oh, yeah! Good boy!" Kobold paws scrabbled on stone, and now Burt was shouting at someone in the distance. "Hey! Hey, Patches found him!"

Gorm fended Patches' affection off long enough to open one eye and look at the Kobold picking his way through the wreckage. His muscles burned, and his mouth tasted of blood.

"Hey, chum." Burt crouched into view, a limp cigarette clenched in his grin. "Guess how long you've been passed out for."

"Not long enough," grumbled Gorm, clutching his head. The blood was pounding in his ears, exacerbating a skull-rending headache.

"Well, it was at least long enough for the shamans to get the waygate open again," said the Kobold. "Otherwise, we wouldn't have had old Patches here to sniff you out. He's getting pretty good at finding you."

"Lucky me." Gorm tried shoving the affectionate dog away again, but Patches easily switched from kissing his face to licking his hand.

Kaitha stepped into view. "There's the hero. Still sleeping it off?"

"I'd like to be," said Gorm, "I take it Jynn won, then."

"Oh, he won all right," Burt said.

"Thanks in no small part to you decapitating the liche," added Kaitha.

"Really?" Hints of memories flashed through Gorm's consciousness, too fast and fluid to make any sense of. "I don't recall that."

"Well, sounds more like you took his body off and left the head behind from what I hear," said Burt. "But there ain't a word for that, and it's the same effect, more or less."

"You did it right after you jumped through a wall, if that helps," Kaitha offered.

"Which one?" It occurred to Gorm that between drinking and berserking, he'd spent a regrettable portion of his life blacked out. He shook his head. "Wait! Did anybody see it?"

"Almost everyone saw the Old Dwarven Kingdoms' army arrive," said Kaitha.

"Complete with Kobolds, Orcs, Goblins, and every other kind of Shadowkin!" added Burt. "Half the city was out on the tiers watching us save them!"

"So Jynn had quite the audience when he took down Detarr," added Kaitha.

"And the army cleared out the rest of the undead?" Gorm asked.

"Well, they definitely would have," said Burt. "If there had been a fight."

"Most of the remaining dead dropped everything and headed east," said Kaitha with a shrug. "There's an odd lurker here or there, but the guild has issued a few quests to clear them out. Should be all taken care of soon enough."

Gorm couldn't stop his own smile from splitting his face. "So it worked then."

"Of course it worked!" Burt interjected. "Listen."

Gorm perked up. Over the blood pounding in his ears, he could detect a distant roaring with an exuberant quality. "Sounds like leverage to me," he said, jumping up. "Come on! Let's go put it to use."

It was often said that nobody knew how to celebrate like the citizens of Andarun, though perhaps it would be more accurate to say that nobody was better situated to throw a party. The city's many tiers formed an inverted amphitheater. Spectacle attracts an audience, but the opposite is also true; the presence of so many eager eyes in one giant stadium of sorts meant that every civic organization in the city was perpetually prepared to put on some sort of show, play, display, or chorus.

Andarun was one big, festive tinderbox waiting for a spark. And Jynn had lit a fire.

The sky swirled with rainbow smoke and bright red and blue ribbons, punctuated by bursts of brilliant fireworks. Chants and songs occasionally swelled, only to be swallowed up again in a cacophony of cheering. Bannermen and civilians lined the walls of every tier and the top of every roof, waving flags featuring Andarun's seven-pointed star and screaming down at the army of Dwarves and Shadowkin.

King Forder's royal tent provided refuge from the oppressive jubilation. The heavy, velvet canopy had been set up near the ruins of Andarun's main gate, next to the deep trough that the Dark Spire had carved through the city streets. Like any good Dwarven tent, the interior was dark, cool, and as quiet as anywhere could be, given the circumstances.

It might have been a relaxing spot, but by the time Gorm and his party arrived at Forder's encampment, members of Andarun's royal guard were already swarming the square. The soldiers barely had time to usher Gorm and his companions into the tent before a herald followed them in and piped the first few notes of the Freelands' anthem on his trumpet.

At the urging of a couple Dwarves, Gorm hurried to take his place kneeling beside Asherzu and King Forder. The rest of the party took up positions behind them, where Darak, Jorruk, Korgen, and a retinue of Dwarves and Shadowkin waited patiently.

The herald set down his bugle and cleared his throat. "All hail His Majesty, the Lord of the Freedlands, King of Andarun—"

"Ha! There's to be plenty of dull ceremony today without the titles, lad! They know who I am." Johan the Mighty brushed the boy aside as he swept into the tent. The king was clad in his typical suit of golden plate mail, but atypically he wore an ornate helm with glowing runes around the Y shaped opening in its face and eagle wings set atop it.

The nonplussed herald tried to rally. "And Guildmaster Weaver—"

"Nobody cares about Ortson," said Johan, dismissing the servant with a wave of his hand.

"Indeed, sire," muttered the rotund guildmaster as he crept into the tent.

The king planted his mailed fists on his armored hips and puffed out his breastplate as he swept his eyes over the room. "King Forder. Orc. And... Ha! Gorm Ingerson! I should have known!"

"Probably," said Gorm. His lips pulled back into a smile-like shape.

"We welcome you, King Johan," said King Forder. "And I appreciate Your Grace's directness. If I may return the favor, I suggest we get right to our offer."

The Human king looked at his advisers, each of whom attempted and failed to shrug inconspicuously. "What offer?"

The Dwarven king held out a hand, and an attendant gave him a circlet of iron spikes wrought at odd angles. "The Crown of Iron Thorns. It would be best for Arth if it was stored in your Great Vault, and as such, I'm willing to sell it at a heavy discount."

"What sort of offer is that?" Johan snorted. "Why would we even discuss such matters today? This will all be settled at the loot arbitration."

"I imagine it will, Your Majesty," said Korgen. "But seeing as Andarun won't be represented at the loot arbitration, all parties agreed to offer ye the Crown for sixty percent of assessed value."

"What?" Johan's voice dropped to a dangerous whisper.

"Ludicrous!" snarled Ortson, his jowls shaking in fury.

"I won't go below fifty-five percent," said King Forder with a slight smile.

"What makes you think the Freedlands won't be at loot arbitration?" said King Johan.

"Why would they be?" asked Forder with saccharine innocence.

"Dwarven heroes completed a Ruskan quest," said Korgen. "The people of the Freedlands need not concern themselves."

"But you saved our city!" snapped Ortson.

"A collateral benefit, I'm afraid," said King Forder. "Regrettably, our force of heroes isn't eligible to participate in quests for the Freedlands, and as they did the slaying, the only quests that could be completed are those of the Old Dwarven Kingdoms and Ruskan. Even if they wanted to submit paperwork for Andarun's."

"They aren't eligible for our quest because they're F.O.E.s!" said Johan.

"Are they?" said Forder with relish. "These Shadowkin were given Dwarven citizenship and enlisted as heroes by my Kingdom's guild."

"We've the paperwork to prove it," said Korgen.

"This is robbery!" snarled Johan.

"Speaking of which, is that not the Wyrmwood Staff?" Weaver pointed accusingly at Jynn. "That's stolen property. It was taken from the Museum of Andarun just over a month back."

"No, it's loot," said Jynn. "I took it from the liche I killed."

Gorm nodded. "Whatever came before that is irrelevant."

Ortson scowled. "That's a flimsy defense."

"Aye, but ye know what isn't?" growled Gorm. "A whole city full of cheering people that just saw us savin' them from the brink of annihilation. Ye think they'll care about the paperwork? Ye think those tired soldiers will go to war with their rescuers over a staff?"

Gorm saw Johan's eyes narrow dangerously behind the slits in his golden helm. "This isn't just about the artifact, is it?"

"No." Forder hefted the circlet with a smile. "As I've often found, a crown isn't everything."

"Fine. Let's deal." Any trace of Johan's typical exuberance had fled from his voice, replaced with hard determination. "What exactly are you hoping I'll give you?"

"The Dwarven Kingdoms might be willing to make an enlarged payment back to the Freelands in their time of need, provided we're allowed to renegotiate the terms of our loans," said King Forder.

"So be it," said Johan. "The clerks can work out the numbers. And then we'll become party to the liche's hoard?"

"Oh my, no," said King Forder. "The loot belongs entirely to my Kingdom, the Ruskan government, and the heroes that slew the liche and his army. You might find a way to tax their considerable earnings, of course, but you'd have to negotiate with them." The Dwarven king nodded to Asherzu and Gorm.

"Bargain with Orcs and criminals? Ha!" Johan's laughter was bitter and cold. "I don't need your gold that badly, Forder!"

Weaver Ortson and a couple of clerks cleared their throats in unison. A trio of Johan's advisors stepped forward to whisper into the king's ear.

"What?" barked Johan, who was to discretion as a rampaging gnurg was to an Elven pottery garden. "Well of course I know what CTOs are. They—eh?… How much? Good gods, the business community must be going mad… Well how could the kingdom have guaranteed that thrice-cursed sum? We can't afford anywhere near that much… ah. Ah, yes, I suppose that is the point. Right… yes. Burn the thrice-cursed gods! Fine!"

When the paladin turned back to Gorm and Asherzu, what little of his skin that was visible was crimson and bulging with veins. "And what exactly do you want, Orc?" the king half-said, half-spat.

Asherzu held up a hand, silencing an angry snarl from Darak and the other Shadowkin. "I am Asherzu daz'Guz'Varda, daughter to Zurthraka, sister to Char and Darak, Chieftain of the Guz'Varda. These are the demands of my people." Burt handed the chieftain a lambskin scroll, which she unrolled with a small flourish. "First, the Freelands will pardon members of the Red Horde for any alleged crimes predating this agreement. Second, the Freelands will recognize the citizenship granted by the Old Dwarven Kingdom to our peoples, and once again accept us as legal residents. Third, the Lightlings of the Freelands will abolish the oppressive NPC system and noncombatant papers in general. Fourth, a public recognition of the innocence of the Guz'Varda Tribe in the recent theft of the Burial Stones of Ogh Mag'herd, known to your people as the

Elven Marbles. Fifth, the Freedlands will cease referring the Burial Stones of Ogh Mag'herd as the Elven Marbles. Sixth, reparations for property—"

Johan threw his arms into the air. "How long is this going to take?"

Asherzu's shrug suggested that the meeting could take a while. Her smile said that she was going to enjoy every minute of it.

Gorm lost track of time as the dealing spiraled into a meandering negotiation. The Shadowkin would be reinstated into the Freedlands. Gorm and his party would receive a full pardon and have their ranks restored. In return, they'd pay taxes as normal heroes, and agreed to exclude any belongings left in undamaged buildings on Andarun's first two tiers from the loot tally. Beyond those terms and several other broad agreements, the exact nature of the deal was too expansive to cover in a few hours.

Proposals were deferred to committees that would be formed at a future date. Of course, that meant that a committee to form the committees was required. The sun was setting by the time the committee to form the committee that would form the committees was decided upon.

Finally, it was time to make good on Johan's chief demand.

"Stand tall," the king growled as they assembled at the entrance of the tent. "Remember that we're all the heroes of Andarun. We all won! Ha! And smile, by the gods. They have to see that we're happy about this." The last instruction was directed at Ortson Weaver, as most of the Shadowkin and Dwarves were already beaming at the terms they'd extracted from Johan's kingdom.

The king signaled, and the tent flaps were drawn open. Gorm walked with the procession out of the tent into a maelstrom of adulation. Lanterns of every hue from amber to lilac lined the ramparts of Andarun's tiers, and beneath them the city's citizens and denizens screamed their adoration down at their leaders and heroes. They made their way to the broad steps before parading up the stairs, flanked by jubilant crowds, sharing the credit for Andarun's rescue.

The victory march had almost reached the Palace when Gorm felt a hand on his shoulder. "Here now, Ingerson, I hope you don't think this is over," Johan growled in his ear.

"How could it be over?" Gorm spoke from the side of his mouth as he waved at the admirers lining the steps. "Nothin's finished so long as ye and I are both still breathin'."

"Ha! Good. So long as we understand each other." The paladin slapped Gorm on the back again before they both returned their attention to the celebration.

Not everyone in the city was reveling, of course. Fallen bannermen and unfortunate citizens needed to be laid to rest, provided they hadn't walked away. And there was little to celebrate for those Base-dwellers whose homes and businesses had been in the path of the Dark Spire. Beyond that, many people were simply exhausted after the most harrowing night of the age.

Feista Hrurk counted herself among their number.

She let Aubren push their way through the crowds. Throngs of celebrants filled every street, keeping their movement to a slow crawl. Rex watched the people pass from the cradle of her arms, his leg resting in a splint provided by a kindly priest at the temple of Oppo. Mrs. Hrurk occupied her mind planning a letter to Mr. Poldo; he'd want to hear how she and the home fared.

The sun was dropping over the Ridge when they finally made it back to the third tier. Mrs. Hrurk was so exhausted that she could barely hold her head up, let alone focus on anything but Aubren's heels. She just wanted to be back at the home, with all her pups and tenants safe.

"Mama, look!"

"Very nice, Rexxar," she said automatically for the hundredth time that day.

"No, look!" The pup grabbed her jowls and swung her head around. The lowest tiers of Andarun glowed in lantern light, framed by the great archway of Malcolm's Gate. Part of the Dark Spire was visible through the rooftops of the second tier, as was the huge gouge that it had carved up the Base.

"It's kind of pretty, if you don't pay the destruction any mind," said Aubren, staring back at the scene.

Even in her half-dazed state, Mrs. Hrurk couldn't help but agree. The lanterns sparkled like a reflection of the stars.

"Still, there is a lot of destruction," added Aubren. "It will take a long time to rebuild the gates, let alone the city."

"And then everything will go back to normal, right, Mama?" Rex said, his tail wagging nervously.

Feista couldn't stop herself from glancing at her son's leg, still bent and buckled in the splint. The priest had been kind and optimistic, but not so much as to lie when Feista asked her frantic questions. Yes, it was bad. No, you couldn't give a child salve, not with the known risks. No, the magic alone wouldn't fix everything; the fracture had been present too long, the crushing of the bones too complete. Yes, the pup would walk again. Would he run again? That was a harder question.

"There will be a new normal," she told her son. "Normal is always changing. But we Gnolls are a strong people. We will find our way forward. Come on. Let's get back to your brother and sister."

Aubren nodded as she shouldered her way through the crowds again. "Well, be that as it may, I'd hate to be one of the poor wretches who has to figure out how to move that big pillar the liche flung sideways into the gate."

Mrs. Hrurk laughed as she followed the girl. "You haven't lived here long enough," she said. "Mark my words, someone will build a restaurant on top of that stone within a month."

Chapter 33

The massive simulacrum of the Dark Spire of Nephan became the subject of intense legal fights. The bannermen annexed much of its northernmost mass to rebuild part of Fafnir's Gate. Meanwhile, the Academy of Mages declared the runes covering the spire to be a magical hazard, and halted any construction near the spire until surfaces could be properly disenchanted and removed. With the property mired in legal battles, the site's developer sold it for residential lots and shattered the dreams of several aspiring restauranteurs.

Still, the entrepreneurial spirit is a resilient one. People find a way forward. A new normal always emerges from the ashes of the previous status quo.

So it was that by early in Fengelde's month, well before the Festival of Sunheight, the rebuilding of Fafnir's Gate was already underway. Bulletin boards posted near the construction showed woodcuts envisioning Spire's Landing, Andarun's newest community of luxury condominiums. The bright illustrations showed how the first weapon to breach Andarun's defenses in ages would be completely paved over by the summer's end.

The Dark Spire's history lived on, however, in the names and dishes of many food-carts clustered in its shadow. Fafnir's Grille, the Spire Diner, and Bonereaper's Roast Ribs served creatively named variations of the city's favorite street foods. The Dark Pile of Enough Ham was a particular favorite among locals.

Fafnir's Gate itself was slated to be replaced with a pair of smaller, more defensible staircases on either side of Spire's Landing, which meant the gates to the second tier at Mycen Avenue needed to be widened. The groove carved by the Dark Spire across the Base was paved with cobblestones and renamed Fafnir's Way, and the buildings along it needed extensive repair. All of this construction and reconstruction brought excitement and industry to Andarun's lower tiers.

Of course, the work brought traffic as well. The streets of the lower tiers clogged with people of every race—when they weren't closed for construction. Confused travelers shuffled along detours and alternate routes throughout the city, asking directions of just about anyone who plied their trade on the roadside.

Some of them should have been more selective.

"Another lost soul!" Ignatius thrust a finger in the air, startling the young Goblin that had stopped by his shrine.

"Um, yes," she said. "It's just that I need to get to the Heroes' Guild today, so—"

"And a fighter at that!" The priest of Mordo Ogg scrabbled over the cobblestones to stare into the eye sockets of the shrine of the god of death. The crimson pinpricks of light in the skull's eyes shone with fierce, prolonged intensity.

"It's just that I need to get my papers this week, and I heard it could take a while." The Goblin tugged at her braid as she looked around with her bulbous, yellow eyes for an escape.

Ignatius leaned in until his nose touched the sculpture's face and stared with wide eyes at the dancing points of light. "Just let go. Just give in," he whispered. "All things end. Time passes. Don't fight it."

The light in Mordo Ogg's granite eyes winked out.

"Ha!" Ignatius cackled, rearing back and pumping his fist in demented victory. "Nobody can resist the call of death!"

"You know what?" said the Goblin. "I think I see it up ahead."

"A Heroes' Guild office?" Ignatius glanced to where the Goblin pointed. "No, that's not—ooh, there goes another! Ha! And another! A two-fer! Double murder, maybe? A suicide pact?"

"I'm pretty sure it's where I need to go," said the Goblin, taking a step back. "I'll just go check."

"Couldn't be," Ignatius said without looking up from the skull. "The nearest one's up two tiers, and then a block Wallward."

"T-thank you," she stammered, and then scurried away at a speed that few but a terrified Goblin can manage.

"See you eventually!" called Ignatius, waving to the retreating Shadowkin. She sped into a mass of other souls, chattering and bustling as they went about their business. They talked to neighbors that hadn't been there once, and who wouldn't be there again soon enough. They worked to rebuild a city that would one day crumble. A beautiful city, and all the more so for being fleeting.

Ignatius smiled and filled his lungs with the musk of the city. Everything was as it should be.

"Or at the very least, it's not as bad as one might expect." Heraldin stretched and cracked his neck as he waited in line at the Heroes' Guild office.

Gaist gave a barely perceptible shrug.

"Oh, don't be so irritable. The guild's doing the best they can, given the circumstances." The bard pointed to the long line of people that ran from the service desks out the door. As he spoke, a young Goblin woman trotted up to join the end of the queue. "They've a ton of work now that so many people need NPC papers."

Chieftain Asherzu's case against the injustices of the noncombatant paper carrier system was well-received in the light of the Shadowkins' valiant defense of Andarun, but her suggestion to abolish the program was a different matter. A bureaucracy is a difficult organism to dislodge from its host, and the NPC administration had deeply embedded itself within the guild and the government. Lobbying against the Orcs' proposal began immediately after King Johan announced it. Clerks and bureaucrats cited dire complications that could come from an end to noncombatant papers, from invalidating a host of standing regulations to trouble reconciling license points with those from Imperial heroes.

Eventually, it was mutually agreed that the only system that was both just and feasible was to require all non-hero citizens of any background to register as NPCs or risk classification as Forces of Evil.

The compromise both pleased and overwhelmed the guild's administration, which found itself flooded with Humans, Elves, Dwarves, and Gnomes of every variety, all eager to get their papers by the end-of-year deadline.

"Even in the middle of the summer, every office is buried in paperwork. Just imagine how much longer it would take to replace these this winter," said Heraldin. He held up his Heroes' License, complete with a woodcut that made him look as though he was about to suffer a violent sneeze. "Gods, let's hope they do a better job this time."

Gaist shook his head and pointed to his own license. Beneath his name and class, it listed his race as "Doppelganger."

"What? Are you still upset about that? Is that what you're trying to fix today?" Heraldin asked. "Everybody knows about it anyway. It's not a big deal."

Gaist looked away.

"No, seriously. You—" Heraldin wanted to tell his friend that you should never hide who you truly are, but realized just in time that it was a stupid thing to say to a shapeshifter. He took a deep breath and stepped in front of the weaponsmaster. "You feel how you want, but as far as I'm concerned, you have nothing to hide, my brother. Nothing."

The faintest hints of a smile were visible beneath Gaist's crimson scarf. He reached out and clasped the bard's shoulder.

"Least of all this woodcut!" Heraldin added, snatching the paper away from the doppelganger and examining the portrait in the corner. "I mean, how did you get someone to render you so well? A flattering pose and good line work? It just doesn't happen!"

Gaist gently elbowed him in the ribs.

"He even shaded you in three-point lighting," said Heraldin, peering at the document. "Did you bribe the artist?"

The weaponsmaster gave the bard a firmer nudge.

"No, I'm serious." Heraldin ran a finger over the woodcut as he searched. "Do you know how many women will ask to look at your heroes' license? An impressive one can mean the difference between going home alone and a chance at—ow! All right, that one hurt!"

Gaist nodded to the front of one of the lines. Heraldin looked and saw a hulking, tattooed figure approaching a desk occupied by a one-eyed clerk.

"Gods, is that Mr. Brunt?" the bard exclaimed. "I thought Gorm killed him at Bloodroot, but I'll eat a dragon's toenail if that isn't the big oaf."

Gaist nudged him again.

"You're right, it definitely is," said Heraldin. "And look, he's in the wrong line. That isn't for NPC papers. If I didn't know better, I'd think he was trying to—"

"Brunt… hero!" The Ogre's rumbling was clear even over the din of the busy guildhall.

"Well, that answers that!" smirked the bard. "I pity the monsters that—"

Gaist grabbed the top of the bard's head with two fingers and gently twisted it five degrees to the left. A pair of mismatched figures swiveled into view as they made their way from the front desks to the door. One was a large Human in hide armor, while the other was a solamancer with a familiar face.

"Oh, is that what this was about?" Heraldin muttered to the weaponsmaster. He waved at the pair and called out, "Laruna!"

"Heraldin? And Gaist!" The solamancer rushed over to embrace both heroes in turn, and she and the bard exchanged warm greetings, followed by the traditional declarations that it had been too long since they'd seen each other.

"I know it's only been a few weeks, but that feels like forever after spending so much time together in the wilds," marveled Laruna. She nodded back to the barbarian, who was reluctantly trotting toward them. "Oh. And this is Hogarth."

Hogarth had straggly hair, a rictus grin, and the wide, wild eyes of a caged animal. He gave a timid wave to Heraldin and Gaist. "Hello!" he said.

"We're a couple now," the solamancer declared. Hogarth winced a little when she said it, but the grin held fast.

"Oh?" said Heraldin, looking at Gaist. "And how did you two meet?"

"We met in a dueling ring back when we'd all split up. It was a normal enough fight, but I could tell there was something special about Hogarth. And he saw something special in me. Right?"

"Oh. Yes. Very unusual." Hogarth spoke with a distant voice and vacant eyes.

"You can just tell, right?" said Laruna. "So after we dealt with the negotiations and I settled back into the Academy, I remembered Hogarth. And I thought, 'Why not go talk to him?' So I tracked him down."

"Tracked me right down." Hogarth shook his head slowly, his eyes transfixed on some past horror.

Laruna set a hand on the brawny man's arm. "So I told him how I felt and what I wanted, and lo and behold, he agreed!"

"Couldn't say no to that!" exclaimed Hogarth.

"It was very romantic," said the mage. "Right, Hogarth?"

"Just… just couldn't say no…" The barbarian sounded close to tears.

"I see," said Heraldin, exchanging a sideways glance with Gaist.

"Brunt… have forms!" thundered the Ogre, clearly agitated.

"Is that Mr. Brunt?" asked Laruna, peering over the crowds. "I thought Gorm killed him."

"Apparently not," said Heraldin.

Laruna nodded. "Speaking of Gorm, have you heard from any of the others lately?"

"Just a couple of meals with Gorm, and Burt was there for one of them. I suspect you've had the same. I think they're trying to keep track of all of us," said Heraldin.

"Anyone else?" asked the mage, making a spectacular failure of trying to look indifferent.

"No, that's about it for me," said the bard, looking at Gaist. The weaponsmaster nodded in confirmation.

"I see," said Laruna, clearly disappointed.

"And you?" Heraldin asked the mage. "Have you heard from anyone else since our last appearance with the king?"

"We had lunch with Gorm and Burt as well," said Laruna. "But mostly I've just seen Kaitha. We try to get together every few days for tea."

"And how is the Jade Wind doing?" asked Heraldin. "I'm sure she's in demand for quests after our recent reinstatement."

"Well, she would be if she was taking on new jobs," said Laruna.

"Oh?" Heraldin raised an eyebrow. "Perhaps she'll use her share of the undead loot to enjoy the simple pleasures of life?"

"Probably not," said Laruna, shifting her weight uncomfortably.

"In triplicate!" rumbled Mr. Brunt. The one-eyed clerk serving him waved a packet of papers up at the Ogre.

Heraldin's voice dropped when he turned back to Laruna. "It's the Troll, then?"

"Yeah, Thane. She's still not over it yet. I mean, I want him to come back too, but at the end of the day, it's his decision, right?" The solamancer sighed. "I tried to tell her to move on, that she can't waste her life looking for someone who doesn't want to be found, but you know Elves. They've got nothing but time. And people do crazy things when they're having a hard time letting go."

The bard and weaponsmaster looked at Hogarth, and then at each other.

"Yes," said Heraldin with careful diplomacy.

The line was beginning to move again, and Heraldin and Gaist needed to shuffle forward if they wanted to keep their place. "We should grab dinner up on the Pinnacle soon," Heraldin told the solamancer.

"Agreed," said Laruna. "I'll send you a sprite when I look at my schedule." And with that, they bade their farewells.

For a moment the bard and the weaponsmaster watched the solamancer and her hapless beau head for the doors. Hogarth intermittently turned back to stare at them with pleading eyes.

"Yeesh," said Heraldin, scratching at his goatee. "I've seen my share of bounce-back relationships, but that one's an Ogre among Goblins, if you know what I mean. It makes you worry."

Gaist shrugged.

"Well, no, of course I'm not talking about Laruna. She'll come to her senses soon enough and move on," Heraldin said. "But she's clearly in a dark place right now, and she was never that perceptive on matters of the heart to begin with. If the solamancer is concerned for Kaitha, you've got to wonder about the Elf."

"It's not crazy," Kaitha whispered to herself as she walked through the long grass. The falling sun cast the world in warm hues, but the ground beneath her was washed in violet. She clutched the burlap bag a little closer and hurried onward.

Crazy was ignoring everything you'd seen and heard. Crazy was letting a chance at happiness pass you by just to return to the same mundane misery that you'd endured for years. Crazy was giving up before you'd given your all.

"It's not crazy," she repeated. "He's out here. People saw him. A Troll was fighting the undead. And I know that rock didn't fall. And that means he was here. So this is perfectly reasonable."

Laruna had disagreed, as had Gorm, as had Kaitha's accountant, for that matter. They did so with varying degrees of concern and understanding, but behind all their pleas she could see the same fear in their eyes; they thought she was losing her mind.

Glowmoths were dancing in the meadow atop the gentle knoll that Kaitha ascended, their graceful dancing occasionally punctuated by a crackle of energy as two lightning bugs encountered one another. Behind the Elf, the tiers of Andarun flickered with amber light. She could hear the burbling of the Tarapin River down by the bank. It was the perfect spot: picturesque, isolated, and high enough to afford her a good view of anyone approaching.

"It's just something I need to do," she said to herself, setting the bag down at the highest point of the small hill. Laruna was particularly insistent that she needed to let the past go, but Kaitha had already let go of a career, a reputation, and her salve habit. Right now, she needed something to hold on to. At least Thane was something good.

She set her bow down next to her and checked her Poor Man's Quiver. Her wrists felt naked without her trademark jade bracers, and she rubbed her hands over the long, thin scars that crisscrossed her forearms. But those bracers had belonged to the Jade Wind, which meant they tied her to a past she couldn't go back to. It also meant they were a part of Heroes' Guild history, which was why a collector had paid a sizable sum for them at auction. The balance from their sale combined with her share of the undead army's loot had given her just enough to finance her plan.

With a deep breath, Kaitha pulled the sack's drawstring. The bag fell away, and the world turned various shades of purple.

Pure mauvium was, according to the salesperson at Luxury Imports of Andarun, mined during sorcerous expeditions to the

Elemental Plane of Violet. Kaitha was fairly certain that was a falsehood spread by aggressive marketers; she'd heard the glowing nuggets were harvested from the spleens of subterranean Umbral Dread Spiders. Regardless of its source, mauvium was brutally expensive, both because it was scarce and because it was the most absolutely purple thing in existence. The presence of so much of it in one place bathed Kaitha and her surroundings in shades of eggplant and lilac; the hilltop shone like an amethyst lighthouse on a sea of summer grass and wildflowers.

She knelt next to the radiant purple, hands in her lap, eyes scanning the horizon for any sign of movement. To the south she could see the dark edge of the Green Span. To the east, the Plains of Aberreth stretched as far as eye could see. Somewhere beyond the wood and the plains was the garden she'd danced in a lifetime ago. The summer evening was cool and dry and regrettably still.

At first she was alert, hopeful. As the evening wore on, she felt worry creasing her face, and her hands wrung at her tunic nervously. By the time the sun had completely set, despair was setting in.

"I'm sorry," she shouted into the wind. "I... I didn't realize what I was doing! And I don't know what to do now." The last words were sobbed as she rubbed tears from her eyes, her voice pleading and earnest. "I just miss you. And I'm sorry. I'm so sorry."

Yet the night remained still, and no reply came.

It was the silence that got Scribe Pathalan's attention.

The High Scribe of Al'Matra was accustomed to new scriptures arriving every night. The Goddess compelled him to write down her holy decrees, or at least her latest thoughts, in a steady stream of transcendental consciousness that usually started just before dinner and lasted until well after midnight. It was his custom to occupy himself with his left hand while his right hand worked away with quill and parchment, recording the Mad Goddess' ranting. The scripture burning across his mind usually faded into the background, like the bustle of the city outside on a summer evening.

Pathalan was working through an acolyte's reports when he noticed the silence. The All Mother's scripture had cut off at some point while he read through a request to fund a contract with the Heroes' Guild to clear the basement; apparently, the lowest chambers of the temple were overrun by Variegated Scargs from the dungeon below. The high scribe intended to suggest that they save gold by boarding off the lower basement instead, but as his left hand reached for the ink he noticed that his right appendage lay still and inert.

Pathalan frowned. He'd grown so used to Al'Matra's mad screeds that the absence of divine inspiration was more noteworthy that the arrival of it. Curious, he looked at the scripture.

It was mostly a list of olives of every imaginable variety, as well as several hundred unimaginable ones. Scribe Pathalan was familiar with olives; the fourth through sixteenth chapters of the Second Book of Pathalan was almost entirely dedicated to different classifications of the fruit. Right after the list of Daellish Sweet Olives, however, the scripture suddenly changed in substance and tone.

I'm sorry. I didn't realize what I was doing. And I don't know what to do now. I just miss you. And I'm sorry. I'm so sorry.

"Very strange," murmured Pathalan, leaning in for a closer look. It wasn't just the near-coherence of the statements; they were also written in the vernacular, whereas the Goddess' scriptures tended to use formal language from the Fifth Age no matter how ridiculous the subject matter. And moreover—

"Looks interesting," said a voice from the door, nearly startling the high scribe from his chair.

"What are you doing here?" Pathalan half-hissed, half-whimpered.

"I've come to see if ye've treated the Books of Niln proper," said Gorm Ingerson, leaning against the doorframe with crossed arms and a face caught between a scowl and a smile.

"I… uh… yes! Yes!" Pathalan fumbled in the drawers of his desk. "The scribes copied them seven times. A copy has been sealed away in the vaults with all of the other scriptures. And I've personally taken care of the originals you gave me." The scribe pulled the leather-bound book from his desk and offered it to the intruder with shaking hands.

Gorm strode into the room and took the book. He flipped through the pages slowly, inspecting them as a merchant looks over imported fruits.

The silence was long and awkward. It was broken only by a low and pained groan from down the hall.

"Did you… did you assault the temple guards?" Pathalan asked.

"They had explicit orders not to let me pass." Gorm shrugged without looking up from the book. "Someone in here must really hate the poor bastards."

Pathalan could feel the blood rising in his cheeks. "I could have you arrested for that!"

"Ye could try, certainly," said the Dwarf, unconcerned. He snapped the book shut. "This all seems to be in order. Good work. Thank ye."

"Wait! Is that it?" Pathalan asked, stumbling after the retreating Dwarf.

"I'll be back if I need anything," the Dwarf said over his shoulder. "Do your guards a favor and tell 'em to let me pass next time."

"You just come in here, beat my guards, take your book, and then you think you'll just walk out of here?" sputtered the high scribe.

Gorm paused at the door and shot the priest an infernal grin. "Well, I plan to visit the sanctuary for a bit."

"T-the sanctuary is closed to the public after dark!" snapped Pathalan.

"Good!" called the Dwarf, already headed down the hall. "I was hopin' for some privacy." With that, Gorm left Pathalan gawking in the doorway to his study.

"The nerve! Who does this sort of thing? And at this hour!" Rathwyne grumbled as he stumbled out of bed. "I was halfway to sleep!"

"He was very insistent, sir," said Marcius. The young initiate of the Fane Amada stood near the door of his master's chambers, holding a decanter of water in one hand and Rathwyne's robes in the other. "Started demanding to see you as soon as he arrived."

"We are the Fane Amada, keepers of the deepest secrets! Whisperers of the most hidden names!" snarled Rathwyne, snatching his robes from the young mage. "One does not make demands of us!"

"That's what we told him, sir," said Marcius.

"And yet somehow he still convinced you to open the gate." Rathwyne struggled to pull the robe over his head.

"Oh no, sir," said the initiate. "That was when he destroyed the gate."

The leader of the Fane Amada paused with his head still buried in gray fabric. "He what?"

"Blew the door clear off its hinges, sir," said Marcius. "I'm surprised you didn't hear the explosion."

"Well, of course I heard it!" Rathwyne finished dressing as he stalked out of the corridor. "I assumed it was another one of Pender's experiments gone bad. Gods! I can't come running every time there's an explosion around here! How would I get anything done? You need to tell me about these things!"

"It's only my second week, sir." Marcius sounded hurt. "And I did come to fetch you straight away."

"Next time lead with 'we're under attack and the gate has fallen,' instead of 'oh, a wizard wants to see you!'" Rathwyne pushed past the initiate and stalked down the hall. "It's like telling me I have a guest for tea if the thrice-cursed Dragon of Wynspar landed on top of the tower."

"Well, he did ask to see you!" insisted Marcius. "And he's not actually attacking anyone. He's just standing in the courtyard waiting to duel you."

"Well, I'm sure he—wait, what did you say?" Rathwyne stopped halfway to the keep's door.

"He's in the courtyard, sir," said Marcius.

"About the duel, idiot!" snarled Rathwyne.

"He wants to duel you," said Marcius. "I feel like that one's fairly self-explanatory."

"As in, to the death?" said Rathwyne.

Marcius shrugged. "I could see it going either way, honestly."

"That's clearly a critical detail!" Rathwyne's snarl was half-hearted, though, as his mind drifted back to the gate. He had fortified the doorway with the best wards he could muster. If the mage at the door could destroy them and still have energy for a duel...

"Did he say why he wants to duel me?" he asked Marcius, trying not to let his voice tremble.

Marcius looked helpless. "Well, no, sir. What he said was to fetch you, which is also what you said I should do if any issues arise, so I did it."

"Maybe so, but people don't just go wandering around challenging other people to magic fights," said Rathwyne. "There must be some motivation behind it."

The initiate shrugged. "I assumed it was to take leadership of the Fane Amada. You know, advancement through duels, trial by combat."

"Ah, see, that's how the Academy does it!" said Rathwyne, grasping at a thread of hope. "Battling for hierarchy may be well and good for the orders of mages, but we are the Fane Amada! We are not wizards—"

The door to the keep blew open with a blast of icy wind. A figure in ornate gray robes stepped into the chambers, flanked by the curious omnimancers of the Fane Amada. His left hand was covered in a black leather glove, and he held a staff with a dragon's claw clutching a large gem at the top.

"Perhaps not, but you will be," said Jynn Ur'Mayan, leveling his staff at Rathwyne. "With my teachings, you will all be wizards and mages."

Rathwyne gulped.

"Ah, ye should have seen the look on his face," Gorm laughed.

The statue of Niln was silent, as was the rest of the sanctuary of Al'Matra. But after a year on the road with Gaist, Gorm was used to one-sided conversations.

The Dwarf once heard that the Sten believed statues could press on the veil between the living and the dead. For the Dwarf, it was enough just to see the scribe's face again, and to have a chance to say what needed to be said.

"Ah, but Pathalan took care of the books, at least. Your scripture is copied and safe in the temple vault." He waved his copy of the Books of Niln at the author's likeness. "And I still ain't sayin' I believe any of this seventh hero nonsense, but I will say this... your words brought me back from the edge, back to the fight. They reminded me of ye and Tib'rin and all the others who died fightin' for somethin' bigger and better than them. Your words saved the world, Niln. You're a hero, true as any."

Niln's likeness was unflinchingly inanimate, but Gorm felt a sense of satisfaction. He was content to imagine that the high priest shared it.

Gorm stood and gave the statue a hearty pat. "I don't know if good Goblins wind up in the same place as the best Al'Matrans, but if they do, tell Tib'rin I said 'gleebek.'"

With a final wave, the berserker left the Al'Matran sanctuary and headed out the front door. He was halfway down the steps when a small figure detached itself from the shadows and scuttled over to Gorm.

"Took you long enough," said Burt.

"Had to have a chat with the guards," said Gorm, cracking his knuckles. "Ye settled on a place?"

"Yeah, come on," said the Kobold.

Burt led Gorm a couple tiers down to a familiar establishment; the Giant Rat was a bar visited by almost every young hero in Andarun at least once. Gorm remembered his own frequent nights in the Rat decades ago, back when he was still trying to make it into the guild. The clientele seeming younger and more foolish to him now, but the tavern was otherwise unchanged.

Burt led Gorm to a private room near the back of the tavern. Inside was a small table with a figure in dark robes seated at one end. Gorm looked into the shadows next to the door and saw a couple of fierce eyes staring down at him.

"Evening," he said.

Darak nodded and turned back to watching the door.

"Were you followed?" said Asherzu softly.

"We don't think so, honored one," said Burt.

"Wouldn't have come if we were," said Gorm. "Last thing we need is Johan findin' out we're meetin'."

"Agreed," said Asherzu.

"And if there's nothing else, honored one, it is getting very late…" Burt trailed off as he climbed up the table and into a fine leather handbag.

The chieftain nodded. "That is all. Well done."

"Aye, thank ye Burt. Off to your purse, then."

The Kobold's hackles rose as he spun on Gorm. "What'd you call it?"

"Uh, I just—"

"A purse!" barked Burt. "Darak, did you just hear what he called your satchel? He called it a purse!"

"It's not a purse," said Darak.

"Do you not see the shoulder straps? The studded bandolier? Do you think Darak would carry a purse around like some Elf?"

Gorm held his hands up. "I'm sorry. I didn't mean anything—"

"Yeah, I know what you meant!" snarled Burt. "You thought I—"

Asherzu cleared her throat, cutting off the Kobold. "I am sure our friend regrets his choice of words, but given the pressing concerns of the evening, perhaps we could let it pass. Just this once."

"Aye, I'm sorry!" insisted Gorm. "I didn't mean anything by it."

The Kobold stared at Gorm with a bulging eye for a moment, then gave a satisfied snort and finished climbing into the satchel. "Yeah, you're right, honored one. Apology accepted. Now, if you'll excuse me, it's time for my nap."

Gorm turned back to Asherzu. "Ye've pressing concerns?"

The chieftain shook her head. "What else do we have, Gorm Ingerson? A wicked man sits upon the throne. The city-states are in disarray. There is tension among my people, tension among the Lightlings, and strife between the two groups. And every day, there are new plots to grind us all back beneath the king's boot."

Gorm leaned back in his seat. "So just the usual stuff, then."

"You jest, but I do not see a way forward," said Asherzu. "Who can say how we will all survive this?"

"An old friend once told me that there ain't always a light at the end of the tunnel," Gorm said. "That's why ye gotta carry a torch."

The Orcess thought for a moment, and then smiled. "Wise words, friend Ingerson. Shall we get to the business at hand?"

"Aye." Gorm returned her grin. "There's much to be done."

Epilogue

"The paperwork never ends, does it?" Duine Poldo asked as he shuffled through the sheaves in his lap.

The Wood Gnomes perched on the carriage's red velvet seats cast shifting shadows in the light of the lantern that hung from the ceiling. One of the Gnomes closest to the Scribkin chirruped curiously.

"Look at what remains for tonight!" Poldo held up a bundle of documents. "Insurance claims to fill out for the undead attack, work orders for the repairs to the home, an issue with an invoice from the General Store, and I still owe Mrs. Hrurk a letter. I'll be lucky if I finish half of it by the time we reach Dunhelm."

The Wood Gnome chittered sympathetically.

Poldo considered the tasks at hand, and opted for the most pleasant. He took out a blank sheet of paper, set it on his lap desk, and began a letter to Mrs. Hrurk.

He hadn't finished his greetings before the carriage lurched to a halt, spilling his ink pot. The Scribkin cursed as he helped the Wood Gnomes clean up the mess. "Well, I assumed I'd have more time than that!" he groused. "How have we reached Dunhelm already?"

The door of the carriage was suddenly pulled open. "Well, sir, the fact is, we haven't," said the carriage driver, a lanky Human with a hawk nose. "Nove's razor and all that."

"What?" said Poldo.

"Nove's razor?" said the driver. "His third principle of universal irony?"

"I'm afraid I'm not entirely sure what you're talking about," said the Gnome.

"Oh, it's a very famous principle," said the driver, leaning against the carriage. "Nove said that when outcomes are uncertain, irony pushes the result against positive expectations. He had this great experiment where he put a cat in a box with a toxic slime and shut the lid."

"So I've heard. It all seems inhumane," said Poldo.

"Maybe, but as long as the lid was closed, the fate of the cat was uncertain, right? It could be alive or dead—multiple possible outcomes! But whenever he opened the box, the cat was dead!"

"Yes," said Poldo. "That's what you'd expect."

"Well, yeah, but…" The carriage driver trailed off, scratching his nose. "No, wait… I'm telling it wrong. Maybe it was that he had a real bastard of a cat, and that was the only one that lived?"

"I'm familiar with Nove's razor!" snapped Poldo. "I'm just not sure what it has to do with our premature stop!"

"Well, whenever you have several possible scenarios, the worst one's the most likely. Case in point…" The driver leveled a large crossbow at Poldo's face. "This is a robbery, actually. Put your hands in the air and keep them where I can see them."

Poldo gasped. Several of the Wood Gnomes leapt to his defense, but the driver snatched one from the air.

"Hang on! Hang on!" he said, lifting the struggling Gnome up over his head. "I like to keep these things nice and neat, but if they need to get messy, I'm not afraid to get a little stain on my boots, if you understand? Squish squish, crunch crunch, yeah?"

"No! No need for that," said Poldo slowly, hands above his head. "Stand down, everyone."

"There's a good man!" said the driver, tossing the Wood Gnome back into the carriage. He guided Poldo down the carriage steps and to the edge of the lantern's light. "I'm sure you understand that in the current economic climate, it's become necessary to supplement my income a bit. Take opportunity as it comes, or so they say! And when a bigwig banker hires my carriage, that's definitely an opportunity. Now, if you'd just stand with your back to the ditch, sir, I think I can do this with one bolt."

Poldo's heart froze in his chest. "I thought you said you liked to keep this clean!"

"Oh, I do, sir!" said the driver cheerfully. "As in, I like to eliminate all the witnesses to my robberies. So if you can manage to drop down amongst those big rocks down there, your body should hide itself without a shred of evidence I ever touched you. And you get a quick and painless death, which is much better than what I'm going to do to you if you try anything funny. Everybody wins, in a way."

"Some more than others," said Poldo.

"Well, you're a banker, right?" said the driver with a dark chuckle. "You should be used to that sort of thing."

"The Wood Gnomes will tell someone," said Poldo, stepping toward the ditch.

"The Domovoy?" The driver smirked. "Anyone they try to talk to is just going to call an exterminator and be done with it. Now if you'd kindly make sure your back is to the stones..."

"What stones?" Poldo peered down into the darkness.

"The huge stones down in the ditch," said the driver-turned-highwayman.

"Behind the bushes?" asked Poldo, squinting. "Those look like shrubs to me."

"Are you blind? I'm talking about the massive boulders sitting at the bottom of the thrice-cursed ditch! They — what?" The driver stopped at the edge of the ridge and stared down at the scrub brush, baffled. "Where could a pile of thrice-cursed boulders go?"

"You have to consider the worst possible scenario," said a voice that sounded like an avalanche.

"What?" said the driver, just before something pulled him up into the darkness. He managed half a scream before he was cut short with an unpleasant, burbling snap.

A hulking figure stepped into the carriage light, the driver's lifeless body dangling from its hands. It towered over Poldo, regarding him with beady red eyes.

"You're safe now, Gnome," said the Troll. "Go."

"Oh!" said Poldo, his heart still racing. "Well, I'm glad you were here. Thank you!"

The Troll's demeanor shifted from cold to confused. "Aren't you going to run away?"

"I should think not," said Poldo. "I wouldn't be able to go far, anyway. Not without this carriage here." He pointed back over his shoulder, to where a few of the Wood Gnomes were desperately trying to calm the horses.

"But I'm a Troll."

573

Poldo shrugged. "And my best workers are Wood Gnomes, and my tenants are Orcs and Goblins, and my... my dearest friend is a Gnoll. Why should a Troll be any different?"

"I don't know." The Troll's hand moved toward his face, as if to touch his eye. "But it is."

"I respectfully disagree," said the Gnome. "My name is Duine Poldo. I used to work in finance."

"Thane," said the Troll, reaching down to shake the Gnome's hand. "I used to be a semi-mythical guardian of the forest."

"Pleased to meet you." Poldo shook the tip of the Troll's index finger. "A guardian, was it? I had a hunch you worked in security."

"Really?"

"Oh yes. The way you handled yourself back there—thank you again, by the way—I could just tell. Quick, succinct, and confident. I especially liked the way you turned the driver's own remarks against him. A very clever quip."

Thane scratched the back of his head sheepishly. "Well, I've heard you're allowed just one."

"Ha! Regardless, it's clear you've done this professionally."

"More of an informal arrangement, really," said the Troll. "Just saving travelers on the roads from bandits, monsters, that sort of thing. Speaking of which, it isn't really safe to be on the roads around Andarun these days."

"That's what I said when I hired a carriage with an armed driver," muttered Poldo. "Well, thrice-curse Nove, I suppose. But it's safer for me out here than it is in Andarun."

He turned to look back at Mount Wynspar. The city wasn't visible from this side of the mountain, but the lights of the tiers formed a halo around the mountain against the purple darkness of the night.

"I probably should have been away from the city sooner," said Poldo. "I just... I just had to stay back and make sure someone would be all right."

"I know the feeling," said Thane. "Now, I know that she's... that everything is going to be fine. But there's still no place for someone like me."

"And you don't want to leave, but staying isn't an option."

"There are just too many reasons it has to be this way."

Troll and Scribkin shared a surprised look.

"Ahem, well, yes, I know that feeling as well," said Poldo. "I, uh… I don't suppose you'd be interested in traveling with me?"

The Troll seemed surprised. "You'd want me to?"

"Oh certainly! I've recently had a security position open up." Poldo nodded to the dead driver. "And you seem like good company. Do you have a standard rate?"

"A what?"

"An amount you usually charge for your work?"

"I… uh, I used to just ask for something purple," said the Troll.

"Ah. That's unusual. And probably illegal, as I think about it. I'm pretty sure Thug and Goon rules prohibit such arrangements, anyway. Are you licensed yet? No, it doesn't matter. I'll just pay you in giltin, and you can buy whatever color stuff you like. Does eighty a week sound reasonable?"

Thane grinned.

TO BE CONCLUDED IN
THE DARK PROFIT SAGA BOOK III:
DRAGONFIRED

About the Author

J. Zachary Pike was once a basement-dwelling fantasy gamer, but over time he metamorphosed into a basement-dwelling fantasy writer. His animations, films, and books meld fantasy elements with offbeat humor. A New Englander by birth and by temperament, he writes strangely funny fiction on the seacoast of New Hampshire. Find him online at **www.jzacharypike.com**.

Glossary

Agekeepers: A sect of esoteric historians who keep and update the official records of Arth. It is the Agekeepers who define when an age begins and ends.

Al'Matra: Technically, the highest-ranked Elven god, as the queen of the pantheon, the All Mother and her followers are really impoverished outcasts. The scriptures say that she went mad after the All Father's betrayal.

Al'Thadan: Once called the All Father, the high god was once the king of the pantheon. He is said to have been Arth's greatest defender against the forces of Mannon until he colluded with the Dark Lord during the War of Betrayal in the Third Age. According to the Agekeepers, Al'Thadan was struck down along with all the Sten at the end of the war.

Andarun: Capital of the Freedlands, built in a cleft of Mount Wynspar between the Ridge and the Wall.

Animancy: The solamancer's counterpart to necromancy. The vibrant magic that gives creatures life.

Arth: A world much like Earth, but with more magic and fewer vowels.

Baedrun: Unlike most Dwarven gods, or most Dwarves, Baedrun is said to be as jovial and curious as he is benevolent. He is the god of mountain springs, underground reservoirs, oases, and other hidden caches of potable water. He is often prayed to as the last resort of men dying of thirst.

Bannerman: The bannermen are the town guard, armies, and other armed officials of the Freedlands. Every branch of every civic organization within the Freedlands is required to maintain some number of armed men who may be called to arms when fealty demands it. Each bannerman is loyal to a such a company, which is loyal to a city, which is loyal to Andarun, which is loyal to the Freedlands. In this way, each bannerman serves his country as well as his city-state.

Biomancy: Biomancy is a field representing all of the disciplines of magic related to life, death, disease, and medicine. Solamancers and noctomancers alike can find work in biomancy, as it often utilizes weaves from both the warp and the weft of magic, such as animancy and necromancy.

Bloomtide: Bloomtide is the farmer's name for Dewen's month, the third month of spring.

Bogling: A catch-all term for the various elementals, spirits, and bipedal creatures that live in Arth's enchanted marshlands.

Boglurk: An unpleasant monster that is more fish than man, more plant than fish, and more smelly than anything.

Bugbear: Neither a bug nor a bear, but instead a rather large breed of Demi-gnoll.

Class: Professional Heroes fall into a variety of classes (e.g. warrior, mage) and sub-classes (e.g. swordsman, pyromancer), largely distinguished by the methods they use to kill monsters.

Crocotrice: Imagine a suspicious-looking log in a swamp. Now imagine it is considerably more suspicious due to having a rooster's crown near one end and a thick plume of feathers at the other. Now imagine it jumps out on six legs and tries to paralyze you with petrifying venom. That's pretty much the last few moments of any crocotrice victim's life.

Darkforged: A derogative term that encompasses the Shadowkin and the monstrous races.

Dawngreen: Leurieth's month is the second month of spring, and the second of Arth's calendar year.

Dewen: The Gnomish goddess of fidelity, patient love, and commitment. Many weddings mention her, but some do not, because her husband joined with Mannon in the War of Betrayal, making Dewen the Betrayed Goddess. She is often associated with melancholy or nostalgia, and is frequently invoked by widows and widowers. Dewen is the Patroness of Clan Dewbell.

Domovoy: *See Wood Gnome.*

Doppelganger: A widely distrusted race of shapeshifters, commonly believed to have been created as infiltrators for Mannon's armies in the War of Betrayal. Doppelgangers would make ideal diplomats, were they not such ideal spies, double agents, and assassins as well.

Dragon: Great reptiles that command the elements, most famously fire. It is well known that dragons slumber deep beneath the ground atop great mounds of treasure, and it is universally agreed that it's always best to let sleeping dragons lie.

Drakes: Dragon-kin that are much like full dragons, except smaller, weaker, and nowhere near as smart. Drakes still pose a significant threat, however, especially when encountered in their native element.

Dwarf: Dwarves are shorter than Elves and Humans, but as Dwarves stand almost twice as wide at the shoulder and are famous for violent grudges, it's generally best not to mention that. Rigid, industrious, and usually stoic, Dwarves live in massive clanhomes dug under the mountains. To the puzzlement of many of the other races, there are no Dwarven women.

Dwerrow: The Gnomes of Clan Erdin, or Hill Gnomes, are often mistaken for Dwarves. They're just a head shorter than Dwarves, but

Continued next page

Continued from previous page

otherwise have similar stocky builds, long beards, and muscular frames. Other key differences from Dwarves include narrower shoulders, rounder features, and (perhaps most significantly), the presence of female Dwerrow. They are also usually heavily tattooed with spiral patterns used to indicate heritage, standing, and fealty.

Elf: The most enigmatic of the Children of Light have sharp, angular features but flowing, graceful movements. They live in tree huts, and many of them have accumulated untold wealth. They are immortal and yet innocent, playful yet powerful, whimsical yet wise. Above all, they are infuriating to almost everyone who is not an Elf. Elves all belong to houses, each of which swears fealty to a Great House. Of course, Elven fealty shifts frequently, and so the Elven houses are forever in flux, playing games of intrigue and power.

Elixir: A miraculous healing potion brewed by magical means, elixir or salve can close wounds, restore organs, and even regrow lost limbs if consumed soon enough after an injury. It's nearly as effective as it is addictive.

Father Tinderhope: *See Fulgen*

Fengelde: Fengelde is the smallest Gnomish goddess, known as a protector of small creatures and a preserver of the natural cycles. She has no temple, though she was worshipped by the druids before their numbers dwindled and faded. She is patroness of Clan Fengeld, the Wood Gnomes.

Fennekin: Fox-like Demi-gnolls with large ears and larger appetites for mischief.

F.O.E.: Short for Force Of Evil, the official Heroes' Guild designation for an enemy of the people and a legal target for heroic slaying

The Freedlands: The most powerful nation on Arth, the Freedlands is a federation of semi-autonomous city-states. The Freedlands has a small centralized government, ruled by a king set in Andarun, that regulates the powerful guilds, associations, and corporations that do business in the Freedlands and beyond.

Fulgen: Fulgen, also called the Underglow or Father Tinderhope, is the Dwarven god of light. He rules over candles in the darkness, purity among corruption, and truth amid lies. Among the Dwarves, he is a favorite of miners and heroes.

Gazer: A horrible creature out of legend said to have been a floating bulb with one cyclopean eye at its center and many tentacles, each ending with a leering eyeball. If they ever existed, they're now long gone from Arth, yet they remain popular in ballads and other artwork to this day. According to folklore, Gazers were said to have been cunning in combat, capable of weaving magic, and adept at avoiding copyright infringement.

Giltin: The currency of the Freedlands, long considered the standard for all of Arth. The common symbol for giltin is G, as in 5G. One giltin is ten silver shillings. One shilling is ten copper cents.

Glowmoth: A lovely, if unimaginatively named, variety of bioluminescent moth that inhabits subterranean Arth. Glowmoths are important in Dwarven and Gremlin culture, and all the more so as they're the holy symbol of Fulgen.

Gnoll: A race of Shadowkin with canine traits, once known as Clan Galden, or the Golden Gnomes. Gnolls were bred for a variety of purposes in the War of Betrayal, and many of these breeds (technically known as Demi-gnolls) are still around today.

Gnome: Gnomes take as many shapes and sizes as the clouds in the sky. While their legends hold that all Gnomes once shared a common ancestor, the great Gnomish clans have all become their own sub-races. Be that as it may, it's proper to refer to any of them as a Gnome, be they a Halfling to a Tinderkin to a Deep Gnome. Said sub-races are often used interchangeably with clan names. All Gnomes stand shorter than most Humans, and most are shorter than Dwarves.

Goblin: A race of Shadowkin that descended from the lost clans of the Dwarves. Goblins are short, scrawny, potbellied creatures. Their skin is green, their limbs are spindly. Stereotypes say that Goblins excel at little except breeding, at which they are amazing. It's true that a handful of Goblins can become a tribe in just a few years.

Golem: Enchanted automatons created by the Scribkin, golems serve many useful purposes across Arth.

Gremlins: A race of Shadowkin with both feline and lizard-like qualities, once known as Clan Remlon, or Moon Gnomes. Gremlins are known for their inquisitive nature, their mastery of bioengineering, and their tenuous grasp of ethics. **Griffin:** It is said that a griffin is a lion with the head, talons, and wings of an eagle, but the Zoological Society of Monchester has determined that a griffin is, in actuality, a giant eagle with a lion's butt.

Halfling: Halflings are Gnomes of Clan Haughlin. They have round features, pot bellies, and curly brown hair (even on the tops of their feet.) While generally good-natured, Halflings are averse to manual labor, or indeed anything that isn't comfortable. Unfortunately, they're often very comfortable with petty theft.

Hardvaark: A ground-dwelling monster with a long, pig-like snout and a thick, metallic carapace. Its tenacious nature made it the namesake of one of the Freedlands' most prestigious universities.

Heroes' Guild: An international organization of professional adventurers who specialize in monster slaying, treasure acquisition, hostage retrieval, and more. The Heroes' Guild is among the largest and most powerful organizations on Arth. Its wealth rivals that of the city-states of the Freedlands, and even some small countries.

High Magic: The elemental energy woven through the universe, high magic is called the great weave. High magic is divided into two distinct orders—solamancy and noctomancy.

Human: Y'know. Humans. Originally mixed-race men, the first Humans were children of Gnomes and Elves and Sten. In time, they became so common that they married among themselves and spread throughout Arth. Now they are the most populous race of man, outnumbering all of the old races combined.

Issan: A legendary Elven champion of Tandos in the War of Betrayal, notable for slaying the Dark Prince's first incarnation.

Khazen: The Dwarven god of war, Khazen is a master of defense and the defender of the home. He is a favored god of guards, watchmen, and militias.

Kobold: Kobolds are a diminutive breed of Demi-gnoll, standing just below a man's knee in height. They have big eyes, a short muzzle, thin limbs, and a severe case of small dog syndrome.

Lamia: The largest and most powerful sept of the Naga, easily distinguished by their flame-colored scale patterns. Two of their matriarchs founded Lamia Sisters, one of the Freedlands' most prominent investment banks.

Leurieth: The Rain Dancer, Leurieth, is the goddess of rain and snow, water from the sky. She's a favorite among Elves and is strongly associated with seasons and the passage of time. She's also associated with the north wind.

Leviathan: A legendary sea monster said to be born of the ultimate evil.

Liche: A mage that rose from the grave through necromancy and extensive planning. Liches are the most powerful form of undead.

Low Magic: The oldest laws of the universe, the rules of life and death, love and hatred, blood and bone.

Mage: A person able to see and weave high magic, usually through years of dedicated study and social isolation.

Magic: The essential forces of the universe, as understood by those who fiddle with them. Magic is divided into high and low magic.

Mankind, Man, Races of Man: Legends say the Creator made the four races of Man—the Dwarves, Elves, Gnomes, and Sten—to make Arth more interesting, and has regretted it ever since.

Mannon: Malice incarnate, the ancient foe of the Creator deceived mankind, created the Shadowkin, and even corrupted some of the gods in ages past. Depending on the temple one visits, it is said that Mannon is either dead, in hiding, or a little bit of him lives in all of our hearts.

.**Manticore:** Large, horned cats with drake wings, manticores are monsters from the War of Betrayal. They're close relatives of chimeras, though not so close as to attend each other's parties.

Meltwater: The farmers' name for Fulgen's month. It's the first month of spring and thus the year.

Mercenary: Killers for hire. Specifically, mercenaries are the killers for hire that are not professional heroes. Assassins, soldiers, thugs, goons: they all fall under the general headline of "mercenary." While more common than professional heroes, mercenaries are less regulated. With some assassins and thugs aside, they're generally thought to be weaker as well.

Monstrous Races: Humanoids bred for various combat roles by Mannon and Noros to fight in the War of Betrayal, the monstrous races are distinguished from Shadowkin in that they didn't descend from the races of Man.

Musana: Musana is the Elven goddess of light and life. She encourages purity and grace, and honors simple living. Musana's high ideals make her popular, especially among the Order of the Sun, but many followers often misunderstand her teaching: Musana's most famous stories depict her humbling those followers who think themselves more pious than others. She is twin sister to Alluna, the Elven goddess of the moon.

Naga: A race of Shadowkin with serpentine traits, Naga were once Clan Nagata, the Iron Gnomes. They resemble green-skinned, scaled men and women from the waist up, but their lower halves are those of serpents.

Necromancer: While all noctomancers can touch the shadowy side of high magic that binds the dead, the word necromancer is reserved for those who have created undead for nefarious purposes.

Noctomancer: A member of the second great order of mages, the Order of the Moon. Noctomancers are Humans and Gnomes that can weave the elements of air, earth, and shadow.

Noros: Once the Gnomish god of dreams, Noros became Mannon's greatest lieutenant.

NPC: A Noncombatant Paper Carrier is a Shadowkin or monster who has secured Noncombatant Papers, removing his, her, or its status as a F.O.E. and thereby preventing professional heroes from killing them (legally).

Omnimancer: A mage who wields both solamancy and noctomancy. Omnimancers once comprised the third great order of mages, the Order of Twilight, but they have fallen from grace. Now, omnimancers are the spell casting equivalent of lepers, living on the margins of society.

Orc: A race of Shadowkin, Orcs were once Elves that sided with Mannon. Hulking, bucket-jawed, green-skinned barbarians, Orcs have a war-torn history and a legacy of brutality.

Order of the Moon: *See Noctomancer.*

Order of the Sun: *See Solamancer.*

Order of Twilight: *See Omnimancer.*

Owlverine: All the deadly ferocity of an owlbear, packed into a beast no bigger than an owlhound.

Ogre: One of the monstrous races, Ogres are like clubs: big, simple, and made for violence.

Poor Man's Quiver: An enchanted quiver that always contains exactly one enchanted arrow, no matter how many are pulled from it. After purchasing one, any man would be poor.

Rank (Heroes' Guild): There's no way to measure the value of a life, except the life of a professional hero, in which case their rank is an effective metric. As a hero attains ranks in different classes by killing things, it's essentially a measure of how deadly, and therefore how valuable, a hero is.

Scarg: A vaguely humanoid bat-like creature, the origins of scargs are unknown. Some say they're naturally occurring monsters, while others say scargs are a monstrous race or a Gremlin experiment gone wrong. They come in many varieties and breeds, most of which are more annoying than threatening to a professional hero.

Scribkin: The Gnomes of Clan Tinkrin, or Scribkin, stand half as tall as most Humans, with stocky builds, bulbous noses, and thick, bushy hair. Industrious and curious, Scribkin are Arth's most innovative inventors, enchanters, and engineers.

Shadowkin: Legends hold that by the Third Age, many of Arth's people followed Mannon or the gods loyal to him. Before launching the War of Betrayal, Mannon and Noros corrupted these lost people into more aggressive, poetically ironic shadows of their former selves.

Slaugh: Imagine a Gnome-sized frog walking on its haunches. Now imagine it has a foul temperament and a fouler odor. Now you know why almost everybody hates Slaugh. Technically, they're Shadowkin descended from the Gnomes of Clan Slaughin, but other Shadowkin are loath to admit as much.

Solamancer: A member of the first great order of mages, the Order of the Sun. Solamancers are Humans and Elves that can weave the elements of fire, water, and light.

Sten: The great traitors. Legends say that members of the fourth race of man were long considered aloof and enigmatic before they followed the traitor god Al'Thadan and colluded with Mannon. Gray-skinned, as tall as Elves, and as broad as Dwarves, Sten were masters of low magic. The Agekeepers confirm that they were wiped out in the War of Betrayal.

Sunheight: Baedrun's month is the fifth month of the year, in the middle of Arth's summer.

Tandos: The Elven god of war and glory, Tandos is the greatest son of Al'Thadan and Al'Matra. It was he who finally struck down his traitorous father, and it was Tandos's servants who defeated the Sten.

Today, he rules over the pantheon as the divine regent in the place of his mother, who is unfit for rule.

Tinderkin: The Gnomes of Clan Kaedrin, Tinderkin are taller than any other Gnomes, standing a little taller than even a Dwarf. They are lithe, graceful figures with sharp, slender features. Tinderkin are nomadic, traveling in small, familial bands. They take their name from the fires they build for nightly gatherings, which are often elaborate visual spectacles.

Troll: Trolls are massive, ape-like creatures, the corrupted remnants of the now-extinct Sten. A Troll is a gray-skinned Shadowkin with a flat, broad-nostrilled face and a shaggy coat of thick fur. They have peerless regenerative abilities and can shrug off mortal blows or regrow limbs within minutes. Originally bred for war and killing, they are regarded as good for little else.

Undead: The bodies and / or spirits of fallen mortals, animated by foul magic to haunt and / or hunt the living. They take many forms, including ghosts, ghouls, liches, skeletons, vampires, wraiths, and zombies.

Undine: Undines are one of the four elemental peoples, most commonly associated with water. Like all elemental peoples, they are uniformly of one gender. All Undines are female, and they interbreed with Sylphs, the people of air. Human legends portray Undines as beautiful and seductive. Undine legends portray Humans as lecherous and creepy. You be the judge.

Ward: A magical barrier, shield, or other protective spell woven by mages.

Wizard: A title given to male mages. Its counterpart, witch, fell into disuse during the Age of Darkness.

Wood Gnome: The most diminutive of Gnomes, members of Clan Fengeld stand just over most men's ankles. They grow long beards, but all of their hair tends to get lost in the tangle of pelts and scraps they

Continued next page

Continued from previous page

wear. They're fiercely territorial and will often refuse to surrender land even after another race has built a city atop it. Their squatting habits have led many modern citizens to regard them as a particularly obnoxious form of vermin, and one that is remarkably difficult to get rid of.

Wust: The Cloudking, Wust is the god of wind. He is legendarily curious; it's said that Wust makes the wind whisper Arth's secrets to him. His drive for knowledge and ingenuity make him a fitting patron for Clan Tinkrin, the Scribkin. He rules all winds, but is most strongly associated with the west wind.

Wynspar: The mighty mountain that Andarun is set inside is riddled with caves, tunnels, dungeons, and various other dark places for monstrous horrors to lurk.

Wyvern: A variety of drake with leathery wings instead of forelegs, much akin to a bat, and a barbed, venomous tail, much akin to a scorpion. It is every bit as unpleasant as it sounds.

Rose Tunic was the only tavern in the town of Dayle, though "tavern" was a bit of a generous term for an old barn with a keg and a pile of hay for sleeping. Then again, referring to a smattering of fishing huts clustered by a lake in the Pinefells as a "town" was more than a little indulgent as well. But the old men of the town, which is to say, the entire population of Dayle, were a generous sort, especially when they'd been drinking. Which was usually the case.

The libations had been flowing freely the night that Bartimus Jakes kicked in the door of the Tunic one summer night. Wind and rain swept in as the old fisherman led a figure with an odd gait into the common room. The cause of the strange walk soon became apparent as the figure unfurled its wings and looked about in a panic.

"Bones!" swore Kelder Dain. The old Halfling leapt from his stool. "Is that a bloody Great Eagle?"

The eagle squawked.

"It ain't one of Gregor's chickens, is it?" growled Bartimus. "Come and help me get him inside."

"It's hurt and it's scared," said Bartimus. "Beyond that, I don't speak Eagle."

"Don't need to talk to see what it needs," said Fergus Ur'Bolan, the Tunic's proprietor. "Come here, lad, let's get you by the fire."

The eagle screeched again. Its eyes darted around the room, but it allowed the old barkeep to usher it over to a crude fireplace set in the side of the barn.

"There now. Some heat and fish'll do you good. And if eagles take grog, you'll have that too," said Fergus.

"He seems pretty worked up over something," asked Bartimus. "Don't suppose anyone here speaks Eagle?"

"Girion does, if I recall," said Dwarven Sven.

"Who?" asked Kelder.

"The young Human fellow," said Dwarven Sven. "The range. Patrols the woods north of the lake."

"I bet you're right!" said Tall Sven. "I seen him talking to animals lots."

"Yeah, but does he understand 'em when they talk back?" asked Kelder.

"It's the best chance we got," said Bartimus. He looked out the window at the clouds swirling ominously overhead. "We'll set out once the storm clears. But that might not be 'til morning."

The eagle screeched.

"Now, now, easy does it," said Fergus. "You stay as long as you need by the fire. And tomorrow we'll take you to the nice ranger and see what this is about, eh? We'll sort this all out. You'll see."

They didn't.

When the fishmonger's ice cart came for its weekly pickup three days later, the driver found nothing left of Dayle but ashes and charred support beams. A report of the damage indicated that the fire wasn't caused by lightning or an accident. Additionally, several travelers on the road from Andarun to Scoria claimed to see a flying, reptilian shape headed north on the evening of the storm. The Heroes' Guild and the Zoological Society of Monchester released a joint report attributing the town's destruction to the Dragon of Wynspar. Shares of the dragon's hoard rose a tenth of a percent on the news.

Printed in the USA
CPSIA information can be obtained
at www.ICGtesting.com
LVHW042323280124
770187LV00032B/598

9 780990 859642